SKELMERSDALE

FICTION RESERVE STOCK

SHARP THROUGH THE HAWTHORN

SHARP THROUGH THE HAWTHORN

Sybil Marshall

MICHAEL JOSEPH
LONDON

MICHAEL JOSEPH LTD

Published by the Penguin Group
27 Wrights Lane, London W8 5TZ
Penguin Viking Inc., 375 Hudson Street, New York, New York 10014, USA
Penguin Books Australia Ltd, Ringwood, Victoria, Australia
Penguin Books Canada Ltd, 10 Alcorn Avenue, Toronto, Ontario, Canada M4V 3B2
Penguin Books (NZ) Ltd, 182–190 Wairau Road, Auckland 10, New Zealand

Penguin Books Ltd, Registered Offices: Harmondsworth, Middlesex, England

First published in Great Britain 1994

Typeset in 11½/13 pt Monophoto Garamond by
Datix International Limited, Bungay, Suffolk
Printed in England by Clays Ltd, St Ives plc

ISBN 0 7181 3797 3

The moral right of the author has been asserted

The lines from 'Just Making Conversation' by
Harry Carlton on page 55 are reproduced by
permission of Trudie Thompson, and those
from 'In Gemma' by H. H. Coward on page 186
by kind permission of Mrs Evelyn Coward.

For my grandchildren,
William, Henry and Catherine,
upon whom the continuity of my family line depends

IN THE FACE OF
THIS CONGREGATION

1

Bells. A full peal of eight tumbling over each other in joyous clamour to announce that George Bridgefoot's daughter Lucy was now the wife of Dr Alexander Marland.

Keyed up to what she called her 'overdrive gear' of sensitivity by the beauty of the ceremony she and William had just witnessed, Fran Catherwood thought of the sound as a flock of silver-winged birds released from the top of the tower to deliver their message to the furthest outskirts of the ancient village and beyond – just as they might have announced Nelson's victory over the French at Trafalgar when that news had at last trickled through to the wide remoteness of East Anglia.

Once upon a time everybody had relied upon bells for news, as well as for the pattern of the daily round. The sound of them was ingrained in those who had ears to hear. She remembered with vivid clarity her own feelings that Sunday morning twenty-five years ago when, after three years of enforced silence, all the bells in Britain had joined in the celebration of General Montgomery's victory at El Alamein – the turning point of the Second World War, and good cause for rejoicing to all British ears. From the day of the outbreak of war till that morning, the sound of bells had been prohibited, reserved to act as a warning that the expected German invasion of British soil had begun. Instead, they had rung out in exultation. The very thought of it caused a frisson up and down Fran's spine, even now.

They had been used as warnings from time to time for other things, like floods, for instance, in the low-lying parts of eastern England, or high tides on the coast, as in Lincolnshire in 1571.

> Play uppe, play uppe, O Boston bells!
> Ply all your changes, all your swells.

3

Fran's head was always full of poetry, especially at times like this.

She followed her own train of thought. Past and present were difficult to distinguish from each other in a place as old as this church. It sat in the middle of the village like an old mother hen among her chickens, clucking with pleasure if there was something good for them, squawking if danger threatened. The old fire beacon that had been lit to pass on the dire news of the approach of the Spanish Armada was still there in full view on top of the tower. The sight of it and the sound of bells made history real. It was only a long process of continuity. William would appreciate that thought, if she could communicate it to him.

They were standing together in the first pew behind the transverse aisle, watching the end of the wedding procession pass before them.

'We may as well sit down again, sweetheart,' said William. 'We promised to wait for Mary and Greg coming down from the organ, and in any case it will be ages before we can get the car out.'

He sat down himself, and taking her hand, pulled her down beside him. She obeyed his gentle tug and made no attempt to withdraw her hand from his, but as she sat she turned to look at the ringers, delightedly watching the sun-browned arms go up and down and the bright sallies rising and falling in rhythm. Her own gardener, Ned Merriman, was among the ringers, and for a split second she was surprised to see him; but of course, he was standing in today for the churchwarden, George Bridgefoot, who couldn't be in two places at once. It was his daughter who was being married, and Fran had seen him, in all the unaccustomed panoply of morning-dress, go down the aisle with the bride on his arm, and come back up it squiring Lady Marland. That would be something new for the village to talk about!

Ring out the old, ring in the new.

'Ply all your changes . . .' Fran wasn't sure whether more change would be welcome. There had already been changes

4

a-plenty in the three years since she had come back to buy and restore for her own occupation the lovely old house that she had known so well as a child, when she and her cousins had spent time there with their grandfather, the last 'old squire'.

She had been prepared for what war could do even to a place as small and remote as Old Swithinford, but not for the more subtle effects of its aftermath. As with the science of campanology the 'changes' that could be rung on eight bells were astounding, so the changes that could take place in a village were almost as many and various. The area of Old Swithinford had not been enlarged, nor had there been, until very recently, much visible change; yet it was not the same village as it had been in her childhood, nor even the same one that she had returned to so little time ago.

'Times have changed' is what people said; but she wasn't sure that they knew what they meant by that any more than she did, or when exactly the changes had taken place. They stole up on you, like the child being 'he' in a playground game of 'Grandmother's Footsteps'.

As her relationship with her step-cousin William had stolen up on her. That had not been part of her plan at all, but it had 'just happened'. So had the sequence of not-so-happy events which had caused such serious upheavals in the life of the village as a whole.

She had had a curious feeling about this wedding from the moment she had first heard about it, though she couldn't then have said why. Perhaps it was that she hoped that an event so out-of-the-ordinary might mark the end of the period of tragedy, unrest and unease as a full-stop marks the end of a sentence.

Listening to the bells had somehow put her thoughts into perspective. What they boiled down to, she concluded, was that nobody with a grain of common sense could expect life to remain static, whatever the circumstances. When organic life stopped moving, it was dying if not already dead. Change, small and insidious or huge and dramatic, was inevitable and ineluctable. If one accepted it as a continuous process, one could always look forward as well as back. The end of the old had to be the beginning of the new. Another era. Whether happy or sad, or both, nobody could foretell; the only thing that anybody could be sure of was that it would be different.

Not that the bells today were telling anybody anything they didn't already know. From the moment that the news of Lucy's engagement had first leaked out, the wedding had been the main topic of conversation everywhere. Coming events in a village cast more than their shadows before them.

'Here they come,' William said, rising to greet the two people coming towards them down the aisle together. One was a small, rather frail but vivid old lady of eighty and the other a most handsome, charming, mercurial man in his early fifties; looking pleased with themselves and with each other.

Both had become very dear to Fran and William in the last couple of years. Mary Budd had been the last of the village's old 'governesses', running the one-teacher school until in the name of progress it had been closed. She had bought the tiny schoolhouse and stayed on there, continuing to do all the other things that in the past had fallen to the lot of the village schoolmistress; which in effect meant that she had kept a finger in every pie. She was loved, revered and/or feared by most of her ex-pupils, because, as she said, she was the one who knew all their secrets as well as knowing them 'inside-out, back-to-front and upside-down'. To Fran it seemed that in her indomitable little body the real soul of the old village still resided. It was she who had kept the community together during the dark days of the war and the even darker days following the end of hostilities. From the moment Fran had met her, she had been aware that Mary's friendship was a priceless gift, and when in the course of time it had been extended to include William, Fran had counted it as among her greatest blessings.

Among Mary's many functions was that of playing the church organ, not only on Sundays but whenever an organist was needed.

It had been a shock to Fran and William when Mary had come to them one day recently, worried because she no longer felt capable of playing the organ well enough for such a wedding as this was going to be. She confessed, for the first time ever, to 'feeling her age', and said she was aware of her diminishing strength and that her rheumaticky old hands couldn't cope properly with the large and splendid organ any longer. Her distress was not on her own account, but because she could not bear to let George Bridgefoot down. She had taught the bride as a child, for one thing, and for another, she had worked hand-in-glove with George in his capacity as churchwarden since the day he had taken over the office from his father.

'They want *me*,' she said, 'but I can't risk letting them down. If only there were another, more competent organist somewhere! George would have a fit at the thought of a paid stranger doing it, and I'm at my wits' end whether to say nothing and risk spoiling the wedding, or to go now and tell George he must find somebody else.'

She looked as if she might have been going to burst into tears, and William insisted that she took some brandy with her coffee; then he came up with a surprising solution.

'There is another organist,' he said, 'though I doubt if anybody but me has any inkling of it. Greg Taliaferro is as good a musician as he is an artist, and the organ is his greatest love of all. He must be terribly out of practice, but there's time to remedy that. I suggest you say nothing, and let them think you are going to do it. If you feel well enough on the day, go through with it; but if Greg were there to take over in an emergency, nobody need ever know.'

Fran was as surprised by William's disclosure about his brother-in-law as Mary was. They had discovered Greg to be a pianist, but somehow since he had come to live among them, his many talents had been kept like wartime black-market goods under the counter, and only brought out one at a time.

'Would Greg agree?' Fran asked, a bit dubiously.

William did not mince his words. 'You know him,' he said. 'We misjudged him because we'd been given wrong preconceptions of him. What you mean is "Will Jess let him?" I'll do all I can to see that she does. My guess is that he'll love it.'

In the event, it had worked out marvellously, on more grounds than one.

Mary had been seen going up to the organ and playing as the guests assembled. Nobody had noticed Greg at her side. Mary had still been playing while the registers were being signed, but when Wagner's triumphant Wedding March had thundered out, Fran and William were in no doubt who was at the console.

As at all village weddings, the uninvited sightseers had gone out first and were now lining the path from the church door to the gate; but the procession of grey-suited men and their ladies was a long one, and Fran had begun to wonder what Greg would do when he came to the end of the march from *Lohengrin*, because it always seemed such a dismal anticlimax for the tail-enders to have to shuffle out meekly to some feeble voluntary like dispirited travellers who had missed the boat. She needn't have worried on this particular occasion. Greg had let the last notes fade into silence, and then almost immediately had set the church trembling again with Mozart's 'Exultate Jubilate'.

'Well done, both of you,' said William, as the two organists reached them. 'We'd better go, or Jess will be wondering what's happened to Greg.'

'It's my fault we've been so long,' Mary said apologetically. 'I've played for far too many weddings here to be hampered by tears at the usual places – but you should have seen me when Greg cut unexpectedly to the "Allelujah". I was so sodden that he had to mop me up with his handkerchief, as if I were six again. It's usually me who has to do the mopping up. I found it a very pleasant change.'

'So did I,' said Greg, and he stopped in the porch to kiss her. Then they all went out into the sunshine, while the bells continued to topple riotous glad sound down on their heads from above.

2

That Fran and William should be attending this wedding as guests at all was one of the sort of changes Fran had been thinking about. In pre-war days, there had still been the remnants of a social hierarchy that had kept 'the old squire' and his family very slightly cut off from the rest, in the same way that his house, Benedict's, stood a little apart from the village.

That was no longer the case, for which the couple from Benedict's were grateful. They had to thank Mary Budd for their re-integration into the social life of the village. By the time Mary had persuaded Fran to attend her annual fundraising effort for the Save the Children Fund, which that year was to take the form of a social get-together, William had also been very much in the picture. It had been on the way home from Mary's 'horkey', that wonderful evening spent together in George Bridgefoot's restored tithe barn, that their love for each other had caught both Fran and William off guard. She had held him off for another whole year, all the same, because he still had a legal wife. The code of 'honour' that had until that evening prevented him from declaring his love for her had continued to exert on her an even tighter grip of pre-war morality simply because she was a woman. The situation hadn't changed since then, but they had. They no longer hid the beacon of their love for each other from anybody, but let it flare out to be seen and recognized for what it was.

That horkey that they had attended together had been a wonderful evening, and it was there in the barn that she had got to know the Bridgefoots and the Thackerays. She had been made aware that night that with the death of the squirearchy, it was the old-established farming families who were now the acknowledged leaders of the village community.

Then, in the last two years, there had been such a sequence of upheaval and tragedy that nothing was quite the same as it had been. It was as if the gods had managed to drop the jigsaw puzzle that had been the Old Swithinford she knew, breaking up the familiar picture and scattering the pieces. It was only now beginning to be reassembled, with some bits – like the entire Thackeray family – irrevocably lost and replaced by new pieces not yet shaped well enough to fit comfortably against those that were left.

With the Thackerays gone, the Bridgefoot family were left

standing among the few other families on the top rungs of the social ladder.

Fran liked the Bridgefoots a lot, especially George, the head of the clan. He was still the sort of man the word 'farmer' conjured up for her, as unchanged from his yeoman forebears as the church itself, though like the church, still at the centre of all that went on. She didn't really know the members of his family as well as she knew George, and had never met Lucy at all. She hadn't expected to be invited, but was as interested as everybody else in the details of her coming wedding, as they emerged bit by bit. As it happened, Fran had a private 'hotline' to them, because Sophie Wainwright, the childhood playmate who had remained unmarried and 'did' for her and William, being as much a part of their household as the furniture, had an elder sister, Thirzah, who happened to be the wife of George Bridgefoot's right-hand man, Daniel Bates.

Sophie was a close contemporary of Fran and William, and when young they had all played together in the happy democracy of childhood, in which social distinctions are adult impositions upon the rights of children to choose their own friends. Sophie's mother, widowed Kezia, had been housekeeper for old Squire Wagstaffe, and in dragonlike fashion had accepted as part of her job the responsibility for his grandchildren when they were dumped on him for long periods by parents either serving abroad or taking long holidays. It was only when Kezia considered that any of her own brood were in danger of overstepping the boundary of 'what was right' that any of the children concerned were aware of such things as 'social distinctions'.

When Sophie had come to work at Benedict's for Fran, taking up, as it were, her dead mother's role again, it would have been difficult to say which of the two women had felt most blessed by good fortune. Their relationship with each other was very much the same as it had been in childhood, except that both now knew how much they depended on each other.

Fran had enjoyed Sophie's gleanings about the forthcoming wedding as much as Sophie enjoyed passing them on.

'Thirz' says as 'ow Lucy's man's father is a lord, or some

such,' Sophie reported. 'And 'im as she's marryin' is one o' them sor' o' doctors as looks after people who ain't quite right in the'r 'eads.'

'Psychiatrists?' Fran hazarded.

'Ah, that's the word, I'm sure. I can't say as it seems right to me, though, for a farmer's gel like Lucy Bridgefoot to be marrying a doctor, let alone one as is the son of a lord. Time was when farmers married farmers and labourers married labourers and such as you married your own sort. We all knowed where we stood then, as you might say. But now nobody knows who anybody is, and it ain't 'ealthy, to my way o' thinking. The Thack'rays would still ha' been 'ere, and that there fire as killed five folk altogether would never 'ave 'appened if Loddy Thack'ray hadn't gone and married that stuck-up wicked woman as 'ad only been a barmaid till then. I don't 'old with such goings on.'

'I think you'll have to get used to it, all the same,' Fran answered, wondering how she could find a chink in Sophie's set ideas to get through. 'The war changed everything. We all had to get through the war together, and when it was over we sort of started afresh. Nowadays it's *what* people are that matters, not *who* they are. If Lucy's husband is a good doctor, it doesn't matter if his father is a duke or a dustman, does it?'

Sophie sniffed. 'Well, you may think so, but I don't,' she said. '"Birds of a feather flock together", as they say, and so they ought. Like you and 'im, I mean.' In Sophie's vocabulary ''im' meant William, as ''Im Above' meant the Almighty. 'If you had told me as you were intending to live out o' wedlock with Brian Bridgefoot or Tom Fairey, you wouldn't ha' ketched me a-coming to work for you, be we never so much playmates when we was little.'

'Why ever not? Brian's a very nice man, as far as I know, quite well educated and I daresay a lot better off than William will ever be. Besides, farmers are top people nowadays. If William hadn't been about I might have done a lot worse than Brian Bridgefoot, I think.'

Sophie was quite unruffled by Fran's teasing, which she recognized for what it was. 'Ah! Well, as long as the Bridge-foots don't get too much above theirselves over this wedding,

I daresay it may turn out all right. But money don't make gentlemen o' folks as weren't born that way. You can't make a silk purse out of a sow's ear, no matter 'ow you try. And money as comes easy, goes easy. Specially wi' farmers. It's usually 'obnails to 'obnails again in four generations. Them as lives longest'll see most. Not that I wish George and 'is fam'ly any 'arm. Thirz' has ketched sight o' Lucy's doctor, and says 'e looks easy-going, like, and not a bit stuck up.'

She left abruptly with a reproving glance at Fran, as if accusing her of wasting their time gossiping. It always amused Fran. She thought for the umpteenth time how prescient Kezia had been to name this particular daughter Sophia. Every crystal of verbal wisdom gained from generations of folk experience seemed to have lodged in Sophie's head, so that an apt aphorism was always ready on the tip of her tongue.

More details of the wedding plans were revealed as the days went by, some of which Sophie gave scant approval to. Fran learned, for instance, that the reception was not to be held in the Bridgefoot house, but at the Franksbridge Hotel, which had been recently opened by the syndicate that had bought up the de ffranksbridge estate, where the disastrous fire had been.

'Seems the way we're all'us done things afore ain't good enough for them London folk,' Sophie said. 'But they are going to have a proper do in George's barn at night, when them posh folk have gome 'ome. I know that's right, 'cos Molly Bridgefoot asked Thirz' to be responsible for seein' to the refreshments, and Thirz' told me as I'd better 'old meself ready to 'elp 'er.'

Fran was conscious of a stab of disappointment that she wouldn't be there in the barn this time. She could recall every moment of the evening of Mary's horkey. She knew it could never be repeated – but then, who was to say it couldn't be bettered?

She was still sitting rather wistfully wishing she could look forward to finding out when Sophie returned with another handful of gleanings she had forgotten to deliver. 'She's heving four bridesmaids, Marge Bridgefoot's twins and two from 'is side about the same age. And young Charles, and Robert

Fairey, and that there other boy o' Jane 'Adley's is going to be ushers – or some such word. I thought as a usher were one o' them gals with a flashlight as showed you to your seat in the pictures, but I'm sure that's what Thirz' said. And she said as they are all going to wear the same sort o' clothes as the men – all dressed in mourning suits, she said.'

Fran showed her surprise. 'Of course – I hadn't thought about that. But naturally the bridegroom's family would expect it to be a formal-dress occasion.'

'What's that then? I couldn't make it out, and I said so. You'd expect mourning suits to be for funerals, not for weddings. It don't make no sense to me.'

'Oh, it isn't that sort of mourning. It's what men used to wear in the morning, I think. Special sort of suits with tailed coats and top hats.'

'Lawks!' said Sophie. 'Well then there ain't no sense in it. The weddin's going to be at two o'clock in the afternoon. I should never ha' expected George Bridgefoot would ha' been party to such foolery as that.'

As it happened, Sophie was very near the mark. She had a most uncanny knack of hitting the nail on the head, sometimes. George had been coerced into agreeing to it only with reluctance.

3

The graveyard was proof that there had been many generations of Bridgefoots in Old Swithinford, land, lore and custom being handed down from father to son as in a timeless game of 'Pass the Parcel'.

George, the present holder, at sixty-seven was still hale and hearty, healthy and handsome. He stood six foot two in his socks, weighed fifteen stone, and was as brown as a berry and still as light on his feet as a cat. He was also as contented a man as could have been found in five counties, more than satisfied with what life had offered him so far. He was an old-fashioned Christian, given to counting his many blessings.

He was doing exactly that, with his pipe in his mouth and his slippered feet up on the kitchen table on the Sunday evening set aside for the family conference to arrange Lucy's wedding. It was just like Lucy to drop such a bombshell on them: not just that she was getting married, but that her husband to be was 'a somebody', well-known and rising in his own right, as well as being the son of a very distinguished surgeon who had been knighted in recognition of his skill. But then Lucy was different, and always had been. She had brought her fiancé to meet them and departed again happily leaving all the wedding arrangements in their hands. Or so George had been led to believe.

He loved to sit as he was doing now, and ruminate. He had only been back living in the Old Glebe where he had been born for a little more than a year. That was one of the changes that had occurred during the upheaval caused by the fire which had destroyed the ancient Hall, the seat of the de ffranksbridge family. The ruined estate of the only aristocrat left in the village, who had died in the fire, had been bought by a syndicate under the direction of a go-getter called Eric Choppen. Where the hall had been there now stood a new hotel, and what land around it had been too poor and neglected for farming was being gradually turned into a modern sports centre. The syndicate had bought up every bit of property they could lay their hands on, tearing up hedges and other familiar landmarks, and turning tiny tumbledown cottages into chocolate-box type residences with all mod cons for holiday-makers. Choppen himself had taken over the complex of buildings that had been the home of George's dearest friends, the Thackeray family, and had restored the Elizabethan farmhouse to a thing of beauty to match what the old squire's granddaughter had already done to his eighteenth-century 'mansion', Benedict's. Then when the old Rector had died, Choppen had bought the Old Rectory, stripped it of its ugly nineteenth-century additions, and given it back its graceful Queen Anne lines. Next, he had cast eyes on the Old Glebe – but no amount of money could have tempted George to sell, even if money had meant anything whatsoever to him now, which it didn't. His bank balance was already so overwhelmingly large that it embarrassed him.

But the offer to buy had given George ideas. There was no reason why he shouldn't restore the Old Glebe House himself, as he had already restored the tithe barn. It had meant asking his son, Brian, and Rosemary, Brian's wife, to exchange residences with himself and his wife Molly, which they had done willingly. In fact, Temperance Farm, which lay out of the village next to the old de ffranksbridge estate, had suited the younger couple better. And so it was that George had come back home to the house where he had been born. It gave him a lot of pleasure to think that if the Old Glebe was not as big as some of the other old houses, it was just as beautiful and undoubtedly the oldest.

Once, when George was a boy, the then Rector had told him that when it had been built four hundred years ago, it had belonged to the church. He didn't doubt the Rector's word, but he knew himself to be the fourth generation of Bridgefoots to be born there. His very first memory was of bottle-feeding a lamb on the worn old flagstones he had insisted on being left *in situ*, when he had been little more than a baby himself.

He had loved the old house then, and he loved it now. It was still a collection of higgledy-piggledy rooms with no apparent plan or purpose relating to the whole. You always had to go either up or down a couple of steps to get from one room to the next, and no room could boast right-angled corners. All the floors sloped and all the ceilings sagged. No piece of furniture would stand without wedges, and any standing against a wall was made doubly secure by a large wooden peg driven into the plaster through a hole in its back made a-purpose. His grandfather's old long-case clock was still both hung and wedged because the kitchen floor sloped so drunkenly, in spite of all its new appointments.

They had agreed to the wedding being early in September, by which time harvest should be well advanced if not completely gathered in. The corn was already ripening in the ear, so it was just as well that the arrangements for the wedding should be started early. Molly had told him the others would not be here till the evening, so he gave himself up happily to looking both forwards and backwards. There was a lot of pleasure in both.

Times had been very hard for farmers when he was young. Once the First War was over the country had soon forgotten its debt to food-producers, and things had slid rapidly downhill towards the agricultural depression of the late twenties and early thirties.

It had been hard, too, to be young and thinking of marriage. His parents had been almost at the end of their tether when he had married Molly Pinner of Temperance Farm. Depressions don't stop people from falling in love, though in those days conditions did make youngsters think twice before settling down and saddling themselves with a brood of children. But he had married Molly and never for a moment regretted it. Their first home had been one of his father's tumbledown stud-and-mud cottages, and there their first child, Brian, had been born, followed swiftly by Marjorie. By that time, the depression was even worse. Molly's father was already in deep water, and neighbouring farmers were going down like ninepins. It was clear that he and Molly couldn't go on producing children at the rate they had begun to. How different in every way things would be now for his only grandson, Charles! In those days, their only answer had been to ration love-making to a minimum and even then be so circumspect about it that it took away half the pleasure. George smiled at the thought. Little minx – she had wanted him every bit as much as he had wanted her.

They still had only two children when Molly's father gave up his struggle against adversity, and died of hard work and worry. Molly inherited a quarter-share of the almost but not quite bankrupt Temperance Farm.

It was then that George had made the daring move that had proved in the long run to have been such a wise one. Against all advice and miserable foreboding, he had borrowed money, and taken the plunge to buy Temperance Farm. His parents stayed on at the fast-crumbling Old Glebe House, and he and Molly with their two children moved into the big

Victorian farmhouse at Temperance. When the Second World War loomed, and the country turned again to the farmers it had neglected so long, his father was dead and he well established with two farms both in good heart to take advantage of the boom.

And boom it had been, with a vengeance; what was more, things were still booming. Money had bred money. Every member of his family could now think in thousands of pounds where he had counted shillings.

Brian had been fifteen and still been at Swithinford Grammar School when Lucy was born, having won himself a scholarship there from Mary Budd's little village school. Marjorie at fourteen had just left school, and was able to stop at home and help her mother. In wartime, she was more use to the country there than she would have been anywhere else. Labour was difficult to get, and women had to work in the fields.

Once the air-raids began in earnest, men who had been out hard at work all day were expected to be out all night as well on Home Guard or Civil Defence duties. The stupidity of the bureaucracy that demanded of George that he leave his own isolated stackyard full of precious grain to go fire-watching on the roof of Swithinford's bank inflamed his normally placid spirit to furious anger and even revolt.

One night when Hitler's *Luftwaffe* pilots, bound for London, had decided to jettison their load of incendiary bombs and make for home while the going was good, he had from his vantage point on the roof of the bank seen a blaze that could only be on his farm. He had not waited for any permission to desert his post, but grabbed his old bike and pedalled off towards the blaze.

It was only in a haystore on the edge of the farm, and swiftly extinguished by the four of them armed with a stirrup pump. At Molly's suggestion he had then gone into the house with the others for a cup of cocoa and a wash before returning to duty.

Back inside the blacked-out house they had realized that they were all as black as Newgate's knocker with sweat, grime and soot. George and the two youngsters made do with a good wash, but Molly went to have a quick bath. George was still drinking his cocoa when she came back fresh, rosy, sweet-smelling and irresistible. He followed her upstairs, and the result was Lucy. It never failed to amuse him that his dereliction of duty had never even been noticed.

From the moment of her birth, Lucy had been different. She was extremely beautiful with brains to match, and, having made up her mind at a very early age to become a nurse, had carved her way without fuss to the large London teaching hospital where she still worked. Where Marjorie had been entirely content to follow the same path as her mother and grandmother, Lucy certainly hadn't. She belonged to the twentieth century. They had all missed her terribly when she had first gone to live in London, but by then all of them, even her parents, had affairs of their own to see to that made them forget how rare her visits home were becoming.

Now they knew the reason why: Dr Alex Marland's attractions were greater than Old Swithinford's. None of them blamed her, and all of them took to Alex. As a baby she had been welcomed by Brian and Marjorie without embarrassment or rancour, and it said a good deal for their family unity that they still regarded her as something special, to Brian and Marjorie more like a member of the next generation than their sibling.

Apart from the late advent of Lucy, other matters in the family had proceeded according to precedent. At twenty-three, Brian had married. The war was over, and prosperity had returned. Financially, there was no reason why Brian should not marry, and for other reasons it made a lot of sense. If anything about it surprised George, it was Brian's choice of a bride.

Brian was not as tall as his father, but quite as handsome, and better educated, with the slight social advantage his years at the grammar school had given him. In fact he was at twenty-three undeniably the most eligible young bachelor in the district, who could have taken his pick from among the daughters of half a dozen up-and-coming wealthy farmers. But his choice had fallen on Rosemary Palmer, who, though born and bred on a farm, had never entered the lists against the others for his attention. She was the same age as Brian, and as comely a girl as any, with a tallish, neat figure that gave George pleasure to contemplate. He disapproved of the craze for women to be, as he put it, 'just straight up-an'-down like a two-by-four plank viewed sideways'. Rosemary had a fresh healthy look about her that owed nothing to make-up, and blonde curly hair that required no expensive hairdressing to make it look artlessly fashionable. She was pleasant and amiable, but always wore an air of timidity that puzzled George. At the least sign of any disagreement or hassle, her cornflower blue eyes darkened with apprehension, beautiful to look at but painful to witness.

When Brian began to press for a very hasty wedding, George had jumped angrily to the wrong conclusion, and tackled Brian about it, because his own ideas about pre-marital sex were on a par with Sophie Wainwright's. He had not expected his son to disgrace him by following the lax ways the war had brought in its train.

Brian's affronted reply had been blunt and honest. His father was way off beam. His only reason for wanting to marry in haste was to get Rosemary out of the clutches of the cantankerous old bitch of an aunt who had been brought in to keep her brother's house and look after his children when their mother had died. Rosemary, the youngest, had then been three. She had lived in fear and terror of the bitter termagant all her life, and did so still. The urgency now was that Rosemary's father had cancer. He had never been able to stand up to his sister, who was making it very clear that she expected to be left everything so as to continue after his death exactly as before. Rosemary's four brothers had been driven away by their aunt's unbearable domination, but Rosemary had been left like a mouse in the claws of a cat.

'She's frightened to death of the old bitch,' Brian had said. 'If I don't get her away quick, she'll never get out of the old gorgon's clutches. She expects Rosy to stay single and look after her – she says so. Rosy won't, if I have anything to do with it. Once she's my wife, things will be different. When I went to see her last night I found her crying because her aunt had called her names I won't repeat when she saw my car draw

19

up, and then had slapped her face in front of me. I'm going to rescue my girl from her if it's the last thing I do – and I'll never have that old besom over my doorstep then.'

None of these disclosures was exactly news to George or Molly, who were well aware of Miss Palmer's reputation as a cruel martinet over her helpless little charges. It was the extent to which she had carried it on now that they were grown up that had shocked them. They agreed that Brian must marry his girl as soon as he could, and they took her to their hearts. In consequence, Rosemary adored all the Bridgefoot family with the pent-up love she had never been able to shower on anybody else.

George had, however, felt he ought to warn his son that, much as Rosemary might love him, she would never be able to shake off the obligation to her aunt that twenty-three years of bullying and brain-washing had engrained in her. 'Let Rosemary play it her own way,' he had advised. 'She won't be happy if she feels guilty.' He had been right about that.

The only fault either George or Molly had ever found with their daughter-in-law was that she had never produced more than one child. As George had been the only son of his father, and Brian of his, so Charles was now the only male Bridgefoot to carry on the name. It was too frail a thread to rely on, but that was how it was.

Marjorie had not pleased either of her parents with her choice of husband. He was of smallholder stock, big and broad and handsome, crafty rather than clever and lacking the warm family feeling that was such a strong characteristic of the Bridgefoots. He had little education and no culture, despising that he was born into and never bothering to acquire any other. His saving grace was that he apparently loved Marjorie to the point of wanting to own her, body, mind and spirit. She seemed satisfied, and with George's financial help they had soon made the farmer grade. She had been no more prolific than her brother's wife, her brood consisting only of twin girls who were now seventeen.

'Here they are, Mother,' George said. 'Both lots together.'

4

They settled down round the kitchen table.

Brian at forty-six was not quite the handsome young man he had been when Rosemary had married him, but he was still a fine specimen of the prosperous farmer type. Not being quite so tall as his father, the weight he had put on made him look a little too thick-set, but otherwise he was a Bridgefoot all over. Except, perhaps, that his face was not so open and amiable as George's.

There was an air of discontent and frustration about him that George never wore. Part of this was occasioned by his feeling of always having to defer to George, who was still the boss, and not nearly as 'with it' in terms of modern agricultural methods as Brian could have wished. With regard to such things as ever-more powerful implements, chemical fertilizers and weedkillers, George had doubts and proceeded cautiously. It got under Brian's skin most when he was in Vic Gifford's company, because Vic operated at the opposite extreme to George, besides being entirely lacking in the matter of tact.

Brian had cherished a secret hope that when he reached sixty-five, George would retire and hand the running of their farms over to him; but such a thing had never occurred to George. Bridgefoots went on till they died. George looked good for at least another twenty years, by which time Brian himself would be sixty-five, and Charles probably trying to elbow him out. He was doomed, he thought, always to be pig-in-the-middle between his father and his son.

That was another of his unspoken grievances. His only son was the apple of his grandfather's eye, and the bond between them was mutually strong. To young Charles, there was no one quite like Grandad. He had found the older man more patient, more understanding, and far less embarrassing to talk to than his father. Consequently, Brian was jealous – of both of them. To do him justice, he tried hard not to let it show, though Rosemary was aware of it and did her utmost to soothe him and play down any difficulties the jealousy caused. She didn't share it because she loved her parents-in-law too much to deny them any part of Charles. Having endured the loveless childhood that had been her lot, she thought Brian's jealousy was rather selfish and a bit silly, but had far too much sense to take sides.

She, too, had put on a little weight, and was a typical example of a well-to-do farmer's wife. She was looking forward to the evening ahead, partly because Marjorie would be there. They had always got on well together.

Marjorie was tall, like all her family. She had inherited her father's placid temperament, which in the circumstances was a good thing, because life with Vic was certainly not all honey. It was a pity she had not made the grammar-school grade, because her intelligence was quite as high as her brother's, and her cultural sensitivity greater.

The chance to meet others of her own kind might have made all the difference to her choice of a husband. When she had first married Vic, she had played down her own likes and dislikes, as well her natural accomplishments, lest she should make him feel inferior. Her love of reading, for example; a cheap daily paper was the limit of his acquaintance with the printed word, and he resented her giving attention to a book instead of to him.

Her self-denial had been lost on him. He *was* of inferior mentality, knew that he was, and like most others with an inferiority complex, bragged and blustered and blew his own trumpet to counter it to such an extent that he made her cringe. The more he showed off, the quieter, more self-contained and dignified she became in contrast. She was not unhappy, because she had much to be happy about (including her beautiful twin daughters), but she missed the touches of the Bridgefoot family's 'natural' sort of culture. Dealing with Vic, always trying to keep the peace and subduing her conversation and activities to match his had made her somewhat sharp of tongue. The only way of getting through Vic's self-satisfaction, when she could stand it no longer, was to say what she had to say in very blunt fashion. But this happened only very occasionally. She preferred peace and quietness to rows. The truth remained that she was often ashamed of Vic, and hated herself for being so. She was consequently a little on edge tonight, because she guessed how he would react to talk about Alex and his titled connections. She could only hope that he would not aggravate either her father or Brian too much.

George smoked placidly, quite willing for Brian to take the chair, as it were, as he seemed anxious to do.

'It'll have to be a formal dress affair,' Brian said. 'Morning suits and top hats and all that.'

'For a village wedding? You won't get me into a top hat,' George countered at once, showing his surprise. 'Whatever would folks think?'

'We've got to keep our end up, for Lucy's sake,' said Marjorie. 'It isn't as if you can't afford it, Dad. I mean, considering who she's marrying ... making such a good match ...'

George cut her short. 'Who says it's a good match? We don't know that yet, do we? Being a doctor and having a father with a handle to his name may seem like a good catch, but a good match is different. I don't care who he is or what he's got or hasn't got as long as he loves her and she loves him. Such as him don't marry farmers' daughters very often. I can't help wondering if it's only because he fell for her pretty face and found he can't get her into bed without marrying her first. But it don't alter the fact that she is only a farmer's daughter, and if he wants to marry her so bad he'll have to do it our way.'

Brian and Marjorie were both looking uncomfortable, and Brian suddenly raised his voice. 'Look here, Dad. It's time you came to terms with things as they are, not as they used to be. We all know, because you've told us often enough, that when you were young such farmers as us crept about touching their caps to the parson and the squire – but times have changed. Any bowing and scraping these days is done to folks with money. That means folks like us. If you won't do what Lucy wants, Alex's folk will arrange the wedding in London. She told me so. So please yourself.'

George was considerably taken aback by Brian's tone, and vexed by what he said. Looking round the group, he saw at once what the true situation was. They were in league against him, and having guessed what line he would take, they had already got everything arranged among themselves. This meeting was just a pretence, to let him think he was in the driving seat. They had probably done what they thought best, but he was riled. They weren't going to 'come one over him' quite as easily as all that!

'It used to be thought common to brag about money,' he said pointedly. 'You wouldn't have seen old Squire Wagstaffe throwing money about just to look big.'

Vic snorted in derision. 'From all I've heard about him, he hadn't got a thruppenny-bit to throw at a beggar. All swank and nothing to back it with.'

Marjorie kicked Vic under the table; George held his tongue only so as not to upset Marjorie.

'Why don't you let me see to it all, Dad?' Brian suggested, more or less taking it for granted. 'There's such a lot to be thought of – reception, guest list, invitations, menu . . .' Faced with his businesslike and purposeful son, George decided to give in rather than risk further unpleasantness.

'Is that all right with you, Mother?' he asked Molly.

She nodded, looking a little wistful. 'All except not having a party when Lucy and Alex have gone. It won't seem like a wedding just for us all to come straight home from the hotel. More like a Women's Institute meeting.'

'Well, ain't we going to have some sort of jollification?' George said. 'What about people like Daniel and Thirzah, and all the rest as have known Lucy since she was born? They won't expect to be sent straight home after the meal's over.'

Brian looked exasperatedly at him. 'Don't be daft, Dad,' he said. 'You can't mix people like them with Alex's folk. It won't be the sort of wedding they'd expect to be invited to.'

They were on dangerous ground now.

'Oh?' said George. 'Who's going to pay for all this show, then? Me, I suppose. So I shall invite who I like. I ain't going to have it said that because we've made a bit of money lately and Lucy's marrying above us, I can spit in the face of folk who've helped me to make it. If Dan and Thirzah ain't good enough for 'em, me and Mother ain't, either. And if Lucy's

24

ashamed of us, let his posh folk hold the wedding where they like. We shan't be there.'

Rosemary had been sitting quietly, anxious-eyed because she had feared just such an outburst. She dreaded any disagreement between her husband and her father-in-law. Now she leaned forward and spoke soothingly.

'I can't see why we can't have both,' she said. 'Let's have the wedding and the reception just as Brian said for Alex's lot, and then have a party of our own in the evening for the rest. They wouldn't want to go to the reception with all the London people. We could have a sort of horkey and a lot of fun.'

Brian's brow cleared. He was regarding his wife with open approval and admiration, as if he was seeing her for the first time.

'Bravo, Rosy!' he said. 'That's a good idea. What do you say, Dad? We could easily clear the barn out.'

Everybody was at ease again. George lit his pipe, and sat back to listen while they discussed things he knew nothing about. He was interested in the 'official' guest list. It included people he would not have presumed to ask, like the two from Benedict's and the new tenant of Castle Hill Farm, whom he had not said more than half a dozen words to, yet. Well, he didn't mind being neighbourly, and he was secretly glad about Fran and William being included. Choppen and his daughter? That did surprise him. He began to understand what his son meant about 'things being different'.

He learned that Choppen's daughter, who ran a London clothes business, had been commissioned to design a model wedding-dress and four bridesmaids' dresses. That would cost him a pretty penny, he guessed, but nothing was too good for his 'little Lucy'.

Everything was going so smoothly now that Molly thought it was time to think about supper, which she had set ready in the next room.

They had gathered up their bits of paper, and begun to chat amongst themselves, when a chance remark detonated the hidden unexploded bomb they had all been so careful till now to leave undisturbed.

Lucy and Alex had been living together as man and wife for at least two years already. Her father and mother had not been made aware of it.

The moment it was out, the others all held their breath to see what effect it would have on George. They had feared this moment all along, knowing how much it would upset him.

They were not prepared for blazing fury. He turned first white, then deep purple, as if he were about to have a stroke. His hands clenched and his neck swelled. He brought a huge fist crashing down on the table, and turned to face them all.

'If that's the truth – and I can see it is – you can forget your plans for any wedding. You all know very well what I think about such things! I never thought to hear it about one o' my own children . . . And you all knowed, and kept it from me? Why do they want to get married now? A baby on the way? And you thought you'd make a fool of me by letting me take her down the aisle of my own church in that condition? Not likely! She can keep her posh man and her disgrace to herself. I don't want anything more to do with her . . . And as for him . . . if I had him here this minute I'd break his bloody neck.' He swayed, sat down heavily, and put his face in his hands. Molly ran to him, terribly afraid. Rosemary, trying to stem tears, put the kettle on. Brian went for a brandy bottle.

Surprisingly, it was Brian who made the first attempt to conciliate him.

'Dad, don't take it so hard. You know Lucy. She's always gone her own way. And she isn't having a baby. They're getting married now because they want one. Don't blame her that you didn't know before, either. She wanted you to know, but we judged it was better not to tell you and Mother. If it hadn't lasted, you need never have known, but it has. She's not the sort of girl to be sleeping round with every Tom, Dick and Harry, and you know it. They love each other. They're right for each other – like the two up at Benedict's. You don't seem to hold it against them. Is there any difference?'

'Yes,' George said, looking his son in the eye. 'Lucy's my daughter. I shan't be asked to take Fran Catherwood up the aisle in a white wedding dress, in front of all my friends and neighbours. Going against what everybody knows I think about the way the young carry on these days. Pretending Lucy to be what she ain't, seeing as she's been living in sin ... would you do it? Or you, Vic? How are you going to feel if your twins start sleeping with their boyfriends any minute now? Brian hasn't got any daughters. He'd think different if he had.'

Brian was keeping admirably calm. 'I don't think it would matter quite so much to me as it does to you, Dad,' he said. 'It's the way things are, now. Look, if you mean what you say, let me take your place and give her away. And if it comes to that, and you won't have anything to do with it, I'll pay for everything as well. Rosemary and I would love Lucy to be married from our house, shouldn't we, Rosy?'

It might have ended peaceably there if Vic had not shoved his oar in, asserting that his twins had been too well-schooled for anything of the sort.

It was not a wise remark, either under the circumstances or because the Giffords as a clan had a reputation far from spotless. The look George gave him would have felled a less ox-like man, but the wrath he aroused fell on Brian.

'Don't aggravate me any more than you need,' George said. 'You may be a big bug in your own eyes, but let me tell you that nobody's going to take my place as head of this family while I'm above ground! You seem to think a bit of money can buy you everything, but when you've lived as long as I have you'll find there are some things no amount of money can buy – like self-respect, for one thing.'

Marjorie was still smarting at her husband's stupidity, and wanted the issue settled.

'Then let Brian do as he says, and give Lucy away,' she said.

George, looking like a bull at bay, was distracted by the sound of Molly's quiet sobbing.

'What is Lucy intending to wear?' he asked. They were all nonplussed by this apparent *non sequitur*.

'Don't cry, Mother. You can tell Lucy from me that I'll do everything she wants as long as she don't wear a white frock and a veil. To folk like Sophie Wainwright, they mean the bride's a virgin. I shall give my daughter away myself, but I won't be made to look a liar or a hypocrite. Let's go and have our supper.'

Brian and Marjorie fell in together. 'Poor old Dad,' Brian said. 'That was a facer for him. He's as out of date as a horse-drawn single furrow plough. Lucy'll be a lot happier that he knows, anyway.'

'We all shall,' Marjorie said. 'We can begin to look forward to the wedding now.'

5

William and Fran were breakfasting together when the postman delivered two identical invitations to the wedding, one addressed to each. They glanced across at each other with amusement.

'We obviously caused them some embarrassment,' William said. 'I suppose Sophie still deigning to come here and "do" for us can on occasion throw a cloak of spotless innocence over us which we no longer warrant, praise be to the gods.'

'I think they are just being tactfully practical,' Fran answered, 'and I don't care how they've invited us as long as they have. I was afraid they wouldn't. I shall have to go and buy myself a new outfit for it, though. Will you come with me and help to choose it? You could see about hiring your funeral suit at the same time.'

He looked at her over a slice of toast dripping with butter and marmalade.

'My dear girl, I should love to – and you know it or you wouldn't have asked. On one condition, though – that I'm allowed to pay for it. A man is allowed to claim conjugal rights by law, I believe.'

'Fancy that!' she said. 'Are you complaining that you don't get your conjugal rights? If you are, I must have been doing a lot of fantasizing. Maybe I ought to consult the bridegroom. He is a psychiatrist.'

He was up and out of his chair, still holding his toast, and urging her towards the bottom of the stairs, before she could escape.

'Stop it, you idiot,' she said. 'I refuse to be seduced at this hour of the morning. I want my breakfast – and besides, you're all sticky.'

'Sorry,' he said, sitting down again and wiping his hands on his napkin. 'It just seemed an invitation too good to miss.'

'It's a working day, Professor,' she said, 'and you have to leave in ten minutes. So if it will settle the question, I will accept your kind offer and let you both choose and pay for my wedding outfit.'

He helped himself to more toast, eyeing her quizzically. 'Do you really suppose that I have managed to reach my advanced age in an outpost of tradition like Cambridge without having to buy myself a morning suit?' he asked. 'I hope you haven't got shares in Moss Bros, because they won't get a penny out of me for many a year to come unless you deliberately fatten me up so that I can no longer get into it.'

'But William – where is it? I've never seen it, so it never occurred to me that you owned one.'

'Left it in my rooms. Whoever would have supposed I should ever need such a thing in Old Swithinford? For heaven's sake remind me to take it to be cleaned. I can't remember the last time I wore it. Are we invited to the barn in the evening as well?'

'Yes. Sophie told me that if we were invited at all it would include the evening. We shall have to come home and change for that. Won't it be fun? Hurry up, you're going to be late again.'

'You're anxious to be rid of me,' he said, leisurely making his preparations for departure, which included coming back twice to kiss her.

Once committed to being guests, they had found themselves more and more involved in the wedding. First there had been Mary's dilemma about playing the organ and William's suggestion that he should try to persuade his step-sister's husband to oblige.

It had proved a little more difficult than William had

expected. Jess was Fran's first cousin, and from the time they had all three been children together there had been an element of 'Two's company, three none' about their relationship. After the war, Fran widowed, William deserted, and Jess marooned on a Scottish island with what had appeared to be an entirely feckless husband, nobody could have possibly foreseen the circumstances that now prevailed. William had been the financial mainstay which had kept Jess and Greg afloat. When, at his urging, they had at last come south again, Jess had not been put into the picture that he and Fran had found their first love for each other stronger than ever for all the years they had been parted, so that when she discovered that they had yielded to it and were living openly at Benedict's as man and wife, she had been jealous to the point of losing her common sense, of which in the ordinary way she had plenty. Though the matter had been resolved, she and Fran had never been quite so close again.

Jess and her husband had been as near to destitute as made no difference when they had come back to Old Swithinford. Their return had more or less coincided with the purchase of the old de ffranksbridge estate by the syndicate of which Mr Choppen was the managing director, and which planned to turn the village upside down with modern methods of farming and tarted-up cottages to promote tourism. The scheme had been a death-blow, quite literally, to some people, and to traditional village life as the older inhabitants had known it. Fran had been as outraged as anybody by the scheme, though it did not affect her personally.

But when Jess, rescued by William and given shelter by Fran, had accepted a job as secretary to the man being held responsible for the upheaval, it had been taken very hard by a lot of the indigenous that one of the squire's grandchildren should have 'gone over to the enemy' so willingly.

It had certainly become a bone of contention between the two women, and for some time their relationship had been more than strained; but 'blood is thicker than water', and in any case they had both made efforts to bury their antagonism for William's sake. They were still fond of each other, but wary.

Especially, as it had turned out, where Greg was concerned. Far from the feeble failure of a man she had been expecting, Fran had found him one of the most mercurial charmers she had ever met, who had, given time and opportunity, proved himself to be a creative artist after Fran's own heart. He had simply dovetailed himself into the family, as far as Fran and William were concerned; but the situation was not as solidly stable as its four legs might have made it because Jess had a streak of possessive jealousy that was always a danger.

The members of the syndicate had learned a lot of salutary lessons, and changed their first ruthless plans to a larger project that caused far less angst among the indigenous village people. William and Fran both acknowledged gratefully that it was Jess's influence over her employer, combined with her deep-seated knowledge of the village and its ways that had contributed largely to the welcome change. But as Greg complained in private to William, Jess herself was different. She was, he said, proving herself to be too good a businesswoman for her own happiness – or his.

Jess declared that her employer, Mr Choppen, was not nearly the ogre or the dictator he had first seemed to be. He had been used to clearing any obstacles in his path with money; he had had to learn that money was too blunt an implement with which to dig up roots a thousand years old.

After the disastrous fire which had put both the Thackeray holdings and the de ffranksbridge estate on to the market, the company of which he was chairman and managing director had been reformed.

New investors had come in, and two of the original ones had departed. They had been made directors because their own holdings had been bought up by the syndicate during its first phase of acquiring property; as traitors to the village and upstarts in the firm, they had been popular with neither side. When the hotel and sports centre had been started, they had been compensated for the loss of their directorships by the promise of posts as manager of the sports centre and manager-ess of the hotel respectively; but Jack Bartrum, a thorn in Eric Choppen's side from the first, had died of liver cancer three months before the planned opening, and his wife, the larger of the two shareholders, had allowed herself to be bought out, making off with her hoard of cash to her native London, much to the relief of the whole community. Sophie had summed it up. 'Good riddance to bad rubbish,' she said.

Choppen would have agreed with her wholeheartedly but for the disruption it caused to his plans for the grand opening, which were already well advanced and had been much advertised. Replacements for Jack and Pamela Bartrum had to be found at very short notice.

In his predicament, Choppen had turned again to Jess, who had consequently found herself personnel manager as well as everything else to the syndicate. She possessed exactly the right qualities of intelligence, prompt and decisive action, a gift for organization, and a liking for responsibility. The change had proved a boon to Eric Choppen, and a bane to Greg Taliaferro, who now barely saw his wife when she wasn't too tired even to answer him when he spoke to her.

Choppen leaned even more heavily on Jess because his own domestic arrangements had broken down: his house-keeper, 'once a Londoner, always a Londoner', had retired when Sophie's niece Wendy had risen to fame as the vocalist in Gavin Choppen's dance-band, and had gone travelling with them. Till then the housekeeper had stayed on to act as chaperone to the girl whose family, except for Aunt Sophie and Uncle Daniel, had disowned her.

Eric Choppen himself needed no more than a personal base, and had solved his own problem by allotting himself a suite in the new hotel, where meals were always available and from which vantage point he could oversee all aspects of the business. He needed his personal secretary close at hand, so Jess's office had also been moved to the hotel. As that lay halfway between the old village and the new town, she spent most of her waking time there, and Southside House became a sort of caravanserai where she fell into bed beside Greg too tired for food, conversation or anything else.

After Mary's visit, Fran and William had issued an invitation to them for lunch on the coming Sunday. They had accepted happily, but when they arrived William divined at once that Jess was tense and her usually ebullient husband very edgy. As soon as the topic of the wedding was raised, it became clear that that was the cause of the apparent coolness between them.

They, too, had been rather surprised to receive invitations to it.

'I can't go even if I wanted to,' Jess declared. 'Our new manageress has only been at the hotel a couple of weeks, and with a function of that size there are bound to be teething troubles. I shall simply have to stay on duty, at hand, as I have promised to. So I really don't see any point in Greg spending a fortune to hire a suit to go by himself. I don't know why they invited us, anyway. We hardly know them.'

'I expect it was because they wanted us,' Fran said. 'I think they simply wanted to be neighbourly. They are such a lovely family.'

'In your case,' Jess clipped back, 'I'd guess it was because they wanted to raise the tone of their guest list by including among their friends a high-ranking academic and a TV "name". Greg and I don't come into that category.'

Fran glanced at William in mute appeal for him to do the talking. Jess's claws were sharpened and at the ready. William understood what Fran was signalling.

'Don't be silly, Jess,' he said, gently. 'If they have any reason for wanting us other than simple friendliness, I imagine it is because George Bridgefoot would think of us as representing Grandfather. They loved him, not because he was "the squire" but because he was the man he was. I think that puts the onus on us to return their courtesy, and that includes you, Jess, as much as Fran and me.'

'Well, I can't. I'm not stopping Greg from going, if he wants to. I suppose he could go in a lounge suit.'

'Yes, I dare say I could, but I shan't,' said Greg, a bit sharply and very firmly. 'If I go at all, I shall go properly attired.'

(Fran could barely prevent herself from clapping. 'Bravo, Greg,' she said to herself. It was time he made it clear to Jess that she no longer wore the trousers all the time.)

'What's the matter, Jess? Don't you want to go? I thought all women loved a good wedding. And it will be fun in the barn in the evening,' William said.

'If I did want to go, I can't be in two places at once,' she said. 'And I haven't worn a dress in living memory.'

'Then perhaps it's time you did, darling,' Greg said crisply. 'I should love to see you properly dressed up again, and out of those bloody ski-pants for once.'

It was plain to Fran that not only did Greg really want to take this first opportunity to be part of the community, but that he was making a firm bid, under William's protection, to get his own way for once.

'Now look, Jess,' said William, taking his cue. 'I know that while you were in Barra you had to count every penny, but you're not going to make me believe that you're worried about the cost of hiring a suit. And as it happens, there's a very good reason why Greg should be there.'

Then before Jess had time to argue, he explained. Fran could tell from Jess's face what she was thinking. If Jess wasn't going, she didn't want Greg to go; the thought of him in top hat and tails among beautiful women dressed for the occasion was more than she could take with equanimity. On the other hand, her devotion to Greg had in it a strong element of the maternal, and like all doting mothers she loved his many talents to be shown off. Fran guessed that one reason for Greg's mood was that at present he had only a mother where he wanted a wife.

She knew how much Greg loved his wife. She threw her resolution to leave it all to William out of the window, and added her persuasion to his.

'Do come, Jess,' she said, coaxingly. 'Get yourself dressed up, and be ready to join us for the reception. Greg can come with us to church, and be there if he is needed. Then we'll come here to take our glad rags off and get into something casual for the evening. It would be so good for the four of us to be there together in the barn. Do say you will!'

She felt, rather than saw, William's appreciation of her affectionate tone to Jess. He turned to Greg.

'So what about it?'

'The very thought of being able to get at that organ sends shivers down my spine,' Greg answered. 'But it's years since I played an organ at all, let alone one like that. If I agree, it will be on condition that the Bridgefoots are told about the arrangement, and that I'm allowed into the church to practise between now and then.'

'No difficulty there,' Fran said. 'The new Rector hasn't yet arrived, and George is a churchwarden. The new Rector is coming to marry them, though, at George's special request.'

Greg reached for Jess's hand. 'Do let's go, darling,' he said.

Fran thought it might be a good idea if she and William went to get some coffee. William waltzed her round the kitchen table in glee.

'Round one to common sense,' he said. 'It would have been like taking a bone from a starving dog for her to have deprived him of the chance of getting at that organ. Wait till you hear him! He'll have you in tears, my softhearted old sweetheart.'

'I shall be in any case,' she said, standing on tiptoe to kiss him and dribbling coffee on the floor. 'I always cry at weddings.'

6

Fran was thinking of that remark as she put the final touches to her eye make-up. She hoped she wouldn't cry enough to ruin it.

She was seated on a low stool in front of an eighteenth-century dressing table in her beautiful bedroom at Benedict's, taking much more care than usual with her make-up. She was dressed as far as her underslip, and regarding herself in the mirror with a sort of rueful satisfaction. Happiness didn't do much for the figure of a middle-aged woman by nature generously covered, she concluded. She had never been slim enough to be fashionable, and she suspected that twelve months of blissful content were having effects on her weight as well as showing in her face. She was happy, and it showed. She didn't want to get fat, but ... she gave her own reflection the expression of satisfaction a Siamese cat puts on when you scratch it behind the ears.

William had said many times that he liked her as she was – so what did anything else matter? She could hear him moving about in the next bedroom, which unless they had visitors, he used as a dressing-room.

Her door opened, and she saw his reflection in her mirror. The sartorial perfection of him took her breath away.

Behind her stood a tall, lithe, handsome man in a grey morning suit of such exquisite cut and fit that she knew at once that she had never before beheld its equal. He had put on his grey topper at a rakish angle over his thick crop of wavy white hair, and his ensemble was completed by a slim black silver-mounted walking-cane.

He was aware at once what effect his entrance had had on her. Their eyes met in the mirror, and the high-voltage current of their love for each other was switched on. He closed the distance between them in two swift strides, tossing hat and cane aside as he went. He stood behind her for a second or two, still holding her eyes with his. Then he stooped to kiss her bare shoulders, running his hands over them to slip off her straps so that he could lift her breasts and bury his face in them. He drew her back close against him, and she felt desire rising in herself as well as in him.

It took conscious effort to pull herself away. 'Oh William, darling! Look what you've done! You've got lipstick on your shirt collar.'

He was straining her against him still, turning her face up to his kisses.

'So what? I've got other shirts, but there's only one you,' he said.

'Darling, do be careful. My make-up will ruin that gorgeous coat and waistcoat.'

'Then let me take them off! We shall never have this lovely moment again. Plenty more, maybe, but never this one again. Can we dare to waste it?'

'We shall have to, because there just isn't time. I have to

dress and you have to change your shirt. You can't go in that one, now.'

'Damn!' he said. 'I suppose you're right, as usual. Can I come back and help you finish dressing?'

'If you promise to behave.'

'I will,' he said. 'But I shan't take no for an answer when we come home tonight.' He let her go, lifting the straps back on to her shoulders and leaving a kiss each side of her neck.

'I love you more and more,' he said to her reflection. 'Do you think it's even possible that Alex-whatever-his-name-is can love his Lucy as much as I love you?'

'*Nee-ooow*,' said a throaty Siamese voice at their feet. They both looked down and laughed, amusement slackening the urgent pull of love between them.

'Quite right, Cat,' said William, and went obediently to put on another clean shirt.

Fran finished dressing in a haze of delight. That was the pattern of their life together. The *tendresse* between them had so many moods, from helpless laughter to deep understanding, from light-hearted foolery to emotional empathy that made them one almost as much as physical desire did. They were incomplete without each other, and always on charge, as it were, for any expression of a love that was so much greater than the sum of its parts.

The couple they were about to watch being tied to each other by church and state could never be more married in the best sense of the word than they were, however irregular by social standards their relationship might be.

It always gave Fran a lot of pleasure just to be among people. She regarded it as something of a bonus that they were obliged to set out early for the wedding, in order to pick up Mary and get her to the church in good time. She was looking bright and smart and relaxed, in spite of her new dependence on a walking-stick.

She eyed Fran and William as they stood at her door with a look of proprietory pleasure, as she might have overlooked a class of children she had trained to perform in public.

'Well,' she said. 'If the official wedding party of "them posh folk from London" lives up to the sartorial glory of its country cousins, I should say this will be the wedding of the year.'

William removed his top hat and kissed her.

'Courtesy to match,' she said. 'That's what I love about you, William – though you make me sad, too. Like the banks and braes o' bonny Doon.' She looked at Fran, expecting both to pick up the reference at once.

Fran quoted, as she knew Mary wanted her to.

> 'Thou mind'st me of departed joys,
> Departed, never to return.

'But no sad memories now, Mary. Don't let's misuse a single minute of this lovely day. Get Mary into the car, William. We've still got to pick up Greg.'

They were greeted by a Greg that not even William had ever seen before, so elegant did his attire make him. William was openly delighted at Greg having so firmly had his own way.

'Who was it who said "Clothes make the man"?' he asked with teasing innocence.

'They make the woman, too,' Greg answered, looking admiringly at Fran.

'I'm not sure I agree about that,' William said. 'I think I agree with Herrick.

> 'No beauty doth she miss, when all her clothes are on.
> But Beauty's self she is, when all her clothes are gone.'

'Well, you ought to know,' said Greg.

'Gentlemen! Gentlemen! Spare my maidenly blushes,' said Mary, twinkling. 'Remember my great age!'

Fran felt suddenly young and gloriously happy. If William and Greg were going to keep this mood up, it couldn't be anything but a day to remember.

They were almost the first into the church, where the four ushers were busy laying out the 'Order of Service' sheets.

'Tell me about them before you go,' she said to Mary.

'You know Charles Bridgefoot, of course. The other two are his friends. The tall thin one is Robert Fairey – from Lane's End farm, Tom and Cynthia's only child. Nearly a twin to Charles with regard to age, and they are as inseparable as twins often are.

The slighter one is the third member of their trio, a sort of protégé of theirs. A bit of a mystery. He was a babe in arms when his mother appeared in our midst as housekeeper to a smallholder out in the wilds behind where Jack Bartrum used to live. She's a strange woman who keeps herself very much to herself. Rumour has it that the boor of a man she keeps house for never pays her a proper wage, which was why he took her in; her part of the bargain was that he never interfered in any way with the way she brought up her son. I never had the chance to teach him, so I don't know him well. But he is most beautifully spoken, like his mother, and extremely well-mannered. His name's Nick – short for Nicholas, no doubt. Nick Hadley. I must go. I don't know the other boy. He must be from the bridegroom's side.'

William and Fran sat down on the first pew behind the transvers aisle, thereby leaving all the front part of the church for the families. Charles Bridgefoot came to tell them that they had been allocated seats much nearer the front, but William explained that they would rather stay where they were because it enabled Greg to come and go as he might be needed.

Fran notched her 'sensitivity overdrive' up even more. It was as if her emotional antennae had greater range, and all her wits had been resharpened. When this happened, it enhanced everything for her, as if she had been given a pair of magic spectacles that enabled her to see in Technicolor, and stereophonic earphones. It happened only when she was happy and excited, and it meant that she was going to enjoy to the full every incident and nuance of this day.

She sat by William's side in great content, soaking up the beauty of the old building and the smell of hundreds of years of history mixed with the heavy scent of the mass of hothouse flowers Alex had provided. As it was the church's own harvest festival the very next day, the exotic blooms were mixed with traditional country decorations, and an intriguing mixture they made. She would never have believed that such opulence and such simplicity could have complemented each other with such striking effect. Alpha and Omega, she thought, the two extremes enclosing all. Was that what the Christian church meant by God? There were times, such as this very minute, when she longed to possess the same sort of faith as Sophie had. She compromised by telling herself that the name of her own god was Love, which included a mystic quality not contained in the practical commandment to 'Love thy neighbour'.

She looked at the ushers again with fresh eyes, especially Charles. He was as tall as his grandfather already, and if ever there was a chip off the old block in tone and manner, Charles was a chip off George. He had inherited every Bridgefoot characteristic except his colouring, which had come from his mother, so that where George was dark-haired, now turning grey, Charles had a mop of thick, fair, curly hair. In his morning suit, worn with such pride for the first time ever, Fran found herself thinking he 'looked good enough to eat'.

Her thoughts were interrupted by the arrival of Sophie with her sister Thirzah and Daniel Bates. All three wore their Sunday suits of black, though in honour of the occasion the women wore grey stockings and low laced-up shoes instead of their usual boots. And wonder of wonders – Sophie was sporting a new white hat with a band of rosy-pink artificial flowers round the brim. It was the first time Fran had ever seen her wearing anything not completely identical to Thirzah's outfit. Thirzah's hat was just her Sunday best, black trimmed with nodding forget-me-nots, the same as Fran was used to seeing on Sophie. It must mean, thought Fran, that Sophie was at last daring to demonstrate the independence the legacy from her dead sweetheart had given her. No wonder Thirzah looked more than usually grim!

William had stood up to greet them. Daniel remarked on the wonderful hothouse flowers, which brought Fran's wits back to the present.

'The screen looks beautiful,' she said, knowing that the sisters were responsible for the decoration of the rood-screen at every harvest festival. 'How long has your family been doing it?'

She put this last question to Thirzah, as being the elder of the two.

The Wainwright family must have been guarding their customary right to the decorating of that rood-screen for generations. Fran wondered who would take it on when Sophie and Thirzah were dead. Their family had run out. The only foothold it had in the next generation was Wendy, the third sister Hetty's child, who had been disinherited of such privileges by producing an illegitimate child before finding fame as a vocalist with Gavin Choppen's dance-band. Neither Wendy nor her child counted, really. The thread was broken and the name of Wainwright lost, like Fran's own family name of Wagstaffe, and that of the Thackerays and de ffranksbridges. Fran sighed. Thirzah didn't answer, and Fran forgot her momentary sadness in watching her strange behaviour.

'Ssh!' said Thirzah in a dramatic whisper, holding the flat palm of her gloved hand before first Daniel's lips, and then Sophie's. 'Here's the new Rector a-coming!'

William sat down, and the other three flattened themselves against the front of the pew to give the Rector room to pass. Fran was having to struggle with an almost unbearable urge to giggle. The aisle was wide enough to take a bridal procession with a lot of room to spare, and even Thirzah's Dutch-barge behind broadside on would have obstructed nobody. But at her bidding, all three seemed to shrink. The new incumbent had met them before, and acknowledged them as he passed; Fran had to grab William's hand to stop the giggle escaping when both the women made a curious bob like the tail-end of a curtsey. How far their mother's candle still threw its beams!

Fran decided she quite liked the look of the new Rector. He was, she guessed, between fifty-five and sixty, fairly tall with a clean-cut, handsome face and hair greying at the temples. Sophie had told her he was a 'widder-man', and 'just hordinary', not like parsons had been when Sophie was young.

He had no money of his own, as the previous Rector had had, and in consequence could not afford to live in the Old Rectory, which was why the syndicate had been able to buy it. He was going to live in a house converted from two old cottages down Spotted Cow Lane. Fran gathered that Sophie felt that the tone of the village had been lowered considerably by such a plebeian parson.

''E ain't the sort of man you can look up to, if you know what I mean,' she had said. Fran guessed that the poor man was being lowered in Sophie's esteem by his address. There had once been a pub called the Spotted Cow.

The church was filling up with grey-coated men and their ladies, though some of the local farmers wore lounge suits. She noted one in particular who came in alone; Fran's delicately tuned perception told her he was always shy and at present acutely embarrassed. She had never seen him before, and guessed that he must be the 'new' man from Castle Hill.

She caught her breath at the sight of the bridesmaids. No wonder Greg raved about Monique O'Dell as an artist, for whom he painted background scenes for pictures of her model gowns, if she could create beauty like that.

Then the bride was in the porch. Fran watched the train being straightened by a neat, compact little person dressed in such a chic outfit herself that Fran recognized her as the designer, who in ordinary life was plain Monica Choppen.

She saw, with a lump in her throat, how George handed his top hat to his grandson and took the bride in his arms to kiss her before leading her down the aisle to give her away to another man.

She wore a gown of deep ivory Ottoman silk with train cut in, and round her head was a chaplet of golden leaves and blue flowers made of silk. Round her neck was a wonderful necklace of sapphires and from her ears hung huge sapphire drops.

Fran watched the bridegroom and the best man move into place, and then Mary at the organ brought the congregation to its feet.

This was the moment when tears were difficult to hold back. Fran felt for William's hand and clutched it as if she never intended to let go of it again, but the tears came all the same. From that moment till the bells began to peal, she felt uplifted, as in the presence of some god of gods, or all the gods she had ever heard of rolled into one.

7

They found Jess waiting for them at the reception, a Jess as feminine in appearance as her taut boyish figure would permit. She had taken great pains, and Fran was surprised to note how stunning a woman her cousin still was. She had fine bone structure that made her face classically beautiful, and when she turned on her scintillating personality as well she could take the shine out of most other women. Fran wished she didn't know that Jess could turn it on and off like a tap, but the fact that she had chosen to turn it on today was a bonus that showed in Greg's face from the moment he caught sight of his wife.

From that moment the reception flowed with a glycerine smoothness that Fran felt was almost too perfect to be true. She was also made a bit apprehensive by her awareness that while Jess was putting on her act of being Greg's beautiful, loving wife, most of her mind was behind the scenes at the hotel, willing all to go well. She wondered how much Greg minded, and guessed that his sensitive spirit was being hurt because in spite of the outward show, the woman who was his wife was actually playing second fiddle all the time to the one who was Choppen's secretary and personnel manager.

They kept Mary with them, and after the departure of the bride and bridegroom, Fran invited them all back to Benedict's for a rest before changing to set out again for the barn.

George was making quite sure that Mary Budd intended to come. She was showing a bit of reluctance, and said, 'Well, if I do, it will be for the very last time. I expect I shall be organizing country dancing on the other side of the pearly gates by the time there is reason for another do in your barn. So yes, of course I'll come.'

Jess noticed that Monique O'Dell was preparing to leave, alone and looking rather forlorn. 'Oh, don't go, Miss O'Dell,' she called.

Fran was quick to take the hint. 'Come back with us till it's time to go to the barn,' she said.

The girl seemed pleased to be asked, but for a business-woman exhibited a reluctance and shyness that puzzled Fran considerably. In the end, she yielded, and joined them. 'But for heaven's sake call me Monica,' she said. 'Greg does, anyway.'

They persuaded Mary to go and lie down, which left the two couples and Monica together. It was as if the wedding had worked some sort of magic, so that William and Fran, Jess and Greg were absolutely at one, just as Fran had envisaged when

Jess and Greg had come home, but which until tonight had never really happened. The strange thing was that the presence of Monica made no difference to the warmth of the little gathering.

'I don't want to break this up,' said William, 'but I think it's time we roused Mary and got changed.'

'I'm almost afraid,' Fran replied, 'in case it doesn't come up to the last time. I wonder who's providing the music? Mary isn't, and I told George it wasn't up Greg's street.'

'Well, I like that!' said Greg. And crossing to the piano stool, he swept aside his grey tails like a concert pianist about to perform a concerto, and dashed into such a Charlie Kunz-like rendering of 'Tea for Two' that they were all stunned, even Jess.

'So who is going to provide the music?' William asked. 'Have they recruited you?'

'No, thank goodness,' Greg said. 'I'm glad I wasn't asked, because I want to dance. Can I book dances with all three of you ladies here and now?'

'Not with me, I'm afraid,' said Monica. 'I'm not coming.'

'You mean you haven't been invited?' The disappointment all round was manifest. 'That's nonsense. Everybody's invited.'

'Yes, I know. But I should hate to be a wallflower or pinch other women's partners. So as I have no partner, I shan't come.'

'Didn't I hear that your brother was home? Wouldn't he come with you?' Fran asked.

Monica's face broke into a twinkling smile. 'He's agreed to be the Carroll Gibbons of the evening – accompanied, I believe, by two plumbers.'

'Now look here,' said William, breaking into the silence her announcement had made, 'you can't just chicken out on us like that! You don't need a partner in the accepted sense for such a gathering as this. That's what's so good about it. It's the East Anglian version of a ceilidh. So off you go and change, and we'll pick you up so that you come in our party.'

When Fran came down from rousing Mary, William was just seeing Monica out. She was saying how much she had wanted to meet them, and promising to be ready in fifteen minutes. Then she left, rather too quickly. Fran could have sworn that in spite of the girl's aplomb, there were tears at the back of her throat. But why on earth . . . ? She knew that Jess had once imagined there to be something more than business between Greg and Monica, but Fran had always put it down to the streak of jealousy in Jess. Surely Monica wasn't carrying a torch for Greg after all?

Her fears were dispelled at once when on opening the sitting-room door she found Jess and Greg clasped in a lover-like embrace that spoke for itself.

'Sorry, Fran,' Jess said. 'It just came over me that once Greg takes that suit off, it will be a very long time before I see him looking like that again. I just wanted him to know how much I love him.'

'Don't apologize,' Fran said. 'As a matter of fact, William had just the same effect on me!'

The two men went upstairs to change, and left the women standing close together. Fran felt that Jess returned her spontaneous kiss with the same warmth as it was offered. The cherished relationship was not broken, or even badly cracked, after all. That knowledge added the last touch needed to make Fran's happiness perfect. In her philosophy, it was most important to know when you were happy, and to make the most of it there and then. To do otherwise was to misuse precious time.

8

In retrospect, Fran was surprised to remember how right her intuition had been that Lucy Bridgefoot's wedding was of some special significance to Old Swithinford. She recalled that she had conceived it as the full stop at the end of a sentence; now that it was over, she was able to see it also as the 'close quotes' of a period that had been opened by Mary's last village horkey. Major events that had changed the structure and ambience of the community had occurred between those two events. Similar in many ways as they were, there were differences too. She recorded them as they happened, with her perception at full strength, but it was only afterwards that she was able to see the differences in perspective.

As soon as they had been welcomed, Mary detached herself from them, and put herself down in the middle of the long side of the barn – on purpose, Fran thought, to be available to any of her old pupils who wanted to talk to her. But at the same time she felt that Mary's detachment was also a deliberate gesture to mark her resignation from the role of leader in the life of the village. Her job was done. Besides, Fran reflected later that whereas the horkey had been a village function, this was a private one. Mary was only a guest. There would be no more village gatherings in that old barn. This was probably the last, because there wasn't likely to be even another wedding. There were no more Bridgefoot girls to be married.

Glancing across at her dear old friend, Fran had the impression that Mary had changed since morning. She looked old and weary, as if the flowering spirit inside her had suddenly withered, leaving her only a dried-up husk of her former self.

There was a difference in the social make-up of the gathering, too. The nucleus of it was the Bridgefoot clan, which in true country fashion had been rounded up right down to what are usually known as 'forty-second cousins'.

All his fellow farmers were there, too. True, George's extended family, those who did or had worked on the Bridgefoot farms were present, but they were mostly the middle-aged or old ones. The younger ones had not come. That was another difference. This was not a cross-section of the whole village; the farmers now constituted a well-off middle class in their own right.

Nevertheless, the celebrations were going as happily as George could have hoped for. Fran had felt his satisfaction while dancing with him, and had told him so. The answering squeeze he had given her told her that henceforward she would be regarded as part of his extended family, too, and on impulse she had reached up and kissed him.

In that instant the social distance between Benedict's and

the Old Glebe had closed like a telescope folding up. Benedict's was no longer apart from the village. There were at least three other old houses restored to rival it, as well as some big Victorian and post-war ones. It had lost its social isolation.

The presence of the Choppen family, including Eric Choppen himself, had been a sort of *bombe surprise*. Fran found it very difficult to believe that the neat, square man of medium height with the slightly embarrassed air who had come in late and been introduced to her by Jess could possibly be the ogre her imagination had created from all the tales she had heard about him in the past eighteen months. Could he truly be the ruthless creature who had ripped the old village in half, hounded old couples and defenceless women out of house and home, and trampled down cherished customs apparently without a single twinge of conscience?

There had been a time when her image of him had been that of a werewolf ravening at the doors of people, like Sophie, whom she loved. He looked tonight more like a lost lamb who had wandered by chance into the wrong fold.

She had had Jess's word for it that he was not really at all a bad sort of chap. Jess averred that he had simply not understood either the situation he had got himself into, nor how to deal with rural people. She had said, over and over again, that he had been badly advised by his one indigenous partner, and was genuinely regretting his initial mistakes. She had added that he was now doing his utmost to make amends.

Fran had regarded all Jess's defence of him as special pleading to excuse her own 'treachery' in going to work for him. But his presence among them now made her think that perhaps after all Jess had been right. However, it had been after his entrance that Fran's sixth sense had picked up warnings that nothing could ever be perfect. Jess, who had been so charmingly natural all day, began to overplay her part. She had put on what Sophie called her 'croodling' voice, as if Choppen were an orphan child in urgent need of mother-love.

(Sophie had once commented acidly on this too-sweet mood Jess sometimes displayed. 'Like treacle, she is, as you might say. A little of it goos a long way, so you feel stickied all over and can't get rid of it.')

Fran found herself feeling sorry for Mr Choppen. He was not a fish out of water, but Jess's attentions were making him look like one. Or, perhaps, like a dog that had strayed into church and which Jess was trying to keep quiet before anybody noticed it and drove it out. If he was ill at ease, it was Jess who was causing him to be so. Her fussing over him was making him the odd man out.

When everybody changed partners, Fran was left standing alone by him. She watched him summon up courage to invite her to dance, and was obliged, though quite happy to accept. He was no great shakes as a dancer, but a very pleasant partner nevertheless. She exerted all her own skill to make him feel less out of practice, and by the time the dance came to an end, she knew she had succeeded. He had lost his embarrassment, and had enjoyed the dance, as well as her company.

'Dad!' Monica had exclaimed, when she rejoined them. 'I couldn't believe my eyes! Greg very nearly had to hold me up when I saw you on the floor. I didn't know you could dance.'

'I can't,' he said. 'Your mother was always telling me so. But Mrs Catherwood would make a lamp-post dance, I think.'

'She must have a magic wand,' Monica said, 'or else she has bewitched you.'

William had claimed Fran for the supper-dance, rejoining the group. 'She's got magic feet, Monica,' he said. 'Didn't you know? Like Beatrice in *Much Ado about Nothing*. Remember? ". . . There was a star danced, and under that she was born."'

'Darling, what a lovely compliment!' Fran said.

It was just then that Lucy and Alex appeared at the barn door, declaring that they had never had any intention of missing the best part of their own wedding.

George's cup of happiness ran over, visibly; but Fran shivered.

'What's the matter, sweetheart?' William asked.

'I don't know. It's all too good to be true. It makes me frightened.'

When he didn't answer her at once, Fran knew that he had been thinking exactly the same thing. He was too much in tune with her to deny it. He was remembering, as she was, that it had been the same at the horkey. And her misgivings had been right then.

'Don't run to meet trouble. Remember what you said to Mary this afternoon. "No sadness today." Let's all be happy while we can.'

Loaded plates were being collected from the long damask-covered table over which Thirzah had been brooding like a dragon until her well-trained team of helpers had magically covered it with a buffet meal of gigantic proportions and mouth-watering variety.

Though they knew Mary would be well looked after, Fran and William went back to her. They found her talking to the farmer from Castle Hill Farm. Fran had noticed him sitting forlornly alone in a corner. How like Mary it was to have managed to engage him in conversation. He rose as they approached, and would have moved away, had not Mary caught him by the sleeve.

'Don't go, Mr Bellamy,' Mary said. 'I want you to meet my two best friends.'

He stood hesitating, a step or two away from them, so terribly embarrassed that the feeling was almost catching. Fran and William, neither of whom had a hand free to offer, for once both looked so socially gauche that Mary laughed aloud. Fran felt the prick of foreboding again. Though Mary had joined in, Fran's ears had detected a crack in the bell of her laughter. Something was wrong.

'They won't eat you,' Mary said to the shy man who was still attempting to back off. Mary appeared to be intent on keeping him with them. Fran supposed she had a reason. William pulled up more chairs, and Mary more or less ordered Fran to accompany Bellamy to the buffet, while she talked to William. Fran noticed how pale Mary was looking, and decided to humour her.

Fran chatted, making use of all the usual pleasantries, but her companion was apparently so tongue-tied that she judged it kinder not to try to make conversation. She was therefore quite startled when he spoke.

'You ought to take your old friend home,' he said. 'She wants to go – now, straight away.'

There were times when Fran wished she didn't know the Bible quite as well as she did. Balaam's ass speaking to him could have caused him no greater degree of amazement than her companion had caused Fran. She also felt indignant, that a complete stranger should be taking it upon himself to put his oar in and presume to tell her what she ought to do.

She replied, rather coldly, that in all probability Miss Budd was overtired after such a long day. He said no more.

Mary waited till they had all sat down, and played with a sandwich while they ate. Then she said abruptly, 'I'm afraid I have inveigled you into a plot, Mr Bellamy. But you couldn't have better conspirators than these two. I need you all to help me. I must go home, Frances. Now, as soon as ever I can. Ssh! Don't make a scene! That's the whole point. You know as well as I do that if I am known to be leaving because I don't feel well, it will spoil the whole evening for the Bridgefoots. I won't do that. So I want you to smuggle me out.'

Fran looked absolutely stricken. All her premonitions had returned. She caught William's eye, and he said firmly, 'Stop looking such a dismal Jeremiad, Fran. Mary's only confessing to being tired. She wants to be allowed to leave without causing a fuss. That's all.'

Mary turned a papery face towards William with her usual wicked little smile in place. 'And I want you, and only you, to take me home, William. Slip out and get your car, and bring it as close to the side door of the barn as you can get it. There's a lavatory out there, and I shall pretend that's where I'm going. Nobody will take any notice. Then you can drive me home.'

'I shall come, too, and see you into bed,' Fran said.

'That is exactly what you will not do, Frances,' said Miss Budd in her most schoolteacherish voice. 'William can be back before his absence is noticed, or mine. If we all three vanish without explanation, we might just as well get Brian to announce here and now that the party's over. You, Frances, are to be what I believe is known as "the cover". And that is where I have to involve Mr Bellamy. Not that I am in the least sorry about that. He's been sitting in the corner all the evening looking nearly as much of an outcast as Mr Choppen did when he first appeared. Now we have made friends, and because he is all alone, he can help me.'

'Come to the point, Mary,' William said. 'The dancing will start again in a minute.'

50

She put her knobbly parchment-like hand into William's, and looked him firmly in the eye. 'That's what we are waiting for,' she said. 'While people are sorting out their partners, you will go out of one door, and I out of the other. And Mr Bellamy will take Fran on to the floor, where everybody will remark upon her dancing with him. If anybody misses me after you get back, you can then tell them truthfully where you have been, and why. They won't suspect that anything at all is amiss, if Fran hasn't gone with you to fuss over me. Please say goodnight to the Bridgefoots for me when you get a chance, Frances. Tell them I just wanted to lie down and relive this wonderful day all over again in my mind.'

Fran was worried, but helpless; she guessed, though, that William had been well briefed.

He whispered, 'Let her have her own way, Fran. I promise you I'll stop till she is in bed, and I'll make sure she has the telephone at her side and all she needs for the night, so don't expect me back for ten to fifteen minutes.'

He was playing it all as lightly as Mary had instructed him. He held out his hand to Bob Bellamy, and then put Fran's hand into the farmer's with a grin of mischief.

'Take care of her for me,' he said. 'I'll relieve you of her as soon as ever I can. She hasn't got two club feet, and has been on a dance floor before.' Next moment, she and her press-ganged partner were left alone.

She found to her astonishment that he was still holding her hand. There was a very pronounced twinkle in his eye as she hastily withdrew it. She decided that there was more to Mr Bellamy than appeared on the surface. She felt as gauche as any fifteen-year-old at her first ball with this unusual stranger, but short of letting Mary down completely, she was trapped.

'This is too bad of Mary,' she said. 'To involve you like this, I mean. I do hope you don't mind. I suppose she took the trouble to make sure you do dance? I'm afraid we really should cause comment sitting out together.'

'Would you rather not risk dancing with me?' he asked.

'Don't be silly,' she said, as she might have done to a teenage brother. 'I had rather you had had some choice in the matter, though.'

'I shouldn't have dared to ask you to dance, Mrs Catherwood,' he said.

The band struck up again, and Fran was disconcerted to realize they were playing a quickstep. She would have loved it if William had been her partner, or any one of several others that she knew to be reasonably proficient with their feet. She prided herself on being able to anticipate what an experienced partner was likely to do, but – well, in the present circumstances all she could hope for was that she and Mr Bellamy would not be made too conspicuous by landing in a heap on the floor. She braced herself to do her best, and found his hold on her comforting. Then they were away, and within five seconds she knew that with William absent, he was by far the most accomplished dancer on the floor. Like William, he became part of the rhythm, or the rhythm part of him, and his feet performed intricacies of twinkling speed and lightness that her own could not better. Moreover, he had that sure clasp on her that forewarned her of every movement he was about to make. Relieved and relaxed, she stopped thinking about anything except the pleasure of the dance. Mary had achieved her purpose, because their expert performance was certainly being noticed.

They finished the dance close to George Bridgefoot, who was beaming on them with the sort of wide-mouthed smile a six-year-old child draws on a picture of the sun.

'Glad to see you dancing at last, Bellamy,' he said. 'You are lucky to get a dance with Mrs Catherwood, I can tell you.' He looked round for William, and it gave Fran her chance.

'Miss Budd asked me to make her apologies to you for slipping away,' she said. 'She was tired, and after supper asked William to run her home. He'll be back in a minute or two. But you were all enjoying yourselves so much she preferred not to interrupt you.' She managed to make it sound convincing enough to be accepted without further comment.

'Thanks for that lovely dance,' she said to Bellamy. 'You might have warned me that you were an absolute expert.'

'I knew you were,' he replied. 'I've been watching you most of the evening. I've always loved dancing – well, till just lately.'

'You haven't enjoyed yourself much tonight, have you?' she said, suddenly feeling quite at home with him, and able to express the friendliness she felt. 'What a pity! This old barn is so beautiful, such a lovely place for neighbours to make merry in on this sort of occasion.'

'Except for the ghosts,' he replied.

'You mean all the ghosts of harvests past, I suppose,' she said. 'That means you're sensitive to places full of history. You ought to come up to see us at Benedict's, and talk to William. He feels like that all the time, sort of picks bits of history out of the air.'

His embarrassment had returned. 'I should love to, if you mean it,' he said. 'I reckon he'd feel a lot of history up at Castle Hill.'

'Then come soon,' she said. She really hoped he would. It was refreshing to meet somebody so full of surprises.

'Would you like to dance again?' he said.

'Yes – except that I'm worried. Why is William taking such a long time? I hope Mary hasn't been taken really ill.'

'Do you know what I think?' he said. 'I don't reckon she's ill in the ordinary sense, but I'm sure she's more than just tired. She's tired of life. She just wants to climb back up the mountain, and go down the other side this time.'

Hairs rose in the nape of Fran's neck. Once when she had been in distress, Mary had told her of an incident in her own life about which nobody else had ever known. *And she had used almost those words.*

Fran put out a hand, as if to stop herself from falling, and Bellamy caught it and held it in a close, warm grasp. She clung to it and shut her eyes – but her feeling of having lost contact with reality was suspended almost immediately by the welcome sound of William's voice.

'Is she trying to escape?' she heard him say. 'You look as if she might be a horse about to bolt! Sorry I have been so long Fran, but I can see you have been well looked after. Did you dance?'

Fran let go of Bellamy's hand and slid her other one into William's. The shock of the farmer's apparently fey reference to Mary's own phraseology when sharing her great secret was already passing. She decided that it simply had to be extra-ordinary coincidence, and as such she was glad to accept it. She recovered herself at once.

'Did we dance!' she said. 'You will have to look to your laurels, Professor. Mr Bellamy's almost as good on a dance floor as you are.'

'Oh. So I have a rival, now, have I? Well, I shall have to show him, that's all. On my way in, I asked Gavin to play a Viennese waltz – especially so that we can show everybody else just how it should be done.'

He held out a hand to Bellamy by way of thanks, and Bellamy took it without embarrassment but with a mischievous twinkle that said plainly, one man to another, 'I'd have a good try at rivalling you in other places than the dance floor if ever I had the chance.' Fran intercepted the message, and most unusually for her, blushed. William laughed aloud.

'Thank you,' he said.

'Thank *you*,' Bellamy replied, and sat down again to watch them perform their star turn. When the dance was finished, he had gone.

On their way home, William stopped the car at exactly the same spot as he had after the horkey two years before. Benedict's still rode like a ship in an ocean of trees, though tonight they had left the outside lights on. A huge yellow moon high in the sky came out from behind a cloud.

'It looks like an ocean liner,' Fran said.

'Taking us on our honeymoon,' William answered, wrapping his arms round her. 'Same old moon that we watched coming back from the horkey two years ago.'

'Same old moon that we watched rise last year from the back door,' she said.

'Ah! So you haven't forgotten that this wedding today is very nearly our first anniversary?'

'I couldn't forget. It was all too wonderful,' she said. 'Just that you were actually back home with me. But you hadn't asked me if I was going to keep the promise I'd made before you went. All I could think of was that song,

We stroll about together, 'neath the magical moon above
Just making conversation when we ought to be making love.'

He was silent, holding her close. 'And I was frightened to
ask. Then when we went in, we found that Mary had decided
to give us a push. I woke up in your bed next morning. What
idiots we had been to need the push.' He turned her face up to
kiss her, and slid his hand down inside her dress.

'You have simply no idea what an effort of will it cost me
not to do this that first time we sat here,' he said. 'I've often
wondered whether you would have held out that night if I had
been man enough to try.'

'Don't look back,' she said. 'In the end it all worked out
for us.'

'Yes, but we tempted fate – sometimes I just daren't think
about it.' His hand slipped lower, and he felt her stir beneath
the caress.

'So let's make it our anniversary. Don't let's waste another
minute making conversation,' he said. 'There'll be time for
that in the morning.'

9

Dawn broke the next morning in streaks of the lurid colour
that country people say denotes a day of 'unpromising'
weather.

George Bridgefoot got up as he always did as soon as it
was light, leaving the rest of the household at Glebe still in
bed. He was feeling as tired as everybody else would be, but
there were things to be done. He took a look at the sky, and
hoped the rain would hold off till all the Harvest Festival
services were over.

Clearing up the barn would be left till Monday, because
since his grandfather's time no work was ever done there on

the Sabbath. Food had been cleared away before midnight last night, at Thirzah's insistence, lest the fourth commandment forbidding 'all manner of work' on the seventh day be broken by her negligence. However, George had to unlock the barn door to allow young Gavin Choppen to fetch his piano out that morning while George was at church.

His first duty was to ring the calling bell for the early service of Holy Communion, for which a curate was coming from Swithinford; and he had arranged for Daniel to help him arrange all the offerings of 'first fruits' sent from village gardens, which had had to be set aside for the wedding, in their usual place before the rood-screen.

Then, because he was a churchwarden, he would have to be back again in church for Morning Prayer at eleven, which would be taken by the lay-reader from Swithinford Bridges – the hotch-potch community much more generally known as 'Hen Street'. For once in his life, George was resentful at having to spare so much time to the church. Lucy and her husband had stayed last night at Old Glebe instead of going back to the hotel. They would be leaving after lunch, and he would have to go to Evensong before they left.

He did not expect the rest of his family to put in attendance more than once. They were all tired out, for one thing. Besides, nobody really wanted to listen to the tall, thin, miserable lay-reader who was having to stand in till the new Rector came.

There were seven people at the early service, including himself, Daniel, Thirzah and Sophie. There had never been so few before.

The women, who would normally have taken pleasure in setting out the produce, went home because it was Sunday, and George found himself considerably irritated by the length of time it took him and Daniel to hump into place all the huge vegetable marrows and piles of scrubbed potatoes and polished apples and traditional loaves of bread made in the shape of wheatsheaves, and all the rest of the offerings. He wanted to breakfast with Lucy and Alex.

He had hardly sat down at the table when the telephone rang. Molly came back from answering it with the look on her face George associated with trouble.

'That was Miss Budd,' she said. 'She is in bed, and can't possibly get to church today.'

'But that'll mean we shan't have an organist!' he said. 'She'll have to come.'

'She can't. She made it quite clear that she was not well enough. I thought it was funny she left so early last night.'

George was tired, too. He had difficulty in contemplating a service without the old Rector in the pulpit and Mary Budd at the organ. How were they going to manage, he asked, as if his family could possibly supply an answer.

'Not just today,' Molly told him. 'Miss Budd's old, and she'll have to give up soon. You'll have to find another organist from somewhere.'

'Would Greg what's-his-name oblige again, because of it being Harvest Festival?' Lucy asked.

'I shall have to try him,' George agreed, clutching at a straw.

So the contagion of 'the morning after the night before' difficulties leapt from Old Glebe over to Southside House. Jess took the telephone call and told George she would ask, but she didn't think it very likely that her husband would agree.

'Not bloody likely!' had been Greg's uncompromising answer. 'Give 'em an inch and they take a yard. Besides you know very well that I don't profess to be a Christian. If I do it once, I shall be expected to turn out three times every Sunday for the rest of time. No! In any case, I don't know the order of the service, or anything about it.'

'Would you do it just for today if I came with you?' Jess asked. 'I used to love the Harvest Festival when I was a child, especially the hymns. We went to church every Sunday, so I ought to remember. You could sightread anything they wanted, and we could check everything with George Bridgefoot first. It does seem churlish not to try to help him today.'

Greg gave in, on condition that it was made clear that it was only just for this once. It was Jess's offer to go with him that had persuaded him. He had felt that they had somehow found each other again yesterday, and he had gone to bed happier than he had been for a long time.

But before they were ready to set out to church, there had been another phone call to the effect that Jess was needed urgently at the Franksbridge Hotel, Sunday though it was. She made no bones about which call had priority in her book.

Greg was both hurt and angry. In the event, it was Daniel who sat beside him and helped him through both services, but Greg's feeling that Jess had come back to him yesterday had been wiped out. Couldn't Choppen do without her just for one day? Far from being closer, at the end of that Sunday they had had a terrible row, and for the very first time in more than twenty years he had made no attempt to make up the quarrel in bed. He blamed nobody but Jess herself, but then she was the one who mattered. He turned his back towards her, and she made no gesture to prevent him.

Sophie had hoped to see William and Fran at the morning service, though they were not churchgoers. She thought that 'the squire's fam'ly' should have made an effort for Harvest Festival. She would tell Fran so on Monday morning, or so she informed Thirzah as they sat waiting.

But when it dawned upon her that her beloved 'Miss' was not in her usual place at the organ, she was seized by panic. She could hardly wait to get the service over, to go round by Benedict's to see if they knew why 'Miss' had not been there.

Sundays were always special to Fran and William. During that last hard year of waiting before Fran had thrown her moral scruples to the wind, they had made a rule that endearments to each other were allowed only on Sundays. They could laugh about the childishness of it now, but it had meant a great deal then.

Their practice was to have early morning tea in bed and then just lie there with her head on his shoulder while they reviewed the past week, and made plans for the next. They discussed each other's latest projects, recounted Sophie's news, expunged any misunderstandings and counted their many mutual blessings.

But the moment she had opened her eyes on this particular Sunday morning Fran had remembered Mary. As soon as William had poured out the tea and climbed back into bed, she had asked him what had happened when he took Mary home, and told him of Bellamy's goose-pimpling prescience.

'It was as if he *knew* the exact words Mary used,' she said, 'while you were away, and she was trying to make me see that I was not being "good" or "moral" by holding you off. I must have told you, surely? She said I was just scared that you might not find me as good in bed as Janice, and that if I didn't give myself the chance to find out, I should have missed the greatest experience life could offer – sex with a partner who was the other half of you. I was so stung by such plain speaking that I snapped back at her and asked her how she could possibly know – a maiden lady village schoolteacher.

'And she told me the secret she had had to keep all her life – of the four days she had had with her lover on his last leave home from the war, the First War. She said she knew what the view from the peak of love was, but she had had to come down the mountain without him, because he was killed soon after. And she said, "But a bit of me stopped up there with him." She told Sophie, too, to make Sophie help her play God to us. She trusted us with the greatest secret of her whole life – for our sakes. And yet Bob Bellamy seemed to know it! He said she wasn't just tired, she was tired of life. Tired of waiting to go back – to her lover on the mountain. William, how did he know? Is he right?'

William held her close, and stroked her hair. His silence warned her, and she asked, 'Is she really ill? Tell me.'

'Well – not in the ordinary sense of any physical illness, but we mustn't fool ourselves. Your new friend must have some sort of sixth sense, I think. Those were exactly the words she used to me last night – that she was tired and didn't want to make the effort to go on any longer. I'm afraid we have just got to accept it. As Sophie would say, "Life's uncertain, but death's sure." Mary will die because she wants to, not really for any other reason.

'I tried last night to persuade her to let me get Dr Henderson, but she wouldn't. She said all she wanted was just to lie and think. She gave up, yesterday. Perhaps it was Greg at the organ, breaking the last ties preventing her from going to join the man she loved. She was very moved by the wedding. She said so.'

Fran turned her face into his chest, trying not to cry. She

had only known Mary for a little more than two years, but she could hardly contemplate a future with an aching gap where Mary's energetic presence had been. William went on comforting, rocking her, and offering philosophy instead of platitudes.

'Don't grudge her her rest just because you – we – will miss her,' he said. 'She hasn't any close relatives to look after her if she lives too long. One can't imagine her in a hospital, or in an old people's home. She knows what she'll miss if she can just give up and slip away. I used to contemplate the chances of being in that situation myself, till I found you again.'

She lay silent for a moment, catching his stroking hand and kissing it. 'Did Mary say anything else last night that you haven't yet reported?'

'Yes. She said she wanted to be left alone to think. She would give us a ring when she was ready to see anybody. I was not to let you go, however much fuss you made. She knows what she's doing, sweetheart. She's a wonderful and wise old lady. We are lucky to have known her. Stop worrying, and tell me more about your new admirer – what's-his-name – Bob Bellamy. He sounds something a bit out of the ordinary.'

She made an effort just to please him. 'Do you know, I'm pretty sure he *is*,' she said. 'I asked him to come and see us.'

'He won't, unless we issue an explicit invitation,' William said. 'We mustn't let him just fade out again. But it will have to wait, I think. We ought to wait to see about Mary first, in case she needs us.'

Fran agreed. Cat came and sat on William's chest, and all three slept again.

They were washing up after a late breakfast when Sophie arrived.

Fran had half-expected the visit, and had discussed with William how much they ought to tell her. She hated to lie to Sophie, who had an uncanny gift of detecting a half-truth. They softened it as much as they could.

'She's feeling her age, all of a sudden,' Fran said. 'It often happens when people give things up – they suddenly know how tired they are. She has been having a lot of pain with her rheumatism just lately. Playing the organ had begun to worry her, as you know from yesterday. She would have had to give it up soon.'

'Nothing ain't the same as it used to be,' said Sophie, wiping tears away.

As Fran said when Sophie had gone, she had summed it up. Nothing was the same, for her or for anybody else. Sophie had a lot to be thankful for, but she would rather have had things as they once were. 'Sophie's one of those who just can't come to terms with change,' Fran said.

'Can any of us?' William asked. 'We have been lucky to be able to cope with our personal lives, but there are other changes I find very difficult to take, in spite of being happier now than I have ever been before. The changes lately have been too sudden. It's like grandfather's axe. If the haft broke, you put a new one in, but it was still grandfather's axe. Then the head broke and had to be replaced, but it was *still* grandfather's axe. But if you threw it away first time, when the haft broke, and bought a new one, all connection with your grandfather had gone. That's the sort of changes we are living through. Historians of the future will see the last twenty years as a great watershed between one era and another. Very few of them will understand how much individuals suffered while all these changes were taking place. It's a case of "For the want of a nail, the shoe was lost" and so on, as far as this village is concerned. From what Sophie says, Mary having to give up playing the organ could undermine the whole tradition at the church. They must have known she couldn't go on much longer, but they shut their eyes to it. Mary is their Canute, proving to them that they can't stop the waves of change from reaching them.'

It was Wednesday before the call they had been awaiting came. Mary said she had had Dr Henderson to see her, and he had been sensible enough to tell her that though there was nothing very much wrong with her specifically, he had no panacea for old age. She was just worn out. 'He's a good man, and a good doctor,' she said, cheerfully. 'He doesn't try to pretend he can make me young again.'

They said that of course they would go to see her though Fran was distressed at the thought of it. 'Why do we all get so embarrassed when people say what they mean about dying?' she asked.

'It's part of the change in society,' William answered. 'It just isn't done to talk about death now. As a topic of conversation, it is as much taboo as sex used to be in our childhood.'

'I'm glad she wants us both. I shouldn't have been much good to her without you,' Fran said.

'I'm never much good anywhere now without you in sight,' he answered.

They found Mary sitting up in bed, wrapped in a lacy bed-jacket and looking pretty, content and, by the look of her, nothing like dying. William kissed her, and told her so.

'Don't try to kid yourselves,' she said, and then went briskly to business.

'I need to tidy up my will, and I should like you two to be my executors. I had left what little I have to be shared out, but I've thought about it, lying here. I have one niece whom I love more than all the others put together. I want her to have everything. But you know what families are, even the best of them, where wills are concerned. Will you act for me? If so, my solicitor will come here when I send for him.'

They assured her that they were honoured by her trust. She looked relieved. 'Let me tell you about Anne,' she said. 'She's my only sister's daughter. She hasn't had an easy life, and it has been worse since she was widowed. She was a fairly successful journalist when she married a widower. Then he died, and left the bulk of his capital in trust for his children, so she gets only the interest. It isn't enough for her to live on, so she still has to do freelance work of some kind. He left her the house for her lifetime, too – which means she isn't free.

'I don't doubt that he did what he thought was fair – but human nature being what it is, his family feel cheated, and aren't very nice to her in consequence. The oldest son is nearly as old as she is. My will as it stands is "fair", but not much good to anybody.

'I can't do much for Anne in the way of income, but this house is mine. If she comes to live in it, she can get out from under her step-children's interference. Her father was shell-shocked in the First War and died very young, so I helped my sister to bring her up. She's almost like a daughter. I'm convinced I ought not to make the same silly mistake as her husband did.

'You can't please everybody, anyway. Of course, she may not want to come and live here but I think she will. She's been here often enough as a visitor in the past. She's just about your age, Frances. I am too sensible to think that I can make you friends, but I can hope. Now – I want to present her with *un fait accompli*, so I have asked my solicitor to come tomorrow. Then I shall write to her, and ask her to come and stay with me till – till then. I know everything will be safe in your hands.'

They could see she was tired, so they left. Fran was inclined to be tearful, but William refused to let her mourn. He turned the conversation to the way Mary had put her accumulated wisdom into practice.

'She's thought of all the snags,' he said. 'That's really why she didn't want anybody to go and see her, and offer advice she didn't want.

'Most people would have made Anne the sole executor, thinking that would be easiest for her – but you heard what Mary said. "You know what families are." She forestalled any of the others trying to muscle in by appointing us, complete strangers to all of them. There's a lot of truth in the saying that "Knowledge comes, but wisdom lingers".'

'I hope that particular source of wisdom will linger a long time yet, in spite of all you think,' Fran said.

'Fran! You don't really mean that, do you, darling? You're just being selfish, you know. You can't possibly wish that, if you really love her.' They had reached home.

'William,' Fran said, gently, 'would you say the same if it were me instead of Mary who was dying?'

When he finally spoke, the face he turned to her was ashen. 'God, Fran! Don't say things like that! I can't bear it.'

'So much for wisdom,' she said, smiling through tears that would no longer be held back.

A TIME FOR EVERY PURPOSE

10

A wet and blustery October followed the hot dry summer; the leaves turned early, and an air of prevailing gloom settled over Old Swithinford. There was general concern over Mary Budd's failing health. She went no more to play the organ in church, and it was taken for a bad sign that she had sent for her niece, Anne Rushlake, to come and stay with her.

The Professor started a new academic year without much enthusiasm; Frances didn't feel like work, especially as she spent as much time as she could getting to know Anne, and keeping Mary company. As Mary constantly told them, she was not ill: she was just old and worn out, and didn't want to make any effort. She was still able to enjoy the afternoons when Fran and Anne sat one each side of her bed while she told tales of old scandals, or Fran repeated Sophie's latest gem of idiomatic country philosophy.

Sophie was taking the change in her beloved 'Miss' very hard. She went about with a sad face, watching and waiting for every omen in her lexicon of rural superstition that foretold death. She and her sister Thirzah came together again in their mutual concern for Mary, and the effect her absence would have on their church. It was noticeable, though, that the power Thirzah had exerted over her sister had never been the same since Sophie had been made independent by the legacy left to her by her childhood sweetheart.

Greg had continued to act as organist once every Sunday, mainly because he was in love with the organ; he had told George Bridgefoot that he would go on till the new Rector was inducted. As it happened, that was long enough, because when the Revered Archibald Marriner moved into his house in Spotted Cow Lane, it was discovered that he had an unmarried daughter who played the organ. For her part, Beth Marriner wished heartily that she had resisted all attempts to teach her any keyboard instrument, because it was taken for granted that her services went with her father's.

Sophie and Thirzah were hard put to it to know what to make of her; she was not what their image of a parson's spinster daughter had led them to expect. She was thirtyish, tall, very slim, good-looking and a forceful personality. She wore her mass of fine, straight, silky-black hair coiled up into a Victorian 'cottage-loaf' style (thus adding about three inches to her already considerable height) – which was not fashionable but distinguished nevertheless among the frizzed and permed heads of those who did follow the prevailing fashion. She used eye make-up, too, which scandalized Sophie, but emphasized Beth's lively, piquant face. She spoke in a cultured voice that could often be heard uttering impatient and none-too-ladylike expletives.

The living was a poor one, but the Reverend Howard had had considerable private means, out of which he had paid for a lay-reader to look after the 'tin-topped' church that served Hen Street, and anybody else qualified to relieve him of as many duties that were officially part of his cure as he could. For the same reason, he had not been unduly concerned about the cost of living in a huge, beautiful though decaying eighteenth-century rectory. Wealthy old bachelors like him were not easy to replace. He and his kind belonged to the past.

Archie Marriner, however, had accepted the living of Old Swithinford with Swinthinford Bridges and had made no fuss about moving into a house converted from two cottages down Spotted Cow Lane. Nor had he jibbed at having to include the church of St Saviour at Honeyhill as well. The lay-reader had been retained at Hen Street, but the new Rector, faced with the choice of looking after St Saviour's church himself or paying somebody else out of his own meagre stipend, chose the former.

This church was situated on a slight rise at the very end of the peninsula of hard clay that jutted out into the surrounding fenland, and upon which Castle Hill Farm stood. There was neither house nor cottage within half a mile of the church in any direction. The church itself was small and beautiful, though now falling badly into disrepair; but a service was still held there once a month. In the old Rector's time he had deputed the reading of this service to any ageing retired clergyman who was willing and whose wife had often been the only member of his congregation.

It was now in Archie Marriner's cure, and he, having no wife, read the first of his services there to a congregation of bats and a stray cat. For music there was the cawing of the rooks in the huge elms of an adjacent rookery. After Lucy Bridgefoot's wedding, comparison between the old and the new Rectors was the main topic of conversation but by mid-November his advent, his peculiarities and those of his daughter had given way to newer topics of interest.

The Franksbridge Hotel had been built, at enormous expense, on the site of the burnt-out old hall, which had stood since the fourteenth century until the fire two years ago. All that had been left of it had been the huge chimney-stacks, one at each end, obviously added long after the original structure. The architect employed by Manor Farms Ltd had incorporated these chimney-stacks into the new building, reconstructing the facade of the new hotel in black-and-white half-timber between them and adding a thatched roof. Even Mr Choppen's worst critics could not but agree that it was most tastefully done.

Behind the facade all was as new and up-to-date as a five-star hotel should be, though the outside of that, too, was painted white, and its roof tiled with old tiles, to be in keeping with the front view. To the casual observer, 'the old Hall' had been miraculously made new.

The garden, once even more splendid than that at Benedict's, had been cleared, but a lot of wonderful old trees were left standing to tone down any brash newness. Behind a stand of larch and dark Scots pine, the new sports centre had been discreetly camouflaged. It contained a gymnasium, a heated swimming-pool, badminton and squash courts and facilities for other indoor sports. Hard tennis courts were being laid behind it, and grass courts planned. Both the garden and the outdoor sports ground ran back behind the hotel into what had been the park and was now taking shape as an eighteen-hole golf course.

All this had been reluctantly accepted, since it could not be prevented even by the die-hards; and some, like Fran Catherwood for instance, positively welcomed the whole venture, not because she had much desire to make use of any of it, but because the hotel and sports complex lay between Old Swithinford and the new town of Swithinford on space which might otherwise have been sold for development and resulted in horrible housing estates. In fact, by the time of 'the wedding' the heat had very largely gone out of the dispute with Mr Choppen and his invisible partners. This was one of the differences that had struck Frances Catherwood on the occasion of the Bridgefoot wedding.

Then, suddenly, the controversy was back in the news again. Mr Choppen had met an obstacle, in the shape of Rosemary Bridgefoot's aunt, who, in the words of a song very popular just then, 'would not be moved'.

What she would not be moved from was her home, a most unprepossessing brick dwelling that stood with its back towards the new hotel, and which until the bulldozers had started work had been separated from the Hall only by a thick and ragged old orchard which was now no more. When Molly Bridgefoot's grandfather had inherited the land, he had had a new house built on it for himself, and two cottages for his workmen. Being a passionate opponent of 'the demon drink', he had called his new residence 'Temperance House'. To safeguard his workmen from temptation, he had had the cottages built for their occupation as far away from any public house as he could get them. They were built at the opposite side of his farm from his own house, sideways on to the Swithinford Road which was about two hundred yards distant and to which they had no access. To get out at all they had to use the cart track which ran through the farmyard at Temperance House.

This pair of strictly utilitarian dwellings stood in a tiny field called 'the Pightle' on the very edge of his farm, where it abutted upon the de ffranksbridge estate. Any man who worked on the farm was required to sign the pledge before taking up residence.

Rosemary's mother had died young, and her father had been very glad of his unmarried sister Esther to come and look after him and his children; but by the time he died, Rosemary was married to Brian Bridgefoot and Aunt Esther had no other home. George and Molly were living at Temperance, and at

George's suggestion, the two cottages on the Pightle had been made into one, and Aunt Esther installed there. It had been her home for twenty years by the time Choppen's bulldozers had ripped up the tangled old orchard that had separated her from the senile old aristocrat at de ffranksbridge Hall.

Aunt Esther demanded that her privacy should be restored. Choppen saw at once that the Pightle was exactly what he needed to complete his scheme; as it already had a dwelling on it, there should be no difficulty in getting permission to build the golf pavilion there, incorporating a self-contained flat for a golf professional.

Like all other farmers, the Bridgefoots were still land-hungry, and not prepared to part with a foot of what they already owned; but Choppen had foreseen this, and pointed out to them that he would buy at development price, because such an ideal plot would certainly be sought by some eager developer sooner or later. So why not sell to him now?

The offer was very tempting, but to George it was a moral issue. Aunt Esther's wishes must be taken into account.

Now in her late seventies, Miss Esther Palmer was a tall, solid, dark-skinned, fierce-eyed and formidable old woman. The Pightle was her home, from which she would not be moved.

As the summer had passed, and Choppen's offer had risen from week to week, Aunt Esther had taken good care to make it a public issue. The price George had been offered had leaked out, and people had started taking sides over something which was no concern of theirs at all.

'Talk about giving apples where there's orchards,' said the envious, such as Kid Bean's wife. 'George Bridgefoot's got more than 'e knows what to do with a'ready. Folks would cry shame on him, if 'e turned that poor old woman out of her home, whatever he were offered.'

'There's no call for nobody to start taking George's character away,' Sophie had retorted. 'I could take my dying oath that no amount o' money would make 'im do a thing like that.'

By November, there was still stalemate. All the Bridgefoot family except George himself had begun to waver, on the grounds that Aunt Esther couldn't live for ever, and their fear that Choppen would soon give up hope and make other plans. You shouldn't look a gift horse in the mouth. His family began to put pressure on George.

There were other interesting topics, too. Everybody had been agog to know what would happen to the de ffranksbridge money when the old woman died in the fire because there were no direct heirs. The executors, a firm of high-class solicitors in London, had given the minimum of thought to it since the death of her husband Hugh de ffranksbridge; the junior partners sent down to see 'the old lady' once a year had brought back such incredible tales of squalor and senility that they had taken a Pontius Pilate-like attitude and more or less washed their hands of their responsibility, though they had been worried that the mean old woman refused absolutely to adjust the insurance. There would be good pickings for them when she died. Only their very oldest partner could remember anything about the will, and until it was needed, it was safe in their charge. It had proved to be a real mare's nest.

Hugh de ffranksbridge had been cheated of an heir by his wife's refusal to take any risk whatsoever of having a child. He had taken to drink and died of it, taking revenge by making quite sure that though he had left her well provided for, she should never pass a penny of de ffranksbridge money on to her own aristocratic, penurious family. He had been very proud of his ancient lineage, and it had broken his heart that his own stupid choice of a wife had caused the line to run out – *as far as he knew*. But there was always that outside chance – so he had made contingency plans.

His executors were given a year in which to trace any possible genuine claimant to the residual estate. But, having been forced to become a realist, he had known that with the Hall and the estate in such ruinous condition, the possibility of anybody but a multi-millionaire being able to restore it or bear the upkeep of it was nil, so he had decreed that on the death of his wife, everything should be sold. If no legitimate heir was traced within the time limit, all proceeds were to go to charity.

None of this had become public knowledge because the syndicate's own legal representatives were quick off the mark. Nobody had been at all surprised to hear that they had bought the ruined estate. They bought every bit of property they could lay their hands on, such as the Old Rectory, for example, which was now in the last stages of restoration to its former eighteenth-century elegance. Rumour had it that Mr Choppen himself intended to move into it.

Then in November, two bits of news on the same day gave the kaleidoscope a shake. Aunt Esther, stepping outside on the first frosty morning of the winter, had fallen and broken her hip. She had been rushed off to the local hospital, and Choppen had gone at once to George with a 'final' offer for the Pightle.

While George still hesitated, because the hip had been set and the prognosis was good, Rosemary had taken a firm stand. It was beyond the bounds of all common sense, she declared, to expect that her awkward old aunt could to go back to living alone. She, Rosemary, would have to look after her wherever she was. She wasn't proposing to shirk her duty, but she didn't see how she could manage if Aunt Esther was more than half a mile away across what amounted to a ploughed field. There was room at Temperance Farm for her. It would be better for her, better for Rosemary, and in any case it wasn't fair on the Bridgefoot family to be done out of a fortune by her aunt, who was connected with them only because she had married Brian. George found the rest of his family inclined to agree with Rosemary, and reluctantly gave in when Rosy revealed her proposition that a few alterations could give her aunt a self-contained ground-floor flat.

('Bad'll become of it,' said Sophie to Fran. 'Time was when every family took its own old folk under their roof, as is only right and proper. But when such old folks are shut away in their own room and ain't allowed to mix with the rest, it never works. There's soon bad blood, try they never so hard o' both sides to be peaceable. Ol' Esther Palmer's never been easy to get on with. Some o' the young'uns still reckon she's a witch. If I was to believe in such things, which I don't, being a Christian, I should think so meself. She ain't a woman I should want in my 'ouse. If they move her out against 'er will, the Bridgefoots'll live to regret it. Specially if they do it for money, you mark my words. She'll git 'er own back on 'em some'ow.')

The other bit of news came like a thunder-clap. An heir to

the de ffranksbridge estate had been traced. According to the village grapevine, which in this case proved to be correct, he was a retired naval officer, in his middle fifties, and unmarried. When informed of his unexpected inheritance, he had promptly visited the village, liked the look of it, and decided there and then to invest his legacy in Manor Farms Ltd, on condition that he should be allowed to buy the Old Rectory for his own occupation.

The fact that Kid Bean the elder brother and former partner of Sophie's dead sweetheart, had at last 'come in for' what had been left of Jelly's win on Ernie had been known since his parents had died; but against the other two pieces of news, the bit that Kid had hoped to astonish everybody with was small beer.

He was about to turn the old muddle of buildings, from which he and his brother Jelly had run their 'odd-job' business, into a brand new DIY store. He planned to open it before Christmas.

It was while these three oddly assorted bits of news were being chased from pillar to post by gossiping tongues that Mary Budd died in her sleep.

11

It was as though a great deal of the grieving for Mary Budd had been done in advance of her death. She had given everybody a couple of months' warning to get used to the thought. Even those who had loved her most felt some sort of relief that the waiting time was over.

'Blessed be they that mourn, for they shall be comforted,' Sophie had said to Frances. Then she had sat down to silent tears, to comfort herself; but Fran had not felt in the least like crying. She could hear Mary's own voice in her ears, in one of her old friend's most queen-waspish moods, denouncing tears as a self-indulgent luxury, especially when shed for somebody who had had as long, as useful and generally as happy a life as she had.

She had not expected Mary's niece Anne to be anything but calmly sorrowful. Anne was a woman of the world. They had got on well together, though Fran reflected that but for Mary they would probably never have sought each other out as friends; but then, Mary had more or less pitchforked them into each other's company, and sitting by Mary's bedside, they had slipped into easy companionship. Fran thought it unlikely that Mary had discussed her with Anne, but she didn't care at all one way or the other. If she had done so, it could only be because she had wished them to continue as friends, and if that was what Mary wished, then without forcing anything, Fran would do her best to make it so.

Fran was surprised that she was able to take the news so well. She knew that William had been right not to wish her to linger, lying in bed immobile and in pain.

Mary was free, and somewhere else. She had no idea where, but she couldn't believe that so-bright life-spark had just gone out for ever. She kept remembering what Bob Bellamy had said about Mary wanting to climb the mountain again and go down on the other side. 'On the other side.' That's exactly where Thirzah would place her. She meant the other side of Jordan, of course. What different interpretation could be put upon four plain, ordinary English words! Even in so narrow a context.

Fran insisted on Anne going to stay at Benedict's. It was there that they disclosed their knowledge of Mary's will, and put her into the picture of her own future.

'I will get the solicitor to come here and read the will to you,' William said. 'Of course, there would be no difficulty in selling that charming little schoolhouse, because Choppen would snap it up like a trout leaping at a fly. But I hope you won't want to sell. I think you'll find us kindred spirits.'

Anne made up her mind at once. She said she would still not have quite enough to live comfortably on, but a bit of journalism or part-time clerical work would give her something to do, as well as close the financial gap.

Fearing that Jess would step in and grab so experienced a

worker, Fran immediately offered Anne work for three days a week at Benedict's, where indeed they had genuine need of her.

Mary had wished to be buried, as she said, among her old friends, few of whom had got round to accepting the idea of cremation. 'George will find room to tuck me in somewhere,' she had said with her wicked little grin. 'Tell him my favourite spot would be under the old yew tree by the door. I seem to have spent half my life watching that door, waiting for brides I taught when they were children to come through it. It's all a lot of silly sentimentality, anyway, and I couldn't care less if you let Ned burn me on a bonfire in your garden. But that would offend the sensibility of people like Sophie, so I suppose I shall have to go along with convention. Spread it abroad that I have made my wish known where I want to be buried, and why; and that I want Greg to be at the organ. He'll understand. That will give them all a lovely lot to shed tears over. They love a nice weepy funeral.'

The spot she had chosen had been used many times in the last five hundred years, but the records showed that it was just over the legal fifty years since the last grave had been dug there, and all George's probing could detect no sign of a coffin, so she had her wish.

The church was full to overflowing. A few of Mary's relatives had been invited, but none of them came, much to Anne's relief. She had asked that the service be in the morning, so that she could get away in the afternoon. She couldn't wait, she said, to move out of the house that she occupied only because her step-children had no choice but to let her, however grudgingly, and into one that was so wholly her own that she could do just as she liked with it.

There were no mournful hymns; George read Mary's favourite passage from the Bible, the third chapter of Proverbs, and William read Sir Walter Raleigh's poem, written when he awaited execution. Only Fran was aware that he had changed a word here and there. Her resolve not to shed a tear was broken at this point, not for Mary but because of the beauty of the poem, and its aptness to Mary's secret, but because William had chosen it and because it was him reading it.

76

Give me my scallop-shell of quiet,
    My staff of Love to walk upon;
My scrip of joy, immortal diet,
    My bottle of salvation;
My gown of glory, hope's true gage·
And thus I'll make my pilgrimage.

Love must be my body's balmer;
    No other balm will there be given:
Whilst my soul, like quiet palmer
    Travelleth towards the land of heaven;
Over the silver mountains
Where spring the nectar fountains;
    There will I kiss
    The bowl of bliss;
And drink mine everlasting fill.
Upon every milken hill.

My soul will be athirst before;
But, after, it will thirst no more.

It caused a lot of puzzlement and some protest among the
congregation. Thirzah was heard to remark that folk ought to
stick to what was right for funerals, whatever they choosed to
do at home; and others asked where it could be found in the
Bible, because they had never come across it before. What did
it mean, anyway?

It meant a great deal to Fran, and took away what little
grief she had left. As far as she was concerned, William's
choice had been perfect.

They sang 'The Old Hundredth' with gusto for the last
hymn, and as the bearers picked up the tiny coffin and started
with it to the gaping hole just outside the south door, Greg
pulled out all the organ stops and thundered into the Mozart
'Alleluia', which Fran thought was just what Mary had expected
him to do.

William escorted Anne to the graveside, but Fran found
she didn't want to go. So she stood alone in church and
listened to Greg, who kept the organ going until the very
moment of committal. Then he came down and took her hand,

and led her out of the other door, where, seated together on an altar grave slab, they waited till William came to look for them.

After a quick lunch at Benedict's, William took Anne to the mainline station and put her on a train. When he got back, it was still only one thirty and the sun had come out into a pale blue sky that promised a frosty night.

'Feel like a walk, my darling?' William said. 'The last thing that Mary would want would be for us to sit about here till you started to feel miserable. I have been wanting to go and visit that little church up on Castle Hill. What about it?'

It seemed to Fran a very good idea.

12

They took the road towards Castle Hill Farm, leaving the farmhouse on their left, and following the rutty track towards the church, which they could see on a slightly higher rise a bit farther on.

'I'm afraid I have given you a long walk for nothing,' William said ruefully. 'There won't be enough light left to see anything inside, now, even if we can get in. It's farther than I thought. You'll be worn out, and you'd had enough before we set out. I think we ought only to give ourselves a breather, and then start back.'

'The walk was just what I needed,' Fran said. 'We can always come again. For today I'm quite content to stand here and stare.'

The church was still ahead of them, its old grey stone mellowed by the late afternoon sun. There was a lichen-covered stone wall all round the churchyard, in which long grass grew over humps that were old graves. Lop-sided, weathered head-stones leaned this way and that. People had been buried there till the churchyard had been declared full and closed. Well, if you intended to pick your own grave-place, Fran thought, you couldn't choose a more serene or beautiful spot.

Behind the church was a massive wood, mainly of elm trees, every one stretching huge arms to hold up and spread out a mantilla of black lace twigs over its own head. Among the delicate tracery of twigs there were dozens of rooks' nests, black patches against the paling sky; and above and beyond and all around a cloud of rooks homeward-bound filled the air with their cawing.

'It's breathtakingly beautiful,' William agreed. 'We must bring Greg up to see it. We might persuade him to paint it for us, as a sort of memorial of our own to Mary. Would you like that?'

She nodded. He was protecting her with his love from sad thoughts, just as he was trying to protect her with his extra height and breadth from the slightly chilly breeze that had sprung up.

'Let's just take a quick look round the other side now we're here,' he said, 'and then go home.'

They went round the east end of the church towards the trees, and found that they were not alone.

Leaning with his back against the church wall, his hands in his pockets and a double-barrelled gun in the crook of his arm, stood Bob Bellamy. His head was thrown back, and his gaze was on the rooks as they glided one by one from the swirling mass above and opening their wings came to rest among the branches.

He looked every inch a robust farmer, thick-set and solid. Fran doubted her recognition of him for a moment, so different did he seem from the twinkle-toed man she had danced with in the barn.

He was wearing breeches and high-topped boots, a warm and bulky hip-length coat, and a pork-pie hat pushed well back on his head. He hadn't heard them, and did not turn his head. Fran was aware of a sense of disillusionment when she saw the gun; she could have sworn he was not that sort of man. But what was his gun for, if not to kill? Shooting rooks could only be killing for the sake of killing. They were no good for the pot, and as far as she knew, did more good than harm on a farm.

William called out a greeting, and he turned, as if coming out of a dream, shyly pulling off his old hat to Fran.

'You caught me at it proper,' he said, smiling. 'Idling, I mean. I come up here most afternoons when I can, to see the rocks come home – though I like it best on windy days, when they're playing breakneck. I reckon they must love the wind, the way they tumble about the sky just for the fun of it. And on a windy day the clouds pile up behind 'em like great mountains and keep changing shape—' He stopped suddenly, shifting the gun about in embarrassment at having given himself away to two comparative strangers.

'You mean you come up here just to watch the clouds and the rooks?' Fran asked. 'Then why on earth do you carry a gun?'

It was out before she could stop it, and she was afraid he would be offended. She didn't want to offend him because she wanted to get to know him better. She was about to apologize, when he suddenly smiled broadly at her.

He leaned the gun against the wall, between himself and William. 'Don't worry, it ain't loaded,' he said. 'I carry it just for show, in case anybody should catch me just looking at things – like you did. I hate killing things, though sometimes I have to. But it's worth coming just to look at, ain't it? I keep trying to paint it, but I never get a picture that satisfies me.'

'You paint?' asked William, sounding, Fran thought, a bit too incredulous for either diplomacy or courtesy.

Bellamy was now covered with shy confusion. 'Not really – I mean I don't know anything about painting,' he said. 'I only do it to please myself and pass the time.'

'I'd like to see your paintings,' William said. 'But we ought to start back home now or it will be dark. I hadn't realized how far it was. Fran's had enough for one day, I think.'

Bellamy's face lit up. He recognized this for what it was – not only genuine interest in his hobby, but a gesture of friendship, because William had said 'Fran' instead of 'Mrs Catherwood'. After a moment, he said, 'Yes, I know. That old friend of yours was buried this morning, wasn't she? I'm sorry. Look – let me take you home. That's my old Land-Rover over there. If you don't mind riding in that as far as the house, I'll get the car out and run you back.'

William accepted without consulting Fran, and she was

glad. Apart from understanding that Bellamy was like a sensitive plant, and that the slightest rebuff would cause him to curl up and wilt, she really was tired. A lift home would be very welcome.

The farmhouse was painted white, and of a most peculiar shape; not at all beautiful, in the way so many other farmhouses were, though larger than most. The light was failing, now, and as they drove up to it, it was silhouetted against the sky, so they could see few details to account for its strange appearance.

As they climbed out of the Land-Rover, Bellamy said hesitantly, 'Will you come in and let me make you a cup of tea? It won't take ten minutes, and there is something I ought to tell you.'

Fran was much too intrigued to refuse even if she had wanted to; and William, willing as always to do what Fran wanted, had no objection of his own to offer.

Bellamy led them into the house through a long kitchen alive with a variety of cats and one huge golden retriever that came forward to be petted. Then Bellamy opened a door, and they were in a room of quite amazing proportions. Fran gasped audibly.

The room itself was more or less cubic, at least forty by fifty feet and two storeys high. One whole side, looking out to the church and rookery, was taken up with floor-to-ceiling windows, side by side with only a foot or so of wall between them. The high ceiling itself was pyramidal, with black beams all converging to a four-foot square at the highest point. A new roof on an old building, obviously, but very much out of the ordinary and of dubious taste.

'I'll put the kettle on,' Bellamy said. 'This is a queer old place, as you can see. Sit down, if you can find anywhere to sit. There's one or two things as I must do afore I go out again.'

He was taking off his outer coat, revealing a well-worn jacket with sagging pockets underneath it.

'I must put my passenger to bed, for one thing.' He was speaking now quite easily, his fenland accent noticeable. Fran was congratulating herself that they had passed his test, and he was no longer shy in their company. She could hardly believe either her eyes or her ears when he began to talk in what

Sophie would call a 'croodling' voice to something in his jacket pocket.

'Come on, my ol' matey,' he said. 'I know you're sleepy, but you'd better have your supper before you go to bed. You'll very like sleep three days next time.' He fumbled carefully in one of his jacket pockets, lifting out with infinite care a little grey bundle that resolved itself in his hands into a bright-eyed squirrel. He held it up to his face, and smoothed his cheek against its fur. 'He's sleepy because of the time of the year,' Bellamy said. 'I found him under a tree one day in the spring. Must have fell out of the drey, 'cos he was only a tiny baby. I fed him with an old fountain-pen filler, so he thinks I'm his mother, and pines if I go out without him. One of the old cats mothers him a lot, but he'd rather be in my pocket, wouldn't you, mate?'

He took the squirrel out into the kitchen where they heard him talking to it, and to the dog. Then there was the sound of water running, as he washed his hands at the sink, and after a while he came back with a tray and a huge teapot surrounded by cups and saucers. He poured the strong tea out himself, and handed them each a cup before pulling up an old Windsor chair and seating himself between them. Fran dared not look at William, lest he should read her thoughts. If the squirrel had produced a large watch from its pocket, and exclaimed 'Oh my tail and whiskers!' she could not have felt more like Alice in Wonderland.

'Now,' said Bellamy, 'seeing as I reckon we are meant to be friends, call me Bob and start asking all the questions you want to know the answer to.'

'No!' cried Fran. 'Not now! Later, when we come again, or when you come to see us. I couldn't take any of it in properly now. I'm already saturated. It has been a long day. But you said you had something to tell us.'

'I don't know as I ought to have mentioned it,' he said. 'I wish I hadn't now, because I don't want you to think I'm off my head. But you'll have to know sooner or later. It's about Miss Budd.'

They looked at each other across him, both out of their depth. What could he possibly know of Mary that they didn't know already? She had only made his acquaintance at Lucy's wedding, and certainly had never seen him since, because she hadn't got up from her bed after that night.

'Go on.' It was William who spoke, though Bellamy was looking at Fran.

'I don't know where to start. I know you belong round here, but do you know anything about the fens – and fen people? Real fen people, I mean, not them as call themselves fen-tigers 'cos they happen to live there. I mean folks like me whose families were there afore the fens were drained.

'They're a queer lot, a sort of race on their own. Living down there on the black land in them little bungalows with no lights and only peat fires made 'em different. They all believe in signs and omens, and fairies, and witches, and ghosts. Some fen folk'll tell you as there's so many ghosts about they can hardly move for 'em! You don't have to believe all you hear 'cos they're good at making things up, and they all like to hear theirselves talk. If you've ever been out in the fen on a winter night by yourself you wouldn't wonder, though.' He smiled, self deprecatingly, and then became serious again.

'But there're some fen folks that ain't telling lies when they tell you about such things. They *can* see ghosts, and such. They've got a sort of gift as old folks call "the gift of seeing". I happen to be one of 'em. They reckon it's because I was born on the very stroke of midnight, but I don't know about that. I don't often see ghosts, but I do sort of sense things, if you know what I mean. And have had some very queer experiences. If you can't believe that, I might as well not go on.'

William shot a warning glance at Fran not to answer, and did so himself. 'A sixth sense is what most people would call it. I'm a historian, and a historian who doesn't keep an open mind doesn't get far,' he said. 'Please go on.'

Bellamy nodded. 'Well, you remember the night of the wedding in the barn – you found me with Miss Budd.' There was a long pause.

'Well, she didn't know me, and I didn't know her. But I'd had enough of just sitting watching other people dancing, so I decided to come home.

'I had to pass her to get out, and as I went towards her she smiled at me, as bright and chirpy as a robin. But all of a sudden she turned white and put her hand out as if she wanted something to hold on to. I thought she was going to faint, so I put my hand out to catch her, and she grabbed hold of it, and hung on. But she wasn't looking at me at all – she was staring at something over my right shoulder. And I guessed that she was seeing something that nobody else could.'

He paused, almost as if unwilling to go on. 'I can't expect you to believe me, but I'm pretty sure that was why she had turned so pale. She was smiling, and I think when she put her hand out and I grabbed it, she was trying to touch whatever it was she could see.

'And then she said something that made no sense, though I know I heard it clear enough. She said, "Over the hill this time". And then she sort of keeled over, and I think she would have fell off her seat if I hadn't been there. I daren't let go of her, so I just stood and waited. But I knew what she meant. I could have told you then that she was going to die soon.

'She was still pale, but when she came round and found herself holding my hand, she laughed and said she thought she must have gone to sleep, because she'd had a lovely dream.' Another long pause.

'She knew very well that she hadn't been asleep, or dreaming, but she didn't have any idea that I knew it as well as she did. I had enough sense not to tell her. She understood what it meant all right, and I could see that she didn't care. In fact she was glad. She pulled herself together and made me sit down with her. I liked her a lot. I stopped with her till somebody else came, and it was you who did.'

Fran couldn't trust herself to speak, but William, as always, spared her.

'Folklorists would say she had seen "a fetch",' he said.

'I'm never heard it called that, but then, I'm only a fenman with no proper schooling. We should just call it a warning.'

He turned to face Fran. 'I hope you won't grieve for her. If you had seen her smile, you'd know it was what she had been hoping for.'

'We did have some sort of inkling,' Fran said, finding her voice at last.

'Ah, well. I'm glad as you believe me. I shan't tell nobody else.'

They sat silent while he got up and cheerfully and methodically made his preparations to take them home, now talking about other things and, Fran noticed, reverting to much more ordinary speech. His English now, though by no means perfect, was quite as good as that of most of the other farmers she knew, though his vowels were still different.

They talked about him on and off all through the evening.

'We have to believe him,' Fran said. 'Nobody else knows about Mary's lover. He couldn't have had any idea at all. And she used the same metaphor about being on the top of a mountain with her William as she did when she told me about him.' She shivered. 'Can you explain it?' she asked. 'I like Bellamy, but that sort of thing scares me. Because I don't understand it, I suppose. Do you think he's a sort of witch, or something – like that chap in the Isle of Man? You know the one I mean – what's his name?'

'Dr Gerald Gardner, was it? The one who set up the museum? No, he was a scholar. Bellamy's just a natural chap who accepts his strange "gift". I don't think he regards it as anything very extraordinary, because his own people accept it. I should say he's a sort of throw-back to earlier times. A shaman. The one selected to be entrusted with the knowledge of good and evil for the welfare of the rest of the tribe. It has happened in a lot of cultures from the stone age onwards. We've got too sophisticated to believe in such things.

'Somebody had to predict whether or not it would be a good day for the tribe to go hunting. The shaman did his best. Now we should believe in the disembodied voice of the weather forecaster over the radio. What's the real difference? Science? The shamans had their own brand of science – dreams, for example – in advance of Freud.

'It all interests me enormously, and if I hadn't such a lot already on my plate, I should love to go into it deeper. Especially the subject of folk memory. Oral evidence. Most historians won't give much credence to anything that hasn't got documentary evidence to support it.'

He went on pursuing his own thoughts, and she followed dutifully, knowing he was trying to take her mind off the events of the day.

It was much later, in bed, that Fran suddenly asked, 'Do you think he lives there all alone? In that extraordinary house?'

'We'll make it our business to find out,' he answered sleepily. 'Forget it now. Go to sleep.'

She tried, but it was a long time before she did. She had never before been so glad of William's arm thrown carelessly across her. Her mind would not let go of the thought of Mary's body lying out there tonight under that great mound of flowers while the real Mary, hand in hand with a tall soldier disappeared for ever into the mist on the other side of the hill with the church and the rookery on it. She couldn't accept it without a frisson of some kind, if it wasn't exactly fear.

But William was there, warm and real, and with her head on his solid shoulder, she slept at last.

13

Plans for Franksbridge Hotel's first Christmas had been laid long before Aunt Esther's slip on her icy doorway had stirred another large measure of ginger into the pot. Negotiations with the Bridgefoots, solicitors, surveyors, planners, architects, builders and all the rest, to say nothing of his co-directors, fell heavily on the shoulders of Eric Choppen, who in his turn leaned heavily on Jess. Not that she minded; having for so long been an intelligent woman more or less forced by circumstances to let her brain atrophy and her capability rust, she was experiencing a great resurgence of vitality. She threw herself with every ounce of her energy into making herself indispensible to her immediate boss in the first place, and through him to Manor Farms Ltd in general. She had tasted power and she liked the taste. The person who was suffering was Greg.

There had been regeneration for him, too, since they had been forced to retreat from Barra, reduced to poverty and low in spirit. Since then, their prospects had changed dramatically. Greg had finished his book of poems and paintings, and was working on another. He had allowed his love of music and his talents as pianist and organist to be taken out of mothballs and now indulged himself whenever possible on Fran's Bechstein grand or the church organ – with the blessing of both parties. He had set up a business relationship with Monique O'Dell to paint backgrounds for her *haute couture* models, and was financially independent as never before – but he was not happy. For more than twenty-five years, the centre of all happiness had been his love for Jess, and hers for him. She had worked at the most menial jobs to keep them fed and clothed when he had sunk into hopeless lethargy; she had shared poverty and disappointment with him, and the humiliation of having to ask her step-brother for financial help to see them through. He not only adored her as his mate, but he also respected and admired her for her qualities as a loyal, faithful and loving companion.

He was enormously attractive to other women, and he had more than once had to run to her for protection, because he could no more stop his charm from attracting them than a flower can prevent its colour or its scent from attracting a bee. This accounted for both her maternal and her possessive instincts towards him. He had never before been given even the slightest reason for supposing that anybody or anything took precedence over him in her life. Now he was not so sure.

Until their disagreement on the day of the Harvest Festival, he had never even considered that Mr Choppen other than as her boss had any part in Jess's life, though her jealous streak had once caused her to accuse him of being more to Choppen's daughter than a business associate. But even that had not amounted to anything once he had her in his arms in bed again. That magic had worked for both of them still, as it had done when they had first met in the spring of 1944. Privation and worry had never spoiled their delight in each other – but material success had begun to tarnish it. They had turned their backs on each other the night of their quarrel on Harvest Festival Sunday, and things had never really been the same since.

Jess was, as Sophie would have whispered behind her hand though the nearest male ears were a mile away, 'in the change' and allowances had to be made for that. She was also working long hours at a very exacting job that carried a huge load of responsibility. She could, with absolute truth and justice on her side, claim to be 'too tired'. Greg had made allowances for all that, and had gone on admiring her more than ever, even though he was suffering more than she knew. But now in the frantic rush of the run up to Christmas and the possibility of a grand opening of the golf course in the spring, he had hardly seen her long enough to talk to, let alone to make love to. In spite of himself, he began to wonder if she was becoming more to Choppen than his secretary.

He brooded, and in his misery, stopped working. He stayed away from Benedict's because he could hardly bear to be exposed to the love between Fran and William. He told himself that they were more or less still in their honeymoon period, because it was only little more than a year since their lifelong love for each other had at last been been consummated, whereas he and Jess had been lovers for twenty-five times as long. He stayed away from Monica because he was in no mood for creative work such as he needed for her 'backgrounds'. His excuse was that he had to do the household chores. Sophie's youngest sister Hetty, who had helped when Jess first went to work, had 'took agin' Jess, whom she blamed entirely for her daughter's success as a pop vocalist, and had refused to set foot in the house ever again.

Greg was honest with himself, and recognized the signs of the accidie he had suffered in Barra. He had to find out the truth about Jess's apparent obsession with her job, before it was too late. He was making up his mind to go and talk about things with William and Fran when Monica rang him about his overdue sketches.

Southside House was part of the complex of dwellings and farm buildings that had once been the Thackerays' homestead. Monica occupied half of the beautifully restored Elizabethan house. It took Greg no more than five minutes to pick up his rough sketches and take them, with his apologies and excuses, over to where Monica awaited him in her cosy sitting-room.

She looked briefly at the sketches, and laid them aside without comment. She was looking at Greg intently, just as he was looking at her. She was wondering why his paintings were not finished or of the usual quality; he had expected a tirade from Monique O'Dell, and was asking himself why the woman he was facing was only a rather spiritless Monica Choppen.

It was she who spoke first. 'Is anything wrong, Greg?' she asked.

'Yes. Everything,' he answered. 'What's wrong with you?'

'Only everything.'

There was an enormous and instant relief in both that there was, apparently, somebody else on the same wavelength.

They laughed. 'Who's going into the confessional first?' Greg asked.

'You. I'm not sure I can "go" at all,' she answered. 'It's something I just can't talk about, not even to you.'

'Same here, really, except that I should have to say "especially to you".'

She sat up, looking more like herself. 'Now we are being silly,' she said. 'We both have problems that are wearing us down, and need somebody to talk to. We've been friends as well as colleagues, and we understand each other. We could wreck the partnership if we don't come clean with each other. So out with it, whatever it is. I promise to take my turn, if you promise not to ask for details. Bargain?'

She went and made tea, and he told her, hesitantly at first and then with his usual eloquence, all that had gone wrong, and why he was afraid to find out why he was now feeling like a dog shut out in the scullery.

'Poor old Greg,' she said. 'What it is to be an artist! I am not suggesting that you're exaggerating, and I think Dad ought to know better than let Jess take so much responsibility that she has to neglect you to cope with it. But I can set your mind at rest on one score. If there is another man in her life, it isn't my Dad. He's as much of a one-woman man as you are. He never got over his luck in getting my beautiful, out-of-the-top-drawer mother to notice him, let alone love him enough to marry him. But there you are, she did. And then left him – killed in a plane-crash, seven years ago.

'He'll never get over losing her. That's why he nearly kills himself with work. I'm pretty sure one reason he thinks so much of Jess is because she doesn't droop her eyelashes at him, or try any other feminine wiles. He feels safe with her. She's a friend now as well as a secretary, and I know that he sometimes talks to her about Mum. And he knows she understands, because he also knows you, and what you mean to each other.

'He fills his life with work, now, and he's really very ill at ease in company, socially that is, where he has to be nice to other women. Though I think he really enjoyed the Bridgefoot wedding. Didn't you feel Jess trying to "mother him" that evening? I could have laughed, if I hadn't been so touched by it. Especially as I could see how it was getting up Mrs Catherwood's nose. Why was that?'

He laughed, feeling better already. 'I think you are too perspicacious for your own good, young woman,' he said. 'Yes, I noticed it, but I know that mood of Jess's very well. I gather that there has always been something of a love-hate relationship between Fran and Jess, dating from childhood, probably set up even then about the pig-in-the-middle, poor old William. He was Jess's brother who preferred Fran's company to hers. I have to admit that Jess does have a too-possessive streak in her. Naturally it used to irritate Fran, and does often irritate me, even when I am the one being "mothered". But Jess has had to accept that Fran now has first right to Bill, so it's only an unconscious reflex from the past. They are really fond of each other.'

'I'm glad,' she said. 'Fran and William are such a lovely couple.'

There was wistfulness in her voice that Greg could not help but remark. He looked at her sharply. 'Come on, your turn now. Why that wistful tone? You haven't fallen in love with William, have you?'

She smiled, but the wistfulness was still there. 'Of course I have,' she said. 'What woman in her right mind wouldn't? I'm in love with you as well, for the same reason. Just what more men ought to be, and aren't – well, most of them, specially the young. But the real reason is that you both remind me of the man I love, and can't have. So, like my Dad, I try to fill my time with work. But every now and then I see him again, and afterwards the whole world is what Hamlet said – "weary, stale, flat and unprofitable". And then I can't cope.'

'And you have seen him recently?'

'Yes. We spent last weekend together, in my London flat.'

'So you are lovers? Then what's wrong?'

'What's right? It isn't enough for either of us. He is married and his wife was my best friend. We both feel horribly guilty, much as we love each other. I know how bad he feels. So for both our sakes I have said "never again". And I mean it. I will not build my happiness on my friend's misery.'

She had got up from her chair, and was fishing for her handkerchief, firm little chin stuck out, but lips quivering dangerously.

Greg leapt to his feet and folded her into his arms, as he might have done a child. After a minute or two, he sat down again, and pulled her on to his knee, holding her head against him. His tenderness was her undoing and she let herself cry.

'Now,' he said, 'suppose you tell me all about it, right from the beginning.'

'Let me go and tidy myself up first,' she said. 'I've got to face up to it, so I might as well start. But thanks all the same. You are a darling, even though I don't think sympathy is good for me.'

She came back, and sat down facing him; but he pulled up an upright chair close to her, to be within reach if she needed contact again. He had already forgotten his own worries in the contemplation of hers. He remembered being as young as she was now, when he had had to leave Jess just before D-Day, and face the fact that he would be lucky ever to see her again.

'So why did he marry the wrong one?' he asked.

She shrugged. 'Why does anybody? It's a sort of game of chance, isn't it, like playing Snakes and Ladders. She and I were at school together – a posh school that Mummy chose, and paid for, because Dad hadn't got much then. We were always together, and went on to art school together in London.

'He was a student at London University. She and I lived together, and he lived in a rented house with four other students. The whole lot of us were just a gang, nothing serious. By the time we had finished our course, and he was taking his finals, the gang had come down to four, two girls and two boys. We were still swapping partners once a week – though I don't mean falling into bed with each other like they do now. I think all four of us were too well brought up for that. Sometimes I wonder if it might not have gone so wrong if we had. Anyway, while he was doing his finals it was me he wanted with him and I knew that I was in love. He has told me since that he knew too. That's how it goes. Luck landed him on a ladder and me on a snake. He did so well that he decided to stay on and do a post-graduate degree. Both us girls got jobs in London – but before I could take mine up, Mum was killed. I had to go home to Dad and Gavin. The other boy went overseas, and my boy and my friend were left together. She helped him a lot.

'From there on it's like a nightmare, one when nothing goes right. We were in such depths of misery at home that it never occurred to me to leave Dad to go up and see them.

'When I heard that they were married, I nearly went mad. I couldn't blame either of them, but I knew I would never love anybody else. I thought he didn't care what had happened to me.

'When Dad came down here, I jumped at the chance to be where I was never likely to meet him again. He still doesn't know I live here, as a matter of fact. He thinks I am always based at my flat, and abroad when I am not there. I expect it sounds silly to you, but you see I still love both of them. It isn't fair! None of the three of us did anything wrong – and we are all utterly miserable now. Why, Greg? Why?'

He took her hand, and held it tightly. 'You must have missed a bit out,' he said. 'When and where did you meet him again?'

'At an Arts Expo,' she said, smiling wanly. 'We just bumped into each other, quite literally, as it happened. He missed his train, and rang her up to tell her he had met me and was taking me out for a meal. We caught up on all each other's news, and he got a taxi to take me back to my flat. Do I need to tell you any more?'

Greg wondered what he would have said to her if she had been his daughter. When he spoke, it was in a serious vein. 'Yes, you do,' he said. 'You are painting him as either a weakling who didn't know his own mind, or a cad who wants to have his cake and eat it. But I don't think you are the girl to let that sort of a man wreck your life. Did you seduce him, or he you? And if he is happy with her, why upset you?'

'Once we were alone, we just fell into each other's arms. Some people are just born to love each other, even if it doesn't work out. The awful situation arises when either or both has thought themselves reasonably happy till they proved what real happiness is.

'We went on meeting whenever we could in my flat, and I think she guessed. I tried to stop it. I suggested that if they had a child it would cement their marriage, and give me a real reason never to see him again.

'That was when I learnt the truth. He had been wanting children ever since he married her, but she refuses point blank ever to consider it.

'He asked her to set him free, and told her he'd been seeing me. She threatened suicide. Oh, I know they all do! But don't forget how well I know her. Both of us are still fond of her. She says she loves him – but how can she, if she won't either give him a child or let him free? Oh Greg – I want his children! I want children of my own, but I can't be satisfied now with just anybody's. I won't marry somebody else I don't love just to get children and make Dad a grandfather, as he would like me to! I want my man's children, and only his.

'But I know her, too. If he comes to me, she will take her revenge, by carrying out her threat. She doesn't want to live without him. We had no chance against her at all. So I quit. Have I done right?

'He wouldn't accept my decision, last week, so after he'd gone, I went straight to an agency and let my flat to a couple of absolute strangers who will only deal with me through them – and gave orders that my whereabouts was not to be disclosed to anyone whatsoever. Then I wrote my last love letter to him at his place of work, and told him I proposed simply to disappear.

'So from now on I shall be here all the time, except when Monique is forced to show her face somewhere. I hope he won't even try to find me. I advised him to tell her all that had happened, so that she won't try to find me, either. And I hope that the scare she'll have had will make her change her mind about having a baby, to give him something else to think about, and show her that if I love him enough to give him up, she ought to love him enough to try to keep him happy. Only I don't really want her to. I want to make him happy myself.

'So now you know. Let's talk about something else.'

He went home relieved of the worst of his own worries, but very disturbed about Monica's. It was up to him to try to put things right with Jess. What was it some poet had said about 'the little rift within the lute'? It came to him as he was setting about making the house as spick and span and homely as he possibly could for Jess to come back to.

Tennyson, of course. Out of fashion now, too sentimental for modern taste; but what a poet!

> It is the little rift within the lute
> That by and by will make the music mute,
> And ever widening slowly silence all.

It was as much his own fault as Jess's that there had ever been any rift in their lute. He just must not let it widen. He hadn't made enough allowance for her age or her tiredness, and had mistaken her sympathy for Choppen completely. It was he, not she, who had been jealous and possessive this time. She must have felt it, and been hurt but too proud to complain. No wonder they hadn't been able to communicate, even in bed. Well, he could try to put that right, somehow. Perhaps if he told her about Monica, who wouldn't mind her knowing, it might serve as the bridge across which they could start out to meet each other again.

He guessed that they would differ about Monica's solution to her problem. Jess would say Monica had done the only thing morally possible. She had never wholly sympathized with Fran and William for solving their problem as they had done. It was still a bone of contention between them in

94

private. For his own part, he was grieved for Monica and both the others too. It was always the same, always had been, always would be. Whoever had first called it 'the *eternal* triangle' had certainly got it right.

It was always cropping up, though society's ideas about such things differed as time went by. Monica and her lover were in the same predicament as William and Fran had been, only turned the other way up; and as far as he could judge, modern sexual emancipation was no better equipped to deal with the emotions inside the eternal triangle than Victorian morality had been.

The young took what they wanted nowadays, and didn't rely on fairies; but they were just as likely as ever to go to bed in a palace and wake up in a vinegar bottle, which is just what had apparently happened to Monica. Greg waited for Jess in a mood both chastened and sad.

14

The Bridgefoot family faced a dilemma. When Aunt Esther had been carted off to hospital in such a hurry, they had had no intention of selling her house; but when, less than three weeks later, she was ready to be discharged, the deal with the syndicate had been agreed, though not signed and sealed. Her house still stood, with all her belongings in it. She was a difficult old woman who had always had her own way. She wanted to go home. 'Home' meant the Pightle.

George's conscience was uneasy. His wife tried to be practical, reminding herself that the old woman was not their responsibility, and that the price they would get for the property, put away for the grandchildren, would provide each with a considerable inheritance; that such a chance would not come their way again; that Miss Palmer had already occupied it for nearly twenty years rent-free, and had no claim upon it whatsoever. In spite of all that, she felt uneasy too; it wouldn't be right to turn the old woman out and hasten her end. It would make far more sense to take her straight back to Temperance Farm. Brian was the one who wanted to do the deal and get hold of the money, and there was Rosemary to be considered. She had suggested the new arrangements, but Brian and her raw-boned, domineering relative had detested each other from the start. It all boded ill.

Nevertheless, in the end George gave in, and the alterations at Temperance Farm were put in hand by the builders Mr Choppen had on the spot. The new arrangement robbed Rosemary of the dining-room, but the unused dairy was converted to a dining-room that had windows giving a pleasant if distant view of the golf course. What had been a large pantry was turned into to a bathroom for Aunt Esther's use only, and the old scullery made into a brand new 'fitted' kitchen. So everything, from the Bridgefoot point of view, was going well.

Nobody so far had dared to broach the subject to Miss Palmer, but there was no need to till she was about to be discharged. It would fall to Rosemary, of course, to break the news. She put it off till the very moment when she and Brian went to fetch the old lady out of hospital.

In the hospital car park, Brian ran back on the excuse that he was badly parked. Rosemary had no option but to face the ordeal alone.

Aunt Esther was dressed, seated at the side of her bed, waiting impatiently. The elbow-crutches leaning against the bed gave Rosemary some encouragement. If her aunt were dependent on them, she couldn't argue that she could manage the stairs at the Pightle by herself.

'You're late, Rose,' she snapped. 'As usual.'

She held up a rocky-jawed face to be kissed. The ward sister came bustling up, to give Rosemary instructions for after-care.

'I am taking her home with me,' Rosemary said. 'She can't go back to her house.'

'Why not? And who says so?'

Rosemary took the plunge. 'We do, Auntie. And Brian's father's sold the Pightle anyway.'

Aunt Esther stood up, without the aid of a crutch, and yelled. '*I will not move!* Do you hear? I will not be made to leave my home. I won't go out of here except straight to my own place.'

'*Ssh!* Miss Palmer,' said the sister with authority. 'You are disturbing the other patients.'

'You shut up!' replied the patient in question. 'Don't you shush me! What's it got to do with you?'

'I'm in charge of the ward. Be quiet, or I shall have to send for the doctor. Just you be a good girl, and listen to what your daughter has to say. She is taking you where you can best be looked after properly.'

'Did you hear what she said?' the old woman inquired loudly of the other patients. 'I shall sue her for inflammation of character! Called me *Miss* Palmer, as is my rightful name, and then in the same breath calls this ungrateful gal as I brought up from a baby my daughter! And me never married on account of having to look after her and the rest of 'em. If she was my daughter, she wouldn't let nobody turn me out o' my home. It's them Bridgefoots. They want to put me in a home.'

The sister tried again. 'Miss Palmer, whoever this lady is, she has looked after you like a daughter. It's her own home she is taking you to. There's nothing to get upset about.'

'That's what you think. Rose, get me out of here.'

'Yes, Auntie. That's what we came for,' said Rosemary. 'May I go and get my husband to help?' she asked.

'No!' roared Aunt Esther. 'He's one o' them Bridgefoots as is selling the roof from over my head. Judases, every one of 'em. Sold a helpless old woman's 'ome for thirty pieces of silver, that's what they've done. I'll never set foot in no Bridgefoot's house!'

She tried to stand up, and tottered. Rosemary rushed to help her, and promptly got her face slapped.

'Now stop it! Miss Palmer,' ordered the Sister. 'If you go on like this, you will give yourself a seizure, you know. Let me help you up. There, that's better, isn't it? You don't want me to have to send for a doctor to sedate you, do you?'

Miss Palmer eyed her with the gaze of a basilisk. She abandoned her helpless old woman role and became the quarrelsome spinster whose tartly expressed opinions were and always had been the scourge of her neighbours.

'You can fetch the doctor and the parson and the lawyer if you like,' she said. 'You can fetch the police and fire service and the Queen's Household Cavalry, for all I care. I know my rights. Nobody's turning me out of my home or taking me nowhere without my consent. I won't leave this hospital till you get me a lawyer.'

A young doctor in a white coat and Brian arrived together. Rosemary, listening while the sister put them into the picture, experienced a moment of wicked glee while watching two helpless males wondering what to do. Aunt Esther addressed herself directly to the doctor.

'I ain't going into that man's house,' she said. 'He's a Bridgefoot. I'm stopping here.'

'You can't do that, you know,' said the flustered young houseman. 'That bed is booked for another patient.'

'Find her another bed. She ain't having mine.'

Desperate maladies need desperate cures. The doctor gave in. 'I think she is too distressed to leave at present,' he said to Brian. 'We shall have to move her to another ward, and perhaps in the meantime you can make arrangements more likely to suit her.'

'Back in my own home at the Pightle,' said the sharp-eared Esther.

Rosemary had had enough. 'You've just said you'll never set foot again in a Bridgefoot house – and whether you like it or not, the Pightle still belongs to them.'

'Thank you, Doctor,' said Brian. 'If you will keep her overnight, we will see about finding her a place in an old folks' home.'

'I told you so! I told you so!' Miss Palmer began to wail. 'I knowed it all along!'

Rosemary wanted to go back to comfort her aunt, but Brian piloted her firmly to the door. She called, 'I'll come again tomorrow, Auntie.'

Once outside she cried and laughed hysterically by turns. Brian, once home, swore and raged; they then went to see George, who neither laughed nor raged. He was very distressed.

After a few minutes of quiet, during which they all suspected that he was consulting the Almighty, he announced his intention of going to see Choppen at once to tell him that the deal about the Pightle was off.

Brian left, to where he could swear to his heart's content. Rosemary hid in the bathroom in floods of self-recriminatory tears. Molly, though disappointed, said nothing; she had never had any real hope that anybody would get the better of Aunt Esther.

George had always found Choppen a hard businessman, but a fair one. He pointed out to George that though the deal had not been signed, he had trusted absolutely to the Bridgefoot reputation for integrity, and had already put a great deal of time and energy into the plans. It would require a lot more to undo them. Was George willing to lose his good name by running back when all was completed but the signing? Was he prepared to make some financial recompense? Would the old lady ever be able to go back there, whatever she felt? Wouldn't it be more sense for them to try and find some sort of compromise? Find out what Miss Palmer would accept?

'It's no good me trying,' George told him. 'She won't talk to me, or any other Bridgefoot. They've made her rooms beautiful for her at Temperance, though I pity them if she ever does go there. She is the awk'ardest old humbug I've ever come across. She's set her stall out, and she'll die of cold and starvation rather than give in to one of us now.'

'Well, shall I go and talk to her myself?'

George could hardly believe his ears, but a drowning man will clutch at a straw, and so it was left.

Choppen took Jess with him, and went to see Aunt Esther next day. She had been moved overnight to the geriatric ward. They were shown to it, and were horrified. The beds filled with human detritus appalled both of them, and the stench was almost unbearable. A television set at one end was blaring a commentary on a horse-race.

Jess left Choppen to deal with Miss Palmer, and walked round the ward, her whole being in a state of revolt. A pair of eyes following her attracted her attention. She went to the side of the bed and stood by it, laying on the bedside locker the grapes Choppen had bought for Aunt Esther. The patient spoke, in a cultured, educated voice. 'It's very kind of you,' she said, 'but I'm afraid I can't eat them. I can't use my hands. Parkinson's.'

'How do you endure that noise?' asked the practical Jess. 'Shall I go and turn the thing off?'

'It would only be switched on again. You get used to it. And the smell.'

'How long have you got to be here, then?'

'Sorry, I can't answer that. Not long, I hope. There's only one way of escape. "The grave's a fine and quiet place,"' she quoted.

Jess couldn't bear it. She fled. It was only ten minutes before Choppen found her sitting in the car.

'It won't hurt that old Gorgon to stay where she is till tomorrow,' he said. 'Probably do the old harridan good! I have agreed to pay for a room in a private nursing home till she'll see reason. We'd better go and find one for her.'

He had got into the driving seat before turning to look at his passenger. 'Jess! Jess, my dear – are you OK? What's the matter? What is it?'

She was shaking uncontrollably, and started to cry. The desolation she had just witnessed had taken out the linch-pin of her determination to be self-sufficient. She felt as if she was falling to pieces inside. She had suddenly seen herself and her new lifestyle as a career women in a different light. That poor woman she had given the grapes to had been a career woman once, she thought, probably a schoolteacher, by the sound of her. No husband, no family. Now in that hell till death released her.

Jess's sobs grew louder and deeper as she let go of her self-control.

The autumn dusk was falling, and the car-park almost dark. Choppen switched off the car's engine, and the lights.

'All right. Cry it out,' he said. 'It was a facer for me, too. I had no idea such places existed.' He seemed content to wait. Jess went on crying, hunched down beside him.

After what seemed a very long time, Choppen handed Jess his handkerchief to replace her sodden one, and turning towards her gathered her into his arms, resting his head against hers. He said nothing. They just sat.

When she began to show signs of calming down, he drew away and said, 'Now tell me what the trouble really is, Jess. You may think me a hard-hearted cuss, after nothing but money, but I do have eyes and ears, especially for those I'm fond of. You haven't been the same woman lately. Why? That ward was only the last drop of misery that made your cup run over. My Annette was just the same – taut and strung-up like you have been lately when anything was wrong. You're a lot like her in some ways –

'Let's go,' he finished abruptly, and switched on the engine, not waiting for an answer. He drove her straight back to Southside House.

Greg, still strung up himself from his interview with Monica, heard the car and flung open the door to welcome Jess, but found Mr Choppen there instead. Jess had not moved from her seat in the car.

Greg's optimism gave way to awful apprehension. Choppen read his mind.

'Jess is OK, but she's all in,' he said. 'It's my fault and I apologize. I have been working her too hard. And I may as well tell you that I have been cuddling her to comfort her, though I didn't attempt to kiss her better. It wasn't my arms she wanted round her, anyway. Come and coax her out of my car.'

They more or less carried her into the house, completely exhausted, dishevelled and still a soggy mass of tears. Greg took her into his arms and held her close. Choppen raised his hat, and turned away.

'Don't go,' Jess said in a croaky whisper. 'I haven't apologized or said thank you.'

He came back and she put out a hand from within the circle of Greg's arms. He took it and held it in both his own. She leaned forward, and kissed him full on the mouth.

'I shall be all right, now I'm home,' she said.

'So shall I,' said Greg.

Choppen tried to speak, but his voice wouldn't work properly; so he left, closing the door softly behind him. He

101

found himself sympathizing with that bitter old woman at the hospital. What a difference there was between living accommodation and a home.

15

Eric Choppen was reluctant to return to his hotel suite, luxuriant in its way as it was. The afternoon's experiences had unsettled him. It wasn't that he had any feelings for Jess other than as an attractive woman who was a reliable, hard-working colleague, and of whom he had grown fond enough to use occasionally as a confidante. But the fact remained that he had not had any woman in his arms, other than Monica, since the morning he had said goodbye to Annette at the airport, and begged her not to stay away a moment longer than she needed to. Holding Jess had brought back too many memories, and they hurt. He didn't want to be alone. He was within a hundred yards of Monica's door, and he turned towards it and her. He went in without ringing, and found Monica more or less as Greg had left her, still sitting by her fire with no other light. He switched on the main overhead lamps as he opened the door, and in place of the brisk, matter-of-fact and companionlike daughter he had been expecting to greet him, saw a limp, listless girl whose eyes were still puffed up and red from weeping.

'Well,' he said, going towards her with slight hesitation, wondering just how unwelcome he might be. 'I seem to have jumped out of the frying pan into the fire. I've just left one woman in tears to come straight to another. How long have you been sitting there in the dark, crying?'

'Hello, Dad. Sorry. I'm glad to see you, really. Since Greg left me, about two hours ago. Who have you left in tears?'

'Jess.' He looked at her sharply. 'There's no connection, is there? I know you and Greg get on well together – and I've noticed that you haven't been your usual self for the last couple of months, any more than Jess has. You haven't been fool enough to start an affair with him, have you? And now he's thrown you over? If that's it, you'll get no sympathy from me. I know better than to try to interfere with what you youngsters get up to out of my sight ... but not in my backyard. And with a married man old enough to be your father, however charming he may be. I thought you were fond of Jess? You must have known that all her husband was after with you was a bit of sex on the side. Aren't there plenty of willing men of your own age? What would you have thought once if a bit of a girl like you had got between me and your mother? You young folk nowadays make me mad! You have no idea what love or loyalty is!'

He sat down, disappointed on his own behalf, and angry with her. He had come to her instinctively, needing comfort. He had expected her to understand when he told her what had happened, but here she was up to her own neck in misery. Couldn't she see that he was upset and needed her for once?

His instinct to go to her had been right, though. She had understood. He never mentioned Annette except under great stress, and that had alerted her. She jumped up and went to him, sitting down on the arm of his chair.

'Poor old Dad! But don't go imagining things just because I've got a fit of the blues. It would be funny if you weren't all so serious. First Greg accuses me of being in love with William Burbage, though I haven't met him more than half a dozen times all told, and then you suggest that I am snatching Greg from under Jess's nose. Why should that upset you so much? You haven't fallen for Jess yourself, have you?'

He remained disdainfully silent.

She hugged him. 'Sorry, Dad. That was mean. I was only getting my own back. I'm very fond of Greg and I think William is a darling, but I do have some sense. You know I wouldn't be sitting here crying for nothing, though, so I shall have to tell you the truth. There is a man involved, and he is married. We've known each other for years, long before Mum went.

'I hadn't seen him since that time, till recently, because I left London then, if you remember. We met quite by chance again – and I knew quite well that he was married. So I knew what I was doing, and that it couldn't last. What I didn't know was how deep it went for both of us . . . how much I love him.'

'And he's gone back to his wife?'

'I suppose so. I don't know. We've been meeting in my flat, but after last weekend I couldn't cope with my guilt – so I scarpered. I've let my flat till the spring. He has no idea where to find me. I'd had enough sense not to tell him of anything here, so he won't try to find me anywhere but in London. I'll work from here and the shop. Don't worry.

'He feels as guilty as I do. And I'm bloody miserable. *You* know how it feels to know that you'll never see the one you love to distraction ever again, don't you? Well, that's how I feel now. Only you did have something of Mum left. You had us, me and Gav – Mum's children. I've got nothing. I've been sitting here wishing I'd had enough sense not to take any precautions. I might have had his child. Would you have cast me off, Dad? Or insisted on me having an abortion? I wonder.'

'So you've been going to bed with him.'

'Yes, of course. Doesn't everybody fall into bed with everybody else now? That's what conferences are for, these days!'

She saw the look of disgust on his face and kissed him. 'No, Dad, not me, and I didn't mean you. I'm just being cynical because I hurt so much inside. You see, I didn't know how much he still loved me till last weekend.

'And I've learned a lot about love. I know now what Mum and you meant to each other. I see Greg with Jess – and William with Fran. They have each other, but they haven't got children. You've got us, but not Mum. It seems you can't have everything. That's what's hurting me most. I always wanted to have children, but I never shall, now. I don't want any other man's children. Or any other man. So that's that. I'm afraid you've got a spinster on your hands, Dad, if not an old maid.' She tried to smile, but it wasn't a success. Her face crumpled, and she began to cry quietly again.

He pulled her on to his lap, just as he used to when she

was a little girl. Annette used to say he spoiled her; he used to quip that she couldn't expect him not to cherish a bit that had fallen off her.

Monica cried herself out. It was what both of them had needed. In the silence broken only by her sobs he had let himself think about Annette.

He had covered his own broken heart with a carapace of work and the business of making money, like a stickleback building its nest by sticking tiny bits of grit to the outside. He had been pleased to see both Monica and Gavin showing his own sort of business acumen, too. He had forgotten how young and vulnerable they were, with hearts as liable to be broken as his own.

Well, there was nothing he could do to help Monica. He guessed she would find her salvation in work, as he had done, but she would find out that it was the work that helped, not the money. The only bit of comfort he could give himself was the knowledge that she still turned to him, and would be 'at home' in Old Swinthinford more now than she had been before. He must see to it that nothing happened that would prevent him from seeing as much of her as she wanted.

When at last she recovered and went to the bathroom to wash the tears away, she offered to make him tea, but he still had to report to George Bridgefoot.

In the ordinary way, he would have gone back to the hotel, and telephoned. The dusk had fallen early and it was inclined to be foggy, as miserable as he felt. Acting on impulse, he turned in to the gate of the Old Glebe, and went to report to George in person.

Molly was as surprised to see him as she would have been to find a Martian standing on her doorstep. She asked him into the kitchen where George was sitting by the fire in the old Windsor chair that had been his father's and his grandfather's.

Molly fussed; George acted exactly as he would have done if Eric Choppen had been Daniel Bates. Hospitality demanded that he be made welcome and given sustenance.

'Take your coat off,' George said, 'and make yourself at home, if it's only for five minutes. What'll you drink?'

As if mesmerized by the warmth and the welcome, Choppen

did as he was invited to do. Then he found himself recounting the tale of Aunt Esther's compliance under his blandishments, and had both the Bridgefoots laughing at his mimicry of her. He hadn't let himself go with anybody like that for a very long time. Molly was glancing at the clock. 'Will you stay and have supper with us?' she asked. 'It's only cold beef and baked potatoes with pickles, and a cold custard tart, because we have our main meal in the middle of the day. But there's plenty and to spare, and you'd be more than welcome. Only we always eat in the kitchen when we're by ourselves, so you'll have to take us as you find us.'

To his own surprise, he accepted. The last thing he wanted was his own company. Nothing his expensive French chef would have produced for him could possibly have tasted so good as Molly's custard tart, heavily sprinkled with nutmeg; but then there is a sort of magic in a farmhouse kitchen that is hardly to be matched anywhere else. It was bedtime before Choppen got back to the hotel, where the receptionist had left a message for him.

Commander Elyot Franks had booked into the hotel in the afternoon, pending the arrival of his furniture at the Old Rectory. He would be glad if a meeting with Mr Choppen could be arranged for the next day.

One way and another, it had been an eventful day.

16

November's blue shadows were falling everywhere. Benedict's was not escaping its share of them. It was mid-term for William and he could not spend as much time at home as he liked to. He was restless, and rather quiet. Fran knew the signs; he had something on his mind. She knew it was no good asking him what it was, because he was as close as an oyster about his own worries. She had found that out long ago, but she hated to feel shut out from anything concerning him, and was touchy herself as a result. Remembering the iconoclastic row there had been once before in just such a situation, she was absolutely determined this time not to ask what the matter was until he told her of his own accord.

Work was the best cure for such niggles. She had plenty to do, though not as straightforward as usual. A year or more ago, while waiting for William to return from the USA she had written her first full-length play. All their mutual happiness had depended on what happened when he came back, and when it had turned out so well she had shoved the play into a drawer and forgotten it. Life with William had become, quite literally overnight, overwhelmingly more important than any fiction could be.

She had recently found the play again, and read it through. It was too good to waste, though it needed editing, shortening and polishing. She had enjoyed doing it, but it was with less confidence than usual that she had dispatched it to her agent. She hadn't told William, and was now anxiously awaiting a reply, with the same scared excitement with which any mother awaits the birth of a first child.

Her birthday fell towards the end of November and she hoped for a celebration with family and friends – though another lesson she had learned was that new friends and close family did not always make a good mixture. What she wanted this year was for both her children to be with her at the same time. With Jess and Greg, who were also 'family', that would make eight, just right for a semi-formal dinner party without running any risk of inviting friends as well.

Her son and his wife had never visited Benedict's yet. She had asked them early, but so far there had been no response. She began to fret in a most un-Franlike fashion about it. *Why* would they never come to see her? She couldn't pretend any longer that it was just by chance that they always had a previous engagement. They were having no more to do with her and William than the frostiest familial courtesy demanded. Fran blamed Sue, Roland's wife, and suspected that her liaison with William was not helping matters. But however much Sue disapproved of that, it could not be the whole cause, because the coolness had been there from the start.

In fact, Fran had been more or less cut off from Roland since the day of his wedding.

The marriage had come as a great surprise to her because she had never heard anything about Sue from Roland till he had telephoned to tell her that he was getting married the next week at a register office in York, and to ask her to be there. Though full of maternal doubts, she had asked few questions. She had showed her surprise, though, and asked who was to be her new daughter-in-law.

'Oh, no worry on that score, Mother,' he had said. 'She's out of the top drawer. In fact, her father's a baronet.'

'Then why the haste, and a register-office wedding, darling?' Fran had said.

'Wrong again, Mum. No reason, except that that's the way Sue wants it. No fuss. Honestly, it's OK, Mum. I've known her for ages. It's always been on the cards. We've just got round to it, that's all. Do come.'

She had gone, and almost wished she hadn't. She had to admit that Susan was a beauty of the very first water, with all the grace and polish that good breeding and expensive finishing schools produce, but there it ended. To Fran she seemed to lack warmth, and was certainly not what Fran had hoped for. Besides, it had been all too plain that Sue had done her best to avoid her new mother-in-law. Fran had been puzzled and a bit hurt. Sue's family were charming and friendly enough, but since then Sue herself had consistently declined any intimacy.

Fran had steadfastly refused to be offended, though she had been disappointed when they had showed no interest in her exciting project of buying and restoring her grandfather's house. When she had thrown in her lot with William, she had been open and honest with them about it, and thought they had accepted it – if not so warmly as Kate and Jeremy.

If her liaison with William was the obstacle, she must try to see it from their point of view; but she thought it queer that her clever, successful and previously loving son didn't seem to care a jot now about her happiness. She cared a great deal about his. Like all students, he had kept his university life and his family well apart. (Sensible parents didn't ask questions nowadays, she had told herself.) Since his marriage, though, she had lost him, and she didn't know why.

She wrote regularly, and phoned at decent intervals, and went on issuing invitations, like this last one. So far, it had been completely ignored. She was letting it upset her, all the more because she didn't feel able to talk to William about it. He was apt to be a bit touchy about her children, leaning over backwards not to come between her and them. Kate and he had set up a marvellous relationship, but he seemed to clam up at any mention of Roland, whom he had not yet met. While he was in his present mood it wasn't a good time to bring that subject up. But her birthday was now only two weeks away.

On a very raw, dark morning Fran woke miserable. Because he had to leave very early, William had persuaded her not to get up before he went, and when she did she felt instinctively as she went downstairs that it was going to be a bad day – as Sophie would say, 'One o' them dark days afore Christmas'.

She heard the postman and picked up the post. Still no letter from Roland and Sue. She was irritated, even angrily resentful. At least they needn't be rude to her.

She went to put William's mail on his desk. There was a letter from the USA – large and official-looking, bearing a logo she didn't recognize. As she put it down, she felt again that old twinge in her diaphragm that spelled fear – fear that Janice, William's legal wife, could still somehow wreck their happiness. She knew this fear to be irrational, but she couldn't always keep it at bay.

She sighed. It would be a long day till William got home. Not that he would tell her what was in that letter, unless it was something good. If its effect was to make him even more uneasy, she would know better than to ask what was wrong, this time.

She went to the kitchen with her own post. Nothing from her agent. The only other letter was from Anne Rushlake, who wrote to say that she had been over-optimistic about her chances of getting back to Old Swithinford before the New Year. In the meantime she was becoming increasingly anxious about the Schoolhouse being left unoccupied, and the garden getting overgrown. Could Fran spare Sophie half a day a week to go and air the house, and Ned to keep the garden tidy?

Fran's hackles rose. She liked Anne a lot, and was glad to have found in her both a friend and a potential secretary; but Anne was not Mary, for whom she would have done anything in her power. She was distinctly irritated at being taken so much for granted. She could hardly ignore or refuse the request; but this morning it definitely irked her. Who was she to give orders to Sophie or Ned as to where they were to go to work? They were not her slaves, as Anne seemed to imply. You didn't tell such people what to do nowadays, you asked them nicely if they would oblige. Anne had a lot to learn.

Fran was missing Mary more than she had ever thought possible. If only Mary had still been here to talk to, she wouldn't have got herself so worked up about either Roland or William. Perhaps that was why she felt irritated with Anne. Nobody could replace Mary; and since Mary had died, she had had no female confidante left except Sophie. Jess was always too busy even if they had now and then returned to the close intimacy of their childhood.

Fran was wondering sadly if she ought to abandon any birthday celebration when Sophie arrived. One look at her told Fran that Sophie was upset, too. As soon as she had gone through the stolid routine of putting on the apron she wore over her overall, she sat down at the kitchen table facing Fran and handed her a letter.

'Read it for yourself,' Sophie said. 'It's from our Wend'. She's a-gooin' to get married! To a man as none of us as ever set eyes on. And none of us knowed nothing about it. Well nobody does still, only me. However shall I tell 'em? Her Mam and Dad, I mean, and Thirz' and Dan'el?'

'Oh, Sophie! Is getting married anything to get so upset about? That's the way things are, these days. She's only doing what others of her age do. It's exactly what Roland did, marrying a girl I'd never heard of.'

'Ah, and no doubt both of 'em'll be getting divorced again afore you can say "knife". I don't know as it makes it any better what other folks do. It's our Wend' as concerns me. I only 'ope as she don't live to regret it . . . going to live in America and all. But see for yourself what she says.'

Fran took the letter. The writing was big and round and

like a child's; to Fran it indicated that 'Sister Anne', the pop vocalist becoming ever more successful, was still the rather immature Wendy Noble she had been when Fran had first met her.

What was there to say? She and Sophie were more or less both in the same boat. Wendy was to Sophie much as Roland was to her.

'Going to *live* in America! That's what I can't get over. I shall never see her no more.'

'Now look, Sophie, that's silly. You have seen William go off to America at least three times, and come back safe. It only takes about eight hours by aeroplane. She'll come and go like he does. And quite likely she'll be on television soon. You'll see quite as much of her, even if she does live in America, as I see of Roland, though he only lives in Yorkshire.'

She hadn't meant to mention her own troubles but disappointment and chagrin had got the better of her. She poured her feelings out to Sophie, who sat with eyes cast down, folding and refolding Wendy's letter.

Then she turned on Fran that deep-eyed gaze that Fran always felt looked right through her. 'Why don't he come to see you, then, like Katie does?'

'I wish I knew,' said Fran miserably.

'Are you certain sure as it ain't because of what goes on here between you and William?' Sophie asked.

'What makes you think that? Are people talking? Kate comes.'

'Well, there is them as have noticed, like, that she comes and 'e don't, as you might say,' Sophie answered truthfully.

Fran was instantly indignant. 'Really! What is it to do with anybody but us? And how on earth do they know? I've never mentioned Roland to anybody that I can remember.'

'There's others as do know about 'im though, ain't there? I mean like Jess – and them. When there were all that talk about Lucy Bridgefoot marrying a lord's son, Jess – I mean Mis' Tolly – told 'em up at the 'otel about your son as were married to a lord's daughter. And the tale got about from that, I daresay. Folks begun to wonder why it were that him and 'is wife 'ad never come 'ere, and then worked it out for theirselves that though you was the squire's family, your son had married above hisself, and her folks didn't want 'im to hev nothink to do with you – specially with you and him a-living together.' ('Him' meant William, in Sophie's vocabulary.)

Fran allowed her indignation to boil over. 'Is that what you think?' she asked.

Again that steady, grey-eyed gaze. 'I should ha' expected you to know me better'n that b'now. You asked me what other folks was saying, else I shouldn't ha'told you. As I said to Thirz' when she told me, it's nothing to do with the likes of us if one o' your children comes to see you and the other don't. And I said to Thirz', it only goos to prove the old saying:

'"A son's a son till he gets 'im a wife.
But a daughter's a daughter all the days of 'er life."

'"I'll take my oath as it's 'er as won't let 'im come," I says.'

Trust Sophie to hit the nail right on the head. They left the matter there.

Fran told Sophie of Anne's letter, and asked what she thought about it. Sophie took her time before answering, then said, 'Well, I shall do it if you want me to, for Miss's sake. But why didn't that Mis' Rushlake keep Olive 'Opkins on? It wouldn't be right for you to set nobody on in Olive 'Opkins's place. Who'll be doing for Mis' Rusklake when she's a-livin' there? She may find it ain't as easy to get folks to work as she expects. She may be Miss's niece, but she ain't Miss. She'll find that out soon enough.'

Fran thought Sophie might be right. Anne was used to living in town.

Sophie was looking down the garden. 'Here's Ned a-coming to the door,' she said. 'I wonder what's the matter. He were right as ninepence when I spoke to 'im as I come in, but there's something gone wrong now, b' the look of 'im. Shall I let 'im in?'

She didn't wait for an answer, but opened the door before Ned got there. He pulled off his cap and stood before Fran. She knew by his manner that he had bad news to impart.

When he was telling her a tale, he would go nearly as far round by Will's mother's to get to the point as Sophie did; but if he had bad news to deliver, he shot it at her at once, as if with a verbal pea-shooter.

'Fox got Oscar last night,' he said. 'Silly old bugger – I mean that daft old fool of a gander – just would not be shut up afore I went home last night, so I had to leave him out. I knowed this would 'appen sooner or later.'

Fran was sorry, because in spite of his display of ferocity, Oscar had become such a feature of Benedict's garden that she hated to think of him as only a bloody mass of feathers. But her concern was much more for Ned than for Oscar. Since Ned's wife had died, he had spent most of his waking hours at Benedict's, accompanied by an entourage of three – Fran's Cat, a pet robin, and Oscar. On them he lavished all his love.

'Oh dear, oh dear!' Sophie was saying, over and over again. 'Oh dear, oh dear!' It was against Sophie's creed to grieve for a creature without a soul, but even she had been fond of Oscar in her way, and she, too, was sorry for Ned. 'Fancy us hevin' foxes about. Nasty smelly things foxes are, to my way o'thinking.'

'Sit down, Ned,' Fran said. 'Poor old Oscar! I really am sorry. Shall we buy some more geese in the spring?'

'That'd be the best thing for the old orchard,' he said. 'But there won't never be another like Oscar for me. But what I come up to say is that foxes ain't particular. You'd better not let Cat get out at night.'

Fran panicked. She remembered that she hadn't seen Cat that morning, since she got up. She had heard William talking to Cat before he left, but that had been while it was still dark. She had been so full of other grievances that she hadn't missed her cat.

'Oh Ned,' she wailed. 'I think William let her out before he left – it was only about seven. I haven't seen her since!'

'No, and she di'n't come to meet me like she does most days,' he said. 'Where did you last see her?'

'Asleep on our bed, between us, where she always sleeps,' she answered, and then realized her gaffe. Both Ned and Sophie were staring stolidly straight in front of them. They were quite well aware that she slept with William; but it offended against all propriety for her to put it into words.

She got up, blushing furiously, and ran away to her study, desperately trying to pull herself together. There was a difference between Cat and Oscar! But there Cat lay, peacefully asleep across the telephone, with her head on her front paws. Fran scooped up the startled little bundle of fur and hugged her, rushing out to the kitchen with tears still on her face and kisses stifling attempted yowls of Siamese protest. The smiles that broke out on the faces of Ned and Sophie told their own story.

'Let's hev a cup o' tea, shall we?' said Sophie not wishing to be seen to care that Cat was safe.

'They say a cat's got nine lives,' Ned said. 'But if I was you I shouldn't risk letting Foxy get one o' them. He'd made a nice mess o' poor old Oscar.'

Fran changed the subject, and again brought up the matter of Anne's letter. To her surprise, Ned for once seemed reluctant to oblige.

Fran felt harassed, and looked it.

'We'll think o' something,' Ned said soothingly. 'There's more ways o' killing the cat than chokin' it wi' butter.'

'Cat!' cried Fran. 'She's gone again! Where is she now? Is she safe?' There was consternation on all three faces, till Sophie went to look.

'She's in the pantry, eating that fish as we was goin' to hev for our dinner,' she said. 'I'll Cat her if I can get hold of her!'

'I don't reckon she'll go far from the fire on days like this,' Ned said. 'Just keep her in at nights for a while.'

He got up to go. Sophie was in the pantry, bent double, clearing up the floor, and looking none too pleased.

'I don't know what the world's a-comin' to, these days, that I don't,' Sophie said. 'You can't eat that fish as is been dragged round the pantry floor, so I reckon I shall have to make some rissoles out o'what were left o' yist'day's meat. Only I should like to git on with it, 'cos I'm still got to goo and find Dan'el and tell 'im about Wend'. I shall leave 'im to tell Thirz' and Thirz' to tell Het. I ain't a-going to be nowheer near when Het goes into sterricks about it. So I shan't be 'ere this afternoon. I don't want no dinner.'

'Nor do I,' said Fran. She was profoundly irritated again with everything and everybody. Just when she needed help and comfort, even her own household couldn't be relied on. Everybody else's affairs were more important than hers, apparently. Even Cat had deserted, and gone to ground in the airing cupboard.

17

Fran went to sit in her chair by the sitting-room fire, still in a mood of gloomy despondency mainly about Roland, not knowing how to pass the time. She had a book in her lap that she could not keep her mind on. William was going to be late home, and there was that letter waiting for him. On any other day, at least she would have had Sophie's company. It was a long time since she had felt so 'blue'. She had almost worked herself into a mood for self-pitying tears when Ned tapped on the door and looked in. 'You've got a visitor,' he said. 'That Mr Bellamy from Castle Hill's at the back door.'

She was undisguisedly pleased. For once in her life the last thing she wanted was her own company.

'Ask him to come in,' she said.

'I did, but he said no, though he didn't want to go without seein' you.'

'I'll come,' she said and got up, following Ned out.

Bob Bellamy was standing at the back door, looking much more of a prosperous farmer than he had when they had seen him outside the church on the hill.

'Mr Bellamy!' she said warmly. 'What a pleasant surprise. Do come in.'

He raised his hat, his eyes shy but smiling. 'I ain't fit to come in,' he said. 'Look at my boots. I only called to see if you'd like a brace o' pheasants as I've got in my car. Shall I go and get them?'

She beamed on him as if he were a child offering his teacher an apple. As he went to fetch them, she thought that his unsophistication was one of the things that made him so attractive to her, except that it made him seem vulnerable. She wanted to protect him, though heaven only knew why, because he was certainly no fool. On the contrary, he was possessed of most unusual gifts, which he was intelligent enough to understand and accept.

He came back swinging the two dead birds from his finger. 'Where shall I put them?' he asked. 'They'll need hanging for a couple o' weeks to be really good eating.'

'Come in and put them on the kitchen table,' she said. 'Ned will know how to deal with them. Oh, bother a bit of mud on your boots! This isn't Buckingham Palace.'

He followed her into the kitchen, and laid the beautiful limp creatures on the table. He ran his forefinger over the glossy green head of the cock bird and then, as if in apology, down the glorious tail feathers. 'I can't eat them,' he said. 'I like pheasant as much as the next man, if it's dished up to me on a plate covered with gravy and all the trimmings – but I'd rather see 'em strutting about alive.'

'Then why on earth do you shoot them?' she said.

He grinned. 'I don't – not if I can miss,' he said. 'Only I happen to be a good shot, and I've got to hold my own among other farmers. There's two more brace in the car you can have if you've got a freezer. I don't want 'em.'

'Come in, and take your coat off,' she said. She sounded like Mary used to when she intended to be obeyed. 'I was just going to make a cup of tea.'

He came without further protest. 'Leave your coat over a chair,' she said, and led him through the hall into the sitting-room, motioning him towards William's chair.

He stood still inside the door, looking a bit dazed. He wore the same appreciative expression as she had watched on Greg's face the first time he had entered that room. His eyes lingered longest on the gold-leafed moulded cornice, and then fixed themselves on the marble fireplace. He sat down at last, and she was handing him his tea when he said, 'What's happened to the picture?'

'What picture?'

'The one that used to hang over the mantelpiece.'

She nearly dropped the cup. There had been a picture there once, when she was very small. An eighteenth-century portrait of the Wagstaffe who had built Benedict's, with his wife and his dogs.

'There used to be a picture there,' she said. 'I remember it, but it's been gone for decades. How on earth did you know? It more or less fitted the space, and it was in a heavy gold frame.'

'That's right,' he said. 'Do you remember the actual picture?'

She told him ... some of her ancestors, a couple in eighteenth-century dress.

'Yes,' he said, satisfied.

'How on earth do you know about it?'

'I've been here before – many a time – though only in a dream. I've dreamt that dream since I can first remember. I used to cry when I woke up when I was little. In my dream I always stood looking at that picture. This room's the one I dream about. You don't know what happened to the picture, then?'

Bewildered and incredulous, Fran shook her head. 'I expect it was valuable, and had to be sold,' she said.

He gave her a most charming, if highly embarrassed smile. 'Well, I know now why I wondered where I had seen you before. The lady in the picture was very much like you, only – if you don't mind me saying so – it's a bit like the pheasants. I'd rather see you alive than in paint.'

She sat down, shivery and goosepimpled, but blushing at his compliment.

He saw, and apologized. 'I did tell you about my gift for knowing things,' he said. 'I didn't mean to be rude, or offend you.'

'You haven't. It's all so uncanny. Does your sixth sense tell you things all the time? Before they happen?'

'I don't tell fortunes, if that's what you mean.'

It was her turn to apologize. 'Mr Bellamy, you know I didn't mean that! It was a silly thing to say – and I wasn't being at all serious. I was only thinking how lonely and miserable I was, desperately wanting company, when you appeared out of the blue. As if you had come like the genie out of a bottle.'

'Perhaps I did come because of that, though I didn't know,' he said calmly. 'When I left the shoot, I wondered who might like the pheasants and thought of you. I didn't want to be by myself. I shouldn't have gone out with the shoot but for that. I don't like killing for the sake of killing. But I wanted company.'

'What's wrong?' she asked. (How funny, she thought. She could ask him that, but she couldn't ask William.)

His reply was just as direct. 'I heard this morning that my wife ain't coming back. I've been expecting it, but I didn't know for certain till now.' She hadn't expected anything so serious; but he didn't appear to expect a rejoinder. He just went on telling her.

'She hated Castle Hill. She never wanted me to take it, but my son did. He's got a degree in agriculture and wanted to come into partnership with me. My fen farm was plenty for one, but not enough for two. John said that with mechanized farming we could make a highland farm yield as much as a good fen farm. It seemed a good idea. So I took a chance and rented Castle Hill.

'But none of the women liked it. Neither of 'em would stop there. They didn't like each other, either. Iris – my wife – was jealous of Melanie – John's wife.'

Fran had long ago accepted that it was her lot in life to be loaded with other people's confidences, but it was something new to be made part of such a difficult situation in a family of more-or-less strangers. She would have tried to change the subject, embarrassed by its intimacy, if he had not been so calm and so matter-of-fact about it – as if he knew exactly what he was doing, and why.

'I couldn't please any of them, let alone all of 'em. I don't blame Iris – I never should have married her, because she ain't the sort to be a working farmer's wife. She didn't want me – I soon found that out – but she could twist me round her little finger. And she'd got big ideas. She went to Spain for a holiday last June, and simply didn't come back. Now she says

118

she ain't going to. Says she won't live with only me and ghosts.'

'Are there ghosts at Castle Hill?'

'I reckon so. There's ghosts everywhere, only most folks don't know they're there. I haven't *seen* any up at Castle Hill – but I've heard 'em. I know they are there. She doesn't – but it's as good an excuse as any other.'

He read her thoughts. Did he mean there were ghosts at Benedict's? He smiled his shy smile. 'If there's ghosts here they won't worry you. I reckon they're just glad to have you back. This is a happy house. That's why I used to cry when I woke up from my dream. You've come back where you belong.'

He had the knack of taking her off guard, catching her unawares. She was very near to tears.

'Oh, Bob – I am so sorry that you aren't happy too. Don't tell me any more if you don't want to.'

'She's been gone long enough now for me to have got used to it. It's Charlie I'm worried about.'

'Charlie?'

'Charlotte, my daughter. She's away at boarding school. I told you my wife has big ideas. Besides, she don't like folks to know she's got children as old as ours are. I reckon Charlie growing up to be so pretty has got something to do with her going. She can't stand the competition. Charlie's nearly eighteen, now. She'll be coming home for Christmas. I hope you'll see her. I don't know what to do for the best.'

'Are you sure your wife isn't just showing a bit of independence? It's the fashion, now. Women do silly things just to prove they are free, not bound like they used to be by a wedding-ring. Some say that a wedding-ring is only a badge of slavery, just to show off. Maybe that's all your wife is playing at. She may well have got over it by Christmas.'

He shook his head. His candour was unnerving. 'She thought I was a simpleton who loved her enough to let her do whatever she wanted, else she'd never have married me in the first place. She's had everything she's ever asked for, till now. I've sent her money every time she asked for it, though it can't have been nothing near enough for the way she's been going on. There's another man in it, must be. More than one, very likely. I had to tell her I couldn't keep it up, so that's when she let me know she wasn't ever coming back. She's got enough sense to know she can only have the cat and its skin.'

'Does Charlie know yet – about her mother?'

'I should think she's got a good idea.'

Fran's heart went out to him. She was furiously angry with his wife for hurting such a sensitive man – hating her own sex for the damage they could inflict on men who loved them. William, Greg, now Bob. Another great change that the times had brought. It used to be the men who went their own way and the women who got hurt; now it was more often than not the other way round.

She had noticed, too, how Bellamy had gradually dropped deeper and deeper into his native dialect as he had told her more and more. She recognized it as a measure of his distress. It was exactly what Sophie always did when she was in trouble. The greater the distress, the stronger the need of the native tongue of the tribe. Words were inadequate anyway, but familiar ones brought the most comfort.

There was a short silence. 'I shall have to go,' he said. 'My family'll be getting hungry.'

'Including your squirrel?' she asked, glad of the let-up.

'Matey's asleep,' he said. 'I miss him. I miss 'em all – Iris and Charlie – and John since he got married.'

'Come and see us again soon, when William's here,' she said.

'Ah, so I will,' he said, and got up. 'I didn't mean to tell you my troubles. You wanted to tell somebody yours, didn't you? Ain't that what you wanted company for? Stop worrying. There's no need.'

He smiled again, then got up and left abruptly, leaving Fran feeling utterly inadequate. She wished at least she had shaken his hand. She had wanted to put her arms round him, to kiss the place and make him better.

She guessed that Iris had failed him in that respect, too. He was a man who needed to be shown affection and she had a feeling that his wife was probably one of those who think the only physical contact that matters is bound to be sexual. It came naturally to Bellamy to express feelings by touch. That

120

accounted for the cats, and the dog and Matey. His children wouldn't have been deprived of hugs and kisses from their father, anyway. Her spirits rose. She had made a friend.

She heard Sophie come in again. Sophie wouldn't go home without preparing William's supper. She appeared carrying a tray with tea for two on it – which Fran interpreted to mean that she had gleaned news she wanted to impart. It also meant that she was feeling cheerful enough again to be hungry.

'It'll save time if I tell you while we have our tea,' Sophie said. 'Shall we hev it 'ere, or shall you come and have yours in the kitchen with me?' Fran went.

Sophie recounted how she had gone to Old Glebe to find Daniel, and had heard the tale about Aunt Esther, and of Eric Choppen's evening with the Bridgefoots. It cost her an effort to admit that there could, after all, be something good to be said about Choppen, but she was too honest not to be grudgingly fair. 'Time'll tell,' she said. 'But you know what it says in the Bible: "Can the leopard change his spots?"'

Fran smiled. Bellamy had made her feel ashamed of being so miserable about nothing.

'Poor Mr Choppen might as well be a zoo,' she said. 'You called him a dog that would always be a dog, and a wolf in the sheepfold. Ned said he was a locust, and William a shark. Now he's a leopard who can't change his spots. I say he's a nice man who went about doing things the wrong way, and ruffled our feathers more than he intended to. I think we ought to give him the benefit of the doubt, now, anyway.'

'And Lucy Bridgefoot is going to have a baby,' said Sophie, dexterously escaping any answer. 'Soon as ever she could, like without causing a lot o' talk. Dan'el says George and Molly are like little dogs with two tails. And you can tell Mis' Rushlake as I'll keep my eye on the School'ouse for 'er till she gets 'ere, but she'd better be looking out for somebody to work for her reg'lar when she comes to live 'ere if she wants anybody. 'Cos Olive 'Opkins is got another job. She's goin' to 'elp Beryl Bean in Kid's new shop. What do they call it?'

'Do you mean the DIY?' Fran asked.

'Ah, tha's it. What's it mean?'

'It stands for Do It Yourself,' Fran explained.

'Seems a funny thing to me for Kid to be using Jelly's money on.' Sophie said, after a bit of thought. 'I mean, if my Jelly hadn't have been killed like he was, him and Kid wouldn't ha' wanted folks to do things for theirselves. They would have wanted to goo and do the jobs for 'em, like they done for you 'ere. Wha's Kid going to do, if folks start doing all the jobs for theirselves?'

Fran felt it was beyond her to enlighten Sophie. Teatime was over, anyway. Sophie was looking at the clock.

'Nobody told me what time he'll be 'ome,' she said, 'so I thought a casserole as wouldn't spoil in the oven would be best for 'is supper. I stopped and bought a chicken on the way back, so I'd better be gettin' it in. And I 'eard another bit o' news while I was at the butcher's shop. You know that there boy as you asked me about at the wedding – the one who's all'us about with Charles Bridgefoot? His mother keeps 'ouse for Bert Bleasby, and 'as done since she come this way with that boy when 'e were only a babe in arms. Well, it looks as if she might be looking for another job soon. 'Cos while I were in the shop, the roundsman come back from delivering, and 'e'd 'eard that when Bert Bleasby come in for his dockey this morning, he just set down in 'is chair and died. So by that her and that boy'll have to get out o' the 'ouse, now as 'e's gone. In the midst o'life we are in death. Where did them pheasants come from?'

'Oh, I had a visitor while you were away. Mr Bellamy from Castle Hill brought them.'

'Ah! I wondered who it were as you'd been givin' cups o' tea to. I didn't know as 'ow 'e was a ladies' man. He hadn't ought to ha' come when you was by yourself. Though I don't see 'ow 'e could ha' knowed as I shouldn't be 'ere.'

Fran laughed aloud. The blues were certainly being chased away. She had once appointed Sophie as guardian of her conscience with regard to William but in the end it had been Sophie conspiring with Mary Budd who had brought them together – in bed. It appeared that Sophie had now appointed herself as watchdog over William's preserves.

'There ain't all that to laugh about, as far as I can see,' Sophie said, severely. 'It was you who was complaining about folks talkin', only this morning. There's no need to go out o' your way to start Kid Bean's Beryl talking. And seein' as 'e's a man whose wife 'as left 'im, folks 'll soon want to know why. We don't want no more scandal about us 'ere than there is a'ready.'

So Bob's wife's desertion was already on the village's tongues. It was incredible how news got about a village.

She let the subject drop. Sophie was still upset about Wendy. Listening to other people's troubles at least had the effect of putting your own into perspective.

'I shan't be a-comin' up tomorrow,' Sophie said. 'I promised Dan'el as I'd 'old myself ready, like, in case me and Thirz' was wanted at Hen Street if Het has sterricks worse'n usual over Wend' gettin' married. You'll be all right till Monday morning.'

Fran had no objection. A weekend with nobody there but the two of them was just what she and William needed.

18

William came in drained and weary. While they ate, she reported the events of her day, omitting her grievance about Roland, and keeping everything on as light a note as she could, even the untimely death of Oscar. She dwelt longest on the account of Bob Bellamy's visit, and his remembrance of the picture. William said so very little that she began to wonder if he had heard a single word she had said.

He had moved his chair a bit away from the table in order to accommodate Cat, who had insisted on sitting on him. His head was bent as he absentmindedly pulled Cat's ears, but when at last he looked up and across to Fran, she was startled by the intensity of feeling in his face.

'Poor old Oscar!' he said. 'No, not poor Oscar. Oscar's dead and out of it. Poor Bob Bellamy!' His voice was so low and tight that she sat silent, almost afraid. Her own throat constricted at its tone.

'Don't ever do that to me, Fran! I don't know how I could have got through today if I hadn't had you to come home to. The thought of Bob Bellamy going back to that great empty house is more than I can bear. Talking to his animals. Listening for ghostly voices . . .' He stood up, pale, tense, suffering. The anger that burst from him came as relief like the first drops of rain in the heat of a coming storm.

'Bloody woman!' he said. 'How could she do that to a man like him?'

Fran ran to him, meeting him at the end of the table. There were tears on his cheeks as his arms enfolded her. She laid her head against his chest, tucking her arms round him under his jacket, and he held her tight, taut and trembling as if he never intended to release her again.

'I just couldn't bear it, now,' he said.

How could she have been so crass as to have reminded him! To have forgotten that he had been in Bob's situation himself, until less than two years ago?

She had to ease the tension, as well as his distress. Danger lay in the chance of his control snapping or of her saying the wrong thing and causing unpredictable havoc. She had to deal with him without letting the situation get out of hand.

'You needn't worry,' she said, deliberately refusing to match his stress with her own. 'I've been as miserable as sin all day, just because you left early and came back late. If I ever did get to the point of walking out on you I should be banging on the door to be let in again before you'd had time to lock it. Darling – if love didn't hurt sometimes, it wouldn't be worth having. But we've been through that stage. We're safe enough now. Sit down and tell me about your day.'

He took the cue from her and loosened his hold. 'Indescribably boring,' he said, kissing her before reluctantly letting her go. 'Nothing worth telling – unless that in itself is worthy of comment. Just a dreadful waste of a long day spent away from you. That's all.'

So whatever was wrong was professional, not personal. She could cope with that. She made coffee, and took it into the sitting-room. He sat down in his chair, following her with his eyes. She poured out a good-sized brandy and set it by his side. She wanted to stay close to him so she sat down at his feet, and leaned her head on his knee.

'Tell me what's wrong,' she said, 'or I shall start guessing. Have you got to go abroad again? If so, where to, and for how long?'

He shook his head. 'Never again, unless you come too. I thought that was understood, though I suppose it is always a possibility. No, nothing in particular. I'm just fed up. Academia has gone sour on me.'

He turned her face up towards him, and looked down at her. 'There – and now you know that, why don't you come clean? Do you think I don't know that you are upset about something? I'm nearly out of my mind worrying about you – have been for the last week. It works both ways, you know. What is it you're not telling me? I've been miserable all day because I had to leave you alone, not knowing what was wrong.'

She laughed, and hugged his leg, rubbing her face against his knee like a cat. 'That's the worst of loving each other as much as we do,' she said. 'We're like two mirrors facing each other. When one goes dark, the other reflects the gloom. While one is bright, so is the other. We need to throw a bit of light on each other. You are fed up with your job; I'm miserable because I haven't heard a word from Roland. He's breaking away from me – from us. I wrote asking them to come and help us celebrate my fiftieth birthday. There's been no reply. I have no idea why. Maybe it's just modern discourtesy, but if that's it, it makes me mad as well as sad. Your problem's much more serious. What's gone wrong?'

'Everything. It's the same old story. Change. Everything's changing – or has already changed – in ways I don't like and don't want to be part of. I'm an anachronism, my darling. I have felt it all this term, but it has been made very clear to me today.'

'Who by?' He smiled at her indignant tone. The bristles in her voice were almost tactile.

'My younger colleagues. There's a new breed of academic

about, and I can't get along with them. I dislike them, and they despise me. We don't belong to the same species any longer.

'There's no meeting of minds, now – no real intellectual contact. We are all just cogs in a machine geared to turning out graduates. That suits my new young colleagues! Whizz-kids, all scrambling to get to the top of the ladder. Resenting me because I occupy the rung they want. But the new breed of students aren't much help. It's fashionable these days for them to buck the system and make unnecessary difficulties. Any system presupposes authority. The post-war young are up against any kind of authority on principle.

'So both sides spend their time at meetings at which nothing gets done. I get filled with the most awful, frightening inertia. Sometimes I wonder if everybody else feels the same, and that's why we waste so much time getting nowhere. Rats' alley. Precious time mostly wasted, as today.'

'I thought a university was the one place in this hectic modern world where time could still be kept in proper perspective,' Fran said.

'There you are! You're an anachronism, too. It used to be like that. Not so long ago, either. We spent time then, we didn't waste it. We used to work together – like masons building a cathedral. Little men with hammers, all doing their bit. Old hands teaching the young the tricks of the trade, and encouraging them. They worked outside themselves, outside their own short span of time, and handed things on to the next generation to continue. Now it's every man for himself on his own little precast pinnacle, and to hell with any overall design for the future.

'I can't go along with them, and I don't. So I'm the odd man out. I just don't fit any longer.'

'You'll be accused of not wanting to give up your ivory tower.'

'Will be? I am! But ivory has a lot to be said for it. It's organic, for one thing, and better than plastic. That's what we are getting in its place. Cheap and nasty, ugly and more or less indestructible. Wait till they try to reverse it again, as of course they will in time. That'll be the day!

'But I feel responsible for the students. Most of them are

good enough youngsters who just get disillusioned and follow the agitators – the few who know it all before they come up, and are intent on wrecking what they call "the establishment". They encourage the rest to "experiment", as they call it, with revolutionary politics – and with drink and drugs and sex. That's "the thing" now – to prove how mature you are.

'I should like to kick a lot of the troublemakers physically on the backside and metaphorically out. But what do my young colleagues say? "You aren't with it, Prof! What's wrong with a whiff of pot? Or alcohol? Or sex? You can't deprive others of the good things of life just because you don't indulge in such things yourself."'

He grinned down at her, better for having let himself go.

'Little do they know,' he said, waving the lovely balloon glass of pale amber brandy round to indicate his surroundings, and fondling her with his free hand.

'Perhaps you should try pot,' she said, catching his hand and kissing it. 'If it's as bad as that,' she said, 'why do you go on with it? Give it up. That's what Lawrence advised, isn't it? If your work has ceased to be fun, *don't do it.*'

'Darling Fran,' – he rested the brandy on his chair arm – 'does that mean that you wouldn't be against my thinking of retiring early?'

'Early? What do you mean by "early"? Do it now! Is that all that has been bothering you?'

'All? I should have thought it was plenty. But it wasn't all. It's you I have been so miserable about. Why do you hide things from me?'

If she hadn't been so surprised, Fran would have laughed. William complaining that she didn't tell him her worries? 'Talk about the pot calling the kettle black!' she said. 'Are you serious about wanting to retire?'

'I don't know. I learned one lesson about wasting time the hard way. I don't want to repeat my mistake. There are so many other things I want to do while I still can. But it isn't an easy decision to make.'

'Why?'

'It would mean a big drop in income, for one thing.'

'Wrong tense,' she said. 'Could, might – not necessarily

127

would. I think we could manage perfectly well – and what we didn't have we'd go without. Like running one car instead of two. All sorts of things like that. But we are both too tired to go into it now. I can't think straight. My day has been like a stew made up of leftovers, a lot of oddments thrown in together.'

'Tell me just a little more about Roland,' he said.

She told him, knowing that now she had his whole attention. 'So what shall I do about my birthday? Shall we cancel it all?' she asked. 'You and I could go and celebrate somewhere by ourselves. But I had been looking forward to a family party.'

'We'll talk about it tomorrow,' he said. 'We are both dropping with weariness. I think I shall have to give my job up just to be able to stop at home and look after you better. Keep other people from loading you with their troubles. We'll think of something in the morning. All I want at this moment is a bed with you in it. The magic balm for all my ills.'

He was asleep before she had had her shower. She lay awake and considered the question of him giving up his job. It would have advantages, not to have to be tied by his academic diary and all the rest that it involved him in. Him, but not her. She was not his wife, and not recognized officially as being anything but his landlady.

She could help him a lot with a freelance career. She snuggled close to him, and made new plans. If there were so many changes in the wind for other people, why not for them, too? As long as it didn't mean leaving Benedict's.

She wriggled her head on to his shoulder without waking him, though disturbing Cat, who protested. 'Ssh, don't wake him,' she said. 'You don't want me to choke you with butter, do you?'

Sleepily she thought what a wonderful bit of idiom that was. Ned wouldn't know a metaphor from a baccalaureate or a papal bull, yet like most real country folk, he used metaphor all the time. It was more than a way of instant communication – it crystallized the countryman's philosophy. Bob Bellamy had choked his wife with butter – and killed his marriage. He would know what it meant, but those young know-all colleagues of William's wouldn't have the faintest idea how deep such language went . . . She slept.

Saturday morning with no Sophie allowed a long lie-in. As soon as Fran roused, she looked at the window to see if she could gauge the time from the light, but it was a very cold morning, with thick fog humping its grey back between her and the garden trees. She loved waking up on summer mornings to bright sunshine and shadowy leaf patterns on the wall of their beautiful room; but on a dark, cold winter morning there was satisfaction in snuggling down again under the covers, and defying the spirits of winter and cold to get at you.

William was still asleep. She lay luxuriating in the warmth, thinking about yesterday. What had caused Sophie's tart remark that they didn't want any further 'scandal' attached to Benedict's? She didn't doubt that her relationship with William was a widow's cruse of village gossip, but there was no malice in it now. She considered philosophically the difference between idle, benign gossip, which was the oil that kept community wheels turning, and the malignant sort of scandal that occasionally grew up like stinking fungi, poisoning the air. Sophie's sharpness of tongue had most likely been occasioned by her fear that Wendy's phenomenal success would tinge any talk of her marriage with the bitter tang of jealousy. And Olive 'Opkins's job with Beryl Bean in the new DIY shop had probably been too painful a reminder to Sophie of the happiness she might have had with Kid's brother Jelly, whose money was financing the venture. If fate had been less cruel . . .

With two notorious gossips working side by side in the shop, no jot or tittle of any new topic would be overlooked. Beryl Bean was noted for getting things maliciously wrong, and even Mary had made fun of the creative gloss Olive 'Opkins could put on to the simplest of statements. Old Swithinford was about to open its own DIY gossip-shop.

Fran smiled at her thoughts. Since she and William had already committed the worst sin in the decalogue under their very noses, she felt that Benedict's was about the last household likely to supply it with a new stock of juicy morsels. If William retired, they would make the most of that, inventing every reason but the right one.

If his job was irking him, he ought to give it up. But was it, truly? He was at his peak as a scholar. The best of his work for history was still to come. Would he do it any better if he were not bound to the prescribed routine of academic professionalism? If he really wanted to get out, why was he hesitating? Of one thing she was certain, that the longer he hesitated, the harder the decision would be to make. 'If 'twere done, 'twere well t'were done quickly.'

The room had grown lighter. She cautiously raised herself on her elbow to look at William. The worn, tired look had gone, and his fine, intelligent face was 'hers' again. She slid out of bed and crept downstairs to make tea.

She set his cup beside him, crept back into bed, and then leaned over to wake him.

'Drink your tea while it's hot,' she said. 'It's a horrid morning and we needn't get up. You look as if your long night's sleep has made a new man of you.'

'Put that cup down and I'll prove it,' he said, reaching for her.

'I've been lying awake and doing a lot of thinking,' she said, ignoring the implied invitation. 'About you retiring. What's stopping you, if that's what you really want?'

He was quick to realize that she was serious. He went to the bathroom and came back showered, shaved and wide awake.

'I really said most of it last night,' he said. 'Tired as I was, I got the main points across. I should love to retire, and follow the delights and desires of my own heart. Why don't I? Practical considerations, such as money. In the past I had no incentive to save much, even if I had been able to. So what it amounts to now is that I can't afford to throw away a very good salary, and the promise of a reasonable pension if I stay the course. I really have no option.'

'Darling, we shouldn't be on the breadline! We're in this together, I hope. Aren't we?'

He didn't answer. Momentary anger with him flared, then fizzled out, and she lay back again within his encircling arm.

'You don't understand, do you?' he said. 'You want to share everything you have with me, but if I let you I should lose something that even you couldn't restore. My pride, sweetheart. Please try to see that. You've given me my manhood back – but you'd take it away again if I let myself become financially dependent on you. It would end by you despising me as much as I should despise myself. I have accepted far too much from you as it is. Don't you think I haven't thought it all out long ago?'

M'm. So they were back again with the old-fashioned notion of honour, the rock on which their love had almost foundered. A man's honour demanded that he be the breadwinner, whatever the overall circumstances. She had some sympathy with him, but not a great deal.

'Look,' she said. 'Apply a bit of common sense. Circumstances alter cases. I happen to own the house we live in. The expense of buying it, and the upkeep of it, would have been the same if I had never set eyes on you. Besides, who is going to know which of us puts what into the kitty?'

'I asked you that once, on a different subject, and what was your answer? "*We should.*" My answer now is that I should. It just isn't on.'

She blazed. 'So now you throw away the happiness we gained by me giving up my so-called honour, in order to save your own beastly pride. All right – keep your honour and your miserable job. Go back to live in your rooms. Be Canute trying to hold back the waves of change! See how you like it.'

'Canute wasn't trying to hold back the waves. He was demonstrating that he couldn't.'

She flung back the bedclothes in absolute fury – and then collapsed into helpless laughter. 'And Alfred didn't really burn the cakes, did he Professor? I mean, is there any documentary evidence for it? Oh, why do sensible women like me have to love idiots like you! Do you require documentary evidence that I do love you? Or will oral evidence do? Do you know what I think?'

He gathered her close to him, kissing away the tears of laughter with anything but pedantry. But his answer was still to the point.

'I wish I had documentary evidence that you were my wife,' he said. 'It would make a lot of difference to my decision. But go ahead. Tell me what you think.'

'I think we might both benefit from you becoming a freelance. You could get on with all those books you want to write now instead of leaving them till you retire. It would mean taking risks. So what? The longer you dither, the harder it will be to decide. Think about it. What about a cup of coffee? The tea's got cold.'

He got up obediently and put on his dressing-gown, still grave of face in spite of her light-hearted mood. She suddenly felt a great upsurge of faith in the future. He stood at the side of the bed looking down at her, unsmiling.

'In lieu of that documentary evidence, there is something you could do to help,' he said. 'Would you promise that if I decide to take the risk, you'll do what I ask without knowing beforehand what it is?'

'Throw down your gage. I'll pick it up.'

He gave a great sigh, as if letting out pent-up feelings.

She called after him. 'There's a lot of mail on your desk from yesterday. Take your time.'

That was only fair; that letter might make a difference, one way or the other. She lay quiet, thankful that they had reached a compromise without one of their occasional tempestuous rows. Those quarrels hurt her badly but she soon got over them. To him they were torture, long drawn-out.

He came back, set down the coffee, and got back into bed.

'I haven't decided – mainly because I feel so much better about everything this morning. I'm not sure now whether I even want to. Being given the option changes the perspective. I think all I really need is a break – a long sabbatical. It's time I had one anyway.'

'So what is it that I can do to help? Does it still apply?'

He hesitated, then made up his mind. 'You told me once that you had a widow's pension. It has been the pea under my mattress ever since. Another man is still providing for you. It makes me feel like a usurper! That I still share you with him. It galls my pride. Couldn't we manage without it?'

She set her cup down, and turned towards him. 'Dear Sir

Galahad,' she said. 'Didn't you give me credit for knowing how you would feel? I haven't touched a penny of it since I became your wife. We didn't need it once you started to contribute. I've had it paid into a special account, as a sort of fund for the grandchildren – who have a right to it. There, my love, my love . . .'

She cradled him as he turned his face into her bosom, overwhelmed. Neither desired anything more but to lie there in wordless togetherness. Both were on the verge of sleep when the bedside telephone intruded on the still silence.

'Our guardian angel at his post again,' Fran said, reaching for the receiver.

It was Katie, almost in tears. Both her children had gone down with some sort of virus. They were not very ill, but the doctor said they could not possibly be allowed to travel in time for Fran's birthday. Fran soothed her daughter and assured her that they would make up for it another time.

William feared that the disappointment would be the last straw for her on this already overwrought morning, but quite to the contrary, she felt oddly relieved. Their guardian angel must have something up his sleeve to make up for it, she thought, remembering what Bob Bellamy had said.

The telephone's intrusion had restored both of them to normality. It was past ten o'clock, so they got up, and tucked into a large cooked breakfast.

'So what about my birthday, now?' she asked. 'Shall we not bother about it at all?'

'No. Let's have a party somehow. Isn't there a story in the Bible about a chap whose first choice of guests couldn't get to his feast?'

'Yes,' she said. 'And the second lot he asked all made excuses, just like Roland and Sue. He sent his servant out to find somebody who would eat what they had got ready. If I remember correctly, he was a bit narked by then and no wonder. So am I. He told his servant to "Go out to the highways and hedges, and *compel* them to come in." Are you suggesting we should do likewise?'

'It isn't a bad idea. We could invite the people we've got to know lately. People like the Bridgefoots, who invited us, and the new Rector and his daughter, to make them feel welcome . . . and your new boyfriend and . . .'

'Make peace with the Choppens?' she interrupted. 'Jess and Greg will be here in any case.'

'Yes, and the chap who has come to the Old Rectory. It's worth considering, honestly, Fran. Any snags so far?'

'Well, one or two. We couldn't get all that lot round the table.'

'Well then, a sumptuous buffet, and a bar in the breakfast-room.'

'And the cost – if we have got to start economizing.'

'So soon? Can't we leave it till after your birthday? Even if I do decide to give up, I shall still have to give a year's notice. And perhaps you ought to take a look at this.'

He handed her the letter she had been so exercised about. It was a royalty statement on the book that had kept him so long in the States last year.

'Look at the cheque,' he said. She did, and gave a gasp that turned into a whoop of joy.

'And that's only the beginning,' he said, stuffing the cheque nonchalantly into his trouser pocket. She could almost hear their guardian angel chuckling.

19

They made a guest list there and then. Jess, Greg, Mr Choppen and Monica, George and Molly Bridgefoot, Brian and Rosemary; the Revd Marriner and his daughter Beth; Commander Franks and Bob Bellamy.

'Not enough of the old to balance the newcomers,' Fran said. 'The young Bridgefoots are very friendly with the Faireys. Add Tom and Cynthia Fairey.'

They drafted invitations, more or less designed individually for the recipients, and wrote them. 'I'm a bit afraid Bob

Bellamy won't come, and will be embarrassed by getting an invitation he doesn't know how to get out of,' she went on. 'And I shall hate it if we get a frosty reply from the Commander. After all, we don't know him. We only know of him, as Sophie would say – by hearsay. Oughtn't we to go and call on him, and deliver the invitation personally? If he's as old as Methuselah or looks like Long John Silver, we needn't leave it.'

'A walk would do us both good,' he agreed. 'Let's give lunch a miss, start now and go up to see your new admirer. We could get back to the village by daylight, and see then how we feel about introducing ourselves to Long John Silver. We'll post the other invitations as we go. Take the bull by the horns.'

'Which of them is likely to prove the bull?' she asked. 'Bob's more like a lost lamb. He makes me want to cuddle him.'

'If you are trying to make me jealous, you won't succeed now,' he said. 'Yesterday it might have been very different. This morning I can only admire any man who has enough sense to fall for you.'

'That's self-esteem carried to its very limit,' she said. 'I'll go and get changed into something more comfortable for walking.' She avoided him neatly. 'No, you can't come and help me. Your coat's under the stairs, where I put it last night. We want to get out while it's still daylight. The fog's all gone, and the sun's shining.'

'Yes, the fog's all gone,' he said. 'Thanks to you. Here – kiss me before you go or I shall follow you up.'

She thought now that he looked much too young to retire, but she had forced him to think seriously, instead of getting moody about it.

They found Bellamy at home, and accepted his invitation into his strange living-room. His easy manner with Fran yesterday had given way to his normal shyness at the sight of William. It made them feel uncomfortable, and Fran had more sense than to produce the invitation, though she was conscious of being disappointed. William, though, had had years of practice in carrying on uneasy, one-sided conversations.

He simply ignored any constraint, and treated Bellamy as an old acquaintance. 'I've been wanting to see this room again,' he said. 'There must be a reason for it being this size and shape. Do you mind if I poke about?' And taking silence for consent, he got up and proceeded to do so.

Fran could see that William's interest was overcoming whatever had been the cause of the glum, self-deprecating mood Bellamy had been in when they arrived. 'What do you make of it, then?' he asked, as William sat down again.

'Well, it's easy to see that three of these walls are very old, probably medieval, and the window-wall and the roof late Victorian. My guess is that this was a fortified manor built round a small courtyard. I'd say it was in ruins till early last century somebody began to patch it up. Do you know anything of its history?'

'I've asked the Bursar at the college who owns it, but nobody there credits me with enough sense to know what they are talking about. Tenant farmers ain't supposed to be interested in history – especially if they come out o' the fens. So I asked the men on the farm if they'd ever heard any old tales about it. One who's lived round here all his life told me a few bits, and I worked a lot more out for myself. Sam says he's heard that it were burnt down too long ago for anybody to remember what it was like till then. And like you say, some bits were left standing. He only remembers it like it is now, but he knows oddments of old tales that get passed down from father to son till everybody's forgot where they started. For one thing, he says he's heard that there's an underground passage as leads from here right up to the church. Well, I reckon nearly every old house as I've ever heard of is supposed to have one o' them, though anybody with a skerrick o' common sense could see that it could only be a tale. But I think it just could be the truth here. It ain't too far, for one thing, and it's all pretty high ground. They wouldn't have had a problem with flooding, or anything like that.

'Then there's a ghost story. According to Sam and his wife, there's a little servant girl as roams about carrying a candle. The tale is that she tried to go down the passage, and got stuck in it. I ain't saying there's any truth in any of it.'

William was genuinely interested. 'Most historians won't trust folk-memory, because it's only oral evidence, but it does sometimes blaze a trail for them to follow. It's something I've always been fascinated by.'

'Have you seen the girl with the candle?' Fran said. She just could not stop herself asking.

He shook his head. 'But . . .' He stopped.

'Go on,' said William gravely. 'This isn't idle curiosity. History is my trade. And we know how right your foreboding about Miss Budd turned out to be.'

'I reckon the bit about there being a fire's true,' Bob said. 'I can show you traces of it on the walls, here and there. But mostly I believe in it because of – other things.'

Fran shivered, and he noticed it. 'What things?' she asked.

He hesitated, but William did not want the subject dropped. 'Don't mind Fran. She believes in you absolutely since you told her about the picture yesterday. Besides, she was the one who asked.'

'Well, I hear things,' he said. 'But you'll have to come and look.' He led them out of the room, down two stone steps and into a square hall that was still a part of the old ruins. In the hall was an incongruous modern door with a half-glass panel, and a flight of ugly wooden stairs, also modern, that went up to a half-landing. The steps ran up by the side of the old wall, turned at the half-landing, and went up again to a passage which obviously led to bedrooms.

'All this bit is new,' Bellamy said. 'Built not long before the war, I should say. I sleep in the big front bedroom, so I have to come up these stairs to get there. It's on this first flight, against the old wall that I hear things. I can't say as I'm frightened, 'cos I've had to get used to such things. But this upsets me more than most.'

They waited. He was having to steel himself to go on and tell them.

'Voices. Little children's voices. Sometimes they're playing – calling out to each other. I can hear 'em better if I put my ear to the wall, but I can never catch the words. I have heard 'em quarrelling and sometimes crying. Often I hear 'em laughing – you could swear they were just the other side of the wall.

And then there's times when the laughing turns all at once to crying, and then to screams – awful screams . . . and then I know what I'm hearing is them being burnt to death, and I can't get the sound out of my ears.

'That's when I hate being here all by myself most. I sometimes make the fire up and sit here all night rather than go on up the stairs again. Nobody else has ever heard anything – well, unless it's old Bonzo – my dog. He sleeps in my bedroom, but on some nights I can't drag him up the stairs.

'And you see this little door here, look, in this bit o' the old wall under the stairs. It only leads down some steps into what used to be a cellar. Bonzo cringes and whimpers and crawls away on his belly if ever I open it. I worked it out that if there ever was an underground passage and the little servant girl did try to go down it, that's where she started from. I can't see any other reason why Bonzo won't go through the door, but he won't. So I don't try to make him.'

He turned, and they followed him back into the big room. Fran wanted to change the subject.

'We came up to ask you if you'd come to a party,' she said. He was dreadfully embarrassed, as she had known he would be. 'Depends who else'll be there,' he said. 'I mean – I ain't used to mixing with posh, educated folks from the university, like.'

'Don't be silly, Bob,' Fran answered. 'You'll know most of the others as well as we do, anyway. And it's William and I who want you.'

He smiled down on her, and included William in his apologetic look. 'I'm touchy today. That's why I'm hesitating. I had enough of being in the wrong company yesterday to last me a lifetime. At that shoot yesterday I was made to feel as if I'd got no sense or feeling. I'm shy enough in company without that sort o' thing happening to me.'

It was William who said, rather as if he didn't believe what he was hearing, 'What happened? Who'd dare to treat you like that?'

Bless him, thought Fran, he knows from dealing with me how much it helps sometimes just to put things into words.

Man to man, Bellamy began, more or less ignoring Fran.

138

'Some chap as has only just joined our shooting syndicate. I'd never seen him before. It happened at dockey time. You see, on a shoot we all take our own dockey with us, and stop at a planned place to eat it. I'm always too shy to sit with the rest of 'em, 'cos most of 'em are rich, posh folks. There's two of 'em with titles, though only one of them was there yesterday. They're all right – well, so are most of 'em. Real gentlemen as go out of their way to see that I ain't left out, as a rule.

'Well, at lunchtime yesterday up draws this new chap's car as close as it could get to where we'd left our things, and his chauffeur carries out a great hamper. Then he opens it up, and starts dishing out grub. I could see it didn't suit none of our usual lot, but they were too polite to say so. I never had the chance, 'cos he just passed me by as if he couldn't see me. So I ate my own sandwiches. Then he opened some bottles of wine, and the same thing happened. I felt like walking away, but I could see it how uncomfortable it was making the others, so I pretended not to notice. But after that, he got a great gold cigar case out of his pocket, and went round with it, passing me by again. That were more than one of the others could take. He refused a cigar and said he preferred his own sort. So he got his cigar case out of his pocket, and a bottle o' champagne out of his own hamper, and come across to sit down aside me, offering me the first cigar and the first glass o' the champagne. Then a couple o' the others come across to us as well and I could see how upset they were on my account.

'The new chap didn't like that, and put hisself out, and said a lot o' things under his breath as the others all pretended not to hear, about not expecting yokels like me to be part of a shoot as had cost him £600 to join. And when we got in line to shoot again, he were next to me, and time after time he took my birds, just to show what he thought of having to mix with such as me. I wasn't going to let him get away with it, because I'm as good a shot as any of 'em. So just before the end, I took two of his birds as well as my own to show him I knowed how to use a gun, and then I told him that the next time I ever see him on my land I hoped it would be down the sights of mine, and he'd better look out for himself. I ain't got over it yet. Quite likely they'll cancel my membership. So after that I reckon it

139

would be wiser for me in future to stop away from where I don't belong. I do know how to behave at a shoot as well as most folks but I shouldn't know how to go on with your friends, likely. Thanks all the same, though. It's done me good to be asked.'

Fran was nearly bursting with disgust and sympathy. Another sign of the post-war era, she thought, that sort of new-rich snobbery. She had never encountered so blatant an example before. It couldn't have happened before the war.

'Whoever was he?' she asked, her voice conveying what she felt. Bellamy, gazing down on her, was seeing not the modern woman in a headscarf who sat in his old Windsor chair, but the elegant great lady of the picture. William warmed to Bellamy as he had done to few other men in this last year or two. He, as well as Fran, would be disappointed if they could not break down Bob's shyness and get him to come to their party.

'He's a property developer,' Bellamy answered. 'My Dad always used to say you could always tell anybody as had been born and brought up on a muckle. Got rich too quick.'

'And you let such a man upset you?' Fran said indignantly. 'Don't be so silly! You can't disappoint us because of him. It's my fiftieth birthday party, and I want you to be there. It'll only be just a party of local friends. We might even push back the furniture and dance.'

'I've been warned,' said William. 'We'll enter the lists against each other.'

'Not à l'outrance, I hope,' said Fran. 'I want both of you.'

She knew that their persuasion had won, so she gave him the invitation, and they left.

As they were passing the Old Rectory, they were lucky enough to meet the new occupier just coming in from a walk. They stopped, and introduced themselves.

Fran thought he looked no more than fifty, though William said afterwards that he must be, because he couldn't have commanded a destroyer at much under thirty, and it was only from the rank of Commander up that they were entitled to go on using their titles once they had retired.

He was as tall as William, with a distinguished bearing and a square clean-cut face that gave the impression of a thinner

man than he actually was. His black hair was only just beginning to show signs of greying on the temples, and he had an
'outdoor' look about him that was very attractive. He was
courteously charming, responding well to their overtures of
neighbourliness. Fran decided to post the invitation.

As they walked homewards, Fran gave William the benefit
of her first impressions of him.

'I kept wondering what it was about him that seemed so
familiar,' she said. 'It's just come to me. He hides it better, but
he's as shy and embarrassed underneath as Bob Bellamy is. I
don't think he'll accept.'

'That's just your fertile imagination running wild,' William
said. 'Will you turn it towards your husband's supper? Gosh,
I'm hungry! But then I'm always hungry when you're about. I
haven't forgotten yet what it feels like to be starving. Especially
now I know I have a rival for your affection.'

They had reached the drive of Benedict's, with its long avenue
of bare and beautiful trees. 'Race you home?' said the academic
who had only yesterday felt too old to go on with his job.

20

Once the invitations had gone out, Fran began to look forward
to her party, and Sophie was in her kind of seventh heaven,
though she greeted the news of it with complaint. There was
nothing she enjoyed more than showing off her culinary skills,
and Fran guessed that her grumbles were only because she had
not been told of it before the plans had already been made. She
would have liked to have been consulted, not told.

'Sixteen people?' she said disapprovingly. 'Tha's more than
one pair of 'ands can do for, 'owever willing. I can cook a 'ot
meal as well as anybody, though I says so as shouldn't. But I
don't know nothing about these 'ere boofies. What sort o'
victuals am I got to get ready, then? Who's a-comin' to eat it?'

Fran told her who had been invited.

'I didn't know as you was friendly as all that with some o' them,' Sophie said, rather severely. 'I never thought the day would come when you'd ask me to cook for that Choppen as wanted to turn me out o' my 'ome, and then robbed me when I was willing to buy it by charging me a lot more than it was worth. And 'im up at Castle 'Ill, as come 'ere that day you was by yourself. Will a man like 'im mix, like, wi' the new Rector? Seems to me as you might as well try and mix 'ile and vinegar! But there, it's your party. As the ol' sayin' is, "Fools make feasts and wise men go an' eat 'em." I can only do my best. No man can do more.'

'We don't know yet if they'll all come,' Fran said. 'Do you think the Rector will? What's he like? I've only seen him at the wedding.'

Sophie's allegiance to the church and everything pertaining to it had been born into her – but so had her obligation to 'tell the truth and shame the devil', which had also been reinforced by her years in Mary Budd's school. She therefore found it very difficult to dissemble, and was placed in a dilemma by Fran's question.

'He's all right,' she said at last. 'I mean 'e's a nice enough man, pleasant like to talk to and not near as stuck-up as parsons usually are. But I can't say as I like 'is preaching a lot. I mean, 'e don't tell us about what 'appened in the Bible, and things like that as we're all'us been used to. He goes on all the while about 'ow wicked we all are now, and 'ow it'll be the ruin o' civilization if young folks don't be'ave theirselves better than they do now' – she dropped her voice to a whisper – 'goin' with each other afore they're married, and such. Makes me and Thirz' feel real uncomfortable, like, 'cos of our Wend' going and 'eving that base-born child. Thirz' is got 'erself real upset about it, 'cos she thinks it's us as he's pointing 'is finger at. "Who else can 'e mean?" she says. And I hev to agree with 'er, sometimes. There's nobody else there as 'e needs to lecture about such things. There's Dan'el and Thirz' and me and Ida Barker what must be sixty if she's a day, and George Bridgefoot and 'is wife, and two or three other old married couples. Tha's about all the reg'lars as go to church now. It ain't like it used to be.'

Fran soothed her by returning to the subject of the party. She knew her Sophie by this time. Having had her say, and applied a bit of verbal punishment for not having been in the plot from the beginning, she would make up for it by working herself 'to the bone' to please Fran. They got out cookery books, and went through them together, spending a whole morning of mutual pleasure together planning the food. Buffet it might have to be, but Sophie had not been brought up helping to prepare harvest suppers without knowing what hearty appetites people had when they were enjoying themselves. In fact, Sophie could have done most of it without reference to Fran at all.

Later the same day Sophie sought her out again. 'There'll be more folks than I can wait on single-'anded,' she said, 'let alone do all the washing up. You'd better let me ask Thirz' up to help. We're been a-doing things like this 'ere together since we left Miss's school. She made sure as we knowed things like how to wait at table, and the right way to go about washing up and such. And me and Thirz' 'as all'us worked together like, so as we know each other's wayses.'

'That would be wonderful,' Fran said, very glad that Sophie had offered it herself. She would hardly have dared to ask.

'And 'e says you're goin' to hev a bar in the breakfast-room.' Fran could detect that Sophie felt that was going a bit too far. However, even her objection to the demon drink had to give way before her devotion to William. If 'he' thought it suitable, it couldn't be as bad as it sounded. 'But me and Thirz' don't know nothink about drink,' Sophie said. 'Miss never teached us how to be barmaids. So I reckon as you ought to ask Ned if 'e'll come up and look after that for you.'

Fran suspected, quite rightly, that Sophie and Ned had got it all arranged to their mutual satisfaction before she was told.

She was impatient now for replies to her invitations. She could not envisage what sort of receptions they would get.

George and Molly Bridgefoot were frankly touched and delighted. Nothing would ever change George. Though now very wealthy, and soon to share a grandchild with a titled surgeon of great renown, it made not the least difference to him or his way of life. His values had been set in childhood, and having money or 'posh' connections was the last thing that would alter them. Like Longfellow's village blacksmith, 'He looked the whole world in the face' in the knowledge that 'he owed not any man'. He loved his land, he loved his church, and he loved his wife and family, which added up to the fact that he loved life. As a consequence, most people he had much to do with loved him. Being the sort of man he was, he also loved a party. Molly warned him that he couldn't expect an old-fashioned country party at a place like Benedict's. He couldn't see why not. Mrs Catherwood had invited them, hadn't she? She knew what sort of people they were. He reminded Molly of how she had kissed him at their Lucy's wedding.

'There's nothing stuck-up about her,' he said. 'Not like some o' the young farmers' wives nowadays. I don't care for their sort of cocktail parties or whatever they call them, where there's no chairs to sit on and all you get is a glass o' sour wine and a soggy biscuit with a bit o' cheese on it not big enough to bait a mousetrap with. I'll bet you a pig to a pound o' lard as we needn't have our supper afore we go up to Benedict's.'

Jess was in Mr Choppen's office with him when he opened his invitation. He passed it across to her. 'Is this your doing?' he asked.

'No!' said Jess. 'It's the first I've heard about a party. The last time I spoke to either Fran or William, it was going to be a dinner party just for the family. They must have changed their minds. Will you go?'

'I don't see how I can get out of it without giving offence,' he said. 'But you know I'm not much of a party-goer. What sort of a party will it be? I hate having to make small talk with people I don't know, with a glass of plonk in one hand and a canapé in the other. Thank goodness you'll be there. I suppose I shall have to accept. Do you know who else has been invited?'

'I don't see much of them these days. I'm too tired, for one thing. Greg goes up now and then to play the piano. I'll ask him to find out.'

She was only telling the truth. She had somehow lost a lot of her vitality. Greg tried hard to be patient, but was afraid they were heading again into the same sort of relationship that they had had once before, when she loved him as much as ever as a husband, while doing her best to escape his attentions as a lover. The doctor had told him that she would get over what was, after all, a very common occurrence during the menopause. It was hard for him to take, because he was not losing any of his desire for her. There was nothing he could do but wait and hope.

One of the effects it had on him was that he worked harder, and went more rarely to Benedict's. It irked him to suspect that William, whom he would once have considered to have only red ink in his veins, was now as lusty a lover as he had been, and indeed still was when Jess was kind; but the occasions were getting rare ... he reflected cynically that it would be William's turn to suspect that his veins were filled with the ox-gall he used for his water-colours.

His work with Monica took him to see her often. She was still very subdued; she had lost weight, and much of her merry bounce.

'How long do you think it is going to take me to get over him, Greg?' she asked one day. 'How long before I either throw myself into bed with every willing man, or become nothing but a hard-nosed businesswoman?'

'I don't think you ever get over that sort of love,' he answered, seriously. 'But most people find substitutes. If I were only your age, I should begin to look for second best. There are still some very nice men about.'

'I have thought a lot about it,' she said. 'At least that way I could have children. I could pretend to myself that they were his – my lover's, I mean.'

Greg hadn't answered. He had always wanted children. He dared not mention it to Jess now, but he guessed that the root of her depression was having to admit that hope on that score was dead.

Monica's invitation to Fran's party stood on the mantelpiece over her roaring fire. He nodded towards it and asked her if she was intending to accept. He was puzzled by her reaction.

She was uncertain of herself, in a way he had never seen before. He thought that for a second or two she looked more like the gauche Wendy Noble before her metamorphosis into Sister Anne, than the suave Monique O'Dell whose designs were becoming famous.

'It's very kind of them to ask me,' she said, 'but I don't want to go.'

'I think you would be silly to refuse,' he said, 'and they would be hurt. I'd take a chance on it, anyway. We shall be there.'

She nodded miserably. 'I'll go,' she said, 'but I don't expect to enjoy it.' Greg thought it was time he gave up trying to fathom the vagaries of women. Were they changing, or was he?

At Temperance Farm, the invitation was received with pleasure, but no surprise. Brian Bridgefoot had only been in his teens when the nation had remembered that it had an agricultural industry, and had turned to it as its saviour with regard to its food supply in wartime. The status as well as the bank balances of farmers had risen with every year that had passed since then. But Brian was old enough to remember the bad times, and the way it had been before the war. He had heard tales about 'the old squire' from his father, including the time when he was so hard up that things from the house had had to be sold to keep him going. Things were very different, now.

'Isn't it nice of them to ask us?' Rosemary had said, already wondering what she would wear.

'Why?'

'Well, they are the old squire's grandchildren, and live in his house. Besides, he's a professor, and she's a writer.'

Brian wasn't quite sure where he stood about her feelings. He was planning to buy young Charles a new car for his twentieth birthday; Marjorie's twins could now be seen riding their own horses, in full riding kit of the finest quality, having been initiated at an expensive riding school.

'That sort of thing's all gone,' he said. 'It's money that counts, now. They came to Lucy's wedding, didn't they? There's no gap between such as them and us, now, like there used to be. If you are going to take that attitude, I shan't go. Nobody's going to patronize me!'

Rosemary flashed at him, anger in every rosy curve of her. 'Don't be any dafter than you can help!' she said. 'You wouldn't use a word like that if you didn't feel that there was still a gap! But you're a worse fool than I thought if you can't see that it's them who are trying to close the gap up. We shouldn't have asked them to the wedding if Lucy had been marrying a nobody, should we? But they came, and they enjoyed it. Now they are inviting us. You'll be the stuck-up one if you go on like that. You know as well as I do that money doesn't count with people like them. You can't make gentlemen just with money. Look at the Baileys, who think a few thousand in the bank has made them into Lord and Lady Muck! But I hope we've got more sense than the Baileys. It isn't my fault, or your mother's and father's, if you haven't. We shall go, and that's that. It's manners that count with folks like them, not money – and don't you forget it.'

'I wonder who else will be there,' he said, trying to mollify her.

She was pleased when Cynthia Fairey rang up. The two couples had always been friends, but the closeness of their two sons, both only children, had cemented them into a sort of extended family.

The Faireys had not seen the alterations at Temperance Farm, which were now more or less completed. 'Bring Tom up to supper on Friday, and see everything,' Rosemary said. 'We can decide what sort of thing to wear at the party, and plan a shopping trip together.'

But by Friday, things had changed. Mr Choppen had written to tell George that as her rooms were now ready for her at Temperance, he was cancelling the room at the expensive nursing home which Aunt Esther was enjoying at his expense, as from the coming Saturday. He was expecting the Bridgefoots to fetch her home and install her as agreed.

The prospect cast a gloom over the supper table at Temperance on Friday evening. So did the absence of Robert, Tom and Cynthia's son. Charles had gone up to Lane's End to spend the evening with him, instead. He was having 'one of his turns'.

'I wish he would let us take him to the doctor,' Cynthia said. 'But he won't, and Tom backs him. Tom says it's only because he grew too fast. He is six foot two, after all, and thin as a rake. But he feels so tired all the time, like today. I'm sure there must be some cause for it. One reason is that Tom works him far too hard on the farm.'

'Hard work never hurt nobody,' said Tom, tucking into Rosemary's treacle sponge. 'It's the only thing likely to give him a bit of muscle. I tell you one thing – your father wouldn't have had him in the forge. He couldn't have lifted the hammer. But then, youngsters today are all the same. There's no real work for 'em to do. Robert did seem to get too tired in harvest time this year, and perhaps it were because I kept him at it working long hours. But with implements costing what they do now, you've just got to keep 'em at work whenever the weather'll let you. He were only sitting on a combine harvester, after all. When I was his age, we had a self-binder behind our tractor, but Dad wouldn't let anybody but himself drive that. So I was one of the team that stouked all day, till my arms were red-raw with scratches and my thighs were so sweat-galled I didn't know how to crawl home. And Dad paid me fifteen shillings a week and my keep. We were always a tall, thin family. Cynth' is remembering her father's side – they were all thickset, like him. Blacksmiths had to be. Robert'll be all right.'

'It isn't natural for a boy of his age to choose to stop in bed, though, is it?' said Cynthia.

'No,' said Rosemary, 'and if he were my son, I should soon get a doctor to him, Brian or no Brian.'

Tom took the hint. 'Well, if he ain't up and about by the time of this party next week, I'll see to it that he goes to the doctor.'

'Next week? So it is! Oh, Brian! Aunt Esther will be here by then. I hadn't realized. What shall we do about her?'

'She'll be all right left by herself,' he answered. 'She knows how to use a telephone, and she'll know where we are.'

'She'll make a fuss, and spoil it for me,' said Rosemary. 'I know her.'

'Now look here, Rosy,' said Brian. 'When I agreed to this

arrangement – to please you, if you remember – it was on condition that she didn't interfere with our lives. We've got to start as we mean to go on. Let the old haybag stop here by herself. She'd have been by herself at the Pightle.'

'Perhaps your Mum and Dad will come and sit with her.' Rosemary said, though not very hopefully.

'Not likely. They're going to the party. Dad's as excited as a child.'

'It sounds to me,' said Tom, pushing his plate away thoughtfully, 'as them folks up at Benedict's know what they're doing.'

Brian and Rosemary fetched Aunt Esther home next morning. She was now walking quite well, though with a stick. As they passed the hotel, and the vacant space where her home had been, she indulged in the luxury of a few tears. 'Money-grubbing Bridgefoots!' she mumbled under her breath. 'Never satisfied. Naboth's vineyard all over again.'

Brian closed his ears and ground his teeth. If there was one thing more than another he couldn't stand about Aunt Esther, it was her ability to turn her knowledge of the Bible somehow to her own advantage in any argument.

21

By that same Saturday morning, Fran had received replies to most of her invitations, in various forms according to the nature of their recipients. Greg had paid them a long overdue visit and enjoyed himself for half an hour on the Bechstein, excusing Jess who he said was trying to rest.

The Bridgefoots and the Faireys had rung to accept; Eric Choppen and Elyot Franks had used the formal acceptance mode; and Monica had written a charming little note. Three people had so far not replied: the Rector and his daughter, and Bob Bellamy. Fran wasn't surprised about Bellamy; she could imagine the war going on inside him between his desire to be there and the fear his desperate shyness created in him. She said so to William.

'Don't press him,' he advised. 'Just leave it that if he comes he comes; if he doesn't, don't be too disappointed. I think us asking him at all has helped him just when he needed a bit of a boost.'

William had moved his study back into the flat, the 'little bit extra' at the back of the house, which for that reason they had christened 'Eeyore's tail'. It was a self-contained set of rooms that he had used when he was only Fran's cousin and tenant. The move meant that he could shut himself away there when he had difficult or urgent work to do, and give his concentration wholly to it – which in effect meant that Fran was undisturbed in her study too except for Sophie's little chats. The room upstairs that had been his temporary study was restored to its former use as another guest bedroom.

Sometimes, as on this Saturday, when Fran sensed his disinclination to work at what must be done, she shot the bolt on her side of the door that connected the flat to the main part of the house. That meant that William couldn't 'just pop in' to see her easily, because he had to go out of the flat's door and round to the back door to get in again. It sometimes actually worked, and kept him at his desk till lunchtime.

When she heard the bang on the old brass lion-headed knocker on the front door, Fran went quickly to open it herself, lest William should be 'knocked off' work by curiosity. She found the Rector standing there.

'Mr Marriner! What a pleasant surprise,' she said. 'Do come in.'

She was aware at once that he was not at his ease, and that he did not fit the picture of him that Sophie had painted, or her own first fleeting impressions of him. Sophie had been a little critical of his casual dress and his way of getting to know his flock – in the pub, for example. This morning, he was meticulously dressed in a dark three-piece suit, which had the effect of making his dog-collar very conspicuous. He wore no hat.

In the few seconds it took for them to pass through the

hall to the door of the sitting-room, Fran tried to think how long it was since men stopped wearing hats.

She knew it could only be in the very recent past, because she remembered so vividly her first trip to view Benedict's when William had met her at the station and driven her out. She hadn't seen him till that moment for twenty years, and when he had lifted his hat to her she had had her first glimpse of the head of white hair that pre-war had been so black. What had recalled that moment to her was that the Rector was somewhat embarrassed by having no hat to raise to her. Men had no substitute now for that little courtesy towards women, except shaking hands. Her present visitor had made no attempt to do that, even if she hadn't had her hands occupied in pulling open the huge, heavy door. But the lack of the courtesy in their meeting together with his severe appearance told her that he was a parson visiting a parishioner, not a potential friend visiting a neighbour.

'Do sit down,' she said, waving him vaguely towards William's armchair by the side of the fire. 'What can I get you to drink? We haven't had the pleasure of seeing you at Benedict's before, though of course we did meet you at Lucy Bridgefoot's wedding. Sophie doesn't always come to us on Saturday mornings, so if you will make yourself at home for a moment, I'll go and put the kettle on.'

He had not accepted her invitation to sit down. He stood rather stiffly in the middle of the room. 'Thank you, but I won't take anything. This is only a very brief visit. I'm afraid it may not be a very pleasant one, either. I have come about this.' He held up his invitation card to her party.

She turned back from the door, surprised and a bit wary, but still a welcoming hostess. 'Oh, you are going to tell me that you can't come to my party! What a pity. We were so much looking forward to having you and Miss Marriner.'

'Mrs Catherwood, it would not be true to say we cannot come. It would have been only too easy to make that excuse, and write to you declining your invitation. But that is not the case.' He was shuffling his feet in embarrassment, and Fran's head came up proudly as she turned back into the room and faced him. She was having some difficulty in believing that her own interpretation of his words could be right. But if it were, she had no intention of letting him off the hook he had impaled himself on. She had the blood of aristocrats in her veins, and she would let him know it.

'You are saying, I think, like Caesar, that "Cannot is false" and that the real reason is that you will not. May I know why? I think you owe that to me, at least.'

A deep red flush flowed from the roots of his handsome hairline, over his face and down his neck. The white band stood out in stark contrast. Fran glanced up at the space above the mantelpiece and became in an instant the great lady Bob Bellamy remembered pictured there. 'Well?' she asked.

'Mrs Catherwood – this invitation is in your name only. But since I have been here you have used the first person plural several times. I am forced to understand that when you say "we" it means you and Dr Burbage.'

'Yes,' she said. 'Your surmise is correct.' Two could play at the game of trying to overawe with language. She was just as capable of conversing in Standard English and a BBC accent as he was. 'Go on. Please elucidate.'

'I am told in the village that the two of you live together in this house.'

'Yes,' she said. 'Why not? We both knew it when we were children. At this very moment, Dr Burbage is at work in his study in a separate part of the house. Would you care to inspect the bolt which separates them?'

He winced at the icy scorn in her voice.

'I think what you are trying to say is that you have heard that we live together here as man and wife. In which case, I have several things to say in return. You are making an insinuation for which you cannot provide a shred of concrete proof. Are you prepared to answer that? It could be construed as defamation of character – not only of me, but of Dr Burbage as well. What is your evidence based on? Village gossip? Not a very strong defence, I fear.

'Secondly, I mistook you for a gentleman. I have yet to meet a gentleman who would dare to take it upon himself to call a lady an adultress to her face when it was absolutely no concern of his whatsoever.'

'Mrs Catherwood . . .'

'Nor do gentlemen interrupt a lady,' she flashed at him. 'Keep your excuses till I have had my say. I quoted Shakespeare a moment or two ago when you were honest enough to tell the truth about declining my invitation. I use the same passage now with reference to myself. I will not deny your insinuation. "Cannot is false, and that I dare not, false." Say Frances Catherwood will not deny it – because it is the truth. Your informants are quite correct. Dr Burbage and I do live here together very happily as man and wife, a state which may very well continue till we are parted by death. Does that content you?'

He was looking quite stunned and disbelieving, not at what she said, but at her proud declaration of it.

'I apologize for what may seem to you bad manners,' he said, 'but I now know I was right to come. I hardly expected you to admit to open adultery in such a fashion.'

'Then what did you expect? That I should anoint your feet with my most expensive face-cream, and dry them with my hair?' She was standing tall, chin held high, and her eyes flashed darts of fiery anger. 'You call it adultery. We call it Love. We don't need such as you to sanctify it for us. This house serves as well as your church. Do you know your Tolstoy as well as I know my Bible? "Where Love is, God is." In which case, you should remove your shoes, because the place whereon you stand is holy ground. But I still fail to see what business it is of yours. Perhaps you will be good enough to tell me that before you leave.'

'As a man, my answer might be different from the one I give as the pastor of my flock. I'm sorry if that sounds sanctimonious but the social part of my calling is firmly based on the ten commandments. I cannot preach them to my congregation, and be seen condoning the seventh by my presence at a party under your roof. I cannot condone the adultery, though I may wish to sympathize. My witness must be by example as well as precept.'

Fran's scorn was evident in the crooked wickedness of her smile. 'Ah, yes, your flock. Your congregation, which I am led to believe sometimes amounts to as many as ten people. Of those ten, two plus one of your bellringers will be in my kitchen next Saturday. Among the guests will be one of the churchwardens and his wife, as well as your stand-in organist. Sixty per cent of your flock, Rector – all condoning an association they know quite well to be adulterous. Is it not your duty to go round to all of them with the message that they cannot come near such pitch without being defiled? I will give you a list of their names.' She turned to pick up the list of acceptances.

'I have no right to interfere with anybody's doings but those of my own household,' he said, suddenly sitting down on the nearest seat, which happened to be the piano stool. As Fran flung herself round to deliver her riposte, she caught sight of William, lounging against the doorpost with his hands in his trouser pockets.

'Then what in God's name gave you the idea that you had a right to interfere in mine?' she said. 'William, darling – Mr Marriner is about to leave. Please show him the door.'

William sauntered across to her and took her into his arms, stroking her hair before dropping a kiss on top of her head.

'Do you know, sweetheart, I think I'd rather show him a glass of whisky,' he said. 'I'm sure he needs it after that. I should.'

He led her gently to the door. 'Leave him to me,' he said in her ear.

She went up to her bedroom, not at all sure she wasn't going to cry out her anger as well as her doubt that he might have spoilt her party. But she was still too angry for soothing tears. She bathed her face, cooled her throbbing wrists and brushed her hair. Then she sat down before her dressing table and coiled her hair into a bun, curling the wet wisps over her forehead, and made up her face. She was still flushed, and inclined to tremble. Her diaphragm was quivering and her mouth dry. She longed for a cup of tea, but she could see Marriner's car still in front of the house, and would not go down till he had gone. She lay on the bed and tried to calm herself by reciting poetry, which usually worked. She was very near to drifting off to sleep when she heard William's tread on the stairs. She sat up on the side of the bed, and he came to sit beside her, drawing her head on to his shoulder.

She could feel that he, too, was trembling. She drew away in order to be able to see his face. He strove valiantly to control it but lost the battle. He swept her back into his arms.

'Oh, my gorgeous Penthesilia! I wouldn't have missed that for all the tea in China!' he said, and gave way to the laughter he had been trying to hold back. He laughed till he was out of breath, shoved his face into the pillow, found his handkerchief and wiped his eyes, and did his very best to stop.

'You were there all the time?' she asked.

He nodded, afraid to speak. 'Outside the door, in case you needed me,' he managed to say at last. 'It was all wonderful, but the Mary Magdelene bit was the best,' he said. The memory of it sent him off into further paroxysms. 'You have no idea how marvellous you looked!' he said. 'Do you know what Marriner said to me as we shook hands at the door? He told me he envied me such a magnificent helpmeet.'

The word 'helpmeet' sent both of them almost into hysterics again.

When at last they got over it, they went down to a long-delayed lunch. William made Fran the cup of tea she was so badly in need of and while they ate he told her what had happened after she had 'swept out'.

'I felt so sorry for him,' William said. 'He had been screwing up his courage to come and be honest with us all the week, and had expected a bit of a fight with me. Apparently, he did have feelings about taking a lady to task, to her face. But when you asked him more or less straight away what he'd come for, he remembered his priestly duty and out it came. The nerve he had armed himself with to tackle me just crumbled. He hadn't expected to do battle with the Queen of the Amazons. Oh, don't let me start laughing again. I want my dinner.'

They left the matter alone till they were sitting down together in the gathering twilight. By this time William had regained his self-control.

'I like him,' he said, simply. 'And he is a brave man, to practise what he preaches, these days. He has a bit of a bee in his bonnet about the commandments, especially the seventh. You see, he believes wholeheartedly that the sexual revolution

155

will undermine the whole fabric of our civilization. As a historian, I'm inclined to agree with him. It's happened before . . . more than once. As the transgressor whose blood he was after today, I'd like to wring his neck, except that he has made me love you more than ever, and I didn't think that was possible. But we understood each other. I led him gently away from his dreadful contrition and apologies, by asking him about the little church on Castle Hill. He told me where to find the key, so next time we go up, we can go in and look round.

'Here's to next Saturday, and our party,' he said, holding his cup up to her. She was glad to regard the episode as over and done with.

It was not over and done with in the Rector's mind. He felt he had made a very bad mistake, though in all conscience he knew that if it came to it, he would do the same again. The hardest thing for him about his job was to weld the man he was with the priest he had chosen to become. They had always been at odds with each other.

When the evening of the party came, he could not keep his mind on the sermon he was trying to write for the next day. He was afraid that he had taken the shine off a happy gathering of friends and neighbours. He decided that he must go across to the church, and try to still his misgivings about his own behaviour in prayer. At the foot of the stairs he met his daughter.

She had piled up her beautiful hair on the crown of her head, making her overtop him by two inches. From her ears swung her mother's long gold and turquoise ear-rings, bright against the dark fur collar of her evening cape. He was filled with apprehension.

'Where are you going?' he asked.

'Out,' she said, lightly.

He caught her by the hand. 'Beth, you can't,' he said. 'I won't let you.'

She pulled her hand away, and put it round his neck giving him a hearty kiss as she did so. 'Daddy,' she said succinctly, 'go to hell! I'm going to Benedict's.'

22

Aunt Esther was installed in her new quarters at Temperance Farm. Rosemary had never had any illusions with regard to her aunt's character and had prepared herself for a lot of aggravation which she determined, as far as possible, to keep to herself and not divulge to Brian or Charles. It was twenty-five years since she had last been so directly under her aunt's thumb, and she had somehow convinced herself that the rock-faced middle-aged woman of whom she had been so scared in childhood and youth would have mellowed a bit with age, besides having enough sense to be a little grateful for favours received first from Brian's father, and now from Brian and herself. After only twenty-four hours, however, she'd begun to understand that if anybody had ever bitten off more than she could chew, she had.

While paying her duty visits to her aunt at the Pightle, she had not been aware of any difference in her aunt from the woman she had always known except, of course, that she was older, and perhaps even more set in her ways. That was to be expected; but she now realized what she had let herself in for. She was going to need the physical energy of a workhorse, the craftiness of a fox and the patience of a saint.

Aunt Esther had fought a battle, and lost. Nothing could have soured her more. She had had to give in; and however much sugar was put on it, she could not come to terms with the bitterness of the pill she had been forced to swallow.

She had always been a hard and bitter woman, with a mannish face and figure, even as a girl. In the aftermath of the Great War, when so many men had been killed, there had been many far more attractive than Esther left without partners. She had had no suitors, but this she never admitted. She chose instead to give the impression that her whole life had been one of self-sacrifice, for which it was only right that she should now be paid in full with compound interest. She had established herself in her widowed brother's household as an oracle against which there was no appeal. When she was left after the death of her brother, George Bridgefoot's kindness in letting her have the Pightle she regarded grimly as only his duty and her due, though it suited her well. She was still master in her own house ... and that was the core of her dissatisfaction now. She was no longer boss nor oracle. She was an elderly dependant, and all the animosity of her aggressive nature was turned in fury against her benefactors.

She had been brought up a Methodist, and the chapel had been the focus of her social life. Her Bible was rarely out of reach, though she hardly ever opened it. She didn't need to, because half-remembered phrases from Bible and hymnal were always at the ready on her tongue, as weapons with which to floor any opponent. Like Sophie, she had been brought up with it in her ears. Unlike Sophie, she understood neither the words nor the meaning of it. She took it ill that her God should have allowed old age and a bit of an accident to put her into her present situation. Since she had no way of getting back at Him, she made the Bridgefoot family her scapegoat. She had always been aggressive, and, having been for a short spell a private patient, had found that she could usually get her own way if she made enough fuss and refused to give in till she had won.

She had, in spite of herself, been quite impressed by her new quarters though nothing would have induced her to admit it. She told Rosemary, with crocodile tears, that it was 'gall and wormwood' to her to think that she should ever have come to this – a burden on her niece and a dependant of the Bridgefoots. 'Church folk at that,' she said venomously, 'as keep all their religion for Sundays. Graven images.'

It added to Rosemary's misgivings that her aunt was going deaf, though she averred that if people would only speak up she could hear as well as she ever had done. She made great play about needing a stick to walk with, though Rosemary had once or twice caught her moving quite briskly without it.

She had made known her avowed intent never to have anything to do with any Bridgefoot. Now her crafty intelligence told her that she was being taken at her word, and that to some extent this had made a rod for her own back. Not that she had ever been gregarious, but she did like to be in the know about what was going on. She soon began to complain that she was being treated like a prisoner.

This had been, however, the one condition on which Brian had stood firm before agreeing to have her in his house. Rosemary saw that she was always going to be pig-in-the-middle, and wondered how long she would be able to keep the peace. It made her apprehensive, and touchy with both of them. She did her best, but after only forty-eight hours she was ready to throw in the towel. That was when she took her aunt her supper on the second day.

She pulled up a cantilever table to her aunt's armchair, covered it with a damask napkin, and set before Esther a plate full of rich shepherd's pie and greens.

Esther picked up her fork and poked the food about, sniffing, the corners of her mouth turned ominously down.

'Rice pudding to come,' said Rosemary cheerfully.

'I ain't heving all my meals by myself as if I was a leper,' Esther said. 'There's no sense nor reason in it, as I can see. Ain't I one o' the family? I'm coming out at suppertime from now on to have my supper at a proper table with the family, like a Christian should. I ain't unclean, nor yet a whited sepulchre.'

'Don't be silly,' Rosemary said. 'Eat that while it's hot. Mine'll be cold if you keep me any longer.'

'What are you having, then?'

'The same as you, of course.'

Her aunt's expression of doubt would have cracked a mirror. 'Nor yet I ain't a kitchen maid, to eat the leftovers as fall from the rich man's table.' Esther pushed her plate away, caught the edge of the table with it, and shot mince and gravy on to the new carpet.

'That's got onion in it. I can't eat onion. You know very well as I can't, especially now I have to walk with a stick. I can't get there quick enough if I eat onion.'

'Rosy! Whatever are you doing? Shall I help myself?' Brian's voice was pitched loud enough to reach Aunt Esther's room.

'Yes,' called Rosemary, on her knees mopping up gravy. 'I'll be as quick as I can.'

'What's he bawling about? Bellering like the bulls o' Bashan. I'd never let no man bawl at me like that! Never have done and never shall. I told you 'ow it would be.'

'You never had the chance,' said Rosemary, under her breath.

'I heard that. That's all the thanks I get. I am like a lamb or a cow that is brought to the slaughter.'

'*Ox*, not cow,' said Rosemary, irritated beyond reason.

'Don't you call me no old cow! How dare you? I won't have it!' She gave Rosemary a painful poke with her stick.

'Rosey!' yelled Brian. 'Come and have your supper! It's nearly cold now.' Rosemary got up and went back across to her new dining-room.

She daren't let Brian see her in tears, but he was too ready for her not to spot them. 'What's wrong with the old bitch now?' he said. 'I told you how it would be!'

Getting it from both sides was too much. She tried to swallow her meal, but despair was almost choking her. Aunt Esther had only been there two days.

There arose a loud tapping from Aunt Esther's room. Rosemary left the table with relief, and ran. Aunt Esther was banging her stick on the floor with all the strength she could muster. 'I want to go over there,' she said, in a hoarse whisper, nodding towards her new bathroom. 'I can't get up with this thing in front of me.'

Rosemary moved the table. 'You'll have to help me up. And I can't manage by myself,' the old woman added.

'Nonsense,' said Rosemary sharply. 'You've been managing to go by yourself till now. And if you are going to want me to take you every time, you'll have to go before Brian comes in for his supper.'

'When the day comes as I have to ask a Bridgefoot when I can go to make water, I shall be as the grass that withereth, and pray to be gathered unto my fathers. There's time to make water even in harvest time, as any proper farmer'll tell you.' In spite of herself, Rosemary smiled at her aunt's discreet rendering of the much coarser agricultural proverb. She must remember to tell Charles, who so far was rather enjoying his great-aunt's idiosyncracies. It was one of her son's many charms that he had a lovely sense of humour.

'Cheer up, Mum,' he said. 'If we don't laugh at her, she'll drive us all round the bend. She'll settle down.'

'I daren't tell her yet about the party on Saturday,' his mother said. 'I know she'll find some way of spoiling it for me. And I shouldn't enjoy a minute of it if we left her here by ourselves. I suppose you and Robert and Nick wouldn't spend the evening in for once, here? I'd leave you a lovely supper, and you could play your records, or anything you liked. As long as you don't leave her in the house by herself.'

'I'll ask them,' he said obligingly. He didn't want her to miss the chance of going to Benedict's and telling him all about it afterwards. 'Only what shall we do if she says it's harvest time?'

Rosemary chuckled. 'She won't. She would wet herself before she would dirty her mouth by mentioning such a thing to a boy, especially a Bridgefoot.'

'I shall tell the others she won't have anything to do with me, so if she does want help it'll have to be Nick who takes her bloomers down. Robert can plead that he isn't strong enough to face such an experience.'

'Do that,' she said. 'Nick's the only one of the three of you with either manners or sense enough to cope with her. Why you two don't learn a thing or two from him beats me.'

She decided not to mention the arrangements to Aunt Esther till Saturday morning, but before she had time to do it, Cynthia Fairey was on the phone.

'Do you think Charles and Nick would come up to sit with Robert tonight?' she asked in an anxious voice. 'He just can't get up again this morning. Tom's mad with him, but I'm really worried. I shan't go tonight and leave him here by himself, whatever Tom says. It's happening too often, now.'

'You must get him to a good doctor,' Rosemary said, and explained her own situation. 'There's nothing wrong with Aunt Esther, only temper,' she said. 'But it would be just like her to set fire to the house or choke herself with an acid drop just to spite me if we did leave her by herself. Oh dear, it is too bad, when we do get a chance to do something a bit out of the ordinary. I don't know what to say. Charles won't agree to stop here by himself and let Nick come up to Robert, I'm sure.'

'I wonder,' said Cynthia slowly. 'I've just had an idea. Nick's mother will be all by herself, won't she? She's got to get out of that place soon, but she's agreed to stop there till after the sale. Besides, she's got nowhere else to go, yet. Since Bert Bleasby died I've been up to see her once or twice, to make sure she's all right. Tom had enough to do with Bert to know he wouldn't care what happened to her, if he died, for all she's worked for him since Nick was a baby for nothing except a roof over their heads and their keep. I don't know however they're managing now, though Nick has got a weekend job. She might be willing to come and sit in your house to keep an eye on Aunt Esther to earn a shilling or two. Then the boys could come up here. What do you think?'

To Rosemary it seemed like the answer to a prayer. If Nick's mother would consent to come once, she might be persuaded to act as a babysitter to Aunt Esther again, at least during the Christmas period.

She told Cynthia what a load it would be off her mind if it could be arranged, and Cynthia said she would go straight away to find out, and then let Rosemary know. It was a good excuse to put off telling Aunt Esther for another hour or two, if nothing else.

When Cynthia reported back, all was well. Jane Hadley was quite willing to help out, providing she could be fetched and taken home afterwards. 'We'll fetch her,' Cynthia said, 'and bring her to you. Then we can all go on to Benedict's together. I shan't be half so shy about going then. I told her somebody would take her home, but I couldn't say how late it would be. But as she said, it didn't matter, because Nick won't be going home till she does.'

The ordeal could no longer be put off. Rosemary chose her time carefully, when Brian was well out of the way.

Aunt Esther's face lengthened, and her eyes gleamed as they had done in the past when she had taken out her grievance against life by walloping Rosemary with that large flat hand of hers. Rosemary could tell that she was wondering whether pathetic tears or a blast of temper would produce the better result. She thought cynically that she was already getting a bit wise to her aunt's tantrums. She busied herself tidying the room, feeling the baleful eyes following her. She had always been frightened of those eyes.

Aunt Esther decided on temper. Tears might be useful later.

'I will not be left,' she said, defiantly. 'You hear me, you wicked gel? *I will not be left!* If you start gallivanting out and leaving me in this barn of a place by myself, you shall be cried shame on. I shall tell it in Gath. I shall tell it in Gideon! Them posh relations o' yours as only want you for your money shall know just what you are. Where is it you are going to, to be out all hours of the night, then?'

Rosemary managed to keep her temper. She ignored the question, and said, mildly, 'But we're not going to leave you alone, Auntie. We've arranged for somebody to come and stop with you. It's up to you whether she sits with you, or in our sitting-room where she can have the television on.'

'Who?'

'Charles's friend Nick's mother. She used to be Bert Bleasby's housekeeper.'

'I ain't havin' her in the house with me. Nobody knows who she is. Come here with that child in arms, didn't she – and never told nobody who its father was. Likely she didn't know. And lived all them years with Bleasby as nobody had got a good word for. I all'us have wondered why you let your boy take up with such as hers – but there, that's none o' my business. But I ain't having a woman of her character looking after me.'

'Aunt Esther,' said Rosemary dangerously. 'You had better be careful what you are saying. And you had better not let Brian hear you making any nasty remarks about young Nick or his mother. We don't know her, but we do know Nick, and we love him. I'll tell Mrs Hadley not to come near you unless you knock for her, shall I? Will that do?'

Aunt Esther sneered. 'Mrs Hadley,' she said. 'She's no more Mrs than I am.'

Rosemary's patience gave out. 'You are a wicked old woman,' she said. 'Nobody knows anything ill of her that I've ever heard.'

'That's what I say. I don't know how you dare have her in

the house, let alone leave me by myself with her. If you find me with my throat cut and all your valuables gone as you bought with the money you got from turning me out of house and home, it'll serve you right. You still ain't told me where it is you're going.'

Rosemary clenched her teeth and closed her eyes against the wish that she might find such a happy solution to the dilemma she had brought upon herself.

'We are going to a party at Mrs Catherwood's, at Benedict's,' she said.

A look of pure triumph crossed Esther's face. 'I might have known it,' she said. 'Money is the root of all evil. I didn't know as you was friends with her now, neither. Another one as is no better than she should be, by all accounts. If you ask me, all the Bridgefoots is getting too big for their boots since they made money. I remember when George Bridgefoot had hardly got trousers enough between the patches to cover his backside. He wouldn't ha' been asked up the old squire's house then, that he wouldn't. And to think as my own niece'll leave me to be looked after by such a harlot while she goes to feast in the house o' such other sinners as them two up there. But what can you expect from anybody married to one o' them Bridgefoots? Cursed be they all, for ever and ever. Amen.'

Rosemary fled, lest her temper got the better of her and she slapped that malevolent old face.

By the time that she was dressed, and Mrs Hadley had arrived with Cynthia and Tom, she had managed to cover up most of the traces of the outburst of weeping she had given way to after leaving Esther.

Jane Hadley was about her own age, and fairly tall, though too thin to be handsome. Rosemary had often seen her about, but had never spoken to her before. She noted a pair of beautiful, calm, dark eyes in a rather worn face, and lovely hands made rough by manual labour; but when Jane spoke, the likeness to Nick was apparent. In tone and quality, as well as diction, her voice could have belonged to Fran Catherwood.

She listened intelligently to all Rosemary dared say of what she was likely to encounter from Aunt Esther.

'I'll cope,' Jane answered. 'I'm not exactly a stranger to difficult people, or awkward situations. Enjoy yourselves.'

'It will be all because of you if we do,' Rosemary said warmly. 'I can't thank you enough.'

With confidence in her new helper, and the prospect of a few hours away from her incubus, she announced happily that she was ready to leave for the party. It was only when they were at last packed into Tom's car that she was able to believe that the Cinderella her aunt was making of her was actually on her way to the ball.

23

So far, so good. The buffet had been a great success, and so, much to Fran's relief and even somewhat to her surprise, was the rather curious mix of the guests proving to be.

She and William had decided in advance to use the down-stairs rooms of 'the flat' as cloakrooms, though a sign pointed the way upstairs to the main bathroom for the use of the ladies. Fran had enough female curiosity herself to foresee that those who had not seen the interior of Benedict's would feel cheated if they didn't get a surreptitious peep into bedrooms.

Jess and Greg had arrived first, willing to be of any help they could. It was a good start. Fran could see that Jess had taken a lot of trouble to look attractively feminine. She really was a most handsome woman, Fran thought, and wondered why she didn't take the trouble to make it obvious more often. Her figure was still that of a seventeen-year-old boy, with just enough bust to prove that she wasn't one. Her low-necked dress showed off the beautiful bone-structure Fran was inclined to envy, and she looked happy. Consequently, so did Greg. He was being his most charming, mercurial self, and helping William with his duties as host. That left Fran free to give most of her attention to those guests she didn't yet know well.

Eric Choppen arrived alone, socially competent enough – and yet? She sought for a word to describe his slight unease

... reluctant. Yes, that was it. He still felt an outsider. She hoped that the party might do something to counter that. She greeted him warmly, and handed him over to the dazzlingly entertaining Jess.

The Commander was more difficult. He was stiff with embarrassment, a fish absolutely out of his own element though correct to a degree. Fran tipped the wink to William, who left Greg to carry on dispensing drinks while he played host to Elyot Franks. She saw that William was answering questions about the house while gently manœuvring his shy companion into the presence of Jess and Mr Choppen. How clever of him, Fran thought. Choppen was the only man in the room that Franks really knew, and Jess would pull out all her extra stops for him. (Later, during the evening she heard the two of them chatting animatedly about naval affairs, and remembered with something of a shock that of course, Jess had once been a Wren officer. Well, you never knew when odd bits of past experience might come in useful. Jess was being a first-class asset tonight.)

When George and Molly appeared, she waited while Sophie relieved them of their coats and then found herself in a bearlike hug. Brian and Rosemary, standing behind, winced at his father's lack of social know-how; but Fran returned George's kiss and led him to William's chair.

'I've been reserving it for you,' she said. 'You stick to it, and don't let any of these others pinch it from you. If there aren't enough chairs to go round they can stand, or sit on the floor.'

William had escorted Molly to Fran's chair on the other side of the fire, thereby fixing a kind of nucleus around which the younger Bridgefoots and the Faireys clustered, feeling safe there. It would be quite a time yet before the social ice melted.

Monica arrived alone, looking extremely chic in one of her own creations. Fran was quick to notice the change in her. She handed Monica over to Greg and went to meet Beth Marriner.

She had been delightfully surprised to get an acceptance from Miss Marriner, noting that it contained no mention of her father. As she moved to greet her, Fran realized that she had never before thought of Beth as a woman in her own right, and not simply as her father's daughter and a sort of clerical dogsbody. Beth was as tall as any man in the room, taller in fact than some, because of the unusual 'cottage loaf' style of dressing her wealth of hair. Her height was accentuated by her slim-fitting, long-sleeved, full-length dress. The beautiful earrings drew attention to a face that could neither be called pretty nor handsome, but was very striking all the same. There was an element of suppressed fire about her, and a feminine elegance that did not consort at all well with Sophie's reports of her, from which Fran had constructed an image of a rather dowdy daughter of the church who showed her resentment at being 'on the shelf' by trying to shock. Fran adjusted mentally to this new Beth, especially in the light of the Rector's recent visit. This intriguing woman in front of her was no more likely to be subdued in the Rector's presence than she had been herself.

She took Beth across and introduced her to William, and then went to the kitchen to find Sophie. Everybody was there now, except Bob Bellamy. She couldn't say she was disappointed, because she had half expected that he wouldn't be able to face it when the time came, but she was sorry. She decided there was no point in waiting for him, and told Sophie they were now ready to eat.

But when they led their guests through to the breakfast-room, they found Bellamy there, chatting to Ned. In the food-selecting mêlée that followed, his presence remained inconspicuous. Fran could not help wondering whether it was by luck or by his own clever timing that he had managed to avoid what to him would have been a round of excruciatingly shy-making introductions.

As she greeted him herself, she gave William a triumphant wave across the room, lifting the arm that bore an exquisite bracelet of antique cameos set in Victorian gold which William had clasped round her wrist in bed that morning. He had teased her that if Bob didn't turn up she would have to make do with him. Over the heads of their guests the message was received and answered. Greg and Monica saw it, and both sighed – one for what he had had and feared he might be losing, the other for what might have been. They returned resolutely to the present, and piled up their plates.

Things were going along easily now, as Sophie and Thirzah, like Dutch dolls in their aprons and with their polished shiny red faces, served coffee in the sitting-room. Fran was conscious that the most difficult time of the evening now lay ahead. She had told William that they would play it by ear as to what they should do to entertain the guests after the meal was over. What on earth could one do with such a mixture? For the first time, she was uneasy lest her party just fizzled out into polite, brittle, enforced conversation between people who had very little in common. That was not her idea of enjoyment. She didn't even know what they expected 'a party' to be. What did they do at their own parties, supposing they ever gave such things? She looked around her in panic, trying to catch William's eye, but for once he was not 'with' her. He was sitting on the arm of Molly Bridgefoot's chair giving her all his attention as befitted the oldest lady in the room, and rapidly enslaving her for ever.

Greg was sitting with Beth Marriner on the duet piano stool. He looked up and caught Fran's eye.

'Play something,' she mouthed at him. He obediently swung his legs over the stool, and opening the piano, put two stiff forefingers down on the keys at the bass end, where he happened to be sitting, and played 'Chopsticks'. Somebody laughed, and Fran breathed again. Next moment, Beth turned herself round too, and played Chopsticks on the high notes. Then after looking at each other, they began to improvise a duet upon the tune with the virtuosity that only a couple of completely confident musicians could achieve. All conversation had stopped, and Fran was beginning to think that her guardian angel must like parties himself, to come so unexpectedly to her rescue, when Greg lifted his hands theatrically, like a concert pianist, to leave Beth with the tune. She took it back to its unadorned origin, expecting Greg to join in, but from William's arm chair came a deep male voice singing,

> 'Oh will you wash a farmer's shirt,
> Oh will you wash it clean?
> Oh will you wash a farmer's shirt,
> And hang it on the line?'

'Altogether now!' said Greg, standing up and conducting for a moment before sitting down again at his end of the piano. To Fran's utter amazement, other voices were raised in singing the silly song, till they all broke down in laughter.

'Surely it should be a soldier's shirt?' said Eric Choppen.

'Of course not. It's a sailor's,' responded the Commander.

'Farmer's,' said four voices, indignantly.

'Well, at least it can't be an academic's,' cut in William. 'That won't fit.'

'I've always thought it was "Oh will you wash your *father*'s shirt?"' said Beth. 'But now that I know, it shall be "Oh will you wash a parson's shirt".' She turned back to the piano to try it out.

'Let's have it once more,' said Jess, 'and all sing our own versions. I shall sing '"an artist's shirt"', because they must take the cake for being difficult to get clean.'

'Right!' said Greg, sitting down again. 'Concert performance, this time. Once through by Beth alone, again by me and Beth as a duet, and then you all come in. Now – ready, Beth?'

She started to play, and immediately all eyes were turned to the end of the piano, where Bob Bellamy was leaning. He had taken from his pocket a mouth organ, and was expertly playing the tune.

'Bravo!' yelled Greg, pounding away happily. 'Now, altogether for the last time.'

All formality had broken down. It was going to be a real party.

'What shall we have next?' asked Greg. He looked at Beth, and then at Bob. 'Something we all know.'

Bob's eyes were full of mischief. He raised the harmonica to his lips again, and began the tune of 'Bless 'Em All'.

'Hold hard,' said Greg. 'Not your own versions, gentlemen – please! – considering we have at least two soldiers, one naval man and one airforce officer here present.'

'Up the Wrens,' said Jess, loudly.

'And the Home Guard,' said George.

'Official version, then. Off we go.'

They went through a repertoire of wartime songs till Greg and Beth called a halt.

'Shove back the furniture,' ordered William, 'or put it in

the hall. Now is the time for dancing, as Henry Hall used to remind us once upon a time.'

'We're not equally matched,' Fran said. 'Eight men to seven women.'

'Seven men,' said Jess. 'Greg will have to provide the music.'

'We'll take turns,' said Bob, taking Fran's breath away. 'If you'll just excuse me for a minute.'

He returned carrying a concertina, a fiddle and a banjo.

'I ain't much good at this modern stuff,' he said, 'except on my mouth organ. But if you want country dancing, or square dancing or even Scottish dancing, I reckon one o' these'll do.'

'A ceilidh!' cried Jess. 'Lovely! Let's start off with an eightsome reel. Oh, never mind if you can't do it. Greg can shout instructions and those of us who know how can push you through. That's half the fun of it. Four couples on the floor, please.'

Molly shook her head, and Cynthia hung back shyly. So did Eric and the Commander. Rosemary, feeling she ought not to desert Cynthia, pleaded that she'd rather watch first time through.

They formed up, with Greg waiting at the piano: William and Beth, Brian and Monica, Tom with Jess and Fran with Bob. William wickedly winked across at Fran, and mimed throwing a glove into the middle of the formed-up square. The tournament was about to commence, and Fran truly didn't know which of her knights she wanted to win. Was it a fair contest? She had no idea whether or not William had ever tried Scottish dancing before but she was sure that neither, both being born dancers, would have much trouble with the steps. It really was remarkable, she thought dazedly, as she began the figures she had learned in her university days, that nobody was bungling it. Jess had lived in Scotland till quite recently; Beth had schooled many a troop of girl guides as part of her duty; Monica seemed to be taking it in her stride. Brian and Tom, though not familiar with actual Scottish dancing, had been put through their paces in English country dancing by Mary Budd, and were quick to learn; but the duel of expertise was between William and her own partner. When the second figure started

Fran noticed that William was adding the correct Scottish footwork to his performance, grimacing triumph to her as he did so. Up went Bob's arm, curved over his head, as he promptly followed suit with his nimble feet. Both of them might just as well have been wearing kilts and sporrans.

They both were expert, and she could not make up her mind which of them surprised her most, the academic or the fenland farmer. Neither, as far as she knew, had the remotest connection with Scotland. William went forward.

'To which of us is the lady of the tournament going to award her favour?'

'To both,' she said. 'I declare the contest drawn.' She took off her flimsy chiffon scarf and wrapped it round William's arm; then she unpinned the orchid from her corsage and placed it through Bellamy's buttonhole, kissing them both. The spectators cheered.

'Greg's turn to dance,' said Jess, firmly. 'And Rosemary's and Cynthia's. Come on, both of you.'

Beth sat down on the piano stool, and beckoned to Bellamy. 'Fiddle?' she asked. 'Can you manage without music?'

He smiled shyly down at her. 'I shouldn't know what to do with it,' he said. 'I can't read a note o' music. I just heir it from my father.'

It was at this moment that Fran caught sight of a worried-looking Sophie at the door trying to attract her attention.

She indicated that she would come out to the kitchen at once. 'Do take my place, Cynthia,' she said. 'I'm wanted in the kitchen.' So away they went again, while Fran left to find Sophie, who was waiting for her in the hall.

'I had to fetch you out,' Sophie began, in a low conspiratorial whisper. "cos I didn't know what to do. While you was all kicking up that row singing and dancing, I 'eard a knock on the front door. So I goos to open it, and finds a young chap standing there with one o' these 'oldall bags in 'is 'and, as says 'e knows you and 'e's come to stop. I asked 'im what 'is business was, but 'e woul'n't say. He just said 'e wanted to see you. He don't look like a bailiff's man – not that I've ever seen one as I know of – nor yet a policeman. But I am 'eard about them private detectives on my wireless, an' I couldn't 'elp wondering if 'e were one o' them as were sent 'ere by William's wife to spy on 'im, like.'

'Where is he, then?' said Fran, amused in spite of a certain apprehension by Sophie's outrageous suggestions.

'Well, I thought as 'ow I'd better not let anybody else see 'im,' Sophie said, 'so I put 'im in your study, seeing as that wasn't being used, and I locked 'im in. 'Ere's the key.' She fished in her apron pocket, and handed the key to Fran. She retreated unwillingly, almost afraid to leave Fran to face the intrusive stranger without support.

Fran's mind was racing as to who it could possibly be that like the fly had apparently walked so innocently into spider-Sophie's parlour. She turned the key and opened the door.

'Hello, Mum,' said the bailiff's man, jumping up from the chair by her desk. 'Happy birthday!'

'Roland!' she gasped, as he hugged her. 'Oh Roland, you came!'

Fran closed the door, looking for Sophie; but Sophie did not need telling to mind her own business, once she knew that Fran was safe. She had gone.

'I didn't know you were having a party,' Roland said. 'I'm sorry to butt in like this.'

'Darling, it's the best present I could have had,' Fran said. 'I wanted you so much! Where's Sue?'

He looked grim. 'She wouldn't come. That's why I'm so late. I had to go out to an emergency meeting today and I went all the way home to pick her up – but she had changed her mind – yet again. She wouldn't budge. Then we had a row, and I told her that if she wasn't ready in half an hour. I should start without her. She went to bed and sulked – so I came. And I'm glad I came! But Mum – I don't feel much like joining the party, and I haven't had anything at all to eat since breakfast. Can you find me some food, and give me a bit of time to collect myself before appearing? There's a lot to explain, but we'll talk tomorrow.'

'Stay here,' she said. 'I'll go and get your supper. Nobody will come in here, but you can lock the door while you eat. Then if you don't feel like meeting a lot of strangers, I'll smuggle you up to a bedroom.'

She went to the kitchen and told Sophie that the stranger was an unexpected visitor who had been on the road all day and was very hungry, asking her to make a huge pot of coffee and pile up a plate for him. 'I can't stop long with him,' Fran said, quite truthfully, 'but he isn't dressed for a party, so I'll take it and talk to him for a minute or two while he eats it.'

Sophie prepared a gargantuan meal, and Fran took it from her. Sophie retired to the kitchen, a bit put out by Fran not telling her more; but as usual, she sensed that there was a good reason why. What she didn't know she couldn't tell. She was glad Fran had not seen fit to satisfy Thirz's curiosity.

In her excitement, Fran had failed to register how long she had been away from her other guests. William was getting anxious, but courtesy required him to stay where he was. Greg was at the piano again, and Jess acting as master of ceremonies. The only one available to send to look for Fran without making it too conspicuous was Monica.

'Fran's been gone so long that I'm afraid there may be a hitch somewhere that she's trying to deal with without letting on,' William said to Monica. 'Would you go and find her for me? Ask her if she needs any help?'

Monica went willingly, and asked Sophie if she'd seen Fran. 'Last I see of 'er, she were going into 'er study,' Sophie said. 'Tha's the room next to the one as you left your coat in.'

Monica found the door, and heard voices inside. She knocked, and Fran opened it a fraction, knowing at once what the matter was.

'Tell William I'm just coming, Monica,' she said. 'Sorry, Roland. I'll be back with Uncle William as soon as ever it's possible. What on earth's the matter?'

Monica, deathly pale, was holding on to the door jamb for support.

'Get out of the way, Mum,' said Roland, pulling her away from the door. 'Can't you see she's going to faint?'

He pushed past her, and caught Monica in his arms, almost carrying her back into the study. 'Look, Mum,' he said tensely, 'lock the door – whichever side of it you like.'

She took the hint, though still as stunned as if she had been pole-axed. 'You'd better lock it yourself on the inside,' she said, 'or Monica won't be able to get out.' She put the key down on her desk and went out, but not before she had seen Monica returning Roland's hungry kisses.

He looked up, and said, 'Go away, Mum. I swear I am as surprised as you are. I'll tell you everything tomorrow.'

Fran stood outside the door, saying 'Well!' to herself, unable to take in anything except that her son was in her house again and that he and Monica Choppen were not exactly strangers to each other. She squared her shoulders and went back to join her guests, wondering how on earth she was now going to explain Monica's absence.

They were just forming up, at George's request, for 'Haste to the Wedding', which had been danced at every village function since long before he was born. George and Molly, Jess and Greg, Brian and Rosemary, Tom and Cynthia, William and Beth. As soon as she appeared, Beth seeing the relief on William's face, insisted that Fran should take her place. In all the circumstances. Fran thought, it would be better to agree; but as Beth turned to sit down, Elyot Franks was on his feet and at her side.

'Will you allow me the pleasure?' he said.

Beth raised her eyebrows in a surprised but delighted smile and said incredulously, 'I knew matelots had orders to dance and skylark, but does it apply to their officers, too? How gallant of you! Thank you,' and she dropped him a deep, stately, straight-backed court curtsey. Bob Bellamy sat on the piano stool, with his concertina on his knees. Only Eric Choppen was left out, seated alone.

Bob had just played a long chord to bid them be ready when the door opened, and Monica came back in. Glancing nervously towards her, Fran saw again the girl with rosy cheeks and sparkling eyes that she had first remarked in the church porch at the wedding. Well, it was all beyond her.

Monica took in everything with one glance. 'Wait a minute,' she called, and ran to pull her father on to the floor. Fran had an extraordinary feeling that a couple of hundred years had been rolled up and they were standing up as they might have done when Benedict's was new.

'It's all been wonderful,' she said to William as they stepped into the dance.

At eleven fifteen, Sophie appeared at the door again, and Fran went to speak to her. If they wanted any more refreshments, which Sophie indicated were all ready on trays in Thirzah and Ned's hands, they had better have them quick, because she and Thirzah would have a job to get all the washing up done before midnight, and work on a Sunday they would not, even for Fran.

'I'll do any washing up as you have to leave,' Ned said.

'There's no call for anybody to be breaking the commandments,' Sophie answered him. Fran took the warning. It was time the party came to an end.

Fran thanked her, smiling. She must remember to tell William of Sophie's discretion, though whose morals were being guarded this time, Fran wasn't quite sure.

By midnight, coats were being fetched and thanks expressed over and over again. Through the happy chatter of the room the telephone bell sounded shrilly. Fran's heart missed a beat. Sue? Or Katie? Who else could it possibly be, so late.

William said swiftly, 'I'll take it,' and lifted the receiver.

'Yes, he's still here. Hold on,' said William. 'Brian, it's for you. Your son.' Rosemary clapped her hands to her mouth to prevent the exclamation that rose to her lips.

'What?' Brian was saying. 'Say that again! Yes, we're on our way now.'

They all looked at him with anxious eyes as he put the receiver down and turned back towards Rosemary. 'Aunt Esther,' he said, and sat down heavily on the nearest chair.

They had to wait till he gained control of his voice.

'When Charles and Nick got back to the farm about half an hour ago, they found Aunt Esther still up, playing "Strip Jack Naked" with Nicky's mother, and saying she hadn't had such a nice evening for years. Then Mrs Hadley went to make her a drink, and she went by herself to the bathroom. She got there all right, and shot all the bolts on the inside, and then fell down with her head shoved up against the door. Charles says he and Nick have tried everything they could think of, but they can't get in through the window, and even if they could pull the bolts back, they couldn't open the door to pick her up, because she's got her stick wedged somehow across her and under the bath, so she can't move. I think we'd better get home as fast as we can, Tom. Nick's just sent for the fire brigade.'

When everybody had gone. Fran made William her loving-cup of chocolate, while he sat in a glow of satisfaction that everything had gone off so well.

'More than you know,' said Fran, and launched into the tale of Roland's arrival, and the extraordinary scene with Monica.

'He was very tired and washed out,' Fran said. 'So I smuggled him off to bed. Let's go and see if he's awake, before we go to bed ourselves.'

They sat reviewing the evening for a few more minutes. 'They all mixed so well,' Fran said. 'That's what pleased me so much. It was a lovely party. Come to bed.'

They stole along the passage to the farthest back bedroom. She inched open the door. Roland's bed was empty.

THOU SHALT NOT

24

Tired as she was, Fran could not sleep. She had to tell William more about Roland and Monica.

'I only had one glimpse of them together, and it was incredible. They both looked thunderstruck, and then fell into each other's arms as if they were starving – but it doesn't make any sense at all. I wasn't drunk, and I wasn't dreaming. I saw it!

'Yet she came back to the party ten minutes later, as chirpy as a bird and as self-composed as one of her own models on a catwalk. I just don't understand it. They didn't expect to meet each other here. They were both absolutely stunned. What do you make of it?'

'Love at first sight. "Haste to the Wedding",' he said, sleepily.

'Oh darling, please be serious. I'm worried.'

'Why shouldn't that be serious? It happens.' He drew her towards him and pulled her head on to his shoulder, but she drew away.

'Because he's my son. And he's married. I hope he has some sort of moral standards. After all, I brought him up.'

'He can't help being a product of his age, all the same. Peer pressure is more potent than mother's good advice. Don't kid yourself, darling.'

She knew he was right, but that didn't satisfy her. She also knew that if he was going to talk at all, he didn't want to talk about Roland. So she lay beside him, restless and wide awake.

He knew that she was listening for a footstep on the stairs or the soft closing of a door. He sat up and put on the bedside lamp.

'Now look here, sweetheart. Are you going to lie awake all night worrying because Roland wasn't in his bedroom? My good girl, I know he's your son but he's out of nappies. He's twenty-seven, with a Ph.D., and his foot on the architectural ladder. And he's been married five years. If he can't look after himself, who can?'

'I know all that. But he was already upset when he arrived. Where is he now? Put that light out, please – I don't want to alert him that I'm awake and on the lookout for him.'

William obeyed.

She turned back towards him. 'And where and how does Monica Choppen fit in?'

'My dear girl, your guess is as good as mine. She's an attractive girl.'

'But darling, he's married.'

'As far as I know, being married is no deterrent to falling head over heels in love. I'm married, too, if it comes to that. Had you forgotten?'

'Yes, if you want me to tell the truth. But this is quite different. Is Monica the cause of Sue's peculiar behaviour? He said he and Sue had had a frightful row when he went back to get her and she wouldn't come after all. Why? Was it because she knows about Monica?'

William recognized the inevitable. She wouldn't sleep till she had talked it out with him. He roused himself to full wakefulness, sat up against his pillows and prepared to give her all his attention.

He pulled her back to his shoulder again and said, 'Now, sweetheart, begin at the beginning and tell me again exactly what happened. But stop torturing yourself till you need. It isn't fair on me.'

There was enough edge on his voice for Fran to detect the twinge of jealousy. The last thing she wanted tonight was to quarrel with him.

'Look, he's your son, but he isn't mine – that hurts enough in its own right without me having to worry about you giving yourself a heart attack or a stroke or something over him. You may be his mother, but you are my wife and my sweetheart first, and it's you I am concerned about, not him. Don't spoil our lovely evening worrying all night about something that may never happen. I agree that it's a mystery. So let's start at the very beginning. Tell me again, in as much detail as you can remember, just what happened.'

Grateful, she began again, and was soon enjoying the telling, adding bits of detail she had omitted in her first brief summary. When he chuckled in the dark about Sophie's mythical bailiff's man she knew that she was safe again from any foolish disagreement with him, and continued her tale in a lighter vein.

He listened carefully, picking up the salient points and registering them as if he were listening to a student reading an essay.

'So he wanted to come, and Sue didn't. That explains why you had no reply to your invitation. Roland has grown tired of making up excuses for her. That should make you feel better, anyway. It proves that any distancing between the two of you is her fault, and not his.'

'I think he had worn her down till she agreed to come, but when he went to pick her up, she just turned stubborn.'

'So he came without her. Good for him! Another point in his favour.'

'Yes. He said they had an awful row. Well, so do we, occasionally. That wouldn't worry me by itself. But why won't she come near me? She never has done. And where on earth does Monica Choppen fit in? Darling – you have to take my word for it – it was the sight of him that nearly caused her, tough and modern young woman as she is, to come close to fainting.

'And when he caught her in his arms, anybody could see that it wasn't the first time she'd been there. If those two haven't been lovers, I'm a Dutchman, as Ned would say. If you'd seen it, you'd know I'm telling the truth. But that's what I can't get over. It's too much to believe they met here tonight by chance. If Monica's the cause of the trouble between Roland and Sue, nobody's happy. But William – where is Roland now, at this hour of night? Why isn't he in his bed?'

'Sometimes I think a fertile imagination like yours is a curse rather than a blessing,' he said. 'Use a bit of reason instead. I agree that it's clear that Sue's avoiding you, and there's some reason we don't know. Roland won't tell you why – or at least hasn't done so yet. There's nothing to go on, so far. Now take the Monica bit. You say it's too much of a coincidence. Life's full of coincidences. If you don't believe me, you should read history. To use a convenient cliché, the world's a very small place, and getting smaller by the minute. The meeting may be pure coincidence, but if they reacted as you say they did, it doesn't take much logic to work out that what they have in common is more than a one-night stand in a Paris hotel. So, extrapolating from what we have so far, my guess is that Roland is for some reason having a tough time with his wife, made a lot tougher for him by the fact that the woman he really wants is still free. History repeating itself? My darling, it always does!

'As to where he is now, I can only guess by putting myself in his shoes where, if my other reasoning is right, I was until last year. Either he is enduring a new bout of torture from having had his arms round Monica again and is striding up and down the spinney wondering how he can endure the rest of his life without her, or he has gone off in his car to climb through her bedroom window. Whether he has a hedge of morality to get through as well, as I did, is open to question. Monica belongs to the post-war era, and you seem to think he's hacked it down at least once before. But either way, it's none of our business. Maybe we shall find out in the morning. Now, cuddle down and go to sleep. And before I forget, in spite of your injunction on the invitation, your new boyfriend brought you a present. He gave it into my hands when the others were all leaving in such a hurry. And in spite of your romantic theories, that's where Roland may be, helping the fire brigade to extricate Miss Palmer from the loo. See what I meant about coincidence? Even you couldn't have thought that up as a note to end such a lovely evening on!'

He could almost see her smiling in the darkness and his arms told him that she was relaxing at last. 'It was a lovely party,' she said. 'My special bit was the eightsome reel. Where did you learn Scottish dancing?'

'I was young, once,' he said.

'Only once? You were young enough this morning.'

'You've had quite enough excitement for one day. Shut your eyes.' She wriggled down with her head on his shoulder and in two minutes they were both asleep.

Before going downstairs next morning, Fran looked to see

if Roland's car still stood outside. It did, and when they went into the kitchen, they found him sitting at the table having made a hearty breakfast.

'Hope you didn't mind, Mum,' he said, perfectly at his ease. 'I looked into the fridge and there were such mountains of food left over from last night that I thought I might as well help myself.' He caught sight of William, and jumped to his feet.

'Hello, Roland,' said William, advancing with outstretched hand.

Fran was watching Roland's face. He grasped William's hand, looking dazed, while a long, slow grin spread gently over his face, as they looked each other over.

'Hello,' he replied. 'Mum told me she would introduce me to *Uncle* William in the morning. I expected you to be at least seventy-five, and bald with pebble-lenses and a hearing-aid. I'm sorry, Mum, but I'm damned if I'll ever call *him* "Uncle". So hello, William. I must say I'm glad to find that my poor decrepit old mother has such good taste in men.'

'You cheeky young devil,' said Fran, relieved that such a sticky moment had passed so easily. 'It's your fault, not ours, that you haven't met before.'

Roland sobered instantly. 'That's part of a long story – and one I must tell you now I'm here at last,' he said. 'Not a very happy one, I'm afraid. But I'd rather not start on it till you've had your breakfast.

'I wish I could have got here earlier last night, Mum. It sounded as if you were all having a wonderful time. But I have brought you a present.'

He handed her a package not very neatly tied up, and Fran's first thought was a glad one that whatever it contained, Sue had had no part in its choice. Her presents always came from the best shops, and were gift-wrapped to such an extent that Fran usually felt a sense of disappointment when she at last got to whatever was inside.

'I picked it up in a junk shop,' Roland said. 'I didn't know whether it would ever be of any use, but I did know you would like it for its own sake.'

Fran unwrapped the queer-shaped brown paper tied with

string, and disclosed a fan-shaped hair comb of fine tortoise-shell, with a crystal bead set into the scalloped top at the end of each rib.

'It's exquisite,' she cried, bending to kiss her son.

'Give it to me,' said William, stretching out his hand.

He took it and placed it in her hair so that the fan sat at a slight angle on the top of her bun. 'Splendid!' he said. 'Next time we go out in evening dress, you will wear that with a flower, and the gipsy ear-rings I got you for the horkey. Fifty, indeed!'

Roland regarded his mother with a somewhat bemused light in his eye. 'May I be allowed to add that I hadn't expected my decrepit Uncle William to have such splendid taste in women, either? Mum, you look fabulous. And as for my ancestral home – it takes my breath away. Do you mind if I go and poke round?'

'How long can you stay?'

'I have to be at work tomorrow morning, so I shall have to leave just after lunch,' he answered. 'But I want to talk to you a bit before I go, if you can spare me the time.'

'After coffee, in my study,' Fran said. 'Will that do? I'm afraid it will mean a scratch lunch, unless William will be the chef. He's quite competent as a cook.'

'Would it be too much to ask that William sits in with us? I think I may need a man's opinion and advice about what to do next.' He took silence for consent, and left them.

'Ought you not to look at your other present?' William asked, when they had finished a very light breakfast. 'I'll go and get it.'

He came back carrying a large flat parcel tied with string, but before the paper fell off Fran knew what it was: an oil-painting, about twenty by twenty-four inches, of the church on the hill with the rookery behind it.

Fran gasped. It was beautiful, though almost too photo-graphically representational in an old-fashioned way for modern taste. She loved it on sight, all the same. Bringing her critical faculties to bear, instead of her emotions, she worked out why. The style was pre-Raphaelite, with every twig and every feather painted with infinite care; yet the whole was just primitive enough to take from it any amateur pretentiousness. It was, thought Fran, as if Bellamy had painted himself, with all his intelligent insouciance, into it.

'My God!' said William, squatting down to examine it closer. 'What an artist the man could be if somebody were to teach him something about tones!'

'Don't you ever suggest such a thing!' said Fran, flaring up. 'That would make him just a good amateur painter. As it is, he's an artist.'

'He seems to be making a fair bid to become your ideal man,' said William wrily, standing up.

She looked at him squarely. 'My ideal man wouldn't be frightened by shadows,' she said, 'nor be jealous of what amounts only to an ingenuous child. And he would know that any hint of jealousy on *any* ground would insult the woman who loved him.'

'Oh Fran, darling, am I so transparent? Forgive me,' he said, looking ashamed and miserable. She reached for his hand, and held it. They were still holding hands and contemplating the picture, when Roland returned. The tiny incident had decided for her that the one place she must not hang it was in her own study.

'Let's try it on the landing,' she said. It took them till coffee-time to find the right place. By then all three of them were at ease again, with themselves and with each other. It gave Fran a great deal of pleasure to have the two men she loved most in the whole world doing their best to please her, though it occurred to her that both of them now felt guilty. Men were all such babies. She remembered Kezia, Sophie's mother, saying, 'Two straws and a half make a baby cry, or laugh'. It didn't take more than three straws to upset or to please most men, either. Yet women were supposed to fall for the he-man, Tarzan type! And men, of course, for women with no shape.

Did they really, or was that peer pressure, too? When she had been in her teens, and much too curvaceous, she had appreciated the wit and point of some lines written by an amateur poet of her acquaintance, about a particularly skinny filmstar.

Gemma's the most ethereal star, I wean,
Of all whose airy thigh-bones grace the screen.
I find her flat as any ale-house bench!
A breastless, haunchless, hipless, hopeless wench!

How silly it was for anybody to try to generalize about affairs of the heart. They didn't always follow fashion. Finding the right one was even more important now that people were living so much longer.

They took their mid-morning drinks into Fran's study and prepared to listen to Roland. It was no surprise to find that it was an affair of the heart he had on his mind.

'This house is a dream, Mum,' he said. 'I had no idea. Who was your architect?'

'Well, I did have one – cost me a fortune and did very little for it. But mostly it's the result of my own ideas, supplemented by William's. He was in it from the start.'

'But why didn't you employ your son? Had you forgotten he was an architect?'

'No, I hadn't forgotten – I thought my son had. He was a long way away and seemed to show so little interest in my venture that I thought I had better not embarrass him.'

Roland flushed, and played with his spoon. Then he looked up, and said, 'Your son has a wife.'

Fran didn't know why she was being so tough, because she certainly didn't want to punish him; but there was a trace of waspishness in her voice as she answered. 'A wife I hardly know. And judging by what I saw last night, he has a mistress too.'

Roland leapt to his feet, the flush deepened now with anger. 'If you're going to take that line—'

'She isn't,' said William, mildly. 'I can assure you of that. People who live in glass houses are careful not to throw stones. But when she found your bed empty last night, she worried herself sick about you. Sit down and let's try to act like three reasonable people. We are all tired, as well as a bit flat after yesterday. Don't cry, my precious one. I can't bear it.'

Fran took a firm grip on herself, and apologized. Roland squeezed her hand, and took the opening her outburst had offered him.

'It goes a long way back,' he said, and plunged into his story.

Lasting friendships are often made during the first few weeks at university. Roland had made one special friend, Adrian, and they went about together, if possible in a foursome with two girls from the JCR. But as it happened, a girl whom Adrian had known at home was at the art school round the corner. They'd gone to look her up, and found a fellow art student with her – her best friend. Monica. (Pause.)

So there they had been, a ready-made foursome, for the next two years; just friends, changing partners all the time. 'Nothing more than friends, honestly, Mum.' She nodded.

By the time all four were facing their finals, both men had begun to show a decided preference for Monica, but the pressure of exams meant that they were not seeing nearly so much of each other.

'When I saw the list posted, and knew I'd got a first, I just rushed round to tell Monica. She wasn't there. Sue told me that Monica's mother had been killed in a plane crash, and she had gone home. She didn't come back.

'I waited in London. I know you were upset, Mum, that I didn't come home for the whole of that vacation, and it was true that it was largely because I had managed to find myself a good vacation job. It had been suggested that I went for a doctorate, and I had started applying. I had to have somewhere to live, and Monica's room in the flat she had shared with Sue was vacant.

'At Sue's urging, I took it – on reduced terms. Sue had found a job, but she wasn't dependent on what she earned. Adrian went overseas and Sue and I were left together.'

William, at a glance from Fran, got up and poured drinks for them all, making Roland's a double whisky. He had written a letter of condolence to Monica, to which she had not replied. He wrote others, but got no answer. Then one weekend he told Sue that he was going to see his mother but in fact went to find Monica at the address he knew. The whole family had moved, nobody knew where, except that it was 'somewhere in East Anglia'. The post office wouldn't disclose the forwarding address.

He concluded that he meant nothing at all to Monica, and that she was deliberately giving him the push.

York University accepted him, and he had some funding, though not enough for three years without work to supplement it. He was on the point of giving up all hope, when Sue had made her astonishing proposal – and proposal was the exact word. Her home was in Yorkshire; her father was a highly respected landowner, and a baronet of ancient lineage to boot. She had money of her own, and with her father's name she'd have no difficulty in getting a job. *Neither, if he were a member of the family, would he.* Two could live as cheaply as one, and in any case they were living, albeit in anonymous London, under the same roof. That wouldn't be possible in her own patch. What she was implying was that marriage to her was his key to a very bright future.

'Mum, don't look at me like that! I wasn't selling my soul to the devil. I had known Sue for three years, and I loved her – or I thought at that time that I did. I suppose I still do. And I was only twenty-two, for God's sake. If I didn't love Sue as much as I ought to have done to think of marrying her, it was because I was too young to know what love really was. She'd always been in the running, but after Monica had gone I think I turned to Sue as second best . . . I reasoned that everybody wants what he knows he can't have. I was piqued, as well, that Monica had turned me down without giving me a chance. You know the rest.'

'No, darling, we don't. All you've told us so far only accounts for you marrying Sue when and how you did. Have you been happy? Are you happy now?'

'To be blunt, no.'

'Then why not, Roland? Why has Sue refused to let you be my son as well as her husband? And how does Monica fit in now?'

'I suppose every pair of newlyweds are happy at first – sex, and all that. But it wasn't long before I found how difficult Sue was to live with, day in, day out. For one thing, she was so terribly possessive. Any other woman who took my attention from her for a single minute was put under a kind of taboo.

'That included you, Mum. And when you took up with William, she played the morality card again, saying that her family could not be seen to be associating with you. I was mad, but I gave in. For Christ's sake, Mum – she had been more or less keeping me afloat till I got my doctorate. What could I do? She had always been moody – we all knew that. When she more or less proposed to me, I flattered myself that her moods had been caused by her jealousy of Monica. As I soon found out, they can be sparked off by the slightest thing, and she sulks for days.

'Then Katie had her children, two babies one after the other. That seemed to send Sue nearly round the bend. I wasn't allowed to go and see Kate or my new niece and nephew – though to be honest, I did. I sneaked away under cover of a conference. Kate's a good sort. She promised me she wouldn't tell you. I wanted children – still do. I was helping to bring home quite a lot of the bacon, so I suggested Sue gave up work and start a family. She refused, completely and absolutely. It was a subject never to be mentioned again.' He paused, looking a bit confused.

William intervened. 'Wouldn't, or couldn't, Roland? Are you sure which?'

Roland looked at him gratefully, for helping him come to the point without feeling too disloyal to his wife.

'Wouldn't. No mistake about that. And from that moment made sure there won't be – the only absolutely safe way.'

'Is she ill? That sounds to me like some sort of irrational fear,' William said.

Fran was suffering remorse at having been so angry with Roland, when it hadn't been his fault at all.

Roland was answering William, glad to be able to talk to a man instead of his mother. 'Yes,' he said. 'I think she's ill. I have begged her to see a a doctor, a gynaecologist, or a psychologist. No hope. She says she's always detested children, never wanted any and won't have any.'

'But she didn't tell you. Was she always so cold – when you were first married?' Fran was keeping quiet, letting William help Roland along.

'Oh no – surely she wouldn't have married me, if that had

189

been the case? I mean, I know there are women who can't bear the thought of sex – but I thought that's what marriage was all about. I had no way of judging – I was an absolute innocent when I married her. I was satisfied, I suppose. Until we had the baby row.' He gulped, held up his head, and looked across at his mother.

'Or, perhaps, until I had been to bed with Monica. I know now what love is. And what sex can be. I shouldn't be satisfied now – but as things are it doesn't arise.'

'How did Monica come back into your life, Roland?' Fran asked.

'Absolutely by chance – or coincidence. Fate, I suppose. I had to go down to London for an Arts Fair – where firms have stands to show the kind of things they do. As the youngest member on our staff, I was sent to mind our stand. It was a pretty boring assignment. I'd got browned off with handing out leaflets and things, and left the stand to get myself a cup of coffee.

'Some clumsy idiot jogged my arm as I was turning from the counter, and I spilt my coffee all over a woman who was just passing. She yelped, because the coffee was hot, so I set my cup down to help mop her up. When she looked up to swear at me – it was Monica.

'We went back to her flat. I've invented several conferences to attend since then. Then about six weeks ago, I found a letter from her waiting for me on my desk at work. It was to tell me that she was disappearing out of my life. She had let the flat, and "gone home". I had no idea where home was. She begged me not to try to find her, and had made pretty sure that nobody told me where to look. She was saying goodbye, though she'd never love anybody else. That letter more or less coincided with your first one about the plans for your birthday, Mum. I've been nearly out of my mind since then.'

There was silence. At last William said, in a voice that let Roland know just how much he understood. 'And yesterday?'

Roland smiled a rather sheepish smile. 'May I tell the absolute truth? I was hurt and I wanted my Mum. I made up my mind to come, whether or not Sue did. As I said, we had the worst row ever. She suspected I'd been seeing Monica again, and I didn't deny it. I asked her if all the blame was mine, and why she'd married me, if she didn't want me or my children. To keep Monica from beating her in the marriage stakes, as she had in every other way. Why had I married her, if I didn't love her? I said I had, and still do; but as she was being so brutally truthful, I was, too. I told Sue how I had tried to find Monica, and couldn't understand why she had never replied to my letters.'

His face twisted with a grimace of despair. 'She told me she had written a letter of condolence to Monica, in which she had also said that we were "going to live together". Well, I suppose we were, in a sense. But not in the sense Sue intended to imply, or the sense she intended Monica to understand. That's why I hadn't heard from Monica again.

'That was yesterday. I left Sue sulking in bed and came. Now I'm in a worse fix than ever.'

Fran was trying to wipe away her tears without either of the men being aware of them. 'And last night?' she said.

'I went to Monica, of course – she told me how to find her. We talked most of the night. Very much like the hoary old curate's egg, actually. She asked outright whether I had any hope for us. I had to tell her that I hadn't: that I had married Sue in all good faith, and that now she was showing signs of instability I couldn't just walk out. Besides, I have obligations to her. She helped till I could stand on my own feet professionally.

'Monica said she was glad, because she wouldn't marry me if Sue divorced me because of her. She had run away because she had felt so guilty. I had to accept it.'

William got up, and began to stride about. He suddenly swung round on Roland, and said almost angrily, 'So you and Monica propose to make yourselves into celibate martyrs, do you? Why don't you take to the cowl, and Monica to the wimple? A fat lot of good that would do anybody!

'Don't be such bloody young fools! Life is made for living. Somebody – I can't remember who – said, "God made man to lie awake and hope but never to lie awake and grieve." Even a dog is allowed one bite before it's put down. Surely men and women ought to be allowed to make one mistake? If they turn into "bolters" as Nancy Mitford puts it, that's a very different matter. It's a question of everybody having to work out his own salvation. Neither church nor law can do it for you. Because your mother and I found our salvation it doesn't mean we can teach you how to. We can only encourage you to go on trying. Maybe I can give you just one tip. Trust Monica. Women are wiser than we, and solve problems their own way.'

Roland, though pale and washed out, was actually smiling. 'She's already done so,' he said. 'She'll welcome me as a lover, as long as I don't leave Sue in the lurch. So you'll probably be seeing a good deal more of me in the future, provided you don't disown me, Mum. I'll be as discreet as ever possible for your sakes.'

(Fran heard Sophie's voice in her ear. 'We don't want no more scandal, like, up 'ere at Benedict's.' She was nearly as prescient as Bob Bellamy.)

'William and I haven't a shred of respectability left to lose,' she said. 'But there are others whose feelings have to be considered. Monica's father, for one.'

He nodded. 'Yes, we went into that. And by the way, Monica asked me to tell you. She says she's turned down some of your offers of friendship. Now you know why. Catherwood happens to be a rather unusual name, and when you mentioned your son Roland, she put two and two together. She daren't run the risk of meeting me here with Sue. Now that you know what she means to me – what she is to me – will you still ask her? For my sake?'

'No,' said Fran. 'For her own. If she can make my son happy, I'll do anything for her.' She got up and Roland met her. William turned away, but Roland let go of his mother and held out his hand.

'William,' he said. 'Thanks for everything. I don't remember my father, but I can't help feeling sorry for him now. Think what he lost by dying.'

William answered him quite seriously. 'Don't waste your sympathy,' he said. 'He couldn't miss what he never had – any more than Sue will. He never had what I've got. That's where the church's laws and man-made morality come unstuck. Love defies legal or moral definition.'

'I'd like to go now,' Roland said, immediately after a quick lunch. 'I daren't go round to see Monica again by daylight; but if you see her, either of you, please give her my love.'

'I shall ring her up on purpose,' said Fran.

25

Aunt Esther's escapade in the loo had far-reaching consequences. She was in no immediate danger, though there was no heating in the bathroom and she lay pinned to the cold floor by her walking stick, with her wet bloomers clinging to her and the November night's temperature falling lower as midnight passed. By the time the party-goers got home to Temperance Farm, the situation had become one of high comedy rapidly turning into farce.

Six firemen in uniform and armed with axes, who had no easy solution to the problem, had decided to wait for George Bridgefoot's permission to hack the window out. There were present altogether George, Brian, Tom, six firemen and two youths hysterical with laughter, as well as Molly, Rosemary, Cynthia and Jane Hadley, to say nothing of the victim who wailed, yelled for help and cursed biblically by turns.

George ordered the women out of the way, and they retired to the sitting-room, all giggling nearly as much as the boys. They had all had a wonderful evening, and more wine than any of them, even the men, were used to. Brian's uninhibited imprecations against the prisoner for spoiling it all for them did nothing to help them suppress a mutual inclination to snigger.

The two boys were told to clear off as well, so they joined the ladies for whom their laughter proved too infectious. They laughed in concert. Only Jane Hadley remained her calm, sober self. Her face was masklike, never changing its expression of rigid control, except occasionally when her eyes softened as they rested on her son. She moved about methodically, heating blankets and hot-water-bottles, making tea for the rest, and waiting at hand for the firemen to get the bathroom door off its hinges.

'What a help she has been,' said Rosemary, whose laughter was mixed with tears. 'Oh dear, I had hoped that if she managed all right tonight I might ask her to come up and relieve me one or two days a week till Christmas is over. But she'll get the blame for all this, and probably be told never to darken our doors again.'

The firemen succeeded in getting the bathroom door off its hinges and lifting Aunt Esther out. She was no worse for her incarceration except for the cold. Jane undressed her swiftly, rolled her in hot blankets and got her into bed. She then asked Rosemary for brandy or rum with which to lace a posset for her patient. With warmth and attention, Aunt Esther's spirits rose rapidly, and Jane announced that the others might come to visit her.

Rosemary was now helpless with relief as well as laughter, and all three women were still finding it difficult to maintain straight faces. Esther detected it.

'Strong drink is raging! Wine is a mocker,' she said sourly. 'Don't you let none o' them touch me! They're drunk. You stop with me.'

'Yes. I will. At least till you're asleep,' Jane replied soothingly, handing her the posset.

'What have you put in this milk? I'm a teetotaller. If it's strong drink, I won't taste it.'

'No, Miss Palmer, of course it isn't. It's sal volatile.'

Aunt Esther sipped, and sipped again. 'I always have liked the taste o' sweet nitre,' she said. 'My mother always used to take it for pain in her kidneys.'

All the others had recourse to their handkerchiefs yet again. Tales of Rosemary's paternal grandmother and her gin bottle had become folklore in the village.

Aunt Esther looked balefully at them over the rim of her cup. 'Like the crackling of thorns in the pot and snow in summer is the laughter of fools,' she said.

The second mangled quotation was too much even for

Jane. She turned her face away, and motioned to the others to leave, which they did as hastily as they could.

When Esther slept at last, Jane crept out, to be made much of. They were all too tired to do anything more that night. Rosemary asked Jane if she would come up on Monday morning to be paid, when they could thank her properly. She and Nick went off at last with Tom and Cynthia. George and Molly left hurriedly, when George remembered that he would have to be ringing the calling-bell in six hours' time.

'It was the best party I ever went to,' Rosemary said.

On Sunday, Rosemary talked to Brian about her idea of asking Jane to help out a couple of days a week.

He snorted. 'Offer her a full-time job,' he said. 'Engage her as a full-time nurse. We can afford it, can't we? I should perhaps get you to myself again, then. I'm getting fed up playing second fiddle to that old humbug. She owes you a lot more than you owe her, anyway, and don't you forget it.'

Rosemary accepted the reproof without offence. She could not get used to the fact that they were now 'monied' people. She had to walk warily with Aunt Esther, as well; it was no good jumping out of the frying-pan into the fire.

When Jane presented herself on Monday morning, Rosemary pretended to the old lady that she had called on purpose to see and ask after her; her offer to Jane would have to be based on her aunt's reaction to the visitor.

It was almost embarrassing in its warmth, but Rosemary's hopes were soon dashed. She was too late. Mrs Catherwood had asked Jane to go to the Schoolhouse, and Mrs Taliaferro wanted her three days a week – if she was able to take the work at all; but it wasn't at all certain that she could. She had undertaken to stay where she was till Bleasby's farm sale was over and the new tenant ready to occupy the house.

'I shall be free to work, then, and very glad of the chance – but we shan't have a home. Nick says he'll leave school at Christmas and get a job of some sort. I've put my name down for a council house, but there isn't much hope. Until I know where I'm going to live, I can't take a job, and vice versa. If I can get somewhere to live, I suppose I could give you the other two days, if it would help you. It would certainly help me – if you didn't mind having me on Saturdays.'

'Mind?' said Rosemary. 'I can't believe it! That's the very day of the week being tied at home irks me most. It would be wonderful!'

Jane damped her enthusiasm. 'Don't get too excited, Mrs Bridgefoot. I may still have to go much farther afield to take a housekeeper's job – though I don't want to move Nick from school till he's done his exams. But beggars can't be choosers.'

There they had to leave it for the time being. Rosemary told her family when they sat down to tea. It was Charles who responded.

'Old Nick is really up the creek,' he said. 'He's set his heart on going to a university, though it was always a long shot. I know he thinks he's had it, now. He's trying to get a job, without his mother knowing. I never realized till lately how tough it must be not to know who you are or anything about your family. His mother won't tell him anything. You can see she's a lady, and you can tell Nick isn't just anybody, can't you – well, by his manners, and things like that. If they have to leave here, I'm going to be the one who'll miss him most. Specially if Robert's going to keep being in bed half his time.'

He looked hard at his mother. 'Mum, what do you make of Robert? I think he's really ill. When Nick and I go up there, he tries to be the same as he's always been – but you can see he isn't. He doesn't fool about like we used to, and he can't concentrate. I'm worried about him.'

'So am I,' said Rosemary. 'And so is his mother. I am trying to persuade her to get Dr Henderson to get her a second opinion. But you know his dad – the Faireys have always been such a tough lot that he thinks it's a sort of disgrace for a Fairey to be ill, especially a young one. I wish I could persuade Cynthia to go behind Tom's back.'

'That wouldn't help old Nick, though. I wish we had a cottage empty.'

'Well, we haven't. There's nothing we can do,' said Brian bluntly.

'Eat your dinner,' Rosemary said. 'I must take Aunt's. Maybe the Lord will provide, seeing that it's for her benefit.'

'And ours,' said Brian.

'And Nick's and his mother's,' added Charles.

Rosemary couldn't see any way round Jane's problem, and lost hope. Charles had made her start to worry about the Fairey family as well.

Charles was miserable. He was resenting his father's 'big bug' mood in general, and his 'I'm all right Jack' attitude towards Nick in particular. His father, having decided that since he could very well afford it, it would make more sense to buy Charles a brand-new car for his birthday and Christmas present combined, rather than 'an old banger', was inclined to be irritated with his son for not showing more interest. He told Charles that it was no good worrying about other people's troubles, especially before they happened.

After a few rather sharp exchanges with his father, Charles went up to be consoled at the Old Glebe. Grandad Bridgefoot at least always listened to what he had to say, and for his grandmother he could do no wrong.

He was soon telling George and Molly everything – about Aunt Esther's latest tantrums, about Jane Hadley's dilemma, about his fear that Nick wouldn't get the chance he ought to have to make the most of his clever brains, and about Robert.

'It isn't fair, Grandad,' he suddenly burst out. 'There's Dad mad with me because I won't decide what sort of a car he can get me, and there's Robert ill though nobody will take any notice, and poor old Nick! I mean – he has hardly ever had anything to wear that hasn't been passed down from me or Robert, and if he didn't have a lot of his meals with us or the Faireys I reckon he'd be half-starved. But I've never once heard him grumble. It doesn't half take the pleasure off what I have, to know what he doesn't get. If he has to go away – especially if Robert doesn't soon get better, I don't know what good my car'll be to me.'

'It is a bad job,' said Molly. 'I do wish there was something we could do for Nick and his mother. I'm sure Cynthia Fairey has enough sense to look after her boy, so stop worrying about that. You'll have to find yourself a girlfriend.'

Charles looked scornful. 'Where?' he said. 'And how? I mean, if I haven't got Robert or Nick to go about with, car or no car, I shan't be going anywhere to meet any girls. We've looked all those at the Young Farmers over already. We were planning to go farther afield.'

George was placidly filling his pipe, packing it firm with a great thumb. He got it going, blowing across the bowl and pressing his thumb on the burning tobacco before he said anything.

'Don't be in too much of a hurry, my boy,' he said. 'It's the most important choice you'll ever have to make – a lot more important than choosing a new car. Us Bridgefoots haven't done too bad in that line so far – but then, when your Grandma married me, I hadn't nothing to offer her only myself; and your Dad hadn't got a lot more to offer your mother. But it's going to be different with you. They'll all be after you for your posh car, and the farm, and this house in the course of time, and your bank balance. Watch it, my son. If you ask me, Nick's the one likely to get a girl who wants him for himself alone. You'll be lucky if you do, and so will Robert. But there, them as lives longest'll see most. You can't put old heads on young shoulders. What about a cup of tea before he goes, Mother?'

After he'd gone, Molly got out her basket of mending, and George stretched his long legs out in front of him and smoked in silence – and thought.

Next morning, he took himself off to seek out Eric Choppen. Since the night Choppen had had supper with them, and in the light of how he had been seen to enjoy himself at Fran's party, George's opinion of him had been modified. Farmers were businessmen – especially since the war; they had to be. But they took their time about things. Choppen had gone at it like a bull at a gate, and had put everybody's back up. George thought he had learned his lesson. He had also heard a rumour that when Choppen had first blundered into Old Swithinford, it was only just after his wife had been killed in a plane crash. George took the rumour with a pinch of salt, but there was usually a grain of truth in a bushel of gossip. It might have accounted for a lot of Choppen's first nastiness. He had certainly softened up a bit, and at the party had seemed as if he was glad to be counted among the others from the village. If the rumour was the truth, Choppen knew something about hard luck.

George told nobody where he was going, or why. Nothing venture, nothing win. He thought Choppen owed him a good turn over the Pightle, anyway, whatever he had paid for it in money.

He found Choppen in his office, with Jess at his side. It was more like a gathering of friends than George would previously ever have believed it could be. Choppen ordered drinks, and George came at once to the point.

He told Eric about the plight of Jane Hadley, and its consequences to her son. He went on to tell them both of the misery at Temperance Farm that Aunt Esther was causing, and the damage to the family he feared she might do. He spoke of Rosemary's experiment in having Jane to look after her, and how well it had worked, and lastly of his own grandson's concern for his lifelong friend, Jane's son Nick.

'It's like finding a little lump on you somewhere, and then if you take no notice of it, before you know where you are, the doctor tells you it's a cancer as had gone too far to be operated on,' he said. 'Jane Hadley was only just over twenty when she arrived here from goodness-knows-where, with Nick as a baby. She'd answered an advertisement for a widow-man smallholder who wanted a housekeeper, child not objected to. Bert Bleasby was a pig of a man but she stuck it out. There's more to that story than we shall ever know. Anybody can see she was born a lady and young Nick's got the breeding of a gentleman. He's been in and out of my house, and Brian and Rosemary's, since the day he first went to school, and we're all as fond of him as if he were one of us. Now if she has to go, he will lose his chance of finishing his education, and God knows what will happen to her. I'd already made up my mind to suggest to Brian and Rosemary that they took Nick in till he'd done his exams, but there's two things against that, as far as I can see. Rosemary's got her hands full with her aunt, for one thing; and that woman as was brought up a lady has slaved like a gipsy for nearly twenty years to give her son a chance – I can't bear to think she's got to be parted from him just when they need each other most. If we could find a roof over her head, none of it need happen. So I've come with a proposition to you, Mr Choppen.'

Jess intervened. 'I've met her – up at Fran's. Mr Bridgefoot's right. She was born a lady – upper middle class, I'd say. And she's applied for a council house. If she could get one in time, she has a job, with me and with Mrs Rushlake at the Schoolhouse, that would at least keep the wolf from the door. But there's a six-month waiting list at least with the council, even for emergency housing.'

'Rosemary wants her as well,' George said. 'She made a real hit with that daft old woman last Saturday, especially after we'd got her out of the bathroom.' He paused, as if to let what he had said sink in. 'Now, Mr Choppen, there's one of your holiday cottages empty. It's very nearly Christmas, and it's likely to stop empty most o' the time till Easter. I know how high the rents are for them places as have been made into little palaces – but I want to take it on a six-months' lease, and you can charge me what you like. I can't see why my money ain't as good to you as anybody else's. So what about it?'

Choppen looked uncomfortable, but again Jess spoke.

'I think you would have great difficulty in making Jane Hadley accept charity,' she said.

George looked at her with a pitying, though gentle expression.

'Mrs Taliaferro,' he said, 'do you really think I don't know that? That's my greatest stumbling block, and why I've come to put it to Mr Choppen to help me. If you,' he said, turning his eyes to Eric, 'will agree to play, nobody else need know. Charge me what you like. Put it about that you're willing to let it to me at half price, with permission to sub-let, till Easter. That'll still be well above her means – but Mrs Taliaferro is here, and I'll go and see Fran Catherwood. If they pay her well enough, she'll be able to raise enough to pay me what I ask, and I'll see she don't suffer in other ways. She wouldn't think a bag o' potatoes charity, if Nick does a little job for me now and then – and things like that.' He looked at Choppen almost pleadingly, and apologetically at Jess.

'She may have her pride, but I'd bet you five pound to a ha'penny it ain't as strong as what them as were born and brought up round here's got. Folks like Sophie Wainwright, or Dan'el Bates – only as it happens none o' them two need charity. I've been a churchwarden, and my father before me, for more than forty year, and I know. There's a charity attached to the church, as were left by one o' the de ffranks-bridges about six hundred year ago, and it's part o' my job to help the Rector to distribute it. We used to have the devil of a job to make anybody take it, before the war. You see, it's called the de ffranksbridge *charity*. We don't have any trouble now – even young'uns'll come banging on my door asking who's had it or what we've done with it. Want their rights, as they say.' The scorn in his voice could have been cut with a knife.

'But we still have to handle the old'uns careful. You can't beat down their sort o' pride without hurting 'em more than you help 'em. But if my guess is right, Nick's mother'll see straight through it, swallow her pride if it chokes her, and accept it for her son's sake. Like the story of Solomon's judgement in the Bible, where the baby's real mother was willing to let the other woman have it rather than it should be hurt. If we can arrange it, pride or no pride, she'll take it, provided it don't smack so much of charity as every old tittle-tattler'll be broadcasting it against her. That's why it can't be let straight to her in the first place. I shall say I wanted it for a workman who's run back from the job, so I've got it on my hands now till Easter anyway.'

'I'd do it for my son – if I'd been lucky enough to have one,' said Jess looking at her boss rather pleadingly.

'Make a contract out, Jess,' Choppen said. 'Make it to George for six months at half the usual rate, and don't forget the sub-letting clause.

'I'll take the responsibility to the board. If anybody is fool enough to deny that any let during the winter is better than none, I'll make up the rest myself, if I have to. I've got a son of my own.'

George went home not only satisfied in his objective, but with other things to think about. He had always had an eye for a good-looking woman, and admired Jess. He liked her husband, too. She had sounded so sad when she said she'd never had a son. Why hadn't she got any children? He thought of his own family, and offered up a little prayer of thanksgiving. He was pleased with himself, too, and the result of his initiative. Eric Choppen had proved that he had got a soft spot if you could find it. You could only find it by probing – like getting milk out of a coconut.

26

It could hardly be said that things were quiet in Old Swithin-ford between Fran's birthday party and Christmas, because village tongues are never quiet; besides, things were happening, even if to the world at large they were barely worthy of comment.

With Christmas looming, Kid Bean had hustled his builders to get a move on so that he could open his new shop in time to catch the seasonal market. As by chance this opening had more or less coincided with the party at Benedict's, the one provided a meeting place for the satisfaction of curiosity about the other. Even Sophie could not resist going to look at the outside of Kid's shop, though she was above going in to ask for a packet of tin-tacks that she didn't need. Kid had certainly gone to town with the residue of his brother Jelly's legacy. The new shop had been created on the site of what had been the brothers' apology for a workshop in the old days; and in Sophie's prejudiced view, it stuck out in a most unseemly modern manner among the other old buildings. It consisted of a double-fronted shop with huge plate glass windows above which a fancy tiled fascia in bright blue carried the legend:

Kenneth Bean and Sons
Do **I**t **Y**ourself

Sophie's lip curled as she gazed at the display of wallpaper, paste, brushes and rollers that occupied one window. As if she hadn't been doing it herself without all that fuss, since she was fourteen! But she stopped looking at it just a moment too long, and got trapped by Olive 'Opkins on her way to do Beryl Bean's housework and then relieve her in the shop.

Sophie was ambivalent in her feelings towards Olive 'Opkins. While Mary Budd had lived, Olive had done her best for her, and anybody who had done anything at all to help Sophie's beloved 'Miss' was protected a little from her sharp tongue; but on the other hand, Olive was an inveterate gossip and now that 'Miss' was no longer there to chide her for making much out of little, she gave full range to her voluble tongue as well as her nosiness. When Olive greeted her and prepared to stop for a gossip and to hear what she had to say about the shop, Sophie put herself instinctively on guard.

She said what was expected of her as well as she could without telling lies, and was preparing to walk on when Olive held her back and began to quizz her about the party.

'I 'ear you 'ad a proper do up Benedict's Sat'day night,' she said. 'Your Thirz' told Win Maskell about it after church yist'day, and Win told me.'

'Ah?' said Sophie. 'Well, if you know all about it a'ready, there's no call for me to be late to work telling you all over again, is there?'

'Funny lot of folks for 'em to ask to a party, if you ask me,' Olive said, immediately taking umbrage at Sophie's uncooperative tone.

'I ain't asking you,' Sophie retorted serenely. 'It weren't my party. They asked who they wanted, no doubt, same as anybody else would.'

'They seem very thick with the Bridgefoots all of sudden. No doubt that's since the Bridgefoots come into all that money by turning poor old Esther Palmer out of 'ouse and 'ome.'

This was more than Sophie could take, partly because of her loyalty to Fran and William, and partly because of her lifelong respect for George Bridgefoot.

'Money won't make no difference to George Bridgefoot,' she said, 'else it would ha' done it a goodish while afore now. And as for them two up Benedict's, they're all'us the same to everybody, prince, parson or pauper alike. They were brought up proper. They was pleased to be asked to Lucy Bridgefoot's wedding, so they asked them back, like, being just as 'ospitable as the Bridgefoots only in their own way, as you might say.'

'Win said Thirz' told 'er as they shoved the furniture out o'the way and danced, even the new Rector's daughter, and 'im as is come to the Old Rectory, and so did that Mr Choppen and all! Doing dances as Mis' Tolly had learnt living up in Scotland. She said as everybody danced only that new chap from Castle Hill Farm, and some other young feller as got there too late to go and dance.'

'Thirz' ought to know better than to let 'er tongue loose to the first one as is nosey enough to ask her,' Sophie retorted, her feathers by now being truly ruffled. 'But she told the truth, all the same. Mr Bellamy didn't dance, sometimes, when 'e was playing the music for the others. And as to the young man who come late, I can't tell you nothink as I don't know. All I done was to open the door to 'im, and then I minded my own business. I wish as everybody else would do the same.'

Olive fired her parting shot. ''Arry Smithers were in the Green Dragon Sat'day night when that young chap put 'is 'ead in the bar and asked the way to Benedict's from there. And 'Arry said as 'e didn't want no swearing to, 'cos 'e were the spit image o' Mis' Catherwood. '"E's her missing son, all right," 'Arry says. There's more in that than meets the heye. You may depend upon it. Win thinks so, an' all.'

Sophie was incensed, and walked away. She was anxious and indignant. She was anxious because she suspected 'Arry Smithers was right about the identity of the bailiff's man, and indignant that Fran hadn't given her more ammunition to use against such as Olive 'Opkins.

But if she wasn't told more freely when she reached Benedict's, she would be far too proud to ask. As it happened, Fran's post had brought a problem that required much telephoning backwards and forwards to London, and William had gone off early and resolutely to start to find out whether there was any chance either of complete release or at least of a long sabbatical. So Sophie, helped by Ned, somewhat glumly set about the task of removing all traces of Saturday's party and restoring the house to its normal swept and garnished precision. Ned engaged her in a bit of speculation about the stranger. 'I reckon as Olive 'Opkins may ha' got something right for once,' Sophie told Ned, ''cos I see one o' the beds upstairs 'as been slept in. So whoever he were, 'e stopped 'ere overnight.'

In the event, they had less than twenty-four hours to wait before Ned brought the story back with the trimmings that had been added on its way round the village. Olive had gone straight in to Beryl with her bundle of gleanings from Sophie, and opened it up. Now Beryl Bean's forte lay in reconstituting scraps of information into new wholes in the same way as a patchwork quilt is made of old garments, and the end product usually bore very little resemblance to the original bits she had had to work from.

'Kid Bean's been doing a roaring trade, by all accounts,' Ned told William in the garden on Tuesday afternoon. 'There can't be many folks left who ain't discovered as they need something like a pound o' candles or a sink-plug or somethink, just to go and get a look in the shop and 'ear the news. According to Bill Edgeley, who did need to go 'cos he'd broke the head off his old hoe, there were a queue outside the door at five o'clock last night.'

Ned looked a bit serious, and William said, 'Go on, Ned. What else?'

'Well – I don't know or not whether you and Mis' Catherwood ought to be told. Bill said everybody as is been in the shop's got a tale about the do we had here a-Saturday night, from Kid's wife. According to the tale that she's put about, neither of you really wanted the Bridgefoots here like, only you felt obliged to have 'em 'cos you'd been asked to their wedding. And you didn't want the Choppens neither only Mis' Taliaferro made you ask them 'cos they'd been so kind to old Esther Palmer when she were in 'ospital. And then there was that young chap as come late and had his supper and went to bed. Seems he asked the way to Benedict's at the pub, and whoever it were told him said there were such a fam'ly likeness to Mis' Catherwood that likely he were her son as 'as never showed up afore, and if he was, why 'ad 'e got 'ere so late and in secret, like? That Beryl Bean all'us has been a trouble-maker. The best thing's to take no notice, only I thought you ought to know.

205

'Oh yes, and another thing as is being said is that you hired the chap from Castle Hill to provide the music, instead o' the chaps from the village. They're right upset about it, accordin' to Beryl.'

'Come in and tell Fran everything,' William said. 'It's about time for a cup of tea, anyway.'

Sophie made tea and all four sat round the kitchen table while Ned repeated his tale. Sophie showed her feelings more and more as the tale went on, till she could bear it no longer.

'That wicked woman ought to 'ave 'er mouth stitched up,' she exploded. 'Telling such a parcel o' lies. I mean Kid's wife, not Olive 'Opkins. She may all'us go round the sun to meet the moon if she's got anything to tell you, but she don't tell lies just for the sake o' telling lies, like Beryl does. An' I reckon it's all my fault for answering the truth when Olive went on about it a-Monday morning.' She set her lips in a straight line and looked Fran in the eye. 'But it weren't me as told nobody as it were your son as slep' in that bed upstairs, or why it were all kept so secret. It's none o' my business, I dare say.'

Fran understood the reproof and accepted it. 'I'm sorry, Sophie,' she said. 'Of course it was Roland – but I was so surprised myself that I lost my wits, I think. I didn't even tell William till after we went upstairs.'

Knowing Sophie's gift for detecting even the smallest suspicion of a half-truth, Fran was glad that she could look at William for confirmation, and get it.

Sophie's face cleared, and Fran added as much as she was prepared to in front of Ned. 'He had meant to be here much earlier, but he had to go to a meeting, and then went home to pick up his things, and by the time he had driven down from York he was so tired and hungry he just couldn't face changing and being introduced to a whole roomful of strangers. So I took him up myself to his room.'

Ned put on his cap and went back to work. Fran told William that he, too, could be excused so flatly that he took the hint and left her alone with Sophie.

'You were quite right about Roland's wife,' she confided. 'He went home to try to persuade her to come with him, but

206

she wouldn't. That's really why he was so late. I'm afraid they're not very happy together, and I'm worried. Roland hinted that he is afraid she may be ill enough to need a psychiatrist – a doctor like Lucy Bridgefoot's husband. But she's quite well physically, I think. She just gets queer ideas. She wouldn't come herself, but he told her he was coming in any case.

'I think we may see him occasionally now, and I feel better because I know he still wants to come and see us. And he fell in love with the house. If he didn't want to see me, he would come just to see the dear old house again. He is an architect, after all.'

'Is he?' said Sophie, with such surprise that Fran had to do a bit of rapid thinking. She must have been very reticent about Roland with everybody except William.

'He hadn't met William till breakfast time on Sunday morning, and of course neither Jess nor Greg has ever seen him. So don't be cross with me that I didn't introduce him to you, will you? And you can tell Thirzah as much as you like. Though she didn't see him at all, did she?'

'Not as I know of,' said Sophie. 'But I shall tell 'er as this tale as is got about is all 'er fault. If she hadn't bluthered it all out to Win Maskell on the way 'ome from church a-Sunday, nobody would have knowed no details about our do. But there, it did make Thirz' a nice evening out. You see, since that row there was down Thirz's place about our Wend' going to be a singer, I'm never 'ad no more to do with our Het. But Mam left 'er for me and Thirz' to look after, and Thirz' wouldn't go back on 'er promise to Mam. She keeps a heye on Hetty and goos to see 'er whenever she can. Thirz' is very worried about her. She has sterricks everyday, now, about something.'

Sophie was healing any possible rift between them with these confidences as Fran was well aware. She had always thought Sophie's sister Hetty only just on the right side of the thin line between simplicity and subnormality. She wanted to let Sophie go on talking, knowing she would talk herself back to normal. Fran rather wished she hadn't invited the report of Hetty's behaviour that Sophie launched into. Hetty was indeed behaving very strangely.

Sophie got up and gave Fran a rather tremulous smile. 'Let

'em say whatever they like, we 'ad a real good do, didn't we? I'm sure Ned and Thirz' and me enj'yed every minute of it.'

She wanted to talk to William about Ned's disclosures, but she had sent him away and he was now at work in his study. She went to her own and sat down to think in some perturbation. There certainly was a difference between benign and malignant gossip; and like a tumour, if it was allowed to grow, the malignant kind could spell death – in this case, to friendships. She couldn't let that happen if there were any way she could stop it. She could hardly wait for William to finish what he was doing and come to talk to her.

27

William was reassuring, except that he foresaw difficulty with regard to Roland's proposed visits. If they couldn't even keep a party in their own house from becoming a verbal football, what would happen the first time somebody – and there was bound to be a somebody – saw him leaving Monica's house?

'"Sufficient unto the day is the evil thereof,"' Fran quoted. 'I just hope none of our guests get to hear what's being said, and take umbrage.'

When the tale was retailed with even more additions to George Bridgefoot, his only reaction was to slap his thigh and laugh. 'Kid's wife needs one o' them old-fashioned gob-stoppers,' was all he said. Rosemary's only reaction was to pray that Aunt Esther didn't get to hear of it, and she was a little surprised at Cynthia Fairey being a bit upset.

'They needn't have asked Tom and me if they didn't want us,' she said. 'Tom's people have been farmers here as long as Brian's or yours have, but I'm only the village blacksmith's daughter, remember. I wish I hadn't gone.'

'Don't be so silly, Cyn,' Rosemary answered. 'Didn't you enjoy it?'

'I don't enjoy anything much these days,' was the unexpected reply. 'And I don't expect to until I don't have to be so worried about Robert. Tom says he won't pay for a second opinion because there's nothing the matter with him, only laziness. I don't know what to do.' And, to Rosemary's dismay, Cynthia then burst into tears, and had a good cry. 'It's bad enough to be worried over Robert,' she sobbed, 'but to be at loggerheads with Tom about it is more than I can bear. It isn't as if we haven't got the money, after all – Tom's made as much as anybody else since the war. But the more he gets, the meaner he gets. What's it all for, if it isn't for Robert? He's all we've got.'

Rosemary, knowing how she would feel if it were Charles instead of Robert, understood Cynthia's problem. There were times when men were useless.

She considered, though, that if it had been Charles, she would have had the benefit of a doctor in the family. Well – 'a little help's worth a lot of pity.' It only took a telephone call to Lucy's husband to set up an appointment with the consultant he recommended. The difficulty lay in Cynthia getting Robert to London without Tom's knowledge.

Rosemary had no option but to take Brian into the plot. She was very relieved that he took it seriously.

'I'll invite Tom and Robert to go with me and Charles to the Smithfield Show,' he said. 'We'll invite Robert, but he mustn't be well enough to come. If we go early by car, Cynthia and Robert can take the train, and they can be back, and Robert in bed again before we leave London.'

Rosemary, though delighted at his ready acquiescence, was nevertheless surprised. She came to a conclusion which she felt it wise to keep entirely to herself. Brian had put himself in Tom's place, as she had put herself in Cynthia's. What Robert was to Tom and Cynthia, Charles was to them. Brian could see the issue clearly, because the boy in question was not his son; Tom couldn't. What was the matter with Tom was not that he was too mean to take a second opinion, but that he was too frightened. He was simply burying his head in the sand.

Luckily, Beryl Bean did not get to hear about it, though her tongue was active with other matters. Jane Hadley's move to the cottage lasted her well because everybody was wondering how it was that she had managed to get a tenancy out of the hard-fisted syndicate. Neither Beryl nor Olive could credit Mr Choppen with being a ladies' man on what they had seen of him, though that appeared to be the only possible explanation. As one of them said to the other, he always had been a dark horse, and after all, a hungry dog will eat any dirty old bone.

'Only she ain't no juicy bone such as I should ha' thought a man with all his money would ha' bothered with,' Beryl opined. 'I mean, she ain't no oil-painting, is she? Thin as a lath, and scraggy with it. And so stuck-up she never opens her mouth to nobody. He's a fast worker, and no mistake. It couldn't ha' started while Bert Bleasby were alive. Besides, that boy of hers is there at nights with her, ain't he? And she works all day and every day except Sunday. We shall have to keep watch to see if his car goes up that way.'

The Commander's apparent lack of any religious allegiance was a pale topic by comparison, though worthy of a bit of comment.

'The Rector went to see him,' Beryl reported to all and sundry, 'and asked him if he'd read the lesson Christmas Day. But he told the Rector to his face that he wasn't no churchgoer. Said so with his own lips! Then our Methodist minister thought as he must be one of us, but he got the same answer. Surely he can't be one o' them Roman Catholics, can he? If he is, it don't seem right to me for him to be living in our Old Rectory next to the church, does it?'

'Miss Budd told me as how our church was a Roman Catholic church once, when it were first built, like,' Olive recalled.

Beryl sniffed. 'There's them as'll say anything as comes into their 'eads,' she said, 'and there's all'us others fool enough to believe 'em.'

The Rector had felt very dispirited to find Elyot Franks so adamant in his refusal to ally himself in any way with the church. After his crushing passage of arms with Frances Catherwood, he felt the Commander's rebuff keenly and concluded that he was failing in his duty.

Before he had taken the living, he had been given a potted

version of its recent history; he had heard that in his predecessor's days, there had been a large and faithful congregation, led by the oldest families, the biggest farmers and the few professionals. The church had a wonderful ring of bells, and had once had a good choir. All this he had been told by the churchwardens, of whom George Bridgefoot was the more voluble, as well as the more truthful. He told the new Rector bluntly that such was not the case now. The old Rector, who had been eighty-four when he died, had more or less given over his cure to a lay-reader some ten years ago. The lay-reader had got into difficulties ('Sins of the flesh!' hissed the other churchwarden into his ear as George paused) and had simply disappeared. Then the leading farming family had been more or less wiped from village history by a disastrous fire.

'It's never been the same since then,' George said. 'Now there's only about ten folk who come regular. Our old schoolteacher used to be a real live wire, and did her best to keep the youngsters interested in the place – but she's got old and can't compete with television. There ain't much hope of building the congregation up again, as far as I can see, and that's the truth. The chapel's got a lot bigger congregation than us, now. Folks say the chapel's better for working men though how that idea got about, I don't know. It runs in families – some are born chapel and some are born church, and that's the beginning and end of it.'

Marriner had formed a rather poor opinion of his upper-class public-school-bred and financially independent predecessor. Such clergymen as Howard were indeed out of touch with their flocks in these post-war times. Five years of shared fear and privation, sorrow and death had levelled out a lot of the social topography.

Marriner realized the need for such as himself to bend a little and go towards the people, but . . . ?

He had found it easy enough in war-time. Twenty years later, it was much more difficult. They no longer wanted him, one way or the other. His attempts at being 'Hail, fellow, well met' in pubs, for example, had not been well received. He had got off on the wrong foot, and he was worried.

He didn't know who to turn to for advice. It was clear to

him that his daughter Beth had very little sympathy. He could not blame her, and he did blame himself. He knew he had used her far too much as a substitute for her dead mother, so that all the tedious social duties that ordinarily fell upon a clergyman's wife had devolved upon her.

She had rebelled by doing outrageous things to show him up, such as using the sort of language he detested, but which had of late become common currency. Now that she was older, she shamed him less but saddened him more. By taking a living in a tiny rural outpost like Old Swithinford, he had, to all intents and purposes, put her irrevocably 'on the shelf'. She was over thirty, well-educated, intelligent and accomplished. She had a highly developed sense of humour, and she could hold her own in most sports open to women; but with regard to matrimony she fell between all the stools there were.

When she had heard from him the story of his visit to Benedict's, she had broken down and cried that he had robbed her of her only chance of making the sort of friends she wanted. In vain he had argued that he had had no choice. It was his duty. It had been an ordeal for him, too, a test of his devotion to his calling, and of his moral courage. He explained to her, as he had done to William, his conviction that the breakdown in sexual morality would lead directly to the breakdown of civilization.

He had been told of the adultery going on at Benedict's – and, like the boy in the Dutch folk-tale, had felt compelled to do what he could to stop the leak in the dyke. He had done only what he felt he must do. Could she not understand?

Yes, she said, she did understand, but she thought him neither a hero nor a martyr. She thought him a wrong-headed fool. 'For all I know, you may be right in your assumption that civilization is going to the devil. But it will take more than a few well-intentioned holy-Joes like you to stop the flood now. You'll only make yourself – and me – ridiculous by bleating about it like a sheep on its back. The dykes have already burst. All you can do is to care for the victims – and I don't mean the people at Benedict's.'

Then she had defied him; in spite of his request, and then his decree that she must decline her invitation, she had accepted it, and had gone. She had subsequently insisted on telling him every detail about it and what lovely people the two scarlet adulterers were.

Well, he agreed with her about Dr Burbage. If there was a man around he would have liked to have as a friend, it was William. So calm, so gentle, so urbane, so – so civilized. But he had blown his chances.

He clung for comfort to the belief that he had been right. He was too honest to invent any other excuse for himself. His prayers that his misjudgement might not be visited on Beth were offered with charity enough towards her, but without either faith or hope. It was the female of the species at Benedict's that he had confronted and insulted (though he hadn't meant to), and such a social gaffe would not be easily forgiven.

The relationship between the two of them in the cottage down Spotted Cow Lane was strained. Sometimes he actually quailed before the set of Beth's mouth and the purposeful gleam in her eyes. For the first time ever he was diffident when telling her what he had planned for her to do in the parish.

'I should be glad, my dear, if you would call on that Mrs Hadley at Revels,' he said. 'Take her a free parish magazine, and have a chat with her.'

'Of course I will,' she said. 'Don't we make that munificent gesture to all newcomers? I'd better put one through the Old Rectory door as well. Commander Franks has a soul to be saved by a parish magazine as much as Mrs Hadley. One mustn't overlook that tiny crack in the dyke, must one? And don't you think we ought to pray for the souls of all the mangled or drowned or blown-to-bits sailors that had only such a heathen as he to read the burial service over them? What chance can they stand of ever getting through the pearly gates? Still, there's one consolation for them – they'll find William Burbage and Fran Catherwood in hell with them, no doubt. That'll be nice, anyway.'

She tossed her head and left him cringing at the scathing bitterness of her ironic tongue. He put on his coat and scarf, and went out. Acting on impulse, he turned towards the path that led to St Saviour's up on the hill. He wanted to be alone.

213

As it happened, Jane Hadley was in no need of consolation from the parish magazine. She was still stunned by her good luck. The cottage was beautiful, with every mod con that Bleasby's miserable house had lacked. The cottage's isolation was an added blessing to her. She had lived so long in isolation that she found friendliness almost too difficult to cope with. Rosemary, Greg and those at Benedict's, where she had to call for her wages, treated her as an equal; her reserve and lack of response was the result of the shell she had had to grow to prevent herself from being hurt too much.

That first Friday, she had been asked in while Fran went to find her handbag, and Sophie had immediately put the kettle on for a cup of tea. When it was ready, Sophie called to Fran and William to tell them so. Jane was astounded at their easy intimacy, as they all sat chatting round the kitchen table. She was sure her ears had not deceived her – but had she not heard Sophie call the professor 'William'?

It was something Sophie very rarely did in company, and Fran noticed the effect it had on their visitor. She apologized for giving Jane her tea in the kitchen.

'We love the kitchen,' she said. 'Of course you wouldn't know, but William and Sophie and Jess – Mrs Taliaferro – and I always had tea in the kitchen together when we were children. We've never really grown out of it. That's right, isn't it, Sophie?'

'Yis! Yis! Tha's right. And Thirz' and our Het. We was all child'en together, like, in this same old 'ouse, only it wasn't so smart and up-to-date in them days. Praise be to 'Im Above as brought us all back to be so 'appy together again 'ere.'

For a fraction of a second, Sophie dropped her eyes to her hands in her lap, as if in prayer. Fran was caught out, amusedly wondering how it was that whenever Sophie did give voice spontaneously in the presence of strangers, her vocabulary seemed to consist mostly of words beginning with an aspirate that she could drop. Jane was afraid she had wandered into a Never-Never Land where she had no right to be. She soaked up every detail to tell Nick. Their new, if only temporary, circumstances were beginning to restore hope in both of them, Nick especially.

The Bridgefoots of all three generations had always tried to make him see the foolishness of giving up his university ambitions till all hope had gone. Hope had now been renewed. It was almost too good that he need not leave school after Christmas.

Christmas was getting close. As Rosemary could now escape on Saturdays while Jane patiently cared for Aunt Esther, she suggested to Cynthia a trip to Cambridge for some last-minute shopping.

They struggled through the crowded town till they were both exhausted, and managed to find an empty table for lunch in one of the more expensive restaurants. Cynthia had enjoyed her shopping, Rosemary thought, and her lunch.

When the waitress brought the bill, both women reached for it, and Cynthia won. 'My turn,' she said triumphantly, and opened her handbag to find her wallet. It had gone.

Rosemary picked up the bill and put the money on the plate. 'You must have put it somewhere in your pocket,' she said. 'You'll find it.'

Cynthia shook her head. 'No,' she said. 'It's been stolen. When we were in that last shop, I found my handbag open, and just thought I hadn't shut it properly. It must have been a thief in the crowd.'

Rosemary was distressed. 'Was there much money in it?'

'Yes, quite a lot. Never mind.'

'Well, I must say you're being very cool about it. Not making half as much fuss as I should. Shall we go to the police?'

'What, about losing a little bit of money? If money's all I'm going to lose, the thief who's got it is welcome to it. He perhaps needs it more than I do.' She paused, her face working. 'Rosy – if I tell you something, will you keep my secret? Robert's got leukaemia, and there's no hope for him. We may keep him a year or so, but no longer, unless there's a miracle. The consultant told me on our second visit, while Robert was getting dressed.

'I daren't tell Tom. If I do he won't be able to hide it from Robert. I've got to let him go on acting to Robert like he's done all along, calling him a lazy young sod and going on at him. For Robert's sake I've got to pretend that everything's all right.

'That bloody thief who stole my wallet has done me a good turn. I don't know how much longer I could have gone on keeping it all to myself. I had to tell somebody. But you can see why I don't care about losing a few pound notes!'

Rosemary stretched her hand across the table to hold Cynthia's. Her throat was too full of tears to let her speak but the clasped hand was more eloquent than words could have been in a crowded restaurant.

'Promise me that you won't tell a soul, not even Brian,' Cynthia said. 'And especially not Charles. I want Robert and Tom to be as happy as they can while they can. What will happen to Tom – afterwards – I daren't think. I won't think. I won't think beyond this Christmas.'

'I promise,' said Rosemary.

Cynthia got up to go. 'It'll be hard on you,' she said. 'You don't know how hard. I do.'

28

Fran and William were going to be alone at Benedict's this Christmas. They had tried it once before, three years ago, and it had been awful. They recalled the experience in bed, where most of their more serious conversations took place.

'Three days on the rack,' William said. 'You wouldn't have put anything else alive through such torture.'

'It wasn't much fun for me either,' Fran said. 'I stood outside the torture chamber knowing I only had to slide a bolt back to put us both out of our misery.'

'But this Christmas I shall have you all to myself,' he said.

'Unless Roland comes,' she replied, a little anxiously.

'M'm. I liked what I saw of Roland, but I don't want him at Christmas. I don't want to share you. I love you too much.'

'That isn't possible,' she said. 'Love's about the only thing you can't have too much of.'

'Perhaps you're right.' He kissed her hair. Then he kissed her cheek, and having got so far his lips sought hers, and the sweet-scented nearness of her made him forget that Roland existed.

She recalled their conversation, though, at breakfast-time next morning. 'I wish Roland would let us know something,' she said. 'I'm not so sanguine as you are about this relationship with Monica. I think he is just being selfish – wanting to have his cake and eat it. And it will involve us, whether we like it or not. We've won our fight – even against that interfering Marriner – but when Beryl Bean gets a sniff of anything between Roland and Monica, we shall get all the backwash. Can't you hear her saying, "Like mother, like son"? And then what will Sophie do? Do you think she'll stand up to another bout of scandal about us? Why couldn't he have found a girl somewhere else, and not on our doorstep? I feel threatened by it – as if it's roused Nemesis to get on our trail for our hubris in being so happy this last year.

'And don't laugh – but I feel unhappy about Sue. She is his wife, and he actually says he still loves her. So what's he playing at? Just using Monica to get what Sue won't give him? It isn't fair on her.'

'No, I won't laugh, but I will say that I think it's just your old puritan scruples raising their heads again. You wouldn't be you without them! But be sensible, my darling. I look at it from Roland's point of view – naturally. You're taking the line of "Don't do as I do, do what I tell you".'

'I did bring him up,' she interrupted.

'You heard what he said – that it was Monica he wanted all the time. If he loves Sue, it's a different sort of love. He cares about her welfare – like I care about Jess's welfare. And just to find another woman for some sex would only complicate matters for all three of them. It would be hell for Roland – married to one woman, sleeping around with others, and knowing that the one you really want is available all the time. You seem to suggest that as long as he gets both constituents of marriage separately he ought to be satisfied. You know you don't believe that. At least I wasn't put through the torture of doing without you once I had broken down your hedge of thorns. I should have gone mad. He's been to bed with Monica. The one thing that he has in his favour that I didn't have is that times have changed. He and Monica belong to the permissive society. We didn't. But the eternal triangle is the same as ever – I expect that started with the serpent in the Garden of Eden. I wish you wouldn't worry – and for heaven's sake don't offer any motherly advice. You're not in any position to do so, honestly, my sweetheart. Concentrate on keeping your son, and let him look after his own morals.'

'I think it's worse because Sue and Monica used to be such close friends.'

'You can't do anything about it. Leave it to the gods – or what Hardy called "the Doomsters", Time and Circumstance. No two cases are ever alike. It always depends on the characters involved. They'll sort it out – and if they can't we shall have to try to pick up the broken pieces. That's all we can do. We have our own lives to sort out. I want to talk about us, not them.'

She knew he was right, and told him so; he knew she wouldn't stop worrying, whatever he said, so he did his best to distract her.

'About the possibility of me retiring. I'm beginning to waver – mostly because nobody takes me seriously. After making me feel an unwanted anachronism for a long time, they now discover that the college needs me. So they're trying to bribe me with the prospect of a year's sabbatical – and heaven knows it's overdue. A rest and a change might work wonders. What do you think? The final decision shall be yours – but you know that. Will you give it some thought during this Christmas vacation?'

She had been half-expecting his change of mind, and smiled.

'If I have a minute to spare,' she said. 'I'm all behind with my deadline, and working for TV isn't like working for a publisher: they'll usually wait, TV won't. I must work solidly right through this weekend, so that I can enjoy Christmas. It's such a pity, because the weather's so good, and I'd hoped we might walk up to Castle Hill. I'm afraid Bob may have heard

218

some of those silly rumours, and be hurt. Besides, I haven't yet thanked him for the picture. If I wrote him a note, would you walk up by yourself and deliver it? You'd be much more likely to get the truth from him than I should.'

'That's a good idea. I'll go this afternoon.'

'Go now,' she said. 'Make use of the light to get a good look at the church. We'll eat tonight, or whenever you get back.'

He set off almost at once, and went straight to the church; he could take as long as he liked, and call on Bellamy afterwards.

To his surprise he found the church door ajar, and pushed it open. The man kneeling at the altar-rail leapt to his feet at the creak of the old hinge. In such a short nave, the two men could not ignore each other's presence. William apologized for his intrusion, and the Rector came forward to meet him.

He was genuinely pleased by William's scholarly interest in the church and told him, rather unnecessarily, about its architecture. William quite understood that the topic was being used as an ice-breaker. They had not seen each other since they had parted after Marriner's visit to Benedict's. The Rector sat down in one of the front pews, and by gesture invited William to join him.

'I come up here whenever I feel depressed,' he said. 'There's a solace in isolation. It puts trouble into perspective to be the only living person among so many dead. Who, no doubt, all had their own problems once. The church needs airing more. It smells terribly damp.'

William wasn't listening very attentively. His eye had been caught by a large stone slab set into the floor. It wasn't a grave stone – but could it possibly be an altar stone? They were very rare, and he'd never heard of this one. Besides, it wasn't where you would expect it to be. He turned rather guiltily back to his companion, registering unconsciously a difference in the tone of the Rector's voice.

'Dr Burbage, I think I have an apology to make. I do not apologize for what I did, but how I did it. I had no intention of insulting your wi— of insulting Mrs Catherwood. And you were so kind to me.'

William's back stiffened itself against the wood of the pew. 'You were about to say "your wife" I think. Which is exactly what she is – in every way.

'The invitation was sent in a spirit of friendship and neighbourliness. It could have been declined a little less bluntly, and we should have understood. As it was, your visit smacked of the nineteenth century and Mr Brocklehurst. We rather expected to be sent to the House of Correction. As it happens, Fran and I both had to overcome nineteenth-century scruples – but we believe that under the circumstances, which only the two of us know, we eventually made the right decision. We make no pretence.

'I'm an historian – but I'm a man first. If I hadn't been, you would have had no reason to make your protest. You are a clergyman – but were you not also a man first? We should still like the man for a friend and neighbout, though the clergyman disapprove of us. Isn't that possible?'

Marriner shifted uncomfortably. 'As a clergyman, I cannot be seen to condone the breaking of the seventh commandment. But in any case I doubt if Mrs Catherwood would receive me now.'

'My wife,' said William, enunciating clearly and firmly, 'is an intelligent woman. She has far too much sense – and charity – to make volcanoes out of molehills.' His proud face broke into its most charming smile as he added, all 'correctness' gone, 'And my name is William.'

'My parents lumbered me with Archibald. I have heard a great deal of you since your party, from my daughter. You hit hard, William – and then salve the bruise. I think I had forgotten what it was to be a man before anything else, since my wife died. But in all honesty, in return for your own, I must confess that I envy you your Frances. While she was tearing me to shreds in your sitting-room, I thought I had never before seen so stunning a woman. I was half-waiting for her to hit me with her riding crop. I was utterly abashed. I'm sorry.'

Into the rather uncomfortable silence came a man's voice, obviously calling a cat.

'Puss! Puss! Where have you got to? It's only me – with

some grub for you and some straw for you to sleep in, 'cos it's going to freeze tonight. Come out, you silly old cat! What's the matter? Oh, I see – there's somebody else about.'

The door was pushed open by a big boot, and Bellamy stood in the porch, a stout ash-plant at the ready in his fist.

'Bob!' said William, jumping up with outstretched hand. 'I was coming to see you in a minute or two. Do you know the Rector?'

'Ah, Mr Bellamy. A great man with a fiddle or a concertina, I understand. Have you lost your cat? I sometimes see a stray one about here. I'm always afraid of locking it in.'

Bellamy pulled off his old pork-pie hat and advanced into the church.

'I reckon that's the same one,' he said. 'She ain't mine, but I feed her. She's half wild. I tried to take her home, but she fought me like a bulldog. That's why I call her Winnie – after Churchill. I bring her food when I come up here in the afternoons. I'll put it in the porch. She'll find it. If you're coming up to the house, William, we ought to go, or it'll be dark before you get home.'

'Wait a minute, Bob. I wanted to ask Mr Marriner if he knows anything about that stone slab on the floor there.' Bob went further in and stood close to them. The Rector was about to speak when William put his finger to his lips; he could see that Bob was not only looking, but listening as well, every sense alert. Then he said, 'This is the first time I've ever been inside here. It's always been locked before. But I shall come again. They like me.'

Marriner raised inquiring eyebrows at William, who shook his head.

'They?' asked the Rector. 'Who are "they"?'

Bellamy came to himself with a start, and, as William told Fran later, seemed to shrink into his huge boots. But he answered. 'The ghosts,' he said. 'What's this about some stone slab?'

William led him to it, explaining that during the Puritan times stone altars had been regarded as symbols of Popish idolatry and most of them had been smashed; but in a few cases they had been left whole and placed on the floor where the people could literally wipe their boots on them if they felt like it. 'I know of one that has been cut down to make a gravestone, and no doubt others came in handy for hearthstones and such. There are tales that some of them were put out in the churchyard to act as altars for black masses. It was, after all, a great time for witchcraft as well as for Puritanism. An age of extremes. One can't wonder, in view of the plague.'

William pointed out some marks on the slab, but it was getting too dark in the church to see well. 'The keys are always here if you want to get in,' the Rector told Bob. 'I come up for quiet and solace, but I don't think I believe in your ghosts.'

They hung the key on a nail hidden among the ivy on the church wall, and said goodbye to the Rector, who had declined Bob's bashful offer of tea.

William and Bob walked side by side, as comfortable as old friends.

'Tell me more about that slab,' Bob said.

'I don't know that I can. What puzzles me is why it was put down where it is, all squashed into a corner. If they'd wanted people to walk on it, they'd have put it down the centre aisle.'

'I reckon them marks on it are where there's been a fire made on it,' Bob said.

'Good heavens! That does sound like witchcraft!'

Bob shook his head. 'No, there's nothing bad about it,' he said. 'I should have felt it if there was. I wouldn't tell anybody else, but I swear I could smell cooking.'

In spite of himself, William laughed. 'So much for my theory,' he said. 'It was probably some old hearthstone put down to cover a hole in the floor, just the opposite to my conjecture.'

'I don't feel so good about the graveyard,' Bob said unexpectedly. 'I've had that queer feeling about it before, just leaning over the wall. You can see that people went on being buried there till about fifty year ago, but there's a patch in the north-east corner without a single grave in it. I get the worst feelings there. Do you know anything to account for that?'

'No – but I'll have a look and start some enquiries. I'll be up again soon. Fran's very hard at work.'

He gave Bob Fran's note, and told him what pleasure they had had in finding the right place to hang the picture.

'Come up soon and see it in place,' he invited. 'I'll get Fran to give you a call. I expect you'll have to be around at Christmas because of all your animals,' he said.

The cloud that passed over Bob's face reminded William of what Fran had said about him being like an ingenous child. 'Charlie'll be here,' he said, 'but nobody else. Iris is petitioning for divorce. I shan't try to stop her. John's wife won't let him come up and she won't come near the place. I still don't know how much Charlie knows about her mother. It's her I worry about. This is a lonely old place when there's only ghosts to keep you company.'

William walked home pondering all sorts of things other than his own future. He was fascinated by the bit of lost history the church represented and turned his trained mind to avenues for doing some research about it. He thought perhaps that in this case research, like charity, might begin at home. He could reason as well as any other historian for documentary proof, but he could not shake off his belief in Bob's sixth sense. It probably grew keener with the sorrow Bob was enduring.

When he saw the lights of Benedict's come into view, his thoughts followed a different tack. There was no wife waiting for Bob, nor indeed for Archie Marriner. One a helpless, hurt, deserted husband, the other a cold, too self-disciplined widower. Eric Choppen was a widower, too, but he coped with loneliness by working too hard. Then there was Elyot Franks, a sort of professional bachelor, whose ships had been his wives. William reflected that he might be the one suffering loneliness worst of all.

Four of them in the same plight, all in one small village. Another sign of the times. You associated villages with old maids, as in *Cranford*; not with unmarried men.

He wanted to shout praise to the gods that he didn't make the number up to five. The thought of Fran waiting for him made him hurry home.

29

There were ten days to go before Christmas. The weather was still mild, even warm.

'I don't care for it, meself,' said Sophie. '"A green Christmas makes a fat churchyard." Everybody knows that. It ain't 'ealthy.'

The word 'churchyard' reminded William that he had questions to ask. Sophie's and Ned's families had been in Swithinford as long as Fran's, and in their cases there had been no break in continuity. Wainwrights, Wagstaffes and Merrimans were all there in the church registers along with Thackerays and Bridgefoots, back at least to the fifteenth century. He could start his research at home, and at once.

'I went up to the little church on the hill, yesterday – St Saviour's, is it?' he said to Sophie. 'Do you know anything about it?'

'Well, no. Nothing you'd be likely to want to know about, I shouldn't think. When we was children, there used to be oxlips in that wood up there and nobody stopped us going to pick 'em by the armful. But Mam never liked us going. She all'us made us promise never to go inside the churchyard, 'cos it wasn't 'ealthy, she said. I don't know why. Only – come to think of it – there is another tale. The de ffranksbridge fam'ly had their own vault up there till it got full. Hugh de ffranksbridge 'ad a young brother as got wounded in the First War, and come 'ome and died. And there wasn't room for 'im in the family vault up there, so his brother said he had to be buried in the churchyard as cluss to it as they could get 'im to the rest of 'is family. And he went and choosed the place. But when he told old Levi Potter, as were the sexton and gravedigger then, he said straight out that he wasn't going to do it. Told 'im if he wanted a grave just there he could dig it hisself. Mind you, all them ffranksbridges thought they only 'ad to order anybody to do anything and it would just be done, but they found out as they were wrong about that. They offered other men twice

224

and three times the money to dig the grave, but none of 'em would. So then they told the hundertaker to get it done, but even 'e couldn't find nobody, not even a stranger, who'd do it. And Mam said as it were on account of a old tale that whoever disturbed that bit o' ground would be dead 'isself within the week. Like digging parsley roots up. You don't never 'ave to try to set a root o' parsley once it's been dug up, 'cos anybody who does is buried theirself within three weeks. I don't know if there's any truth in that, 'cos I'm never yet knowed nobody fool enough to try it. But Mam said a lot o' folks was upset at 'im wanting to bury 'is brother just there, and some went and complained to Parson Howard about it. And 'e took their part, telling Hugh de ffranksbridge as 'ow there must be some reason for it never being used, like, and per'aps there was something in the s'ile. He advised the fam'ly to respect folks's wishes, and leave it alone. So by that, the soldier were buried in our churchyard. You can't find 'is grave now, though. That old woman as were burnt to death were too mean to have a 'eadstone put up to 'im. But nobody cares now, anyway. The fam'ly's died out.'

William was intrigued; it already appeared to bear out a theory he was forming. He sought out Ned, whose version was slightly different.

'There's some sort o' mystery about it,' he said, 'as I heard from my Grandad when I were an old boy. They told us never to go into the churchyard, but o' course we did. We all believed a tale as had got about that the de ffranksbridges had buried their money and jewels and stuff there in their vault while Cromwell's war was on, and laid a curse on anybody who tried to dig it up. Us old boys were all'us a-making plans to go and try to get it, but when it come to it, we daresn't 'cos o' the curse. None of us would be the one to dig the first spadeful out . . .

'And there were another thing. When I were learning the bellringing, and got interested in it, like, I asked if there was any bells up there. 'Cos to stop us going there as children they used to tell us a ghost story about bells ringing o' their own accord with nobody to pull 'em, though the sallies would still be swinging. Nobody I knowed had ever heard 'em, so I thought I'd settle it. If there wasn't no bells there, it could only be a made-up tale or one has had got moved from another place. So I asked the old Rector and he said yes, there were six beautiful old bells there, but they daresn't ring 'em, and hadn't done for as long as anybody could remember, in case the vibration brought the tower down, like.

'But I all'us wondered why the church were there at all. 'Cos apart from the Castle Hill farm and two or three little cottages on it, there ain't no more houses. Who used to go to church there, do you reckon, when it is so far away from everywhere, like?'

'I don't know,' said William; 'that's why I'm asking you. I just happen to like historical puzzles. If you think of anything else, you will tell me, won't you?'

They had given him a good start; the next thing was to have a good look at a six-inch Ordnance Survey map. He went inside to ask Fran if they had one, and found her just putting the telephone down.

'Jess,' she said. 'Asking what we are doing for Christmas. I suppose that means they hope they will be invited to lunch up here on Christmas Day. Not that I mind. I love it when there are just the four of us, especially when they're on good terms with each other. I hate it when Jess flies off the handle and gets at Greg. I just don't know why she does it. Perhaps that's why they would rather not be left *à deux* all over the holiday.'

Fran's premise was wrong. By post the next morning came an invitation to them to spend Christmas Day as Eric Choppen's guests, along with Monica, Jess and Greg, and Elyot Franks, in his private suite at the hotel.

'We can't refuse,' Fran said, rather dismally. 'I'd rather be at home.'

'So would I – but I like all the others who'll be there, now that we know them. We can always eat our own Christmas dinner the next day, and call Sunday Boxing Day.'

'Other way round,' she said. 'Then we can have Jess and Greg up here to help us eat it.'

That fixed, William found his map, and had a pleasant half-hour with it. Then he told Fran that he was off up to the church again, if she didn't mind.

'Get Sophie to pack you a sandwich,' she said, barely lifting her fingers from the typewriter keys. 'If Bob's at home, he'll give you a cup of tea.'

As he strode by the Old Rectory he had a glimpse of Beth Marriner, peeping through the letter-box – or at least, that's what it looked like until he saw the pile of parish magazines under her arm. The sight of it jolted him into thinking about her – that fascinating, lively woman who had matched Greg's musical skill with her own had been the perfect guest for a party and had even enticed the rather stiff Commander on to the dancing-floor with her. What on earth was a woman of such accomplishment and fire doing wasting her life pushing little homilies meant for the Thirzahs of this world through letter-boxes? He guessed she was about thirty. Did she already think of herself as 'an old maid' – and being her father's daughter, quite literally so, like Sophie? If so, was it by chance, or because of some tragedy in the past that had robbed her of her mate? He couldn't make himself believe that it was by choice. She was too full of latent vitality. It might be a misplaced sense of duty to her father's calling, of course, or by his wish or decree. He wouldn't have expected the girl who came to their party to have submitted to that without a fight.

He found himself wondering what sort of a father he would have made himself, if he and Fran had married each other when they ought to have done. Parent–child relationships were no easier to cope with than any other sort, as far as he could see. Fran was still worried about Roland, and no doubt if Eric Choppen knew the truth, he would be just as uneasy about Monica.

The little church was now in sight, and he paused to enjoy the view.

He reflected wistfully that he would have risked the pain of dealing with their grown-up troubles if only fate had been kind enough to let Fran's children be his children too. He tried not to let Fran guess the ache in his heart it caused him that they were not. Jess and Greg. They had been married young enough – why hadn't they had any? There couldn't have been a more virile man than Greg! And Jess—?

At least Fran had got children, even if they were not his.

He was glad that Janice hadn't wanted her fun stopped by any such encumbrances. They would have complicated his life.

As it was, he did have a vicarious half-share in Fran's children, and grandchildren. If you never had children, you missed out on grandchildren too. So he was better off in that respect than Greg, or Elyot; maybe than Eric, because Monica wasn't very likely to produce any, under the circumstances. Nor was Beth Marriner, so he had to include her father, too. His thoughts had gone full circle.

What was it Sophie had said? 'The family's died out.' He was the last Burbage of his line. Ned's line had ceased when his only son had been drowned. The Wainwrights' relied solely on Wendy's illegitimate son and the Taliaferro and Catherwood names looked like coming to an end as well as 'the family' that Sophie had meant, the de ffranksbridges, whose only representative now was a middle-aged bachelor. It was the historian in him, rather than the man, that felt the sadness about all that. History relies a lot on continuity. Well, the Bridgefoots and the Faireys and one or two other families still had sons. So had Bob Bellamy.

He decided to go up to the farm before going on to the church, in the hope that he might find Bellamy free enough to go with him. With his knowledge of history allied to Bob's intuition, they might get a good start.

Bob had just finished his midday meal, and welcomed him sincerely. William produced his packet of sandwiches and asked Bob for a cup of coffee.

In wonderfully easy companionship, they finished their meal, with Bonzo lying between them and cats everywhere: sleek, beautiful, fine-whiskered cats that looked human beings in the eye and trusted them. Well, any animal could trust Bob Bellamy, William thought. He's at one with them. As much part of nature as they are. They know it. He's a real pagan, literally. That's what Fran meant, a child of nature – that's why he's open to messages from sources inaccessible to most of us.

They set out together, and on the way William told him his theory about the patch of 'cursed' ground. 'There's usually a tiny scrap of truth behind most folk-tales,' William said. 'In this case, I expect the curse covers some other valid cause. My guess is that it was a communal grave-pit for victims of the plague. Approximately three hundred years ago – thirty years to a generation – only ten generations. Ned remembers his grandfather, who would in turn remember his. That's five generations out of the ten. Sophie said her mother had thought it was "something in the soil". My guess is that she was right. Rotting corpses in the soil, barely covered because there were so many of them, and too few left to bury them. Bodies still contagious. It was only common sense to get them up here and as far away from the village as they could. I can't say I blame the sexton who wouldn't dig new graves there.'

Bob was standing still, listening but pursuing his own line of thought.

'Except I don't think they were brought up from as far away as that,' he said. 'They must have had a grave pit of their own down there, surely? And how did it happen that this church was so conveniently out o' the way for 'em? Churches mean people. I reckon that where there's a church there must have been people as well. Besides, I know there's been houses round here, 'cos I keep on ploughing bits of stone up as you can see have been shaped for building. I daresay if you could get one of them photos took from an aeroplane, you'd be able to see the foundations of a lot of little houses between my farm and the church. It ain't the church that's been built away from the people – it's the people as have gone away from the church. I reckon they all died.'

'Well, *of course!*' William said. 'There are records of whole villages being wiped out in the Black Death. Why not in the Plague? Probably nobody's ever done a thorough investigation here. Where a record was kept in the church registers, it is easy enough to trace – like at Eyam in Derbyshire. I wonder if anybody has ever looked at this church's registers? Let's get the key and go inside. I'll ask the Rector about the registers, though they may be in the archives somewhere by now.'

'Let me give Winnie her grub first,' said Bellamy. 'If you go inside, she'll come out and show me she's all right.'

William began to poke about. It was only a matter of minutes before Bob sat silently down by his side.

'Ned says there is a ring of six bells in the tower that are never used now – though apparently they ring themselves faintly now and then. Have you ever heard them?'

Bellamy shook his head. 'I've heard such tales before – that's an old one. And the bell-ropes are always swinging.'

William laughed. There was something extraordinarily refreshing about Bellamy. He reflected that if Bob had not been entirely genuine, he would have fallen for that opening.

They went to the slab. William was pretty sure that it was the top of an old altar. Bellamy was prepared to believe anything William the Historian told him.

'I don't get any bad feelings from it, though. And I swear those marks are the marks of burning. I can smell it.'

William looked up, doubting. 'After three hundred years?'

'I don't know about that. Somebody could have had a fire on it lately. Hippies, perhaps, who found the key when nobody was about here, before I took the farm. The marks may just as likely be three hundred years old, though. I just get the feeling of fire.'

William had the grace to be ashamed, and apologized.

'And about them bells,' Bob said. 'I don't doubt there's bells up there – look at the size of the tower. Plenty big enough for a bell chamber. But how did they get up into it?'

'Well, there must have been a series of ladders, or something. Besides, before the Puritans got to work, parsons often went up some steps and read bits of the service from over the top of the rood-screen. Sometimes the bellringers' way into the belfry was just a continuation of the steps. This tower's so big and the church so small, it can't have been designed like that in the first instance. It must have been rebuilt at some time. Maybe they had to improvise. Let's look for the steps.'

'They'd have to run up behind the pulpit,' Bellamy said. 'That's the only place there's room.'

Ten minutes later, they had found the tiny staircase.

'Too late to go up today,' William decreed conclusively. 'And not safe unless somebody else knows where we are. In any case, I wouldn't presume to trespass without the Rector's knowledge and permission. Let's call it a day now. I'll get in touch with the Rector, and ask him to come with us. But I'm still puzzled by that altar slab. I should like to know what's under it. Could you bring some crowbars with you next time, if we are allowed to investigate? Three of us ought to be able to prise it up, heavy as it is. I wonder why it was moved. I think it was in the aisle once, where that stone to Jethro Tomson is now. But why did they bother to put it down again, where it is? That's what puzzles me.'

They locked up, and hid the key. 'I don't know whenever I've enjoyed an afternoon so much,' Bob said. 'Come in for a cup of tea.'

William held out his hand. 'I'd love to,' he said, 'but . . .' He stopped, embarrassed.

'But you've got somebody waiting for you at home,' Bellamy said. 'If I stood in your shoes, the devil himself wouldn't stop me getting back to her.'

All William's social training had no rubric for dealing with a statement like that. He put out his hand again, and the other man took it. After a minute Bellamy said, 'Don't worry about me, William. Iris would never be satisfied with me, now, anyway. She wants a new man every week, I reckon – like the young'uns today do. Sex mad. It ain't got a lot to do with love, if you ask me. I shall get over it. I've still got my old dog and six cats. I don't reckon they'll desert me.'

He turned abruptly and went into the house. William decided he would not report that bit to Fran; she had too soft a heart, sometimes.

When he was nearly back to the village, he fell in with Elyot Franks, who had also been out walking. They continued together to the gate of the Old Rectory, where Franks said, 'Will you come in for a drink?'

William hesitated. He wanted to get home, but there was a sort of plea in the Commander's voice that made it difficult for him to refuse, apart from his desire to show neighbourly courtesy.

'Would you allow me to phone Fran?' he said. 'I've been away rather a long time.'

'Of course. I need advice. I would be grateful if you could spare me a few minutes.'

Stuck in the door was the parish magazine. 'Hello, what's this?' A frown crossed Elyot's face as he threw it aside. 'I've put my foot in it with the Rector,' he said. 'He's intent on saving my soul somehow. Even with the parish magazine.'

'I saw Beth putting it through the door as I went by this morning,' William answered. 'You must have taken a pretty long walk.' Franks didn't answer. William used the phone in the hall while Franks put on the lights and found drinks.

His sitting-room was a man's room, newly furnished, but with just enough old pieces to make it feel homely.

The fire soon burned brightly, and William sat down with his drink, not at all sure whether he was in Harrods furniture department or a naval captain's cabin. Franks read his expression correctly. 'I think it will settle down together before very long,' he said. 'Thirzah Bates is so finicky about the new stuff that I hardly dare use it; but I won't let her touch my old bits so they just get dirtier and shabbier. Of course, it may be a case of "never the twain shall meet".'

There was a boudoir grand piano in one corner of the vast room, polished till everything else was reflected in its glossy surface. 'Are you a musician?' William asked, surprised.

Elyot shook his head. 'Harrods,' he said. 'I just told them to furnish the house as they thought fit. They put the piano in to fill the corner up, I think. They instructed me never to polish it, but you might as well try to stop a battleship with a cobweb as Thirzah Bates with words. It doesn't really matter. Nobody ever touches the keys.' He took a sip of his whisky and went on hesitantly. 'I told you I needed advice. I'm out of my own element in a place like Old Swithinford. I don't know how to handle the people, or situations – such as this.'

He handed William his invitation to be Eric Choppen's guest on Christmas Day. 'I don't want to go, but how do I get out of it? I'm not really made for parties and merrymakings. But I don't want to be rude.'

'You came to us,' said William. 'Was that against your will? You pleased us by coming – and you seemed to be enjoying yourself.'

'To be honest, it was against my will. But the company changed my mood.'

'Then accept this, and join us again. Fran and I will be there, and Jess and Greg, and Monica.'

'I suppose I must make the effort.' Franks stood up. 'What worries me is that I may say I'll go, and then be incapable of facing it when the time comes. If I am in one of my "black dog" moods, as Churchill used to say, I simply couldn't face anybody, let alone a Christmas party. I thought maybe getting right away inland might help. It hasn't done. The moods are worse than ever.'

'The war?' suggested William.

Elyot looked up sharply. 'Yes,' he said. 'The naval equivalent to shellshock, I imagine.'

'What happened?'

Franks took his time, filling his pipe and lighting it, though William thought he was only making up his mind whether to answer or not.

'We were sunk. Torpedoed and on fire. When everybody who could had taken to the boats, I went the rounds to make sure there was nobody left who could possibly make it.

'I found a youngster, an ordinary matelot who had been asleep when the torpedo struck. He'd come up through the fire in his underpants, across burning decks in his bare feet. I shoved him into the boat that was waiting for me, and we got away. Just in time. His burns were awful – far worse than anybody else's, though most of them were beyond help.

'There was only one young sub-lieutenant and me still more or less whole. We were adrift for days – water running low, sun like hell by day and freezing by night. One by one the others died and we put them over the side – with me reading the burial service. Such bloody awful twaddle in that sort of circumstance! All the others listening and praying they'd be the next . . . The only one who wouldn't die was the kid I'd rescued. He never complained, though he must have been in worse pain than anything hell could offer. He just followed me about with his eyes, till I couldn't stand it. I nearly went mad. You see, if I hadn't saved him, he would have gone down with the ship and been dead in three minutes. I wanted to strangle him, just to put him out of his misery. I kept saying to myself, every time I looked at him, "Die, damn you! Die!"

'The young sub was marvellous – until he went berserk

and threw himself over the side. Then there was just me and that boy. Somebody's son. Might have been mine, for all I knew – you know what sailors are. I went into the navy straight from school, and had spent all my life learning how to do *that* – to other people's sons. I had my revolver for myself, but with those eyes following me, I couldn't use it on him.

'I had hoarded our medical supplies at first, hoping we'd be picked up quickly. The longer it went on, the more we should need them. There was some morphia still left, when all the rest were dead. I gave him the lot, and then held his hand till he died. I pushed him over the side all by myself, and read that fu— that damned burial service over him, and watched him sink.

'Then I got my revolver out – and a plane from a small carrier appeared that very minute out of a cloud, came down and wiggled its wings at me, and flew off. Just too late to save that beautiful boy. I felt by that time that he was my son, whatever bastard had fathered him or whatever sort of a tramp his mother had been. But they couldn't have been that sort. He had the public-school label on him. I loved him. But if that is what fathers do to their sons, I'm glad I never married. He haunts me. I just can't forget . . . *Damn and blast you!* Why am I telling you all this?'

William's face was pale and tense, and his fingers round his glass showed white at the knuckles; but his voice was calm, and low, and matter-of-fact.

'Probably because you had to tell somebody, if you've been brooding on it all day,' he said. 'And possibly because you thought I might understand. I do. I have my nightmares, too.'

Franks sat down abruptly. 'Tell me!' he ordered.

William did not resent the command. He had to prove that he hadn't been offering facile sympathy.

'I was a Spitfire pilot. We were used to scrambling six planes and only landing four. But in wartime friendships made overnight could be more than ordinary – they went deeper and deeper the longer both parties survived. There were two of us who seemed to have as many lives as a cat. A chap who had been a classics man used to call us Castor and Pollux – the heavenly twins. We began to feel like twins. We almost lived each other's lives, flew with each other inside each other's cockpits, fought each other's dogfights – as I say, nearly became each other. We knew the luck couldn't last for ever, but we were – I think – both quite convinced that the day a Messerschmitt got one of us, he'd get the other as well.

'We'd been out just over the Channel, and were making for home again, flying high for obvious reasons and keeping each other in sight . . . till I saw black smoke trailing from Mac's kite. I kept close – just willing him to be able to control it till we got close to land and he could jump. We made it – I'd never been so glad to see that sandy coastline beneath me before. I flew close and he gave me the thumbs-up sign, so I got out of the way to give him room, and I watched him bail out.

'Roman candle. His parachute didn't open. I saw him fall. Castor was dead; and like in the old story, Pollux was left.

'Until about three years ago, I used to go outside every clear night and look up at Gemini – and pray to the gods to let me join Mac. Nightmares always – of that eternity it took him to hit the ground.'

A long silence reigned, unbroken but for the puffing of Elyot's pipe, and the occasional sound of a glass being put down on a hard surface.

Elyot's voice seemed dragged out of him. 'Do you still have them? The nightmares?'

William didn't shirk the truthful answer. 'No – not in this last year. Not since I could put out my hand and feel Fran there beside me. I can rouse and bring myself out of it before he jumps. Fran doesn't know. I've never told her about it.'

'That remedy's denied me. You don't know how lucky you are. I'm too old – and a murderer.'

'Good God, man! Aren't we all? All of us who fought "upon St. Crispin's Day"?'

Franks shook his head. 'Not in the same way. I wanted my boy to die. I planned his murder, and I carried it out. There'll never be anybody beside me but his ghost.'

William got up, and left without speaking again. Elyot had turned his back, and William did not want to see his face.

He had told Franks the exact truth: he did still often start to dream, but before it became a nightmare, he could pull out of it and wake just by making sure Fran was within reach. But telling Franks had brought it all too close again, and that night his remedy didn't work. He was sweating, shaking, shouting 'Bloody Roman candle! Oh Christ! Mac! Mac!' when Fran woke him up. She had never heard the story, but she knew quite well what 'Roman candle' meant.

She sat up on her pillow, and pulled his head towards her, wiping off the sweat and holding him till, wide awake but still trembling, he cried the whole story out into her breast. She rocked him and soothed him until the horror left him, and he began to drowse again, exhausted, into sleep. His last waking thought was for Elyot Franks, a man beyond hope, who had tried himself at the bar of justice and had condemned himself. Against such judgement there is no appeal.

Fran lay awake and held William till her arms went numb and she thought her back would break. She couldn't reach her handkerchief and feared that her tears falling on him might rouse her sleeping child. When that unimaginable nightmare had been actuality, he hadn't been much more than a boy. Younger than Roland was now.

30

Nobody loved Christmas more than George Bridgefoot, and this year it promised to be extra-special. He loved all aspects of it, as a committed Christian, as a family man, and as a good neighbour who truly did wish peace and goodwill to all men. At Christmas dinner this year his whole family would be together again: Brian and Rosemary, with Charles; Marjorie and Vic, and their seventeen-year-old twins, Poppy and Pansy; and Lucy, three months gone with his fourth grandchild, and Alex.

'Eleven of us,' George said to Molly. 'We can't count the baby, yet.'

'Twelve,' said Molly. 'You've forgotten Aunt Esther.'

It was true. He had. Some of the brightness went out of his Christmas dream, and he sat down heavily, at war with himself. Christian charity bade him make her welcome, and it was certain that she could not be left up at Temperance alone. But every thread of instinct and common sense in him was against including her.

She would be the wicked fairy at any feast; intuition told him that the presence of Alex would be enough to make her raise her scorpion's tail. Molly decreed that they must make the best of a bad job, because there was no solution.

He went to visit Rosemary. She started to cry the moment she saw him, guessing why he had come. Esther was her relation, not his. When the subject of Christmas had been broached Esther had declared flatly that she would not eat at the table of the ungodly. Rosemary and Brian could leave her, like they had done once before, to go and feast with republicans and sinners. She would cry shame on them, and curse the lot of them, down to the third and fourth generation.

George was fond of his daughter-in-law, and worried to see her looking so unhappy, subdued and wan. He wondered if Brian and Charles had been 'getting at her' because of the presence of her aunt always in their house. He told himself that it was his fault; he should never have been coerced into agreeing to the sale of the Pightle. He told Rosemary so, too.

'Aunt couldn't have stopped there by herself. But she won't come up to Glebe at Christmas, and I can't leave her. So please – *please* – will you help me to persuade Brian and Charles to let me stop here while they come up to you? I shan't enjoy this Christmas, anyway.'

He didn't understand, and asked her to explain, but all his questioning gave him no clue to her uncharacteristic depression.

She could not and would not betray Cynthia Fairey's secret, but the inevitable event at Lane End was casting dark and frightening shadows around her, too. Her son was as vulnerable to the random shafts of fate as Cynthia's. Brian had planned to have a brand new car delivered to their door on Christmas morning, though a pretence had been kept up that

Charles's Christmas present was to be money from everybody to buy himself as good 'an old banger' as he could get with it. She was living in dread, and would have held Christmas Day off for ever if she could have done. She almost hated Brian for insisting that he wanted to spend some of his extra windfall on giving Charles the best. She could see the new car only as a terrible threat to them all. Brian pooh-poohed her fears. 'He's been driving on the farm since he was ten,' he said. 'You've never minded him driving our car since the day he had his first licence. A new car is safer than an old one, and it isn't a sports car. I had more sense than to buy him a hot-rod, however much he would have liked it. Don't be silly.'

George knew nothing of her fears, and put Rosemary's tears down to her disappointment about Christmas Day. 'I don't suppose Jane Hadley would come again, would she?' he said.

'What, and give young Nick the alternative of spending his Christmas Day alone, or here with Aunt Esther?' said Rosemary, witheringly.

'Let Nick come up to us with Charles,' he said. 'With Pansy and Poppy there'd be four youngsters to amuse each other. I'll go and ask her.'

He didn't add that he had already thought about Nick, who had neither father nor grandfather to indulge him, and had included him when he put new £50 notes into envelopes for his grandchildren. It was always at such times as this that George felt guilty about his own good fortune. He was very fond of Nick, anyway.

He went straight to the point with Jane, offering her enough money to make it possible for her to give Nick something worth having. He appealed to her common sense, too, saying that she knew Aunt Esther well enough by now to understand their dilemma. Jane's unbending reserve and her unnatural calm were beyond his understanding, but there was something about her that earned his respect. She would not refuse to do a kindness where she could. George appreciated that.

He told her she was the only woman he had ever known to earn praise from Miss Palmer, and that only she could save his family's Christmas from ruin. Nick protested, but George got his way.

He was very pleased with himself when he told Molly, and a bit disappointed at her none-too-pleased reaction. 'That'll make twelve, with Nick,' she said. 'Are you sure we can't count Lucy's baby? 'Cos if we do, that'll make thirteen sitting down together, and I won't have that. You know what that would mean. One of the thirteen wouldn't be alive next Christmas. Suppose it should be the baby! I should never forgive myself if Lucy lost it.'

'Now look here, Mother,' he said. 'Don't go looking for trouble. What with Rosemary looking as if she's been ate and spewed up again, and you worrying yourself to death because there's twelve and a bit sitting down to Christmas dinner, anybody'd think it was a funeral instead of Christmas. If ever a family had reason to be glad and thankful, it's us.'

Molly said no more, and George went off singing to himself. 'Gl-ad ti-i-dings of co-om-fort and joy, comfortandjoy, Gla-ad ti-i-dings of co-om-fort and joy.' Molly contented herself by making quite sure that she knew exactly where the little silver cradle had been inserted into the Christmas pudding, so that Lucy would be sure to get it.

'I don't envy you your day,' Nick told his mother, as they set out.

'Nor I you yours,' said Jane. 'You go and have a lovely day. Think how much better it is than last year. Make the most of it.'

Charles's car had been delivered, drooled over and then garaged at Charles's own suggestion, so as not to invite comparison. There would be plenty of time to share it with Nick and Robert later.

Not even George could have wished for a happier Christmas Day than his turned out to be. After lunch, the two boys and the twins set off to visit Robert Fairey, whom they found feeling better. By the time they got back to Glebe, Nick had fallen for Poppy and Robert had had more than his fair share of attention from Pansy.

Charles was horrified. 'They're not girls,' he said. 'They're my cousins.'

Nick was not to be put off. 'The twins have changed since the wedding,' he said. 'I hardly noticed Poppy that day.'

By the time he was at home and in bed, it had occurred to Nick that it might be himself who had done the growing up. His mother was right: everything had altered. Last year there had been so little hope. Now every avenue seemed to him to be bursting into bloom for him.

William and Fran were a bit ambivalent in their attitude towards the invitation to join Eric Choppen's lunch party.

Though little had been said about it, the recurrence of William's nightmare had pushed their relationship up yet another notch. To be able at last to let the full horror of it break over him within the circle of her comforting arms had been absolutely cathartic; it had also relieved him of a feeling of guilt that by withholding from her his memories of the war years, he was somehow cheating on her. He could not have said why he had not shared them with her before, as he had shared everything else. On the morning after that nightmare, he had just let himself go and told her all sorts of things, including bits about Janice and his friendship with Mac.

The mention of Janice had caused no adverse reaction. That, he now understood, was what he had been shying away from. Afterwards he had felt washed and cleaned and warmed and wholly at peace with himself as well as with Fran.

Fran had lain awake most of the night, because once he had gone to sleep she would have suffered torture rather than that he should wake again. With 'dead' arms and a crick in her neck she felt would never again come out; sleep had been impossible. She had had to lie and think. So there were still things she did not know about him! She could hardly believe that he had been carrying such a load of pain and distress she had not even suspected. Why hadn't her instinct told her how much he was still hurting? She thought it must have been selfishness; her own happiness had dulled her sensitivity to him. But it would be all right now. It surprised her to think how they could have believed themselves so completely at one with each other before his nightmare had brought about their final surrender to Love. Fran, looking down at the face that had been so haggard in his dream now sleeping on her breast as relaxed as a baby's, felt fulfilment and content as never before, in spite of her physical discomfort.

Afterwards, they were both wholly satisfied in body, mind and spirit, almost languid with peace and content. Their own home was where they wanted to be.

Sophie voiced it for them. 'Folks should be at 'ome with their own, come Christmas,' she said.

'Jess and Greg are our own,' Fran replied. 'And what about loving thy neighbour? Ought we not to share a time like Christmas with friends?'

Sophie produced such a dramatic sniff that it had sent Fran scurrying to the shelter of her own study to laugh. To Sophie, the Choppens did not come in that category.

Fran wished she dared tell Sophie how much Monica was already in a sense 'their own', but that would be asking for trouble. She was still worried.

William, dressing on Christmas morning, also wished he could stay at home, yet for some reason he was looking forward to the gathering at the hotel. He stood brushing his hair before the mirror as the truth dawned on him. Talking of his days in the RAF had reminded him what camaraderie there could be among men. His student days and his academic life had been spent amongst colleagues mostly male; but colleagues are not necessarily friends. Friendships in wartime had cut across all boundaries — age, class, background, education, everything. In Old Swithinford, it was like wartime without the stress. He had made men friends again.

He wasn't quite sure yet whether they included Eric Choppen. Though they had all been in different branches of the armed services, with Greg and Elyot Franks he shared that wartime experience, and it was an invisible bond holding them together. Eric Choppen was the same age as they — so what had he been doing through the war years? Making money?

William was immediately ashamed of his snide thought. He didn't know Eric well enough to make any such judgement. Choppen was a very forceful man who at the same time was both retiring and timid — like a lost dog wanting to be admitted to somebody's warm hearth, but afraid of being kicked. That didn't necessarily point to shame or guilt. It was much more likely to indicate that he had been kicked badly in the past, and was still wary. One didn't get over wartime experiences without scars.

As he continued to think about it, William saw Eric in a different light, and with a flash of insight he felt sure was correct. There was an air of instantaneous decisiveness about Choppen and of expectation that his commands would be instantly obeyed. William had met exactly the same characteristics in Commandos. Commando training applied to business could have made Eric act as he had done, and do the things that had set people against him. He had had to learn to change his manner. William now felt quite certain that there would be four ex-service men together at lunchtime today. Four new friends wasn't a bad bonus for a Christmas morning. Plus, of course, Bob Bellamy.

Again, William caught himself up. In his own way, Bob had been through the war as well. It was all too easy to forget that the war had left very few untouched and unscarred. Fran had been a war widow: what had she had to face, left so young without a man to help her bring up two children?

It was more than twenty years since hostilities had ceased, but the war wasn't over yet for any of them who had lived through it. It was still there in their subconscious, still very near the surface of their thoughts. Whatever experiences had been piled on top since then, they could still feel its influence. It would be at least another generation before it could be called 'history' and tucked, dry as dust and reduced to fact and statistics, between the covers of a history book. It still affected them all in personal ways.

His thoughts returned to Eric. Was that lost look Eric sometimes wore the result of personal tragedy? Eric has lost his wife. William himself had been in danger of retreating into nothing more than a stuffy academic recluse when the war was over and Janice had left him. What would it have been to lose Fran? His diaphragm contracted with pain at the thought.

He owed everything, including his new friends, to Fran. He had an urge to rush out and buy her something special, like a flag to set on the peak of their Everest.

He grinned at his own reflection in the mirror, remembering that so far he had done everything in the wrong order. He had bought her a wedding ring when he had had nothing more than vague hope to go on; he had followed it with an eternity ring to mark their 'marriage'. She had never had an engagement ring. He made a resolution that one day, when occasion served, he would buy her one, a broad band of gold with the biggest ruby he could find set into it.

She opened the door and came in, dressed and ready to go. Too plump for modern fashion, too healthy to need make-up, too open-faced for female intrigue or artifice, too clear-eyed for seduction – yet wholly, enticingly feminine. And she was his. He put on his jacket resolutely, knowing that if once he touched her they would be very late for lunch. He wanted desperately to bury himself again in those comfortable curves, just to make sure she was still there, still his – even if it was only four hours since ... he wrenched his thoughts into another channel. How had he survived without her? How was Eric surviving? What about Elyot, and Bob? And even Greg – was he losing out, just lately?

He had not felt free to tell Fran Elyot's confidences, but he was a little apprehensive about Franks' admission that 'when the time came' for him to honour his acceptance of Choppen's invitation, he 'might not be able to face it'. William now felt a friend's obligation to make sure he did. He had a premonition that it was important for Franks to be there.

His faith in Fran's intuition allowed him to act on his own initiative. She made no demur when at the end of the drive he turned the car towards the village instead of towards the hotel, though she wondered why.

He pulled up the car outside the church gate, and got out, going round to open the door on Fran's side. 'I took the loop road to go and make sure Franks had transport,' he said.

She raised her eyebrows – was that the truth, a prepared white lie or the first thing that had come into his head? He obviously had some reason for it, and thought she wouldn't know he was being devious. When she turned her face towards him, she was laughing at him; the twinkle in her eye told him that as far as she was concerned his subterfuge was as transparent as a plate glass window, or as a child. He responded with a chuckle, and bending his tall back he leaned inside the car and slipped his arms round her. The lingering kiss he gave her was so unchildlike that when she looked up from it to see Beth Marriner standing at the gate, Fran felt the flood of colour rising to her cheeks. William had not noticed Beth, and was already on his way towards the Old Rectory.

Fran pushed the car door further open, leaned out and called 'Happy Christmas, Beth.'

For a moment, she thought Beth was not going to answer. She stood by the lychgate tall, erect, proud, aloof. Her face was so white and set that Fran was afraid she must be ill and about to faint. As Fran began to scramble out of the car, Beth's pale features broke into a wan smile.

'Are you OK?' Fran called.

'Just frozen with cold,' Beth said. 'You are looking splendid. Whither away, at this time on Christmas Day? I thought all women except me were basting turkeys and whipping up brandy butter.'

'I'm excused. We are being Eric Choppen's guests. William has just gone to see if Elyot Franks wants a lift.'

Fran was taken aback at the bitter grimace that Beth didn't try to hide.

'Lucky old you. Have a lovely time,' she said. 'I'm late, and I shall be in disgrace. Cinderella must get back to her chimney corner.'

She slammed the car door shut and was gone while Fran still had her mouth open. What was the matter with Beth?

31

Beth herself would have answered 'Everything.'

She was just about at the end of her tether as far as her new life in Old Swithinford went, but that was only the latest phase of a long period of unrest. Christmas only made things worse. It was supposed to be a time of peace and joy and goodwill, but she was cynically aware how little of that kind of Christmas spirit was left in her now. She was no longer a child and her Christianity was wearing thin. She felt rebellious but she no longer enjoyed rebellion for its own sake, as she had done once, deliberately teasing her parents by knocking down middle-class shibboleths. She had given in, long ago, when her youth had come to a sudden end.

Just as she had finished her course at a college of music, and was preparing to step out into the world on her own feet, her mother had died. Her father had then been only forty-five. Beth loved him desperately and had given up all thoughts of a career for herself to go home; to be with him, to grieve with him, to support him, to try to fill the gap in his life.

He had not wanted to accept that sacrifice from her, but it had seemed right, then. Now she knew what a mistake it had been – for both of them.

Twelve years later, the mistake could not be rectified. Time is inexorable.

Her father had tried to assuage his grief by working harder than ever before, and she had thrown herself wholeheartedly into his work with him. She had tried to fill her mother's place, but she couldn't make him the happy man he had been. Children are notoriously wary of attributing any sexual activity to their parents and it had come as a shock to her to realize that there was one gap she couldn't fill. It was only when it was far too late that she had understood how significant that particular gap was. Too late, sadly, for her.

She had been too young, as well, to understand that her father already had problems with regard to his ministry. The war had shaken his faith, but it had not destroyed it. Once hostilities were over, he had thrown himself with all his still-youthful vigour into the social side of his work, helping to pick up the pieces. Loving thy neighbour as thyself in the bombed-out slum where he had taken his first post-war living had not been easy; but he had had his wife at his side, doing more than her share of the work – and always there to go home to. Whatever doubts and difficulties he faced outside his home, once there he was happy. The couple had regarded the antics of their teenage daughter with amused tolerance; she was a lively, intelligent and gifted girl, and her rebellious tantrums had only made them laugh.

The suffering he had found in his slum parish had done nothing to restore his weakened faith, but it had bolstered his calling. His task was to ameliorate physical hardship with spiritual comfort and at that he was good – all the better for having had to deal with broken soldiers.

What he found most difficult to come to terms with was the hopeless disillusionment, and the resultant crumbling of pre-war codes of morality. He was appalled by the violence and the blatant abandonment of sexual codes of behaviour. That one led to the other he understood, and he worried about its long-term effect on society; but he had been far too busy doing the next job that came to hand to bother too much about the distant future.

Then the blow had fallen. His wife's heart, weakened in childhood by rheumatic fever, had given out. What had he done to deserve that?

He had been guilty of losing faith; and he had sympathized and even condoned the growing tide of immorality, instead of preaching against it. He had been a good social worker, but a poor priest. He had been too sorry for the sinners in his care to condemn them. He could only regard his bereavement as punishment.

By the time the first edge of grief had been dulled, he had become a man with a mission. He was convinced that all the other ills of post-war society stemmed from the rampant sexual permissiveness; surely civilization's only hope was a return to the commandments of the Supreme Authority whose servant he was. 'Duty' instead of Loving Kindness became his guide. And Duty, like Charity, had to begin at home, within himself and in his own household.

For if gold rusten, what shall iron do?

Beth had tried to follow, but the change in him worried her. She noticed that the parishioners who had loved him so much in the past were avoiding him. They attributed the change in him to grief and forgave him, but they no longer took their troubles to him.

Life centred round duty rather than charity became very difficult for Beth to take. Her father kept her so hard at work that she had little time for herself but it dawned on her that she was being deliberately kept away from male society, though as far as she knew, she had never given her father any reason to suppose she was likely to seduce the curate, or engage in any other sort of sexual misdemeanour. As she told herself bitterly after several years had passed, chance would be a fine thing.

It occurred to her that her father was subconsciously transferring discipline meant for himself to her – making her his whipping-boy. She began to be worried about the state of his mind. He was becoming obsessed with his belief that 'man's first disobedience' in the Garden of Eden was at the root of all evil. She urged him to see a psychiatrist.

No one, he had angrily assured her, who had faith in Christ was ever in need of a psychiatrist. After which dogmatic statement, he had promptly slid into the nervous breakdown that she had been fearing. It had taken him two years to recover. He had been in clinics and retreats gradually picking up the threads of faith and self-respect again, and she had been left alone, a woman who was already 'out of the swim'.

She had done what she could about it; her mother had left her a small legacy which her father had forbidden her to touch, but now she used it, buying herself feminine clothes and having her mother's fine pieces of jewellery mended and refurbished. By the time her father was recovered, and his bishop had suggested a quiet country living, she had regained a lot of her *joie de vivre* and some of her youthful personality.

Three months ago, when they had moved into Spotted Cow Lane, she had been full of high hopes. They had tried to pick up their relationship with each other but both were changed people. He had regained physical health and she had become an attractive woman again. Neither of them knew where to start to heal the past or plan for the future.

One unforeseen difficulty was that neither had any experience of living in a rural community. She sometimes thought that he had expected to find his new cure taken straight from the pages of Trollope. Indeed, in some respects it might have been, because most of her father's congregation, such as Thirzah and Sophie, had hardly moved on since then. In other respects, it was already changed. The odd mixture of old and new made walking with circumspection imperative.

Beth was quick to learn that she had to wait to be welcomed into the village. Her father, conversely, had made every mistake in the book. He had expected to 'be looked up to', but only the oldest of the indigenous retained that sort of reverence for his cloth. Even his churchwardens were men of wealth far above his own means. He had been shocked and disillusioned to discover that even in this, a last outpost of rural England, wealth was already the measure of worth.

So he had tried the other tack, of 'being one of the boys'. Beth had known instinctively that that would be a mistake, and it was. He had alienated both sides by that false move. The old and the unsophisticated, like Sophie, had been scandalized, while the young he had been hoping to entice back to church had seen through the false *bonhomie* and laughed.

At the Bridgefoot wedding, she had glimpsed the sort of society she could hope to be part of. In November had come the invitation to a party at Benedict's. It had been to her like seeing the sun again after a long, hard winter. She had gathered that Benedict's was 'the big house', and that Mrs Catherwood was a writer. Nobody had informed her of its far-from-hidden secret, though tongues had wagged vigorously to the Rector. He had lost none of his conviction that sexual permissiveness was the Devil's secret weapon for the destruction of God's creation. Though he had not expected to have to begin his crusade here so soon, or at the top, he would not shirk the issue.

When she learned what her father had done by visiting the adulterous couple and putting them out of bounds, Beth had been absolutely appalled. She had told him that he had lost his sense of proportion, and that far from being a pastor he had become a bigot.

She had seen the incident as a test case for her freedom, and she had defied his decree, setting her at odds with him and warning her of difficulties to come. For a few hours, she had felt young and happy again, but afterwards her world had seemed bleaker than ever.

By Christmas, her relationship with her father had deteriorated. She loved him still, and indeed admired him in many ways, but she saw him all too clearly as a man with an overwhelming obsession, and because of his previous breakdown, she was afraid for him. She saw also that in a rural parish he was a fish out of water, even without his crusade.

He had expected her to take up as his secretary, housekeeper and general parish dogsbody where she had left off. By doing so, she had labelled herself from the beginning as only an appendage to him. She had, metaphorically, put herself back into pawn, if not into bondage.

She had no life of her own, and unless she did something drastic about it, she never would have. She resented being taken so much for granted, but saw no way of escape.

The more his sense of failure, the greater his unhappiness and the sterner with himself he grew. He became an austere and uncomfortable companion, who was deliberately distancing himself from her.

She reciprocated, in small but telling ways. She no longer referred to him as 'Daddy', for example, as she had always done before, to keep the filial bond between them strong. Instead, she called him 'Father' – partly to remind him that she was no longer a child, but also with irony, sniping at his stiff clerical bearing towards her; and after one particularly sterile evening she had gone to bed with a nagging feeling that he would rather be alone. Had she become an obligation to him? A spinster daughter it was his duty to house? Did he want to escape, and if so, why?

Since she had defied him about Fran's party, it was clear that matters were coming to a head. With Christmas looming, she had hoped there might be other invitations, but Christmas had come without a single invitation or gesture of friendship from anyone.

She had not wished her father a happy Christmas, nor he her. She would do the duties he required of her, but she was not at all sure that duty would stand the strain much longer.

She had been up just after seven o'clock on Christmas Day

to prepare their lunch before attending the eight o'clock communion service. The church had been cold and the service long. She wondered how many others of the six people present had had nothing at all to eat or drink before setting out, as had been decreed for her. When she reached home she had prepared breakfast, but her father refused bacon and egg, and abstractedly munched dry toast. Beth ate heartily; eating was one of the very few physical pleasures left in life and, since it was not overtly connected with sex, a sin he overlooked. It was lucky for her, she thought, that there was no chance of her running to fat, because she knew that she was eating more than she ought, to comfort herself.

She had a lot to do before setting out for the church again to take part in a special children's service that her father was inaugurating this year.

'I really don't know what line to take with them,' he said, looking up at her at last. 'I shall of course dwell on the meaning of Christmas – but it is difficult to get it across to excited children who have found laden pillow-cases full of cheap toys by their bedsides only an hour or two before. I know I ought to disabuse them of the Father Christmas myth. It is condoning a lie not to do so. When they do find out that they have been deceived by their own parents, they never believe them again. Especially with regard to such things as the existence of God. Christmas is the celebration of the birth of God. Yes, I must do it today.'

Beth spilt her coffee. 'Father! You can't! You mustn't! You have absolutely no right to interfere between little children and their parents.'

'On the contrary, I have every right. They are souls in my care. It is my duty.'

'Then damn and blast your bloody duty! If that is the line you are going to take, I'm not coming. But I don't think you need worry. I doubt if there will be a child in sight.'

'How dare you use language like that in my house? Or to me? Or anywhere else! If no children come, you and I will still hold the service in memory of your mother and your own innocent childhood.'

Still harping on the question of her innocence, as if she

were thirteen instead of thirty-three. He could only mean sexual innocence. Why did he want to ram the question of sex down her throat at every opportunity? Just to remind her that she was a dependent old maid who would never know any experience of it?

She had been right about the absence of children; so she had sat on at the organ while her father had waited, until it was too late to go home again before morning prayer. She had reached the conclusion that to save her father's sanity as well as her own, she must get away from him at least for a time. But where could she go? She had gone on sitting, alone, after the morning service was over, cold and stony-hearted, imagining the dining-room at Benedict's – warm from its great log fires, warm with music and joy and peace, warmest of all with love. If such were the wages of sin . . . ? Her jaws set, and her cold hands clenched.

She was frozen in body, mind and spirit when at last she made her way out of church to the gate – just in time to see William bestow that blatantly lover's kiss on Fran. The pain inside her was physical, like a gripe. Fran had everything that she had missed.

In an attempt to hide her envy, she had gone to speak to Fran, only to be told that they were on their way to a gathering of people, all of whom she had met at Benedict's. The tears were prickling under her eyelids as she caught sight of William running back. She could not endure to meet him.

'Sorry. Must go,' she said, and ran away.

Though she dished up their dinner, neither of them ate anything. The afternoon and evening stretched ahead of Beth like the wastes of Antarctica.

She got up abruptly, put on her warmest coat and announced her intention of going for a walk.

'In which direction?' he asked suspiciously, as if he had every right to know. The last strands of her self-control gave way. 'What the hell is that to do with you?' she asked, and went out, slamming the door behind her.

He barely heard. The Devil had appeared again, not as a ravening monster but as Lucifer in all his angelic compelling glory, and to him, personally. He had noticed how white and

251

strained Beth had been during the service and when she had not gone straight home, he had felt obliged to go back to make sure all was well. He had got there just in time to see William kiss Fran, and had slunk home again in torture.

Punishment was for once fitting the crime. The psychiatrist at the clinic had told him that his obsession with modern sexuality was due to his own repressed sexual desires, he having admitted proudly to being celibate since the death of his wife. He had also been told, to his horror, that his subsequent over-protection of his daughter was in fact a sublimation of incestuous feelings towards her. He had repudiated such information as utter nonsense – though he had taken care to draw away from Beth, appalled by the thought that others might draw the same terrible conclusion as his counsellor.

Installed in his new living, he had at once made it plain that his first objective was to put up a fight against the rampant devil of sexual permissiveness wherever he found it lurking. To that end he had 'set his stall out' and in that cause he had paid his visit to Benedict's. Since then he had had no peace. The Devil was after him.

For twelve years, he had been gently but successfully resisting the blandishments of eager young ladies and repulsing the advances of widows and spinsters. None of them had stirred his blood at all. The psychiatrist must be mad.

Then he had paid that visit to Benedict's, and come face to face with Fran. Her fiery contempt of him, and her blazing defence of Love in the face of all convention had pierced right through his carefully constructed moral armour. He had reasoned with himself, scourged himself with whips of shame, schooled his thoughts like a frightened schoolboy and intensified his war on modern sexuality as proof to himself of his own innocence. Fran was an adultress, whom he must prevent from contaminating others.

But he could not forget her, or William's reminder that he was a man. He had even admitted his admiration of her to William, who had been so magnanimous and who in any other circumstances he would have been so proud to claim as a friend. Fran was a widow, and but for William . . .

He had been vaguely conscious that Beth was disturbed,

and knowing from experience what often happened to maiden ladies, had decided that she must have fallen in love with William. He was angry with her, but guilt and duplicity in himself stilled his tongue. If, this morning, she had seen the kiss (as he guessed she must have done) . . . They were both in the same boat. And there was no way out. They should not go on living together. They no longer liked each other, however much love there still was between them. She was an obstacle to the realization of his dreams, and he to hers. She stood between him and the chance of ever having any other woman, as he had prevented her from finding herself a man. He didn't want her in his house, but what could he do? He could hardly turn out an ageing spinster, who was also his daughter, and who had been his slave for so long. What would become of them – both?

After she had slammed the door behind her, he admitted to himself that the psychiatrist had been right, though not, as far as he could judge, about his feelings towards Beth.

Except that if he had been possessive of her, even as a daughter, it was because she had been 'his', standing in as dummy until his fantasy-woman appeared. Now the fantasy had a name and a shape. He put his head in his hands and confessed to himself that he had never in his whole life desired a woman as he now desired the one he had watched William kiss.

He fell on his knees, and prayed that he might be relieved of such a burden of sin, until he fell asleep. He had resolved to tear Fran's image out of his heart, but even in his sleep he had seen her face glow under William's caress. He woke to pray until in pure exhaustion he slept again. When it grew dark, he crept across to the church, resolved to kneel in prayer before the altar all night if it took that long to wipe Fran out of his mind. His heart was as cold as the stones on which he knelt by the time his battle was won. It was only then that he began to wonder where Beth was.

32

The luncheon party at the hotel was a great success, much more so than Fran had expected. They found Jess, Greg and Monica there already when they arrived.

Jess was wearing a dress and looking decidedly feminine and beautiful. She turned her charm on Elyot Franks, and all the rest amusedly watched him succumb. Monica, looking as beautifully chic as she always, did, sent a different sort of message to Fran. There was about her an air of serenity that acted as an antidote to Jess's mercurial brilliance. Fran guessed that it was the result of Roland's reappearance in her life, and was a little anxious; but she watched William being at his most enchanting to Monica, shrugged off her worries and gave her attention to her host.

He seemed to be at ease with them all, a man among his friends, and Fran felt guiltily how much they had all misjudged him. The lunch itself was perfect in every way, and with coffee they settled down to that sort of comatose cosiness that comes over such a gathering: a sense of well-being after a good meal and excellent wine, and with time to waste.

It had been a surprise to Fran when Eric said, rather tentatively, 'Would anybody object to my smoking my pipe?' It was difficult to think of him as 'just a man' without his business-executive cloak on. The pipe quite changed him.

Then Elyot also fished shyly in his pocket for his own pipe, and Jess and Monica had both accepted cigarettes. Greg produced a cigar, and Fran and William had raised eyebrows at each other across a haze of blue smoke.

It was a glance of interrogation. Neither had ever smoked in the other's presence, and both were wondering now whether the other had been abstaining entirely out of courtesy. Fran exploded into laughter.

'No, William, I don't smoke, and never have done. How extraordinary that you never asked before! What about you?'

'Tried it as a student, of course, and smoked off-duty

during the war, but gave it up long ago.' The incident had caused a good deal of fun and a lot of chaffing from the others. It helped to meld them all into a very comfortable group.

Fran wondered how long they were supposed to stay, once the pipes were finished. She didn't want to break the party up, but – one must never overstay one's welcome. It was Monica who read her intention to gather her things together, and begged them not to leave yet. Eric added his plea. 'I don't want you to go. This is the nearest thing to a proper Christmas Day we've had since – since Annette was killed.'

So of course they stayed, and at Jess and Monica's urging, spent the entire afternoon engaged in a round-robin tournament of children's games fetched from the hotel's children's play-room. It ended in a draw between William and Elyot, and Jess, acting as referee, declared that there had to be a play-off. Eric dispatched a waiter for a bottle of Rémy Martin for the prize. The others gathered round to watch with the sort of eagerness that might have been accorded to a knightly passage of arms. Fran found herself perched on the arm of Eric's chair. He slipped an arm round her to make her comfortable, as unconcernedly as William might have done. It was into her ear that he said, 'I've just come to a decision. Tell you afterwards.'

Elyot won, and Fran had the honour of presenting him with the prize. She took the bottle of brandy and put it into his hands, then pulled his head down to kiss him, and called,'Quick Jess! Your turn.' Jess sprang to take her place, and in turn held him for Monica. Elyot's reddening face broke into an embarrassed but delighted smile. He hadn't noticed the kissing-bunch of mistletoe under which he had taken his stand.

'Not fair!' cried Eric. 'That wasn't part of the prize.'

Fran turned towards him, pulled him up, and repeated the process while Greg and William voluntarily lined up behind him. Then they all collapsed into chairs, laughing like a lot of over-excited children.

'That was fun,' said Eric. 'There won't be nearly so much Christmas spirit – except the sort that comes out of bottles – in the ballroom downstairs tonight. I guess we never really grow out of being children, though it takes a brave man to show it.'

'Four brave men,' Jess said. 'I congratulate you all.'

The afternoon had slipped away. They were all surprised how late it was.

'Ring for supper, Monica,' Eric said.

'What a lovely suite this is,' Fran said. 'And just imagine being able to say in such a lordly fashion "Ring for supper". As in a baronial hall.'

'M'm,' said Eric. 'But this is the first time ever that it has felt remotely like a home. That is what I meant. Gavin has just taken on a long tour of the States with the band. I have decided that I shall move back into his part of the farmhouse. We'll keep an office here, Jess, but I'll have a proper home of my own.'

Fran's heart missed a beat. So the lovely day was not going to end without a note of worry, after all. With her father in the house, what could Monica do about Roland's visits? She felt her own face flushing as she stole a nervous glance at the girl, but Monica was hugging her father with obvious delight.

So the party broke up, with Fran issuing invitations to Benedict's the next day for 'a second Christmas dinner' which, as she said, had got to be eaten if only to prevent Sophie from being offended.

Fran and William settled down to a cosy evening, still at intervals reviewing the unexpected pleasure of the afternoon.

'Jess and Greg both looked happier than I've seen them for ages,' Fran said.

'You looked happy, too,' he said.

'Well, don't I always? I am. I have good reason to be. Damn! Whoever can that be?' The telephone was shrilling. William got up to answer it, while Fran, as always, sent panicky thoughts round her family, wondering which of her children was in trouble. William put the phone down.

'Elyot,' he said, 'in some sort of agitation. Wants us to go straight away.' He was already on his way to fetch warm coats.

While they had been indulging in innocent Christmas foolery, the wind had turned to the north and the temperature had fallen below zero.

33

They were no more than five minutes getting there. Elyot's car was facing into his double garage, with its lights still on. He came out of the garage to meet them.

'Thank God you could come!' he said. 'In here. . . . I just didn't know what to do.'

They followed him. The double garage was very large, empty where his car normally stood. The other side housed all the tools needed for Ned and Bill Edgeley's onslaught on his garden. Among them stood a wheelbarrow, and in the wheelbarrow slumped a figure, covered with Elyot's own coat and some car blankets.

'I went straight into the house,' he said, 'and waited till the fire had got going before coming back to put the car away. Then I saw her. I thought it was a tramp crawled in to die – but when I went to investigate I found her, only unconscious. Flat out. Dead to the world. I can't rouse her. I could have carried her inside the house, I know – but it didn't seem wise. It isn't her physical welfare I'm concerned about. My instinct was to keep quiet till I got another woman here. Sorry, Fran. Naval experience isn't much good in a situation like this.'

'She?' asked Fran. 'What do you mean? Who is it? A drunk pushed out of a passing car? Surely it's the police you want.'

'No – nothing so simple,' he said, rather grimly. 'It's Beth Marriner.'

Fran pulled off the coverings. Beth was curled up in the wheelbarrow, with her head on a sack of fertilizer. She still had on her warm coat, a woolly hat and thick gloves, and she had spread some old sacks round her legs, which were very wet and muddy. It looked as if she had settled herself down for the night. Her face was deathly white, but her breathing was deep and regular.

'Exhausted and frozen through,' William said. 'Let's get her inside.' They picked her up and carried her into Elyot's sitting-room, where Fran pulled the new settee from Harrods round to face the fire.

'You see why I hesitated to send for help,' Elyot said. 'As William says, she appears to have collapsed just from cold and weariness – but why on earth in my garage?'

'She can't be drunk, can she?' Fran queried.

'No. Felt ill suddenly, probably, and crawled in here hoping to be able to rouse me?'

'No,' Fran said. 'She knew you wouldn't be here. I told her so. Besides, she was very nearly home. And she wasn't too far gone not to cover herself up as well as she could. Perhaps she couldn't get in at home.' She knelt by the couch, chafing Beth's cold hands.

'Get some hot-water-bottles, Elyot. And William, open that bottle of brandy. We've got to get her warm. I suppose we ought not to have moved her. It may have been a hit-and-run accident. Oughtn't we to get a doctor?'

'Fran, my darling,' William said, 'don't start to panic. I'm sure Elyot's right. She's in no physical danger, unless it's from pneumonia. He's just trying to prevent a lot of unnecessary talk and conjecture. We'll find out what's happened before we alert anybody. Can you get those wet stockings and things off her? The moment she comes round we'll get some brandy down her. And then I'd suggest a hot bath.'

Warmth and massage were bringing colour back to Beth's face, and as soon as she opened her eyes they forced some brandy down her. She coughed, and looked round, but failing to recognize where she was, shut her eyes again.

'Clear off, you two men,' said Fran. 'Go and run a bath, and find an old dressing-gown and some blankets.'

'Shall I call her father, first?' Elyot asked.

'No,' Fran ordered emphatically, remembering how strange Beth had been outside the church. 'My guess is that he is at the bottom of all this. In any case, we've already done everything wrong by the book already, so there's no point in us changing tack now.'

Next time Beth opened her eyes, she found Fran's arms round her, holding her and stroking her face. She began to cry.

When she had slammed the door behind her in Spotted Cow Lane, she had simply wanted to get out. She had no idea where she was going, but after walking a while she had struck one of the many linked paths that went right round the long clay peninsula that stuck out like a pointing finger into the surrounding fens. Sometimes the paths petered out and she had to scramble her way through bushes and briars, but she was incapable of thinking or feeling. All she wanted was to keep walking away from home.

She went on till she came to the wood on the end of the finger of highland, and ploughed through the trees till she came out under the rookery by the little church. She had been crying though she hadn't known it . . . with grief, temper, rebellion and despair. The tears had dried on her face in the cold wind.

The sight of the beautiful little church restored her memory of what day it was, and why she was where she was. A fresh outburst of weeping sent new tears chasing after the old, bitter tears now of loneliness, envy and longing.

She had cried first for her love for her father, love now so damaged and broken. The second outburst was for the sort of love she had never known. She had missed out on everything that made a woman's life worth living. Because she had thought her father needed her, she had let that sort of love pass her by. Now nobody needed her, her father least of all. She had been blind not to understand. When her father was pronounced cured, she had rejoined him with hope that they could take up again the pleasant if not exciting sort of life they had had before depression had defeated him. A fresh start in such pleasant circumstances must surely be what they needed. But she had felt she was taking up residence with a stranger, because both of them had changed. She had regained a lot of her former verve and personality, but he had become altogether more sober, sterner and more autocratic. His battle against the prevailing sexual permissiveness had become a challenge against impossible odds. He was only a puny David appearing on the battlefield when Goliath had already triumphed, Beth thought cynically.

Physically, he looked well. He was still handsome, energetic, young for his fifty-six years. What could have altered him so much?

His constant harping on the breakdown of sexual morality worried her; it was so out of character that she began to wonder if 'treatment' had done more harm than good. He appeared to resent her. Did he see even his own daughter as a temptress? The thought made her smile. Some temptress!

His behaviour about their invitation to Fran's birthday party had been a turning point. He appeared to regard even the most innocent social intercourse between the sexes as an attack on civilization, especially, as he had pointed out to her, among people who were just the sort that ought to be providing moral leadership, but who were openly and blatantly flouting all sexual morality. Till then she would have given in rather than upset him; but her newly regained independence would not now accept a dictat from a man whom she feared must have a kink in his brain. So she had defied him, and had gone to Fran's party.

And there at Benedict's she had met Love in the flesh, as it were. She had never before felt it so palpably in the air around her. She had noted the wonderful patina of happiness that Frances Catherwood showed even in middle-age. It wasn't fair.

She sat down among the dead leaves at the foot of a tree and looked up at the old nests in the bare branches. She wasn't nearly as old as Fran. Why should she regard herself as a has-been, or, more accurately, as a 'never-was'? She knew herself to be an attractive woman still. Why should she be made to spurn as Sin what even her father's God must have intended. Why else were the rooks above her head created male and female?

She had in church that very morning listened to him expounding the miracle of the virgin birth. How could a religion, ostensibly one of love abounding, be based on anything so sterile? So sanitized? So inhuman? It didn't make sense. Then she had gone miserably out, only to see William kiss Fran – like that. Sin, said her father. Holy, holy, holy, said her heart. The memory of it stirred her yet.

In the shelter of the rookery she tried to come to terms with her situation. She sat so long in the wood that the damp soaked through her coat, and she was very cold. It had also grown dark. She got up and stumbled her way past the church on the hill, but missed the track and found herself in a ploughed field. She had begun to feel faint with hunger as well as disorientated by the turbulence inside her. It took her a long time to find the path again, but at last the lights of the village came into sight. She had no option but to go towards home.

It was more than five hours since she had left. Had her father been worried? She wanted desperately for him to care that much about her. He would have been worried, once; but now, she thought, he would only be full of dreadful suspicion. He would accuse her of having broken the fifth commandment, of not honouring her father, if not actually suggesting that she had slipped out to some immoral assignation. She could almost see him accounting for the mud on her coat in his own way. His mind ran on only one track – yet they had said he was 'cured'. She doubted that . . . He would keep coldly aloof from her tonight, when all she craved was affection.

The cold wind had numbed her feet in her mud-clogged stockings and shoes; her mind was almost as numb as her feet. She couldn't decide what to do. She had hoped she would meet her father out looking for her, but there had been no sign of him. Would she be let in when she got home? She could see the outline of their cottage from where she stood, but there were no lights in the windows. She felt faint and dizzy, and unable to face the issue just yet.

The gates of the Old Rectory stood open and she stumbled through them to sit down in the garage to wait. If he came out to look for her, she would be able to see his torch from there.

The longer she sat, the colder it grew. She was desolate. Nobody wanted her, not even her father. She had no family, no friends and now no home. Bodily fatigue robbed her of the power to move, and despair of the will to make further effort. She sank back into the wheelbarrow, and oblivion.

It was a very different Beth who sat in Elyot Franks' room an hour later. Once warm again, she regained her hold on common sense. The brandy she had been made to drink, and the long, luxurious hot bath they had insisted on her taking had restored her strength, except for a rather delightful feeling of languor. She didn't want to have to think. In any case, she had to see her father before making irrevocable decisions. It couldn't be done here and now.

Fran would not allow her to put on her own wet clothes again, so for the time being, she was marooned. She had been wrapped in one of Elyot's dressing-gowns, which was none too long for her, but swamped her in every other dimension. Fran had coped with its excess of width by tying her own brightly coloured silk scarf round Beth's slim middle.

She had brushed her long hair, and braided it into a plait which hung down over one huge camel-hair covered shoulder. When she looked at herself in the bathroom mirror, she had even recovered enough to raise a smile at her reflection. Her face was flushed with heat after being so cold and shone as if her skin had been polished, but there was no make-up at hand to tone it down. To complete the incongruous picture, her legs and feet were bare. But her courage had been restored, and hope reborn. She wasn't going to quit of her own accord.

Her spirits had been thawed more by Fran's practical kindness than by anything else. No one had asked her how she came to be where they had found her, or why she had been in such a state. 'If I had been a stray dog they would have acted just the same,' Beth reflected. They wouldn't have expected the dog to explain anything; they were too well-bred to ask her any questions.

But she owed them an explanation and would offer it when a chance arose. The day had been so long; it seemed like a complicated dream in which nightmare and farce had become inextricably muddled.

'Are you ready to go down?' asked Fran from outside the bathroom door.

'Fran! Looking like this? I can't!'

'You look absolutely beautiful,' Fran said. 'A cross between Pooh Bear and "La belle dame sans merci". Come on. It's only William and Elyot, both anxious to see how you are.'

She followed shyly as Fran led her into the sitting-room, where both men leapt to their feet. The courtesy, in view of her ludicrous appearance, almost reduced her to tears again. Fran guided her back to the Chesterfield. Then Fran looked pointedly at her watch.

'Elyot,' she said. 'Haven't you got anything eatable in your larder? Because I don't know about anybody else, but I'm starving. There's plenty of food up at Benedict's, but we can't take Beth out again just yet. I suppose William could go and fetch it.'

Elyot looked blank. 'I don't know,' he said. 'I leave all such matters to Mrs Bates. There's bound to be iron rations if nothing else.'

'Well, don't stand there like a couple of helpless idiots,' Fran said. 'Go and see what you can raise for us all – on our laps here in front of the fire. And plenty of hot coffee,' she called after them.

'Men!' she said scathingly to Beth as they went, glad to be excused. 'They should have remembered their Homer. He was always so practical about food. Especially after any sort of trauma. I really did think one of them would have had enough sense to have guessed you might be hungry, and got something ready for us.'

'Hungry?' said Beth. 'I'm famished! Like the beggar at Semmerwater, "I faint for lack of bread." I haven't had anything since breakfast.'

She caught Fran's eye. 'I quarrelled with Father,' she said. 'I ran away, I suppose. Then I couldn't make myself go back. Fran – did you know he had had a nervous breakdown, before we came here? I'm afraid he's going to be ill again. His mind is still all kinked up. He's turned against me for one thing. I must go home, of course. He needs me if he doesn't want me. But I've been giving in too much. I've had no life of my own at all, since we came here, and today I just snapped. I'm so sorry to have caused you all this fuss. It was all very silly of me, but I felt that if I didn't establish my independence at once, we should both be heading for a loony-bin.'

'Oh dear! We had no idea. Thanks for telling me. We'll keep it dark, so don't worry about that. We all get to a breaking point and . . . Ssh! Here they come with food. Ward-room or RAF mess-style, I wonder? Do you mind?'

'Would Odysseus have cared?' she said. How fortifying it was to have a bit of intelligent conversation again! That's what she had been missing most and had nearly gone round the bend because of the lack of it. She tucked her bare feet up under the folds of the voluminous teddy-bear dressing-gown, and looked eagerly towards the food.

There were ham sandwiches, nicely made by William. The hunks of bread and cheese were much more basic, but all the better for that. A large fruit cake, the exact twin of one still uncut up at Benedict's, was obviously by Thirzah out of Kezia. Coffee from a solid silver coffee-pot poured into half-pint mugs completed the meal.

'Well,' said Elyot. 'Life is full of surprises. I didn't expect my first Christmas here to be as jolly as this. Who's for another brandy?'

'Do you,' asked Beth, 'always serve your guests – invited or uninvited as the case may be – with Rémy Martin?'

'Well, no. I like good brandy, but I don't often run to this. I won it, as it happens, this afternoon, from William.'

'Poor William. It must have cost him a fortune. But at least he's getting a little of his own back. How did you come to win it?'

Both men looked sheepish, and neither answered her. 'A bet?' she hazarded.

Fran had begun to giggle. It was one of her most endearing characteristics that when anything caught her funny-bone, mirth bubbled out of her like champagne when the cork is released.

'I'll tell you,' she said. 'Because they won't and you'd never guess the answer in a million years. *Playing tiddly-winks!*'

As Rupert Brooke said, laughter is the very garland on the head of friendship. They were still laughing when a peremptory knock sounded on the front door.

Elyot went to answer the knock, leaving the sitting-room door open.

'It's Father,' said Beth, colour draining from her face.

Fran caught her hand. 'Sit still!' she ordered. 'Let Elyot deal with him.'

'I am looking for my daughter,' Marriner said, offering no further explanation. 'I saw that you had been out in your car, and wondered if you might have seen her anywhere?'

'She's here,' Franks answered. 'Do come in and join us.'

Fran sought William's eye. She had not seen the Rector since her Queen of the Amazons act. She didn't want to meet him. Beth watched incredulous as Fran disappeared through the door that led to the kitchen, followed swiftly by William. They shut the door behind them, and Beth was left alone.

The Rector was still wearing his clerical gear and dog collar. He was pale and taut from his own spiritual ordeal, and cold from his long, long vigil in the church. It had led him to the conclusion that he had been wrong, and the psychiatrist right. The priest in him had suppressed the man, but the man had refused to die. His feelings towards Frances Catherwood had made him admit it. But with the admission had come a great relief. To know your enemy was half the battle.

He understood now how lucky he had been that it was Fran who had caused the crisis. It would have happened sooner or later, possibly with consequences utterly unthinkable. It helped that he knew her to be unattainable, widow though she might be.

When he had risen from his knees, he had doused the fire inside himself by prayer. His task still was to do his best to prevent the modern sexual contagion to which he had so nearly succumbed himself from wreaking havoc elsewhere. His own experience would make him more tolerant, though no less fervent.

His heart was sad, but he felt cleansed of guilt – as far as Fran was concerned. He could not absolve himself so easily with regard to his recent behaviour towards Beth. He had forgotten that she was a lively, healthy young woman who had feelings of her own.

She had changed, though. He was suddenly afraid that his neglect of her might mean that she now had a secret life of which he knew nothing.

Had she gone this afternoon to meet a lover?

Chilled inside and out, he had left the dark church and gone homewards to find her and apologize. The cottage was dark, the fire had gone out, and the food uneaten from their Christmas dinner still stood on the table. Filled with panic, he grabbed a torch and, without stopping to put on a coat over his cassock, went out to look for her. He didn't know where to start. The village streets were deserted, his parishioners all inside eating Christmas supper before settling down to watch TV or whatever. For that he was grateful. If he found her, nobody would be any the wiser about the day's events.

She had it in her power to undo him. He had today sacrificed his feelings as a man on the altar of his priesthood, resolved in future to give his whole heart to his calling. What if his own daughter had already been infected by the contagion of promiscuity? If she had let him down, he would have no standing, either as a moral crusader, or as a father. He would have failed himself, his daughter and his God. There would be nothing left at all for him. He felt fear; he had to find her, not least because he needed human company.

It was with enormous relief that he saw two cars standing in the front of the Old Rectory, and lights above the front door. He forgot his quarrel with Franks. Another unattached man, especially one who was not yet part of the village, was the best help he could have. The emotional crisis he had been through had not left him incapable of rational thought.

But when at Elyot's invitation he had followed him into the sitting-room, reason deserted him. There, on a voluptuous Chesterfield, plenty big enough to hold two, lay his errant daughter, wrapped in her host's dressing-gown, with her hair down her back and her feet bare.

He pulled himself up in shock and horror, and found his voice.

'Will you kindly explain the meaning of this?' he said.

Elyot, mystified by the tone, replied, 'The meaning of what?' and turning, took in at a glance what his visitor meant.

Beth's eyes, dark in her pale face, were set on him, huge eyes, pleading, filled with pain and fear. Anger rose in him before any other feeling had time to register itself. He roared, as he might have roared orders from the bridge in the middle of a battle.

'Sir! Do you dare to insinuate that your daughter is in any sort of danger in my house?'

Listening outside the door, Fran clung to William and choked. But William stopped only long enough to push her into a chair. 'Stop there. This is serious,' he said.

266

Wondering, she watched him prepare to make his entrance on to the stage. He opened the door nonchalantly, stood as if surprised, half withdrew, and then strode forward with hand outstretched.

'Archie!' he said, grasping the Rector's hand 'How on earth did you know where to find her? We were just about to ring you. On our way home from the hotel for a drink with Commander Franks, we found Beth lying on the side of the road. She was wet and cold, and unconscious, but apparently unhurt. The most obvious thing was to get her dry and warm.' He raised his voice, and called. 'Fran! Fran! Where are you?'

She took her cue. If William could put on an act, so could she.

'Sorry, William, coming— Oh, I see. Good evening, Rector. Have you been worried about Beth? I'm afraid that's my fault. I insisted on her having a hot drink and some food. She isn't injured – just knocked out, we think. I was just wondering how we were going to get her home – though she needs care. William, why don't we take her back to Benedict's with us? I can lend her some night things, and Elyot will have to do without his dressing-gown till tomorrow.'

She spoke as if it were all settled, the Lady of the Manor giving orders. 'That's all right with you, isn't it, Rector? I promise I'll look after her. And we'll bring her home in the morning.'

She gave Marriner no time to answer. 'Are you ready, Beth? Oh, of course you can't walk, without shoes. Bring the car to the door, William, as close as you can get it. Elyot, I have taken a blanket. I was just getting it when William called me.'

By this time, the others were mesmerized by her performance. Once or twice Marriner tried to speak, but she always got in first. He could not object to her proposal without making a complete fool of himself.

William played up to her, only he having any idea how perilously close to popping the champagne cork in her throat must be. She was getting her own back with interest. William fetched the car to the door while she wrapped the blanket round Beth.

Beth stopped on the way to the door to kiss her father. 'Goodnight, Daddy. I'm sorry if you have been worried. Tell you all in the morning.'

The Rector attempted once more to speak, but Fran broke in yet again.

'Oh – wait a minute, Beth,' she said. 'You can't walk out barefoot. We shall have to carry you. Come on, Elyot, do your stuff – she's not a heavyweight like me.'

Dazed, Elyot swung Beth into his arms and stalked out with her, Fran following. She wished he didn't look quite so much as if it were a sack of potatoes that he had swung over his shoulder.

The moment the car door was shut, William let in the clutch. He dare not speak, yet. But Fran was far from the laughter he had been expecting.

She turned in her seat to look at Beth. 'Beth,' she said, 'if you want to go home now, of course we will take you. But you are in no state to face another row with your father tonight. I know it's no business of mine, but my hunch is that if you are ever going to make that stand for independence, you've got to do it now. I think a night spent worrying about you will do more for your cause than a week of argument. It's up to you.'

'I'll take you home very early in the morning,' William said, 'before anybody else is up. I'll ring your father when we get in and say you are in bed and asleep, and ask him to make sure the door is open. Nobody but us will ever know.'

They tucked her up in a warm bed with a posset of hot milk and more brandy. She was asleep within five minutes.

'What a day!' Fran said, as they sipped their own hot drinks.

'You didn't half hit poor Archie Marriner hard,' William said.

'Pompous ass,' Fran replied. 'And a bigot into the bargain.'

'No, sweetheart. For once you're wrong. He's a man who was an idealist and thinks he is watching civilization going to pot before his very eyes. I'm afraid he may be right. His mistake is in thinking he can stop it. Be magnanimous, my darling. We can afford to be, can't we?'

'I don't want to think ill of anybody. It's been a lovely day. We were like the ingredients of a Christmas pudding this morning – all separate from each other. Now we've been mixed and moulded into one group of friends.'

'Trust you to hit on a topical analogy! But you're right. Though it's the top end of the village that's doing the melding. I wonder if the other end is, too? It would be a pity if there was a cleavage between the two lots of us.'

'History in the making, Professor?' she said. 'Even on Christmas Day?'

'Cicero said that history is a witness of the times,' he answered. 'That's all I am.'

'And didn't some German philosopher say that a historian was a prophet with his face turned backwards?'

'I can't win, can I?' he said. 'When did you read German philosophy?'

'I didn't,' she said truthfully. 'When I hear anything I like, it just sticks in my head and I don't forget it.'

'As long as you don't forget that I love you, I don't care who or what else sticks in your head. As Ned would say, "You're a cough-drop."'

34

William delivered Beth home before eight o'clock on Boxing Day. He left a note for the Rector, asking for an interview with him to see the registers of St Saviour's Church.

Fran had time to remove all trace of Beth's having stayed there. She hated having to keep secrets from Sophie, but Sophie's close connection with the church made it necessary. Not that she need have worried. Sophie was glad to be back to work, and wanting to know how Christmas at the hotel had gone off.

'Who's a-coming to dinner today then?' she asked. ''Ow many am I got to cook for?'

'Oh Sophie – I'm afraid I don't know! When we were about to leave yesterday, I sort of threw out a general invitation – but I can't remember what anybody said. Jess and Greg will certainly come, and possibly four more. Can you manage? Or shall I ring to find out?'

'That turkey's big enough to feed a rigiment,' Sophie said. 'Thats why I come so early, to get it in the oven. And I can make a apple pie for them as don't like plum pudding. I know a lot o' town folks won't eat it. It's them vegetables as is worrying me.'

'Cook plenty. If nobody comes, we shall have to keep hotting them up.'

Sophie looked disgusted, and said, 'If you know a way o' 'otting Brussle sprouts up so as even a starvin' dog would eat 'em, you could make yourself a fortune, 'cos I don't.'

Greg and Jess came, and Eric and Monica. William slipped away into his study and rang Elyot. 'Sorry, William,' said Elyot. 'Black dog.' William put the phone down. No mention was made of Elyot's absence. It was a quiet day for which Fran was thankful. Conversation flowed gently and easily, and late in the afternoon Greg sat down at the piano, and the rest sat quiet and listened. All except Fran; her mind refused to give up wondering what was happening in other places. It pleased her to have Jess in such a happy frame of mind, and even Sophie had smiled once or twice at Eric. Yet there was worry, even there. She felt guilty that while she and William were welcoming Eric as a friend into their home and their circle, they were withholding from him a vital piece of information about his daughter's relationship with her son. Coming silently behind her to replace a log on the fire, William leaned over her and whispered, 'Don't run to meet trouble. It may never happen.'

Then late that evening, Roland rang. He was spending Christmas with Sue's family, and had slipped out to a call-box on the excuse of packing the car for an early start next morning. Sue was staying a few more days with her parents. She was being very difficult, but he was doing his best – to please Monica. 'Mum,' he said. 'I have to see Monica – to talk to her. If I come to see you tomorrow, can we see each other at your house? Just to talk – I promise nothing else. I don't want to be seen at her house just at present. She knows – I've just rung her. It's really rather important.'

Fran was glad to oblige, and to see her son; but as she said to William, it looked as if previous decisions were about to be overturned.

'It's Monica I'm worried about,' she said. 'I hope he's not running back on her now. She looks so happy and contented.'

'My dear girl,' said William, 'you really will have to make up your mind what you do want! He can't have it both ways, and you'll feel guilty whichever way it goes. Haven't you learned to trust your guardian angel yet? He hasn't let you down so far, has he?'

She had to agree that all the worry in the world wouldn't change things; what would be would be, and she was grateful for William's interest and advice; but it was a man's advice. She longed for Mary's clear-sighted common sense. There were times when she missed the female company of Mary more than she dare say.

Young Charles Bridgefoot got up early on Boxing Day, and slipped out before anybody else was up, to try his new car on the road. He knew that his mother was worried about him driving it, so he didn't want her to know.

He backed the car out quietly, the new engine purring so softly that he could hardly hear it himself. He didn't want to go towards the Old Glebe, or through the middle of the village, lest he be thought to be showing off. He couldn't go along the direct road towards Castle Hill (which had the fewest houses on it) because that led past the cottage where Nick and his mother lived, and Nick was the very last person he wanted to show off to. So he branched off before he got to Nick's home and took a side road that he had known from boyhood. It was actually only a track across a grass field, and ran along by the side of a hedge, petering out to a muddy lane after about half a mile. He knew that at the end of the gravelled bit of road there was a gateway where he could practise a three-point turn. He had been driving for years, but he had never before been in charge of a brand new car that was his very own. He was handling it with all the respect such an expensive new toy deserved. Once he'd got the feel of it, he would let it rip.

Charles was a very happy young man that morning, and aware of his good luck. To count your blessings was something his grandad had drilled into him. He had a conscience about Nick, who had so little when he had so much. It wasn't fair.

Good old Grandad! It evened things out a tiny bit that Grandad had treated Nick yesterday exactly as he had all his grandchildren. The thought struck him that if Nick kept up his sudden craze for Poppy, Uncle Vic and Aunt Marjorie wouldn't be at all pleased. They'd have higher hopes for their daughters than penniless nobodies like Nick.

Was Nick a nobody? It had never bothered Charles before, but as he sat in his car in the gateway, he thought about it. Malicious gossip had it that Nick was a bastard, and certainly there was no father in evidence. Nick had none of the things that Charles took for granted – no roots, no family, no proper home, no prospects. What he did have in plenty was brains, manners, and enormous charm. God only knew where they came from, because his mother couldn't have been poorer, or more retiring. Nick certainly hadn't learned his social graces from that old boor of a man in whose poor home they had taken shelter of a sort until he'd died. Charles wondered if Nick knew who his father was . . . he never referred to his own family.

It crossed Charles's mind that if Nick got a place at the University, he might be acceptable to Poppy's family. Grandad Bridgefoot was not one to hold Nick's origins against him. He was always reminding them all that it only took four generations from hobnails to hobnails again.

Nick hadn't bothered much about girls till now, though among the three friends the subject was a constant one. Nick being Nick, though, it wouldn't simply be a passing fancy about Poppy. Charles didn't want to give his friend up to any girl yet, let alone his cousin Poppy. Charles supposed, with the arrogance of the heart-free, that she was 'all right', but nothing to turn anybody's head. He had yet to learn that Love is no respecter of persons. Well, he'd go back now, and later today he'd pick Nick up and go down to Lane's End to see Robert. If Robert was well enough, they might all go out together.

Charles was reversing into the gateway when he glanced into his driving mirror, and saw disaster approaching, however swift his reactions were.

Coming up a slope on the other side of the hedge was a horse at full gallop, with a rider intent on jumping the old gate. She was lying low on the horse's neck, and Charles saw with horror that it was a girl riding bareback. His only chance of avoiding a collision was to tread hard on the accelerator and pray that he could move fast enough for the horse to land behind his car and not right on top of it.

The horse caught a gleam of reflection from the car's shiny new polish and shied. It refused the gate, reared, and swerved abruptly to the left. The girl lost her seat, went over the horse's head and fell on his side of the gate, landing heavily just behind his rear wheels. He screeched to a stop. He couldn't believe but that she must have broken her neck. He scrambled out and went towards where she lay on her back. He was stunned by shock and paralysed with fear, and his first thought was that there was no help anywhere close at hand.

Chaotic memories of basic first aid began to seep through his mind. 'If you suspect severe injury, don't attempt to move the person.' He didn't suspect injury; he suspected that she was already dead. He was terribly tempted to drive off and leave her to be found by somebody else.

Nick and his mother were nearest. The thought steadied him. Nick would neither lose his head nor run away. Charles clenched his fists, beat down a spasm of terrible nausea, and forced himself forward. The girl groaned, opened her eyes, doubled herself into a ball, and rolled from side to side. She wasn't dead – yet.

Charles had a glimpse of a pair of huge dark eyes in a face grimaced with pain as she strove to draw breath, and when she rolled over again he had a back view of a long mane of chestnut hair tied at the nape of her neck. Weak with the relief he concluded that she wasn't even badly injured. Badly winded and perhaps concussed, possibly with a broken limb or shoulder-blade.

He stood over her, hoping she would come round enough to understand that he was going for help. She began to breathe again, and struggling into a sitting position, turned two electrifying eyes on him and began to curse.

'Beelzebub and the pit,' she said. 'You God-almighty bloody fool, what were you doing there? You startled him. He's never refused the gate before. God's teeth – I might have been killed! Is my horse OK? *Zut!* Don't just stand there, you stinking bastard – go and look for him. No – don't bother about me. *Sacré bleu*, you flaming idiot – I'm all right, I want to know if my horse is. Go and look! *Entrañas de Dios* – can't you hear? I'm OK, I tell you! Go and see to Ginger.'

Charles went. The horse had bolted a little way, stopped, and was now gently trotting back to the gate. He made no attempt to get away again when the boy caught his trailing halter and tied him to the gate.

The girl turned the fury of her oaths on to her steed, though the force had gone out of them. '*Ventre de biche*,' she yelled, turning to Charles again. 'Help me up, can't you? If you're not the village idiot, you must be his twin brother! Get me back on that horse so that I can go home. Oh, *madre de Dios*, spare me from any more fools.'

Charles gave her his hand, and she tried to stand up, but the effort only produced another string of curses in four separate languages, as far as he could judge; then to his dismay she sank down again, turned her head away and began to sob.

'Go and fetch your help, then,' she snuffled. 'I can't stand. I think my ankle's bust.'

'I'll take you home,' he said. 'But what about your horse? He's fine, but we can't leave him tied up here. Tell me what to do with him – or shall I see to you first?'

'If you just take his halter off, he'll go home,' she said. 'He knows the way. If you bring your car closer and help me to stand up. I can hop to it.' He untied the horse, secured its trailing halter, and slapped its rump.

He reversed the car as close as he dared to the girl and got out to walk towards her. She crawled to the car, but could put no weight on her left foot. She yelped with pain when she tried, and wiped her tear-stained face with a muddied hand, while a fresh string of multilingual curses flowed from one of the prettiest mouths Charles thought he had ever seen. They gave out at last, and she said, 'Well, here's a bloody how-d'yer-do!' in a much milder tone.

Emboldened, he said, 'Let me help you,' and wound an arm round her waist. The world lit up in psychedelic colours at contact with her. He hadn't been slow in the last year or two at trying out his luck with the girls he had met, though he had never ventured much farther than a shy kiss or two. Not that they hadn't encouraged him to take his exploration farther – but he hadn't wanted to. Well, not enough to rid himself of the echoes of his grandfather's gentle prohibitions about sex.

He and Robert and Nick talked of little else, when they were alone together. Robert was the boldest and most experienced of the three, and the one who had the most advanced and modern outlook on matters concerning sex. Nick was the romantic one, full of day-dreams that he didn't want tarnished till he found the right girl; he was the only one of the three to have read any books that could claim to be literature, and talked wisely about 'relationships'. Charles knew what was holding him up from 'going all the way', though he had never told the other two. It was the knowledge of how much it would hurt Grandad, if he ever found out. His grandfather's love for him was like a silken rein that guided and controlled without hurting. He had never yet resented the rein, nor been tempted to bolt.

But any other girl he had ever touched had been but a lump of putty compared to this jewel. Her face was covered with mud and blotched with tears, but he was already entranced by her eyes, which were still sending out red sparks from their velvet depths. Her hair had come loose from its tie, and was hanging thick on to her shoulders, so that she was shaking it back in fury like a red setter coming out of a pond. A strand of it brushed across his eyes and he was blinded. She had assaulted his ears so far with nothing but imprecations and curses yelled in a voice that might have belonged to Aunt Esther at her worst, but the thought of what the same voice might sound like in other circumstances made him dizzy. And the feel of her – she sent shock waves through him like a live electric wire. In that instant, the boy became a man. Every sense he had was now sharpened, and as he helped her into the passenger seat he caught such a heady scent of horse mixed with expensive perfume that his head swam. He was bemused, able only to rejoice that the first ever passenger in his car was found to be a gorgeous stranger whom chance had catapulted at his feet.

Her ankle was already swelling. 'Tell me where you live,' he said, 'and I'll take you home.'

She shook her head, and angrily wiped unbidden tears away. 'That's no good,' she said. 'There's nobody there. God rot the lot of them.'

'But,' Charles stammered, completely out of his depth, 'I mean – it's Boxing Day. Christmas. There must be somebody at home.'

'Well, that's all you know, *espèce d'imbécile*! There's only me.'

'All by yourself – at Christmas? I don't believe it.'

To his dismay, she began to cry again, no longer tears of anger, but real tears that slipped down her muddied cheek and filled him with an insane desire to lick them off.

'Dad's gone to see my brother and his simpering fool of a wife. I can't stand her, specially just now. So I wouldn't go. While Dad was out feeding his animals I sneaked out and made off on Ginger – that's why I didn't stop to saddle him up, though I usually ride bareback when I'm mad. I didn't care if I did kill myself, this morning, anyway. Christ al-bloody-mighty, my ankle doesn't half hurt!'

Charles closed the car door, and went round to get in beside her. He was not capable of clear thought, except that he hated to see her tears, which continued to flow unchecked. She was brushing them off with her sleeve. How many times had his mother read the riot act to him for refusing to use a handkerchief – but nobody but namby-pambies carried handkerchiefs these days, as he had told her. He wished he had one now, though, to offer his passenger. There wasn't even a bit of rag in the new car. He was helpless.

'Why are you crying?' he asked. 'Because your ankle hurts? Or about something else? I don't know where to take you till you tell me.'

'How would you feel if you came home for Christmas to find that your bloody mother had gone off with a dago and wasn't coming back? And that your father had known about it for months and hadn't told you?'

He couldn't answer because to him it was an impossible scenario. 'Look,' he said. 'Tell me who you are, and I'll introduce myself. We can't just sit here.'

'Charlie,' she said, her voice still muffled by tears.

A dull flush of hurt embarrassment crept over his face. Nobody had ever called him Charlie, except in derision as 'a proper Charlie' when he had done anything silly. How did she know his name? And in what sense was she using it? 'Nobody ever calls me Charlie,' he said. 'Specially my friends. My name's Charles.'

'Now you are being an idiot,' she said, though in a much less scornful tone. 'My name's Charlie – short for Charlotte. Charlotte Bellamy, from Castle Hill Farm.'

'Then where have you been till now? I've never seen you before.'

'At school, of course. Boarding school.'

'Where you learned to swear, I suppose,' he said, unbelieving. 'I can't even swear properly in English. My grandfather doesn't encourage it. He's a churchwarden. I'm Charles Bridgefoot.' He said it with pride.

'Hello, Charles Bridgefoot,' she said, and smiled.

Charles sank, drowning, in love. 'Hello, Charlie Bellamy,' he said, and to his own amazement heard himself say, 'May I kiss you?'

He was even more amazed at her reply. 'Yes please,' she said. 'I've been wanting somebody to kiss me better since I got home ten days ago. Dad did his best, but in the end I had to kiss him better instead. It's bloody hell about Mum.'

So Charles kissed her, gently and soothingly, and licked a tear away, not needing any instruction other than what instinct told him. When he let her go, he was able to think again. He was feeling protective.

'It's no use taking you to your home if there's nobody there,' he said, 'though I suppose we can get your father on the phone. You need a doctor, but it's only still early – and Boxing Day. Old Dr Henderson won't be up yet.'

His first plan had been to take her to Jane Hadley, but he

changed his mind. He had been against giving up his friend to a girl, but he was more afraid now of losing his damsel in distress to his friend's charms. Not that Nick would approve of her language, any more than Grandad would. He wondered if he dare warn her.

'I shall take you to my Grandad's house,' he said. 'We can phone from there. I must let Mum know where I am. She'll be having fits with worry already.'

'Lucky you,' she said, her face crumpling up afresh.

Charles put his arms round her, and kissed her again.

She smiled, and pushed him away. 'I like you,' she said. 'I'm sorry I swore at you.'

'I'll forgive you if you'll tell me how you learned all those ferocious-sounding oaths,' he said. 'Not at school, I know.'

'Well, not exactly. But we're very hot on languages, all the same. I do French and German and Spanish. It was all too much for me, until an Italian who works on my Dad's fen farm gave me a tip. He said he'd had to learn several languages to stay alive in the war, and it was always best to learn the swearwords first. So I did – from him. Then at school we formed a club to see who could find the most swears in all four languages. It does help – honestly. You never know when you may need them – like I did this morning.'

Charles laughed, still sitting looking at her in delight.

'God's guts!' she said. 'Aren't you ever going to get me to a doctor? Or at least somebody to bandage my bloody ankle up?'

'Yes,' he said, his mind made up. 'At your service, Miss Bellamy.'

Five minutes later, he was driving up to the door of the Old Glebe. The family were all still at breakfast round the kitchen table. 'Sorry about this, Uncle Alex,' he said, 'but I've got somebody in my car who needs a doctor. Or maybe only a nurse, Aunt Lucy – I don't know which. I picked her up when she went over her horse's head, and her ankle's bust, I think.'

They were all outside before he'd finished, fussing over Charlie. She was carried away to the bathroom, and brought back clean, tidy, bandaged and demure, Alex having pronounced the injury only a bad sprain.

Molly insisted on giving them breakfast, and Charles ate his in a complete daze of pleasure and bewilderment. Charlie was conversing easily in voice, tone and the sort of English he associated only with people like Uncle Alex, Nick's mother and Mrs Catherwood. He caught Charlie's eye and wickedly mouthed 'God's teeth!' at her. She ignored him except for a bewitchingly mischievous smile that brought a dimple to the corner of her mouth. He had the most strange feeling that his heart was dissolving, like sugar in a cup of tea. Grandad was telling Charlie that he knew her father, and would ring him up to tell him where she was.

'But we're all going up to Marjorie's to dinner,' Molly said. 'Everybody except Rosy, that is. She can't because of Aunt Esther.'

Charlie said that if Charles would take her home, she'd be quite safe till her dad got there. Molly was saying that it wasn't fair on Rosemary, but they couldn't ask Jane Hadley to leave her son for two days together. Charles came down to earth, desperation giving him ideas. Let him go back and see Mrs Hadley, he suggested, and if she would look after Aunt Esther again, why couldn't he then go and collect the twins and Robert and take them down to Temperance Farm, so that all the young ones could spend their day together? He knew that his mother had plenty of food prepared.

'It would be such fun for us, Grandad,' he said. 'Especially for Robert. May we? Aunt Esther and Nick's mum will be there. And I'll promise to take care of Charlie, honestly. Tell Mr Bellamy to pick her up there.' He could hardly believe it when they all agreed.

When Bob called for his daughter in the evening, Jane led him into the sitting-room, where Charlie sat in the best chair with her foot on a cushion and Charles at her feet gently massaging her swollen ankle. There was a record-player on, very low, but none of the youngsters was really listening. Nick and Poppy had their heads together over a book, and Robert and Pansy sat twined around each other on a settee in the shadows. Charlie looked happier than he had seen her since he had had to break the news to her. He didn't want to break up the happy gathering, and felt a twinge of guilt when he picked up Charlie and carried her out. Such trustful, innocent happiness was a scarce commodity, to be valued for its own sake while it lasted. He wished he didn't know so well that it was also too good to be true.

35

Beth had been shocked at the sight of her father. He seemed to have aged ten years since breakfast time on Christmas Day. He was pale and drawn, and looked defeated, but he was no longer aloof. He made no reference to her having been at Benedict's all night, and she thought, with rising irritation, that his line was going to be that the incident was past and therefore over. Well, it might be so for him; it wasn't going to be so for her, because she wasn't going to give up an inch of the ground she had gained.

He told her nothing of his vigil in the cold church, and his spiritual victory that had left him half a man but an even more fervent crusader. He did, however, confess that he knew how badly he had been treating her. He apologized for making her a drudge and expecting her to accept the role without protest.

His contrition almost broke her resolution, but she held out. 'I don't mind being a drudge, as you put it, in the least, Daddy – if it will help you. I do mind not being allowed to make my own friends. Till now, my friends have always been your friends first. You've chosen them. If I wait for that now, I shall never have any, because you're so out of touch with the times. Those who rescued me yesterday when I was very near to giving up altogether are broadminded enough to accept people as they are. You want to make everybody go your way, Daddy. They won't! So where do we go from here? Do you want me to stop and keep your house for you, or would you rather I got out and found a job of some sort?'

He flushed with guilt. So she had picked up that he had

been finding her presence unwelcome? He sighed, and felt more contrite than ever. She wasn't an obstacle to the fulfilment of a dream now because the dream no longer existed. He was wide awake, and knew only too well who would be the loser if he lost Beth too.

It cost him a great effort to tell her that he had been afraid he might be slipping back into another breakdown, but he thought he had now come to terms with the cause of it. He asked her to stay.

She kissed him, and said how glad she was that he had voiced what had also been her fears for him. 'But Father, it's no good curing yourself by sending me into a breakdown, is it? If I stay and we go on as we are, it will have to be on one or two new conditions. The main one is that I go where I like when I like. And I hope you won't make yourself ridiculous again like you did with Fran Catherwood and William. Think about me if you don't care how silly you make yourself look. I know how sincere you are – and so will they if you give them a chance. They'll honour you for it – if you'll let them.'

She smiled at the remembrance of the scene last night. 'So stick to your guns, Father – but don't go firing them as trigger-happy as you were with Commander Franks last night. He fired back. You won't frighten people like him or Fran Catherwood.' She got up and dropped another light kiss on his forehead.

'There, I've had my say, so now I'll get us some breakfast. I'm hungry. How long is it since you ate? It's a holiday, remember? I bought you a book you've been wanting for a Christmas present. Forget yesterday, and put your feet up by the fire, and have a good read. Even a crusader has to rest from his labours sometimes.'

He was still sore at heart, and smarting, but he was also relieved. He accepted the book with real pleasure and hugged her as he hadn't done since he had returned from his 'treatment'. She was thinking how old he looked; he was thinking that she looked ten years younger than she had done yesterday morning. They ate their breakfast amicably together, and she was glad that he asked her no questions. When she had made sure that he was comfortable by the fire, she gave him William's note. For the first time for several weeks, it led his mind away from the state of his own soul or his task of saving civilization from itself. He had no idea where the registers of St Saviour's were. He began to wonder how to start to find out.

Beth set about clearing up the ruins of yesterday and getting things back to normal. When she looked in at her father, he was fast asleep. She crept quietly out, rolled Elyot's dressing-gown into a large parcel and set off to return it.

The man who answered the doorbell was almost unrecognizable from the one who had roared at her father the night before. He was unshaven and haggard. His eyes were heavy with dark shadows beneath them, and unsmilingly weary. The moment he saw her, he fumbled with the open neck of his shirt, as if to somehow conjure up a tie round his neck. He was creased and rumpled, with only a threadbare pair of old carpet slippers on his feet. Her appearance on his doorstep was so obviously unwelcome to him that if he had hit her it would not have caused her much more of a shock.

She had prepared her speech in advance, feeling that the embarrassment would all be on her side. 'I just came to thank you for being so kind to me last night, and to return your dressing-gown.' she said. She pushed the parcel into his hands, and turned to go. 'I do beg your pardon for disturbing you. I should have rung to see if it was convenient. I'm sorry.'

He took the parcel from her, attempting to pull himself together.

'Miss Marriner! Won't you come in? For one thing, my telephone's ringing. Don't go before I have answered it.'

She followed him into the room that had seemed so full of warmth and friendship last night. He had a telephone extension by the side of his armchair, and turned his back towards her while he picked it up. The fire was out, and an empty whisky bottle and a whisky glass stood on the occasional table by his chair arm. Beth was conscious of both shock and disappointment.

He listened for a moment, then said, 'Sorry, William. Black dog,' and put the telephone down. Disgust rose in her. Black dog? A naval euphemism for a lone drinking session? Her years in the slums had made her well acquainted with alcohol, but if there was anything that made her gorge rise in utter distaste it was the sight of 'a gentleman' who had had too much.

'That was William, asking me up to Benedict's for lunch. I'm afraid I'm in no mood for company.'

'Then I'll go away,' she said.

'No. Please don't. Not at least till you've given me the chance to apologize for my appearance and this shambles. I haven't been to bed.'

She was nearly as tall as he, holding herself erect and almost visibly withdrawing the hem of her garment – looking like a caricature of the vicar's maiden daughter that in reality she was. Her eyes, that had looked at him so pleadingly last night, now registered nothing but scorn.

'So I see,' she replied, looking pointedly at the empty bottle.

For some reason, that made him smile. 'Didn't I make it clear enough to you and your father last night that you were in no danger in my house? Then allow me to repeat it. I did have a couple of glasses of whisky last night – or at least in the early hours – to see if it would help me to sleep. It didn't. Please forgive me. I hope you are no worse for your exposure yesterday.'

Beth's mind was working at great speed. Black dog – Winston Churchill – mood of deep depression – sleepless night – no fire in the grate – Boxing day – no Thirzah Bates – no breakfast – not drunk – *ill*.

She pulled off her coat and headscarf, and threw them in a chair. 'Sit down,' she ordered. 'What you need first is some hot strong coffee. Where do you keep the rum?' She had found it before he had registered her intention, and disappeared kitchen-wards before his protest reached his lips.

He sat down because he didn't know what else to do. He knew now why he had had the worst night he had had since he had come to Old Swithinford. He remembered that when her father had appeared last night, she had looked up at him with eyes too much like the eyes that haunted him.

It was always the same; he was all right till something or other triggered the memory. He had begun to drown in it last night almost before the cars had drawn out of the yard and left him alone.

Beth was soon back with a tray of coffee and two cups. She had already poured his black, sweetened it heavily and laced it liberally with rum. 'Be careful. I've heated the cup,' she said. 'Drink it. Don't talk.'

He obeyed, grateful for the stimulant, but more than grateful for the company which was already beginning to chase the ghastly waking nightmare away.

When he set his cup down, she said, 'One good turn deserves another. Tit-for-tat quite literally, in this instance. Here's your dressing-gown. Go and have a bath while I clear up. Sorry, sir, but like Mr Maryk in *The Caine Mutiny*, I'm relieving you of your command until you are fit to resume it again. You can have me court-martialled at your leisure, but for the moment I am the captain of this ship. The bathroom, I believe, is upstairs.' She pointed, and he went.

He came down shaved, dressed and feeling incredibly shy. He found her on her knees before the grate, having swept and garnished the hearth before lighting a fire with the kindling Thirzah had left ready in the kitchen. Chairs had been straightened, cushions plumped up and all traces of alcohol removed.

'Now come and have your beakfast,' she ordered. 'In the kitchen – I didn't know but I guessed you usually breakfasted there.'

He sat and watched her deftly fry him a huge English breakfast of sausages, bacon, eggs and fried bread. When she had put a rack of toast before him, she went out to get her coat and headscarf. He jumped to his feet but she sat down again on a chair facing him. 'I won't go till you have finished eating,' she said, 'or you won't finish it. Then I'll go and let you take over. But may I ask one or two questions?'

'Of course.'

'I don't need telling that this is a relic of the war,' she said. 'I've seen too many of my father's nerve-shattered lame ducks not to recognize the symptoms. I'm asking no other questions – but please tell me, do you get these "black dog" moods very often?'

'I'm afraid so – quite often enough,' he replied.

'I'm truly sorry. And I want to apologize for my insinuation about the drink,' she said. 'We used to live in the East End slums. I know too much about drunkenness, and reacted stupidly. I ought to have known it would take more than a bottle of whisky to make a naval man the worse for wear. Forgive me.'

He held her eyes. '*I* forgive *you*?' he said. 'Miss Marriner – what an apt name you have – Miss Marriner, I am asha—' She was holding up an imperious hand and he stopped in mid-sentence.

'Beth,' she said.

He stood up, tall and straight, now overtopping her by an inch or more; she moved resolutely to the front door where she turned to give him her hand.

He bowed low over it, as if she might have been royalty on his quarter-deck.

'You may resume your command, Captain,' she said.

He let go of her hand, and saluted briskly. He caught the gleam of the twinkle in her beautiful eyes. 'What's amusing you so . . . Beth?' he asked.

'I was just thinking how much I should have loved to see you in your full dress uniform,' she said, and ran off, turning to wave at the gate.

She was free. She had proved it to herself. She had said and done whatever had come into her head without examining it through her father's eyes first; and she would not feel obliged to tell anybody where she had been this morning, nor what she had been doing, nor why she had done it. She had been her own woman, and would never again be simply an appendage to her father. It had been a painful process while it lasted, but at the age of thirty-three she had been born again.

36

Roland arrived at Benedict's before lunch the next day. As it was Sunday, it saved Fran the discomfort of having to prevaricate with Sophie. She said so to William.

'Why on earth should you have to worry about Sophie? Can't a man go to see his mother at Christmastime without causing comment?' It wasn't like William to be 'spiky' with her, and Fran took notice of the red flag that this rejoinder unfurled. On the subject of Roland and his predicament, she couldn't rely wholly on William's sympathy. He wasn't jealous, but it did irritate him that she should be caused worry and anxiety. All part of his devotion to her, of course, but it did nothing to ease the strain on her to have to watch her tongue with William. Well, 'A soft answer turneth away wrath,' she told herself.

'It isn't his visit,' she said. 'It's what's behind it. It's a case of us knowing either too much, or not enough.

'Thus conscience doth make cowards of us all.'

'We haven't long to wait,' he replied.

So over lunch, Fran asked Roland to put them into the picture a bit before Monica arrived. She told him that they had lit fires in the flat so that he and Monica could be completely private, but she would be less anxious if she knew a little more.

'I can't tell you much more till I know what Monica wants to see me about,' he answered. 'I seem to have got myself into no-man's-land between two lots of barbed wire. To put it bluntly, Monica won't have me as a lover unless I stay Sue's husband. She says she won't steal me from a friend. I can't make her see that she wouldn't be. According to her reasoning, if a former friend's dog found its way to you and wouldn't go away, you'd have to let it starve to death or be accused of stealing it. Sue doesn't want me, as far as I can see, except to keep me from Monica. I'm beginning to feel like a starving stray dog!'

'A plague on both their houses?' asked William.

'No, not really. I haven't quite got to that stage yet. I thought we had worked out a possible *modus vivendi*, but it seems we haven't. I haven't seen Monica since your birthday, Mum. I've told Sue about meeting her again, but not where she lives or that it's nearly next door to you. I don't want Sue tailing me here, for your sakes. Which she might – she's acting very queer. Her mother's worried, but they can't make her take medical advice any more than I could. What I'm dreading today is that guilt has got at Monica, and she's decided to give me the push. Going to tell me that after all she has decided to marry some American millionaire and clear off, – if only to end the present stalemate. God only knows what I shall do!'

William was making coffee. 'Your Great-grandfather Wagstaffe used to say, "Never run to meet trouble." You seem to have inherited your mother's ability to sprint towards it. What Monica does have to say may turn out to be exactly the reverse of your gloomy expectations.'

Fran was looking thoughtful. 'I think William may have a point,' she said. 'We've seen a lot of Monica in the last two days, and if ever a girl looked happy and contented, she does. I was the one feeling guilty because I thought I knew why, while her father was still in the dark. I would have said she was quite satisfied with your *modus vivendi*.'

'More likely that she's found another man to take my place. One who is free to marry her without any guilt.'

'Stop being such a moral coward,' William said, quite sharply for him. 'I agree with you, Fran, darling. If ever a woman looked happy, Monica does. Wait and see. She'll be here soon, and that's good. Benedict's has a guardian angel who's proved himself an adept at cutting barbed wire, so far. Give him a chance.'

'William's right, Roland. And you know we're on your side.'

Roland got up, and excused himself. A few minutes later they saw him striding up and down the garden, hands deep in his trouser pockets.

'Here's Monica,' William said. 'I'll go and meet her and send her to him out there. Then we'll make ourselves scarce in the sitting-room with the door shut. What happens from now on is between the two of them.'

'Really, William! My maternal instincts may be engaged but they haven't yet turned me into an interfering maudlin old fool, I hope! You needn't be afraid I shall put my big feet into anything. But I think somebody's going to get hurt, probably Roland. I just wonder why it should always have to be like this.'

'Perhaps, my darling, because it can make the ultimate outcome all the happier. That's what you used to tell me. Let's go and do the washing up. What you need is occupation.' He pulled her up from her chair.

'What I need is you to keep me sane,' she said. 'But Sophie got it right, I think, with one of her sayings the other day. When she was discussing Wendy she said, "Little children, headache. Grown-up children, heartache". I shall be glad when this afternoon's over.'

The afternoon was long and strained for Fran. She thought irritably that wherever you were these days and whichever way you turned your thoughts, you came up against some preoccupation with sex. Once upon a time it had never been mentioned – within the middle-class, at any rate.

It used to be what Shakespeare called 'the deed of darkness'. There was nothing hidden about it these days. It was on everybody's mind, if not on their tongues. She didn't suppose that human nature had ever altered much; it was fashions and attitudes that had changed, and not always for the better. The war had demolished the bad with the good, the good with the bad. Slums as well as palaces, palaces as well as slums. Replaced too quickly with ticky-tacky, that all looked just the same, morals as well as buildings.

She had had to fight her way through the ruins of Victorian prudery and had come out the other side happy. But she still thought that the modern obsession with sex must eventually do more harm than good. Hadn't Mary Budd held that opinion? Wasn't that what Archie Marriner preached? Didn't William half-agree with him? Didn't she herself believe that you shouldn't separate sex from love?

She couldn't keep her mind from those two in the other part of her house. Their difficulty seemed to be that they *wouldn't* separate sex from love, not that they did. Sue was anti-sex, for some reason, even with a husband like Roland. All three appeared to be too 'old-fashioned' to shake off other obligations, as most of their contemporaries were doing.

What she feared was that like any other animals caught in a trap, they would turn vicious and harm each other, or them-

288

selves. It cheered her a bit to look across to William and think that real Love took a lot of killing.

It was past six o'clock before Roland knocked hesitantly at the sitting-room door and came in. William took one look at him, and went to get drinks. Fran sat up on the edge of her chair, tense hands gripping the arms, while she tried to read her son's face. He was pale, a bit tousled, and Fran could have sworn she detected traces of tears on his face; but his eyes belied any signs of distress. They were brilliant, and in them shone a light that she could only interpret as triumph.

'Monica's gone home,' Roland said. 'She asked me to apologize to you that she couldn't face you tonight – partly because in spite of ourselves we broke a promise I'd made to you if you let us meet here. She's all in, anyway – and Mum, so am I. Row with Sue last night, long drive this morning – with snow over the Pennines, incidentally – and then seeing Monica this afternoon. Thanks, William, I need that.

'So if you'll let me, Mum, I'm going to bed. I've got to be in London by nine o'clock tomorrow morning. I can't tell you any more than that, mainly because I still don't know what's likely to happen. It's Monica who has to make some final decisions. But we have set a time limit – next Friday. New Year's Day.

'We thought it would only be fair that you two and Monica's father should know what the outcome is. So I am to invite you to supper with Monica at her house that evening. If you see her father before then, please say nothing about today. Whether I shall be there or not depends what decisions she comes to. I've got a lot of thinking to do, as well. If I don't go to bed now I shall collapse at your feet, so I'm going. Same room, Mum?'

He kissed her, shook hands with William, and went.

'Well, really!' said Fran indignantly. And for once William had nothing to add to what his expressive raised eyebrows were already saying.

37

Sophie never took more than the "Oly Days' off work if she could help it. She was back at work on Monday morning, full of questions about Roland's brief visit, comment on Fran's guests on Boxing Day and scraps of other people's Christmas doings. 'George Bridgefoot and them had a proper fam'ly party, like it should be,' she said. 'Even Lucy and that grand 'usband of 'ers come from London. And Brian Bridgefoot bought that boy of 'is a brand new car. Times is changed. When my Dad as died when he were gored by one o' old Bridgefoot's bulls were a little'un all 'e ever got a-Christmas mornin' were a orange. But there, farmers is got more money than they know 'ow to get rid of, now. It's to be 'oped young Charles don't kill 'isself in it like my Jelly did in 'is'n. I don't 'old with making boys think they're men afore they are. 'E's only twenty.'

'They all grow up quickly, now,' Fran said. 'It's a different world.'

More news trickled in via Sophie once Beryl Bean opened her shop again. Choppen's car hadn't been seen going up the lane past the shop, but Charles's new one had. 'Goin' to show off to 'is friend Nick, so Olive 'Opkins thought. 'Owever, 'alf a hower later they see Nick walking the other way and it turned out as Charles 'ad been up to Castle Hill. That Mr Bellamy left 'is gal all by 'erself a-Boxing Day, and she fell off 'er 'orse. Young Charles were the one who picked 'er up, took 'er to Lucy's 'usband to be seen to. So by that, so Olive 'Opkins told Ned, they reckoned he'd been up to see 'ow she was. She'd only sprained 'er ankle, though.'

This was the sort of gossip that kept everybody in touch. Sophie did not indulge in the other sort. Fran listened to please Sophie mainly, though she admitted to herself a sneaking enjoyment of it. It was a sort of communion wine. She had learned from Sophie today that Bob had had Charlie home for Christmas, although she had had the bad luck to sprain her ankle. She wanted to meet Bob's daughter. It would while away some of the restless, seemingly endless days till Friday if she could persuade William to walk up to Castle Hill with her.

Ned was working full time in Elyot Franks' garden with Bill Edgeley. Fran and Sophie agreed how much they missed Ned 'being about' at Benedict's. Sophie had met Ned on Monday, and he'd said he was worried because somebody had been in the garage at the Old Rectory over Christmas and shifted a lot of their things about. 'Mind you,' said the ever-truthful Sophie, 'Ned said as there weren't nothink missing. Only put back in the wrong places, like, so as they 'ad to waste time looking for 'em. I don't know whoever could ha' done such a thing.'

It must be true that you couldn't sneeze in a village without everybody knowing.

'I expect it was Commander Franks himself, looking for something,' Fran said. 'It is his garage, after all.'

Sophie sniffed, which she always did when she sensed that Fran had intended a slight rebuke. It usually meant that she still had what she would have called 'a crowner' of information left to deliver.

'Do, that must ha' been a-Christmas Day, then,' she said, ''cos 'e ain't been well since then. Thirz' don't goo up there Mondays. But when she went yist'day, she could see as he wasn't hisself. For one thing he hadn't been to bed. She asked 'im why 'e'd made his bed 'isself, and 'e told 'er 'e 'adn't, 'cos it hadn't been slept in it since she made it afore Christmas. So then Thirz' says as 'e couldn't have 'ad much to eat, neither, 'cos where was the dirty crocks? And 'e said as Miss Marriner must ha' done 'em. So by that Thirz' thought, like, as 'e was light-headed with whatever it was the matter with 'im. But when she went out to put the ashes in the dustbin, she found a hempty brandy bottle and a hempty whisky bottle as well as one that 'ad 'ad rum in it.' Sophie's voice dropped to a dramatic whisper as she came close. ''E were drunk! I doubt if Thirz'll goo to do for 'im no more, once 'e's got uvver this bout.'

Fran had difficulty hiding her amusement from Sophie. If ever Sophie had offered a sprat to catch a mackerel, the mention of Beth was the bait. However any bit of information had leaked, Fran could not even conjecture. Poor Elyot, to have his reputation besmirched for ever on the strength of three empty bottles!

The next thought sobered her, though. Better Elyot's reputation than Beth's. If he had mentioned Beth to Thirzah – and heaven only knew why he should have done – it would be accounted for by him being supposedly the worse for drink.

She repeated Sophie's story to William later the same day, and was surprised at his concern. He told her, knowing that now she would understand, about Elyot's 'black dog' moods and the cause of them.

'It must have been worse than usual, to stop him from going to bed for three nights,' he said. 'I'll bet that scene with Archie Marriner upset him. I ought to go and see him. Will you come?'

'Wiser not, I think. But I'll ring Beth and see if she'd like to come for a walk. She's probably suffering after-effects, too. Only I don't want to have to speak to her father.'

'I do, as it happens, so I'll ring,' he said. 'I'll ask Beth.'

They found Beth waiting for them at the end of Spotted Cow Lane, so Fran and she didn't wait for William.

Beth told Fran about her visit to take the dressing-gown back, and how she had found Elyot still sitting in his chair. (There was a germ of truth in Thirzah's tale. Fran said nothing to Beth, but she hoped that it might never reach Beryl Bean's ears.)

When William caught them up, they decided it was too late to go on to visit Bob Bellamy.

'Archie says there are no old registers,' William reported when they were home. 'The present ones only go back to 1878. A pity, though not unusual. He's a stickler for doing things by the book. Not at all keen on letting me peep under that stone, without proper permission from the rural dean and Old Uncle Tom Cobbleigh and all. I suggested he should come and watch Bob and me raise it just an inch or two, and put it back again. Tomorrow, if Bob's willing. I only want to make as sure as I can whether or not it's an altar slab, before I set up a proper bit of research.'

'I wish you joy of his company,' said Fran. 'He'll expect to find a couple making love – as they call it – underneath it. As Sophie would say, his beads are all threaded on one string.'

'He's not exactly your favourite man, is he?'

'No. But he won't put me off coming with you tomorrow. I want to see Bob and his daughter. And I don't want to be left by myself till Friday's over.'

William had rarely felt so helpless. He cursed Roland and Monica silently, his wish only to be able to shelter her from grief. In this matter of her son, all he could do was watch and hope. He could not bear that she should suffer.

She looked up, and knew what he was thinking; she smiled a loving, grateful smile at him, and he was comforted.

38

William had arranged by phone for Bob to meet them at the church the next afternoon. Fran and William walked up, the Rector promising to follow in his car. 'He probably has no more desire to be in my company than I in his,' she said. 'Besides, he could hardly afford to be seen out walking with notorious adulterers.'

'I wish you wouldn't say bitter things like that, Fran. It doesn't hurt him. It only hurts me.'

She was all instant contrition, which he knew was genuine; she asked herself why she had said it and knew the answer. She was being bitchy because she was so much on edge about Roland, Monica, Eric and the general outcome of tomorrow. Whatever happened, somebody was going to get hurt; probably all of them. But that was no excuse for her hurting William.

She stopped, and put her arms round him. 'Sorry,' she said.

He responded, at once, holding her tight, and kissing her. Neither had noticed Bob Bellamy leaning in his usual place on the churchyard wall. He had turned his back by the time they reached him. Fran went straight to him and called a cheery greeting. He replied, but his voice was flat, and his face was dark, without its usual shy welcoming smile.

'Sorry about that exhibition, Bob,' William said, coming up. 'We were just making it up after a few sharp words. We don't often do it in public.'

'You might just as well,' Bob said. 'You can't hide anything.'

'And neither can you,' said Fran. 'Something has upset you. Is it Charlie? We heard she had had an accident. Are you worried about her? Would you like me to go up and see her?'

'No, it ain't Charlie. Now she's got over the shock about her mother, she's as right as rain, though I can't make her promise she'll go back to school. She says she won't leave me – but that's only an excuse. It's young Bridgefoot she doesn't want to leave. He picked her up. You may depend his dad expects he's at work now, instead of sitting up here drooling over Charlie. I come out of the way, so as he could make sheep's eyes at her all he liked – and run straight into you two acting as if you were only eighteen. I wish I was either eighteen or eighty.'

'What's wrong?' asked Fran. 'What's happened?'

'Only something that happened this morning as I can't forget. Careful with my gun – it's loaded today. I'm waiting till that bu— till he comes over that rise and within range. Then I'll blow his bloody head off.'

Fran was horrified by the red blaze of fury in his eyes and the hatred in his twisted face. He really did look murderous. She was frightened.

'Bob,' she cried, 'don't look like that! Do you mean that man who insulted you once before? What's he done now? Stop being so silly! He isn't worth one of your cartridges. William, do something! Go and warn them. Stop them!' William had already seen the fury in Bellamy's glittering eyes, and thought Fran's advice wise. He began to run towards the top of the hill.

'Unload your gun Bob, please. Now, this minute, before it's too late! You can't – you mustn't – what *did* he do to make you behave like this? No, Bob, *no*! Don't – leave it where it is!'

Misreading his intention as he reached for the gun, Fran flung herself at him, winding her arms round him, putting herself between him and the gun. 'What are you going to do?'

He pushed his old hat back in a dazed fashion, the searing flame of temper suddenly burnt out. William was back again, having found nobody in sight. The surge of relief at seeing him set Fran trembling, but she did not unclasp her arms. Bob put both his round her, to keep her from falling.

'What am I going to do? Nothing that would upset you, my pretty,' he said. 'Here, William, come and take her away before I kiss her. I was only going to unload the gun.'

She went to William, still trembling and clinging, and watched Bob break the gun and put the cartridges in his pocket. Then she went back to him. Cuddling up beside him on the wall, she put her head on his shoulder. 'Thank you,' she said. William joined them, and they sat on the wall with Fran between them.

'It was a good job for him that you came when you did,' Bellamy said. 'I don't often lose my temper like that. I reckon you are about the only folk who could have stopped me killing him if he had come into my sights.'

'What had he done?'

He hesitated, then plunged in. 'Well – it ain't a very pretty story. It's another instalment of the same one. The shooting syndicate didn't cancel my membership, so I had notice they were coming. I didn't want to go, but I thought I ought to show up to tell them as had invited me that I appreciated it. But I wasn't going to shoot with him. So I went across early to the gamekeeper's cottage, right the other side of the wood, where they usually start from. If that chap hadn't been there, I should have stopped with 'em till they had their dockey, and then left to come up to meet you.

'While I stood talking, out comes the gamekeeper's little girl, Patty, with a cat in her arms. It was one of Winnie's last year's kittens as I give her, and it had growed into one of the prettiest cats I've ever seen in my life. She could do anything she liked with it – she told me as she dressed it in her dolls' clothes and wheeled in about in her dolls' pram.

'Anyway, all the others had turned up, so we went off

towards the edge of the wood and the gamekeeper was lining the beaters up and giving 'em orders, and Patty come along to watch the start, with the cat in her arms. I hung back, when I see him, and decided not to go after all. There was a fair amount o' bustle going on, and that cat got frightened and jumped out of Patty's arms. It run straight in front o' the beaters, and she'd started to run after it when that bugger' – he looked at Fran but this time there was no apology – 'that bugger took aim and fired and blowed her little cat to bits right in front of her eyes. Her father daren't do nothing, 'cos his job depended on it. She run to me and I tried to cover her eyes up and run off with her. The others just stood. They couldn't believe it.

'"We didn't want that bloody thing scaring the birds," he said.'

Bellamy had started to tremble, and his face under its tan looked almost blue. 'I'd left my gun behind when I decided not to go, or I should have killed him there and then,' he said. 'I carried Patty back to her mother, but I don't reckon she'll ever get over it properly. She'll never be able to forget. More shan't I.

'I went home to change – and there was my Charlie with young Bridgefoot mooning over her, looking so happy, and all my own cats purring round my feet . . . I just couldn't bear the sight of 'em. I picked my gun up and come up here to wait for him – only you got here first. I reckon you saved his life. And mine.'

There were tears on his face that he brushed off roughly. 'I shan't ever forget Patty's screams,' he said. 'And that little cat's head with its eyes still open laying there in front of her.'

'Here's the Rector,' William said, low-voiced. 'Stop here with Fran till I give you a call.' He left them.

It took no more than five minutes' careful examination to convince the Rector that the slab was an altar top. He was shown the hidden steps behind the pulpit that William and Bellamy had found for themselves, and heard all the theories William had formed about the disappearance of a village that had once centred around a fortified manor-house that now formed the basic structure of Castle Hill farmhouse.

'Are the plague years recorded in Old Swithinford's registers?' William asked. 'Is there any evidence that you know of? As soon as term starts, I'll begin on some research – but in my experience it's always a good idea to start from something you know. This place is fascinating because the church must have been rebuilt some time – anybody can see that.

'By the way, I want to ask permission to go up to examine the bells. I'm told there are six which can't be rung because of danger to the tower. May I organize an inspection – complete with authority and the best advice available? I'd arrange it through the University.'

Marriner was becoming intrigued, though somewhat agitated. He found William's enthusiasm catching. He agreed to take the steps necessary for it to be formally approved. Both agreed that nothing much could possibly be done until the Easter vacation.

'There remains the question of that altar slab,' William said. 'I can't work out any reason for it being put down where it is. I've asked Bob Bellamy to bring up some crow-bars. May we, with your permission, do a little bit of off-the-record investigation? All I want to do is to just lift it enough to see what's underneath. Perhaps Fran had better stay outside. Bob Bellamy says he gets no premonition of evil there. I'd like to try it today because he's already in a wrought-up state, and is likely to be more receptive than usual because of that, I think.'

'You puzzle me, William. Surely you can't believe in such primitive stuff? A trained academic historian?'

'That,' said William, 'is just what makes me give some credence to it. If a trained researcher starts with an absolutely fixed mind, all he's likely to do is to add to what's already known. He has a duty to examine any new leads, and accept any possibility until he can prove beyond all reasonable doubt and by every known method that it cannot be possible. Negative evidence only can't be final. What looks silly may lead you to a key bit of positive evidence. I try to keep an open mind on what I don't understand – but in the case of Bellamy's sixth sense or whatever you want to call it, I do have personal experience of two examples I can't refute.

'In this particular instance, I can range as freely as you will let me. I'm doing it only because it interests me, not because my future prospects depend on finding anything, let alone publishing a thesis on it. I can please myself, and Bob may be a great help. What we want now, though, is his physical strength, not his sixth sense. May I call him in?'

Bellamy was the one who applied all the common sense, giving reasons for everything he suggested to avoid breaking the slab. They needed to move it only an inch or two, so that if nothing interesting was revealed, they could simply slide it back into place. Under his practical guidance, the other two heaved and strained against the weight of stone until it moved.

Fran, watching from the door, saw them all three recoil, and a thrill of fear ran down her spine. Then Bellamy stepped forward and squatted down by the crack they had made, and sniffed.

'Smoke,' he said. 'Burnt timbers. And it's hollow underneath. Let's move the slab an inch or two more.'

Twenty minutes later, they knew they had solved one question. Through the gap they had made, William's torch showed them a set of four or five steps leading downwards, ending in a collapsed heap of rubble.

'It's the other end of the passage that starts in my cellar,' Bellamy said. 'And there's no doubt now about the fire. I reckon that poor little servant girl is somewhere down there as well, burned to death, like the old tale says. She wouldn't stand much chance, caught in the middle of a tunnel of fire.'

William was white with excitement. 'Archie,' he said pleadingly, 'will you agree that for the time being we keep this our secret, and not let anybody else in on it – especially the press? Just till I've had time to find if there is any written evidence anywhere?'

Bellamy was standing looking into the hole, his nose quivering like a pointer's.

'Can't see anything,' Bob said. 'Only rubble. But I told you I could smell fire,' Bob said.

'You said cooking,' William corrected him.

Bob grinned. 'Same thing, perhaps. Let's put the slab back.'

Archie Marriner was uneasy about any sort of concealment

and already regretting his silent acquiescence. It was his duty to report the find. William pointed out that he had done nothing more than move a slab. Marriner did not doubt his scholarly integrity, so they compromised. William would keep Archie informed of all the steps he took and of any progress made. He would not disturb the slab again, and would bow to the Rector's decision about the timing of any revelations. There was no other honourable course open to William. But he was disappointed, and knew that Archie was taking the wrong line. Duty was all very well – but William knew Bob wouldn't see the Rector's dilemma. The Rector was once again alienating instead of making friends with another of his parishioners.

Once outside, they began to disperse. Fran hugged Bellamy and said she'd be up to see Charlie before long.

'Take her home, William,' Bob said. 'Unless you want to swop her for my gun. I ain't got no use for it now.'

Fran breathed a sigh of relief, and smiled a brilliant smile that told Bob she had understood what he was telling her.

Marriner was out of his depth. He envied them all the warmth of their relationship and easy companionship, but he couldn't begin to understand it, especially Fran's part in it.

39

Friday came. Fran had never before been inside the old Monastery House. It was as beautiful as she had expected, and if she had not been so apprehensive, she would have loved to just sit and absorb its Elizabethan atmosphere. As it was, she was more concerned with people than with houses, however old and beautiful.

Eric Choppen was already seated by the fire in Monica's sitting-room when they were shown in, and, much to Fran's surprise, Jess and Greg arrived almost at once. She searched her mind for any reason why they should have been included in what she had understood was to be an intimate family gathering to thresh out a knotty personal problem. As far as she knew, she and William were the only ones who knew what it was all about.

Monica looked very much her usual self, pretty, purposeful and as chic as always, placidly playing the charming hostess, though Fran thought that perhaps her usual merry twinkle was a bit subdued. She was probably very nervous, in spite of her apparent *sang froid*.

They sat through the usual pre-supper drinks and a delicious light meal in Monica's equally pleasant dining-room in a spirit of cosy companionship that made Fran begin to wonder if she had completely misunderstood Roland. To all intents and purposes, this could have been merely the last of the round of get-togethers to mark the Christmas season. Roland was not in evidence, which made Fran even more uneasy.

She knew, though, that she had not misunderstood. The scene was being set for a drama to be enacted before the evening was over. Left by herself for a few minutes while they rearranged themselves again in the sitting-room after supper, she went into her overdrive gear, able to act on one level and think on another at the same time.

Eric handed her coffee and a liqueur. Then he sat down beside her, stretched out his legs, and prepared to enjoy his glass of port. He had offered her the big chair nearest to the fire, but she said she preferred a more upright chair, and he didn't argue. He was relaxed, happy and comfortable. He made no attempt at small talk, seeming content to let the pleasure of the company flow over him. Fran was glad, because it gave her a chance to register undisturbed her thoughts about him and all the others.

She always felt some guilt, since they had got to know him, about the way they had at first misjudged Eric – though at the same time refusing to let go of her belief that he had asked for a lot of the opprobrium he had got. He had exhibited far too much disdain for his new rural neighbours, indicating that he held the inbuilt belief that all country people were inarticulate tom-noddies. Fran stole a glance at him sitting by her side and decided she was being unfair if she did not acknowledge his ability to admit that he was wrong, and adjust. Eric was rapidly adjusting.

Though it had never been confirmed, she thought William was probably correct in his guess that Eric was an ex-Commando. His manner when he had first come had borne that idea out. Then from Greg she had learned that just before his arrival, his personal life had been shattered. So in that period when he had seemed so hard, so blind and deaf to the feelings of others, he had been numbed by his own grief and the bleakness of life without his wife. Jess had revealed how much he had let himself be influenced by the one man among his new partners who was not typical of the village community. Altogether, he had got off to a bad start; but it took a real man with a strong character to admit his mistakes and not shrink from attempting to change his image. She realized how very much she liked him.

She had always liked his daughter. Monica was still dispensing coffee, with both William and Greg attendant upon her. An image of Roland rose before Fran, and a pang of regret caught her like a stitch in her side. If only he hadn't married that cold, beautiful aristocrat, how she would have welcomed that strong, independent, warm-hearted, merry-eyed girl as a daughter-in-law!

And why, she wondered, had her guardian angel let her down by allowing Roland to take the gilt off the gingerbread for her now?

She was philosophic enough to see that life could not be all sunshine – there had to be clouds and shadows as well; but her feelings about her son even William could not properly understand.

William was sharing some joke with Greg. Fran knew quite well that when the curtain went up and whatever the raising of it revealed, in spirit he would be by her side wherever he happened to be seated at that moment. She was the least 'alone' of any of them.

How much William had revised his estimate of Greg, too! She remembered asking him once what was worrying him, and he had replied 'Jess and that hopeless husband of hers', thereby creating for her a mental picture of a long-suffering woman tied to a completely worthless and unprincipled man. She had discovered for herself that Jess was by no means long-suffering, and that Greg's only drawback, if it could be classed as such, was that he was an artist with an artistic temperament. William and Greg were now good friends.

And what of Jess? Fran wished that she was able to categorize Jess as easily as she had been able to sum up the others, but she couldn't. As Sophie was always saying, 'Blood is thicker than water.' Jess was the nearest thing Fran had ever had to a sister, and in childhood they had loved each other. Nothing would, or could wipe that out.

She admired Jess. She admired the slim middle-age dignity of her cousin, and the wonderful bone-structure of her face that somehow reminded Fran of Queen Nefertiti; she admired Jess's business acumen and her capability – in plain language, the guts that had kept them going till Greg could find his own feet again. She loved Jess's brilliance of personality, when Jess was in the mood to show it . . . Yet there was still a reservation. She didn't feel safe with Jess. There was, as there always had been, a streak of possessive jealousy in Jess that made her dangerous in the same way that a playful kitten is, when it suddenly digs sharp claws and needle-pointed teeth into you for no apparent reason. Fran had felt both claws and teeth. Greg was as uxorious a husband as any Fran had ever met, but very often Jess's attitude towards him was more like that of an old hen with only one chick than an equally adoring wife.

Jess was seated directly opposite to Fran in the circle round the fire, watching her husband and her brother paying courteous attention to their hostess. Jess was laughing, yet she reminded Fran of a hungry feline tensed to spring. Her presence in the group tonight, under the circumstances, increased Fran's uneasiness.

'Has everybody got coffee?' Monica asked. 'And drinks? Do sit down, you two! No – I'll stay here, where I can see you all.'

William sat down beside Jess, but glanced across at Fran. His look said, 'This is it. I'm here if you need me.' Greg pulled up two chairs for himself and Monica, though she didn't sit down. Turning towards them she said, 'I'm so glad you could all be here together tonight, because I have some news for you.

For one thing, I'm going back to live in the flat again, at least for a little while. I'm sorry about that, Dad, just as you plan to come back to live here – but if all goes well I shall soon be back again. That depends to some extent on you. I'm afraid all sorts of things may have to be changed, and that's where you come in, Greg. I'm going to ask for more of your time than our present arrangement demands. But again, what happens now now depends to some extent on you. You see, I'm pregnant.'

Recalling that moment afterwards, Fran always thought that they must have resembled the people of Pompeii, petrified into immobility. Nobody moved. The shock, like lava, ran over them all.

William watched Fran, ready to spring to her side, but her only thought was for Eric. She had been expecting some sort of pronouncement, though this possibility had never crossed her mind. Eric had had no inkling that anything was likely to happen. She saw his left hand tighten round the stem of his glass, and the one that lay on the arm of his chair clench itself into a ball. Instinctively, fearing an outburst, she laid her own hand on it. The fist opened to take hers and cling to it. He shut his eyes, and the pressure of his fingers almost made her cry out with pain. Then he regained his composure. She squeezed the hand that still held hers, and felt the answering pressure. He did not want her to withdraw hers.

The first to move was Greg. He turned towards Monica, took her hand and pulled her down gently into her chair. His mobile face was showing the depth of his feelings, and his beautiful eyes were full of tears he made no attempt to hide. 'My dear girl!' he said, leaning over to kiss her. 'My dear girl!'

Fran digested Monica's words and their implications; William was willing her not to worry, and not to say anything. Her antennae went on working, more sensitive than ever because of the shock.

Greg's reaction was just what she would have expected of him. He never had inhibitions about showing his feelings in public. Over his shoulder Monica was looking towards her father.

Fran turned her head to watch for his response, and caught sight of Jess. The crouching cat had leapt. Jess's face was contorted with a grimace of pain and bitterness such as Fran had never seen there before, not even on the occasion of the terrible quarrel they had had about William.

'Good God!' she said to herself, feeling revulsion like a spasm of nausea. 'She thinks the child is Greg's! How can she?'

'Dad?' said Monica.

Fran's hand was crushed again, till he found his voice.

'I suggest another drink all round,' he said. 'Gregs would you oblige?'

Having thus adroitly got Greg to his feet, he heaved himself out of his chair and went over to take Greg's place by Monica's side. William lost no time in crossing over to take the chair by the side of Fran. With the tray of drinks dispensed in silence, Greg sat down by Jess's side; her icy face and bitter contempt froze his into an expression of incredulity and fear. She refused the hand he held out to her, and turned her back.

Eric sought and found his daughter's hand, and Fran saw her relax. Eric could not wear his heart on his sleeve as Greg did.

When he spoke, his voice was absolutely under control. 'We all appear to have survived the blast,' he said. 'If I heard what you said correctly, Monica, you propose to go away to hide your condition while you work things out. That means you intend to go through with it alone. I take it because the lover you told me about is already married. Right? And it depends on me what you do – whether you stay away, or ever show your face here again. Is that it? You don't want to disgrace me?'

She nodded. Though he dropped his voice, intending it for nobody's ears but those of his daughter, the room was so still that Fran heard every word.

'Do you think I would let my darling girl's baby and my Annette's grandchild be born anywhere but in my home? Stay with me, Monica. What do I care what folks think or say?'

Monica was crying now, quietly, wiping tears away as they slipped from her eyes. William had reached for Fran's hand and his touch was communicating his thoughts to her. Only Jess and Greg still sat apart, detached from each other as Fran had never seen them before.

Eric was aware of it, too. He had been about to raise his glass and ask for a toast to his first grandchild, but he thought better of it.

'You certainly made a very dramatic announcement,' he said smiling at Monica. 'And you'd obviously planned it carefully, so that your friends had the same chance to take it or leave it as you gave me. But you're not really being very fair to them. I already knew that there was a man in your life who wasn't free to marry you. You asked me then what action I would have taken if you had done what you wanted to, and had his child before you gave him up. I thought you had decided against it, and hoped you would get over him. You obviously couldn't do that. So you've seen him again. Does he know? You've been so frank and honest with us so far – is there any chance that you'll tell us a bit more? It may not matter to the others, but it does to me. There's no need to ask him for anything, my dearest, but I'd like to know what sort of a man is responsible for my first grandchild's existence.'

Fran opened her mouth, but William's hand warned her not to interfere. Eric was not asking for his own sake – he was asking it for Greg's. William's hand tightened on Fran's almost as strongly as Eric's had done a few minutes before. He had seen the door opening, and behind Monica's chair now stood a man, immaculate in well-cut lounge suit, with collar and tie; tall and broad with thick brown hair falling over the forehead of a strained but proud young face.

He placed a hand on Monica's head, and, holding his head high, said clearly, 'I am.'

Monica caught his hand and kissed it. He didn't move.

William let go, and Fran sprang to her feet. 'Eric, Jess, Greg,' she said, 'may I present my son Roland?'

40

The gathering broke up very soon afterwards. Greg and Jess were the first to take themselves off, Jess being perfectly sweet to everyone except Greg. Fran had other things than Jess's mood to think about, but she was irritated on Greg's behalf.

Jess had hurt him badly by showing him her suspicion, and he was not making his usual gallant efforts to placate her. Now she was punishing him for that. Fran was heartily glad to see the back of both of them, and be able to give her attention to the other three.

There was a lot of explanation to be done among the parents, and a lot for Monica and Roland to say to each other.

'Eric,' Fran said, 'I think William and I owe you an apology, though I hope you'll take our word for it that we are just as surprised as you about the baby. We've all been put through the mill a bit tonight, especially Monica and Roland. I suggest we leave them alone, and you come home with us. Then we can tell you as much as we know. Will you?'

He agreed without fuss, and kissed Monica goodnight as if nothing at all out of the way had happened. Roland hugged his mother and said, 'I'll be in my bed before it's daylight in the morning, I promise you. Don't worry on that score.'

Back at Benedict's, they filled in the background picture for Eric. 'They met here last Sunday,' Fran explained, 'but we were told nothing. Of course we know now why she had asked him to come. She had to tell him – which means that the baby must have been conceived the night of my birthday party. He wasn't in his bed when we went up, but we had no idea where he'd gone till he told us everything the next morning. Just as we've now told you.'

'Monica had told me about her lover,' Eric said. 'I'm afraid I tore her off a strip – told her that I didn't expect to control her doings but she was not to play any games in my backyard. Which she has since done quite literally, it seems. She said then that I needn't worry, because she never wanted any other man or any other man's children. She actually said she wished she hadn't taken any precautions when they had met for the last time.'

'She meant it,' Fran said. 'She didn't intend ever to see him again. He was nearly round the bend about it. They were both taken absolutely by surprise at meeting each other here, though she did know her lover was my son. That's why she has been so cool towards us – she felt she was cheating. I think that was the last straw that made her throw him over. She just couldn't cope with the load of guilt about cheating on all of us, poor child. But he went to her that night of my party and all either of them cared was that they were together again. We know the result. Eric, I must say you were splendid about it!'

'I'm glad I said what I did before I knew,' he said. 'I meant it – it wouldn't have made any difference whoever he'd been – but my God! What a blockbuster it was! That did nearly knock me over.' He looked at Fran as if he'd never seen her before. 'To think that he'll be your grandson as well as mine.'

'And mine,' said William. 'Let's drink to him.'

'Or her,' Fran said. 'It may be a girl.' They were all feeling the strain now, and glad to sit silent with their drinks, each pursuing their own thoughts.

'It's going to have a lot of repercussions when the news breaks,' Fran said at last. 'We've got to be prepared for a lot of talk. William and I are already black sheep, and there are still a lot of people willing to get a dig at you where they can. I can just hear Beryl Bean saying that what's bred in the bone will come out in the flesh, and Archie Marriner telling his congregation that they can't go near pitch without getting themselves defiled. Poor old Sophie will get the brunt of it if she stays with us in such a depraved house.

'It's all so – so *wrong*! I can't forget the look on both their faces tonight – it was like seeing something holy. But our new grandchild will still be labelled "base-born" by such as Thirzah Bates, and "the fruit of adultery" by Archie Marriner.'

'You're doing it again,' William said, going to her and seating himself at her feet as he so often did when they were alone. 'Running to meet trouble. I mean. Have you forgotten your guardian angel? No. I mean *our* guardian angel. Think what he'll do for young whatever-its-name-will-be. He's at work on it now, because if ever a baby will be welcomed into the world, it will be this one. There's already five of us drooling about him.'

'Six,' said Fran. 'Count Greg in.' William opened her hand and planted a kiss in her palm. They took no account of Eric's being there, which pleased him. He was remembering Annette, and trying not to show how it affected him. 'Not Jess as well?' he asked. Neither of the other two answered.

'Maybe I understand Jess better than either of you can,' Eric said. 'Don't be too hard on her. I don't know what it is or where, but there's a sore place inside her that just won't heal. If it's touched, she can't hide the pain. I've had one, too – but mine is gradually healing over, with time. Jess's doesn't seem to be. Maybe she needs some drastic surgery. She's helped to cure me, but I can't help her – for one thing because I don't know what caused the wound. I wish I could help, though if Greg can't, nobody can.' He looked straight at William. 'What was the matter with her tonight?'

'She's got a jealous streak in her,' William said. 'That's what Fran and I have had to contend with. She jumped to a wrong conclusion.'

'Yes, I thought so, too. Poor old Greg is far too attractive for his own safety, and Jess too possessive for her own good. She doesn't realize how lucky she is. You do, Fran. That's the quality that makes you shine in the dark.'

'Eric!' Fran exclaimed. 'That's one of the loveliest compliments anybody has ever paid me.'

(The ability to communicate without words, or without even looking at each other, was in action between her and William. Each knew what the other was thinking. 'No, not anybody. William's called me his lighthouse, many a time.' She sent him a message that told him she had not forgotten – but then, he was not 'just anybody'.

'She does give off a kind of light – fancy Eric being aware of it! Not his lighthouse, preventing him from being wrecked, but a tiny beacon guiding him through a very dark patch. Especially tonight. Keep it up, my darling.')

She put out her hand, and Eric took it. She was made to think clearly at that moment of something that was so instinctive to her that she had never before considered it – the importance of physical contact in everyday relationships. Just another of those precious things that had been so cheapened and prostituted lately. There were sexy 'clinches', and meaningless cheek-to-cheek pecks wherever you looked; political handshakes with forced smiles and a lot of filmstar posing. All visual sound and fury, signifying nothing.

But this warm handclasp was not a formality – any more

than the warm hug Greg often gave her, which spelt not only affection but trust; the reaching of her own hand over the table to Sophie when words were not enough; William's finger under her chin long before the words he wanted to say could be spoken; Roland's hand resting on Monica's head tonight. And if it meant so much — as it did to her — how could people do without it? How long was it since Eric had held anybody's hand for comfort and support, as he had clung to hers this evening? How long since Elyot Franks had experienced that kind of touch? Bob Bellamy was quite different. She had had no inhibitions whatsoever about bestowing kisses on him — but then he understood. That's why he had a squirrel in his pocket, a dog at his side, cats within reach. She kissed George Bridgefoot just as naturally. When the time came and she could kiss Eric Choppen, it would mean his wound had healed, even if there would always be a scar. She left her hand lying in his, as they returned again to the problems of the present and immediate future.

A conference between the respective parents, including William, and Roland and Monica was imperative.

'At my place, tomorrow afternoon,' Eric said. 'Nobody takes any notice of people dropping into a pub.'

They stood together in the lighted doorway to see Eric off. His thoughts were centred on getting himself back into Monastery House as soon as ever it was practicable. A home, even without a woman in it, was a step towards becoming human again.

Sophie arrived next morning before Roland was up, though she had seen his car in the forecourt. By the time she went home at lunchtime, he had won her heart.

'It ain't right,' she said to Fran on the quiet, 'for 'im as is the rightful heir to this when you are gone to live so far away as 'e can't only come 'ere now and again. And it's to be 'oped that wife of 'is will soon come if she's ever going to. It's time as we knowed, like, that the fam'ly ain't going to die out like so many others is doing. There was a time when such as 'er thought it was their duty to make sure a old fam'ly kept going.'

'It's uncanny,' Fran said to William as they watched her plodding homeward up the avenue that ran through 'the front cluss' of Benedict's. 'She's very nearly as much on the ball as Bob Bellamy is. She does it all the time, as if she picks things up out of the air.'

'No – she doesn't sense things. She just applies plain common sense and works things out,' William replied. 'But she's hit the nail on the head again this time. Illegitimate it may be, but Monica's baby means descent through the male line – and that's what people like Sophie understand. She'll probably convince herself that it's the will of 'Im Above. I think it would be wise to take her into the secret as soon as we're allowed to.'

'Darling,' Fran said. 'It *is* the will of "Im Above", isn't it?'

They heard what proposals the young couple had to put forward that afternoon. Roland explained his position *vis-à-vis* Sue. Neither he nor Monica were willing to do anything to worsen her condition, so there was no hope of legitimizing the baby. All the same, it would make it easier for everybody if Monica went back to the flat for the time being.

Eric suggested that he should take over the whole of Monastery House again as the Choppen family home, where either or both of his children would go to visit or stay as long as they liked. He hoped Monica would return there in time for the birth. He saw no reason why anyone else should know any details.

Fran said she knew village life better than to expect that such a secret could be kept long; but if that's what Monica and Roland wanted, she wouldn't argue. They would do their best to keep gossip to a minimum; but she and William would like to be allowed to tell Sophie the truth soon.

Monica said that since her dream was coming true she didn't care who knew and how much talk there was, as long as it didn't make things more difficult for Roland. He had to deal with Sue.

Then she went on to say that she had never felt more creative in her life than she did now, and ideas for designs were coming thick and fast. She had let the business slip just lately, so she had some leeway to make up, which she could do better from the flat. She thought it might be a good idea to offer Greg a small share in the business if he were willing to be 'the leg-man' when she could no longer risk long journeys or take the pressure of too much work – dealing with the retail trade and the shows and so on. He would be acting as her representative but in his own name, which was already connected with her designs. She would put the proposition to him, anyway.

It was over tea in Eric's suite that William tentatively raised another topic. They had been discussing names. 'We must have something to refer to it by,' Eric said. 'I object to my grandchild being reduced to "It".'

Monica giggled. 'I asked Roland that, last night,' she said. 'He'd been reading an old magazine while he waited in the kitchen to make his entrance, and answered "*Zinj anthropos*" at once. That's the name the archaeologists gave to the latest find of the earliest human skull in Africa. I'm afraid the baby has got a nick-name already. He's "Zinj" or "Zinjie" now.'

William was looking seriously thoughtful. 'Roland,' he said, 'have you given any thought as to the baby's surname? What name you will register it in? Choppen? O'Dell? Catherwood? Or what?'

Eric intervened. 'I wouldn't wish a name like Choppen on a dog,' he said. 'That's why Monica used her mother's name for her business. But Roland may want his son – his child – to bear his name. Can that be done? Or in a case like this, does the child have to take its mother's name?'

'You can call yourself anything you like,' William said, 'and with a little trouble you can make it legal. I know I'm the one who has no right whatsoever to have any say in this – but as it happens, I care. It's my fault that Fran is still legally Catherwood, but even if I had been able to change her name to mine she would still have had to be Frances Catherwood professionally, because she was that before I came back on the scene. The new member of our family hasn't got a name yet. Eric doesn't seem to mind it not being a Choppen; I'm sure he wouldn't mind it being O'Dell, because O'Dell hurts nobody. Catherwood does hurt me.

'Roland doesn't remember his father, though he may be

proud to bear his name – I don't know. If so, I'll say no more. But – Catherwood isn't native to Old Swithinford any more than Choppen or Burbage is. I'd rather not be reminded all the time of Roland's father's share in the baby. It struck me that a name which does belong to Old Swithinford in general and Benedict's in particular is Wagstaffe.

'If Monica were to have her name changed to Wagstaffe by deed poll while she is living in London, nobody here would be any the wiser; and little Zinj would have a legal right as well as a blood-line to the name.'

He got up suddenly and went to look out of the window. He had had no intention of interfering, nor of being so frank about his own feelings. He hoped he hadn't upset Fran or Roland. 'Forgive me, Roland,' he said over his shoulder. 'It really isn't any business of mine – it was something Sophie said recently that made me think about it. I'm sorry. Forget it.'

Fran couldn't trust herself to speak; Roland was holding Monica's hand, and looking at her for an answer. She nodded.

'William,' said Roland, 'would you care to have a look at my business card? He took one from his inner pocket, and handed it across to his mother, who got up and took it to where William still stood.

He looked down at it. 'Roland W. Catherwood, RIBA.'

'What do you think the "W" stands for? It is part of my name already. Zinjie has a perfect right to it, without me being disloyal to my father.'

William turned back to the table, and sat down again, somewhat overcome by the result of his outburst. He felt an explanation was due.

'Sophie was regretting the way old family names are dying out,' he said. 'She was mourning the passing of the Wagstaffe name with Grandfather's death, even though Fran is a Wagstaffe by blood.' He paused, thinking. 'Do you know, I'm not at all sure we haven't hit by chance on something that may be helpful?

'A lot of the inevitable talk when the news gets out will be toned down quite a bit by genuine interest and the speculation that there might one day be a Wagstaffe back at Benedict's again. People like Beryl Bean still have a sort of inherited interest in what goes on there – look at the talk after Fran's birthday party. It's part of village tradition, anyway, a human interest that doesn't die easily. A hundred years ago there wasn't much romance in the lives of people like the Wainwrights or the Benns, so they got it vicariously. The squire's philanderings and his choice in women, as well as the line his wife took towards them, put a bit of spice into their own lives, gave them something to talk and take sides about. The same sort of thrill as going to the cinema gave them later, between the wars.

'There's another thing, too – it will make Jess an ally rather than a danger. She's a Wagstaffe, as much as Fran is. How? Grandfather's first wife died soon after Fran's father was born; then he married my mother. She was a widow – my father had been killed on the Somme, before I was born. So though I have no Wagstaffe blood, I was brought up by and with the Wagstaffes, as often at Benedict's as Fran or Jess. I don't want the Wagstaffes to die out any more than Sophie does.'

The idea appeared to have taken root. When the talk became general again, William told them he was hoping for some sabbatical leave. 'One of the things I plan to do with it,' he said, 'is to trace the history of the Wagstaffes as far back as I can. I've been thinking of it for ages, but I shall have a good reason to spur me on, now. So take good care of young Wagstaffe, Monica. Come on, Fran. We must go home.'

It seemed a very hopeful note on which to start another new year.

THIS MAN AND THIS WOMAN

41

January was cold and dank, with no snow and no sun. The temperature stayed just above freezing, with a cold north-westerly wind that brought miserably cold rain but had hardly enough strength in it to move the low grey clouds.

'You'd 'ardly think as it was weather for folks to want to move 'ouse,' Sophie said, divesting herself of her wet coat on the morning that term started and William had already gone off to work before it was properly light. 'I daresay it ain't no news to you as Choppen is fed up with the 'otel and going back to live in Thack'ray's old 'ouse, seein' as you're so thick with 'im now.'

The weather seemed to be getting on top of Sophie as much as it was affecting everybody else's spirits. It was no time for Fran either to take offence at her tone, or to confide in her.

'Yes, I did know. He decided on it at Christmas, when he knew that his son was going to America and his daughter back to her London flat. It would have been silly to let that lovely old house get damp and unlived in. But he's hardly moving house! All he has to take are his clothes and his personal belongings. I think he's going to change its name again, back to Monastery House.'

The news mollified Sophie a little. 'It never were the Manor,' she said, scathingly. 'Calling it that were Jack Bartrum's doing. 'E liked to think it made 'im Lord o' the Manor, like. Cock o' the dung'ill, more like. You can't make a silk purse out of a sow's ear.'

Fran changed the subject. 'There's a letter from Mrs Rushlake. She's coming back to live in the Schoolhouse next Monday. I thought I'd suggest that she comes on Friday and stays here to be on hand when her things arrive. She isn't bringing much furniture, either. She's keeping Miss Budd's house much as it was.'

Sophie's spirits definitely moved up a notch or two. 'I'm glad to 'ear that,' she said. 'I were afraid as she'd hev a sale, and I should hev to see Miss's things all sold to strangers, very like, things as I remember from the time I was a child and used to be sent to the house for things as Miss had forgot. We used to think her 'ouse were so pretty, wi' carpets instead o' oilcloth on the floor, and suchlike. We only 'ad pegged rugs and bits as was throwed out from 'ere. Which bedroom shall I get ready for Mis' Rushlake? It's to be 'oped as that Jane 'Adley is kept the School'ouse well aired. I ought to ha' gone there meself, but there's a limit to what one pair o' 'ands can do.'

'I've got a key,' Fran said. 'If it stops raining, we'll go down together and see for ourselves. But I'm sure Mrs Hadley will have done whatever she's been paid for. Jess says she's good, and Mrs Brian Bridgefoot is very pleased with her.'

'It's just as well she 'as got something to be pleased about,' Sophie said. 'Don't, she'd ha' soon wanted looking after 'erself, from what I 'ear. What with heving to deal with Esther Palmer day in, day out, and worrying about young Charles night and day into the bargain. She all'us used to be so cheerful, but she's worrying 'erself to death now, by all accounts.'

This was news to Fran. She hadn't been face to face with Rosemary since the night of her birthday party. 'Really, Sophie? I'm sorry to hear that. What's the trouble? Why should she be worrying about young Charles? I thought it was Robert Fairey who was ill.'

Sophie didn't answer. She was wielding a broom ferociously to sweep out corners that had no speck of dust in them and keeping her head bent low so that Fran should not see her face. Fran knew the signs so well that Sophie might as well have hung out a sign saying 'No further bulletins will be issued'.

Fran understood that this was not Sophie's ordinary reluctance to passing on gossip that she could not substantiate, but quite the reverse. She was in the know about something that had not yet reached the distribution point of the DIY shop, and she wasn't going to be the one to get the blame for it leaking out. She had already said more than she intended. Fran knew quite well how Sophie came by titbits about the Bridgefoot family, Thirzah's husband Daniel being so constantly in and out of The Old Glebe. Very few things concerning George were kept secret from Daniel. Things that did matter were as safe with him as with the Bank of England, but he passed oddments of what he called 'women's talk' on to Thirzah, who told Sophie 'in confidence, like'.

Sophie stood up, having made up her mind. 'If I tell you,' she said, 'you'll hev to keep it to yourself. In my opinion it's all old Esther Palmer's doing. It's all very well to say you don't believe in curses and such, but once you get things like that in your 'ead, you can't get 'em out. There's a lot o' folks as still call 'er a witch.

'It appears that as soon ever she knowed she weren't gooin' back to the Pightle, she took again all the Bridgefoots, from George hisself down'ards, and said she'd lay a curse on 'em. Nobody took no notice of 'er, till Christmas. Seems Brian was set on buying that boy o' their'n a brand new car. His mother were ag'in it from the first, 'cos she was scared as 'e'd come to grief in it, like my Jelly did in his'n.

'She got 'erself so worked up as she begged 'er 'usband not to buy him it, and they had a real row about it. Brian bawled at Rosy till she run away crying, but that awk'ard old woman 'eard 'it, though she pretends to be deaf. She told 'em it was 'er curse on 'em was beginning to work. They was only falling out with each other yet, she said, but they'd soon find out what other troubles laid ahead of 'em. Then Rosemary told Brian as her aunt must mean Charles wouldn't be safe driving a new car. But Brian 'ad got 'is temper up, would hev 'is own way. They used to be such a 'appy couple, as never 'ad a cross word, till that old woman went to live with 'em. But say it I must – Brian Bridgefoot ain't the same man 'e were afore they made so much money. It's gone to 'is 'ead. Dan'el says 'e never used to goo ag'inst 'is father, but now 'e's as bad-tempered as a bear with a sore be'ind. If you was to ask me, I should say 'e's as worried about that there curse as any of 'em, only 'e won't be seen to take no notice of it, 'im going to the grammar school and all that.

'But that wicked old woman knows she's got Rosemary scared, and keeps 'arping on bad luck coming to Charles. "You're only got the one son," she says, "and you'll never hev no more now. Bad'll become of 'im 'cos o' that car. Like what 'appened to the young man Absolom in the Bible, whose father couldn't do enough for 'im and got paid out for it." Well, so Thirz' told me. Esther went on about it, reminding Rosemary of 'ow Absolom used to wear 'is 'air long just like they do now, and 'ow in the end 'e got 'ung in a tree by 'is own 'air.'

'Oh Sophie! Poor Rosemary. Is Miss Palmer really as nasty as that? Charles doesn't wear his hair long, does he?'

'No, but that don't make no difference. Molly Bridgefoot told Thirz' 'erself 'ow it is. Her aunt goes on at Rosy all the while, wearin' 'er down, like. Saying things as there ain't no answer to, like, "You'll wish you'd never 'ad that ill-got gain to fool away on your son like you 'ave done, same as King Solomon wished 'e 'adn't made such a fool o' 'is son. God don't pay 'is debts wi' money", she says. "God knows as them Bridgefoots never should ha' turned me out o' my 'ome. 'Vengeance is mine,' saith the Lord." Molly Bridgefoot says Rosemary looks like a ghost as is frit of its own shadder. She can't think o' nothink only about the curse falling on young Charles.'

Fran shivered. Whether Miss Palmer knew it or not, this was exactly how the modern sort of witchcraft worked – brainwashing and mindbending like the propaganda for Fascism or Communism or anti-Semitism. Ideas that were sown in other people's minds so often that some of them were bound to take root and then multiply, like mushroom spore that could make a green field white overnight, or as modern psychedelic drugs could make addicts see everything in different light. The danger was that such ideas put into Rosemary's head might become self-fulfilling.

Fran gave herself a mental shake. She was letting Sophie's chatter frighten her, and that was silly. She spoke briskly, trying to restore common sense. 'I shouldn't have expected Rosemary to be so silly,' she said. 'Charles has had the car a month now, and hasn't killed himself or anybody else in it.'

'No,' countered Sophie. 'But Brian and Rosemary are at logger'eads about it all the while, and even George and Molly and them are miserable. And then there's that gal o' Bellamy's.'

'What on earth has she got to do with it?'

Sophie gave her a sharp look, unbelieving. 'Lawks!' she said. 'Whatever are you been doing as you ain't 'eard about that? Everybody else 'as. But there, you ain't been like yourself for the last little while, else I should ha' told you. All'us shut up in your own room or mopin' about as if you was sickening for something. I was feared that you might be quarrelling with 'im about something, do I should ha' asked you what was the matter. And I thought seeing as you're so thick wi' Bellamy, you'd be sure to know all as there was to know.'

Fran had had no idea that she had let her anxiety about Roland show. And of course Bob had said that since Charles had picked Charlie up from her fall on Boxing Day, he had been going up to Castle Hill to see her. But what on earth was wrong in that? She said as much to Sophie, in a slightly sharper than usual tone.

'It's all part and parcel o' the same thing,' Sophie said. 'If 'e hadn't have had that car, he wouldn't ha' met her. Now 'e's gone crazy about 'er. Brian is so aggravated about it that him and Charles don't speak to each other no more.'

'Why? What's Brian got against her?'

'I told you as Brian's got swelled-'caded. She ain't good enough for 'im. 'E's got big ideas for 'is son. Set 'is 'eart on Charles marrying some big farmer's daughter, so's when the Bridgefoot land is put with the gal's, it'll make 'em into landowners, like, instead o' just farmers. They didn't find no fault with the gal 'erself – Molly said she talked like a lady and be'aved 'erself beautiful that day Charles took 'er for Lucy's 'usband to see to 'er ankle.

'But 'er father's only a tenant farmer as don't own no land. Tha's why Brian's puttin' 'isself about so much. 'E don't want young Charles to get tangled up with her. And Bellamy's a queer, shy sort o' man, as they don't know properly. Come up out o' the fen, so they say.

'Besides, wheer's 'er mother? Accordin' to Beryl Bean, she's gone off with a foreigner, and there's going to be a divorce. The Bridgefoots wouldn't want to be mixed up in no scandal like that.'

Fran was almost choked with anger. This malice stemming from that cantankerous old woman up at Temperance Farm was infecting everybody, even invading her own kitchen. She was furious with Sophie for retailing the story, and wanted to slap her down, like a king who killed the messenger that delivered bad news. How dare anybody turn on Bob Bellamy just because he was a fenman? It wasn't true, anyway, that he owned no land. He had a fen farm of his own – he had told her so. But she knew why he had been picked on; it was because he was suffering already, and therefore a ready-made victim for slanderous tongues. Could Sophie be right, that having made money had really changed Brian Bridgefoot so much? It was a side of him she had never seen – but then she wouldn't, would she? She and William were already in the social league he was trying to aspire to, if Sophie was right. She had thought such snobbery was dying if not dead. At the present moment it seemed to have a new lease of life.

She made up her mind that Brian would never be invited to Benedict's again, only to change it again immediately. She couldn't deny that she and William had always acknowledged that being Wagstaffes had made *noblesse oblige* in some ways obligatory to them, for instance, with Sophie. But she didn't act on her own privileged position, and had no intention of punishing Rosemary for Brian's *nouveau riche* nonsense. By Sophie's account she had enough to put up with already.

Sophie, reading Fran's face correctly, looked as if she might burst into tears. Both of them hated the very rare occasions when, as Sophie would have phrased it, 'they got off hooks with each other'.

'I'm sorry if I have been a bit glum just lately,' Fran said. 'I do feel sorry for Rosemary Bridgefoot, because I can sympathize. What's wrong with me is that I'm worried about my son, too. I'm afraid things may be coming to a head between him and his wife, and there's another woman involved now. So please don't be cross with me, Sophie. I'll tell you all about Roland another time. Not today, because we are both too upset already. Let's have a cup of tea, and then we'll go up to the Schoolhouse, shall we? I think the rain has stopped.'

42

Rosemary's distress was not all Aunt Esther's fault. It had begun with Cynthia Fairey's disclosure about the seriousness of Robert's illness. The awful knowledge in its own right weighed heavily on Rosemary, and she was under even greater constraint than Cynthia to keep it to herself. Cynthia had released a bit of her agonized tension by telling her friend. If she had been able to confide in Tom, Cynthia felt she could have borne it better but she knew him to be incapable of dissembling well enough to hide it from Robert. What she didn't realize was that she had loaded Rosemary not only with the secret, but with awful dread.

Rosemary, already unhappy with the way things were going at home, became a prey to foreboding. Like Cynthia, she had but one son. Why should Cynthia's son be taken from her, while her own was left? Charles might be the healthiest specimen of a young man in all East Anglia, but he was just as vulnerable to accident as anybody else. He was a Bridgefoot by birth – and Aunt Esther had cursed all Bridgefoots.

No. Of course she did not believe her aunt to be a witch, or to have any evil power! She was just a nasty old woman bent on making trouble. Rosemary told herself so ten times every day . . . but as soon as Charles was out of her sight the insidious, superstitious fear crept back. It centred itself on the car Brian intended to give Charles for Christmas, and there it stuck.

A year ago, she would have told Brian, who would have listened to her, laughed at her and told her she couldn't wrap a boy of nineteen up in cotton wool. This year, his temper was frayed beyond endurance by the presence in his house of an old woman he had never liked, who hated him, and who took vindictive pleasure in upsetting his domestic happiness.

Rosemary had told him many times how much under the thumb of her aunt she had spent her childhood and youth, but until now he had never understood how strong her domination over his wife really was. He put all Rosy's apprehension now down to her aunt's constant nagging, and set himself to counter it. He would let the old so-and-so know who was boss. She should not dictate to him, either directly or indirectly through Rosemary.

In her present state of apprehension, it only made things worse for Rosemary. Brian knew it, but persuaded himself that once Christmas was over and things had had time to settle down, they would get back to normal.

They didn't. All three blamed Aunt Esther, but Time was also having a hand in it. In his relentless fashion, Time had turned three boys into three men. Everybody knows that this change must come: parents wait for it, and then fail to notice when it happens.

Christmas had been the turning point. For the last few years, the main topic of conversation among the three boys when alone had been sex. Their approaches to it in the flesh had been as different as were their personalities.

Robert had the lusty vigour of a line of sturdy farmers inherited from one side and an even lustier line of village blacksmiths on the other. Both his grandfathers had had many a tumble in the hay long before they reached the age that Robert was now. Though he lacked their physique, the insidious disease from which he had been suffering in the last year had strengthened his biological urges, and he had boasted a good many times to his two less adventurous friends what it was like. That he had never yet quite 'made it' he kept to himself, hating having to admit it, though he didn't fool either of them. Girls might be more emancipated, but they were also more sophisticated than the village maidens his grandfathers had encountered, especially well-educated farmers' daughters with their eyes on the future and a good marriage.

Charles was not only more diffident in female company than Robert, he was also a good deal more inhibited. The only person who had talked straight to him about such things had been Grandad Bridgefoot, who though he had never once mentioned the word 'sex' to him, had left no doubt about his meaning. Charles had been led to understand that he was the only one left to carry on the Bridgefoot line, and the upright, honest name and reputation that went with it. George let Charles know that it was expected of him to keep the name that way, and not drag it through the mud of any scandal with a bit of a girl who only was after his money. Charles would have flown into a temper if his father had dared so to prohibit his doings or his choice of girlfriends, but Grandad was different. He wouldn't let Grandad down for any girl he had so far come across. Having no grandfathers, neither Robert nor Nick quite understood Charles's diffidence, and Robert teased him unmercifully for being so slow.

Nick was the youngest by almost a year, but in all-round maturity well ahead of the other two. His youthful longings were as painful for him as any other normal adolescent's, but he had grown up having to get used to waiting for, or even doing without things he wanted. He was capable both of thought and introspection. He knew that he lacked the material advantages of the others, so it was up to him to make his own way. His future prospects depended on his getting a place at a university. It would be a long hard slog before he could hope to match his friends in taking acquaintance with any girl beyond casual friendship. He was inhibited by his circumstances, and by his acquaintance with serious literature.

His constant reading had given him some vicarious experience with which to balance the biological urges of adolescence. He could not but wonder about his own origins, but his love and respect for his mother had prevented him from asking questions, even in the early days when he had gone home from school crying and smarting at the crude jibes of his nastier classmates. He had always been a reader, and through books he had explored a good many human relationships, and reached some conclusions. One was that there was no way he could risk any sexual experiment until he had achieved his goal of getting into a university. Whatever mistake it was that had been the cause of his mother's life of drudgery and his own life of deprivation, he was not going to repeat. There was more to love than capitulation to Mother Nature's commands.

Or so he had thought until Christmas Day, which caught him off guard against Poppy as they walked to see Robert.

Somehow the four had become two twos. Charles and

Pansy, acting like the healthy young animals they were, had started a bit of cousinly horseplay, chasing each other and throwing clods of earth at each other, tussling and scrapping as they had done since they had been toddlers. Nick and Poppy had fallen behind.

Nick had known the twins always. They had even been in the same form as he at school, until their parents had conformed to the prevailing fashion for farmers to spend their increasing wealth on having their daughters educated 'privately' at local independent schools. They were keeping up with the Jones's by giving themselves and their offspring this bit of cachet, though to be fair, many parents like Vic and Marjorie truly believed that they were only doing what was right by giving their children 'the best', and chances they had not had themselves.

The twins had left their school last July, having been turned into well-spoken young ladies whose only interest in life seemed to be horses. Nick had met them at intervals since, but they had not interested him. He did not like 'horsey' girls, because once the horse-bug bit them, they appeared incapable of talking about anything else whatsoever. He had been prepared to listen politely if Poppy insisted on telling him every detail about the proposed riding stables their father had promised to set up as a business for them this year. She began on the subject as they followed the other two.

'I shouldn't have left school but for that,' she said. 'I really wanted to stop on and do my A-levels. Pansy didn't want to, and wouldn't. It's the first time ever we've really wanted different things. We started pulling different ways last year. I liked school, but Pansy didn't. Dad wasn't prepared to fork out for a riding school for one of us, but he would for both. I couldn't let Pansy down, could I? I had to give in. I don't mind horses, but she hated school. I miss it. I should have been doing the same A-level English as you – *Twelfth Night* and *Sons and Lovers* and *Modern Poetry*.' She sounded so wistful that Nick stopped to take a look at her.

She wasn't just a dim-witted, horsey girl. She wasn't just the Poppy he had been eating Christmas dinner with an hour ago, either. She was pretty, with a head of short dark curls, a dimpled face, a straight little nose, a mouth that Nick suddenly wanted to kiss and eyes – what was it that poet had said? Something about eyes being so dark that they draw one trembling near.

Nick wondered with jealous trepidation what sort of an institution her school had been. All girls, thank goodness, and a boarding school too, so its pupils must have been under more supervision than those at his own co-ed day school, where the girls were competing not to be the last to wear the golli-wog brooch indicating that they had forfeited their virginity.

Too many of them wore it for it to be the truth, Robert had informed him – a lot of the girls sported badges who had never been offered the chance to earn the right to wear one. Poppy wasn't wearing one, anyway. Nick cheered up, and in a tumult of feeling such as he had never experienced before, continued to discuss literature with her till they reached Lane's End.

Within a week, six individual youngsters had formed three couples. Such is the power of Time. The advent of Charlie Bellamy into the life of Charles Bridgefoot had given the kaleidoscope yet another shake.

The identical twins had been difficult to tell apart, but now personality had begun to differentiate them. Their father was a somewhat stolid type without much sensitivity to commend him, other than his devotion to his wife and family. He was proud of having 'done well', giving the credit to nothing but himself. It pleased him to show his financial success to the neighbourhood. Pansy took after him. She made the most of her looks, her private education, her good seat on a good horse and her expensive riding gear. She took it for granted that when she was ready, there would be a suitor of the kind her father envisaged lined up for her. In the meantime, she liked having Robert at her feet, which he was.

Their mother was too much of a Bridgefoot to go along altogether with her husband's complacency, and without a twinge or two of the modesty he lacked; but she liked a quiet life, and let him call the tune. She had noticed that Pansy was growing up faster than Poppy, but it had not bothered her.

Pansy had been born first, and had been the bigger baby. She had always been more advanced than Poppy, except at school. As long as they were together, Marjorie didn't worry. Pansy led, and Poppy followed.

In the week after Christmas, Pansy suggested another visit to Lane's End, to see the 'new' used car Robert had been given for Christmas. They found Nick with Robert, but no Charles.

Robert took Pansy off in his car for a run, giving orders to Nick and Poppy to keep it dark that they had been left behind. They had no objection. They found a strawstack more or less sheltered from the gentle rain, where they sat down and talked. Nick held Poppy's hand, and she put her head on his shoulder. Nick regretted for the first time that by next week he would be back at school with his books.

Pansy returned flushed and excited. She knew that if she wanted to go on meeting Robert, she had to resort to subterfuge, with Poppy as cover – but that must not include Nick. She was playing with fire herself in meeting Robert, because although as another farmer's son he might be just about acceptable to her father for her to flirt with and cut her romantic teeth on, he was not what her father had in mind as a match for either of his daughters. Nick the Nobody was completely beyond the pale.

Pansy told her sister so, making it quite plain that Nick was as unacceptable to her as he would be to her father when he found out that Poppy was 'mooning about over a beggarwoman's bastard'.

Poppy had as much spirit, if not as much false pride as her sister. She retaliated. 'He won't find out, because there isn't anything to find out,' she said. 'You're the one who's got to look out. If it ever comes to that, I can spill a lot more beans than you can.'

The secrets they had always shared now became a sort of mutual blackmail. Only confidences whispered from bed to bed in the darkness registered the difference in the course of their first real 'love affairs'.

The weather was unkind. On the last day of his holidays, sitting under their sheltering strawstack, Nick told Poppy that he would not be seeing her again. She had expected it, and didn't argue; but she snuggled closer. His few kisses till then had been furtive, tentative schoolboy efforts; but when he saw the pain in the well-depths of her dark eyes, and felt her draw in her breath against his throat, he forgot he was only a school boy.

She fell back into the straw as he kissed her again, and he felt her yielding body clinging to his. Perhaps it was lucky for them both that at that very moment the gentle rain turned into a heavy downpour of cold slanting arrows.

Within seconds it had sought out their refuge and soddened the straw.

Laughing, perhaps even relieved, they sprang up and ran for cover. Neither of them needed telling that next time it might not rain.

'But we can still be friends, can't we?' she said, her mouth quivering, when they had reached the shelter of Robert's garage.

He nodded. 'We should have had to stop if your dad had found out. It would only have made it harder to bear, the longer we had gone on meeting. Besides, I shan't be here always, like Robert and Charles will. If I don't get a place in a university, I shall have to go away to get a job. There's my mother to be considered as well. She has only me to help her. You'll soon find somebody else. I shall have to try not to care.'

'I care,' she said, pointed chin held high.

Nick clenched his hands. 'So do I,' he said. 'I love you. Too much not to know that I have to stop seeing you.' They sat hand in hand till Pansy and Robert returned, and Poppy walked as far as the gate with him. The rain mingled with the tears on her face, but Nick did not look back. He went home to books that for the first time he had lost interest in.

Later that evening, he told his mother about Poppy, and what he had decided. Poppy told Pansy. Poppy cried quietly a lot of the night, but not so tragically as Jane Hadley did. Pansy had other things to think about. She had to find a way of seeing Robert without Poppy as chaperone.

Nick felt terribly empty. He was also lonely. A great gulf

was widening between him and his friends, Robert and Charles. Like Pansy, they had other things to think about. There was no help for him but to go on as he had done so many times before. He had learned to accept everything else, but this time it was not so easy. He felt ten years older than he had done before Christmas.

Charlie Bellamy was still nursing a painful ankle and a heavy heart. Charles went at least once every day to see her. He had been shy of meeting her father again, but Bob usually made himself scarce and left them alone together.

Charles was completely under her spell, as enchanted by her many-sided personality as by her beauty and her educated know-how. She was an exotic creature of many moods, as changeable as a chameleon; but whatever the colour of the mood he found her in, he loved her best like that.

Some days she would be hopping about dressed in ragged old jeans and a Sloppy Joe sweater, trying to make that extraordinary room clean and homelike. Then he, who had never done a chore for his mother without a great deal of fuss, took orders from her without protest and helped her till they were finished and could sit down together. On those practical days she treated him only as the mere acquaintance who had happened to be the one to come to her rescue. He did not take it as an insult; had he not also been the one to comfort her? Hadn't she let him kiss her?

The next day she would be thundering to meet him on Ginger, be-jeaned and riding bareback; or by contrast so point-device in jodhpurs and boots that she filled him with a terrible sense of inferiority, though he was proud to walk beside her holding on to her stirrup, mentally comparing her with Pansy and Poppy. They had been taught to ride; she had been schooled in horsemanship. When she alighted beside him and took off her riding hat, and her chestnut hair escaped its fastenings, his hand lifted itself involuntarily to stroke it. She swore at him, interlarding good old English curses with foreign ones, and commanded him to unsaddle Ginger while she went to change. That did not distress him, either; that was the Charlie he had first seen, and he had loved that one on the spot.

Ten minutes later, he barely recognized the girl wearing a soft green silk dress with hair caught in a slide on her crown, from where it cascaded down over her shoulders. She put her arms round his neck, and he was enmeshed. 'Kiss me,' she said. 'Why do I have to ask?' He needed no second invitation, but he dared not venture further.

He began to be able to distinguish her fiercely independent, angry moods from her alluringly feminine ones when she needed the comfort of his caresses. He took no liberties, knowing by instinct that what she wanted was just to be held and petted and stroked as if she were the dog which had its head on her knee, or the cats that clambered purring over them both.

Gradually she became less like a beautiful but lost and hurt wild creature, tamed by his presence and his love for her. He ventured to suggest that he should take her again to see his grandparents.

'Why not to your home?' she said, immediately on the defensive. He didn't know the answer; he only felt sure that for some reason it would be unwise.

He made Aunt Esther his excuse, and told the girl about her. He was rewarded by peals of bell-like laughter that made his heart ring with them. He had never heard her laugh like that before. Even Aunt Esther had her uses still.

He had put his grandparents in a dilemma, but they had been on his side. Thereafter, it had all happened much as Sophie had told Fran – though so far the troubles came only in single spies.

43

The weather worsened into continuous heavy rain. William left every morning in the dark, and it was dark again before he came home. Sophie arrived wet, and grimly declared that it would be February fill-dyke black this year, and no mistake. They regretted that the bad weather was stopping Ned and Bill Edgeley from getting on with the Commander's garden. The heavy rain and the dull skies prevented anything in the way of casual social intercourse. Fran always hated the first weeks of term when William had to be so much engrossed in his work; this year she needed him more than usual, because he was the only one with whom she could discuss the Roland-Monica-Sue-Zinj situation. She had begun to worry again, particularly on the grounds that they had all been foolish to go along with the idea of trying to keep Monica's pregnancy secret. It would have been so much better to let the bombshell explode and get it over with, she thought.

'They're hoping for some sort of miracle, I suppose,' she said to William. 'But as you once said, we're too old to believe in them.'

'Perhaps,' he replied. 'I did say so, I know – but our miracle happened all the same. Though I really don't see in this case what purpose secrecy can serve. Except that there may be a danger that it could be the last straw that will send Sue into a real nervous breakdown, and Roland is trying to prevent that. But pregnancy can't be hidden very long.'

'It's just feeling cut off from everybody that's getting me down,' Fran said. 'I hate having to keep secrets. And this weather is enough to drive *me* into a nervous breakdown.'

The awful weather was in fact acting like a lid on a can of seething worms. Things were happening in other places besides those connected with the Bridgefoots, but because of the weather, for once they had not become common knowledge overnight.

Eric Choppen, having moved into his son's half of Monastery Farm, had changed his mind about doing his work from the hotel, though he hoped Jess would split her time between him at Monastery Farm and the office he would still maintain for her in the hotel. It was necessary for somebody to be on the spot there, he said, at least till the sports centre including the golf course was completed and in action. As their main block of offices was already in what had been Michael Thackeray's house, and Jess lived in Lawrence Thackeray's new house only the other side of the old farmyard from it and from him, everybody could be on the spot most of the time. It was all more flexible and comfortable than anyone would have dared to hope or forecast in the days of its difficult beginnings.

Monica had wanted to see her father well settled into the farmhouse before she left him alone. He still wanted her to stay, to let him help her and share with her the preparations for the birth of his – and as he constantly reminded her, Annette's – first grandchild. But as she reminded him, Roland also had some interest in the baby, and if she were in London he could visit her and keep his eye on her while she kept her eye on her business. Until she left the farmhouse, she would be teaching Greg about those aspects of the business she proposed to hand over to him altogether in six months' time.

Fran had kept in touch with Monica by telephoning in the evenings when Sophie had gone home, but she had seen none of them. She couldn't go visiting casually, either to Monica or up to Castle Hill, in weather like this, without causing the comment they had been asked to avoid as long as possible; in any case, Anne Rushlake arrived at the end of the first week of William's term.

She and Anne had got to know each other reasonably well before Mary had died, but the rather long break since Anne left had caused them almost to have to start all over again. Fran remembered those afternoons spent one each side of Mary's bed with a queer mixture of pleasure and regret. She knew why she and Anne had not become close friends in that time; they had really only communicated through their mutual pleasure in Mary's peculiar brand of wise, witty, stringent, nostalgic, philosophic conversation. Their feelings for and about each other had been, as it were, strained through Mary's sieve. Now that had been removed and they were face to face.

Anne looked younger than Fran had remembered her. She was slightly the elder of the two, but showed no signs yet of middle age except that she wore spectacles for reading. She was fresh and vigorous and full of energy, much more so than Fran, who was forced to conclude that perhaps she had been too content for her own good, until this business of Roland had cropped up. She had got lazy.

Anne was quite a mine of energy in comparison, and could hardly wait to get at the Schoolhouse garden herself. While there was still a certain amount of reserve between them, by the time Anne was ready to go and live in her own house, Fran was rejoicing that there was a potential female friend in view.

She had invited Jess and Greg up to Benedict's on Sunday to renew their acquaintance with Anne. Fran was somewhat taken aback when Jess boldly suggested that she and Anne should talk business, in view of the very changed circumstances that now pertained to Mr Choppen's offices.

'My dear girl,' Greg had protested, 'let Anne get her breath back before you pounce on her to come and start work. She hasn't even moved into her house yet! Besides, she knows nothing of what has happened. Isn't it Fran's privilege to tell her when she's ready?'

'It's mine as well. My boss is involved as much as Fran is. While he stops at home fussing over Monica, the extra work falls on me, and if there's one more straw it will break this camel's back.' She wasn't looking at Greg, but Fran and William knew her too well not to see that she was really hitting out at him. While William was preparing to intervene, Jess added, 'Especially as my husband is also involved, away three days of every week now instead of being at home to help me. So I'm involved in it, too, willy-nilly. I'd like to know as soon as possible whether or not Anne wants the job somebody's soon got to do before I go under.'

William's voice was like oiled silk, which informed Fran that he was irritated to the point of anger, but keeping himself wholly under control.

'You're making it sound as if the whole affair is a conspiracy against you, and that you want Anne as an ally before anybody else sees her as reinforcement,' he said. 'It's still a family matter, mostly for Fran and Eric, but it won't be much longer. As Sophie would say, "Truth and murder will out".'

Fran knew that what William was doing was to chide Jess gently enough to stop her from using her whiplash tongue on Greg again. She supposed Jess would take the hint and let the matter drop, but she was wrong. Jess snapped back, 'So will pregnancy.'

Fran, Greg and William were stunned into silence by the tone of her voice. Jess turned on Anne the insinuating smile of a female Iago, forcing her to make some sort of rejoinder.

'This all sounds tantalizing,' Anne said, 'but I'm afraid I don't understand. I gather that the usual routine has been upset by somebody becoming pregnant – but that happens all the time. What has any of it to do with the possibility of me getting some work somewhere? I thought I had been offered some part-time work for Fran if and when she needed me. So what's all this about?'

Fran decided that the stage was hers, rather than Jess's, and briskly and succinctly explained the situation to Anne.

Jess, not to be outdone, also became very brisk and business-like.

William took the hint. 'Come on, Greg,' he said. 'Let's leave them to it, and go and have a nice quiet drink in my study.'

'Cowards,' said Fran, relieved into laughter. 'Like cock chaffinches. When the weather gets stormy, they vamoose and leave the hens to cope as well as they can.'

'Do they, honestly?' asked Anne, intrigued.

'Yes. Didn't you know? Then the females all flock together, and see each other through till mating time comes round again. I believe the cocks all make for the woods, but you can very often see a flock of hens in the garden. I counted twenty-two from that window one morning this winter.'

The change of topic had cleared the air. The two men went, and the three women left alone were much more at ease, 'chaffinching' together. As time went by, and the three spent more time enjoying each other's female company, they all referred to their talking sessions as 'chaffinching'.

Jess, having no Greg to cut at, became much more reasonable, and explained the situation she was in. The hotel and sports centre were taking off in a big way, and bookings for the future were coming in thick and fast. 'I just can't cope with it all, now,' she said, 'especially having to make important decisions because Eric isn't always on the spot to make them himself. I need a full-time second-in-command. Not just a bit of typing, but somebody who can answer letters about bookings, for instance, without reference to me or Eric, and take a bit of responsibility, and so on. Ideally, we need a linguist, but that's asking too much, I suppose. My French is passable, and Eric has a smattering of schoolboy German, but that's all we've got at the moment.'

'My languages are rusty,' said Anne, 'all except French which I have kept up. But I did German and Spanish at university. I dare say they'd soon come back.'

Jess was looking disbelieving. 'You're on,' she said. 'How soon can you start?'

'But I promised Fran—'

Fran cut in. 'All I need is a copy-typist. If you want a full-time job, take what Jess is offering you quick.'

'It would make me more financially independent than I've ever been since Stanley died,' Anne said. 'Would Mrs Hadley still do some of my housework for me?'

'She's suddenly very much in demand,' Jess said. 'Eric wants her more often when Monica goes. And I need her, too. I've got used to her. She's a rather strange character. Never speaks except to answer a question, never makes a comment, doesn't respond to any advances. We work on a strictly employer/employee basis. I started by calling her Jane, and asked her to call me Jess, but her face told me that I'd overstepped the mark. So Mrs Hadley she remains. You simply can't get anywhere near her.'

'I think she must have been very badly hurt, some time or other,' Fran said. 'I expect she's kept a strict guard on her tongue so as not to give anything away about herself. She's as well educated as any of us, and it's plain by her voice and diction that she wasn't born to be a charwoman.'

'She lives in one of the firm's cottages now,' Jess said. 'Surely she has enough sense to know which side her bread is buttered on?'

Fran was looking worried. 'You can't take her away from Rosemary Bridgefoot,' she said. 'Well, not just at present.'

'Why?' asked Jess, bluntly.

'Sorry, I can't tell you. But I assure you there is a good reason.'

'I must say I never believed Aunt Mary about a little

village being such a hotbed of intrigue and deadly secrets,' Anne said. 'It seems I was wrong.'

'Then it's a good thing you're learning quickly,' Fran said seriously. 'If anybody knew what village life really is, it was Mary. As Thomas Hardy said, it's like the pattern on a carpet — you can follow one colour or one design by itself, but sooner or later they all touch each other. Everybody knows everybody else, and most of their business too. Jane Hadley has achieved the impossible, keeping her past dark for so long. But I happen to know that if anybody really needs her just at present, it's Rosemary Bridgefoot. Take my word for it.'

'Business overrides such village affairs,' Jess said.

Fran spun round on her, hackles rising. 'I thought we had finished with that argument,' she said. 'Don't stir it all up again for no reason.'

'Eric Choppen doesn't belong to the village,' Jess said.

'No?' answered Fran. 'I'm willing to take a bet that this leopard can and will change his spots. May I make a suggestion about Jane Hadley? If I were you, Jess, I would talk to Eric about her. Persuade him to let her stay on permanently in that cottage on condition that she goes on to the firm's payroll, as it were. Make her job a five-day-week job, going wherever she's wanted most each day. I think it would work. It would give her a sense of security, and the flexibility of the conditions would probably suit everybody. She could still look after Aunt Esther when Rosemary needs her. I'm sure Eric would agree if you were to put it to him, Jess.'

'I think he'd probably listen to the lady of the manor better than to me,' Jess said. 'Especially now they are about to share a grandchild.'

'All right, I'll ask him,' said Fran serenely. 'Jess, do go and tell those two poor exiles they can come back again . . .'

Jess went. Anne caught Fran by the sleeve. She looked really worried. Fran knew she was disturbed by the sudden barbs there had been in Jess's voice. 'Take no notice of Jess,' she said. 'I've let her upset me for no reason many times before, but I think I understand her, now. There's an old country saying about people like her, that if they can't be first horse, they won't pull at all. She's always afraid that she may

337

not be first horse – especially where Greg is concerned. She doesn't like him agreeing to work with Monica. She's afraid now of my new relationship with her boss – because of this baby. She'll ask him, believe me. I shan't have to interfere. If only one knew *why* she had these sudden moods— Ssh! Here they come.'

44

The rain was nearly driving Beth Marriner to distraction. It was defeating her, taking from her all that she had gained by the trauma of Christmas Day. She had told herself then that she was free, that her father could never again dominate her life as he had done before; but the terrible weather meant that neither of them could escape each other's company for more than an hour at a time, and as the dark, dull days went by, both found themselves slipping back into old routines, old expectations of each other, old modes of address – everything, in fact, that Beth had thought she had got rid of for ever by her act of rebellion and despair.

Nevertheless, there was a difference, even if it did not show very much in their daily dealings with each other. The Rector had turned colder with an internal coldness that made him feel he would never be warm again. His vigil in the cold church on Christmas night had ended in a great victory of the spirit over the flesh. In tearing the image of Fran Catherwood out of his heart, he had seemingly destroyed the whole fabric of his physical needs. He was now only two-thirds of a human being, running on the two cylinders of mind and spirit. He had no interest in food, no pleasure in comfort, no desire for any company, Beth's least of all. He read most of the time heavy, scholarly books of philosophy, religion, Christian doctrine and psychology. His sermons, which always had been above the heads of his very rural congregation, now lacked even the warmth of his crusading spirit. The constant cold rain that kept him pinned in his home also prevented him from coming face to face with either the sinners or the righteous. His crusade was becoming an abstraction, lacking the warmth of life-blood as he did himself. He could but suppose that while it lasted, the rain was damping down the lusts of the flesh in everybody. Even his enemy was obscured by the rain and mist.

The one interest he had in mind other than his resolution to save civilization from its headlong rush over the Gadarene cliff of promiscuous sex concerned the one man he did not particularly want to meet yet – William.

He had been genuinely intrigued by William's theories about St Saviour's church, and had done what he could by writing and telephoning to find out what had happened to the registers. Nobody knew anything, not even George Bridgefoot. All he had been able to elicit from anybody was that it was about a hundred years since a crack had been noticed in the tower, and orders had been given that the bells should not be rung till it had been made safe. The restoration had proved too expensive, and had had to be abandoned. The crack had not worsened, so it had never been mended, but the bells had never been rung again. Sad as it was in itself, even Archie Marriner could not persuade himself that it was of very great significance to a church that had no worshippers other than a stray cat.

Beth had reacted in exactly the opposite way to her adventure at Christmas. She had almost forgotten the cause of her escapade because of the extraordinary and almost farcical way it had all ended. Imprisoned by the weather in the small cottage with her silent, morose father, mending or knitting or trying to keep her mind on her book, she went over every detail of it again and again in her mind. Once, her father had looked up from his perusal of *Confessions* of St Augustine – to ask her what she was laughing at. She had lied that it was a funny passage in her book, though in fact it had been the memory of herself being given a fireman's lift over the broad shoulder of Elyot Franks, with her bare feet clasped to his chest and her long plait hanging down his back.

Very different emotions were aroused by the thought of

him red-eyed from lack of sleep and punctiliously kissing her hand in farewell as she had left him the day she had returned his dressing gown. She had not seen him since.

From the side window of her home she could see the imposing front door of his; she often wondered what he was doing to while away these long days, when even Ned Merriman and Bill Edgeley were not near enough for him to speak to. Of course, he had a car, and was able to get out if he wanted, up to Benedict's, for instance, or to the Hotel; but she hadn't once seen the garage doors opened. What she had seen was Thirzah Bates, mackintoshed and sou'-westered, complete with Wellington boots that refused to go over her sturdy calves and were consequently turned back like seaboots, splashing through the puddles to go to 'do' for him one day. So he was being cared for after a fashion.

In spite of everything, her father included, the memory of all that had happened on Christmas Day kept her in optimistic mood. She knew she would be welcome at Benedict's whenever she chose to visit. Fran and William held the key to a bit of social life for her, providing she was able to nourish the little plant of friendship there before it died for want of attention. Time was still young, in spite of each of the rainy days seeming so long; the rain would stop, and the sun would shine again. Her cheerfulness on occasion seemed to be the last straw of irritation to her father, so that once when she found herself singing 'Messing About on the River' as she did the housework he had shouted at her to be quiet, or if she must sing at least to make it something worth her singing and him having to listen to. She sighed. There were times when the thing she longed for more than anything else was the piano that had had to be sold because there was no room for it this smaller dwelling.

On the fourth consecutive day of complete incarceration, it came to her that if Thirzah Bates could brave the elements in the course of duty, she could also brave them for the sake of her own health and sanity. She was a perfectly healthy young woman who would not melt in the rain, though she might very well become comatose if she didn't soon get a breath of fresh air or die of ennuie if she soon didn't see something else other than her father's head in profile half-hidden by a book. Rain or no rain, she was going out for a few minutes.

340

She was as tall and thin in her rainproof outfit as Thirzah was short and square. She rather hoped they didn't meet and have to stop even long enough to pass the time of day. The sight of them together would have made the cat laugh. As it happened, they did meet. Thirzah had obviously left The Old Rectory earlier than usual, since it was only just after eleven o'clock and they came face to face at the end of Spotted Cow Lane. Just as they met, a car with its windscreen-wipers barely able to deal with the downpour sloshed through a puddle and sprayed them both. Beth had a fleeting glimpse of Greg's laughing face at the wheel.

'Well!' said Beth. 'Wait till I see him again.'

'I doubt if 'e expected anybody in their right mind to be hout in this,' Thirzah replied. 'Only them as 'as to be, like. I might as well not 'ave bothered, meself. I 'ope as it ain't the 'flu as 'e's sickening for. 'E told me 'e didn't want nothink done, 'e only wanted to be let alone. Told me to go 'ome and leave 'im to 'isself.' She inclined her head sideways towards the Old Rectory, disgruntled, and a cascade of cold water ran from the brim of her sou'wester down the front of her ample bosom. 'Good-day,' she said shortly, and went, planting her booted feet wide of puddles right down the middle of the road.

Beth stood under the hedge in the rain, thinking, very undecided. She knew quite well what was the matter with Elyot Franks, and why he didn't want Thirzah's disruption of his solitude. If it had been an attack of physical illness, she told herself, she would not have hesitated to go and see if there was anything she could do for him; but dare she attempt to deal with a man of his temperament in one of his 'black-dog' moods?

Calling herself a moral coward for looking up and down the road to see if anybody was likely to see her, she crossed the road and rang the bell. There was no answer. She tried the door, and found it would open, so she went into the front porch, and divested herself of her wet things, even her shoes. Then she quietly opened the door into the sitting-room.

He was sitting in his chair, staring into the fire, hands clenched into fists lying on his chair-arms. She saw at once that he was fully dressed and newly shaven – no doubt because he had expected Thirzah. He turned his head at her entrance, but looked away again at once, without speaking. She had seen enough in that instant to know that he had not slept for a long time, and that he had shut his eyes as if to cut off the sight of her, while his face had crumpled into a grimace of what seemed like unendurable pain.

Beth stood still. She had met this kind of reception before, in slum dwellings where a child had died or a husband been sent to gaol, when she had gone as her father's representative to offer both practical help and comfort. It had often been very difficult, and she had sometimes stood her ground only because some sort of instinct had told her she was needed if not wanted. Never, though, had she dealt with the situation when the one needing help was her own equal socially, of the opposite sex and considerably her senior. Reason told her that in this case she must apologize, excuse herself at once, and leave. Nevertheless, her instinct pulled against reason.

'I beg your pardon, Elyot,' she said. 'I'm sorry I disturbed you. I'll go.'

'No,' he said, in a thick voice, without moving his head again. 'Don't.'

'Can I do anything for you?'

'Yes. Stay. But don't come where I can see you. Stay out of my sight.'

She thought he might as well have hit her; but he was used to being obeyed.

She had two choices – to sit somewhere behind him or to go to the opposite end of the big room and find a seat in the furthermost corner where the old, protruding porch would cut off his view of her. She chose the latter, wondering if whatever it was that had happened to him had so affected him that in these fits he was barely responsible for his actions. Why on earth should he not tell her to go, as he had told Thirzah? He needed another human near but not in his sight. Thirzah would not understand that. Her heart was wrung with pity, as it would be for a wounded animal or a winged bird.

She chose a chair, from which she could see his profile, turned slightly away from her. His eyes were still tightly closed.

'You haven't been sleeping much, have you?' she asked gently.

'Not at all,' he replied gruffly.

'I am going to take the telephone off the hook, and then sit down again here. If you are not asleep in half an hour, I shall creep out.'

He didn't answer. She turned to make herself more comfortable and prepared herself to wait silently.

Among her many gifts was that of remaining tranquil when she needed to. She neither moved nor made a sound, just sitting with her hands in her lap. After the first ten minutes, she noticed that there was less tension in him. She moved noiselessly to the piano stool, lifting the lid as she did so. Then, as if acting under some distant compulsion, she began softly to play. She could never recall afterwards what she had played, except that she had chosen simple, quiet, rhythmic, sleep-inducing melodies. Lullabies suited to a mature adult. There was no reaction at all from the figure in the chair when she began, except that his hands unclenched and with one he began to stroke the leather on the arm of the chair. When that hand stopped moving, she stopped playing. He was almost asleep, but not quite. The only thing breaking the stillness now was the ceaseless lashing of the relentless rain against the windows.

Her watch told her it was already past their normal lunchtime, and she began to fear a repeat of her father's performance when he was looking for her on Christmas Day. Her stockinged feet made no sound on the thick carpet as she moved like a cat from the piano, across the room till she stood behind his chair to see if he really was asleep. He had moved his head to a more comfortable position, his neck now being supported by the leather that had shaped itself to fit him years ago. He gave no sign that he knew she was there. His breathing was deep and regular, but twitching eyelids told her that his sleep was not deep enough for her to risk leaving. She placed her hands on the back of his chair, but he did not move. Still acting on impulse, she began to stroke his forehead, gently massaging his temples and the strained muscles under his eyes with her fingertips. Only when she saw his lower jaw unlock itself and drop did she steal out to go home.

As she crossed the road, she felt a glow of triumph. She had bent his will to her own, and *made* him sleep. She had not only quietened him, she had outfaced the black dog, and beaten that, too. She felt elated, happy to be needed if not wanted. Still battling against the cold rain buffeting her in wind-blown torrents, she paused at the cottage gate, warm and breathing hard. Her heart was banging against her ribs, and she gasped as she wondered how much that was due to exertion, and how much to the remembrance of that grizzled, furrowed brow as it had relaxed under her soothing hands.

'What bloody nonsense,' she said to herself, 'for him to be so alone and helpless, when there are friends at hand!'

If only her father would show that he needed her sometimes, and make her feel more like a woman and less like an automaton designed to play the church organ and distribute parish magazines, how much happier she would be.

She went inside, to face his cold, deliberately incurious silence. She would have preferred interrogation, as of old, and thought guiltily that in order to save herself, she had perhaps killed something in him. He had lost the common touch that had once made him so popular.

In spite of the rain, life went on. Beth did not risk going to The Old Rectory again and she did not expect Elyot to remember much of her visit. However, about three days later, she heard the clatter of the letter-box, and a car driving away. She picked up a rolled piece of paper which resolved itself into a water-colour sketch of herself and Thirzah talking in the rain. What a darling of a man Greg was – and how extraordinarily gifted. He was spending a lot of time these days with Monica, which was why his car went by the end of the lane so often. Beth knew that Monica's father was now living in the farmhouse with her, so there must have been other changes that she hadn't yet heard about. She didn't show her father the sketch, but pinned it over her bed. It seemed to her like a talisman.

By the end of January, everybody was aware that Anne Rushlake was working for Choppen, that Monastery Farm was now the nerve centre of his enterprises and that Jane Hadley worked full but flexible time charring for them all.

The wet and blustery weather still persisted, but the village began to come back to life in spite of it. Beryl Bean kept her eyes open, and what she didn't see she heard from Olive 'Opkins. They had to make do with very mundane bits of news.

Beth plucked up courage to go across to The Old Rectory one morning on her way to practise on the church organ, found Thirzah there, and hurriedly invented a fictitious message from her father as her excuse for calling. Elyot's eyes shot her a wicked little twinkle that almost made her blush, so aware of Thirzah's scrutiny was she.

'Miss Marriner,' he said, giving her the rather stiff inclination of his head that marked him out to Thirzah as 'a real gentleman'. 'Thank you so much for your kind inquiry about my health when Mrs Bates reported to you that I had a bad cold. She told me that she had passed you in the lane and that she told you I had sent her home. I am sorry I was not able to get up to answer the door to you.' Beth, thinking what a polished liar he was, was nearly undone by amusement.

Somebody must have seen her go to the door. She wondered if Thirzah had looked back and seen her cross the road. Well, if so, she wasn't getting much change out of Elyot. Beth did actually colour a little as she answered demurely that she had not minded in the least; she had called again today to deliver her father's message on her way for her daily practice on the church organ.

'I have to keep my hand in,' she said. 'We haven't a piano I can practise on at home, now.'

'My dear Miss Marriner! And I have one which nobody ever plays! I think Mrs Bates is finished in this room. I was just going to make myself some coffee – may I make you some, too? Then I have work to do in my study. Can I persuade you to take pity on a good piano which the tuner tells me must be played to keep it in good tone? I don't think it has been opened since it was put in here. Why not come and use it on the days that Mrs Bates is here, and do me a good turn?'

She was having much to-do to keep a straight face as she gracefully accepted. Thirzah understood her role perfectly. 'I shall be a-gooing in about half a hower,' she announced pointedly.

'I shall be busy. Miss Marriner can let herself out when she's ready,' he said.

'So by that,' Sophie told Fran, 'She goos in and out now as she likes when Thirz' is there. Thirz' says as 'e is a real gentleman, and never stops nowheer near while she's there playing. But there's times when she does stop after Thirz' goos. Thirz' don't think as she ought to, but I told Thirz' to mind 'er own business. 'Er father is a parson, I says, for one thing, and for another 'e's old enough to be 'er father. If you was to ask me, I should say as Thirz' misses hevin' me and Het to talk to. She never used to gossip like that, once.'

Fran replied that it wasn't gossip to report the truth, and what a sensible arrangement it was. She would have been delighted to know that as soon as Thirzah's back was turned, Elyot sneaked in to listen to Beth playing, and that often she went out of her way just to play for him, long after they had been left unchaperoned. Her visit on the black-dog day was never mentioned between them, and with Thirzah's help, the situation was accepted as 'a good thing for the church as 'e'd come round, like, a bit towards the Rector'. Poor topic as it was, it provided enough of a smoke screen, in these dull times, to obscure the growing tensions in the Bridgefoot family.

45

The Bridgefoot family was a close clan. Like every other family, they occasionally had internal squabbles, but in general they stuck to each other, and took their tone from George. Even at the time of Lucy's wedding, they had managed to hold together and be happy, in spite of having to override all George's misgivings. None of them would or could have believed that five months later the seams of their family unity would be giving way.

It was Brian who broke the first stitches. The month-long

rain was giving him a lot of anxiety about his crops, which his father didn't in any way seem to share. He said so to George.

'It's no use you throwing yourself about,' George had told him. 'As far as I know there's only one harvest as is never been got in, and that's this year's. And if it don't turn out quite so well as we've been used to for the last year or two, we shan't starve, shall we? We ain't done bad this last few years. Take the rough with the smooth, like us farmers have all us had to, my boy. Grumbling about the weather won't do a bit o' good.'

'If you'd listen to me, we could still do a lot better,' Brian retorted. 'We're behind the times compared to all the others. Look at Vic, look at Tom Fairey, look at Choppen's lot. We don't get nearly as much out of our land as they do!'

'Don't you start telling me how to farm,' said George, riled. 'It's still my land, for one thing. And for another, I want it to be in good heart when Charles and Charles's sons take it over. The way them others are going about it, they'll ruin their land for ever, sucking it dry for every ha'penny to put in the bank. Treat land fair and it'll treat you fair. But you young'uns today are never satisfied. While I'm above ground, I shall have things done my way.'

Brian's temper these days was on a very short fuse. 'You made me a partner,' he said, 'and that gives me a few rights as well. It's time you put your feet up and let me run the show, with Charles as a junior partner and you a sleeping one. We could do as well as the rest then.'

'Don't let's go into all that again. You've had your say, now, and I hope you feel better for it, but you know how I feel. There's never been a Bridgefoot yet that I know of who's give up before they planted him in the churchyard, and I ain't going to be the first. You want us to be gentleman farmers. I don't. I'd rather go back to where I started. I'm happy enough as I am. Your turn'll come – though it seems to me as nothing 'll ever satisfy you. You're like everybody else, now – wanting money for its own sake. You know what the Bible says about that. "The love of money is the root of all evil."'

'I didn't come to be preached at.'

'Then what did you come for? Out with it before Mother wakes up.'

Brian was afraid he had already upset his father by saying things he hadn't meant to. He did think his position between two other generations was not an easy one, but there was nothing he could do about that. His father could very well last another twenty years, and by that time Charles would be forty. He doubted if he would ever really be boss of the outfit, and it irked him that he couldn't be as up to date and mechanized as others with holdings smaller than theirs. But that was a built-in, long-term problem, not an urgent one.

Most of his present mood was the result of the prevailing uneasiness at Temperance Farm, where for so long he had enjoyed every comfort a married man who still loved his wife could want. But Rosemary had lately lost her 'go', her rosy contented bloom, and to some extent, her equable temper. She was always on edge, and Brian was irritated by the change in her, rather than worried. He put it down, of course, to the presence of Aunt Esther in the house, but he was wise enough not to say so to his father. He knew that George's conscience was anything but clear over the sale of the Pightle for cash that was surplus to any requirements, and wanted only to invest.

He had no such inhibitions where Rosemary was concerned.

'For God's sake, why doesn't the old bitch die!' he had yelled at his wife that morning after a more than usually acrimonious passage of wordy warfare with her. To his dismay, Rosemary crumpled into a tearful heap, sobbing incoherently. It surprised him that she should be so upset. He gave her a long, hard look, and saw her as something more than a bit of furniture for the first time for weeks.

She was pale, though until Christmas she had been as rosy as her name; she was haggard and thin where she had always before been plump and serene; and she looked old. He was considerably jolted.

She looked up at him. 'Oh Brian!' she wailed. 'Take that back! Don't wish death into the family! He might get the wrong one.'

What was she on about now? She knew quite well he hadn't meant it! As if he didn't have enough to deal with, without having to watch his tongue as well. If she was ill, why

348

didn't she tell him, and do something about it? He was aggrieved, but that was mainly because he also felt guilty. He left Rosy crying, and went up to the Old Glebe, only to find himself at loggerheads with his father.

George was smoking his pipe with his stockinged foot up on the kitchen table, making the most of an enforced idleness, and Molly was snoozing in her chair. Brian took a conciliatory tone. 'I wish I could put my feet up and not have to worry,' he said.

'What's the good of worrying? It'll stop raining all in God's good time,' said George. 'Why don't you go home and put your own feet up?'

'Because there's neither peace nor comfort there since that damned old woman moved in with us!' Having begun, he told his father his troubles.

Molly slept on, and George listened. 'I've seen how pale and tired Rosy's got,' he said, 'I thought things would be better when she got Mrs Hadley to give her a bit of help.'

'Made no difference,' Brian said. 'Rosy's so touchy you wouldn't believe it. Starts to cry if I raise my voice at the cat. I don't know what's come over her.'

George looked across to Molly to make sure she really was asleep. 'Ah! So that's it. Trouble between the two of you, is there? Are you sure it's all her fault? You're pretty touchy yourself. What's got between you? Is Rosemary against you wanting to set yourself up to be a new Lord Muck, like me and Mother are? I knowed there'd be trouble if we sold the Pightle. I never expected it to work, 'cos I've knowed Esther Palmer all my life. If you poke a stick into a wasps' nest you expect to get stung. Rosemary only agreed to it 'cos she thought you wanted the money. She's doing it all for you. Money's dangerous stuff, my boy. The more you have of it, the more dangerous it is – like dynamite. Anybody can see it ain't making any of you happy.'

George took his feet off the table, and laid down his pipe. He eyed his son lovingly, thinking of sticky patches in his own life before the upturn in their fortunes. When he spoke, it was as man to man, not father to son.

'If I were in your place this afternoon, I know what I

should do. I should go home, lock the door on that old witch, and take Rosy to bed. If there's anything wrong with our Rosy that you can't cure in bed, then it's time for us all to start to worry.'

Brian was startled, and a bit disturbed by his father's insight. He had been neglecting Rosemary lately. He'd been bad-tempered with her, always getting at her about her aunt. He hadn't even been nice to her when there was no reason not to be. She wasn't his cosy Rosy any longer. And his father had put his finger on to a tender spot. As far as he could remember, he hadn't attempted to make love to her since Christmas – or even before that. He couldn't remember the last time. He did remember that when he had looked at her as they had danced at Fran Catherwood's party, he had thought how pretty she was, and how he would tell her so once they were home and in bed. Instead, they had fallen into bed back to back in the early hours after rescuing that bloody old woman from the lavatory. The coolness between them had started from that night.

He didn't know how to go about putting it right now without having a scene with Rosy and making a fool of himself. He was touchy now about losing face with anybody, even his own wife.

What if she rejected his advances? Dare he risk following his father's advice? He wanted to do just that.

George had misinterpreted his silence. 'You haven't been fooling about with another woman, have you?' he asked. Brian was flabbergasted and affronted. Did his father really think that of him? Worse still, did Rosemary? Was that what was the matter with her? Well he could and would soon put that right!

His reaction had set George's mind at rest. 'You've still got a lot to learn, my boy. You take my advice. Don't you see that you are letting Old Esther do just what she wants? Show her she can't get between you and Rosy. Back Rosy up at every turn, and show her how much you still love her. Then perhaps she'll tell you what it is she's really worried about. It isn't young Charles, is it? Mothers often don't take kindly to their sons falling in love.'

'Neither do fathers, when it isn't the right girl,' Brian answered. 'I want a word with him myself about that. Where is he now? I sent him up to clear the big barn up. Is he there now, do you know?'

'I doubt it,' said George complacently. 'I reckon if you want to find him at this time on a wet day, you'd better go up to Castle Hill.'

The fire of anger that George's previous advice had damped down flared up again.

'I'll break the young fool's neck if I catch him,' he said.

'What, for being young and in love? Don't be daft! Didn't you do the same? Seems to me that I remember a time when you spent more time on Palmer's land than our own.'

'Things are different, now. He could take his pick of any girl in the county – like Sir Martin's daughter, who's heiress to the biggest holding in the district. I'm not going to let him throw himself away on the first bit of a girl he hasn't known all his life. I've got better plans for him than that.'

'What's wrong with her? She seems a nice enough girl to me.'

'What's right about her? She's nothing and nobody. Bellamy's only a fen-tiger tenant farmer, and her mother's a tart gone off with some foreigner, by all accounts. I shall have to put a stop to it.'

'You can try,' said George drily.

'She's a lovely girl,' said Molly suddenly from her chair. 'I couldn't wish for anybody nicer for him.'

'How on earth do you know?' Brian asked, wondering how long his mother had been awake. 'You've only seen her once, like I did, for about half an hour on Christmas Day.'

'Yes I have. She's been up here to tea with us three times already.'

Brian was incredulously infuriated. 'Do you mean you've been letting him bring her here behind my back?'

'Why not? It's our home and he's our grandson.' This was George, fearing Brian's tone would upset Molly. 'It's no credit to you that he had to bring her here instead of to you, if you ask me.'

'I'm not asking you! That's what's making me so mad. You didn't ask me, either, did you?'

'No,' said George, getting up and facing his irate son. Of

351

the two, he was the taller, and far the more imposing. His face had lost its normal look of contented benevolence, and he caught and held the other man's eyes with the gleam Brian hadn't seen there since he was a boy himself.

'No, I didn't ask you, Mr Bighead, but I'm going to tell you. There are some things in this life that you can't buy and you can't get by brag and bluster either. One of 'em's your own way as to who your children choose to fall in love with. As far as I can see, you've got nothing against this girl except that her father ain't good enough for you, and her mother's left him. I don't know anything at all about her mother, but I'm sorry for a girl who hasn't got one, or has got one like she has, if the tales are true. I don't know anything more than you do about Bob Bellamy – but I do know that a man who's good enough to be a friend of Fran Catherwood and William Burbage is good enough to be a friend of mine. I don't know the girl you've got your eye on as a daughter-in-law, either; but if her father's got a handle to his name as well as being a big landowner, I doubt if I ever shall. Even your son wouldn't be good enough for her. Would she be good enough for him is what would worry me. Would she soil her ladylike hands making him a meal? Bellamy's daughter would. Let me tell you what happened here last Sunday afternoon. Charles brought his girl to tea, looking every inch a lady and behaving like one – and when tea was over, she offered to wash-up, and your mother had enough sense to let her.

'Then I went out in the rain to have a look at one o'the ewes due to lamb early, and I could see she was going to need help. I come back to the house and told Charles to ring for the vet, and then come and help me as quick as he could with her. But when I got to the door, Charlie Bellamy was there before me in her boots and mackintosh. We got there only just in time. Between us, we'd saved triplets and the old ewe before Charles could reach the vet on the phone. That girl was as pleased as punch and I told her I could see it wasn't the first time she'd helped with lambing. Do you know what she said? "We're all mad about animals. My brother's got a degree in animal husbandry. I want to be a vet."

'If that ain't good enough for you, what is? She's good

enough for Charles, though. He's head over heels in love with her and will be all his life, I reckon, whoever he marries in the end. I'm afraid it won't be her. What has he got except himself to offer a girl with her guts and her looks and her brains? Who can speak three other languages already as well as you or me can speak our own?

'You don't know her yet. She's as proud as she's pretty, and in my opinion she's got a right to be. If she suspects you don't think she's good enough for you there'll be one of two outcomes. One is that you'll lose your son, who'll never forgive you if she throws him up over to please you. The other is that she'll settle it her own way, and make him man enough to decide for himself. I'd lay my life that the two of them are as innocent as a couple o' kittens, yet. But you stand in his way with your big ideas, and see what happens! You'll find yourself looking down the wrong end o' Bob Bellamy's double-barrelled gun, and me and Mother'll be putting a bit by for our first great-grandchild. You know very well how I feel about such things, and I don't want it to happen that way. But by God, if it did, I should be glad to know I had a proper man for a grandson, and not a stuck-up money-grubbing milksop running where his father tells him to go.'

He sat down suddenly, looking exhausted. Molly had never heard him make such a long speech before, and Brian was so shaken that he was glad to find a chair as well.

Molly looked from one to the other of them. 'Shall I make you both a cup of tea?' she asked, itching to do something to break the silence.

'No,' said George. 'You can make me one when Brian's gone.' He turned towards his son again, and said, 'Well. I've had my say. And now, no doubt, you'll go and do just as you think fit. All I want is for the boy to be well and happy.

'Don't keep Brian here drinking cups of tea, Mother. The sooner he gets back to Rosy and remembers what it is to be young, even if you have to do without handles to your name, the better. Charles is her son as well, after all.'

Brian left without another word. Molly put the kettle on, and made the tea. 'You ain't cross with me, are you, my old duck?' he asked her.

She shook her head. 'No, it was time somebody took him down a peg or two. I'm sorry it had to be you, but he'll get over it. I'm afraid we're in for a lot of trouble with the grandchildren for a while, though. They're at the awkward age.'

'Not all of 'em,' he said. 'Lucy's ain't. Don't you worry. Whatever happens, you've still got me. Give us a kiss.'

46

On one of the wettest days in mid-January, Vic Gifford announced to Marjorie at breakfast time that as he couldn't get on with anything else, he proposed to go and see his bank manager about setting up the riding stables for the twins. Pansy was still what her father called 'titivating' herself upstairs, but Poppy was at the table.

'Don't count me in, Dad,' she said. 'Do it for Pansy if you like, but I don't want anything to do with it.' She was calm and cool, though Marjorie knew that any obstacle to his decision would bring an outburst of anger from Vic. As with all other farmers, the weather was affecting his temper, and he didn't take kindly to interference with his plans in any case.

'What'd'you mean? Ain't that what you decided you wanted?'

'Not me,' said Poppy. 'It was Pansy who got round you to do what she wanted. I don't like horses all that much.'

'Well what do you think you're going to do? You'll do as I say, and go into it together. You can't sit around being a lady while Pansy does all the work. I won't have it.'

'You'll have to, if I won't join in. I want to go back to school.'

At this point Pansy came in, and there was a free-for-all row of gigantic proportions. Knowing she had her father's support, and consequently expected her mother's, Pansy threw herself about in a temper derived from all the same sources as

354

Vic's own. He was a bull-like man who was reasonably docile most of the time, but dangerous when aggravated. His mind didn't reach beyond the immediate present, except with regard to making more money and thereby gaining more prestige. Pansy 'took after him' in that respect.

'What the hell's got into her?' he asked Pansy, glaring at the subdued but still undefeated Poppy.

'I know why she wants to go back to school,' Pansy sneered angrily. 'It isn't what has got into her, it's to do with what she'd like to get into her.'

'What on earth is that supposed to mean?' Marjorie asked.

Poppy looked straight at Pansy. She mimed opening a tin, and then turning it upside down. There was an angry gleam in her eye and a set to her mouth that frightened Pansy. She was used to getting her own way, especially with Poppy. Both parents watched the pantomime in complete bewilderment, and were more than surprised when Pansy suddenly subsided into sulky silence, blushing furiously. It wasn't like her to give in. The two girls glared at each other, but it was Pansy who dropped her eyes first.

'Let her do as she likes,' she said, after looking at Poppy's stubborn face again. 'I'm not going back to bloody school for anybody or anything.'

The trouble with Vic was that when he did lose his temper, he was liable to revert to violence of some kind, though not against his womenfolk. Last time it had happened, one of Marjorie's most precious possessions, her grandmother's Crown Derby soup tureen, had been reduced to smithereens. She tried reason and a soft answer.

'Poppy's always loved school, Vic. You know she has. Why shouldn't she do what she wants as much as Pansy? They don't *have* to do the same as each other. What do you want to do, then, Poppy?'

Poppy looked gratefully at her mother. Two against two was different from three against one.

'I want to go back and finish my A-levels,' she said. 'If I do well enough, I should like to go on to university; if I don't I'll be a nurse or something. I don't want to spend my life messing about with horses.'

Vic slung himself outside to his more compatible surroundings of the farmyard. Pansy went back upstairs. Marjorie and Poppy stayed where they were.

'We don't know that they would have you back at school,' Marjorie said.

'If Laburnum Court couldn't take me back,' Poppy said, 'I think Swithinford Tech would have to. I've got eight O-levels. Then Dad could spend all the money on Pansy's riding school.'

'You'd better not suggest that!' her mother said. 'You know how proud he is to be able to send you to a private school.'

'Really, Mum,' said Poppy scathingly. 'You're as much of a snob as he is. I thought you knew better.' She got up and went to fight a pitched battle in their bedroom with Pansy. Marjorie heard them quarrelling, and wiped her tears away. It didn't happen often, and upset her when it did.

Vic decided he would go and talk to Brian about it. Brian had wanted Charles to go to a university and been aggravated when the boy wouldn't. He might have more idea what Poppy was talking about than he or Marjorie had. They had both left school at fourteen. They left the girls still quarrelling, and Marjorie, having decided that a talk with Rosemary might do her good, went over to Temperance with Vic. It was at times like these that the Bridgefoot clannishness came into its own.

Marjorie was shocked to find her sister-in-law so low in spirits, but poured out the story of the morning's row.

'It's Aunt Esther's curse on the whole Bridgefoot family,' Rosemary said. 'It's starting to work on you, now, as well. You are a Bridgefoot if Vic isn't. She's managed to spoil everything here. Charles and Brian don't speak to each other, and I can't do anything right for either of them. Now it's the twins' turn. They've got Bridgefoot blood, as much as Charles has.'

'What's the matter with Charles?'

'He's lost his head over that girl from Castle Hill Farm – Charlotte Bellamy. Brian thinks it's the end of the world.'

'You can't blame your aunt for that.'

'Oh yes I can! She's putting us all against each other. Looks as if that's what she's doing to you as well.'

'She can't do anything if we don't let her,' Marjorie said stoutly. She was very much her father's daughter. 'I mean, you expect 'em to fall in love when they're Charles's age.'

'And Pansy's and Poppy's,' Rosemary countered. 'Are you happy about Pansy seeing so much of Robert Fairey as she does?'

Marjorie opened her mouth, and shut it again. All sorts of bits of this morning's row suddenly fell into place. She knew exactly what sort of a mad bull that bit of information would turn Vic into, but she didn't question the truth of what Rosemary was suggesting. She had been blind because she hadn't tried to see, and Poppy had helped Pansy keep the wool over her eyes. Rosemary watched the revelation sink in, and was immediately apprehensive at her own foolishness in letting the information out.

'See? It's different when it's your own. It's all very well for other people's children to do as they like, but not your own. I remember when we had to tell Brian's dad about Lucy living with Alex before they were married, and he asked you what you'd do if the twins started sleeping round. You said you thought it was something you'd have to get used to. It looks as if the time's come. Or does it make any difference who it is they're sleeping with? Not that I'm suggesting anything like that about Pansy, only when everybody else does . . . Dad swears that Charles and his girl aren't, but Brian would believe anything because he's so mad with Charles for seeing so much of her. It isn't what they do, but who they do it with that seems to bother him. I don't believe it of Charles – I can't and I won't. And yet I've got enough sense to know that my son is no different from anybody else's, when it comes to the point. If he is at it like all the rest, I'm glad it's somebody like Charlie Bellamy, and not some frizzed-up kid from Swithinford.'

'I don't believe it of Pansy, either,' Marjorie said. 'Are you sure she's been seeing Robert Fairey a lot? I mean, he's not well enough to be out in this weather. And Poppy's always been with her.'

'Are you sure? They may start out together. And Robert's got a car.'

'So has Charles,' said Marjorie. Rosy didn't answer. That

car symbolized all her fears, and she had a twinge of guilt that she might have been disloyal to Cynthia Fairey. Vic called Marjorie and she left, a wiser if not quite so sanguine a mother as she had set out.

Rosemary, all her fears and worries renewed, was at her lowest point ever when Brian came in, and proceeded to put his father's advice into practice. He couldn't have chosen a better time, and he found it worked as well as George had predicted.

Marjorie kept all she had learned from Rosemary to herself, and wisely allowed the row to get well over before she broached the subject again to Vic. Brian had managed to make him see that a good education carried a lot of cachet these days, and Marjorie clinched the matter by saying that one never knew where it might get Poppy in the marriage market – look what had happened to Lucy.

Vic's argument was that it might be all very well for Poppy, but what about Pansy? What was she going to do? 'Let's wait and see,' Marjorie had said diplomatically. They told Poppy that they agreed she could go back to Laburnum Court if they had room for her. Poppy dug her heels in again. She didn't want to go back to boarding school; she wanted to get into Swithinford Tech. Made to give her reason, she gave one of two true ones. 'I don't want to be parted from Pansy any more than I need,' she said. 'I could come home at nights. We could still be together then. We should both be lonely without each other.'

'The day will have to come,' their mother said.

'Two years doing different things will give us a chance to get used to the idea,' Poppy answered, and so it was arranged.

Poppy went back to her A-levels. Pansy messed about at home for a couple of days, and then told her father outright that she wasn't going to be a prisoner just because Poppy wasn't about to go with her, and would go mad if she couldn't get out soon to see some of her old school friends. Could she sometimes borrow the car to visit them if they were too far off, or the weather too bad for her to ride?

Her school friends were the sort of girls to take Pansy into the right sort of society, so Vic agreed willingly, and Pansy set out almost every afternoon alone, rain or no rain.

Much refreshed by the rather sudden resumption of a loving husband's attention, Rosemary had cheered up. They avoided mentioning Charles as far as possible, and Brian found that to be on good terms with Rosy again was having a delightfully souring effect on Aunt Esther. She hadn't failed to notice that he had found an antidote to her poison. It was, to some extent, this small victory over her that eased his grudge against his son. The rain went on, though January had now given way to February.

Rosemary hadn't heard from Cynthia for some time. The passing of each day, let alone the end of each month, must be torture for Cynthia, Rosemary thought. She dreaded having to face her, but a friend who isn't a friend in need doesn't deserve the name. She rang Cynthia up, and told her that Temperance Farm in the rain with nobody about but Aunt Esther was driving her round the bend. Could she come up to Lane's End for a cup of tea, and if so, when?

She could tell at once by the flatness of Cynthia's voice that she was miserable, but there was no doubt about the welcome she got when she went. Cynthia was there alone, and they were soon sitting with tea beside them in front of a roaring fire in what Cynthia still called 'the parlour', because that's what it had been since the first Fairey had taken his bride there.

'Tom's gone into Swithinford to fetch a spare part for the tractor,' she said. 'I wish this rain would stop. Sometimes I think I just can't bear things another minute, and feel like drowning myself. Did you know the floods are out all over the fens? The rivers must be pretty high everywhere – honestly, Rosy, I can't take much more.'

'Robert?' asked Rosemary, sympathetically. Cynthia nodded, and tears ran into her tea. She pulled herself together.

'I wonder if I ought to take them some tea up?' she said, looking up as if she could see through the ceiling into the bedrooms above.

'Oh dear! Is Robert in bed again?' Rosy asked.

'Yes. Has been for nearly a week. I sometimes think Tom must have some inkling of how bad things are by now, but if he has he doesn't let on to me. As soon as Robert's a bit better, I'll try to smuggle him up to London to the specialist again, though I know he can't do anything. But I have to keep up the pretence to Robert himself. Sometimes I think he guesses. He gets low and miserable and lonely.'

Rosemary was unhappy. She knew Charles had found very little time for his friend since Christmas.

'Does he get visitors?' she asked. 'You said you wondered about taking tea to "them",' Rosy said. 'If Robert's in bed, who's with him? Nick?'

Cynthia lifted her tear-stained face to her friend. 'No, Pansy.'

Good. If Charles was deserting, he had a family stand-in. Rosemary smiled. 'It's a good job Beryl Bean didn't hear you say that,' she said. 'It sounded as if she might be in bed with him.'

Cynthia bit her lip, and shook away the tears. Then she looked Rosemary straight in the eye. 'I dare say she is,' she said. 'In bed with him, I mean.'

Rosemary blanched. Cynthia went on, her voice flat and expressionless, knowing that she was risking the friendship she valued by being as truthful as her upbringing and her schooling at the hands of Mary Budd had made her; but she could not, and would not, lie.

'About a week ago,' she said, 'the first day that Robert couldn't get up, Pansy came to the house and asked for him. Well, I knew they'd been meeting each other ever since Christmas, so I let her go up to sit with him. Then when I was making a cup of tea, I took some up for them, and pushed the door open with my elbow – they were too busy to have heard me coming. Making love. I wonder I didn't drop the tray – but I crept away and left them to it. I'm sure it wasn't the first time, and it certainly wasn't the last. She's been coming up almost every day since. So now you know.' She held her head high, and her chin was jutting forward as hard and firm as her father's anvil.

Rosemary was appalled, her mind racing. This wasn't Beryl-type gossip that might or might not be true. It was first-hand knowledge. And she was involved in it, right up to her neck, with all its ramifications. Pansy was one of the family, a Bridgefoot. Rosemary had good reason to love all her in-laws, who had made up in overflowing measure to her the sort of love she had never had as a child, George and Molly, especially. If George heard about this, it would be enough to give him a stroke. He would never be able to cope with it. And Vic – what wouldn't he do! Poor Marjorie! Need they ever know? Was it too late to prevent anything worse happening which couldn't be kept from them? She had been able to keep Cynthia's other secret, but would she be justified in keeping this one? She would have to warn Marjorie ... what other secret? *That Robert was dying.* She turned a strained, white face towards Cynthia, to be met by a pair of flushed cheeks and angry, defiant eyes.

'I can tell exactly what you're thinking,' Cynthia said. 'You're blaming me for not walking in on them and putting a stop to it there and then. Well, just you put yourself in my place! By next Christmas, Robert'll be dead and in his grave. I've kept that fact to myself, even from his father, so that while he is alive he can live as ordinary a life as possible. He may look like the Faireys, but he's more like my side in a lot of things. I know what most boys of his age in my family would want most. So do you. Do you think I didn't know what his car was most likely to be used for? Do you think I cared?

'Then when he started getting fond of Pansy, I stopped worrying about it. I didn't think the twins were that sort of girl, and they were usually about together, anyway.

'Then Poppy went back to school ... And I found Robert and Pansy at it ... in my house ...'

She turned away, and then swung back, eyes blazing. 'Do you think that I would have spoilt *that* for my dying son? It was too late to save Pansy's virginity, even if it was Robert who took it. But who knows that, besides the two of them? The Faireys are as strait-laced as the Bridgefoots are about such things, but that girl isn't all Bridgefoot any more than my Robert's all Fairey. It was six to one and half a dozen to the other, I dare say. The Giffords have always had a reputation for being that sort. If it had been your Charles with Bellamy's daughter, under the same circumstances, would you have given him away? You know you wouldn't! You're his mother!'

'But Cyn ... suppose she gets pregnant?'

'Do you think I haven't thought of that? Vic Gifford would hush it up and send Pansy off somewhere for a month. But sometimes I wish she would. It would save my Tom from the worst, when Robert goes, if there was another Fairey to carry the name on and inherit the land. I'd sacrifice her for that! And if that's wicked, I can't help it.'

'I don't know that it's wicked for you to think like that, but I do think it's unfair,' cried Rosemary. 'She's Marjorie's daughter as much as he's your son. Oughtn't I to warn Marjorie? I wish you hadn't told me.'

'What's the good of worrying her, now? It might have done some good before it was too late – but if they stop her from coming up or seeing Robert now, he'll just die all that much sooner. You can't do that to me and Tom, Rosy. You can't.'

'I can't decide, Cyn. I must think about it. But I'd better go now before Pansy sees me and knows I've been here.' She put her arms round her friend, and held her. 'I'll be here if or as soon as ever you want me,' she said, and went as quickly as she could.

As she drove home, it came to her that her best ally at the moment would be Charles. He would be likely to know more than any of her own generation. She found him in the kitchen taking off his boots and, fearful of losing her courage, tackled him straight away.

'Charles, did you know that Pansy was sleeping with Robert?'

A beetroot flush spread all over his fair skin, but after a pause he looked up and said, 'Yes. He told me. But how on earth did you find out?'

'His mother told me.' Anger rose in Rosemary. The young now were so unfair, to be so bloody selfish. 'And I suppose you are sleeping with Charlie Bellamy, and exchange confidences with Robert about her,' she said scathingly.

Charles finished drying his hands on the roller towel behind the door, and then came back and stood facing her.

'Take that back, Mum,' he said, 'or I walk out, and never come back. I don't care what you think about me, but you shan't say such things about Charlie. I love her. I intend to

362

marry her as soon as I can do as I like – if she'll have me. If not, I'll wait till she will. But she isn't that sort of girl.'

Rosemary knew he was telling the truth; she was pleased and proud of him, but that settled nothing of her present predicament. 'And Pansy is, I suppose?'

Charles was out of his depth, discussing sexual matters with his mother, but he could see she was not going to be put off.

'I don't know, Mum. But if she weren't my cousin, I should say yes, she is. She takes after Uncle Vic. Not Poppy, though – she's different.'

'Did Robert tell you that, as well?'

Charles writhed under his mother's disgusted scorn. He had to explain. 'No. He only told me about Pansy because – so that – because somebody is going to have to deal with her if he dies. She may need a lot of help.'

'Charles! What are you saying – about Robert dying, I mean. *He doesn't know how ill he is, does he?*'

'He's got a good idea. He asked that London doctor a lot of things he wasn't prepared to answer. Robert isn't daft, Mum. He drew his own conclusions. He doesn't think anybody else knows, though, except me.'

'His mother does, and she told me. Nobody else. She thinks he believes he's going to get better soon. He isn't.'

'I know. So you see why Pansy matters so much, don't you, Mum? He hasn't got any time to waste.'

'Oh, Charles! And I've been thinking you didn't care about anybody but yourself and Charlie Bellamy. I'm sorry. But I wish I didn't know about Pansy. I feel so bad about your Aunt Marjorie. What if Pansy gets pregnant?'

'She won't. She's on this new contraceptive pill.'

'She can't be! Doctors won't prescribe them except in medical cases.'

'Robert is a medical case.'

'Robert isn't taking them. You mean to tell me that their doctor . . . he'd want Uncle Vic's consent.'

'I know what I'm talking about, Mum. It wasn't their GP.'

'Charles, please tell me what you know, for God's sake. It will make it easier for me to keep their secret . . . I suppose you want me to?'

'I should want you to if I were in Robert's place.' He was begging her to stop the interrogation, but she couldn't, not now.

'Oh dear! Can't you see what a spot that puts me in? It's my friend and your friend or the Bridgefoot family. I've got to let one lot or the other down. Everything's suddenly gone wrong – like a plague among us. I can't bear to think what it would do to your Grandad Bridgefoot if he found out.'

Charles squared his shoulders, and pushed her gently down to a chair by the table. Then he sat down and faced her. 'Then don't think,' he said. 'Grandad knows already.'

She was robbed of speech, and even of the power of thought. 'Mum, if I tell you all I know, will you promise absolutely to keep it to yourself? Not tell even Dad? Or Robert's mother? On your honour?'

'Cross my heart,' she said.

'Well . . . when Robert told me, I felt awful, like you do now. Except that I'm only nineteen – I just couldn't deal with it by myself. So I went and told Grandad – out in the big barn one day. Just the two of us.'

'What happened?' she asked in a whisper.

'He's the only one who really treats me like a man. He said I had to stop worrying because I had been right to tell him, and it was his responsibility now, not mine. Then a few days afterwards he told me what he had done about it. You think nobody else knows – but I know, Grandad knows, and Mrs Catherwood knows. Grandad said he couldn't tell Granny, but he had to have advice. And it was no good going to the Rector, because he can't think straight about anything to do with sex. It wouldn't matter to him that Robert was dying. All he'd care about would be saving his soul from such a terrible sin.' The scorn in his voice hurt Rosemary. It was Robert alive that mattered to Charles.

'Grandad said Mrs Catherwood was wonderful. She simply said that if she had a doctor in the family, she'd know what to do. So Uncle Alex arranged it.'

Rosemary was limp with conflicting emotions. One of them was that she hardly knew this young man who was her son.

'Shall I make you a cup of tea, Mum? Don't let you-know-who see you crying. We're in this together with Grandad and Uncle Alex and Aunt Lucy – and Mum, I am glad you know. It's been awful.'

Yes, Rosemary thought, it was awful. Far worse than Charles yet realized. Poison spreading among the branches of their family and even down to the roots. Killing all trust between the different branches of the Bridgefoot tree, as that old witch, her aunt, intended.

'Try not to worry, now Grandad's in charge. He's not afraid to do anything for anybody he loves. He loves us all. I love him. I love Robert. I love you, Mum. I love Charlie. Will you let me bring her to see you?'

47

Fran had been very touched by George Bridgefoot's turning to her, and appalled by his confidences. She had the same immediate reaction as Rosemary had had – why Cynthia's son, and not her own? Monica had gone back to London, so she wasn't likely to see much of Roland, because whenever he was able to leave York, naturally he would want to spend his time with Monica. She was still uneasy about it all being kept so secret. The only person 'in the know' that she couldn't trust absolutely was Jess, but surely Jess wouldn't want to get on the wrong side of Choppen?

Fran detested deception or subterfuge, and thought that they were all silly to be playing silent donkey about it for no reason, because it would all have to come out into the open eventually. By contrast, she saw the need for everybody's silence about Robert and Pansy only too clearly. In bed on the night after George's visit, she poured his story out to William.

'Another bloody secret to keep,' she said. 'I can see why Cynthia wants to keep it from Tom, for Robert's sake; but

Robert knows anyway. It would be a lot kinder to Tom to give him some advance warning. Jess said pregnancy will "out" – but you can't hide death easily, either. It's terrible for them all. Especially poor old George. What a great character he is – the very model of what a real yeoman farmer used to be before the war. He's honest and upright in all his doings, like Kezia or Sophie, based on the commandments. Yet he'll go against all his principles for the sake of somebody else's son. He hates this modern sex among young folks, but he comes to tell me – of all people – about it, and lets his own granddaughter go on with it rather than add one iota more trouble to what Cynthia's already enduring. That's what I call Christianity. But where's the God he believes in? A God who could let such tragedy happen to people like Tom and Cynthia? How can they possibly bear it? Poor young Pansy!'

William held her, silently thinking.

' "There remain three things," ' he quoted. ' "Love, hope and charity . . . and the greatest of these is charity." Do you remember *The Railway Children*? When Perks's wife went to the parson to ask if the children's birthday gifts to Sid were "charity"? He told her that the true meaning of "charity" was loving-kindness. George Bridgefoot's just a living example of it.'

She nodded. That was it. William kissed her hair.

'And you wonder why he came to you? Like recognizes like, my darling. It wouldn't have been much good him turning to the present Rector, with a tale like that.'

'Do you know, he actually said so?' she answered. 'I had forgotten!' She shivered. 'Oh darling, I'm frightened. Hold me tight. It's as if the foundations of the village are being shaken. When is it going to be our turn? Our luck can't hold for ever.'

'Sh! You're forgetting our guardian angel,' he said. 'He won't desert us unless we give him good cause – like losing our faith in him. Don't you remember telling me once that we'd paid in advance for our happiness?'

He wrapped his arms tightly round her, and when she stopped trembling, he went on. 'Perhaps the foundations of the village are being shaken,' he said. 'But earthquakes don't only throw things down. Sometimes they bring old things up to light again. George Bridgefoot came to you, because he knew you'd understand. But I think that in lieu of the church, his instinct would be to turn towards Benedict's. We're all conditioned to look upwards for help and comfort, and if we don't find the god we happen to believe in available, we latch on to something that is.'

'Look up? To Benedict's? Most people would have a fit to hear you say that, now,' she said, surprised. 'They'd give you chapter and verse about how the poor detested the squirearchy.'

'Sweetheart, do you really want a history lesson tonight? You have to be precise about what you mean by such terms as "the squirearchy". There was the agricultural revolution, and there was the industrial revolution. Both created a race of rich top-dogs. In the country, the top dogs became the sort of squires you and I mean, like Grandfather, who was one of the last of them. They belonged to the land – many of them were yeomen farmers who had made good while their neighbours were slipping down the social scale. Like in *Tess of the D'Urbervilles*. They understood country ways. But it was *their* sons who rushed off to volunteer in 1914 – and were killed in their thousands. Their breed was wiped out, and their places taken by the new-rich of the industrial revolution, who didn't care at all about country ways, though they lived in the houses the others had left. They were the sort who were given titles for turning out munitions from their factories – fish out of water. It was that sort that put people's backs up. George Bridgefoot remembers Grandfather – who better to turn to in trouble than a Wagstaffe?

'It makes sense, my love, though in these days nobody will admit it. I like to know that such old ties still hold. It was what my father and his generation thought they were fighting and dying for. But there, I told you – I'm an anachronism.'

'So is my guardian angel, then,' she said. 'I think the bees have been at work, cross-pollinating him with you.'

He chuckled. 'Now just what do you mean by that? You know perfectly well I'm not a homosexual! Do you want proof of it?'

Her laughter was fairy-music to his ears. He hated and

even feared her getting upset by worrying about other people's troubles, though he knew she always would. She was still smiling when he willed her to close her eyes, and cradled her into drowsiness and sleep.

In spite of her niggling worry about Roland and his affairs, she had really been very happy in the last two weeks. The new arrangements down at Monastery Farm were working splendidly.

In Monica's absence, her sitting-room became a sort of rest room for Jess and Anne to get out of the office atmosphere, and they usually met there, often calling Eric in to join them, for coffee in the morning or tea in the afternoon. The 'business' side of things was no less important now than it had always been, because it was growing all the time; but it had become less like a Commando raid, and more like a well-planned strategic campaign. It took its new tone from Eric, as Fran was well aware.

With such miserable weather and William immersed in his own work, and with a lot on her mind she didn't want to stop at home and think about, Fran had got into the habit of 'dropping in' at Monastery Farm around afternoon-cup-of-tea-time, for half an hour's 'chaffinching' with Jess and Anne. In this case the old axiom that 'two's company, three's none' seemed to be reversed. Anne's presence brought the two cousins closer than they had ever been since Jess's return from Scotland. Some of it was because Jess was less tired, now that Anne could take a good deal of responsibility off her shoulders; but Fran thought that perhaps Jess might be a bit lonely, now that Greg spent three days of every week in London. He went up and back every day, but it was still a great change for Jess, because till now he had always worked at, or from home. And occasionally he had to stay the night in town. Then Jess had no need to hurry home, and 'business hours' didn't concern her very much. The chaffinching sessions grew longer on those days.

Jane Hadley had been a sort of catalyst in the new arrangements, too. Given a full-time job to arrange as she liked, she had organized herself to work at Southside House and the Schoolhouse in the mornings, and at Monastery Farm every afternoon. This meant that she was responsible for the fire in Monica's sitting-room, and the production of tea at three thirty for whoever happened to be there.

A secure job, a home of her own and more money to spend were making changes in her. She had lost her gaunt, rather haggard look already, and was less angular than before. Fran noticed particularly that her hands, which had been previously so work-hardened, showed the change most, being looked after well now, even to a touch of clear, protective nail-varnish now and again. They were long-fingered and thin, but strong and capable. Fran decided that hands, rather than faces, were pointers to character. Jane's face was still set firm, her mouth nearly always unsmiling. The other three had asked her more than once to stay and have tea with them, but had always met with polite refusal. She was as silent and uncommunicative as ever.

'It's almost as if she were learning proper charwoman's ways from Sophie,' Fran said on one occasion. 'Sophie would say primly, "No thanks. I know my place." Jane just does it by setting her mouth in a straight line and sticking her chin out. We probably offend her by trying to be kind to her. She has set her stall out, as Sophie would say, never to be the object of charity. It's kinder to accept her at her own face value, I think.' So they did, though always with a little extra courtesy.

Then on an afternoon in the third week of February, Eric landed Jess and Anne with a problem. The hotel was getting booked up for conferences well into the future, and Eric was more than pleased to be moving into the international scene. Anne's languages were proving an enormous boon to them all. But it was Eric himself who brought into the middle of their chaffinching session a letter addressed personally to him, which he laid on the tea-tray with a grin. 'There you are, ladies,' he said. 'Which of you can solve that Dutch puzzle? No, I can't stop for tea. I just popped in to see if any of you knew how to deal with that.'

'Dutch it certainly isn't,' Anne said. 'It's Arabic. Not a hope.'

'I shall have to take it to a translator,' Jess said. 'It's unusual – most of the letters we get are in English, however much we have to guess what they mean. The Japanese are the worst. They might just as well be in Japanese, for all the sense they make.'

'I know,' said Fran. 'I've got a beautiful modern mah-jong set, made in Japan. We very rarely get round to actually playing because the rules – in English – can't be resisted. They are as good as reading Mark Twain on "The Awful German Language". We can't see the tiles for laughing."

Jess stretched out her hand to retrieve the open letter as Jane leaned over to pick up the tray. She glanced up in time to catch a flicker of interest in Jane's eyes as they looked down at the letter before Jess was able to get it. Jess paused, surprised, and watched a flood of crimson embarrassment flood over Jane's face.

'I beg your pardon,' Jane said, very low, to Jess.

'No need,' said Jess, smiling. 'It's nothing personal.' Then a thought like a stone from a random sling hit her. 'You can read it, can't you?'

The hands that held the tray tightened on it. 'Yes,' said Jane. 'I haven't spoken it for more than twenty years, but I can still read it. Can I be of service to you?'

While Fran and Anne held their breath, Jess handed back the letter to Jane. 'It's from a chess addict asking what the terms and conditions would be for a regional Egypt-versus-England match over a weekend some time next summer,' Jane said. 'Not very professional, I'd say, because the way it reads makes it sound as if this man's only just thought up the idea of a weekend's chess-based holiday, but hasn't put it forward till he found out if such a thing were possible. He probably daren't trust his English.'

'Well, well,' said Jess, who knew Jane much better than either of the other two. 'What a dark horse you are, Jane.' She said it jokingly with a delightful smile to accompany it. Up went Jane's head, and back came the withdrawn look as she set the tray down again.

'I'm sorry again,' she said. 'I must have reacted to the sight of the Arabic script. I give you my word that I am neither spy nor secret agent. Just somebody who happens by chance to know Arabic ... And now I have to ask you, all three of you, to forget. Please keep it a secret, especially from my son. It is truly very important to me, though to nobody else.'

They felt guilty, overawed by her dignity and her calm, fatalistic tone. Hastily, they all gave her their solemn word.

'Thank you,' she said, picking up the tray. 'I believe you.'

They were still sitting as if chained to their chairs when they saw Jane stride out in the rain to go home, twenty minutes later.

'Gosh!' said Anne. 'I felt as if I were facing the Almighty on Judgement Day. What do you make of that?'

'That Nick's missing father was an Arab?' said Jess. 'He doesn't look as if that could be but it might. She wouldn't be very popular if that is the case. It could account for a lot.'

'Still *another* secret to keep,' said Fran. 'It would be funny if it weren't so serious for the people involved.' She caught herself in time – the other two knew about Monica's secret, but not what George Bridgefoot had told her. She didn't want anybody to ask questions as to what she had meant. She got up and collected her things.

'When shall we three meet again
  In thunder, lightning, or in rain,'

she asked lightly.

'I don't see much chance of thunder or lightning,' Jess said, 'but you can rely on old England for the rain, by the looks of it. Tuesday?'

'Next Tuesday as ever is,' said Fran, and left. She was destined not to keep that appointment, though.

The next day's post brought her a letter, postmarked York, but in a hand she didn't recognize. She was afraid to open it, and heard her own voice saying to William, 'When will it be our turn?' It could only be something in connection with Roland and Sue.

Dear Mrs Catherwood,
    You will probably guess at once the reason for this letter. I am sorry that we have never got to know each better in the last few years. It would have made things easier for me now.

I am very fond of Roland, but the fact remains that something must be done about the situation with regard to his marriage to Susan now that his mistress is expecting a child.

I have this information from Roland himself. Susan has said nothing of it either to me or her father.

I am sure that you, like me, only wish for the outcome to be as civilized as possible, and cause as little pain to all three of them as can be managed.

I propose to come down to London on Monday next for as long as I need to be there. Would it be possible for you to meet me for lunch at my hotel and discuss the matter with me?

I should appreciate your compliance with my request a great deal and hope that some good might come out of such a meeting.

Yours sincerely,
Bernice Woodstone.

Fran read it through several time before she could take it in. She was reluctant, to say the least, to interfere in any way whatsoever with what was, after all, her son's business. Mothers should not take it upon themselves even to give advice, unasked. She had made up her mind to say so in reply to Lady Woodstone, but there was something rather strange about the wording of the letter that intrigued her. It had been very carefully crafted so as not to throw any blame on anybody. Fran appreciated that. She would, as always, consult William before she made up her mind.

The second letter was from her agent. Her play had been accepted for production by the BBC in a rather big way. He needed to see her urgently, and was willing to come down to Old Swithinford, soon. But a great deal more could be done to push the business on if she would be willing to come up to London for a few days, and see people and their proposals for herself before any contract was drawn up.

At any other time she would have gone whooping through the house to find somebody to tell the great news to. This morning it only had one significance for her. If she went next week, she could meet Sue's mother without fuss or causing any suspicion.

She did, as always, consult William first. He thought she should go, on both counts, but pulled a wry face.

'It will be the first time over you have left me alone,' he said. 'It will seem an awful long week.'

'Well, I like that! How many times have you gallivanted off to the States and left me for weeks – even months – at a time?'

'We weren't married, then,' he said simply. 'I expect I shall survive. Of course you must go – and not least to meet Sue's mother. I think we must keep that dark, though. It might be construed as interference, and we can't risk that. See what happens, and tell Roland and Eric afterwards if the need arises.'

'Yet another bloody secret? I'm running over with them!'

'Well, at least I haven't got any secrets from you, now,' he said.

She wished she could say the same. She had not broken her word to Jane Hadley by mentioning that incident of the Arabic letter, even to William.

He put her on the train, promising to be there to meet her on Friday afternoon. As the train noisily ground its way out of the station, the sun broke through the clouds for the first time for about six weeks and the rain stopped at last.

If there was one thing she hated above all others, it was being in London alone, especially on a wet day.

'I can't help being me,' she thought. 'I have got a country bumpkin mentality. M'm. In more ways than one.'

48

The spell of wet weather had lasted so long that everybody had begun to get used to it, even Beth Marriner. Every day was the same as every other, except that on Sundays she still had to go and play the organ for the six or so stalwarts who braved the elements, Sophie, Thirzah and Daniel usually constituting fifty per cent of them.

Weekdays were varied by the comings and goings of Thirzah. Beth watched so as to get over to the Old Rectory as soon as she saw Thirzah squelching through the mud, thereby preventing Thirzah from polishing the piano, and providing herself with a chaperone at the same time. She often deliberately practised scales while Thirzah hovered round, to make her hurry and get the sitting-room done. Then she played for her own sake, and discovered how therapeutic these peaceful, musical sessions were. She wondered how she could have got through that awful period after Christmas but for the chance that Elyot Franks possessed a piano. The terrible distress that had driven her to such extremes had receded. She would not have said that she loved her father any less than she had always done; but now, when familial duty had been observed, they left each other to their own devices. The warmth that had showed a little after Xmas had evaporated. He appeared completely indifferent. Well, if that was how he wanted it, so be it. At least she had won herself freedom to come and go as she liked, and promised herself she would make good use of it as soon as the weather would let her.

Sometimes, thinking as she lay in bed, she wondered how she could have let herself get into such a state – but she usually ended up by reliving the pantomime of Christmas night. She had a well-developed sense of humour, and the remembrance now caused her only amusement and a glow of warmth at the friends her rebellion had secured for her.

She began to hate the days when Thirzah did not go to 'do' for Elyot, by inference precluding her from going there either. Then one day Elyot had come in and more or less ordered Thirzah to go home and leave her to play as long as she liked. He had then tactfully gone away till Thirzah's square figure was out of sight, after which he came back to sit quietly and listen.

That had been the thin edge of the wedge; if her reputation was not in danger from being alone with him while she was at the piano, why should she be dependent on Thirzah's presence?

There was a tacit agreement that she should go whenever she felt like it.

It suited her to go across most mornings. Sometimes Elyot would not even attempt to go away, but brought her coffee and biscuits, leaving them at her side and retiring to his own chair, almost always with his back to her. That puzzled her, but she asked no questions. She thought it was a bit like getting to know a baby or a new pet – the more you ignored it, the more likely in the end it was to come to you of its own accord.

Ten days passed before there was the slightest hint of the black dog to upset things; but the next Monday morning she saw that he was not in his chair when she arrived, and when he did come in he barely looked her way, sitting down without speaking. Little blobs of lather behind the ear that she could see informed her that he had just taken a hasty shave – which must mean that his normal meticulously disciplined routine had been neglected. His face, as usual, was resolutely turned away from her. She stopped playing.

'Isn't it my turn to make the coffee?' she asked, and without waiting for an answer got up and went to the kitchen. She was carrying the coffee in when he said curtly, 'Put it down. I'll get it when I want it.'

Rebuffed, she did what he told her to; but she had seen his face, ravaged and red-eyed from lack of sleep. She hadn't seen him since Friday. She guessed that he hadn't been to bed for three nights.

She began to pack up her things to go, but he spoke, still without turning his head towards her, and, almost as an order, said, 'Don't go. Keep on playing.'

She sat down again on the piano stool, and began to play from memory the same sort of soothing pieces that she had used before. When he spoke again, his voice was his ordinary, cultured, friendly one.

'Can you let yourself out? I'm sorry to be such a boor, but the headache I've had for three days is just beginning to fade a bit and I'm afraid of setting it off again by moving.'

She packed up her things and put them by the door. Then she went back, careful to keep behind him. 'Close your eyes,' she said. 'You don't have to look at me.' He had no wish to open them to look at her, and wished she would go. But he was not sorry to feel her hands on his forehead again, on his temples, on his clenched jaws and where his headache hurt most, up the back of his neck – her touch was magic. He didn't want to go to sleep and miss it, but when he woke up, the dusk was already falling, although it was still only late afternoon.

Thirzah came next day, but not Beth. Nor the next. He concluded that he must have offended her, and that she would not come again. There was a great hollow somewhere under his diaphragm that nothing, he thought, but her playing would ever again soothe. He missed it as he had never missed anything before, not even his ship when, after a long spell in a naval hospital, he had been given a shore job till he was retired. The house was so deadly quiet that even Thirzah's broom bangings and crockery rattlings were welcome. He had never been particularly fond of music – but perhaps that was because he had never listened properly before.

He looked towards the empty piano stool, and a thought came to him like a torpedo striking him amidships. It was not the music he was missing. It was Beth herself.

The black dog was upon him again that night, worse than it had been since Christmas. Wherever he looked, even when his eyes were closed, he could see her eyes – or were they the eyes of that suffering boy in the boat? His head raged.

She had come, not sent by a benevolent Lady Luck to comfort him, but by a malignant fate to add to his torture. Damn the woman, why had she chosen his garage to faint in? He'd been all right till then. Now he would never be free of his ghosts; time had been gradually wearing down the memory of the boy, until she had looked up to him from his settee with the same pair of eyes. He wasn't going to get the chance to forget anything here – not with her living no more than two hundred yards away. If she had to be there at all, then why hadn't she come to play his piano? Why hadn't she come to him, when he needed those cool hands on his head so much . . . ? He started up, with a sense of foreboding. Perhaps she was ill, or had gone away. Perhaps even for good. He had to find out.

He staggered upstairs and into the bathroom, with some vague idea that he must go across to her home and ask. He washed and shaved, and dressed as well as he could, the raging headache almost blinding him. He was halfway down the stairs when he heard the first soft notes as she ran her hands over the keys before starting to play what she had chosen to bring to practise. She had made up her mind to memorize something new, to take her mind off thinking how his head had felt under her fingers.

He sat down heavily, uncertain what to do next. She crossed the room as lithe and silent as a cat, and began the massage. Neither spoke. It had been going on for five minutes when he put up one of his hands, without warning, and took one of hers in a strong, firm clasp, holding it close to his cheek. She wondered that he didn't hear the tumult in her own heart through the thick leather back of his chair.

'Elyot,' she said, making no attempt to withdraw the imprisoned hand. 'Why will you never look at me?'

'You remind me too much of somebody else,' he said.

The emotion in Beth's breast which had never really resolved itself before into anything recognizable flared up, fluttered and sank.

'Your wife, lost somehow or other? I am sorry. Do you want me to go?'

'No,' he said, clasping her hand tighter, and transferring it from his cheek to his lips. 'I never had a wife. And I don't want you to go. But it would be better if you did, all the same. Better for us both.'

She leaned over him, looking down. 'Then who, Elyot?' There was a note of insistence in her voice. 'Who, if not another woman?' He opened his eyes, and looked up at her, first with an expression she had never before seen in any man's eyes directed at her, and then immediately with such a look of agony that she could not bear it.

She closed his eyes with her fingertips, and held his eyelids down. He put up both his hands to hold hers there. It was a long tense moment before she bent her head, and kissed the deep furrows of pain on his forehead.

'Then who, Elyot?'

He let go of her hands, and drew himself away to stand up and face her.

'The man I murdered,' he said. 'Now go.'

That was on Monday, the last Monday in February, when the sun at last broke through the clouds again. It cheered Fran on her journey away from home and to a strange meeting that not even her imagination could invent a scenario for.

It shone on the end of the cafeteria of Swithinford Technical School, where Poppy and Nick sat with a coke and a bun, as they did every Monday afternoon, and told each other of the week's doings, or compared notes about a passage of Shakespeare or a poem they both liked. The cafeteria was so nondescript and crammed with other young people that nobody had ever noticed them. Nobody, not even Pansy, was aware that they met each other in this innocent way, to keep their friendship going. Poppy's desire was to keep abreast of him educationally, so that he should never have cause to reject her on those grounds. Nick's aim was to get the university place that could, would, must put him, in the long course of time, into a position where he could be more than a friend to her if she still cared for him. He had never for a single day forgotten that moment in the straw before the rain came down and stopped them forgetting everything else but each other.

The sun soon set all farmers except one rushing about like the ants in an antheap kicked over by a horse, so much work was there to catch up on. The exception was Tom Fairey. He stood for hours in the corner of one of his fields farthest away from the yard, ash-plant in hand, and looked back towards the house his grandfather had been born in, and his father, and himself, and his son.

His son. They had tried to keep it from him, but he was no fool, and just lately he had had to acknowledge that Robert was getting no better. It was inconceivable to him that the boy would die . . . but fear would not be kept at bay.

He decided that he must take more notice of Cynthia and let the boy off lightly with regard to work this coming summer. That would perhaps set him up again – that and Pansy Gifford. Tom approved wholeheartedly of Robert's

378

courtship of Pansy. He could have asked for nothing better than alliance with a Bridgefoot – but then, he was a simple man without high ambitions.

He had set his own heart on the village blacksmith's daughter when they had both been together in Miss Budd's class, and had never wavered. She had satisfied him in every way except that he had expected a whole brood of children, and there had never been more than one. But one was enough, provided he found himself a wife and begot another generation of Faireys to take over Lane's End. Pansy would do very well. She was the robust one of the twins, even if she was the hoity-toity one. She had that look in her eye that he associated with good-breeders.

Vic Gifford was not nearly so pleased about Pansy's interest in Tom Fairey's son; but he could afford to bide his time. When the summer season started again, he intended to buy Pansy a horse worth showing, and at gymkanas she would soon get herself into the 'horsey' set that included the real gentry's sons. She'd know which side her bread was buttered on. She had always been his favourite and he watched her blossom from a girl into a very fetching young woman with the same appraising eye as he looked over his cattle or pigs. She was what was called in farming parlance 'a good doer'. There was no need to worry about her having a bit of a fling with young Fairey.

Marjorie the placid took a long time to adjust to the fact that she had two separate daughters instead of one double one. She accepted it only when Poppy demanded that they should have separate bedrooms. Poppy wanted to work in hers, she said, which was a good enough excuse. The real reason was that she did not want Pansy's whispered confidences, or the burden of knowledge of what Pansy was up to; besides, she had nothing to offer in return. She daren't even tell Pansy of her meetings with Nick in the cafeteria. She was wise enough to know that Pansy would be completely unscrupulous about giving anything away if it would serve her own purpose.

There was quite a lot of strength in the sun when at last it did get through the clouds. Floods receded, puddles dried up, and flowers like aconites and primroses, crocuses and grape hyacinths appeared from nowhere – having been quietly getting on with their annual cycle in spite of the rain.

Bob Bellamy, leaning on the church wall that same Monday afternoon, was enjoying himself. It hadn't been worth his while to stand there in the rain, but it was now. The old elms were no longer dark against the sky; where the afternoon sun caught them today they showed deep red from the myriad tiny flowers and the rooks were building and restoring with such caw-ful activity that his every sense was satisfied. He felt the old cat rubbing up against his legs, and picked her up, nuzzling her against his face.

'So you've been at it again,' he said to her, severely. 'Who do you think I'm going to be able to palm this litter off on?'

Having Charlie at home made a difference to him, even if he didn't see a lot of her. Charles Bridgefoot had taken her home with him, and since then she had seemed to spend as much time up at Temperance Farm or at the Old Glebe as she had done with him at Castle Hill. He was glad for her sake that Charles had come along just when he had, because it had helped her to get over her mother's desertion of them. Her presence had helped him in the same way. He had put Iris behind him, but he had not made Archie Marriner's mistake of expecting Charlie to take her mother's place in any way at all.

He saw how besotted Charles was, and loved the boy for it, even while feeling sorry for him. It wasn't that he doubted Charlie knowing her own mind – the trouble was that she knew it too well.

She wanted to be a vet, and she wanted to make use of her skill with languages. She couldn't do either from Castle Hill. Both meant her leaving home again, for an unforeseeable time, and with unforeseeable consequences.

'But I don't want to leave you by yourself,' she said.

'Don't bother about me,' Bob had answered. 'It's your life. But what about young Charles? Doesn't he come into it?'

She sat on the hearthrug at his feet and hugged her knees, looking up at him. 'Yes,' she said. 'I think he does, Dad – but not for years yet. I want to be sure, before I give up everything else just to stay where he is. He might drop me at any minute for the next girl who falls at his feet like I did.'

'Not he,' said Bob, stroking her hair. 'He's got it bad. It's you I'm not sure about.'

'I'm not, either. I'm not sure that I don't love him just because he's so much like you. He's so kind, so – sort of humble. He never asks for anything, never tries anything on. I have to ask him to kiss me, even! I'd rather be with him than any other boy I've ever met – but I feel more like his sister than his girlfriend. So how do I know whether I'm in love or not? I think I've got to go away to find out.'

'What would you do if you found him kissing another girl?' he asked, laughing at her ingenuous answer.

She rolled over on her back and thought about it, pulling Bonzo's ears while she did so. Then she looked up at her father. 'Kill her,' she said.

'You'll do!' he said. 'That's your old fen pride coming out in you. He's probably frightened to death of upsetting you, and I don't wonder. But I reckon he won't lose anything by waiting a bit for you. Do just as you think best.'

'But what'll you do, Dad? Would you have Mum back now, if she withdrew her divorce petition and wanted to come back? She's been writing to John. He told me – asking him for money, because she's run short. She hinted that she might try coming home to you again.'

That was no great surprise to Bob; he had been expecting some sort of difficulty to crop up for the last week, so uneasy had his mind been. His intuition plus a knowledge of his wife's character had warned him from which direction it was likely to come. He had already done a good deal of thinking about it.

He hated to be alone, without anybody to love; but Iris had never supplied him with what he meant by love, and wouldn't, ever. He'd had more real love from old Bonzo than he'd ever had from Iris. But once Charle had gone . . .

'What do you think about it?' he asked her.

'Is she better than nobody?'

That was the question he couldn't answer. 'If the divorce goes through,' he said, speaking thoughtfully, 'she'll no longer be my wife. But she'll still be your mother, and John's. I'd take her back for your sakes. I'm not sure that I would for my own.'

'Don't have anything to do with her for my sake!' she said,

sitting up and staring at him. 'I loathe the woman. I don't want her. She's never wanted me. But she does love John. So don't count me as a factor in your equation at all. Ask John. If you want her back, I'll clear out.'

She took herself off, and left him with two cats on his knee and Bonzo's head in his lap. She looked in on him before setting out to meet Charles, and saw that he was asleep, so she didn't wake him.

He was not only asleep, but dreaming, back in his old childhood dream of the house with that lovely room in it, where he was standing looking up at the picture. Then the dream faded, and he woke to find himself alone, except for his animals, but no longer with a problem. He knew where to find that house of his if not the picture. The woman in the picture had been his ideal – but she was unattainable, gone with past years. He could see and speak to her reincarnation in Fran, whom he could call a friend. But she was as unattainable as the other had been, or as the moon.

A loving friend though; he had had more of what he called love from Fran in the course of friendship than he had had in twenty years of marriage to Iris, who didn't understand anything but sex.

He was now quite sure that he did not want Iris back. If ever he bothered himself again with any woman, it would have to be one who came within striking distance of his ideal in the picture. 'Some hope' he thought, as he put on his old cap and went to see if Matey had stirred with the change in the weather. He didn't really mind having to go on living with only a dream. There were no high-born ladies available, and if there were, they wouldn't look his way. But he was a man who knew the value of dreams. He'd rather have pleasant dreams than unpredictable reality.

The afternoon sun shone on the the newly restored front of the Old Rectory, and the soft warm tones of Benedict's deep-pink-coloured rendering. Both houses had porches held up by imposing columns, and huge heavy wooden doors.

Beth looked out at one through tears she could not control. She knew she would never be let through that door again, even if she could forget what Elyot had told her, and could persuade herself that it made no difference. And her father preached about a loving God! What kind of a God would have tortured her into the state of misery she had been in in at Christmas, teased her by all that fantasy, tempted her by those lovely mornings spent at Elyot's piano with him in sight, let her fall in love for the first time in her life, and then knocked the whole edifice of his creation down at a blow like a child playing with building bricks? There was no God. There was nothing, nothing except the knowledge that she loved a man who was a self-confessed murderer. As he loved her. That was why he had put his reputation as a gentleman – and perhaps even his life – in her hands.

William did not register how beautiful Benedict's looked in the sunshine either when he got home that afternoon. The dusk was already falling and the low sun was making golden glory of the coloured wash, but he hated the thought of having to use his key in that massive door. It was locked against him because there was no Fran inside. When Cat came crying to meet him, he understood just how she had been feeling all day, as deserted and bereft as he felt himself. He cuddled Cat and fondled her little pointed ears, which always made her purr. She was satisfied with him as a substitute for Fran, but it didn't work the other way round.

He thought guiltily of the many times Fran must have felt just like he did now, when in the past he had left her alone for weeks at a time.

'She'll be back on Friday, Cat,' he said. Funny, though, what a long time off Friday afternoon seemed to him now. Like trying to see to the other side of the horizon.

49

Fran's agent had booked her hotel for her, and was there to meet her, having set up such a programme for her that it would be Wednesday at the earliest before she could arrange to see Lady Woodstone. It was agreed that they would meet for tea at Lady Woodstone's hotel on Wednesday afternoon.

She ate her dinner in solitary state, hating every moment, and retired as soon as she could to await the call William had promised. She thought telephones one of the worst evils modern science had inflicted on ordinary people, but blessed the telephone's inventor that first evening as soon as she heard William's voice. He spent quite a lot of time telling her how he missed her and how much he loved her, and a considerable amount of money into the bargain making sure that she reciprocated all his feelings. She felt considerably better when at last she put the receiver down, after being assured that he would ring again tomorrow.

'Will there be anything to say?' she had asked.

'Nothing that I haven't said tonight. But I don't mind having to repeat myself,' he said. She laughed. 'Nor I how many times you do. But don't forget to tell me if anything exciting happens. London's a dreadfully dull place after Old Swithinford. All these faces and not one that you know – let alone know what their owners are up to!'

'You can always invent what you don't know,' he said.

'We don't have to invent things at home. They happen. Till tomorrow then, my darling.'

She would have things to tell him on Wednesday evening. She asked him to leave the call on Wednesday till after ten p.m., when she would be in bed and could take her time to recount what had happened at the meeting.

The two women had only ever seen each other once before, on the occasion of the marriage. Fran's first impression was that Lady Woodstone was older that she had remembered, but not a whit less elegant, though her eyes, Fran thought, looked decidedly weary. Lady Woodstone's first opinions were the direct opposite. Mrs Catherwood had definitely put on weight, and was therefore not so elegant nor so well dressed as herself; but if anything she looked younger than she had done, and though at present a little apprehensive, in general wore an aura of contentment.

They ordered tea, and sparred verbally in the polite way of well-bred women till they had taken each other's measure, and the waitresses were out of hearing.

'Thank you for coming,' Lady Woodstone began. 'I'm afraid we have a rather difficult time ahead of us.'

'Do you mean this afternoon, or the general future?' asked Fran.

'Possibly both.'

'Then I think I ought to say straight away that I have no intention of interfering with my son's life,' said Fran firmly. 'I had no knowledge of Susan before Roland married her and have never been allowed to get to know her since. I do know the girl you refer to as his mistress, because her father bought property in our village, and I met her by chance. I had no idea until last November that Roland knew she existed. I have hardly seen Roland since his marriage. I'm terribly sorry it has turned out as it has, but quite honestly I don't see what either of us can do. I have only heard Roland's account. There are usually two sides to most questions.'

Lady Woodstone heard her out with a patient sort of smile. 'I think you may be barking up the wrong tree,' she said gently. 'I'm very fond of Roland, and it's to do my best for him that I'm here. I can't bear to see him suffering for something that is not his fault. And being so good about it. If his devotion to Sue and all his own misery would do any good, it might be worthwhile, but I'm afraid it can't.'

Fran was so surprised that for once she floundered for words. She had expected a sort of queen-bee put-down, and had made up her mind not to enter into any sort of verbal battle. She hoped she wasn't expected to reciprocate out of politeness, and stick up for Sue, because she wasn't going to. However, she did apologize for seeming stupid, and asked for explanation.

'I'm afraid it's a long, sad story and a personal one. I don't know that you knowing will do much to help except that you may have some influence on Roland. You have my permission to tell him as much or as little as you like. And there may be the tiniest glimmer of hope somewhere ahead. In which case, I should need you to persuade Roland to agree to divorce. At present, he will not consider that option.'

Fran struck in. 'He is still very fond of Sue – and she was Monica's best friend. Monica has made it quite clear to him that she will not build her happiness on the ruin of her former friend's marriage. She's expecting Roland's child, but is asking nothing of him. I can't be very proud of his behaviour, but I truly think it would never have happened if he had had a wife in more than name. But he is a young and healthy male . . . and Monica loves him as much as he loves her. I am in no position to throw stones at anybody, Lady Woodstone, as you know. I'm glad to know my son has something to look forward to. Susan, apparently, refused to have children. He wanted some.'

Lady Woodstone nodded agreement. 'That is what I must explain,' she said. 'Roland was unfairly treated, but not with our consent. The story goes back to my own marriage to Susan's father. To Susan's birth. We had hoped for a boy, because of the title – but we thought there was plenty of time.

'But I began to be ill and – to cut a long story short, I am epileptic. Hereditary, apparently, though I had no idea. I had a son, but he died soon after birth – in a convulsion. No, I don't know, but the implications were clear. The risk was too great. My husband preferred that the title should pass to his brother, who has four sons, than to an epileptic one of his own.

'There was a war on, of course, and my husband went back to his regiment of the Guards. Our sex life had had to be extremely circumspect – I expect you can guess the rest. He fell in love with the woman who has been his mistress ever since. I would have divorced him, let him free to marry her and have the son he wanted, but – I don't want to sound bitter or snobbish – she isn't the sort his sort marry. He still needed me as hostess and cover for his respectability. Besides, we both had to take Susan's welfare into consideration. It may have been sensible, but it wasn't happy. I can't bear to see it repeated.'

'Oh, please Lady Woodstone – must you tell me any more?'

'I came expressly to tell you all of it. Naturally, we kept a close watch on Susan, and by the time she was seven she did begin to show some symptoms; but we fooled ourselves, I think, because both of us felt guilty that she didn't have a happier home environment. In the event, we had to seek medical advice, and sure enough, she was suffering from *petit mal*. The treatment was wonderful. I thought it was being kept absolutely under control by the latest drug treatment.' Lady Woodstone paused, and steadied herself with another cup of tea.

'When she was going to the art school, our dear old family doctor was asked to explain her condition to her – including the risk of having children. She appeared to take it very well, though the moods she had always been given to since adolescence were more frequent and worse. She was in London, of course, and things being as they were at home, we didn't see a great deal of her. Then came news of her romance with Roland – and plans for a hurried wedding.

'I was horrified. I begged her to tell Roland the truth – even threatened to take it on myself to tell him. My husband wouldn't let me. He said Sue had a right to her own life, and that young people nowadays knew perfectly well how to take care of themselves. Besides, she wasn't marrying a baronet. What did it matter? The new pill could make sure she didn't have children and Roland need never know.

'When she began to get very difficult, and her drug dosage had to be increased, I guessed the reason. The marriage was in difficulties because Roland thought it time for them to start a family. She refused – of course – but didn't tell him why. He still doesn't know. The rest you do.'

Fran was having difficulty in holding tears back – not for Roland or anybody else but the sad woman the other side of the table. (She heard William's voice in her ears again . . .

'As flies to wanton boys, are we to the gods;
They kill us for their sport.'

They didn't kill cleanly, either. They tortured first or else made mad.)

'If only she had let me, I would have told Roland, and suggested sterilization on medical grounds. He would have been disappointed, but he would have understood. Instead, she chose to make him suffer by keeping him at bay – and fate sent Monica across his path.

'That was the last straw. Sue is quite impossible now – as nearly mad as makes no difference. If Roland hasn't told you details, he's an even better man than I gave him credit for. She adores her father, so I persuaded him to coax her to see the very top man on such brain-associated complaints. His opinion was that there was latent epilepsy, held in check by the drugs; but the strange behaviour and the uncontrollable moods could be a side-effect of drugs taken over so many years. The choice was plain. She could either come off the drug, with God knows what effect, or go on getting progressively more impossible to live with.

'It is not her fault; but that's no reason why her condition should spoil three other lives. Sue herself cannot be more unhappy than she is – in fact, I think she might even be better if some of the guilt she carries could be lessened. She knows she is spoiling Roland's life, and Monica's, and the baby's chances of having two parents. The power she has over him induces her to exert it in ways that are mad: the guilt reduces her often to a state of suicidal depression. He must be made to see that his self-sacrifice is doing no good at all. It may do a lot of harm. Will you try?'

'If I am ever given a chance, yes. But I can't and won't interfere. Monica asks for no more than she's got. She is in a sort of heaven that she never expected to know, and is satisfied. Roland tries to do his best for them both. What was that gleam of hope you mentioned?'

'For twenty-odd years now, I have been no more than a housekeeper to my husband. For his reputation's sake, I have put up with the knowledge of his affairs – the permanent one and a good many others. There have been no compensatory liaisons for me. But time brings changes, whether we want them or not. I am now beyond the age at which there could be any possibility of me passing on my genes, and I have taken a lover who wants to marry me – a widowed American states-man. I have asked for a divorce, and Manfred – my husband – has agreed. We discussed the whole business in a very civilized fashion. Manfred is still only just over fifty. If he can bring himself to make his mistress redundant, he still has a very good chance of remarrying and producing the heir he still so much wants. His only argument against my request was that he still loves and respects me – as Roland does Sue, which really means no more than that he has got accustomed to my face.

That he needs me, as he says he does, is much nearer the truth. What will he do for a hostess at his high-powered dinner-paries and the like without a competent and experienced hostess? But that's where the gleam of hope lies – where Sue comes in.

'Susan has always been his ally. While with him, she rarely throws a fit of depression or one of her raging, destructive moods. She could do my job for her father as well as I can, and I think would soon be so absorbed in it that she would forget that Roland or Monica existed. She is extremely beautiful, you know, and if we can persuade her to be sterilized, she might yet make a good, happy, honest marriage with an older man who neither needs nor wants children. That is my hope. Conversely, my husband-to-be and I are prepared to take her with us to the States, for new medical opinion, or if nothing more, to start a new life.

'So far, she will not be moved from her present position of power over what she considers an erring husband, or budge an inch to let her rival have him. He has grounds to divorce her on desertion – though it would mean washing her dirty linen in public. My opinion is that he would only have to threaten, and she would put a petition in herself, on the grounds of his adultery, at once. Neither is a pleasant prospect – for you and me. Their generation take divorce after marriage like aspirin after a hangover.'

'I can only promise to do my best as you have done,' Fran said, warmly. 'Thank you. I do hope you will be as happy in the future as you deserve to be.'

'Thank you,' Lady Woodstone said, holding out her hand. 'I shall always regret that we didn't meet sooner, and that your new grandchild will not be mine as well. I envy you your son.'

Fran got herself back to her own hotel in record time, and had time before dinner to let her riotous emotions settle down. William would not ring for another three hours, but there was no reason why she should not ring him.

She began to dial at eight forty-five, but at eleven o'clock there was still no answer. After a restless night of worry and conjecture, she tried again at six thirty the next morning. There was no reply.

She did not want breakfast, but sent for coffee in her room. 'Tell the porter to fetch down my things, and I want a taxi for Liverpool Street as soon as possible,' she said. Something must be dreadfully wrong at Benedict's, and she could not get back there quick enough. Any other business could be held over. She was going home.

50

Because Fran wasn't there to greet him, William stayed late at work and dealt with a lot of odd correspondence before going home. He was almost an hour later than usual on Wednesday evening, and was surprised to find Sophie still there, waiting for him. She never wasted time, so she had prepared his supper and had it on the table for him as soon as he had got his coat off and greeted Cat.

'Now tell me what's the matter, Sophie, please. Has Fran rung you with a message?'

'No,' she said. 'As far as I know there's nothing the matter with 'er. But some'ow I couldn't rest easy after I met Thirz' when I went to the butcher's. Seems she went to the Old Rectory as usual this morning, being Wednesday, and found the door locked. She 'as a key of 'er own to get in with, like, when 'e ain't there, so she tried it, but it wouldn't work 'cos the big old key were still in the lock the other side. In the end she 'ad to come away. She were a bit worried, 'cos 'e does 'ave them bad days. She don't goo there a-Mondays, being as it's 'er own washing-day, but she did goo yist'day. But she never see 'im at all. He must ha' gone downstairs and opened the door for 'er, but she never set eyes on 'im. 'E'd left 'er a note telling 'er not to goo nowheer near 'im, do 'e didn't want nothing only to be left alone and quiet. So by that she come away as soon as she could.

'But get into that 'ouse this morning she could not, not

no'ow! And she thinks as 'e must be 'aving a real bad turn, 'cos the last she see of 'im were Friday. So I said if she'd let me 'ave 'er key, I'd wait till you got 'ome and tell you, and per'aps you could get in even if you 'ad to get the police to 'elp you. 'E may even be laying there dead, for all we know – Thirz' says 'e 'as terrible 'eadaches when them bad turns are over.' She produced a large key and laid it before him on the table.

'Thank you, Sophie,' he said, 'and Thirzah, too, for being so thoughtful. I will go down, as soon as I've finished my meal, though if Thirzah couldn't get in with that key I don't suppose I can. But I think I'd better keep it. I might be able to push the inside key out of the lock if I go prepared.'

He was pretty certain that Elyot was merely having a 'black dog' mood, and didn't blame him for avoiding Thirzah. She was hardly the sort of uplift a man in that condition needed. He didn't wonder that Elyot had taken precautions against her letting herself in.

Elyot would probably be feeling better by now, and if so it would while away a tedious evening for them both if he and Elyot could spend it together, though of course he would have to get home by ten o'clock to ring Fran as they had arranged.

The first foreboding that there might be anything truly amiss came only as he drove into the yard at the Old Rectory, and saw that there were no lights on anywhere.

He left his own car's sidelights on to provide a bit of illumination, and went to the front door to ring the bell vigorously. There was no response. He tried the door, but it was as firmly locked as Thirzah had found it, and he had no more success with her key than she had had.

Perhaps Elyot had been called away at short notice; but it was strange, if so, that he hadn't communicated with Thirzah somehow. William began to feel distinctly apprehensive, and took thoughtful stock of the situation. It was always just possible that Sophie's gloomy prognostication might be right. He had only Elyot's own word that the dreadful attacks of depression were no more than just that – it could be that there was a physical cause that he had not disclosed. He might, indeed, be very ill, if not dead. There was no sense in raising any alarm until he knew. Elyot was not a man who cared for others minding his business for him.

William decided that his first duty was to investigate alone as far as he could. He tried to think logically and calmly. If Elyot had gone away, his car would not be in his garage. He found the garage doors unlocked, and pulled them open. The car was there, facing the doors, having been backed in. He didn't know why he should find that sinister, but he did. It smacked of preparation for a quick getaway. The idea was ludicrous, but then, the whole situation was beginning to seem like the prelude to either farce or tragedy, with the garage as the *mise-en-scène* again. On Christmas night when he and Elyot had carried the unconscious Beth into the house, they not gone round to the front door with her, but through a door at the side of the garage that led directly into the back of the house. He felt his way in the dark over a pile of gardening tools, and located the door. To his enormous relief, it opened. He pocketed Thirzah's key, and squared his shoulders against the task ahead of him. Whatever he was about to find, it was better for Elyot that it should be found by a friend.

He switched on the light, and went cautiously into the main part of the house. There was a meticulous neatness about it all that he associated with Elyot, and no sign of disturbance or panic. Elyot liked things shipshape, and of course, Thirzah had 'done' the downstairs rooms on Tuesday morning. He crossed to the door of the sitting-room, and unlatched it gently.

'Elyot,' he said into the darkness. 'Elyot? Are you there? May I switch the light on?' As there was no answer, he put the switch down, expecting to see an unshaven, dishevelled figure in the big leather chair. The room was as empty and prim as one in a show house on a new estate. The big chair had not been sat in since Thirzah had plumped the cushions yesterday.

There was certainly something wrong. People were often found dead in bathrooms – especially suicides. Why on earth had he thought that? There was the kitchen, the dining-room and Elyot's study to be searched first. He took them in that order.

Elyot's study was as neat as the rest, but there were signs

here of fairly recent activity. Papers lying on the desk. William was now faced with another dilemma. It was unthinkable that under normal circumstances he would have pried into private correspondence – but it might be that Elyot had left those things there expressly to be found. If so, better again that it be a friend who found them. Reluctantly, he moved forward and looked down at them. A pile of bills with cheques paper-clipped to them. A fat letter in a sealed envelope, addressed to Beth Marriner. And an unsealed legal envelope, marked on the outside 'WILL OF COMMANDER ELYOT FRANKS, RN (RTD) DATED . . .' but there was no date.

William's mind began to race. Elyot had made a new will, but it had not yet been signed or dated. That could only mean that wherever he was, he was still alive. With a great sigh of relief, William resumed his search. He concluded that Elyot had made careful preparations for departure somewhere. Either finally, by suicide, or for ever out of their lives by simply disappearing. And the cause of it had to be Beth. That letter was probably a farewell, meant only for her eyes. The new will, though he had not seen its contents, in such circumstances told its own tale.

But what was there between them – if anything? He felt an irrational twinge of anger against Fran, for not being at hand when so badly needed . . . he wondered if she knew anything she had not told him. He was instantly penitent, knowing his reaction to be the result of his own feelings of helplessness and inadequacy in a situation that above all called for the utmost discretion. Had Elyot made advances to Beth that had been rebuffed? He couldn't believe that – because he would have staked his life that Elyot would never make approaches to any woman. Had he not told William so? Then had Beth herself been making the running? Equally impossible to believe. He pushed conjecture aside. It was pointless anyway, until he had found Elyot. He took a grip on himself, and regained his composure. Whether he liked it or not, the gods had chosen him to be his brother's keeper. He was surprised to discover in that moment how much Elyot Franks had come to mean to him, as one of that little group of brothers-in-arms who were linked closer than blood brothers by their shared experience of war. He began to run upstairs, taking them two at a time.

Elyot lay on his back, only his head visible above the eiderdown, breathing heavily. On a chair by his side, a large black briefcase stood open. William saw that it contained pyjamas, underpants, a shirt and a toilet bag containing razor and other toilet necessities. The pocket in the lid contained a chequebook and another envelope full of identification papers, driving licence and so on. But the clothes were weighted down by Elyot's service revolver, William guessed loaded. As he had got there in time, it didn't matter, so he didn't stop to find out.

The bedside table held an alarm clock set for five a.m., an empty gin bottle, a bottle of Angostura bitters and an empty glass.

Well, no wonder Elyot slept so soundly. William's relief was so great that he smiled at the thought that only a naval man would have been able to get drunk, go to bed and trust himself to be awake and alert the moment the clock roused him. He picked up the clock and switched off the alarm. At least he could spoil that bit of Elyot's preparations.

How long had Elyot been asleep? He had bargained on being awake and clear-headed by five a.m. next morning. It was now getting on for eight p.m. By calculating backwards William guessed that he must have been at work on the letter and the will in his study when Thirzah had tried to get in; he had locked the door against her to make sure he was not disturbed while writing that letter. The chances were that he had not been to bed the night before, or had much to eat. The letter and the will probably took him all the morning. But he had bathed and shaved before starting to drink as a way of forgetting, and of sending himself to sleep, leaving everything ready for instant departure before it was light next day.

Everything, that is, except the will, which still lay on his desk downstairs. It ought to have been in the briefcase. Elyot had most likely intended to get it looked over by a solicitor and duly signed and witnessed, leaving instructions for it to be forwarded to his bank. The letter to Beth might have been meant to be found where it was, or dropped through her letter-box *en route*. Elyot must have started drinking around lunchtime. He had used his razor before packing it, and while doing so had remembered the will but decided to pick it up in the morning. That could be why he had left the briefcase open, to remind himself not to go without the will. He must then have finished the bottle of gin in bed.

At a rough guess, William thought, he had been asleep for five or six hours. Long enough for so seasoned a man to have slept off the worst of the gin's soporific effect. In which case, William decided, he might as well rouse him at once. He sat down on the bed, leaned forward, and pressed the ends on his fingers hard just below Elyot's left ear.

The supine figure opened its eyes, jerked itself up unto a sitting position and was wide awake at once. William watched the dawn of pained remembrance in the heavy eyes, which in spite of their weariness were instantly on the alert. They took in William with a puzzled frown.

'What the hell are you doing here?' Elyot asked.

'Stopping you from making a worse bloody fool of yourself than you already are,' William retorted.

'Who sent you, and how did you get in?'

'Nobody. Fran's away and I was lonely. I just walked in.'

'Then walk out, damn you! I have too many problems of my own to play nursemaid to a love-sick twirp like you.'

'So I have observed. Things requiring an early start, a new will that hasn't been signed yet, and a loaded revolver.'

If Fran had been watching, she would have known by William's relaxed posture and his calm voice that he was keyed for swift action if need be. Though taller than Elyot and younger, the other man would be more than a match for him physically. He would have to rely on Spitfire reactions if the injured animal in front of him reacted with violence. Elyot growled and threw off the covers, but sank back holding both hands to his head, the growl turning itself into a groan.

William got up. 'You need some strong black coffee, which I shall go and make. Go and put your thick head under the cold tap,' he said.

Elyot got out of bed, and needed William's steadying arm to guide him to the bathroom.

Ten minutes later, William returned with the coffee and some dry toast.

The cold water had worked wonders on Elyot, though his

head was still thumping like a pump. He thanked William, amd apologized.

'If it had to be anybody interfering, I'm glad it was you,' Elyot said.

William said lightly, 'It takes one to know one, so they say.'

'What are you implying by that? You won't change my mind or my plans.'

'Perhaps not. There are still nine hours to the time set for execution. I'm prepared to spend the whole night with the condemned man if necessary. And what I meant was that it takes one love-sick fool to recognize another. Think yourself lucky that it was me and not Thirzah Bates who found a way in. Do you want to talk here, or shall I go and put a match to the sitting-room fire?'

The dull red flush under Elyot's tan told William that his shaft had gone straight home, though the look of despair hurt him. Both accepted that either too much had already been said, or not enough.

'Here,' said Elyot. 'I don't want to look into that sitting-room ever again.' He closed his eyes, remembering. His dear old chair, and the piano stool with Beth on it. His dear old chair, with Beth standing behind it, cool hands on his aching head. His hands on hers, holding them to his lips – she hadn't withdrawn them. His head against that familiar old leather, and her lips on his forehead, kissing one pain away but leaving in its place an agony which nothing could ever cure.

The coffee cup rattled against the saucer as he tried with trembling hands to set it down. William took it from him, and watched him shiver as if in a cold draught.

'Get back into bed,' William ordered. 'Tell me if you want to. I realize it's all to do with Beth – but what, I can't imagine. You don't need my word that I will tell nobody – not even Fran if you say so – but I can't let a friend destroy himself without making some effort to save him. I don't know what is between the two of you, or why it should be such a tragedy that you back off and run without firing a shot on your own behalf. And what about Beth? If she's in the same state as you are, it will be Fran and I who have to cope with her. What's it all about? If it's anything at all serious, are you really intending to skedaddle and leave here to face the music alone?'

('Clever William,' Fran would have said. That pricked where it hurt – his pride.)

Elyot lay back, and began, a bit incoherently, to talk. It was all as William suspected. 'It's partly your fault,' Elyot said, 'because I think it all began at your party, though I didn't know then. I've never been in love before. Oh – I had my fling when I was a youngster – what sailor doesn't? But that wasn't love. And once I'd got my own ship, she was my wife and my mistress combined. Sex, as far as I was concerned, was a wartime disease. Then I went unwillingly to your party, and saw you and Fran together. To be in the same room with you made me think what I had missed. Jess and Greg too, and even George and Molly Bridgefoot. Love was sort of in the air, that evening. Besides, I never have been able to resist a challenge. That smashing girl with no partner, and two old stagers sitting out like maiden aunts, me and Eric Choppen. An old bachelor and a lonely widower. One of us had to dance with her, out of courtesy. I got there first. First bloody mistake.'

'You fell in love,' said William simply. 'Was that such a mistake?'

'I should have gone there and then, if I'd even suspected it. I didn't know. Then there was Christmas Day – she had to come and faint in my garage. Fran made me carry her out to the car! And her eyes, so full of pain and despair, expecting me to be able to help her – just like that boy in the boat . . . The sight of her tortured me . . .

'The black dog came back next day, because she reminded me – and it kept coming. Then I wanted her more, to cure them. She could, just by being there. She can get rid of the migraine as well, by massaging the pain away. She's been coming to use my piano, and . . . well, that's it.

'There's no future in it, William, and you know why. I'm fifty-five, for one thing, and she can't be more than thirty-five. I can't stay where I can see her, and not want her. I should kill Eric Choppen if he ever got his eye on her. I've got to get away. It's settled, as far as I'm concerned. There's nothing you can do. Go home and wait for your woman. Find out how it feels to want her so, and not be able to take her. I can't face the future always wanting Beth. So I'm quitting, one way or another. You won't change my mind.'

'You don't have the monopoly of such feelings, Elyot. I waited thirty years for Fran – two of them in your sort of torture, before she'd come to me. And I never thought of you as a quitter. Well, not without putting up a fight. And what about her? Have you any idea at all how she feels about you?'

Elyot didn't reply, so William went ruthlessly on. 'Have you any right to think of saving yourself by breaking her heart? I don't believe any man could get himself into the state you're in without a whiff of hope or encouragement. Certainly not a fifty-five-year-old chap whose career has depended on sound judgement. When did you last see her?'

'On Monday. I was nearly blind with a migraine. She . . . she kissed it away.' He rolled over in the bed, and turned his back on William.

'And what did you do?'

Elyot sat up, hands clenched and eyes blazing. 'I did the only thing open to me, as an officer and a gentleman. Or as a man who loved her better than he loved himself. I told her to go home and leave me alone. I also told her I was a murderer. She won't bother with me again.

'And if you must know, it's because I think she's already half in love with me that I've got to go now, before she gets hurt worse. She may be a bit upset, but she'll get over it. There's always Eric to step in. My mind's made up and no man on earth can change it. So don't try, William. You can't reach me. You've been the best friend I've had since I lost my ship – and my boy. Please leave me alone. I mean it . . . you can't help.' He turned away, and refused to speak again.

William could only humour him, or at least pretend to. He set the alarm clock again, put some fresh water in the glass and left, closing the bedroom door.

He had lost the battle, and felt deflated and angry. He had lost a lot of his sympathy with Elyot for creating such a storm, but that didn't absolve him from responsibility.

He was involved, whether he liked it or not, in what might yet prove to be a matter of life and death, to say nothing of what a guilty conscience he would have if he did what he felt like doing, which was to go home and leave the silly fool to do as he pleased. Besides, there was Beth to be considered. Till he knew how she felt about Elyot, he had some sort of duty to her, before it was too late. He was smarting on his own behalf at the thought of losing a friend in such a ridiculous, melodramatic fashion. Since Mac's death he had had few friends he cared about so much as those made in these last happy years. He went down the stairs slowly, his thoughts in turmoil.

The man he had left upstairs was no longer hungover, and knew what he was about. If he suspected that William was only retreating to gather reinforcements, or to make any other sort of plan to divert him from his purpose, he would wait only till William's car was out of sight before getting up and leaving. At the foot of the stairs William paused.

It had been a battle of wills: his own against that of a tough mariner inured to hardship and discipline, a lonely, hurt man who was hardest of all on himself. Would the result have been the same if it had been a battle of wits?

Elyot had declared that no man's words could break his resolution – but it occurred to William that a woman's could, especially if the woman were Beth.

It was past nine p.m. The Old Rectory was only two hundred yards away, but William could not be sure Elyot was not already at the window, watching. He had somehow to stop Elyot from making his getaway before he had time to consult Beth. He acted on impulse, creeping silently round all the doors, removing the keys after locking them. On his way to the front door through the sitting-room, he dropped the keys into the duet stool. He banged the heavy front door as he went out, to let Elyot know he had gone, locked it from the outside and pocketed the key. It could only be a delaying tactic, but the golden rule was to put yourself in the enemy's place. If Elyot had the sense William credited him with, he wouldn't send for the police or the fire brigade to release him. Nor would he risk being seen climbing out of a window. He'd get out somehow, but in a way that didn't damage his dignity. William calculated that he had about two hours to bring the silly, stubborn idiot to his senses, by hook or by crook.

Beth's father was his worst obstacle. It was too late for him to be calling on the Rector, with some made-up excuse for speaking alone with Beth. He deliberately let the car roar as he went towards home.

He had never before, to his knowledge, broken a promise to Fran, but tonight she would have wait. He had to ring the Rector's cottage, with a fictitious message from Fran to Beth if need be.

His relief on hearing Beth's voice made him almost dizzy.

'Beth,' he said urgently. 'This is William. I must talk to you, now, tonight. As soon as ever possible. Without your father knowing.'

Her voice showed her surprise, but she kept it low. 'He's gone to bed. We don't sit together very often in the evenings, since Christmas. But why on earth – and how and where?'

'Can you slip out to meet me? I'll be waiting in the car, without lights, in the church gateway. Don't carry a torch.'

He could almost see her smiling. 'Ah! Cloak and dagger, is it? Eminent Professor of History in clandestine meeting with Rector's daughter. Alas for your reputation, William, and mine. What are you playing at?'

'Beth – I'm sorry, but I can't take time to explain. I'm afraid it's deadly serious, or I wouldn't ask you to play such silly games. And every minute counts. Can you be there in ten minutes? It's about Elyot.'

He heard the sharp, indrawn breath, and there was a long pause. 'Beth,' he said. 'He's in trouble, and I need your help. Will you come?'

'Yes,' she said. 'Is Fran with you?'

'Fran's in London. That's one reason it has to be you.'

'I'm on my way.'

He was there before her, the car pulled under trees in the darkness. He opened the door and she got in. 'I don't want to move the car where I can't see Elyot's house,' he said. 'If a car comes by, slide down so that you can't be seen. And the quicker we can be, the better.'

He took her hand, and held it while he told her. There was no time for subtlety, diplomacy or anything else but the bald and brutal truth. 'I left him awake and sober, with a loaded revolver within reach. I have too much respect for him to think he will take that way out. But – he insists that his love for you is hopeless, and his life worthless. Worthless without you, that is. I can put myself in his place – I've been there. What I can't answer for is how you feel about him. He's twenty years older than you, for a start. He may mean no more to you than Daniel Bates does, or me. Don't fool yourself that you have to do anything . . . except tell me the truth. You couldn't fool him if you tried pretending. Tell me the truth, and let me decide what to do next.'

She leaned against him, and he put his arms round her, feeling the tenseness that made her almost rigid. Then she spoke out of the dark silence.

'I do love him, William. I love him as I never expected to love anybody. I think he knows I do. That makes no difference, because he's keeping a dreadful secret. He ordered me out of his house – because he said *I reminded him of the man he murdered.* William, is that true? Do you know? Not that it matters to me – I'd go to the gallows with him if he'd let me. But now that he knows I know, it would always be there between us. He's right. There isn't any hope for us. And I love him more than I love life, too.'

She didn't cry, but laid her head on his chest. He felt the tremors running through her as if they must break her, waves breaking up a grounded ship.

'And they say there's a God,' she said at last, bitterness overflowing like bile.

'So there is, Beth. His other name is Love. Relax and let me tell you a story. About a great man called Elyot Franks, and the boy he accuses himself of having murdered. He had almost forgotten, till he fell in love with you.'

The clock in the tower above them struck midnight before his tale was finished. She was crying, now.

'Thank you, William,' she said. 'I'll go home now. Can I have the front door key to get in to him tomorrow?'

'Go early – very early,' he said. 'And call me if you need help.'

He drove home worrying about Fran. The only bright spot was that he could be sure of her forgiveness when she knew why he had failed her. He'd ring her at breakfast time tomorrow.

Elyot still lay where William had left him, drained and inert, sadness and longing robbing him of the will to get out of bed. His heart ached for what he was losing, and his conscience pricked him for hurting such good friends. But he had no choice.

It was going to be a very long night. Five hours till dawn, at least. He let himself think about Beth, yearning for one more glimpse of her to remember . . .

He heard the creak of the stairs, and shut his eyes tight. William should have known better than to come back.

He made no move when the bedroom door opened, pretending to be asleep. Then he thought he had been to sleep, and was dreaming. That faint, elusive perfume drifting over him couldn't be William's aftershave.

He felt the covers being gently lifted, and held his breath to keep the dream from fading; but she had slid into bed beside him, and was whispering his name. Before he could escape, she had wrapped her arms round him, and pulled his head towards her. 'My love, my love, my love,' she was crooning, kissing the nape of his neck.

His will gave way in spite of himself, and he turned, filling his empty arms with her softness, and his desolate heart with the kisses she was returning as passionately as he was giving them. His last waking thought was that after all there were more ways to heaven than by pulling a trigger.

At exactly five thirty next morning, William's car was outside the church again, with his engine still running. From there he could watch the front of the Old Rectory without being seen himself. If Elyot's car came out of the garage, he would have time to barricade the gate with his own and make one more attempt to reason with him, even if it meant betraying Beth's confidence.

The light above the front door came briefly on, alerting him, before being just as swiftly switched off again; but his eyes were now being assisted by the first grey glimmers of dawn. Two figures stood in the old porch, one tall and slender,

and one like a teddy-bear in a huge camel-hair dressing-gown.
William watched them merge into a close embrace before the
slender one disengaged herself and slipped into the shadows
down Spotted Cow Lane. William felt the elation of triumph.
He had won, after all.

Elyot stood by the door till she was out of sight, then
gently closed it on everything but himself and his incredulous,
riotous emotion.

William dared not risk putting his car lights on. He drove
without them till he was round the bend in the road. Keeping
vigil was one thing; snooping was another.

At eight thirty he dialled the number of Fran's hotel and
asked for her. She had just left for Liverpool Street station in a
taxi, he was told. He wondered if Elyot could possibly be a
happier man than he was himself when the message had sunk
in. Fran was on her way home, a day earlier than he had
expected her.

51

William decided that there was no valid reason why he should
not take French leave for the day. He had been up most of the
night, and it had all been quite stressful into the bargain. He
wanted to tell Fran about it, and hear how she had got on with
her own affairs and with Sue's mother. So he rang his secretary,
waited to tell Sophie they would both be home to lunch, and
went to meet Fran.

She hadn't rested well, either. When they had unburdened
themselves of their respective stories, they both sat somnolent
in their chairs, facing each others, until Sophie served up
lunch. William told Sophie he had found Commander Franks
with a very bad migraine, and had stayed with him till he was
sure there was nothing more he could do.

'I think you ought to tell Thirzah,' he said. 'Migraine
attacks often come in batches, several one after the other, and

then months may go by before the next. It's really quite a common complaint, but attacks can be very bad. I should advise Thirzah not to bother if she finds the door locked, for a little while, in the next week or two. Tell her if she does that it would be better if she just went home again. She'll get paid all the same.'

'Ah, I will,' Sophie said. 'Mam had a cousin what used to hev' them megrims. She'd be so bad-tempered when she did as you daren't goo near 'er. If one of us child'en were cross and mardy, like, Mam would say, "Leave 'er to git over it. She's as bad as Cousin 'Tilda with the megrims".'

They dared not look at each other till she had gone.

'Oh William! That really was wicked of you,' Fran said, catching the laughter in his eyes and trying to stiffle a giggle that she feared might still be heard.

'Why? I told nothing but the truth, did I? It is a common enough complaint old Elyot has got, and a severe attack at that. Enough for Thirzah to find the door locked against her often just at present, I'd say.'

'Poor Cousin 'Tilda,' Fran said, gravely. 'To be remembered chiefly because she had the megrims so bad.'

William gave way to his laughter. 'Ssh!' warned Fran. 'Sophie'll hear.'

'Damn Sophie,' he said. 'For once we could do without her. There's nothing I should like better than to go to bed with the sort of megrims Elyot's got. I thought megrims was a disease sheep get.'

'Not that I know of. It's just the old-fashioned country version of migraine, I think.'

'Well, there's no doubt poor old Elyot's got it. He thinks he caught it at your party.'

'I never 'eard afore as it was catching,' said Sophie, coming in at the door again. 'I wonder if our Het caught it from Cousin 'Tilda?'

'I hope I haven't caught it from the Commander,' William answered her. 'Short of going to bed, I should say the best prevention would be a walk. Do you feel like it, sweetheart?'

'Which?' she said, avoiding his eyes. 'Both or either. We can't just waste the afternoon.'

*

404

'That was playing with fire,' Fran said, as they made for Castle Hill. 'She'd be so hurt if she thought we were laughing at her.'

'We weren't,' he said. 'She'll know perfectly well what it was all about when the truth comes out – which it must before long. What mustn't come out is that the honeymoon preceded the wedding. After all, that was mostly my doing. The least I can do is to provide Elyot with a bit of cover till everybody catches on that love is in the air again, as the song of our dancing days had it.'

'There's her father,' Fran said. 'Whatever happens, he mustn't ever find out the truth about last night. That isn't funny at all, really. I couldn't bear it to be spoilt for them, now.'

They caught sight of Bob Bellamy at the door of his house, and made for him instead of the church. He was divesting himself of outdoor clothes, ready to go indoors. Fran thought he looked a lot less cheerful than when she had seen him last.

'Come in for a cup of tea,' he said. 'Charlie's making some now, before young Charles has to go home. She's going with him, but insisted on getting my tea first.'

Fran still hadn't met the girl, and was glad of the chance. It was one of Charlie's 'spruced-up' days. Her jeans were whole, clean, well-fitting but not, Fran noticed, too tight. She wore a white blouse under a multicoloured pullover, the crisp collar turned out. Her hair was brushed back into a thick, springy pony-tail, and her manners were prettily perfect. Charles was the silent, somewhat embarrassed one, taking his cue from her all the time. Fran was enchanted at the sight of such sweet and fresh young love. When the youngsters had left, she said so to Bob.

'She's beautiful, Bob! She's got William hooked – he couldn't take his eyes off her. Could you, Professor?'

'There's no doubt she's a winner,' William replied. 'I don't wonder young Charles is head over heels.'

'So what's the matter, Bob?' Fran said, changing her tone. 'Aren't you happy about Charles?'

'I should be, except I'm so afraid he's going to get hurt,' he replied. 'All she wants is to be loved and petted, like a kitten. That's why he's so right for her just now. That's the way he treats her, as well. But kittens grow up to be cats, specially if they're as clart as she is. When they're hurt, they scratch. And because he's closest to her, it'll be him she'll claw.'

'Why should she get hurt? She looks happy enough.'

'It'll upset you if I tell you,' he said.

'We're friends, Bob. Isn't that what friends are for?'

'It's her mother. Stirring everything up. Charlie's never got on with her, but John couldn't do wrong for Iris. She's been asking John for money, and he's been getting it out of me, using Charlie as the go-between. John's having to keep it from his wife, 'cos her and Iris are like a couple of strange tom-cats with each other. Charlie thinks the world of John and is trying to protect all of us. She's scared that her mother might come back if she runs out of money, divorce or no divorce.

'I could see very well that Charlie was upset about something, but I didn't know what. Then John wrote to me – though he sees me three or four times a week. With all this upset about Iris, his wife's been at him again to get her out of the fens, so without telling me he's been applying for jobs. He's got one – in Australia. They'll be going soon.

'I haven't told Charlie, yet. I don't know what to do. I shall have to put a man in down on the fen farm, because I shall have to stop here till my lease runs out. But I can't expect Charlie to stop. Besides, she's set her heart on being a vet. She'll go sooner or later, Charles or no Charles. There'll just be me and the ghosts again soon, I reckon.'

Fran tried to find something to say. 'And your animals,' she said. 'Bonzo and Winnie and Matey and all the other cats . . . and the rooks.'

'And my dream,' he said. 'Don't you fret about me. The only thing that I'm sure about is that I mustn't let Iris come back. I reckon there's a lot o' misery to come yet. But I shall get through.'

Fran took his hand, and held it. The only way to comfort him was by human contact. He looked terribly shy, but she knew she had done right.

He turned to William. 'William,' he said. 'I reckon as I'm found something as'll interest you. Only you won't have to split on me to that stiff-as-starch parson. You see, what with this rain stopping me from getting out on the land, and being worried to death about what's happening, I had to go somewhere to be by myself and think. So I let myself into the church. I like it there, anyway. But one day last week I were so miserable I thought it wouldn't matter to anybody, not even Charlie, if I were to get myself killed ... so I went up them ladders to the bell chamber, all by myself.

'I wished you'd been there. There's them six great bells all covered with cobwebs and bat-droppings, all left with their mouths turned upp'ards. If anybody ever does hear 'em ringing o' their own accord, it'll be 'cos one or more o' the ropes has perished and broke. But there's all sorts up there. I poked about as much as I dare, and found the old church chest, covered up with rusty cassocks and things, up in one dark corner. I tried the lid, and it opened. It were full o' junk – but I found the registers. I left 'em there – but I know where they are. Only ... there were another book, not with 'em, but wrapped up ever so careful in layers and layers of canvas, and bound round wi' leather thongs, right at the bottom o' the chest and under the rubbish as had been throwed in on top of it. It were the same shape and size as the registers, but I don't think it can be just another. I reckon it's something special. Do you want to see it? I brought it back with me, because I could swear nobody but me has seen it in living memory. I haven't unwrapped it, so I can still put it back if you say so.'

Desire and scholarly rectitude were at odds. It was so tempting that William almost gave in and asked Bob to produce it, but in the end academic conscience won.

'What have you done with it?' he asked.

'Well, I had enough sense to know that I couldn't just let the air get to it too sudden, 'cos if you ask me, I should say it's been there a hundred years or more, maybe two hundred. So I wrapped it round with oilskin as I happened to have, and then tried it in the Bible box as my grandfather left me. And it fitted as if it had been made for it. So I locked it up, and there it is.'

'It's absolutely fascinating – but I think it will have to stay there till I've had a word with the Rector, and possibly the local archivist. It might be wiser, too. You know my idea that St Saviour's is a plague church? Well, there are several known cases where people saved themselves from the Black Death – and the plague – they were the same thing, anyway – by hiding in churches. By the time of the plague they did have some idea that it was contagious. Caught by contact. And it was cloth in one or two cases that caused it because the fleas that carried the disease were in the seams of the clothing. If you say this book is wrapped in canvas, I don't think we can be too careful. Leave it where it is till I make some enquiries about such things.'

Bob nodded, accepting his decree; but there was a twinkle in his eye that Fran hadn't seen before during that afternoon.

'You're the scholar,' he said. 'I mean, I'm only a higorant ol' fen-tiger, as don't know a big A from a bull's foot. But if there's fleas still alive in that canvas after three hundred year I reckon it'll be the Natural History Museum that'll want that parcel. It's as good an excuse as any to get you off the hook, William. I'll accept it – and take the blame for keeping the parcel till you can square your conscience. It's safer now than where it was, anyway. Any hippy or thief breaking in could have found it, and such as you would never have got a sniff at it, let alone the plague from handling it. Still – I don't let no professor tell me how to farm. Why should I think I know better than you about such things?'

Fran looked from one to the other with amusement. William was having the grace to colour. Bob was laughing.

'Well fielded, Bob. And a well-aimed throw-in as well,' she said. 'You were run out, Dr Burbage.'

She went towards them, holding out a hand to each. From the shelter of William's possessive arm she leaned forward and kissed Bob. 'I can see why you must never have Iris back again, Bob. She thinks your head is as soft as your heart. Next time, choose a wife as quick-witted as you are yourself.'

'Next time?' he said. 'That's too much to expect. I don't.'

'Then there may be a church up there, but there's no god in it,' she said.

He was suddenly as serious as she was. 'I think there is,' he said. 'That's why I feel so much at ease there. I don't know what it is I can feel round me there, but somehow it gives me hope. I shall be all right. Come and see me again soon.'

'Isn't he an extraordinary man?' Fran said as they started home.

'Don't break his heart, darling – or mine. Don't get too fond of him.'

'You're not at your best today, my love,' she said. 'It must be because last night was such an ordeal. Bob's one of the George Bridgefoot type. He wouldn't pinch even a spent match from a friend. He feels safe with me because of you. And I understand him. That's all.'

'I've had three days and three nights without you. Perhaps I've got the megrims,' William said. 'In fact, I'm pretty sure I have. Let's go home.'

They hadn't been in long before a very embarrassed Elyot phoned. 'I saw you go by, so I know Fran's home again,' he said. 'Can I come up? I've got to talk to you both.'

'Of course. Soon as you like,' William answered, adding, 'Damn and blast! No cure for my megrims yet.'

Fran laughed. 'He doesn't know you were snooping this morning,' she said. 'So have we got to pretend we don't know what happened? Poor man! He's gearing himself up to the worst ordeal he's ever faced. I think you ought to save him the ordeal of telling us, by getting in first. Put him out of his misery.'

William agreed, and met him in the hall before taking him in to Fran, who was waiting with outstretched hands.

'I've told her,' William said.

'It's absolutely wonderful, Elyot. I just can't tell you how glad we are for both of you.'

He was incoherent, a confused mixture of shock and fear.

'It can't be true,' he said. 'William, how drunk was I last night when you left me? Bad enough to have been blotto and dreaming? I must have dreamt it all! It isn't possible. A girl like Beth Marriner – actually in my bed? I'm frightened – afraid that I've been gradually going off my rocker ever since the torpedo, and that this is the last step. I know I was nearly mad all day yesterday. God knows what might have happened but for you, William. But I must have gone right round the bend after you left. It's pretty hard to face up to.'

He sat down heavily, doing his best to act normally.

William and Fran looked at each other rather helplessly. The awful thought had occurred to them both that perhaps he didn't want it to be true; in which case, William had created a mare's nest that it was going to be very difficult to get out of.

'Which part don't you want to believe?' William asked.

'I dreamt — I could have sworn — that Beth Marriner came to me in bed. Sorry, Fran. That isn't the way a gentleman should talk about a lady, especially in front of another. But how can I find out?'

William opened his mouth to speak, but Fran caught his eye.

'And that's the bit you don't want to be true?'

He grabbed her hands, and held on to them. 'I'd give my life just to dream the same thing again, let alone believe it could actually have been true. But it's ridiculous. Out of all reason. Such things can't happen — especially between a parson's daughter and a man of fifty-five. I've either gone mad already or shall go mad now, wanting her. Help me, Fran.'

'Elyot,' she said, firmly and slowly. 'I wasn't there. But William has just told you that he saw Beth leaving your house at daylight this morning. Isn't his word good enough for you?'

'I can't believe! I daren't believe! If it's true I have ruined her reputation. She can only have done it because William told her what I said — that I was going to use my revolver when I had seen to one or two other matters. If I didn't dream it, she was acting under a sort of blackmail. That's even worse.'

'William,' said Fran. 'Please go and ring Beth. Ask her to come here at once. If you need an excuse, tell her that I'm ill or something. Don't tell her Elyot is here.'

She waited until William had gone. 'Look at me, Elyot. Swear to me on your oath to tell me the truth. Do you love Beth, or don't you?'

'Love her?' he groaned. 'How do I know? I only know I don't want to live without her, and that I'd die for her! That I never knew before how much love could hurt, because I would never have believed I could ever want any woman as much as I want her. But I want her only on condition that it's what she wants, too. And that's the impossible bit. She can't!

I've been two days in this state, Fran, except for the drunken dream last night. I can't take any more.'

To Fran's dismay, he hid his face in both his hands, and wept. She heard William coming back. 'Bring the brandy,' she called.

William took the scene in at a glance, and went back for the brandy bottle. Fran went out to him, and whispered. 'You take that to Elyot, and make sure that he drinks it. I'm going to wait at the front door for Beth. If I bring her to him, you come out.'

It seemed to Fran like a year before she heard a car on the gravel. She opened the door and let Beth in, putting her arms round the girl and holding her tight. 'Ssh,' she said. 'Keep your voice down. Elyot's here. If William is telling the truth, you acted very courageously last night. You may need just as much courage now. He's in a pretty het-up state. I'm sorry to have to ask, Beth, but I must. Was what you did last night done out of love, or pity?'

Beth was taller than Fran by a couple of inches. She drew herself up, her face aflame, but her eyes as defiantly proud as Juno's might have been.

'Do you dare ask, Fran? You, of all people – do you *need* ask? Where is he?'

Fran reached up and kissed her. 'I'm so glad. I think it's up to you now. Don't give in,' she said, and led Beth to the sitting-room door. Elyot, still white and shaking, leapt to his feet as Fran appeared in the doorway. She waited there till William had time to cross the room to her and then stood aside.

She had a fleeting glimpse of Elyot's face, and his arms flung wide to take Beth in. Her ears caught Beth's whispered words, 'My love, my love, my love,' before she closed the door.

Fran laid her own head on William's chest a moment before pulling him into the kitchen.

'Whew!' she said. 'I don't want to go through that again.'

'What now?' he asked.

'Remember your Homer,' she said. 'Food, and lots of it. I'll bet neither of them has had a bite all day. Thanks to

Sophie, we can always produce some sort of a meal at short notice. Make some coffee while I cut sandwiches. What else can we raise?'

'Pancakes,' he said. 'I'll make them. Don't you remember the night I brought you Cat? I knew after that night that whatever Shakespeare may have said, the real food of love is pancakes.'

'So did I,' she said. 'But neither of us said so.'

'We weren't free,' he said. 'They are.' The wistfulness in his voice made a lump come into Fran's throat. It still mattered to him that he couldn't offer her everything.

They went together to make sure all was well. The dazed look on Elyot's face and Beth's blushes told them all they needed to know.

'Drinks to celebrate, William,' Fran decreed. 'Then supper.'

She was right about them both being hungry. William's pancakes were an enormous success.

'I advise you both to learn to make pancakes,' William said gravely as he handed Beth her second. 'Fran and I have proof that they are the food of love.'

Fran thought that Beth and Elyot wouldn't have argued if he had said it was grey flannel. They reminded her of Charles and Charlie, so shyly tender were they to each other.

But when the meal was over, William brought all four of them down to earth again.

'I think perhaps we ought to apply ourselves to practicalities,' he said. 'You might as well face them first as last. What about your father, Beth? It's all too sudden for any of us to take it in easily. Will you tell him at once? Or let the possibility dawn on him first?'

'I'm too old to play pussy-foot just to please him,' Elyot said, suddenly looking square of jaw and naval again. 'Besides, as you know very well, it's too late for him to raise any objections. There's nothing he can do, now.'

Beth was blushing furiously and delightfully, but her eyes were appealing to Fran.

'We live in a village, Elyot,' Fran said. 'For Beth's sake, you can't rush things too much. And you may have to be a bit altruistic towards Beth's father. Beth won't be happy if he goes into another nervous breakdown because of her. And if she isn't happy, you won't be either. I'd say hold your horses till Easter.'

'Another month?' said Elyot aghast. 'Fran, I can't.'

Beth's shy laughter was like golden bells. She took Elyot's hand, as if for moral support, and said, 'I don't somehow think Fran is suggesting complete Lenten abstinence. I can still come across to play your piano, can't I?'

Elyot relaxed, kissing the hand he held.

'But as it happens, Fran, there are other things I have to face up to Father about. Not for his sake, but for my own. I can't go on being a hypocrite to please him any longer, and I've known that since Christmas. I can't go on sitting on that organ stool pretending I believe what he believes, when I know I don't. I was going to have to tell him that, anyway. Now I shall feel worse than ever, with . . . with old maids like Sophie and Ida Barker thinking I'm still one of them.'

Her chin was up and she didn't falter. 'I nailed my colours to Elyot's mast last night. I'm Elyot's wife, now, not Father's daughter. But I must be as kind to him as I can. Can you all leave it to me?'

'Isn't it up to me to tell him the truth?' Elyot said. 'Let me spare you that.'

'No,' said Beth. 'Please! The cards are in my hands, and if it comes to it, I hold the ace of trumps.'

Elyot leaned over and kissed her. Fran was thinking that there were some things nobody had to be taught how to do. She smiled at the thought, at which William promptly kissed her.

'And the young think they have the monopoly of this sort of thing!' he said.

52

There was no doubt that Charlie had charmed the Bridgefoots, even Brian. He gave up his high hopes of Charles making a well-to-do marriage reluctantly if at all, but in the meantime he looked on Charlie with an admiring and even fond eye. She had the knack of making herself at home with whatever company she was in.

Rosemary was impressed by her down-to-earth understanding of life in a farmhouse, and her ready and capable help at mealtimes. Brian found he could talk animal husbandry to her without the least bit of embarrassment, and even learn from her. She treated Molly with the polite courtesy due to age, without ever suggesting that Molly was past doing anything that she could do herself; she simply threw herself at George and hugged him.

The first time she addressed him without thinking as 'Grandad', in the sitting-room at Temperance, he slapped his thigh with delight while she turned the colour of a boiled beetroot and bolted. Charles went after her, and tried to coax her to come back. He caught her in the new passage at the back of the house, and he folded his arms round her.

'I'm so sorry, Charles,' she said. 'Whatever will they think?'

'Nothing. They're all tickled pink by it. Dad says it was what Uncle Alex would call a Freudian slip. He's my Grandad, so why shouldn't he be yours – one day?' He kissed her, far more like a lover than he had ever dared to before, unable to believe that he had made what could be taken as a proposal and had not been sworn at for daring so to take anything for granted.

She clung to him, and returned kiss for kiss till his head spun with unbelievable delight that there might be hope for him, some years before he had ever expected much more than their present relationship. They stood silent, their arms round each other.

'Charlie,' he said, breathless. 'Come on now. It'll be all right. I promise you.'

'Are you sure?'

'Can't you trust me to know what I'm doing? I love you, Charlie. Kiss me again.' She did, still wanting time before having to face the family again after her gaffe. The more Charles kissed her, the more she responded. Neither had heard Aunt Esther's door open.

'Come on, now,' Charles said. 'If we don't show up soon they'll all be suspicious of what we're up to.'

The rest of the family were tactful, and Charlie soon regained confidence.

Later, over the supper table, she told them about her brother's new job in Australia, and that she mustn't be too late going home because she knew her Dad was upset. 'It means I can't leave him, yet, to do what I had planned,' she said.

'What had you planned?' asked Brian, fearful that it was marriage. She was only eighteen, and Charles only just twenty.

'To be a vet. A small animal vet. It means at least three years at a university – I had hoped in France or Germany. I shall have to wait, though. I can't and won't leave Dad alone.'

'Can't you do the course in Cambridge?' Charles asked, stricken with awful doubt and fear.

'If I have to,' she said. He breathed a great sigh of more than relief. His spring idyll was in no immediate danger. He felt grateful to her brother, thinking that perhaps in the meantime he could change her mind.

George looked at his grandson with a terrible ache in his heart. He had seen too much bright spring promise cut down by a June frost. Robert Fairey would have no summer, and Pansy . . . he couldn't guess what would happen to her. Maybe it wasn't all that sinful for the young to make hay while the sun shone in this modern uncertain world. Nobody who had lived through two world wars could fail to remember how short young life could be, and temper moral judgement with sympathy.

The spring sun had a surprising amount of heat in it, and was generating energy everywhere. Work that had got so far behind on farm and garden was for a short while being tackled with a will that left everybody too tired to mind anybody's business but their own. But in the last week in March, Monica paid her father a visit, and with her pregnancy at half-time, even her own carefully designed maternity wear couldn't quite disguise the slight alteration in her compact, trim figure. The two-piece she had created for herself being such a success had inspired her to others of the same kind for the market, and Greg had excelled himself in producing the watercolour picture as background for an advert. The model wearing the dress stood on a low bridge over a canal, on the further bank of which was a row of houses, one of which had a Dutch gable and a chimney on which perched a tiny but unmistakable stork. He had been delighted by Monica's reaction to it. She had asked him specially to have the original framed for her.

It was when he had collected it from the framer's that Jess first saw it.

'So you have had to lower your standards to the commercial aspects of your job after all,' she said, after examining it carefully. 'It's cheap. A clever bit of advertising, but not art. Without the stork, it would have been a nice bit of painting. But East Anglia doesn't breed storks.'

Greg was nettled. 'Why on earth should it be East Anglia?' he asked. 'People in Holland have babies.'

'It could just as well be East Anglia. Man-made waterways and Dutch gables, flat landscape and sky.'

He looked back at his original and refused for once to take her evaluation of it. The composition was right, the atmosphere was right, the painting was excellent. You could have wetted your feet in the water under the bridge. A lovely peaceful place for a baby to be born in. He tried not to mind her criticism, and said, 'I'm just going to take it over to Monica. Are you coming with me to see her?'

'No, not now. I shall no doubt see her before she goes back. Some of us don't drool over babies like you and Fran do.'

'I never had any to drool over, as you put it, before. Please yourself.'

Roland was spending the same weekend at Benedict's, ostensibly his Easter visit to his mother, though Easter was still two weeks away. Fran suggested a 'family' lunch on Saturday, with Eric and Monica, Jess and Greg. Sophie insisted on coming to do the cooking.

'I wish she wouldn't,' Fran said. 'She does rather inhibit the conversation on an occasion like this.'

'Darling, it isn't our business, any more than Beth's and Elyot's is. Stop worrying.'

To stop worrying now was beyond her, however much William tried to boost her. It was all very well, and quite flattering in its way, to be the one to whom others went in trouble, but the weight of keeping their secrets really wasn't fair on her. Apart from the insane desire to tell when you knew you mustn't there was always either grief or apprehension connected with such confidences – why otherwise would they be secrets?

She had William to share everything with, but he was a man. He worried more about her reactions than he did about the principals. She came to the conclusion that in this particular instance, his philosophy was right. She only made things worse for herself if she gave him reason to worry about her.

But the present load of secrets was getting too heavy. Worst of all was her knowledge about Robert Fairey. She welcomed every sunny spring morning until it brought Robert to mind, because George had said it was very unlikely the boy would ever see another spring. And if she felt like that, what did Robert's mother feel? George himself, too, because of Pansy's part in it.

That led her thoughts to Monica, and with Monica came the nagging worry about Roland. Her son. Had he told Monica the secret he was now sharing with his mother-in-law about Sue's epilepsy? How awful that was for all of them, including Sue herself – but she cared most for Roland. What was he to do? As far as she could determine, he had done nothing for which he deserved a lifetime's punishment. She could be glad of his affair with Monica, because she knew from her own love for William what compensation his visits to Monica must provide, even though they added to his present dilemma. There was his unborn baby, too.

Now there was Beth and Elyot. How on earth would that business be resolved? She knew Bob Bellamy's sad predicament, too, and even that had a secret in it if he had not yet told Charlie of her brother's plans. Lastly, her too-sensitive antennae were picking up uncomfortable warnings of a deteriorating relationship between Jess and Greg.

As she sat waiting for Sophie's arrival on the Monday morning following their 'family' lunch the previous day, she felt depressed and full of foreboding. If only Mary Budd were still alive to be talked to! She enjoyed the 'chaffinching' sessions with Anne and Jess, but neither was a confidante, Anne because she was still too new to everything and everybody, and Jess because – because she was Jess. Like a hedgehog, Fran thought – always ready at the least provocation to roll herself into a prickly ball.

Greg had arrived alone yesterday, with apologies from Jess who had got up with a sick headache. What was wrong with her now, Fran wondered? All the same, the lunch had been really enjoyable, and once Sophie had left, they had talked freely. Greg had by that time excused himself.

Monica was in excellent health, still very busy. The baby was due towards the end of August. She said she planned to stay in London and book herself into her obstetrician's private maternity home. There was wistfulness in her voice that she could not disguise.

'Away from us all?' Eric had asked, bluntly. 'Why?'

'Safer,' Monica said.

'Medically, or to save talk do you mean?'

'You won't safeguard Sue if you give birth in a home for fallen women,' Roland said, a bit brusquely. 'And wherever you are, I'm going to be there – or close at hand. It's my child, isn't it? If Sue chooses that day to throw herself over a cliff, I shall still be where you are. Her mother and I are agreed about that. She's promised me she'll cope. We both suspect that Sue can induce attacks when she wants to – and on this occasion I agree that she may have cause. But you stop being silly, Monica. Her condition isn't your fault.'

(Oh dear! thought Fran. They have had this over several times before. It must mean that Sue had no intention at all of letting go of Roland, and he wasn't going to force the issue. Even if there were time, now.)

Eric knocked his pipe out into the ashtray William had set at his side, looked round the group as if silently soliciting support, and spoke directly to Monica.

'You're not giving birth to my Annette's first grandchild anywhere but in my home,' he said, and the tone was that of an order. 'Since Roland, through no fault of his own, has not yet the right to be masterful with you, I'm the one who has. Don't come any feminist arguments with me! They won't work. A woman wants her own round her at a time like that, not a lot of doctors in white coats, and a posse of starchy nurses. I'm remembering the time you were born. Wartime, but I had got leave, and was at home. So was Annette. There wasn't room in hospitals then for such a natural thing as childbirth for anybody who had a home of their own left standing.

'Babies ought to be born at home, anyway. If I have my way – and I shall – this baby will be born up at Monastery Farm, in your own side of the house, with the best medical help money can provide standing by in emergency. And Roland and Fran and William and me and Old Uncle Tom Cobbleigh and all can be in my side of the house waiting for the good news with a bottle of champagne ready to wet the baby's head – if they want to be, that is. If not, Roland and I will drink it together. And that's settled.'

'Bravo, Eric,' said William. 'If I were lucky enough to be in your shoes with regard to my first grandchild, that's exactly the line I'd take.'

It was extraordinary, Fran thought, how everybody suddenly relaxed. The Commando officer was in charge.

'Who,' said Monica, trying to break the overcharged silence, 'is Uncle Tom Cobbleigh in this case? I suppose you mean Greg, bless him, and Jess?'

'Greg, certainly. He's your partner, now, isn't he? I don't know about Jess. I wouldn't be at all surprised if she has a sick headache again.'

Fran was going over it all in her mind when Sophie arrived. Sophie's mood did not match the spring sunshine. Fran was almost glad of a chance to turn to Sophie's woes in lieu of her own uncomfortable thoughts. She asked what the matter was.

'Only six people again at church yist'day morning,' Sophie said. 'I don't know what things are coming to, really I don't. That great old place as used to be full, with only three others besides me and Thirz' and Dan'el yist'day, and one o' them the churchwarden! It all'us feels so big and bare in Lent, wi' no flowers on the altar an' such, and when there's no organ either ... And the Rector preached another of 'is sermons about the commandments, as if we didn't know 'em quite as well as 'e does. I don't know why 'e should think such as us need to be told to honour our father and our mother, I'm sure, nor George Bridgefoot. Sometimes I think the Rector must hev' queer turns, like.'

Fran was putting two and two together. 'Why was there no organ?' she asked.

'We wasn't told. Only that 'is daughter wouldn't be coming. She didn't come last week. I thought I'd told you.'

'Perhaps she's ill.'

'Not bad enough to stop 'er going across to the Old Rectory and playing the piano there,' Sophie said flatly. 'Thirz' is a'most ready to give 'er notice in, what with 'er being there most days so Thirz' can't get on, and other days when she can't get in 'cos 'e's got the megrims. Funny way o' going on, if you ask me.'

Fran said nothing.

'And Thirz' asked me if I knowed whether it were right that Choppen's daughter's in the fam'ly way. Seems Beryl Bean see 'er getting out o' Choppen's car, and says she'd swear on 'er Bible oath that she must be four or five months gone. "Who's the father o' that one?" she says to Thirz', nasty like. She never loses a chance of a slare at us about Wend', still.'

Fran still made no reply.

'When they first come about 'ere,' Sophie went on, 'folks said as she 'ad a man in London. Seems they was right.'

Fran could take no more. 'Oh, for heaven's sake, Sophie,' she snapped. 'What has any of it got to do with Beryl Bean, or Thirzah, if it comes to that? If you are asking me what I know, ask outright and I'll tell you. As it happens, I do know. They are right – on both counts. But you are not to repeat it.'

Sophie sat down by the table, and looked up at Fran, who for once had lost her composure, and was angrily trying to find something to do with her hands to stop them giving away her desire to cry.

'There's no need for you to keep secrets from me,' Sophie said with enormous dignity. 'Especially if it's about you or any o' yourn.'

Fran sat down facing her, feeling humble and very ashamed

420

of her outburst of temper. When every other female friend failed, Sophie was always still there, staunch and loyal and even open to reason and sympathy these days.

'I shan't tell nobody nothing, you know that. Nor I shan't be giving in my notice. You ain't been the same woman since Christmas, though I thought as you was a bit better after you come back from London that time, till now. I shan't never forget 'ow you stood by us in our trouble. It don't take a lot o' working out for me to know as you're mixed up in this some'ow.'

Fran nodded.

'Ah, I thought so. When Thirz' said what she did yist'day, it were all as clear as daylight to me. "If she's got a man in London as is the father of 'er child," I says to myself, "what were young Roland doin' a-kissing 'er in the pantry yist'day when they didn't know as I were just come back into the kitchen? There's more to that than meets the heye," I said, "and I don't wonder as Fran's been worried."'

'Only I thought as you would ha' told me. I'm never give nothing away as goos on in this 'ouse yet, nor never shall.' There was such gentle reproach in her voice that Fran's tears began to slip down her face. She was genuinely sorry, and thought how stupid she had been not to avail herself of the solace Sophie could provide almost better than anybody, failing Mary. She could not break anyone else's confidence, but about Roland and Monica she told Sophie the whole truth.

'You mustn't think we mind about the baby,' Fran said. 'There will be a lot of nasty gossip – especially because of me and William – but we are only concerned about Roland being so unhappy. Me especially. He's my son! Mr Choppen is being marvellous – we all misjudged him terribly, you know. He would rather Monica had been married, but he's prepared to do everything he can to help her. It will be his first grandchild. He's hardened to gossip. I suppose if it gives such as Beryl Bean a lot of pleasure, we ought not to mind – as long as it is only the truth they're telling. It's when they put things about that have no truth at all in them that it's really harmful. It isn't really our business. It's Roland's and Monica's. So just let them talk. Times have changed so much that it's only in places like Old Swithinford that anybody would be interested.'

'More's the pity,' said Sophie mournfully. 'Can't Roland get a divorce and marry her afore the baby's born?'

'I didn't expect to hear you advocating divorce,' Fran said, smiling.

'I shouldn't ha' done once, only you and 'im give me such a lot to think about. When Miss Budd were talking to me about you two, I said as I didn't believe in divorces, because of what the marriage service says – "Them whom God as j'ined togther, let no man put asunder." And she says to me, "Do you believe in God, Sophie?"

'"Yes, Miss, I do," I says, "and I all'us shall."

'"Then do you think that if God j'ined a couple together," she says, "as any man *could* put them asunder?"

'"No, Miss," I says. "I don't. Nobody can undo God's work."

'"Ah," she says. "So you believe as God 'as j'ined William to 'is wife for ever, though she's left 'im and gone years ago?"

'"No," I says. "I reckon God j'ined William and Fran together when they was little. They've all'us loved each other," I says, "and nobody knows that better than me as was their play-mate."

'"Then use your 'ead, Sophie," she said, just like she used to in school. "You can't hev it both ways." And I could see what she meant. Besides, it ain't as if Roland's got a proper wife now, from what you say. They don't j'ine together in proper wedlock no more. But all the same, that poor little innocent'll be base-born same as our Wend's little ol' boy. Nothing'll alter that.'

'Except for one great difference,' Fran said. 'Wendy hated that man who seduced her. Roland and Monica really love each other, like you and Jelly did, or William and I do. Don't think of Monica's baby as being "base-born". Think of it as "a love-child", because that's what it is.'

'Poor young things,' said Sophie sadly. 'Roland and Monica, I mean. It's too 'ard on them a'ready for the likes o' Beryl Bean to make it 'arder.'

Fran kissed her. 'Thank you, dear Sophie,' she said. 'Are people in the village talking about Beth Marriner going to play the Commander's piano?' she asked, as Sophie prepared to set

422

about her work. 'I mean, is Thirzah telling people what she told you?'

'Well, she is only telling the truth as she finds it,' Sophie said. 'It's more 'er not playing the organ no more as is making folks talk. But then, they'll all'us find something. They'll talk about Monica and Miss Marriner till the next thing turns up.' She shook her duster, and departed.

53

It was the spring sunshine to blame for not letting either Monica or Beth run their full course as topics for speculation. One difficulty was that it was only speculation. Nobody actually knew that Monica was pregnant; they knew only that Beryl could and would take her Bible oath that she looked so; and nobody was sure why there was no music at church on Sundays – but considering what other queer ideas this Rector had, it was surmised by the knowledgeable that he had of his own accord added music to the list of things to be abstained from during Lent.

On a particularly bright morning, Rosemary Bridgefoot was startled to find Aunt Esther standing by the front door dressed in her outdoor clothes, and armed with a stout walking stick. Rosemary, though still worried about the Fairey family and Pansy's part in the tragedy still to come, had regained a lot of her cheerfulness. The knowledge that George had the matter in mind – and therefore, as far as the Bridgefoot family was concerned, in his hands – had taken from her some of the load of dread anticipation. Then Brian had been so much less touchy, and had been getting on so well with Charles, that he was her Brian again; her husband, in fact, because he had not been slow to take his father's advice about the way to cure her depression. She didn't know why he was so loving towards her again all at once, and put it down to the ripening friendship between Charles and Charlie taking place under his very nose, as it were. If she had ever had any high hopes of Charles 'marrying well' she was quite prepared to relinquish them for a girl like Charlie. Peace had descended on Temperance Farm – a fact that Aunt Esther had not failed to notice, or to resent. It irked her that she seemed to have lost her baleful power over them.

'Whatever are you doing, Aunt?' Rosemary asked. 'Do you want me to go round the garden with you for a breath of fresh air? I don't wonder. It's a lovely morning and we've all been cooped up so long by the rain.'

'I am going *out*,' said Aunt Esther.

'Out? Where to?'

'I'm waiting for the bus. I may be forced to be as a slave in the house of the ungodly, but you can't keep me in if I want to go out. I want to hear all the news.'

'The bus won't be along for an hour yet. Wait till I put my coat on, and I'll take you wherever you want to go in the car. You can't manage the bus by yourself. I daren't let you try.'

'The Lord shall control my goings out and my comings in from this time forth – but not a chit of a girl as I had to bring up whether I wanted to or not – and even for evermore. I shall go where I like, and when I like. And you can tell him so.'

'Tell who?' said Rosemary, losing her bearings. Aunt Esther was quite capable of telling the Lord what she wanted Him to know. Surely she hadn't suddenly gone senile and lost all reason? Rosemary was usually well-versed in translating her aunt's biblical utterances into some sort of sense, but her knowledge that nobody else was about to help her cope rather scared her. She was genuinely worried at letting the old woman out alone for the first time for about six months, but decided that it would be best to humour her.

'Nobody wants to stop you going out for a chat, Auntie, but I wish you would let me take you.'

'You can take me down to the village. I want to see some of my friends from the chapel. They would have come up to see me, if you and him had let them. "I was a father to the needy, and now I am their song, yea, I am only their by-word,"' she added.

'If they had come to see you, we should have been pleased for your sake, and made them welcome,' Rosemary retorted, stung into answering back in spite of her resolution. 'I suppose you mean Brian,' she said. 'He has been good to you, and so has his father. I won't argue with you. I'll go and get the car.'

Aunt Esther was having some difficulty in recalling enough texts to fit her aggressive mood. She was somewhat out of practice, it now being a long time since she had had her memory refreshed from the chapel pulpit once at least every week.

She was stiff and her bad hip was awkward. It was only with a lot of patience and difficulty that Rosemary eventually got her installed in the passenger seat, and that proof of her helplessness had done nothing to sweeten her aunt's temper.

'"I have been young, and now I am old," saith the Lord. "I have seen the wicked in great power, spreading himself like the green bay tree."'

'Oh, do stop it, Auntie. Brian can't hear you, anyway.'

'"God is in heaven but thou art upon earth. Set thine house in order."'

'What do you mean by that?'

'"A wise son makes a glad father, but when pride cometh then cometh shame. You should not have spared the rod. The father has ate the grapes, and the son's teeth are on edge." I heard 'em and I see 'em at it, with my own eyes, in the passage outside my room last Saturday night. "Pride goeth before a fall. There is death in the pot." That boy o' yours shall bring down his father's head with sorrow to the grave. Serve him right. Never did I think the day would come when I should be dependent on such as them Bridgefoots!'

'I shall put you down here, Aunt Esther. You can get home by yourself.'

'Here' happened to be just outside Beryl Bean's shop. Beryl was the one member of the chapel congregation Miss Palmer most wanted to see.

They made much of her in the shop, finding her a chair against the counter, and making a cup of tea to drink with her. Neither Beryl nor Olive liked Miss Palmer any more than most folks did, but Beryl had the crafty astuteness of the unintelligent 'on the make'. The shop had raised her and Kenneth up a rung or two from the simple odd-job men Kid and Jelly had been previous to Jelly's windfall and death before he had had time to marry Sophie.

Beryl had been sent to the chapel Sunday school from the time she could toddle by her older sister's side, and remembered what joy it had given all the congregation when the tall, hard-faced woman who had come to live under George Bridgefoot's patronage at the Pightle had appeared at the evening service the first Sunday she had lived there. She had been a thorn in the flesh of all the established regulars from that day, but at the same time they felt somehow that she was a sort of trophy won from the church. Moreover, she was a conduit through which news of any event concerning the church reached the ears of the chapel congregation, sometimes even before members of the church's own knew anything about it.

Now that Miss Palmer was there in the flesh again, recent doings at chapel were recounted in detail, which naturally led on to those of the church. Aunt Esther had to admit that she had not heard before about the defection of the organist for the last two Sundays.

'Well, we shall know come Easter Sunday whether it's only on account of it being Lent,' Beryl said. 'Though I know for a fact as she were there the first Sunday in Lent. But there, he's a queer'un, the new Rector I mean, by all accounts. I have heard tell as he's been seen going about at night with a torch, shining it into the back seats o' cars. There is them as think he's a bit barmy, specially about what goes on between young couples these days. Won't have nothing to do with them two up at Benedict's, so they say.'

'It puzzles me about them altogether,' Olive put in. 'Miss Budd were very thick with 'em, wasn't she? And why Thirzah Bates'll go and help 'em at parties and such, I never have understood. Or why Sophie Wainwright still goes to do for 'em.'

'Soph's a dark 'orse,' Beryl said. 'We all' us did think there should ha' been more money than there was left when Jelly got killed. There's them as think Soph' were the one who had all the rest. But Jelly wouldn't ha' left her thousands o' pounds

426

for nothing, would he? Stands to reason, don't it? Daylight robbery, that were, her taking it out o' the mouths of his family. But there, that's church folk for you, all over.'

'There were a time when no Bridgefoots would ha' been asked up to Benedict's,' Olive said. 'But Soph' told me herself as they were there at that party they had afore Christmas.'

'Left me by myself,' Aunt Esther said, 'with that woman o' Bert Bleasby's. Not that she ain't as good as any Bridgefoot.'

Heads closer together, voices dropped. There was no need for Aunt Esther to resort to quoting the Bible with these two avid gossipers. From the party to the company, to Choppen, to Monica, to Beryl's suspicion, to guesses who the father might be. Beryl had heard of Greg's weekly visits to London. They agreed that it looked fishy that he had only started them 'regular' when Monica had gone back to live there.

'There's your young Charles just gone by on his way up to see that gal o' Bellamy's,' Beryl interrupted. 'Same time, every day. I 'ear she comes up to Temperance now.' Luck had played right into Aunt Esther's hands.

'She's all'us up there,' she said. 'I don't know what that niece o' mine can be thinking about. Such goings on!'

'What, up at Temperance?' prompted Beryl.

'Them young'uns think as I'm blind and deaf,' Esther said. 'When my door ain't quite shut I can 'ear every word they say. That's where they meet to plan things. Right outside my door. That gal o' Choppen's won't be the only one, afore long. But there, as the twig is bent, so shall the tree grow, as the Bible says. That boy's all'us had what he wanted and nobody's ever said him nay about nothing. That girl didn't say him nay, either. I heard 'em planning what they'd do that night when he took her home.'

Beryl was a past master at the craft of wheedling details out of those who hinted. Esther was soon regaling her hearers with the story of the meeting in the dark passage outside her room. Many partly deaf people irritatingly insist that what they thought they heard was what was actually said. What Esther thought she had heard was supplemented by pleasure at holding the centre of the stage, and her animosity to any Bridgefoot. 'There they was, wound round each other like a couple o' dogs as couldn't separate, slopping and kissing, and I could 'ear every word they said.'

Beryl and Olive leaned closer.

'"I can't," she says. '"It'll be all right," he says. "Are you sure?" she says. "Can't you trust me?" he says. "I'll take care of you. Come on! If we don't go quick they'll wonder what we're up to now."'

The poisonous mushroom spore was not long in spreading right round the village. It blew into the ears of the Rector, Brian Bridgefoot, Bob Bellamy and, via Sophie, into William's and Fran's.

It was Brian who told George. George went straight to the source and asked Charles outright.

Charles went red with embarrassment, white with fear at what it might do to him and Charlie, and then red again with anger. Clear-eyed and indignant, he refuted the charge, and George believed him.

'It's that damned old woman,' Charles said. 'Nobody but her would hint such things, about me and Charlie! Oh, yes, Grandad – I'm a man all right now, and I want her like that. I'll marry her if she'll have me, one of these days, whatever anybody says. But you needn't worry. I can wait – and anyway, she wouldn't consider getting married yet. Any fool who knows the situation would see that. I do . . . and I know her. I love her, Grandad. I'll wait for her for ever, if I have to. I thought you'd understand me.'

George thought he had never been so proud of his grandson as he was at that minute. 'I do, my boy, I do. And I've been young myself, though things were different then. But stick it out if you can till you're married. Keep something to look forward to. And if you only try to do that you can rely on me to back you if ever you should need me. Go on taking care of your girl. You'll win in the end.'

'But people are talking about us, and it isn't true! What can I do about that?'

'You can't stop folks talking. And women'll always keep their eye on other folks's daughters instead of their own – always have done, always will. You can't stop 'em. Men make mucky jokes about it, and boast and brag about their own performance. Mostly lies. Not in front of me though, they don't. But there's only one way to deal with that sort of talk and that's to take no notice of it at all. If it ain't the truth, just laugh at it. That takes some doing, and I know how it hurts, but it's the only way. What was that we all said when we were kids? "Sticks and stones may break my bones, but words'll never hurt me." You've got to let 'em know you believe that. And you've got to make yourself believe.'

'I don't care what they say about me,' Charles retorted. 'What I don't know is how I can stop 'em talking about Charlie.'

'You can't my boy, you can't. I wonder where it all started.'

'I don't,' said Charles. 'I know! Thanks, Grandad. I'm going home, now, to sort something out.' Before George could reply, he turned and went off without a backward glance.

As it happened, Brian was there when he got to Temperance. Charles strode in, and confronted his parents with the tale, asserting that there was no truth in any of it, and that he was going to 'have it out' with Aunt Esther.

'That day she went down to the shop,' he said. 'Mrs Bean and Mrs Hopkins were standing with her at the shop door waiting for the bus when I went by, so I stopped and picked her up. She didn't speak even to thank me, but I could see she was excited, and guessed she'd heard a nice bit of gossip. You can tell by the way she twists her mouth. I wondered who she'd been getting at. Us Bridgefoots, of course, we're used to that. What I didn't know then was that it was all lies about my goings on with Charlie.'

He turned and faced his father, head held belligerently high, face flushed, chin thrust forward. 'Is she going to leave Temperance, Dad, or am I? It isn't big enough to hold both of us.'

Rosemary quailed. Brian, taken by surprise, looked stolid, but didn't answer.

'Mum believes me, I know,' Charles went on. 'I can see that you don't. Because you don't want to. So it's up to me. I'll give you till Easter to make up your mind which of us you want. Get her out, or I go. And I don't care where.'

He was very near to tears, now, and slammed himself out of the house without going near Aunt Esther after all. Well, she could wait.

Rosemary put her head down and cried. 'Brian, he's our son. My son!'

Brian only glared at her. They were back again where they had been before.

Brian went to tackle Aunt Esther. She was forced to answer him, Bridgefoot though he was.

She repeated to him what she had heard in the passage outside her room, with enough truth but enough twists in it to make him doubt Charles – partly because it suited him to, as Charles had said. He had hoped his son's infatuation with the girl wouldn't last, in spite of liking and admiring her.

Charles found Charlie, when he got to Castle Hill that evening, curled up in a chair, crying. Her father was nowhere to be seen.

'Where's your Dad?' he asked, standing just inside the door.

'I don't know. Walking about the farm somewhere, I should think. Why?'

'I want to talk to him,' Charles said. 'What's the matter?'

He went closer to her, and decided her father could wait. His anger gave way to a great wave of tenderness for her as he took in the depth of her distress. He pulled her out of the chair, sat down himself, and took her back on to his knee and into his arms. He stroked her, soothed her, kissed her gently, held her tightly. She put her face down on his chest and cried till his shirt front was wet.

Never had he felt more adult, never wanted her more. Never had he let it excite him less. His grandfather's advice had taught him his role as a protector. The helplessness of his usually so independent and fiery companion deepened his love for her to a pitch he had never known before. He had to be everything to her that she needed except the lover that he longed to be.

'What's this all about, my lambkin?' he said, the endearment his grandmother had so often used to him in his childhood coming, it seemed, from nowhere.

It got through to Charlie as nothing else could have done. She smiled through her tears, and held up her face to be kissed.

'Dad, mostly. He's so upset. John came up to say goodbye to us today. I don't think Dad really believed he'd go. He thinks he'll never see his son again, because once they are there, Melanie won't let him have much to do with us. She's just taking him away from us — Mum especially, but from me and Dad as well. Poor old Dad! I wish I knew where he was. He's been gone since dinner-time. What did you want to see him for?'

'To tell him there is no truth in the tales that are going round the village about you and me,' he said, kissing her again. 'And to tell him that I shall ask you to marry me, one of these days. Will you?'

'I don't know,' she said. 'Not for years and years yet, anyway. I like you best of all the boys I've ever met, but I don't know if I ever want to get married. Marriage means sex. I know too much about animal sex — I hate to think about people doing it. I mean, look at my mother! It's all she thinks about.' She made a face of tearful disgust. 'I want to be loved, not mauled. I want to be cuddled, like this, not raped. That's why I do love you Charles. I feel so safe with you.'

'I want you, though,' he said.

'Yes, I know. Sometimes . . .' She stopped, and blushed. His heart turned over. 'But I'm not ready to commit myself to anything,' she said, firmly.

'I shall wait till you are,' he said. 'I'll never want anybody else. When that time comes, I shall ask you to marry me.'

'How will you know?' she asked.

He looked down at her, still lying in his arms, her head on his chest. The swell of her breast was within reach of the tips of his fingers, and all his young manhood urged him to reach out and touch . . . but her eyes held no invitation. She was as innocent of any sexual provocation tonight as the lambkin he had called her.

'If I wait long enough, my lambkin,' he said, 'I think you'll tell me.'

She sat up. 'Charles, please don't say anything to Dad tonight, if you see him. He's too upset already. I'm really worried about him. Will you stay with me till he comes in?'

431

He felt about twenty years older than he had done that morning. He nodded.

'I don't know that it's wise,' he said, 'considering what they're already saying about us. If anybody saw me come up here, and then I'm seen going home in the middle of the night, you'll probably have to marry me, or I shall have to marry you to keep your father from shooting me.'

'I wonder where he is?' she said. The concern in her voice warned Charles to take her worries seriously.

Bob had left the house full of trouble. He was already very angry at the rumours about Charlie which had reached his ears. He was not bothered that they might be true. He knew they were not. He hoped she would never know. But he didn't want to lose her yet, one way or the other. She was the only thing left, close to him, except his animals. Even Matey, rousing more often, showed signs of restlessness that Bob understood. He put the little creature down at the edge of the wood, and said, 'Go and find her then . . .' but he was afraid that a predator would find the squirrel first.

He called, and Matey came scampering back – and then off again. That was just like Charlie, he thought. She wouldn't leave him just yet, if she didn't get in one of her tempers because of the gossip. If she did, she would take up the offer she had already got of a job as an au pair to a vet's family in Brittany.

Then there was John. John had always been Iris's son more than his, because she had used the clever boy for her own ends, to boost her social standing. It was she who was driving him to the other side of the world now – to get away from her.

He wandered by habit towards the rookery, standing under the trees and watching the young rooks trying their wings. He wondered if their parents cared as much as he did when their children left the nest. He went to lean on the church wall, still with one eye on the busy activity of the rookery, wondering what was disturbing the birds so much. For a few minutes, he forgot his own misery in speculating on the reason for the noise, the general air of frenzy, the unusual number of black bodies among the budding branches.

And then, as if at a signal, the whole mass of them rose like a black cloud above the wood, circled once or twice, and headed away. He knew at once that they would never return.

The hair rose on his arms and at the back of his neck. He had never seen it happen before, but he had heard of it, and knew what it meant. When rooks left their rookery, it was a dread omen of fear, of death and destruction – for their rookery itself, for the location, for somebody in it. Perhaps for all of those things; perhaps for him. Well, he had troubles enough now. He had already lost both his wife and his son.

He turned away from the empty trees, and stumbled about to search for the church key among the ivy. He let himself in and locked the door from the inside, secure there from any intrusion, alone with his ghosts. Ghosts of his own past, spectres of an empty future, phantoms of what might have been if Iris had never crossed his path and he had found the sort of woman who had loved him for himself, and not for what she could get out of him. Somebody he could have lavished his love on, as William lavished his on Fran. That thought hurt. He had lavished love on Iris, and it had slid off her like water off the back of a duck. It had never got through to her . . . She had never given any of it back in the way that Fran reflected William's. It hurt him to be in their company, while it warmed him at the same time. It pleased him to know that of all other men, he, the simple uneducated fenman, was the only one who could rouse jealousy in William. Not because he wanted to hurt his friend, or had designs of any sort on Fran. He could no more have tarnished their relationship with each other than he would have destroyed any other thing of beauty – strangled a kitten, or pulled a rosebud to pieces. That he could raise jealousy in William was a proof that they both understood his need of what they had.

Only his animals had ever accepted what he had wanted to give. Iris never, John never. Iris had seen to it that Charlie had been sent away from him so young that until recently he had never had long enough with her to find out how much she would accept. He knew how much she had to give. She had been giving to him and to young Charles Bridgefoot a lot, just lately. She was learning how to give; but he was not at all sure she was learning to accept so readily, either from himself or the boy who wanted to give her his life,

He put his hand into his jacket pocket to feel for Matey, but the pocket was empty. Empty as everything else.

He put his head down on the back of the pew in front, and wept. He wept the pent-up tears of many years, those he had held back when Iris had spurned him in bed; when his faithful old gun-dog bitch had died giving birth to dead puppies because he had not been there and Iris hadn't even sent for the vet; when John had gone to boarding school; when John had gone to college, and showed how much he despised his fenland origins by never bringing a friend home; for Charlie whom her mother had never wanted, and whom he had allowed to be sent away when she was even younger than John had been; for the kitten that bugger Bailey had blown to bits in front of his eyes; for the empty rookery; for his empty pocket. For Matey. For himself.

He had no idea how long he had been there, except that it had grown pitch dark inside the little church. He had no more tears left to shed. He felt emptied, stranded, purposeless, with no will to do anything but just sit there.

His thoughts turned to Charles. Poor boy! He couldn't save Charles from pain any more than he could save himself. If Charlie insisted on leaving, he didn't know which of them would suffer loneliness most. He rested his head again on the pew in front to think, but this time he slept.

When he woke, he still had no idea what the time was, but his first clear thought was that it must be past midnight, and that Charles must have left Charlie alone in that great ghost-ridden room long ago. He felt much better, and lost no time in locking up and going home. When he opened the door into the big room softly, the log fire was still giving out a soft glow of light. Charlie was fast asleep on Charles's lap.

'Ssh,' Charles said. 'She didn't want me to leave her till you came in.'

'But it's nearly two o'clock,' whispered Bellamy, aghast.

'Too late for anybody to see me go home. Don't worry. I wasn't going to leave her alone.'

They looked at each other. Charles could see the ravages of his lonely ordeal still on Bellamy's face.

434

'You needn't worry about anything,' Charles said. 'She's been as safe with me as she would have been with you.'

Bob smiled. 'I never worry when she's with you,' he said.

Charles felt as if he had been knighted. They didn't put the light on for fear of waking her. Somehow Charles managed to transfer her from his own arms to her father's without fully rousing her. She put her arms round her father's neck and kissed him, snuggling down again on to his chest.

'That was meant for you,' Bob said, smiling.

'I hope so,' Charles replied. 'This is meant for her, anyway. Tell her so when she wakes up.' He leaned over her as she lay in Bob's arms and kissed the top of her head.

'You know I love her, don't you, Mr Bellamy?' the boy said.

'I thought so. If anybody's welcome, you are.'

'Nobody is, yet, really, with her,' Charles said. 'But I can wait. Goodnight . . . sir.'

Bob's back straightened up, and his courage returned at the boy's gesture of respect. He carried his daughter up the stairs and tucked her into bed.

Charlie had not been in the least concerned to learn from Charles or from her father that she was the main topic of scandal for the time being. She had a completely clear conscience, for one thing, and for another she had not been at home long enough since she grew up to know how virulent such gossip could be. She was inclined to regard it as a joke.

She was much more sophisticated in her outlook than most girls of her age – Charles's twin cousins, for instance. Her education was streets ahead of anything a small local independent school could provide.

Her knowledge was different from theirs and her manners and deportment perfect, when she wanted them to be; she had been educated among the daughters of the upper middle-class who took what they were for granted. Her schooling had not included the element of snobbery for which Pansy and Poppy's father had paid. It had cost Bob Bellamy more for his one daughter than Vic had paid for both his, and there was an element of snobbery about it – for Iris's benefit, not for

Charlie's. The overall result was that while the twins put on airs to show their difference from state-school pupils, Charlie was only ever herself, or one of her many selves, according to her changing moods.

It was only when she went to Temperance that she became aware of a coolness towards her that had not been there before. Rosemary, on edge again with Brian and afraid that Charles might carry out his threat to leave, wished with all her heart that Bellamy's daughter had never appeared in her son's vision. She tried hard to be the same with the girl as she had always been, but did not succeed. Charlie was too astute not to see through her pretence.

Brian was angry that Charles had dared to bring the girl to his house again while the talk about them was still rife. He didn't try to be nice to her. Charles was miserable, embarrassed and apprehensive. He knew Charlie too well to think that she would accept the change of attitude meekly and without explanation. Nor did she. Left alone with Charles for a minute or two, she asked what it was she had done wrong. He pretended he didn't know what she was talking about.

'In that case, I'll find out for myself,' she said.

Rosemary had barely got back in the room before Charlie said, 'Charles, I would like to go home, please. Will you get my coat?'

Rosemary began a rather feeble protest. Charlie waited politely while she finished. 'I would prefer not to stay where it is so obvious that I am not welcome,' she said. 'May I be allowed to know what it is I have done wrong?'

Charles was back. 'It's my fault, Charlie,' he said. 'I thought my parents had more sense. They are ashamed of us. They choose to believe that the tales about us are true. Have you heard the latest?' His question was addressed to his mother. 'The latest is that the Rector caught us at it in the back of my car when he shone a torch on us. Don't look so shocked, Mum. You apparently accuse us behind our backs of indulging in sex, but think I'm vulgar to mention it. That's just hypocrisy ... Aunt Esther's sort of morality. As it happens, Charlie doesn't need telling about the birds and the bees. Ask Grandad. She wants to be a vet ... and she hasn't got your small mind –

or your nasty one. Say what you like. Believe what you like. It won't do Charlie any harm.'

'Don't you dare to speak to your mother like that,' Brian bawled at his son, having come back in the middle of Charles's angry diatribe.

'Take me away, Charles, please,' said a very haughty Charlie in her most ladylike voice, disdain in every line of her.

Esther had heard the raised voices and crept along the passage to listen.

'It's that old witch who started the tale going,' Charles said. 'She's got her way. She's turned you against Charlie by her lies – because lies they are, and you know it. And she's turned me against you. I did warn you.'

'No, they ain't lies neither,' said Aunt Esther, stepping into the room. She held up her hand like a witness in court. 'May the Lord do unto me and more also if I didn't hear them two talking their filthy talk outside my door. And you should ha' seen the way they was carrying on there. In your own house. No wonder other folks knows what they get up to. You can smell it on them. They stink like tom-cats in spring.'

Charlie's persona changed. She turned towards the old woman, forgetting her ability to swear in French, German, Spanish and Italian. Her English served her quite well enough.

'You bloody lying old bitch!' she said. 'May the Devil collect you and roast your guts in hell! Spit your damned curses. They'll only blow back into your own ugly old face. You may scare the simple-minded, but you're only farting against thunder with anybody who's got an ounce of brain. They know the truth, and that's what a wicked old bugger you are. You don't scare me, you evil-minded old she-devil.'

'Charlie! Charlie!' Charles was pleading.

'So this is your well-educated young lady you've been bragging about, is it?' sneered Brian. 'Get her out of my house.'

'This,' said Charles, 'is the girl I shall marry as soon as she'll have me.'

Charlie had turned herself back into a proud young woman with the air of a duchess buying clothes-pegs from a gipsy at the door.

'You may keep the change,' she said to Rosemary. 'And your son, if you can. I have no use for him yet. I'll whistle for him when I'm ready for him. As now. Come along, Charles. Thank you for your hospitality.' She turned towards the door.

Wait, Charlie,' called Charles urgently. 'Wait in the car for me. I won't be long.'

Charlie went out with her chin high, reached the car and broke into tears, swearing in every language she could lay her tongue to.

The room she had left was silent except for Rosemary's sobs, the grinding of Brian's teeth and Aunt Esther's malignant mutterings.

Rosemary looked up when Charles appeared carrying two suitcases and other things over his arm.

'Where are you going?' she wailed.

'To Grandad and Granny,' he said. 'If I ever come here again, it will be after your sainted aunt's gone, and then only if you beg me to . . . with Charlie at my side.' He slammed the door on his home and his parents, secure in his Grandfather's love.

Molly grieved, and George suffered; for all of them, but this time, mostly for Charles . . . and himself. His family had come to pieces in his hand.

54

Beth had declared that she needed to talk to her father herself. She left it till the following Saturday. The Rector was aware that she had been visiting the Old Rectory to use the piano, and had made his disapproval of even that innocent acquaintance very clear by refusing ever to mention it. Beth had supposed his stance due to his previous brush with the Commander, though it had crossed her mind that he also regarded it as unseemly that the daughter he was so obviously writing off as an ageing spinster should appear to be putting herself forward in the path of an unnattached man. In her present mood of almost delirious happiness, she could afford to laugh at him. Poor Father. He had so often in the past been the quarry.

Her conscience with regard to Elyot was not troubling her at all, not even about those mornings when Thirzah had found the door locked. She examined the whole situation as clearly as she had done her own before Christmas. She had never thought of herself as 'an ageing spinster' by nature – only by circumstance. And she was aware that what she was feeling now was not an old maid's craving for sexual experience. She could tell herself with truth that if Elyot's diffidence had been on account of injury or impotence, she would have wanted to marry him just the same (though she was honest enough with herself to blush at her remembrance of his virile proof that it wasn't). Looking back, she felt that she had always known, from the moment he had so gallantly stepped forward to partner her in that eightsome reel, that that incident had only been an instance of a coming event casting its shadow before it. She acknowledged that perhaps her despair at Christmas might have been in some part due to disappointment that her intuition seemed to have played her false.

Her conscience had been troubled for a long time on a very different matter, about which she would have had to confess to her father if Elyot had never existed. What had now happened made it necessary to bring her confrontation with her father about her loss of faith in his brand of Christianity forward.

Even before the onset of her father's breakdown, she had begun to be troubled by her lack of commitment to the church. She hadn't been then, and still wasn't prepared to substitute the concept of Christianity as a whole for 'the church' in this context. She still believed, she discovered, in Something or Somebody who 'had the whole world in his hands'. What had happened between her and Elyot in this last week had made that belief stronger, because she now wanted to throw herself down before whatever this power was in paeans of joy, 'lost in wonder, love and praise'.

Her duty towards her neighbour had never been in doubt.

Before her mother had died, she had thought her father the very epitome of what a parish priest should be, his compassion and tolerance towards frail humanity balancing the doctrinal aspects he preached from the pulpit. But during his illness, and since he had become Rector of Old Swithinford, the balance had been lost. He was no longer tolerant nor compassionate, especially to the young, and his sermons had become dogmatic to a degree she could not accept.

She had been rapidly approaching the point of no return when he had started on a series of sermons based on the commandments. Kneeling for the general confession one Sunday morning, she had listened to her own voice making declarations which were simply not true. Bearing false witness, in fact. She examined her conscience with regard to the Commandments other than the ninth. The fifth? Guilty. She still loved, but no longer honoured the bigot her father had become. The tenth? Guilty again. She had certainly coveted the sort of love she had encountered a few times in her life, most recently at Benedict's. The sort that left a fragrance in the air and sprinkled drops of happiness over anyone in contact with it for a few minutes – till the envy set in.

As she waited to face her father, she wondered how it could be that the god of the commandments who, according to the second, showed mercy into thousands of them that loved him and kept his commandments should now have seen fit to shower so many on her, who wasn't keeping them very well. Such blessings as Elyot's love.

Well, they hadn't broken the seventh commandment, anyway, because neither of them had, or had ever had, other spouses. So what sin had they committed? Any or none? They had offended against the holy laws of society as laid down by Victorian prudery . . . but? Try as she might, she could recall no absolute biblical ban on sex, even when disguised as fornication, in its own right. Most of the taboos laid down to the Hebrews of old were matters of hygiene rather than sin. Try telling that to Thirzah Bates, though!

Whether or not she had now committed the worst of all sins she didn't really know, and she cared less. She did care very much that she should not have to regard herself as a liar or a hypocrite by continuing to attend services her conscience would not allow her to participate in, even without her new secret.

At her father's entrance, she steeled herself to say what she must as calmly and firmly, though as kindly as it could be said. She glanced across to the house where Elyot was, and felt his love for her with her, by her side, above and below her, before and behind her, round about her and inside her. The bleak wastes of Antarctica had melted. She was no longer alone.

'Father,' she said. 'I need to talk to you. I hope what I'm going to say won't upset you too much, but I have decided I don't want to play the organ at church tomorrow. Perhaps no more at all.'

He laid down the newspaper he had just opened, and looked towards her. 'What nonsense is it now?' he asked testily as if to a fretful, demanding child. No. As if to an irritating spinster of uncertain age whom he suspected of suffering menopausal instability. It had the effect of making her more forthright.

'Not nonsense at all. I just can't go along with your sort of Christianity. I'm asking to be excused from having to pretend that I believe in things I don't.'

'Oh, very well,' he said, opening his paper again. 'It is Lent. We can do without music till you come to your senses. I shall expect you to have had second thoughts by Easter Day.' And with that he dismissed her and began to read, exactly as if he had done his duty by ticking off a naughty choirboy detected in singing his own ribald version of a hymn. He took it absolutely for granted that she would obey him if he now humoured her.

With only eight days left to Easter, she tried again.

This time he showed his anger. 'What did you say? Of course you will do what is asked of you, especially on Easter Day. You will help to celebrate the Christian year's most holy festival.'

'No, Father, I can't and I shan't. You must try to understand.'

'I do understand, only too well. This comes of me giving you too much rein since we came here. As I predicted, you

441

could not come near pitch without being defiled. Your so-called friends . . . your new acquaintance . . . whose company you are making yourself riidiculous by seeking out under any excuse . . .'

He got no farther, staring up at her as she leapt to her feet, turning eyes blazing with temper on him.

'How dare you criticize my choice of friends, even if I had any other choice! What on earth do you think gives you the right to choose my friends for me? I'm no longer a child. I'm thirty-three, and you don't own me. You think you do because you are responsible for me whether you like it or not – your dependent daughter to whom you have a duty. Since the episode at Christmas, an embarrassing duty, because you fear I may be mentally unbalanced. The pot calling the kettle black?'

He was on his feet now, standing to face her. 'That is quite enough,' he said, coldly.

She laughed. 'Why don't you send me to bed without my dinner? Look at me. I am your daughter, but you don't own me. I'm not dependent upon you. I don't owe you anything. I've earned my keep three times over. First as your loving daughter and your constant companion – while you wanted it that way. And for all these years the domestic slave who has looked after all your creature comforts. And I've been your assistant, overworked like my mother till the weight of her duties killed her. She was only doing what she had promised when she married you – obeying you. I've never made you any such promise. I'm not my poor mother. I am me! For whom you are not responsible, body or soul.'

He spoke mildly, as to a screaming child. 'Sit down. You are beside yourself.' His tone infuriated her.

'I haven't done yet,' she flashed back. 'I suppose by my defiled friends you mean your *bêtes noires* up at Benedict's? And that the acquaintance you suppose me to be chasing is Elyot Franks?' She paused. She was very nearly as tall as he, and her contempt seemed to diminish him. 'More than my acquaintance, Father. Unless, of course, you are using the word in its archaic sense, in which case you are quite right. My dear acquaintance. My friend, my lover, my husband-to-be.'

He tried to push her down into a chair, but she held her ground.

'My poor child,' he said. 'Have you any idea what you are saying? What repressed adolescent day-dreams you are now putting into words? I have seen it happen before, not once, but several times. I did not understand until my own illness brought me into contact with psychology. Would you like to go away somewhere for a while? I will arrange it for you as soon as I can.'

Her response to that was to sit down rather suddenly and start to laugh. She had never felt so free of him and all he stood for as she did now.

'You don't understand even now,' she said. 'I'm not going round the bend. I'm just telling you the truth. Let me say it all again, in plain words. I have been sleeping with Elyot Franks. I've only hidden my relationship with him for your sake. We were hoping you need never know what I have just told you, and that we could give you time to get used to the idea of my ever getting a man of my own. Any other father would have guessed the nature of our relationship, I think. You didn't see because you didn't want to. But perhaps you understand now why I would rather not be sitting on the organ stool while Daniel Bates belts out Easter hymns – though I'd very happily sing "Alleluia!" If you still think I'm a sex-crazed old maid having sexual fantasies, let me ring up Elyot and ask him to come over – as he wanted to. He's old-fashioned enough to want to ask you for my hand. Oh Daddy, I had hoped to spare you this. Honestly, we were doing what we could to keep our own secret until he could make an honest woman of me – no, perhaps till we could both make an honest man of you!'

His face was distorted with incredulity and pain. He drew back his hand and struck her across the face with all the power anger could give to his arm. 'Harlot,' he said. 'You are no daughter of mine! *Get out of my house!*'

She reeled from the blow, clasping her stinging face in her hands, but took them away and straightened her back to outface him again. Her voice was low, and quivered, but she had it under control.

'Did you really mean that, Father?'

'By the God I serve, I did! That my own child should deliberately shame me, and in that particular way! *Get out of my house.*'

'Yes,' she said. 'I'll go. Perhaps by the morning you may have had second thoughts about giving Mrs Bean a new topic for scandal and act with a bit of reason. I still hope so.'

He raised his hand again.

'I wouldn't, if I were you,' she said, her voice now tipped with steel. 'The bruises will show by the morning, and they won't be a very pretty sight to a lover's eyes. I imagine Elyot would prove a pretty tough customer in a mix-up. He happens to be old-fashioned in that way, too – gentlemen don't take kindly to a man striking a woman, whoever she happens to be.'

'Get out! Go to your friends!'

'To my affianced husband, Father. Just give me time to collect my night things.'

55

As Fran said afterwards, looking back on the events of that incredible week that led up to Easter, the whole village seemed to have been playing a game of deadly serious musical chairs.

By the time Sophie had come to work on Friday morning, she had heard through her usual hotline to the Old Glebe of the arrival of Charles asking to be given shelter there, and the cause.

'Dan'el's worked for the Bridgefoots ever since 'e left school,' she told Fran. ''E's never knowed 'em to quarrel afore – well not bad enough for anybody else to 'ear about it. But George were so upset 'e went out and told Dan'el everything. Charles won't speak to 'is father, and George is betwixt and between 'em. Rosemary won't go nowheer near Old Glebe, and that's upset Molly, 'cos she thinks, seeing as the real cause o' the trouble is 'er aunt, she should be the one to goo and try to make peace. Not that there'll ever be any peace, if you ask me, while that old woman is there. Mind you, I don't know the ins and outs of it, but it were all to do with that gal o' Bellamy's as young Charles is so crazed over. It's all over the place that the Rector caught 'em – in the back of Charles's new car. Shone 'is torch right on 'em, accordin' to Beryl Bean, and see what they were doing. But George says he'll believe 'is grandson till 's got somebody else's word besides Beryl's. Seems as if Brian's prepared to believe anything to do with that gal. 'E's set 'is stall out and won't give in. It's a pity that Bellamy didn't stop where 'e belongs, in the fen.'

'Really, Sophie!' Fran said, bridling at Sophie's tone. 'What on earth have you got against him? I know you're fond of the Bridgefoots – so am I – but I'm fond of Bob Bellamy as well. And as far as I can see his daughter is an extremely nice girl. It isn't fair to take sides just because the Bellamys are strangers.'

Sophie put on a rather grim face. 'I 'adn't forgot as 'e were such a good friend o' yours,' she said, and went off to get on with her work, offering no chance of further discussion.

She left Fran anxious. There was no brooking the implication in Sophie's voice that she, at any rate, thought Bob was too good a friend. But Fran was worried about him, all the same. He must be worried by Charlie getting involved in the Bridgefoot row, apart from Beryl's tales. And he was already unhappy. It must be very near to the time of his son's emigration. She hated to think of him having nobody to tell his troubles to; she ought to go to see him.

Second thoughts overruled her impulse. The anti-Bellamy tone in Sophie's voice was on William's behalf. It amazed Fran to think that a man of William's age, intelligence and character, as utterly devoted to her as she was to him, should ever allow himself to exhibit a streak of jealousy strong enough for Sophie to have picked it up. Yet there it was. She knew he was ashamed of it, and that she ought to be flattered; but this morning she wasn't. She was merely irritated. William knew perfectly well that he wasn't threatened by her special place in Bob's life; he just hated the thought that anybody but himself should have any special place. She had felt the same once, though, about Jess's special place in his. Darling William – she certainly wouldn't do anything so foolish as to go up to Castle Hill without him. But now that the thought had occurred to her that Bob might need her, she couldn't put it aside. As Sophie would say, 'There's no sense in doing a kindness if you leave it a day too late.' Fran picked up the telephone, dialled, and asked to be put through to William's office. Luck was on her side. He answered it himself. She explained.

'It's Friday – supposed to be my research day,' he said. 'I'll cancel an unimportant meeting or two, and be home for lunch. Then we'll go up straight afterwards. Will that do?'

'Thank you, William,' she said, putting as much love into the commonplace words as she could. He laughed. 'No need to be so circumspect, my precious. Everybody else here is having their extended coffee break. I was working through mine so as to be able to get home early, anyway. Darling – thank you for not going flying off to Bob without me. I'm fond of him, too, you know. Just fonder of you. I'll be with you in about two hours.'

She hadn't said a word about her reason for deciding not to go alone. It was the ability to read each other's thoughts at work again, and she was relieved. So was Sophie, as her face showed, when Fran told her William would be home to lunch. 'I know as it's nothing to do with me,' she said, 'but it wouldn't ha' done for Beryl and Olive to see you gooing up there without 'im,' she said. 'It's as if them two 'ave been sowing seeds o' scandal broadcast. The trouble is that some of 'em'll be bound to grow.'

It was Fran's turn to feel a sense of shame. She should know by now that Sophia and Wisdom were the same thing.

They took the car as far as the farmhouse, expecting to have to walk up to the church to find Bob, but he called to them to come in. Fran saw at once how right her instinct had been. He was certainly 'not himself'. Depressed, she guessed, and tinged with some immediate anxiety.

'Is anything wrong, Bob?' she asked, going straight to the point. 'We thought you might be at work this fine day, so we were going to wait for you up at the church.'

'I ought to be at work,' he said, 'but I ain't got no spirit for it. John went yesterday. I don't expect I shall ever see him again.'

There was such finality his statement that she was prevented from offering any of the usual platitudes. 'Come out,' she said coaxingly. 'Let's walk up to the church and watch the rooks come home.'

He looked at her with eyes full of tears. 'The rooks have all gone, as well,' he said. 'Just empty nests left. I have a job to make myself go up there to feed Winnie, but she's got kittens, so I must.'

Fran thought she could not have heard him right, and asked. He described what had happened. (How good he was with words, when he wasn't thinking about himself.)

'It's an omen as most country folk know of,' he said. 'I've never knowed it to happen before, though I've heard of it. It means calamity – sort of general bad luck all round. And there's death omens connected with it. I've been going to the church a lot lately, and letting myself in, 'cos I felt better just sitting there by myself. But I don't go now the rooks have gone.' He glanced at the grandfather clock in the corner. 'I wish Charlie would come back. She's been gone since we finished our dockey.'

That was the anxiety Fran had sensed. He believed in omens of death.

'Where is she?' Fran asked.

'I wish I knew. She won't go near the village, and won't let young Charles come up here, so she's perhaps meeting him somewhere. But she went off on Ginger, bareback, like a mad thing. If he were to put his foot in a rabbit hole— And I've let Matey go. He won't come back, either. None of 'em will. I miss 'em all so.'

He fished in his jacket pocket for a large handkerchief and hid his face in it. Fran sent William a mute appeal to clear out and let her deal with Bob alone. She felt just like she used to when Roland, as a toddler, suffered from earache. She couldn't stop the pain, but to be in contact with her had always soothed him. She daren't attempt to cuddle Bob, much as she would have liked to, so she reached for his free hand and held it.

No words were spoken until he dried his face, turned it towards her and squeezed the hand that held his. He looked more like himself. 'Lucky William,' he said, squeezing her hand again before letting it go.

'He hasn't always been, you know,' she said. 'He had years and years just as much alone as you are now. Except that he had nobody but a half-sister in Scotland. You've got Charlie.'

'Not for much longer,' he said. The awful thing was that she couldn't contradict him. His prescience was too strong.

They heard voices, and William came in with Charlie.

'Dr Burbage has been tearing me off a strip for getting you worried, Dad,' she said. 'I'm sorry. I never thought. I tore round on Ginger till I felt a bit better, and then tied him up and walked down to the post office to post some letters. I hoped I might meet Charles, but I didn't. I just wanted him to know I'm sorry. I'm going to miss him more than he'll miss me, I think.'

She excused herself prettily, and went off to do her hair.

'They'll make it up,' Fran said. 'It's only a lovers' tiff with a bit of parental interference thrown in.'

Bob shook his head. 'You heard what she said. I'm pretty sure she means to get right away from him so that he can make it up with his father,' Bob said. 'When she's gone, there'll be nobody.' He got up suddenly, and went out.

William did his best to comfort Fran. What was hurting her was her own helplessness. 'I'm not sure,' he said as he kissed her tears away, 'that the obligations of friendship aren't heavier than those of love. Lovers have a way of healing each other denied to mere friends.'

She nodded. 'The ultimate human contact,' she said. 'That's what Bob needs. That's what I can't give him. If I had a god to pray to, I'd pray that he would listen to me on Bob's behalf.'

'Don't forget our guardian angel,' William said. 'Look what he's done for Elyot and Beth. He may be listening.'

'In this doom-filled place?' she said, sceptically.

'Even here, my sweetheart,' he answered firmly.

'He's got a lot on his hands already,' she said. 'But I'll try to believe you.'

56

Just after lunch on Saturday, William answered the telephone. He came back to Fran looking worried. 'It's Beth,' he said, 'ringing from Elyot's house. She sounds nearly frantic, and is asking for me to go – without you. It doesn't sound too good. Sorry, darling, but I think we ought to do just as she says, don't you?'

'Of course. It sounds as if Elyot has run back. There's no point in speculating. Get off.'

He saw that Fran's surmise was wrong the moment that in answer to Elyot's call, he opened the door and went in. Elyot was sitting in his own huge leather chair with a tearful Beth clasped in his arms. At William's entrance, she turned her face into Elyot's chest and cried again.

'He'll have to see it, my love,' Elyot said, 'and it was you who asked him to come, you know. Come on, tell him why you rang him. I'm not likely to floor William, however mad I am.'

He kissed her, and tried to put her away from him, so that he could stand up. She resisted, pleading. 'Promise, Elyot? Promise – not till you've talked to William, anyway?'

'Yes – I'll promise that much. Now do let me get up, please.'

She rose, and turned towards William. The left side of her face was swollen, her left eye was already blue beneath the lower lid, and the imprint of fingers showed red against the pallor of the rest of her face.

William went forward and kissed her gently, holding out his hand to Elyot at the same time.

'Who on earth . . . ?' he said, and stopped, fearful that the answer might be that an enraged or fearful Elyot might be the culprit. It could be Beth who had run back. But the way they were looking at each other made it clear to him that there was no rift in that particular lute.

'Her father,' Elyot answered. 'The swine! You're here to

449

prevent me going to turn him into pulp. Sanctimonious, bloody bastard!' His hands were clenching and unclenching, and the muscles at his jaws showed prominently square as his chin jutted forward. 'She wouldn't have been able to stop me – except that if I had lost my temper and killed him she would have had nobody left. William, tell her I must do something! Make her understand how I feel!'

William was still holding Beth's hand and felt that she was tense and ready to spring towards the door to bar Elyot's way if he should make one move in that direction.

It was one of William's virtues, born of long practice in outfacing belligerent and frantic students, that he could and very often did use the ploy of a soft answer even while raging inwardly with fury himself.

Remembering Marriner's visit to Benedict's, and his own anger as he had watched Fran deal with him, he sympathized wholly with Elyot; but Fran was not the Rector's daughter. Beth was.

'Sit down, Elyot,' he said. 'And calm down. I can't even begin to give advice till I know what's happened. I can see that the attack on Beth's only very recent. Let her go and bathe her face. Cold water, Beth – and arnica's still as good as anything for bruising. I promise not to let Elyot out of my sight till you come back.' He guided her towards the hall door, whispering, 'Leave him to me.' Reluctantly, she went.

'Now, Elyot, tell me quickly what caused it all. I suppose he found out.'

'She tried to talk to him sensibly – though not about us – and he chose to insult her. She says he treated her like a mad old maid – actually told her her that she was suffering mental instability because of her age, and suggested he should get her into a psychiatric clinic. In the end, she told him the truth, and he lashed out at her. He would have hit her again, but she had the presence of mind to threaten him with what I should do to him if he dared. So he ordered her out, instead. She came straight across to me, of course. The reaction only set in after she'd got here.

'I think what made him so fighting mad was that she didn't show herself afraid of him – and the long and short of it now

450

is that she's afraid *for* him. He's her father and she loves him. You see, she's just told me that he's already been round the bend with a breakdown once, before they came here. If he goes off his head again, he's done for. But she's mine now, and nobody's going to treat my woman like that. It isn't as if he's an old man! He's nearly as old as I am!' He sat down again, face working. 'I guess I'm out of my mind because I'm scared of losing her, one way or the other. I'm not sane enough yet to see what to do next. I tried to stop her from involving you again, but I'm glad now that she did. I still want to go and kill him.'

Beth came back. The bathing hadn't improved her face much, but it had calmed her. She looked apologetically at William, and then bent to kiss Elyot full on the lips.

'I heard that,' she said. 'You're never going to be able to lose me. Forget any such nonsense. We must all be sensible. If Father doesn't do anything more than usually silly, no notice will be taken of me not being at church tomorrow. Nobody but he knows I'm not at home, and nobody but you knows where I am. For the moment, we're safe; but with Easter Day coming up, I just daren't think. I'd made up my mind to tell Father I just couldn't go on pretending to believe everything that he does. That's all I meant to tell him today. I knew he would be upset – but, well, we quarrelled. Now he knows I have been to bed with Elyot, he's threatened to denounce me from the pulpit as a harlot.'

Elyot growled – for all the world, William thought, like a St Bernard dog whose tail has been trodden on. William could see that his own first task was to prevent Elyot from making matters worse.

'Listen, Elyot. I know how you feel – but Beth's the one we have to consider. And her father's got to be handled sympathetically as well. I know him better than you do – he's a good chap with a wasp in his armour – but he is still the Rector. This matters to a lot of other people besides you and Beth. If he flips about this, it could have very far-reaching consequences.

'It's no use you growling at me, Elyot. I'm trying to be objective. How do you think Beth would feel? Would she ever forgive herself if she sent him back into the loony-bin? Or forgive you? You can't risk it. You've got to face that fact, Elyot, and accept it. It's just the way it is.

'I doubt if he is responsible for his actions just at present. We've got to concentrate our efforts on preventing him from doing anything silly or irrevocable. Beth, I think you hold the key for the moment. I imagine he is waiting for a contrite daughter to creep in and throw herself at his feet, begging forgiveness. He can't conceive of you as anything but his daughter. That's always been pretty plain. You must stop playing that role. The sooner you are Elyot's wife, the better. Any objections, Elyot? Beth?'

'Sounds wonderful in theory, William – but Easter's coming up, and I know him. He won't dissemble in any way. Unless I'm there at the organ with everything normal, he'll resign and everybody will know why.' She looked at Elyot. 'Not that I care, except for his sake.'

'All right, be there. Elyot's wife, not his daughter. He couldn't denounce you for that.'

'Now you're getting carried away, William. Easter Day is tomorrow week. And by that time I shall be a scarlet woman on everybody's tongue. They'll have my father's word for it.'

'That's unthinkable,' said William shortly. 'There must be a way out. But it may mean you going back home again, Beth, if your father will have you, that is.'

'No,' growled Elyot. 'Over my dead body.'

'I don't think Beth would have much use for your dead body, now,' said William wrily. 'Don't lose your common sense, Elyot. I think we may have to indulge in a bit of cover-up. We, including your father, Beth.'

'He wouldn't, William. He's conducting a one-man crusade against sexual permissiveness. It's an obsession – it just grew on him during his illness. He read a lot of psychology to try to help himself, and somehow he channelled it the wrong way. The congregation has noticed that he's always preaching about the modern attitude to sex. The men in the pub make jokes about it, I'm told. There's even a rumour that he goes round with a torch in the dark to catch courting couples in the back seats of cars – not true, of course, but it shows how they've cottoned on to him.

'That's what caused this, yesterday,' she went on, holding her cheek. 'In all my life, he's never hit me before. When I told him what I'd done, he cracked up. If I'd stolen the church silver or drowned a baby in the font he'd have made excuses for me. But I've committed the one sin he can't forgive. I'm sure he'd much rather get me certified by Dr Henderson as a hopeless pyschiatric case than see me anywhere near Elyot, married or not. In his eyes, we've sinned against all he holds dear. He'll never get over it.'

In spite of brave resolution, she began to cry again. Elyot pulled her back on to his knee and tried to comfort her.

William held to his purpose. 'That remains to be seen. With your permission, I am going across to see him, Beth. It's all right, Elyot. You just look after Beth. It's just possible that he'll talk to me, and listen to reason. I can but try. Beth, would you please ring Fran and tell her not to expect me till she sees me? Tell her just enough to stop her from worrying about me. She's got a lot on her mind already.'

He didn't wait to answer Elyot's angry objections to letting Archie think he held the whip hand; he trusted Beth to pour balm on Elyot.

There was no answer to his knock at the Rector's door. After the third knock he opened the door and walked in. Archie was sitting at his desk in the study, writing. He turned angrily to glare at William, very surprised to see who it was. He did not get up from his swivel-chair, but turned it towards his visitor, angry and full of suspicion.

'This is an unpardonable intrusion, Dr Burbage. I am very busy, as you can see. I don't walk into other people's houses without being invited. I respect privacy.'

'I don't strike defenceless women,' William replied bluntly. 'I respect them.'

Marriner turned white, and said nothing. Then, controlling himself with an effort, he said, 'Ah! So you have come from my daughter and her seducer as an emissary. I ought to have expected it.'

'I have come as a friend, and at my own request,' said William, sitting down unasked. 'There's so much you don't know, Archie. You are condemning them without trial. You didn't give Beth a chance to speak for herself, even if she would have done, did you? We can't undo what's done – but with a bit of common sense we can prevent it from mushrooming into a tragedy. Look, I'm not speaking now as the prisoner's friend. I'm a historian with an interest in the welfare of a village he loves trying to reason with the Rector of that parish. A wrong move at this point could be disastrous.'

'I am no longer Rector of this parish. My letter of resignation is already written and signed.'

William jumped to his feet. 'Then you're a bigger goddamned fool than I took you for!' he exploded. 'And the village is well rid of a bloody pig-headed bigot with a maggot in his brain.'

He towered over the sitting Rector and let himself rip. It was not often that he allowed himself to lose his temper, and in general he despised men who had to resort to bad language to make their points. Nevertheless, he had not served in the RAF without acquiring a fair vocabulary, much of which he would have sworn on oath that he had forgotten; but the crass stupidity and self-delusion of the man before him, combined with the memory of Beth's pathetic swollen face triggered off in him such fury that it spilled up and over like boiling tar.

The effect on Marriner was to rob him of speech. He just sat neither attempting to interrupt or to stop the flow.

'And you can thank that bloody old tyrant you call God that I got here before Elyot Franks did,' William said. 'You'd probably have been on the way to hospital by now if I hadn't got here first. *He didn't seduce Beth. She seduced him*, for which I must take most of the blame. That's what I came to tell you, you narrow-minded bloody fool . . .'

Words failed him, and he sat down suddenly, surprised at himself, but strangely elated. In fact, he grinned across at his victim, half-triumphant, half apologetic.

The Rector rose. 'Well done, Professor,' he said scathingly sarcastic. 'I don't think I've ever heard that bettered, even in my days as an Army chaplain. Have you finished? Whisky?'

'No, Archie, to both questions. Not unless we can drink as friends again . . . when you have come to your senses. Is that your letter of resignation to the Bishop?'

Marriner nodded. 'My position is untenable. Beth has left me no option.'

'Balls,' said William crudely. 'There are options galore, but only if you can think as a man and a father, and not as a lily-livered Victorian curate.'

He stood up swiftly, lithe as a cat, and grabbed the sealed letter from Marriner's desk. Then he placed it carefully in front of the clock on the mantelpiece, where both could see it. 'Let that be our gauge till we settle this. Not as the friends we were, nor as historian and cleric, but as men. I want to tell you what happened. I shall be wasting my breath unless you will hear me out. Will you listen?'

Marriner inclined his head.

'Will you promise to reconsider before you post that letter?'

'Till Tuesday only. I cannot and will not take the Easter services while my daughter is living in sin with my neighbour.'

'It's ridiculous that we are having this argument all over again. Last time you admitted to being a man as well as a parson. This time you seem to have made up your mind to be the Levite, and pass by on the other side. So who is thy neighbour?'

'Let me get that drink,' the Rector said. 'I need it if you don't.'

William did. The fire had gone out of him, and he felt exhausted; but his task was only just begun. He accepted the whisky and began to talk.

He told the story, beginning from Boxing Day when he had first found out about Elyot's black dog. 'So you see,' he concluded, 'I forced Beth into that terrible choice. To break the moral code you have instilled into her and hurt you, or to destroy a fine man who had been through hell and was just beginning to see hope on the other side. A man who loved her enough to sacrifice that hope for her sake. Do you really think I would have involved Beth at all if I hadn't known, because she told me, that she loved him in return more than she loved life without him? If there was any sin, it was mine. It was the only way to save him. I know that sort of desperation myself. I thank the god I believe in that my strategy worked.'

Marriner sat silent. 'She at least had a choice,' he said. 'I haven't. I know where my duty lies. She has shamed me.'

'Nobody need know. What's so wrong, even in your eyes, if they can now marry straight away? Before Easter, if possible. By special licence?'

The Rector smiled, a wan disparaging smile. 'Don't be silly,' he said. 'You have no idea what you're talking about. Even if that would make any difference to me, such an idea is quite impossible. It means approaching the Archbishop of Canterbury, who must be given reasons for the request, and character references which must in turn be supported by the incumbent of the church in which the couple ask to be married. I couldn't give them that support. It would be an insult to His Grace and to my cloth. It wouldn't change the facts. Nor would I be a party to such blatant deception.'

'But Beth's your daughter, man,' William pleaded. 'Nobody but you, Fran and I know what happened, or why. Don't you care about her reputation? Enough to shield her from every gossiping tongue? It could be done with your help. There's just about time. The fact that he's so much older than she is would provide all the excuse they need – he is a very shy man. Everybody else would love such a romantic event, Oh, come on, Rector! What was it Shakespeare said in *The Merchant of Venice?*

To do a great right, do a little wrong.

Surely, for her sake –'

'Forswear myself, William? Never!' It sounded as final as the trump of doom, but at least he had reverted to calling William by his given name. William finished his drink and backtracked on his thoughts. Marriner couldn't stop Beth marrying. He must find a way that didn't require the Rector's co-operation.

'Then may Beth come back under your roof till she goes to Elyot as his legal wife? She can, of course, come to us at Benedict's, but that would cause speculation and set tongues wagging almost as much as her staying where she is. At least offer her that protection. And think about what you're doing.'

'You are only postponing the inevitable,' the Rector said. 'I believe you propose such a desperate remedy sincerely, and as much for my sake as hers. But it is a ridiculous one in which I will have no part. Suppose it ever came to light that I had condoned in my own daughter what I condemn in others? However, I see your point. This is her home; I will agree to her returning until I post that letter . . . If I do that, it won't matter under whose roof she is. Tell her she may come, but to keep out of my sight as much as possible.'

'She may not accept the condition,' William said. 'I can but give her the option.'

The thin edge of the wedge, William told himself as he went back across to the Old Rectory and reported. What he had to say did Elyot's temper no good at all, but he could see how relieved Beth was. He also had a glimmer of hope that one glimpse of Beth's distorted and discoloured face might do more good than all his argument.

To prevent any unfortunate sightings of her, William drove her home, going straight on to Benedict's. He really had not the faintest idea how to straighten out the coil; William was very conscious of an obligation to rescue the Rector, as well as Beth and Elyot, from an extraordinary situation. William wanted Fran's help, and felt he couldn't get home to consult her fast enough. He also needed to consult a law compendium that had accompanied him for most of his academic life. It was outdated, but at least it would supply basic information. Laws changed all the time, but he felt fairly safe in his intuition that anything relating to the church would be the least likely to have changed drastically. He had kept his eye on the divorce laws for a very personal reasons. It amused him a little to think he had never thought to check changes in the marriage laws.

He was thwarted on both counts. He found George Bridge-foot with Fran, pouring out his troubles to her. He had no alternative but to join them.

57

Apart from the bare bones of each story, they were both too tired to tell each other much after George had left. William blessed the fact that it was the Easter vacation, and Sunday tomorrow.

Flat on his back with Fran's head on his shoulder and Cat on his chest, William described his visit to Archie Marriner.

'It's the gods interfering again,' he said. 'We thought they had done with us, and they haven't. We ought to have known better. I think they must be jealous of you and me, because they seem determined to involve us. Two of our friends fall in love with each other, which ought to cause us nothing but pleasure. And what happens? I have two sleepless nights, one playing pander and the next wondering what on earth I can do to stop Samson pulling down the pillars of the temple round our ears.'

'Funny how you somehow take clergymen for granted,' Fran said. 'I'd forgotten he'd had a nervous breakdown. But he's hardly a Samson, is he? What do you mean by him being likely to pull the temple down? I mean, it's nasty for Elyot and Beth, but to hear you it sounds as if there's likely to be an earthquake about it.'

'He isn't acting rationally; that's why I'm concerned. It's too close to home. It's as if he's two people in one skin. You can't reason with one because the other gets in the way. Beth let on that during his breakdown he got hooked on psychology. Trying to heal himself, I suppose, and focusing all he read on his own situation as a parson. He lifted the emphasis of modern psychology on sexual matters out of context. He's turned sex into a devil he imagines it's his duty to subdue. It's become his personal Apollyon, an obsession that's warped his judgement and made him lose all perspective.

'He seems never to have considered Beth as a marriageable woman, let alone one that some man might actually fall for. He won't think of her in any sexual context. On the other hand, because of all the psychology he's read, he blames sex for everything – like attributing what she told him about Elyot to her having menopausal fantasies, though she's only just over thirty! Could be wishful thinking, I suppose. If she were past it, he wouldn't have to worry about her doing anything to worry him on that score, let alone disgrace him. But with my help, she goes and does just that. So now I feel responsible for him, as well as for her. That goddamned one-track-minded fool *is* capable of pulling the place down round our ears.'

'Why? How do you mean?'

'You know how vulnerable places like this are to change – we've already experienced one bout of that and survived, more or less. But we can't afford another, especially one aimed at the church. With the school closed and the hotel taking pride of place over the pub, the church is the only leg the old village has to stand on. Just think what could happen if he carries out his threats. He denounces Beth publicly, playing the martyr because she's his own daughter. Then he resigns. God only knows what would be made of it. That's the sort of story the gutter press loves to get hold of. Just imagine what that would do to our star-crossed pair of lovers!

'But it wouldn't stop there. If Archie sends that letter of resignation, it will be accepted like a flash, and he won't be replaced. The living will be added to St Crispin's at Swithinford, and the lay reader from Hen Street would take over except for the sacraments. Old Swithinford might as well disappear under a reservoir.'

He lay silent, stroking Cat till she choked herself with purring.

'The church has always been at the centre of village life. It's the centre of gravity, as it were. Even if people don't go to church, they still want it to be there . . . for the rituals of birth and marriage and death. Ritual is atavistic. The early Christians had enough sense to take over pagan ritual. Humanity can't do without ritual – you know that, my sweetheart. That's why you cry at weddings.'

He sat up. 'Go away, temptress. We must get up, because I've got a lot to do. I don't want to have to give up an idea I had last night. And I must hear all that poor old George told you.'

459

'His family is falling apart. Brian wants to be the new sort of squire, partly because he thinks all the money puts him in that league, but he wants to climb the new social ladder by marrying Charles into a posh family. Lucy's already made the grade, and apparently Brian hates being left behind. Charles is a throw-back to George, and won't play. Marjorie doesn't care as long as her children are happy, but Vic intends his daughters for the landowner, horsey, show-off rural set. Brian's ready to break Charles's neck because of the rumours going round of his goings on with Charlie Bellamy, who it seems has given Aunt Esther the rough side of her tongue and proved herself no lady.

'George declares that Charles and Charlie are still as pure as the driven snow, but he has to keep his temper and his perspective because of Pansy and young Fairey. So he no longer knows where he stands. He would have taken the same line on sex as Sophie used to, but like her, he's begun to think for himself. He's stopped trying to swim against the tide altogether, like the Rector's doing.

'But I gathered that George is more worried about what to do with Miss Palmer than any of the other problems. He blames her for breaking up the family and himself for putting her into a position where she could. Oh, darling, is that really happening? Or likely to happen? Old Swinthinford has seemed such a haven against such things. I can't bear to think of it changed altogether.'

'We're safe enough at Benedict's, my sweetheart, as long as you and I don't change. But the romantic idea of the village idyll with roses round every door never has existed except on chocolate boxes. People are people wherever they live. A pretty rural environment doesn't save them from anything. Any more than an ugly urban one is responsible for all their ills. It's always been the same. As Shakespeare said, hawthorn hedges don't provide shelter from cold winds.'

'"Sharp through the hawthorn blows the wind,"' Fran quoted. 'I've never really thought what it meant before.'

William leaned over Fran, looking down at her. 'Your hedge of thorns flowered, my precious one. It keeps out all sharp winds from me.' He kissed her lingeringly, and let her go. 'All right, Cat, I am coming. What with you and Archie Marriner . . .'

Over breakfast, they tried to be practical.

'I told Archie that he owed it to Beth to help us with a cover-up for her reputation's sake,' William said. 'What I suggested was a wedding by special licence. Nothing doing. He won't play, and they can't get the licence, apparently, without him. Elyot would settle for a civil marriage, but that wouldn't solve the problem as I see it. What it boils down to is that unless we can get her married in time, the loss of Beth's virginity could wreck a thousand years of traditional village life. If you with all your creative genius can think up a more dramatic scenario than that, I'll eat my hat!'

'You haven't got one,' she said.

'Oh yes I have. My topper. Don't you remember the effect it had on you? I would have loved to wear it again as Elyot's best man.'

She suddenly became serious again. 'About Elyot,' she said. 'I don't think you should be scheming anything without consulting him first. And he ought not to be left alone all day today, calling up his black dog. I don't trust him not to do something silly. He's knocked sideways, and very angry. Beth's in the same boat – but she'll cope. Men are such idiots in a crisis. Get him here, soon as you can. Ring him now, this minute. I want him under my eye. Besides, what is it Ned says? "Two heads are better than one if they're only sheep's heads."'

'If Beth's wearing a wedding ring by next Sunday the only person who could possibly cause trouble is her father. Would he really do that? As it's Easter Sunday, we might even show up ourselves, and make Elyot go with us. That would put what George calls a gob-stopper in Beryl Bean's mouth. And I'd pray that it would choke her.

'It's the rats in Archie's attic we're up against. He knows Beth's no longer a virgin. Ten marriages now won't wipe that from his mind. He can't see anything but his daughter's "sin". He's got to be brought to reason somehow, to make him see all the consequences of the line he proposes to take. I'd want him to do it for Beth's sake, anyway, because if he ruins

461

himself she'll feel it's all her fault. If she has a guilty conscience about him, Elyot won't be able to make her happy. I know about women with consciences!

'Go and ring Elyot, then. We'll think of something. I want a hand in writing a happy ending, but my prime motive just now is the lovely thought of getting my own back on Archie Marriner.'

Elyot arrived at Benedict's very soon. William was in his study, so Fran greeted him. He had not got rid of his anger.

'I'm not used to taking orders from anybody, or pussy-footing round a lot of old biddies like your Sophie,' Elyot said. 'If I had my way I'd storm in and carry Beth off over my shoulder, like a Viking.'

'I hope you'd look as if you were enjoying it more than you did on Christmas Day,' Fran countered. 'No, Elyot, don't flare up at me. I'm well aware that it's no laughing matter. But you must keep a sense of proportion. If we can keep your secret from those old biddies, as you call them, till you can get a ring on Beth's finger, they'll be your greatest allies. Thirzah in particular will take all the credit for "seeing which way the wind was a-blowing". Beth doesn't care about anything but you – but if she can have you with her father's goodwill, and save him from another spell in a clinic into the bargain, she'll have all that and heaven too. That's what William's hoping for.'

'I resent her father having anything whatsoever to do with it,' Elyot said. 'She isn't a child! I warn you that I shan't agree to anything just to please him – or William.'

'Or Beth?' asked Fran.

He looked at her almost angrily, hurt by the question. 'I would pledge my soul to the devil to please her,' he said. 'Don't worry, Fran. I hope I've got more sense than her father has. Hello, William. What sort of a plan are you hatching now?'

William had come in carrying a large book. 'This may be out of date, so I warn you,' he said. 'But it looks interesting. Marriner was absolutely right about a special licence. You couldn't get one without a reference from him. So that's out. But there are other ways. There's something called a "registrar's licence" which you can obtain after only one day – I presume twenty-four hours. This is a "combined certificate and licence", and if I have interpreted it right, it is both marriage and registrar's licence in one. With it you can be married in a register office by civil law – so there's no reason why Beth shouldn't be Mrs Franks by next Sunday morning. That's a last resort though. It wouldn't solve the real problem. Archie said he wouldn't go along with any marriage, knowing what he did, and we can't hope to hoodwink the village folk. They'd smell a rat at the Rector's daughter having a register office wedding.'

'Damn them,' said Elyot violently. 'I won't be made to do anything just to save God Almighty Marriner's feelings. We'll be married when and how Beth wants, and not before. Let 'em talk. There's plenty of time.'

'Not to save Beth from wagging tongues, Elyot,' said Fran earnestly. 'You don't know village life like we do. And besides – forgive me for being so personal, but – a self-declared celibate bachelor and the virgin daughter of a village parson are hardly likely to have been carrying contraceptives in their dressing-gown pockets. Has it occurred to you that Beth may find herself pregnant?'

The effect on both men was startling. Elyot half rose, sank back into his chair and covered his crimson face with both hands. William lowered the book and looked at Fran over it, the first time ever, she said afterwards, that she had ever seen his jaw actually drop. She repressed with difficulty a desire to giggle. Men! Didn't they know the basic facts of life, one of which is that Nature is no respecter of persons?

Elyot was still floundering in a morass of very mixed emotions. William closed his mouth and the book he was holding.

'That settles it, Elyot,' he said. 'Archie has agreed not to post his letter of resignation till Tuesday – I can only guess to give it time to take effect before Sunday, though I have no idea at all how such things work within the church. You will have to get a licence somehow tomorrow.'

'Where do I start? I'm in such a state I couldn't even buy a packet of razor blades,' said the erstwhile Commander of a Royal Navy destroyer.

'I'm coming with you,' William said. 'I do at least know my way about Cambridge. I also have a solicitor friend there; and if there is need to pull any strings, I daresay I could find a few ends to pull. At least it will give us both something to do. Is there any hope of lunch, Fran?'

That, Fran thought, was intended as a diversion. She knew William too well not to believe that he was either shelving the matter for the moment or pushing it aside till Elyot recovered himself a bit. They ate the cold lunch in comparative silence, each pursuing his own thoughts. Fran felt she could almost read Elyot's. There would be no real peace of mind for him now till he had seen Beth again, and that was not going to be possible for at least a couple of days.

It was she who returned to the subject. 'Elyot,' she asked, 'have you any means of communicating with Beth?'

'Only if she can ring me while her father is out. Why?'

'She mustn't be told a whisper of what has been said here today,' Fran decreed. 'Not about anything. She would hate to know we had been discussing her behind her back, but it has to be cloak-and-dagger conspiracy. Nobody must be given an inkling that anything at all is either wrong or afoot. But Beth ought to know you won't be around tomorrow. If she rings and you don't answer she'll be in such a state that by one word out of place she could blow the plot sky-high.'

'She promised to ring me this afternoon while he is taking evensong,' he answered.

'Good. Well, tell her that William has asked you to go with him to some male University lunch tomorrow, and that you will be gone all day and she is not to worry. So you must go now, to make sure you are at home when she rings you this afternoon. But promise you won't say a word to her . . . about anything.'

For the first time that day, Elyot produced his slow, charming smile.

'What do you take me for, Fran?' he said.

'A man, therefore an idiot. Moreover, an idiot in love. Capable of any idiocy under the sun. A darling idiot, second only to William. But all this secrecy and guile is really women's work, you know.'

'Don't kid yourself that she is plotting and planning on your behalf,' William said solemnly. 'She has her own ulterior motive. She's been waiting for the chance to rub Archie Marriner's nose in the mud since November last year. It's a personal vendetta as far as she's concerned. You've got a good ally in Fran.'

Elyot left, looking very tired but far less strained than when he had come.

'I'm glad he had to go,' William said. 'I've lost a lot of sleep on his behalf already, and I had been nursing a hope that an afternoon in bed would be a good idea.'

'Off you go then. I'll clear up.'

'You don't get the message. I need putting to sleep. I also need to talk to you, on my own account and on Beth's and Elyot's. We always talk better in bed.'

'Take the telephone off the hook,' he said, as she slid in beside him. 'Even our guardian angel would ring again if it was really urgent.'

'And what is it you want to say?' she asked.

'Everything else can wait, but . . . my darling, you did give me an awful jolt! Beth and Elyot couldn't have been less prepared than we were that night I got back from the States and found that Mary had played God to us. You risked much more for me then than Beth did for Elyot. He's free to marry her. You risked everything! And I want you to believe me, but the thought never even occurred to me! I just let you take the risk!'

'I didn't let it bother me, either, at the time,' Fran said. 'It was what happened to Monica that made me think about Beth now. There really wasn't nearly as much risk for me. Even Beth's fifteen years younger than I was then.'

He gathered her up. 'I daren't think about it,' he said.

She left him asleep and crept downstairs to prepare an early tea that could wait till he woke. It was almost seven o'clock when he appeared again, bathed, refreshed and hungry. 'Are you prepared for another bout of guile?' he asked. 'Because I have still a lot to tell you. And we may need another ally.'

'Fire away,' she said. 'I'm at your service.'

465

'Don't be too free with your invitations,' he said, raising crooked eyebrows at her. 'I feel like a new man after that sleep.'

58

'We've got to pick up where you stopped me in my tracks by suggesting Beth might be pregnant,' William said, when after supper they turned their thoughts back to the problem. 'I've always thought it must be nice to be old Zeus sitting on his mountain playing chess with us poor mortals, but I'm not so sure, now. It looks as if I'm about to find out what it's like. Poor old Elyot doesn't know what's hit him. I've got to do his thinking for him. He's "mazed", as Sophie would say, by being in love. But I don't know how he'll react. I can't put myself in his shoes.

'I'm pretty sure this is the first time he's ever actually been in love. How can *I* know what he wants to do about it? I've been in love since I was about fourteen. When you turned up again it was nothing new – only the same condition a lot worse. I can't just take it for granted that he will want to do what I would. But there's more to it than that.

'None of the three of them can understand why it isn't just their own affair and nobody else's. They've got to be made to realize that a village isn't just a conglomeration of nice old houses that make desirable residences for retired wealthy people, or easy cures for sick clergymen. A village like this has got a life of its own, and they've chosen to be a part of it. They've got to find out that living in a small community has two sides to it. They may have their own ideas and principles, but so has it. They don't understand how it works, but you and I do. That's why we're involved.'

'It may be why *you're* involved,' Fran said, 'but I'm involved because I want my two new friends to be happy. You seem to be adopting a historian-cum-philosopher attitude to it, with a touch of the squire thrown in. The sort of paternalistic role Grandfather would have played mixed with your passion for history.'

He smiled delightedly. 'You couldn't have paid me a greater compliment than that,' he said. 'I am concerned for the very same reasons that Grandfather would have been. But first things first. It's all very well to be academic about it, but I have to be practical as well.

'I'll do my best to see that Elyot gets a registrar's licence tomorrow. I think he ought to decide to use it as soon as he can – just in case Beth is pregnant. But for anything more we're going to need an ally inside the church. George Bridge-foot's the answer, of course. For one thing, he's a church-warden. My guess is that Archie's conscience will oblige him to tell the churchwardens first if he does mean to resign.

'I think George ought to be prepared for him, armed with the truth. And that's where you come in, my darling. You'll have to go and tell George the whole story, tomorrow.'

'Count me in,' Fran said succinctly, 'and stop waffling about as if you were counsel for the defence not wanting the prosecution to know what you've got up your sleeve. If I have to brief George, I must know as much as you do.'

'Well, I just hope I'm right. As far as I can make out, a registrar's certificate permits marriage after one day's notice, providing one of the parties has a fifteen-day residence qualifica-tion. In this case, both of them have. It doesn't state that the marriage has to be a civil one. It does say that a parson can't be compelled to marry a couple if either has a former spouse living, which I take to mean that apart from that restriction it is possible for the licence to be used in church. It also appears to indicate that the incumbent has no option but to marry the couple in whatever church they choose. If he won't, he is committing an ecclesiastical offence and is answerable to his bishop.

'If Archie would only use common sense, it could all be plain sailing. I think we might have had trouble with Elyot but for your reminder that sex can have consequences. He would have been stubborn, said it was nothing to do with anybody but the two of them and that he wouldn't be hurried by anything, least of all her father's touchy morality. But he has enough sense to know they daren't risk leaving it even a month. Every old woman would be counting on her fingers, anyway.

'So what happens if they declare that they wish to get married here next Saturday? Archie will either have to get out or give in. Perhaps if George were to face him with the situation as we see it, he might think again. If he won't bend, I've got to find some other church and a parson willing to oblige. We've got to support Beth and Elyot. Either way it looks as if it will fall to me to give the bride away.' He caught her eye. 'Not wearing my topper, alas! I rather liked the effect it had on you.'

He might look mischievous, Fran thought, but she was beginning to understand the seriousness of his concern.

'Isn't what you're saying tantamount to moral blackmail on the Rector?'

'Isn't his attitude to Beth blackmail – with menaces? Sex between adults above the age of consent isn't a criminal act. It isn't even regarded as a particularly immoral one these days, except by people like him. He's got an obsession about modern sexual permissiveness, which makes him not just difficult, but dangerous.'

William got up and walked about, all concentrated thought. 'I share his concern, but not his obsession. Apart from that, he's no more mad than I am. But people will think he is if he refuses to marry his own daughter to a man like Elyot. He would have to give his reasons. Can you see any sane man exposing himself and his only child to that amount of scandal and his church to such ridicule? Or being so silly in ordinary terms? Elyot may be middle-aged, but just look what he's got to offer a wife. It isn't as if Beth is in her teens. Besides, apart from the bee in his bonnet, Archie's a fine man and a good parson, as far as I know. Sweetheart, I'm relying on you to go and tell George the truth, and my part in it. I hope that he'll apply charity to the sinners and a bit of pressure on Archie. He may be able to make the Rector see what a sex-based row could do to the church. If he can persuade Archie to perform the ceremony, it would give the church – and him – a real boost. The village would have an Easter they would never forget. "All the world loves a lover." '

'Isn't Beth having a hard time? Faced with consequences of actions she didn't intend, she has to defy her father's principles to get her own way. Is that fair?'

'Life isn't fair. And there's nothing new in having to choose between parent and lover. That situation's as old as the hills. Sweetheart, it was *I* who made Beth choose – between her own principles and Elyot's probable breakdown if not suicide. Besides, I don't believe in the nonsense of Archie's sanity being at risk . . . though I think his pride is. And where would his pride be if Beth did produce a child too soon after marriage? Just think of what Beryl Bean and old Esther Palmer would make of it! They'd drag the whole lot of them through the mud, the church as well. The mud would stick to us all. Why are you playing the devil's advocate? What's worrying you?'

'Having to involve poor old George,' she said. 'He's got enough problems of his own. But I will. Leave it to me.'

59

Fran couldn't work. There were far too many things on her mind, besides the task immediately ahead of her. She felt out of touch with everything and everybody. She hadn't seen Jess or Anne for almost two weeks, mainly because they had been too busy for chaffinching. She missed those afternoon chats a lot.

Since her meeting with Sue's mother, it was as if Roland's affairs had gone into a state of suspended animation. She hadn't heard anything from anybody. Monica, she knew, was making the very most of her last few weeks of activity in London before handing all the personal contact side of her business over to Greg and retiring to Monastery Farm till her baby was born. Fran felt aggrieved that she hadn't been

469

advised when Monica was coming back. Monica's pregnancy was real, not merely a shadowy possibility. What was more, the baby was her grandchild. If Eric knew when to expect Monica, why hadn't he told her? Because he expected her to know as much as he did, probably, which might be exactly the case. Maybe neither of them knew.

She suddenly felt a wave of disgruntlement. Here she was, forced into playing a part she certainly wasn't going to enjoy to protect Beth Marriner's reputation, while she could do absolutely nothing to counter the barrage of scandal that would be aimed at Benedict's when the paternity of Monica's baby became known.

Roland and Monica had decided that if it could be done without sending Sue into a clinic when the time came, they would simply let the truth be known. As Roland said, he wasn't going to be hiding in London and miss the birth of his baby.

Considering her own liaison with William, Fran couldn't argue against their decision; but in the meantime the paternity of Monica's child was yet another secret to keep, and she was fed up with having to guard her tongue.

(She looked at her watch for the third time in irritation. The minute hand was crawling from one mark to the next like a centipede with ninety of its legs broken.) She who hated secrecy was continually being forced into it, getting more and more involved as one matter overlapped another, like George's revelations to her now tangling with what she had to tell him. She thought of Kezia, Sophie's mother, quoting

O what a tangled web we weave
When first we practise to deceive!

She wished Kezia would stay out of it – and not always be right!

This waiting was almost unendurable. She was suddenly angry with William, who she thought was making a mountain out of a molehill. She still thought he was exaggerating everything because he felt responsible.

William was waiting when Elyot arrived next morning

looking as if he hadn't slept much. Fran noted with relief, though, that his stubborn, angry look had been replaced by a rather bewildered, helpless air. William noted it too, and became pleasantly purposeful.

'Have you got proof of identity, Elyot? And your cheque-book? Then let's get off.' He turned to kiss Fran and whispered, 'Good luck, my darling.'

'And to you,' she said.

Elyot turned back to say, 'Thanks, Fran. God only knows what I should have done without you two.'

Fran wanted a chance to think clearly before she rang George Bridgefoot; but Sophie appeared from the kitchen, hoping, Fran thought, to be told where the two men were off to so early. For once she was afraid of Sophie's uncanny ability to sort out the grain of truth from any bushel of talk. She decided to lie boldly, though in the ordinary way Sophie was the last person she would have either lied to or prevaricated with.

'They're off to some male-only do,' she said. 'William wouldn't have gone alone, but it is nice that there's another man free to go with him, now that Greg is so occupied with work. I hope the Commander will enjoy it.'

'He might ha' told Thirz' as 'e was going to be away today,' Sophie replied a bit disapprovingly. 'She don't reckon to goo there Mondays, but she could ha' got a lot done with 'im not there nor the Rector's gel neither, seeing as she ain't well.'

'Is Miss Marriner ill?' Fran asked, astounded that any leakage however tiny or inaccurate could have occurred so soon.

'She wasn't at church again yist'day, and when somebody asked the Rector about 'er 'e said she was keeping to 'er room. So by that we thought as she couldn't be well.'

So Marriner wasn't above prevaricating. That made Fran feel better.

Sophie was telling her something. She recovered her wits, and listened.

'So as long as you remember as it's 'Oly Week. 'Cos I shan't be 'ere a-Friday, and if you want anything extra done, I

471

shall have to get forrard with it. But if you want me, I'll come a-Sat'day instead. Are we got any visitors coming?'

'I don't know until I've made some phone calls,' Fran answered. 'I shall know better by tomorrow what the plans are, I think. Will that do?'

She had no idea yet what the weekend might bring. She wanted to escape Sophie's eye, so she said she had things to do and went to her study.

It was still only just past nine o'clock. George would be out on the farm; better leave her call till he went in for what he called ''levenses' at about ten thirty.

Another glance at her watch. Still fifteen more minutes to go before she could ring George. She went up to the landing window. The church tower just showed above trees sprouting their first spring greenery. Fran thought wistfully how nice it would have been to have been preparing for a conventional wedding there, with the whole community engaged in such a romantic affair. Instead of which she had the task of arranging a hole-and-corner one which might still have to take place in a register office. Looking out on the church at the very centre of the village made her appreciate William's anxiety. He didn't want Archie to cut the church's throat as well as his own. To be at one with William again made her feel much better as she went down to ring up George.

She was lucky in her timing, and George himself answered the phone. She explained as briefly as possible that she had an urgent problem on which she wanted advice. 'I'm sorry,' she said. 'I know you've got plenty of problems of your own. But I'm afraid you are the only one who can help.'

'Can it wait till tonight?' he asked. 'Do you want me to come up to Benedict's?'

'No, I'm afraid it's really very urgent. And please don't come here – it's a very delicate and personal matter, and I can't risk sharp ears, at either end. Could we meet somewhere now – at the church, for instance?'

His manner altered, and she heard the concern for her in his voice. 'My dear girl,' he said. 'Are you and William in trouble?'

'If we were,' she said, 'we should only have to come to you

to be straightened out. But no, nothing's wrong with us. He kissed me goodbye only a couple of hours ago when he left to do some business in Cambridge, but he did make me promise to try to see you before he got back. All I dare tell you now is that he's involved, and that we need you. Please say you'll give me a bit of your time.'

'You've given me plenty of yours,' he said, 'and I'd give you the rest of the day if I could, but I've promised to meet the Rector in church at half-past twelve.'

Fran panicked. She had to get to him before Archie did.

'Then please let me must see you first,' she said. 'I must talk to you before the Rector does. I think the two things are very likely connected.

'All right,' he said. 'I'll be there in a half an hour.'

Now she had the problem of getting away without telling Sophie where she was going. Her scruples about prevaricating had gone out of the window. She told Sophie she was going to the post office, and would perhaps call and see how Beth was.

'Ah. It's to be 'oped she'll be well enough to play the organ Sunday. It ain't like it used to be when the old Rector was alive and Miss were playing the organ. Things is changed, and not for the better.'

Trust Sophie to say something right to the point. 'We shall all be lucky if things don't change more than that,' Fran said, and left before Sophie could read her mind or deduce anything more from what she left unsaid.

She walked, so that her car might not be seen, and visited the post office on the way. In spite of her delay, she got there before George, and went into the church. She sat, deliberately, where she had sat at Lucy's wedding, and remembered how beautiful the old building had looked that day. Now it was bare, cold and unwelcoming, almost stark in its Lenten nakedness. Would it still have to remain as bare as this on Saturday, if ... how stupid and depressing that would be. But she supposed Christian custom would have to take precedence. She longed to put some pagan touches in it, for a wedding that would celebrate pagan Eostre, the raising of the dead land to life again, the spring after winter for Beth, the dawn after a long cold night for Elyot.

Ah, here was George. He sat down beside her, and took her hand. What an enormous man he was! The very sight of him filled her with comfort and hope, though she saw at once that his face was grave.

'We haven't got much time,' she said. 'I must start my tale straight away, in case the Rector comes early. It concerns Beth . . . and Elyot Franks.'

He didn't reply, so she plunged in and told him everything she could.

She was rather dismayed when he let go of her hand, stood up and went to sit down in his own pew, marked by the churchwarden's white wand. Then he knelt, head on the pew in front. Fran sat motionless. If there were any sort of God in this place they called His house, she thought He must surely listen to the prayers of a man like George Bridgefoot. She wished she could pray as he did.

He had barely risen from his knees when the door opened, and Archie Marriner came in. He was not wearing his dog-collar, and he looked white and thin, almost, it seemed to Fran, to the point of emaciation. He was very much taken back by her presence.

He inclined his head stiffly towards her. 'Mrs Catherwood,' he said. 'Is it I that you wish to see? I'm afraid I have some important business with Mr Bridgefoot. Another time?' He held the church door open for her.

'No,' said George, standing up in his pew. 'You can't have anything to tell me as I don't know a'ready, Rector. And I know it 'cos Mrs Catherwood has just told me. If you want my help, either or both o' you, say what you've got to say in front of each other.'

The Rector did not offer Fran the courtesy of speaking first. 'Very well,' he said, his face set and expressionless. 'I have come to tell you that I have made up my mind to resign the living. The reason you apparently know from Mrs Catherwood. My daughter has been playing the harlot. I am disgraced and no longer fit to be a priest. I wish to be released at once, before I am asked to take one more service of any kind here. My reason is mental illness.'

'That is not true,' said Fran, loudly and distinctly. 'You are

474

not mentally ill, and you know it. It is only an excuse. Doesn't lying to God matter?'

'It is none of your business, Mrs Catherwood. Please leave. Please get out of my church.'

Fran sat down again, making a very deliberate show of it. 'It isn't your church, even if you are still the Rector. I'm a member of the parish. The door is open, and if I choose to sit here, I shall. May we return to the matter in hand? Both you and Mr Bridgefoot know exactly what caused Beth to do what she did. Love for a man at the end of his tether. Doesn't that excuse her?'

'As I understand her, and Dr Burbage, it was not just love. It was sex. Unhallowed sex. I am appalled, disgusted and utterly disgraced. I will not discuss her, excuse her nor defend her. Nor will I have anything more to do with her. I have no purpose left here, no place in this village. My wish is to get away before the coming weekend. I came to ask my church-warden's help. I have nothing more to say to you.'

George had still not spoken. Fran felt terribly sorry for him. She looked at the Rector, feeling that she was confronting a graven image.

(Kezia's voice again:

> 'You might as well kneel down and pray
> To blocks of wood and stone
> As offer to the living God
> A prayer of words alone.')

Bless Kezia, this time! That was it! It was no use bandying clever words with this man. His feelings were covered in moral concrete, but there was just a chance that it might not yet have set too hard to crack. She had to go on trying to get through it. She had to show the Rector not what she thought of him, but how much she cared for Beth and Elyot, and how much it meant to the community, to people like George.

She softened her attitude towards him. 'Come and sit down, Rector. I know you would rather not discuss such things with a woman, but I am only here because William can't be. I'm here as Beth's friend, too. When William and I caused you difficulty, we tried to understand your point of view. It helps us to understand how you must feel now, that you think we are aiding and abetting Beth. It isn't really like that. Don't hold Elyot wholly responsible, either. It was a crisis, and William did the best he could. He and Elyot have gone today to try to get a licence for them to be married before the weekend. Beth doesn't know yet. If William succeeds, will you marry them? And keep their secret?'

'No. I will not perjure myself in the sight of God. To marry them after unhallowed sex would be to condone it. I am not expected to marry those who have been divorced, because that is to condone unhallowed sex. I see no difference. I would have thought I had made my position on such matters abundantly clear to you.'

She ignored the personal barb. 'Do I understand you correctly?' she said, 'Do you mean that if you knew a young couple had been to bed together before they came to you to arrange their wedding, you would refuse to marry them?'

'Yes. I should advise a civil marriage. That is still open to Commander Franks and my daughter.'

'Which he knows, of course. But he happens to love Beth very much, and he also knows how much she wants your blessing, and that of the church.'

'Why? She told me that she no longer believes the doctrine I preach.'

'She still loves you, though. And she still loves the church. Think of all the other couples she has played the wedding march for. Beth and Elyot are not foolish youngsters, but they are just as much in love. Won't you help us to make them happy?'

'I cannot go back on my word. I cannot and will not allow myself to condone sexual promiscuity just because my only child chooses to indulge in it. Cannot and will not. Couples who desire the church's blessing on their union must get it before, and not after the fact.'

'Are you aware that you are obliged to marry those who wish to be married in church providing there is no other impediment?'

'Quite aware, thank you, Mrs Catherwood. That is exactly

why I am trying to relinquish the living at once. I regard what has happened between my daughter and her lover as an impediment. I wish to leave before I have to refuse to marry them.'

'With the knowledge that your resignation is based on a lie? That Beth must be terribly hurt? And Elyot turned against the church for ever? Your faithful congregation, like Sophie, left to endure the scandal without you? Headlines all over the local rag, and even in the national dailies? Please, Rector. Please think again! Weren't you ever in love? Think of Beth's mother – would she have taken the same line you are doing?'

Fran had quite forgotten George. She had forgotten everything but her sudden, overwhelming pity for the man at her side. Her anger had evaporated as she had pleaded and registered the rigid set of his back, the quivering hands clasped together in his lap and the suffering in his eyes.

She'd been too angry with him before to notice signs of his distress; besides, she had seen him wince at something she had just said. Instinctively, she put out her hand to him, laying it on his arm, offering what was to her the greatest of comforts, the warmth of human contact. He drew away as if a bee had stung him, leaned forward, and covered his face with both hands.

Fran was afraid he might be going to pass out. She didn't know what to do, and looked around to summon George's help. He was no longer there. Soft-footed as a cat he had left them. Her ears caught the sound of muffled voices in the church porch.

Then he came back and stood, tall and grave, before them. Marriner sat up, having regained control.

'Rector,' he said. 'I reckon you came here to tell me what you intended to do, not to ask me. That's what's been wrong with you all the way along. You're too fond of telling other folks what they ought to do, or not to do. I ain't telling you, I'm asking you. So is Fran. Like it says in the Bible, expecting you to act like a father towards his child. Asking you to forgive her her trespasses. When she asks for bread, not to give her a stone.

'I'm only a simple farmer as has lived here all his life, and served this church like my fathers before me. Them Bridgefoots as 'as all lay a' one side o' the path you walked up today. They wouldn't ha' liked what goes on today no more than you do. No more than I do. But things don't all'us go as we want 'em. You preach often enough about the way God forgives us for our sins. And if God can do it, so can I, and so can you. I've had to. How many weddings have you took in this church since you come here?'

Fran was looking up with a kind of awe at her friend. Though in his distress he had reverted to his country speech, she felt she was hearing the voice of God himself. He had pulled himself up to his full height, and in his working clothes seemed to her to be clothed with the garments of truth, far outweighing any clerical robing. His dignity was awesome. Even the Rector was listening, his eyes fixed on George's face.

'None,' he answered. 'One before I was inducted – your own daughter's.'

'Yes, my Lucy's. My daughter who had lived in sin – if that's what you call it – with her man for two years before that day. I was hurt when I found out, quite as bad as you are now. I couldn't believe it. She was my baby. I couldn't stop loving her, could I? So I had to think it out.

'I loved her enough to keep her secret and to do all I could to make sure she'd be as happy as me and her mother have been. She'll have a child soon, conceived and born in wedlock. But according to what you say, you wouldn't have married her if you'd ha' known. What good would that have done? What harm might it have done? To me and mine above all, but to a lot of others beside.

'And I ain't got time now to stand and plead with you, 'cos of something else waiting for me to do. To toll the passing-bell for young Robert Fairey, who died about an hour ago.'

The tears began to course down his face, and Fran's heart felt so squeezed with grief that she could hardly breathe. But he still held that leonine old head high and looked down at the shocked clergyman.

'His family'll want him buried outside among all the other Faireys on the opposite side o' the path from us Bridgefoots. There won't be no more of 'em, now. Are you going to agree to bury him, Rector? Because I'm going to tell you something else that I hope'll never go outside these walls. That poor boy has knowed he was going to die for the last six months or more, and he wanted to be a man while he could. He's been sleeping with my granddaughter Pansy since he found out for himself what nobody could bring theirself to tell him. And I've known about it, all the while. I was party to it. You see, I loved him, as well. He's been in and out of my house since he were a toddler, nearly like a twin brother to my grandson. And every time I pull that rope in a minute I shall be grieving for him – and thanking God that somebody else ain't doing it for our Charles.

'So are you going to take the burial service, knowing what I've just told you or have I got to arrange for somebody else to do it? Because as I see it, if you do agree to bury him, you ain't got no case at all for not doing the other and marry your own girl. Ask yourself if you would bury her, if it was her I was just going to toll for.'

He began to move, slowly and heavily, down the aisle towards where the sallies of the bells hung. Fran sprang up and threw herself into his arms. She knew by the way he clasped her that he was as glad she was there as she was that he was. He kissed her and put her away from him, striding sadly towards his heartrending task. She fled, anxious to get home to Sophie and share the distress she knew would greet her there. Neither George nor she looked again at the Rector.

She was more than halfway home before the first stroke of the great tenor bell boomed its sad message across the grief-stricken village.

60

Sophie was still at Benedict's when the two men returned. She and Fran had absorbed some of each other's grief, but gloom still hung over the house, and a hushed, frightened silence over the village. Sophie, who had been glad of Fran's company, was not up to facing the stranger she still felt Elyot Franks to be, and soon went home, for which the others were thankful. Yet even without her presence in the house, it was difficult to put the death out of their minds and discuss those things that had been paramount the same morning.

Fran persuaded Elyot to stay to an early supper with them so that both sides could report progress – or otherwise.

'You first,' Fran said. 'Because you probably have made some headway, and I haven't resolved anything. The news of Robert's death just put everything else out of mind. But it was all rather fraught. How did you get on?'

Elyot apparently expected William to do the talking. 'No real fuss about the certificate. It can be picked up on Wednesday morning. Legally, we have the means and enough time to make Beth Mrs Franks by Sunday. But as Elyot reminded me, she's had no say in anything so far. The next step must be to get at her somehow. But until we are sure what line Archie is going to take, we can't do much more.'

Fran reported her visit to the church and the Rector's obstinate but plainly deeply felt opinions about marrying couples who had been engaging in any sexual activity before, as she said, 'to use his expression, it had been "hallowed". I told him that he was answerable to the Bishop if he wouldn't perform a ceremony requested of him, providing there was no other impediment, but he knew that already. He was one step in front of us. I gathered that his plan was to have pleaded illness – by which he meant another mental breakdown – and given up there and then, before he could be asked or expected to do anything more at all.

'I told him that would be a lie, but I might as well have been talking to a clothes prop. He looked like a dead man walking. I think he probably hasn't eaten anything since Saturday. Then we heard about Robert, and I ran home to be with Sophie. I knew how she'd feel. She was at school with Cynthia and Tom. There's a sort of bond between them that even such as we can't share. It makes us feel outsiders. So really, that's about it. No farther forward, I'm afraid.'

She couldn't bring herself to tell William, in Elyot's

hearing, of George's personal disclosures. That part was for William's ears only, when they were alone.

When anything as shattering as Robert's death occurred, the village closed ranks. The indigenous stuck together, even though as individuals they might have been at loggerheads for donkey's years. Then there was another circle, outside the nucleus, made up of people like Fran and William and Jess, plus a few others such as the doctor who had spent most of his life caring for their physical welfare. All the rest were outsiders.

It was a different sort of hierarchy, one that had nothing to do with class or wealth. Fran kept on coming back to her own metaphor for it: a sort of country dance. It was the same mixture of people all the time, but the groupings changed according to the figures of the dance. Those born to it understood it; but it took real newcomers, such as Elyot and Archie Marriner and the Choppens a very long time to understand and come to terms with it. That was why they were looked on as 'furriners' till they had been in residence for seven years. Any countryman would tell you that.

As soon as Elyot had left, she sat down on the arm of William's chair and told him what it had really been like down at the church that morning. He wrapped an arm round her when she got to George Bridgefoot's intervention and her feelings about it.

'He was as tragic as . . . as King Lear,' she said. 'An old man who had had to learn that his ideas couldn't always be acted on even if he still thought he was right in principle. So noble and so humble at the same time that I could hardly bear it. And then the news of Robert's death – and that first awful hollow sound of the bell following me home, while I kept thinking of George counting the strokes with the tears dripping off his cheeks and his heart aching for Tom and Cynthia . . . and the awful thought that it might have been Charles instead of Robert.

'And all the time Archie Marriner just sitting there. I wondered how it was affecting him. It was so queer – I had got the impression that until then he hadn't *felt* anything at all. As if as far as he was concerned, the whole issue had only been

481

in his head. Like the prince in a fairytale, I thought – his heart had been turned to stone. I reached across and touched him, to make some point or other and . . . darling, I know it sounds silly, but he jumped as if I'd given him an electric shock. And just for a minute, after that, I thought we might be getting somewhere, but then George came and took the stage, and I ran away. It's just possible that Archie was beginning to feel enough for what George said to sink in. But much as I wanted him to give in, I can't bear to think it took Robert's death to get through to him.'

She was near to tears, and all he could do was hold her, without speaking.

In the long silence, he was thinking that he knew why her touch had had such an effect on Beth's father. She was responsible for his petrified heart; but that, of course, she must never be allowed to suspect. As he now stroked and soothed her, William realized that perhaps he had known intuitively all the way along what had made Marriner so much worse lately.

He thought that maybe he, William, hadn't wanted to admit it, even to himself; but the knowledge had been there. He was glad now that he had been patient and sympathetic with the other man, at any rate till last week. It was fairly clear to William now that the 'man under authority' had torn the ability to love out of himself lest he continued to yearn towards temptation and the impossible. He had numbed his heart to such an extent that his rejection of love had included even Beth. It explained a lot.

William had jested that morning about playing at being Zeus: but surely it must have been some god or other who had arranged for it to be Fran on the spot when the crux came? Perhaps in time.

Fran was getting up. 'I must write to Cynthia for both of us,' she was saying. 'Anything more would be an intrusion. No outsider should gatecrash grief as great as that.'

He pulled her back. 'Try to turn your thoughts away from it now,' he said. 'We knew Robert was bound to die soon. I don't know whether that makes it better or worse, but life has to go on. It hasn't altered the other problem. While you were having such a tragic time, I was having a rather comic one. I took Elyot shopping, to a jeweller's. We only went in to buy a wedding ring, in case of emergency. What's the old saying? "A lover's purse is tied by a cobweb." It was a good thing I was there to stand surety for his solvency! We looked at every engagement ring in the shop, and a bracelet for a wedding present, and a pair of ear-rings to match it, and then there was a necklace that couldn't be left behind because that matched as well – we were so loaded with valuables walking back to the car that we weren't safe, either from muggers or the police.

'We had a lovely time – except that I was jealous. Jealous that he could do what I can't, and buy his wife wedding presents, when I love you so much, quite as much as he loves Beth, and more. Oh Fran, why can't I, when I love you so much . . . ?'

They both raised enquiring eyebrows as the heavy knocker on the front door clattered and broke them apart.

'That bloody guardian angel of ours at it again,' William said. 'Who can it be as late as this? Sit still, I'll go.'

He came back almost at once with George Bridgefoot.

Fran jumped up and kissed George. She had begun to regard herself as part of his family. He was apologizing for disturbing them so late, but as he said, there had been all sorts of developments during the day.

'You'll be glad to know as the Rector's promised not to do anything till after Robert's funeral,' he said. 'I reckon he was a bit ashamed. He didn't expect God to take the decision out of his hands like that. He just went on sitting all the while I was tolling the bell – and I think he'd have liked to go on talking, but I wanted to get away, for one thing 'cos I was so worried about young Charles.

'It was him Molly sent up to the church to tell me that Robert had gone. He's took it every bit as bad as I'd expected. When I got home he was up in his bedroom, and wouldn't let me in. Then he saw his father's car coming, and wouldn't stop to face him. He went out of one door as Brian come in the other, and drove off somewhere. He hasn't been back since.

'I've been up to Lane's End. Rosemary's there with Cynthia. I don't know what'll become of Tom. They want the funeral Friday – Good Friday, but that's for the Rector to decide. I don't know as there's anything against funerals, Holy Week or not. Most parsons don't like weddings on Holy Saturday, though some allow it because so many folks want Easter weddings and they all seem to want to be married on Saturdays now. Not like when I were young – no woman would have a Saturday wedding then, 'cos o' the old rhyme. You know, they were all superstitious about such things. They all'us said:

> 'Monday for health,
> Tuesday for wealth,
> We'n'sday the best day of all.
> Thursday for losses
> And Friday for crosses
> And Saturday no luck at all.

'But there you are. Folks don't take notice of them things, now. They want Robert's favourite hymns – at times like this folks expect the church to be like it all'us has been before. But with all this to-do about the Rector and his daughter, as I can't tell the Faireys nothing about, whatever can I do about getting somebody to play the organ? That's really what I came to ask you.'

Rambling though it had been, Fran had taken in much more than George had actually said. She had seen a sliver of hope, like the first thin thread of the new moon through a mass of heavy clouds. If Archie was going to bury the boy, it was because he was grieving with the Faireys. Perhaps his heart had started to thaw.

She was recharged with hope, bringing confidence and energy with it. Ideas stormed through her head. She could almost feel her antennae rising and scanning the horizon for possibilities.

'You've got too much on your plate already,' she said to George. 'Leave finding an organist to us.'

He nodded, looking so relieved, that for the moment he was 'done up'.

William noticed. 'Sit down, Mr Bridgefoot. However much of a hurry you are in to get back home, what you need now is a drink.'

George made no protest as Fran pushed him into her chair and sat on the arm of it. He took a swig at the drink William handed him, and almost at once became his usual self again.

'I must get home,' he said. 'Molly's nearly out of her mind about Charles. She wants me to go and look for him, but I don't know where to start.'

'Try Castle Hill first,' Fran said.

George stood up, impatient to be gone. 'You do your grandfather proud,' he said. 'Both of you. I wish you wouldn't call me Mr Bridgefoot. It don't seem right.'

When she had seen him out, she was aware of William's quizical gaze on her.

'You really are "a cough-drop",' he said. 'Here we are up to our necks in problems already, and you land us with another of producing an organist out of thin air. Greg's no good, this time. He can't get home till late on Saturday at the earliest. Monica's arriving on Friday for Easter. We met Jess this morning and she told us.'

'Beth will have to do it,' Fran told him, confidently. 'I take it that one or both of you men intend to go and pick up that registrar's certificate on Wednesday morning? We dare not risk leaving it till after Easter, in case she is pregnant. And she won't face up to playing on Sunday unless she's wearing a wedding ring.

'Men! You're right about one thing, though. We mustn't let our sympathy for the Faireys spoil things for Beth. Elyot's preparing to load her down with jewellery like a raja's elephant, but of course neither of you has thought about clothes. Her tiara should look marvellous over a black eye and a creased old frock dragged out of a suitcase. She's been shoving her wardrobe together in case her father turns her out again. So, while poor old George plans a funeral, we plan a wedding. A proper wedding, even if there has to be a register office one first. Leave it all to me, though of course I shall need your help. It'll be your job to bring Elyot into line. Maybe Archie, too, though I'm hoping against hope that Beth will be able to do that. And if necessary, I'll have another go myself.'

William lay back in his chair and eyed her with admiration.

He hadn't any idea what she was planning, and to tell the truth, he didn't care much. The beacon in his lighthouse had begun to flash again.

61

Fran had been right in her surmise that Charles would make for Castle Hill. Charlie had forbidden him to go there, but even if he couldn't see her, it was somewhere far enough from home for him to be alone, not only with his grief, but with his first ever close encounter with death. He discovered that he couldn't take it in. He had never seen a dead human being. He tried to visualize Robert lying dead on his bed in the room where they had romped together since he was old enough to be allowed to go up to Lane's End alone. He either couldn't visualize it, or was terrified by what he saw when fleeting imagination momentarily showed it to him.

As he turned up the lane towards where he had first met Charlie on Boxing Day, another fear came to him. The Easter holidays had begun, and Nick would not be at school. He had to pass the cottage where Nick lived – but the one person he could not bear to meet today was Nick. Himself and Nick together, without Robert? That had recently quite often been the case, but it was different now. Without Robert *ever again*? He trod on the accelerator and sped past the cottage.

Had he but known, Nick was inside thinking very much the same thoughts and not wanting to see Charles. He was feeling guilty because since Christmas, he had rather left his friendship with the other two boys to look after itself. The change in his mother's circumstances had allowed him to give all his attention to achieving his ambition of getting a university place. He was better fed, better dressed and happier than he had ever thought could be possible till he could earn his own living. He had neither the means nor the desire to go 'girlhunting', besides being too busy with his school work. There was Poppy. They were friends, and had kept it that way since he had kissed her in the straw in a deluge of rain. He dreamed long-term dreams in which Nick Hadley, MA. would ask an equally well educated Poppy to marry him, but he recognized them for what they were, just dreams. Life and literature had both warned Nick that dreams and hopes were not the same thing.

He had also been brought much nearer to the reality of death than Charles had ever been. He had been there when they had carried Bert Bleasby's dead body out of the house which had been the only home he had ever known till then.

As Sophie turned to her Bible, Nick turned to Shakespeare: Claudio facing death in *Measure for Measure*:

> Ah, but to die and go we know not where,
> To lie in cold obstruction, and to rot . . .

That was too much for him. He was glad there was nobody else there, to see his tears for Robert.

Charles drove straight into the yard at Castle Hill Farm, and came immediately face to face with Bob Bellamy.

The boy's face told the man that something was very wrong. He knew it wasn't Charlie, because he had seen her only a few minutes before, going across to the building he had given her for use as her tack-room.

In his usual shy fashion, he held back from asking, but the look he gave Charles communicated a question as well as words could have done.

'Did you know that Robert Fairey died this morning, Mr Bellamy?' Charles said. 'I . . . I wanted to tell Charlie.'

They stood side by side, each glad of the other's presence. Charles felt that putting the awful truth into words had helped him come to terms with it. He didn't need telling how moved by the news the older man was.

Charles followed Bob's gaze up to the white clouds being wind-blown across the vast blue sky, and then across to the church and the abandoned rookery beyond.

When Bob, still silent, began to walk that way as if impelled, Charles kept pace with him. When Bob leaned on the churchyard wall, Charles stood close by, at a loss to know what else to do, and still drawing comfort from the farmer's presence.

Bellamy turned, and went towards the trees. Charles followed. Once under them, Bob looked up into the delicately greening elms.

He turned to Charles. 'The rooks have all gone,' he said, speaking for the first time. 'I knowed that was a warning of a death to come soon – but you all'us go on hoping that such things are only old wives' tales. Or if you can't help believing in 'em, like me, you hope as the warning's meant for somebody who's had a good life and is ready to go. Not somebody with his life still in front of him, like young Fairey. His father's only son.'

He kept his eyes up on the empty nests. 'I reckon the rooks will come back next year, and start building again. It's hard for anybody to understand death. I like to think it's only really a part of life. Just going back to nature to start again. Like spring always comes again after winter. You can't have spring without winter. Young Robert's gone back to nature, whatever the church makes of it. Remember that when you're watching 'em letting his coffin down. *He* won't be there. It's only like burning last year's haulms.'

He began to walk on, through the elms and farther into the wood, only stopping where the whole expanse under the trees was covered with oxlips, their heads so heavy with pale, primrose-like florets that they appeared to be holding each other up.

'Look! There's spring for you! You don't see a sight like that everywhere. Only where there's been cowslips and primroses left to grow together year after year undisturbed. They get mixed, like old families in villages used to, till now. It won't be long before somebody'll say they ought to be sprayed, or ploughed up. But not while they're on my farm.'

He stooped and began to pick the flowers till he had as many as his big hands could hold. He held them out to Charles. 'Here, my boy, take these to Charlie. I reckon she can't know they're out yet. You'll find her in the tack-room.'

Charles took the flowers, murmuring thanks, and walked

away. He found Charlie in her large tack-room, stretched on a couch made of two bales of hay. She looked up at him, surprised to see him, and anxious when he failed to find his voice.

'Charles? What's the matter?'

He stood over her, clutching the oxlips. Her eyes were great dark pools, first of apprehension, and then of sudden intuitive understanding that he was in trouble, struggling against some deep emotion. He laid the flowers in her lap.

'Robert,' he said, but he could not go on.

The pools grew even larger, filling with tender sympathy. She held out her arms to him, and he knelt down by her side, burying a wet face against that soft young breast he had never even dared to touch before.

She understood his need, all feminine instinct, and herself undid the buttons of her high-necked blouse that was preventing close contact between them.

She cradled his head and stroked him, murmuring words he had heard in his dreams but not expected to hear in reality till in some distant future in a fairy realm where dreams came true. Even when she turned her murmurings into French, their meaning was just as plain to him. He hardly dared to breathe lest he break the magic spell, and lay like a child being solaced and comforted. She was running her fingers through his blond curls when at last he lifted his head. A tiny patch of smooth silky skin swelling above the lace trimming of her bra was just beneath his lips. He bent his head, and kissed it.

He heard her gasp, and magic faded into reality.

Resolutely freeing a hand, he slowly and deliberately did up the buttons of her blouse. Then he got up from his knees, and sat down beside her, taking her into his arms, and kissing her with such tenderness that it was she who began to cry.

'I love you, Charlie,' he said 'I love you far too much to . . .'

She nodded, to show him she understood. Too much to take advantage of her sympathy for him, or of what the shock had done to her. Too much to treat her in any way that his grandad wouldn't have thought right.

'Will you marry me, Charlie – one day? When you're ready?'

Her eyes were bright, with tears still standing on her lashes. 'Yes,' she said. 'I expect so, some day. I'm like my dad. Sometimes, I know things. I know I shan't ever love anybody else the way I love you. But you'll have to wait ages. I think I know that, as well. Will you wait?'

He closed his eyes as he remembered the feel of the contour of her breast under his lips, and wondered if he would dare ever again to put himself into such temptation, or have the strength to resist it if he did. She felt him trembling as he struggled with desire that was now far more than a boyish need to experiment with sex. Death and life were at war in him, one urging him to make up for the other. Winter and spring. However long the winter . . .

'I'll wait for ever,' he said at last. 'But, my lambkin, don't make for ever too long.'

He let her go and picked up the oxlips. Their sweet scent wafted all around them. They stood close, looking at each other, with the oxlips between them.

'Your dad said we always had to have winter before it could be spring,' he said. 'It will be winter for me till you decide it's spring.'

From the house, her father watched them come, holding hands; the boy looked as relaxed and comforted as he had hoped, but he could see by their faces that whatever had happened between them had left both as fresh and innocent as the flowers she was carrying. All the same, there was a look there that he had never seen on his tomboy daughter's face before. He glanced with envy at Charles. He had never once seen that sort of look on her mother's face, though he'd caught it on Fran's once or twice when her glance had been resting on William.

The sight of the two youngsters lightened his own heavy heart. He felt that the two beautiful youngsters were like heralds of spring to him: a sign that his own dark winter couldn't last for ever.

The telephone was ringing and he moved to answer it.

'Yes, he's here and he's all right now. I'll send him home. Charles,' he said, 'that was your grandad. They're worried about you.'

'I must go,' the boy said. 'I can face them all, now.'

He kissed Charlie with a proprietory air that made Charlie blush.

'Don't worry, Mr Bellamy,' he said. 'That'll probably have to last me a long time. Till Charlie decides it's spring.'

'When she can set her foot on nine daisies?' Bob said, understanding perfectly what he was being told. Charles handed her over to her father, holding her hand till the last possible moment before letting go.

'Goodnight, my lambkin,' he said, and went.

Bob eyed Charlie questioningly. To his surprise, she flung herself into his arms, and began to weep despairingly.

'I can't help it, Dad,' she sobbed. 'It just came over me how I'd feel if I were Pansy Gifford, and knew that Charles would never call me his lambkin again.'

Charles was greeted at the Old Glebe with such relief and love that it embarrassed him and almost undid him again.

'Your mum is stopping with Rosemary tonight,' his grandad said. 'And your dad's been ringing up about every ten minutes. He wants you to go home. Will you?'

'On one condition,' Charles said. 'Tonight I asked Charlie Bellamy to marry me – some day – and I know I shall never ask anybody else. Not to please Dad or anybody. If Dad's prepared to accept that, and will let me take Charlie home occasionally, I'll go now, this minute. I want to go home. Will you tell Dad that for me, Grandad?'

George went discreetly to another telephone. Molly let her tearful gaze rest on Charles. His grandfather had looked just like that, at twenty.

George came back. 'Off you go, my boy,' he said.

62

On Tuesday morning, Fran told Sophie that she would be having a lunch party on Saturday, and would be glad of her help. She didn't yet quite know for how many, but a maximum, she thought, of eight. She was sure, she said, that she could leave Sophie to get on with it, because she was going to be very busy, one way and the other, for the rest of the week.

Sophie was gratified. A weekend that lasted from Thursday night till Tuesday morning was not at all to her taste, especially with a funeral in the middle of it. They spent a happy morning selecting menus to last over a long weekend, as well as a special lunch on Saturday.

Sophie didn't ask who would be coming, which was strange; but Fran guessed that Sophie was just as glad to have something to take her mind off the Faireys as she was herself.

That settled, Fran told William after lunch that she proposed to take herself down to see Beth that afternoon. He raised his eyebrows, but she didn't wait for him to raise any objections.

'She's not in prison, is she? Her father's a parson, not a gaoler. He can't be rude enough to me not to let me see her if she wants to see me.'

She was banking on her intuition, and what George Bridgefoot had said, that the Rector must have reconsidered his position a bit. She had made up her mind that boldness had to be her friend.

The Rector answered the door to her, and coolly but courteously invited her in. She asked to see Beth.

'I haven't actually seen or spoken to my daughter for four days,' he said. 'She is keeping to her room – you know why. Will you go up to her, or shall I tell her you are here?'

'I'd rather you did,' Fran said. Then she launched herself directly along the course she had decided to try. 'You can't really go on like this much longer, you know,' she said. 'It's quite ludicrous! Somebody's pride's got to give. I need to ask you both about Robert Fairey's funeral, to help poor old George. Why not take this opportunity of breaking the ice between you and Beth?'

He bowed his head slightly in her direction, nonplussed as to how to deal with so matter-of-fact an approach. To avoid having to answer her, he went up the stairs, and she heard voices. Well, at least she had made him speak to Beth, who called to her from the top of the curved cottage staircase.

'Come up, Fran,' she said. 'I'm not really fit to come down.'

Beth was in her dressing-gown, fresh from the sort of long, luxurious bath that in the ordinary way she never had time for. Her thick braid of hair hung down over her shoulder, and Fran saw at once that the black eye now only looked like a bit of smudged eye-shadow.

'He spoke to me!' Beth said. 'In fact, he apologized for hitting me. What's happened to him?'

'Something or somebody's made him think,' Fran said. 'Did he tell you it was about Robert Fairey's funeral I had to see you? Well, so it is. I've promised George Bridgefoot that you'll play the organ. You can't not, for the Faireys' sake, can you? But will your father agree?'

Beth pleated a fold in her dressing-gown, looking down at it before speaking. 'Would they want me, if they knew what you do?'

'Do you think anybody but your father will give you a thought when they are burying a twenty-year-old boy?' Fran asked.

Beth flushed.

'That's what I meant,' said Fran. 'It's too late for you to start being "missish". Unless your father makes an exhibition of himself, how is anybody else to know anything at all? He's the only danger. That's why we've got to spike his guns. He couldn't do a thing if by Friday you are already Elyot's wife.'

Beth turned white, and sat down rather abruptly. Fran launched into the tale of the registrar's certificate. Beth gasped.

'Now,' said Fran, very cool and businesslike. 'There can't be a wedding, even in a register office, without a bride. The men can't go any further till they have your consent. As soon as I get home, if you agree, they will fix it up with the registrar. William and I will go with you as witnesses, probably on Thursday.

'The church will be crowded for the funeral, and the whole village mourning with the Faireys. Until that's over, there really mustn't be anything to detract from it. Do you see? So if your father raises any objection with you about playing, show him your marriage certificate, and shut him up. If not, keep quiet about it. In this instance, the Faireys' feelings come before everything else.'

Beth nodded, but she was very quiet. 'Fran,' she said, appealingly. 'May I talk to you – about how I feel? I've had such a long time up here alone to think. You know how much I love Elyot. How much I want to be his wife. But – does he really want to marry me? Or is he just being a gentleman and saving what's left of my reputation? I couldn't bear that! I won't have him forced into a wedding he doesn't want. What happened happened. I shall never regret it – but he doesn't have to marry me. Can we get that straight first?'

'I think if you ran back now,' Fran said, 'he really would use his revolver. On himself. Do you think William would have done what he did, if he hadn't known Elyot to be out of his mind with love for you?'

'I can't really believe it,' Beth said. 'It's so wonderful . . . But Fran, I want to thank Somebody. I'm a parson's daughter, and still a Christian. Oh, I know what I said – and some of it's still true. Daddy's God isn't – or wasn't – the same one as mine. But I shan't feel *married* in a register office! If only Daddy would agree to bless us afterwards! I'm sure he won't, and if he would I don't expect Elyot would agree, after what's happened. But I'd always dreamed that if I ever did get married, it would be in a church full of flowers – like Lucy Bridgefoot had. I know that can't be, now – but why do we have to be in such a hurry? Daddy might come round in time to agreeing to a quiet church wedding.'

Fran tried not to be exasperated. She thought of all those jewels Elyot had bought for a willing bride who had already proved herself a worthy bedmate. Beth was having what in Victorian times would be called 'a fit of the vapours'. She decided to be forthright.

'And what happens, in the meantime? Elyot goes off his head waiting, while you play the simpering, shilly-shallying miss? Or do you sneak across to go to bed with him until somebody sees you and sets the village alight with the best bit of sexy scandal for years? Be your age, Beth! You've got your father over a barrel because of this funeral. But there's another reason. Sex means babies. How do you know you're not already pregnant? When will you know?'

Beth coloured and fidgeted.

'Well? Don't tell me you hadn't thought about it.'

Beth bridled. 'I'm not a child, Frances,' she said. 'And I haven't lived in a London slum for nothing. I have been praying that it just couldn't be. It'll be two weeks more before I can be sure.'

'And what are you proposing to do if you are? Drown yourself? Abort Elyot's child? Slink off and bring it up unknown – like Jane Hadley? Kill the baby's father as surely as if you shot him, and put your own father into a lunatic asylum as well? Cause endless anxiety to friends like me and William, who love you? God, what fools these mortals be! Especially when there's any question of a bit of sex. As if God didn't know about sex. He arranged it that way didn't He? Stop mooning and think.

'How long is it since your honeymoon with Elyot? Five days. It may seem like six months to you, but it's only from Thursday to Tuesday. Even Beryl Bean couldn't cast aspersions if you are a married woman before this week's out. Stop being Victorian and be practical. As you say, what's done is done. And if you are going to have fits of conscience about not having the church's blessing, I suggest you leave everything to me and William.'

She was hitting too hard, and softened her tone.

'You may not believe it, but William and I do know how you feel about wanting some ritual – in your case Christian ritual – in your wedding. But I think . . . in fact I'm sure, that the most important thing of all is for you to make it up with your father. Don't let the ice that's been broken this morning have time to freeze over again.

'Come back here to sleep in any case till Holy Week's out.

It won't kill Elyot to wait a few more days once he knows you are his wife – though I expect he'll either sulk or throw himself about. I've never seen a man more in love, you lucky girl. Except perhaps William.' She smiled. 'It gets them bad in middle age. So far it's been William doing all the plotting to make you happy. Now it's my turn. I've got ideas I intend to try to put into practice if you'll let me. What about clothes? Have you anything suitable for a civil ceremony? Let's go shopping tomorrow. You need something special in hand for a quiet little country wedding. Yes, a wedding, not a blessing. You and Elyot are both free. There's no reason why you shouldn't get your wish. I'll go to work on your father, and persuade him to marry you if I can. If I can't, somebody else will have to. But my guess is that he will. Now get dressed and come down to make him and me a cup of tea. But not a word to him. He knows the facts of life, too. Let him do a bit of thinking and worrying. Just show him how much you care for him. And I advise you to stay away from Elyot, so as not to rub your father the wrong way. I'm going down to talk to him now. Not about you. Simply as one of his parishioners, or as your friend.'

She kissed the bewildered Beth. 'I'll l'arn him,' said Fran, looking both wicked and dogged. In spite of herself, Beth laughed.

Because Beth had been immured upstairs for the last five days there was nothing to offer with the tea, and the Rector was considerably embarrassed. He offered apologies over and over again, and actually said to Beth, in quite a commonplace, fatherly voice, that he was looking forward to some of the oat biscuits she was so clever at making.

Fran caught Beth's eye, and dropped an eyelid. Who would make his oat biscuits for him in future?

Fran pushed the business on by asking about the arrangements for Robert's funeral. He was not anxious to discuss it, but said that as it was Good Friday, he had requested that the interment be in the morning.

'Is it usual to have other sort of services in Holy Week?' she asked.

'It is entirely at the discretion of the priest,' he answered.

'In all my years as a parish priest I have never been asked before to hold a funeral on a Good Friday. But this is a very special case. His parents have been absolutely adamant about keeping his body at home. The boy died on Monday morning. It would have been impossible to delay the burial beyond Saturday, and his mother wanted it on Friday. She insists on sitting beside the body, day and night, I'm told. Mrs Brian Bridgefoot is with her, and George Bridgefoot is doing what he can for poor Mr Fairey. I don't know the family at all well but it's clearly an old one by the evidence of the churchyard. George tells me that both parents were only children, so there are no uncles, aunts or cousins. Robert's death means the end of the family. Very sad.'

Fran felt a wave of anger, and then of guilt. This family needn't have died out, and some of it was her fault that it had. She had given George advice on which he had acted. If Robert had made Pansy Gifford pregnant, what a difference it would have made now to Tom and Cynthia! But of course, the Rector knew about Robert and Pansy, though not of her part in it. She had been there when George told him, in the church, and he knew that she knew. George must have pierced his armour. Beth, of course, knew nothing about that.

A silence fell. Where could the line of sexual morality be drawn by anybody, in such a case as this? Certainly she was in no position to judge anybody: herself and William; Roland and Monica; Beth and Elyot.

Robert and Pansy belonged to the present. They had probably not thought 'having sex' wrong at all. They had been doing only what most of their peers did, anyway. Was it wrong? If she and George and Alex had kept out of it, nature would have possibly kept the Fairey family going. Surely, that eventuality must have been *right*? As it was, there was no knowing what the outcome might be.

Yet to Archie, sex was the sin of sins. What did that really mean? Were Adam and Eve 'married'? However one read that creation myth, it looked as if the Creator didn't know His own mind, or else wanted it both ways.

William the historian agreed with Archie that promiscuity could threaten civilization. Like alcohol or drugs, he said, it was 'excess' that caused harm. But you had to qualify 'excess', surely? By quantity or quality?

She began to gather her things together, ready to leave. 'William has some business or other to see to tomorrow,' she said to Beth. 'He says we ought to get away to keep the tragedy in proportion. I thought I'd go shopping. Will you come with me?'

'Thank you, I should love to,' Beth answered demurely.

'Thursday as well?' Fran asked. 'William thought you had been cooped up long enough, and suggested we took you out to lunch that day. He's already booked the table.' Not waiting for answer or protest, she left.

63

'You may kiss your wife, Mr Franks,' said the expressionless registrar.

Elyot obeyed in the reluctant, timorous fashion of a small boy commanded to kiss an ancient great-aunt of whom he was scared, and whom he didn't like the smell of. Beth allowed herself to be pecked on the cheek. She was almost as tall as her new husband, straight and willowy as he was thickset and square-shouldered. Both were moving like marionettes.

There were handshakes all round, and they went to the car park. William was driving, and the newlyweds sat in the back seat, still looking robotic.

William had thought it wise that Elyot should go to town early in his own car that Thursday morning, and meet them at the register office. He had therefore not seen Beth since William had taken her back home on Saturday, until she had arrived at the appointed time at the register office. Bride and bridegroom both looked embarrassed and bewildered. Nevertheless, the deed was now done.

Fran understood very well why Beth wouldn't feel properly

married, in spite of the ring on her left hand. She doubted if she would have done so herself had she been in Beth's place. The register office had been much nicer than she had expected, the registrar very kind; but however well it legalized the union, it was still more like a business transaction than the joining of two lives into one. It was a contract, with no element of ritual about it. She decided that ritual was what it had lacked.

Always able to think on two levels at once, she was following up that thread of thought as they waited for William to bring the car round. It was on Beth's father that her thoughts centred – Archie Marriner as he represented the Church, that age-old established institution caught willy-nilly in the process of change, and doing its best to resist it. Especially with regard to divorce and remarriage, and the sexual behaviour more or less forced on the young by the war years. Hadn't William said something to that effect, on that wonderful day they had spent together in Hunstanton? 'When you expect to be killed before tomorrow morning, you don't stop to ask yourself what you are doing.' Then George Bridgefoot in the church only three days ago: 'He wanted to be a man while he could.'

How could anyone, parson or not, condemn them? Wasn't mercy and charity expected of a clergyman as much as of any other father? The war had been over for twenty years – but those who had been through it and survived, like William, Elyot, Greg and Eric, couldn't be expected to regard it simply as a bit of history. They bore invisible scars, as much as those who could show wounds. So did a whole multitude of women who were now being expected to 'put it behind them' and forget what they had lost.

She found it very difficult to come to terms with Archie's attitude towards Beth and Elyot. It wasn't that he didn't know, or understand what William had told him of Elyot's scars. He had lived through the war years himself. He couldn't be either blind or deaf – or incapable of feeling. He must somehow have blinkered himself, and stopped his ears. The church as a whole was yielding a little before the tide of social change, but rigid, hidebound individuals like Archie weren't really doing much to help to save the ship. Fran smiled to herself as her word-filled mind provided her with an analogy. He was like the captain of the *Nancy Lee*, the hero of the popular pre-war song, and was 'climbing up the rigging as the ship went down'. She told herself that she had got to try again to make him see that.

She was watching the couple in the back seat surreptitiously through the vanity mirror on the back of the sun-screen she had pulled down on purpose, a little alarmed at the woodenness of the event so far, and afraid that Beth's doubts about Elyot being dragooned into marriage against his will might be rising again.

'What now?' she asked William, when the silence had become unbearable.

'I booked us a special table at the Garden House,' he said. Fran glanced again into the mirror to see if this announcement had any effect.

She heaved a great sigh of relief when at last Elyot sought and found Beth's hand, stripped off her glove, and looked down at the ring. Then he picked up the hand and held it to his lips, and next moment Beth was in his arms.

'Don't mind us,' said William, adding under his breath to Fran, 'I think I'd better drive round a bit, don't you, darling?'

Fran agreed, and they did several circular tours round the city, before William judged it safe for them to make a dignified entrance to the hotel.

They toasted the couple discreetly in champagne, and William made them an elegant little speech that Fran guessed cost him a lot. She knew how deeply jealous he was that the ring on Beth's finger was not on her own. It didn't matter to her to anything like the same degree as it mattered to him.

Elyot made an equally elegant, if impromptu, reply.

It had been left to Fran to break it to him that he was not going to be allowed to take his bride home with him that day. The result was what all the others had expected, and as William said afterwards, it might have been extremely dramatic, if it hadn't been staged in a high-class hotel. As it was, after Fran had explained, the four just sat staring at each other, Elyot too irritated for speech, Beth tremulously tearful, William embarrassed and Fran struggling with that bubble of mirth that so often threatened to choke her in situations where she couldn't allow it to escape in laughter.

She managed to smother it, and spoke directly to Elyot, knowing she could rely on William for support. 'Try to understand why, Elyot,' she said. 'All we have done today is to clear the decks for action. In all the circumstances, it really was a very necessary precaution. But it has to be kept secret — mainly because of what is happening tomorrow. It's going to be awful . . . everybody will be grieving with Tom and Cynthia, united in sorrow and sympathy. Do you honestly think it could be like that if people knew what we've been doing this morning? With Beth in sight? Please, Elyot, allow us old villagers to know best! I give you my promise that you shan't have to wait longer than Saturday to take Beth home with you.'

'What have you got up your sleeve?' William asked, because they hadn't actually planned any further than they had now got.

'I haven't planned anything. But if it's at all possible, I hope to be able to make Saturday a real wedding day for Beth to remember. It depends on her father, and what happens in the next forty-eight hours. Elyot, I haven't done anything so far without Beth's agreement. I know you want what she wants, don't you? I'm going to try to arrange a church wedding as well.'

Elyot, though disappointed, knew by Beth's face that Fran was speaking for her. Though still reluctant, he agreed and left them to go and pick up his own car, looking wooden again. Beth was inclined to be miserable, in spite of Fran's determined assurance that all would be well.

William held Beth's hand, and tried to make light of it. 'He's having his first experience of having to take orders from a woman,' he told her. 'I promise not to take my eye off him between now and Saturday, and if I hear a single growl from a black dog, I shall come for you to deal with it. But I know of old that when Fran gets an idea into her head . . . Trust her to see it through, Beth. I would.'

'Let's get back home then,' Fran said. 'I've got a lot to do and no time to do it in. The first thing is for me to have another go at the Rector. I'll drive you home, Beth, and if he's at home, I'll tackle him then and there. If I need you, William, I'll phone. I suggest that we don't let him know about this morning, so you'll have to take your ring off, Beth. Elyot can put it back on on Saturday, whether I succeed or not. Leave me alone with your father for half an hour. If he's still as stubborn, I'll ring William to collect Elyot and we'll face him with the fact. But let's hope that won't be necessary.'

Since Monday, the Rector had had no peace. He had been undergoing a spiritual equivalent to the pain felt when sensation at last returns to hands or feet numbed by cold, the condition known in East Anglia as 'the hot-ache'. As the blood flows back into cold extremities, the pain is indeed 'hot' in its medieval sense of being so intense as to be well-nigh unendurable.

It was not his extremities that had been numbed, but his heart. The pain was all the greater for that, when at last his numbness began to wear off. Monday afternoon's experience in the church had reconnected his mind to the rest of him, and with every hour that passed the pain of remorse grew worse. Desperate contrition and regret gnawed at him. He was having great difficulty in making himself believe that the whole affair was not a particularly ghastly nightmare.

At first he had tried to persuade himself that Beth's declaration about her affair with the Commander existed only in her mind. William, Fran and George had disabused him of that bit of wishful thinking. He was up against reality. Until Fran's visit, he had not set eyes on Beth since William had taken her home on Saturday, but he had to face facts. Fran would not have involved herself without good reason. He didn't need telling what her reason was. She had appealed to him to marry his daughter to the Commander, and he had refused. Shaken to the core by George's words, he had left the church asking himself *why* he had refused. Whichever way he looked at it, his own dogmatic reaction no longer made sense to him, but he had no way out of his dilemma.

He spent Tuesday trying to come to terms with himself; with the past few years, and with the future. He felt adrift, where until Monday he had been so certain of his bearings and the course he had charted for himself. He was also absolutely alone.

Alone, alone, all, all alone, alone on a wide, wide sea.

Coleridge's lines kept running through his head . . . but then Coleridge had been drugged on opium half his time. That set him off on a new tack.

He had been on drugs, too, though the treatment had been finished some time before he had come to Old Swithinford. They had told him he was cured – but had the cure had side effects that he was only just becoming aware of? Was this terrible remorse the beginning of a belated return to sanity? If so, it was too late. He had alienated his daughter, his potential friends, his congregation and his parish. Personally and professionally, he was a failure.

Then, later in the afternoon, Frances Catherwood had visited Beth, and stayed to tea. After she had gone, and Beth retired again to her room, he carried on his self-examination.

During Fran's visit, he had acted normally, just as he might have done before his breakdown. The truth that dawned on him was unpalatable, but plain. He had been suffering side effects from his breakdown. He'd gone on treating himself after his counsellors had discharged him, and poisoned himself with an overdose of their remedy.

They had tried to restore his self-confidence. It had resulted in him posing as a David against the Goliath of social change, except that he had no sling and no stones. How on earth was he to find a dignified way of retreat?

Beth had been magnanimous. There was a difference in her. She was alive, vibrant and showing her independence. Against his own wishes, he had had to conclude that it was because she was so happy. He was ashamed that it had been he who had made her so unhappy.

On Wednesday she had gone shopping, as arranged, with Fran. Frances Catherwood. He had to face up to his crazy obsession with her. He had made her into the living embodiment of Sin, adultress and temptress in one. His shame at the thought brought him out in a cold sweat.

All she embodied now was womanhood at its best, with her head in the air, her feet on the ground and her heart full of love for her neighbour.

As his ought to have been, for sinners as well as for the righteous. He had a duty to his neighbours now, which was to visit the grieving parents at Lane's End. Already in distress himself, he was more vulnerable than usual to that of others. Used as he was to this duty, he thought that never before had he ever encountered such depth of wordless, tearless grief.

He had been invited to see Robert in his coffin, and had felt utterly inadequate, both as man and priest. His heart, for so long anaesthetized against emotion, was stabbed by the boy's mother with pain so terrible that it rendered him incapable of uttering the few words of prayer he had intended; but even her grief did not affect him as badly as the dumb suffering of Tom Fairey.

He was very glad that Rosemary Bridgefoot was still there to help him discuss with them the details of the funeral. It was clear that it was taken for granted that Beth would be the organist. Well, so be it.

He bent over the coffin to look at the serene young face, and felt tears begin to slide off his chin. They were needed to wash away not any sins the boy might have committed, but his own.

Back at home, the suffering continued, till he fell asleep in his chair. Beth was not back when he woke up, for which he was glad.

His mind was clearer than it had been for many days, but he was utterly exhausted, physically and emotionally, and went to bed.

Beth came down to breakfast with him on Thursday morning. They tried, not very successfully, to be natural with each other. He felt that he had forfeited all right to her confidence; besides, his mind still boggled at his knowledge that she was no longer his maiden daughter, but the Commander's – er – what? Even, possibly, already carrying her lover's child.

She, on the other hand, was flushed and pale by turns, sometimes near to tears and the next minute radiating such a glow of happiness that he could make no sense of her mood.

When William's car drew up at the gate, she picked up her handbag and gloves, went to the door, waved to William to show him she was ready, and then came back.

'I'm having lunch out, Daddy,' she said, and waited. He found himself politely standing up, till it struck him that she was waiting for some sort of gesture from him. When he made none, except to wish her a pleasant day, she leaned forward and kissed him, and then ran out.

He was instantly contrite. She had wanted to make it up with him, to reach, at any rate, a meeting point at which they could discuss what must be faced between them. He had failed her again. Well, she would be back by teatime, he supposed. He would talk to her then. It suddenly became very important to him that he should get things back on a loving footing between them before they set out for that poor boy's burial tomorrow morning.

The day seemed inordinately long to him, and he felt weary to the bone, physically tired and drained mentally and spiritually. When he had completed all preparations for his part in the funeral tomorrow as well as his normal Good Friday services, he longed to seek the solitude and comfort of his bedroom, but he had made up his mind to wait for Beth. When he opened his eyes again, it was not Beth who sat before him, but Fran.

He jumped to his feet, but she waved him back. She had been studying his face as he slept, and it had told her a great deal. She, too, was strung up emotionally, and at her most sensitive to the smallest nuances. William's sleeping face had taught her more about him than his waking one, and she had had a chance to study the man in front of her as never before.

She was rather surprised to discover how much she liked him. He looked drained, but not strained, a tired man who had, for the moment at least, sheathed his crusader's sword. She was filled with courage and hope.

'Beth's gone up to her room,' she said. 'We didn't want to wake you, because you looked so tired. Do you mind talking to me for a few minutes?'

'I'm glad of the chance. I went up to see the Faireys yesterday. It was a gruelling experience that I haven't really got over yet. It made me think. So did you, Mrs Catherwood, on Monday. And George Bridgefoot. I want to apologize for my rudeness to you. On Monday, and . . . before. I was wrong to think I had any right to interfere in your lives, whatever my principles. You offered friendship, and I refused it. Forgive me. I'm sorry.'

'That's all in the past,' she replied. 'Don't call me Mrs Catherwood, though. I'm Fran to my friends. And you never even dented your friendship with William, did you? Wasn't that proved the other night when he swore at you? Not that I blame him. I wanted to swear at you myself on Monday. George didn't need to swear, though, did he? I hope you have decided to let Beth be there at the organ tomorrow.'

He nodded. 'They took it for granted,' he said.

'I'm so glad,' she said. 'Anything that will ease grief tomorrow will help us all through it. But Archie . . . Saturday is another day. Can't it be a case of joy coming in the morning? For obvious reasons, we must get Beth and Elyot married as soon as possible. Elyot has a registrar's licence. I've come – completely of my own accord – to ask you again to consent to marrying them on Saturday, so that on Easter Day Beth can be at the organ wearing a wedding ring. I'm asking for her sake, of course, but for yours too. And for all of us. Nothing can help the Faireys except time . . . but the rest of us need something to put into the balance against such awful sorrow as young Robert's death. What could be better than an unexpected wedding? And such a romantic one? Don't you see that once the news is out, all Old Swithinford will be thrilled by it? It would bind us all together again as we haven't been since long before you came.'

She got up and went to sit close to him. 'Please do,' she said, and without thinking put out her hand to him, just as she had done in church. This time he took it, and closed his own over it.

'Why does it matter so much to you?' he asked.

'Because I don't want the village to fall apart, for one thing. But on personal grounds, because I want Beth and Elyot to have the ritual that is denied to me and William,' she said. 'Because Beth is my friend, and I know what it would mean to her to have your blessing. Besides, think what it will mean to you both in the future, to be on happy terms together. You don't know Elyot yet, so you don't know how lucky you are, either.

'And it may also give you something that I have, and William hasn't, nor ever will have, now. A stake in the future. That's something Elyot never hoped for, but Tom Fairey confidently expected and has been robbed of. By me and George Bridgefoot. Perhaps I'm asking you to help me expiate my sin with regard to Tom and Cynthia.'

'I hate to disappoint you,' he said. 'But even if I can agree, it couldn't take place on Saturday. Though the ultimate decision is my own, in general we avoid weddings on Holy Saturday. There could be nothing but a plain, unadorned marriage service, and even that would be against the Bishop's advice.'

'It wouldn't satisfy Beth, in any case, that way,' she said. 'But if you're willing, Love can find a way.'

He smiled at her, a gentle, friendly smile. 'Your confidence is infectious,' he said, 'but I don't follow you.'

'Well, as it's too late to make it a full-scale grand affair, it would be best to keep it as quiet as possible, especially in deference to the sadness still in the air and Holy Week into the bargain. So why not hold it in your other church, St Saviour's?'

He was silent for what seemed a very long time.

'Frances, I don't know whether you are a saint or an enchantress. That little church has been my refuge and my strength on many occasions just lately.'

'Not only yours,' she said. 'It's a sort of magic place. That's what would make it so right. Well?'

The pressure on her hand grew tighter. He closed his eyes and sat silent, then opened them, and nodded.

She returned the pressure of his hand. Neither of them could find words.

'It's very short notice for me to do anything about the arrangements,' he said. 'My duty to the church this week must come first. What do you want me to do?'

'Nothing,' she said. 'Because you will be performing the ceremony, William and I will be acting *in loco parentis* to Beth, if you'll let us. Will you leave it all in our hands? We'll arrange a meal at Benedict's after the ceremony, though there'll be nobody there except the wedding party. Can you possibly not let Beth know anything till tonight, to give me a chance to tell William first? You must meet Elyot, too. Bring Beth up to Benedict's for drinks tonight. About eight o'clock? Ssh! Beth's coming down. Just say I asked you and you didn't want to be rude to me again! I'm going before she sees me. I couldn't keep my face from telling her that something's afoot. I want it to be a surprise for her to see you meet Elyot tonight.'

She was gone before he had a chance to make any objections.

'Ah, Beth, my dear,' he said. 'Did you have a nice day? I have told Frances you will play for the funeral tomorrow. I hope you will agree. And we have been asked up to Benedict's for coffee tonight.'

William was waiting impatiently for her. He was as overcharged with emotion as any of them, though long years of keeping himself under control made him show it less than most. He wished he knew what Fran had in mind. Part of his own restlessness was a fear that she would come back defeated and upset. He was at a loose end, and he hated her to be out of his sight when his mind was not engaged directly with anything else. It was as though she carried a bit of him with her wherever she was, and he never felt completely at ease when he was separated from her. But most of all he suffered when he could not protect her from worry, sorrow or disappointment, as he feared now. If ever he did feel irritated with her, it was usually because she allowed herself to be weighed down with other people's troubles and sorrows. He wished that occasionally she would say no to somebody, if only for his sake. Couldn't she see how he worried about her? Not that he would have her in any way different . . . Here she was, home at last.

She left her car in front of the house and almost ran to the door, calling his name as she opened it. He went to meet her in the hall. As he put his arms round her, he was reminded of what it felt like to catch a bumble bee in a handkerchief and hold it in your hand while you got it to an open window to set

508

it free: the vibrations of its wings come through however many layers of cloth there are round it. He could feel the vibrations of energy and purpose in her, and was aware that she was making a beeline for all sorts of aspirations she had not so far disclosed to him.

'You're quivering with suppressed energy like a frantically buzzing bee,' he said teasingly. 'Can't you calm down for a moment now you're home? Isn't a wedding and a high-class lunch enough for one day?'

'Gosh!' she said. 'Was that only this morning? It's a good job we ate well at lunchtime, because I don't think we're going to get any supper. We've got visitors coming for drinks at eight o'clock, and you have to go and persuade Elyot to come.'

She explained as quickly as she could how she had succeeded in persuading Archie to go along with her idea for the wedding on Saturday – so far.

'But it could all become a terrible fiasco if Elyot is still anti Archie and vice versa,' she said. 'They've got to meet somewhere before they do in church on Saturday. So I've arranged for them both to be here tonight. We shall need all our skills in diplomacy, I fear. You must warn Elyot not to let on about them already being married this morning – but remind him not to come up tonight without that beautiful engagement ring you told me about.'

'Must you go on trying to play God now, my sweetheart?' William asked anxiously. 'You'll wear yourself to a frazzle and worry me to death. If the wedding is on, arranged with Archie for Saturday, what else is there for you to do? Can't you spare me just a few minutes of your time?'

She sat down in her chair, inviting him to sit on the floor beside her, as he so often did just to be in contact with her. She tried to simmer her excitement down.

'I get too many big ideas,' she said. 'They'd never come to anything but for you. But this time, my darling, the two of us won't be able to deal with it all without other help. Archie can't take the service and give his daughter away at the same time, so you will have to take Beth up the aisle. But who's going to be Elyot's best man?'

'Then there's the question of getting the church nice. Not just swept, but garnished, and full of flowers. That's a part of Beth's dream I'm determined she shall have. There's only tomorrow afternoon to do it in. It's Good Friday, so it's no use asking Sophie to do anything. I had thought of Ned, but Sophie put me off that idea without knowing. She warned me to expect Ned "not to be himself, like" because Robert's death has brought back memories of his own son getting drowned. She said he had told her he didn't know if he could face going to the funeral, but he'd have to for Tom Fairey's sake. So he's out as far as any help tomorrow is concerned.

'There's only one solution, as far as I can see. We've got three hours from now till our guests arrive, and in that time you have to go and get Elyot here if you have to tie him up and drag him. And I must go to see the only other person I can think of, Bob. If you'll go to get Elyot, I'll go and tell Bob the whole story. I'll ask him to help us get the church ready tomorrow afternoon, and act as best man on Saturday.'

She leaned down and put her cheek on the top of his head, caressing his face with her hand. 'He'll love it,' she said. 'He's the biggest romantic of you all – worse even than Greg.'

'Too much so for my liking, where you are concerned,' he said, getting up from the floor and sitting down again on the arm of her chair. She looked up at him anxiously, reading his reaction in his face.

'What's wrong, my darling?'

'If I'm jealous, it's because I'm insecure. I let you out of my sight, and you come back and tell me how you have bewitched Archie Marriner. Eric Choppen eats out of your hand. Bob Bellamy worships you. Where do I stand? All three of them are free to offer you the one thing I can't.'

'Are you afraid I shall break my marriage vows?' she said, catching his hand and holding it to her breasts. 'Didn't you marry me on Hunstanton pier? That bit of ritual was worth all the church weddings in the world to me. And if I'm playing God to Beth and Elyot, it's only in gratitude for what Mary and Sophie did for us. Remember? What more can I do to stop your silly jealousy from spoiling this for us all?'

Contrite, he kissed her and let her go. 'Nothing,' he said.

'At least until bedtime. All this love in the air is bad for my nerves.'

'I'll drop you off at Elyot's place. I don't want him to turn up tonight half cut because he's so mad with chagrin and disappointment. It's your job to see he acts like a gentleman.'

'No problem,' he answered. 'He is one. And if he's mad because he can't get at his wife, what about me? Dare I let you go up to Castle Hill without me?'

She laughed, knowing that the danger had passed, and kissed him, but she dare not linger in his arms. 'We must go,' she said. 'But if only Beryl Bean knew where I was going and what for! By Monday she'd have me married to Bob and you hanging yourself in the rookery, while Archie cuts Elyot's throat and then goes off to give himself up at Broadmoor – so Beth runs away with Greg and Jess has to marry Eric. A nice derangement of all the characters concerned, don't you think?'

'Write it up for one of the independent television companies,' he said. 'They'd love Beryl Bean's version. I like the real one better.'

She looked at him and thought that, like Beth, she sometimes needed Somebody to thank.

She spent a delightful and very rewarding hour with Bellamy. He listened to her story like a child listening to a fairy tale, with no intimation of anything but delight in making the lovers happy. That was what was so good about him, Fran thought. Other people understood with their heads. Bob understood with his heart first – about all sorts of things.

'I'll see to getting the church swept and cleaned tomorrow morning,' he said. 'The Faireys won't miss me at the funeral. I know that Charlie's going, to be there if young Charles needs her. There's another real love story for you . . . only I'm afraid there's a lot of suffering for Charles, first. But maybe I'm wrong to worry about them. Did you say you want flowers for the church? Where are you going to get them from? It'll be Good Friday, and all Swithinford's florists will be run out of flowers, making so many wreaths for the funeral. Wouldn't greenery and wildflowers do? I reckon if it was me getting married there, I'd rather have wildflowers than hothouse ones. But there, it ain't my wedding. I'll do whatever you want.'

'You're absolutely right,' she said, astounded once again at his insight.

'Leave it to me to find you what I can. You can arrange it tomorrow how you like.'

'You realize you'll have to be Elyot's best man? Do you mind? I just want it to be a happy ending to what could have been a very sad story. So of course you must come up to Benedict's for the wedding breakfast afterwards.'

'I'd do a'most anything you asked me,' he said, simply, 'but I don't know about sitting down to a meal with Starchie-Archie.'

'This business of Beth has taken a lot of the starch out of him,' she said seriously. 'Come to please me and William.'

He stood and watched as she drove off. She had wanted to kiss him, but that would have meant a confession to William, which in his present mood it was wiser not to risk. He had no need to be jealous of any man, but least of all of Bob. Yet if any man needed love, it was Bob who did. Real Love. She found herself wishing she had a Supreme Power she could beg to arrange it for him. With sudden insight, she saw that his greatest need was for somebody to lavish his widow's cruse of love on; he would ask nothing, but to be happy he had to be able to give. What a lot of different kinds of loving there were!

She was relieved to find William there when she arrived home, and Elyot with him. They sat together in the kitchen eating ham sandwiches, as far as she could tell, completely relaxed. Fran snatched a sandwich as she passed to go upstairs and change. The day wasn't over, yet.

Archie and Beth arrived punctiliously on the stroke of eight, and Fran's heart dropped as the old misshapen lead weight of the grandfather clock did when the worn ropes gave way.

Archie wore his dog-collar with a dark suit, exactly as he had done on his first and only other visit to Benedict's. He also appeared to have shoved a ramrod up his jacket. He must have changed his mind since she left, she concluded, and had come as arranged merely to tell them so.

Beth was so pale that she gleamed like moonlit marble. Perhaps they had had a dreadful row? All the buzz went out of Fran. She was suddenly so weary that she didn't care what happened next. She wasn't God, or even one of His errand boys. As she mechanically welcomed the Rector and his daughter, she asked herself why on earth she had got herself involved. Elyot and William had both risen at Beth's entrance, while Fran was still in the doorway of her sitting-room. And there the projector jammed.

Nobody moved, nobody spoke. Fran viewed the silent 'still' before her, and her sense of deflation flared into anger. Why were they all leaving everything to her?

Because the whole caboodle of them were thinking of nobody but themselves. Archie had put on the garments of his calling, as if arming himself against letting love conquer him. Beth was probably afraid, seething with feelings of guilt about her deception of her father concerning the wedding ring now worn round her neck on a gold chain instead of on her finger. Well, thought Fran bitterly, at least she had not given Beth hope that was now to be dashed. Elyot was still angry and frustrated, not understanding why Fran was taking the line she was taking, apparently with William's approval. Fran read his expression. He had the certificate of his marriage to Beth in his pocket. Beth was his *wife*. Why, then, were they being asked to play this infantile charade? Fran looked from him to Archie, and felt her confidence ebb away still further. What had she been thinking of, trying to produce a springtime play with such a middle-aged cast as this? Even William seemed a long way away from her, she guessed because he had still not conquered his envy, besides wanting to know what had passed between her and Bob, which she had not yet had time to recount.

While time and action stood still, she examined her own motives. She could see herself very clearly, among those still figures.

She was a female counterpart of Bob Bellamy – insisting on giving whether the recipients of her gifts wanted them or not. She was an interfering busybody. That's what William, as kindly as he could, had been trying to tell her.

But in all fairness to herself, there was another reason, and one that at least William shared. She closed her eyes for a moment, recalling the picture of her ancestress that had once hung over the marble mantelpiece which still provided the backdrop of this set. Of the group gathered there, *only she and William were concerned with the question of continuity.*

Her strongest motive had been her desire to keep the village whole and undivided. Not to allow outsiders like the other three to dig up her roots, or Sophie's, or Beryl Bean's, or George Bridgefoot's. Now she understood the significance of William's history lesson. In the village's end was its beginning. Her unseen ally had been Robert Fairey, who had perhaps given up his life to some purpose after all. But for his death, the scenario would have been very different.

She opened her eyes, and found William's, watching and agonized, upon her.

He had seen her eyes close, and believed she was about to faint. He crossed the room to her in two strides, but as he moved she came out of her trance and became aware how Time had tricked her. Thought and Time had no correlation at all. The other three had not even noticed her abstraction, nor anything whatever out of the ordinary, except perhaps the slight social stiffness they had all been expecting anyway. William clasped her hand, and her internal projector started the scene moving again. She and William entered the room together.

'Rector,' William said, 'I know you have met before, but may I present Commander Franks to you in his new role as your son-in-law? Beth, my dear girl – how wonderful you look!' He kissed Beth, as he did so urging her gently towards Elyot. Then he turned back to Fran, taking her hand and pulling her back towards the door.

'We'll go and find some coffee,' he said. 'Do sit down and make yourselves at home.'

'Better leave them alone,' he whispered to Fran in the doorway, but she found that her feet didn't want to take her away until she had some idea what was going to happen next.

Elyot had stepped forward, holding Beth's hand. He made a slight sort of inclination of his head towards the Rector, and then said 'Mr Marriner, it is my pleasure as well as my duty to request your daughter's hand in marriage.'

William heard Fran draw in her breath, and his arm round her told him that Elyot's outdated correctness had drawn the champagne cork of her mirth.

But she wasn't going to miss its effect, or Archie's reply on which everything still hung.

She looked at Beth, whose blushes were making her face seem like a rose on a very long stem. Archie returned the stiff bow before speaking, though his face was anything but stiff or stern.

'As far as my observation informs me, Commander,' he said, 'you appear to have got it already. Beth, my dear, I hope you will be very happy.'

Beth ran to her father, and William firmly closed the door. 'Now you can laugh all you like,' he said, kissing Fran. 'You've won!'

She ran kitchenwards. 'Champagne, first, William,' she said. 'Coffee can wait.'

But then her champagne cork popped, and she let her delight out in peals of laughter, in which William joined as she clung to him. They both knew that the thick old walls of Benedict's would prevent any sound of it from reaching the sitting-room as long as the door remained closed. There was no longer a whisker's breadth of difference between the two of them. Laughter had always been their best medicine.

But they had the duties of hosts to perform. They took champagne from the fridge and the tray of glasses William had prepared back into the sitting-room. The three they had left there were now seated, Archie on one side and Beth, with Elyot by her side, on the other.

William handed round the glasses, and took up his position on the hearthrug to propose a toast. The others rose, silent and with due solemnnity. William raised his glass, and prepared to speak.

'Hang on, William,' said Elyot, frantically searching his pockets. 'I forgot something.' His inside jacket pocket at last gave up its secret, and the relief on his face set the whole circle aglow with smiles. The almost Victorian naval officer of a few minutes ago had been metamorphosed by the incident into a boy, Fran thought, no older than Charles Bridgefoot. What did his age matter? He was a man in love.

He picked up Beth's hand again, and slipped on to her finger the hoop of five emeralds that William had described so accurately to Fran. Beth gasped with surprise, delight and disbelief, and in front of them all she turned her rosy glowing face to kiss him.

Fran wanted to cry. She nudged William.

'To Beth and Elyot's happiness,' he said. They drank.

To her enormous surprise, it was Archie that Fran found herself kissing, while William saluted Beth. Then Beth returned to Elyot, and Fran dragged William out of the room.

She cried on his shoulder in the kitchen as they waited for the coffee to get hot again. At least, that was the excuse they made for being so long gone. As William had said, Love was in the air again.

IN DUE SEASON

64

Discreetly dressed, Fran and William set out to walk to church next day. The calm mid-April morning was almost too beautiful to contemplate, Fran thought, looking up through the filigree of tender green leaves to the cloud-patterned blue of the sky above the avenue across the 'front cluss'. The world was vibrant with life; what could Death have to do with a morning like this?

She was dreading the occasion, and had been since the moment she had opened her eyes. She had had to attend funerals before, though she was not, and never had been, one who cared much about the trappings of death. Was that reprehensible in her? No – she thought of Mary Budd's funeral, which was the last one she had attended, and remembered that 'trappings' was a word nobody could have applied to that. Certainly not 'trappings of woe'.

Her mind began to range backwards. It depended, surely, on all sorts of things how one felt at a funeral. It struck her with surprise that apart from Mary's, she had not attended the interment of anybody who had meant a lot to her alive, except perhaps those of her parents-in-law.

Both her mother and father had died and been cremated abroad while she was at university; Grandfather had died in wartime, when she had been too far away to think of getting home, even if she had been able to leave two small babies. There had been nothing left of her husband to bury, and at the memorial service for him and all the colleagues who had died with him, her whole concern had been for his parents whose prop throughout that terrible ordeal she had had to be. They had depended on her from the news of their son's death till they had died themselves. She had missed them then more than she had grieved for them, because they had been so dependent upon her. Though she had always got on well with them, they had not been particularly dear to her.

In any case, when they died it was she who had had to

undertake all the arrangements, and there hadn't really been time to grieve if she had wanted to.

Looking after the survivor as well as everything else had left her no opportunity for philosophizing about anything.

When the second of them had gone, the result had been to set her free – to come 'home' again. To her roots, to Benedict's, and to find William.

For her, she thought now, their deaths had meant her resurrection. That was the message the Christian church tried to get across at Easter. Well, you either believed, or you didn't. She couldn't herself find much comfort in thinking of young Robert being resurrected in his body on Domesday.

Until last night, she hadn't been able to see a single gleam of anything in his death other than pain, and (in her own mind) anger against the god who had decreed that he should die.

Yet something inside her was responding to the hopefulness of this spring morning. There, all around them as they walked in unaccustomed silence side by side, was 'life everlasting'. The earth and everything in it was constantly resurrecting itself. Every spring *was* a resurrection.

Symbolically, at least, the church's doctrine was comforting.

As they drew nearer to the church, they met others in twos and threes all converging on the church. It was only then that she began to consider what rural etiquette demanded of them.

'William,' she said. 'I know, because Archie told me, that most of the arrangements have been left to the undertakers. I wonder what we are expected to do? Do we go into the church, or wait outside to follow the coffin?'

He had not considered it. In their childhood, the coffin would have been carried by six neighbours, and everybody else would have walked behind, many of them gathering at the house of mourning to start with the corpse from there. But in these days, the motorized hearse went too fast to follow on foot, so the family mourners were conveyed in gleaming black cars. The bearers were strangers employed by the undertaker. Friends and neighbours congregated at the church and met the coffin there.

Therein lay Fran's immediate dilemma. She knew from her experience at Mary's funeral that the past would not let go of the present when it came to custom, tradition and ritual. Friends and neighbours used to the old ways wanted to follow the coffin; so they waited in a group at the churchyard gate, and when the hearse and the cars had discharged their passengers, they fell in behind the cortège, walking in pairs. They filed down the aisle behind the bearers, taking places wherever they could in pews behind the chief mourners.

Others, whose slighter acquaintance with the deceased required their attendance for the sake of courtesy, or who felt that they could not presume too much on new friendship, went into the church and waited there. It was to this group Fran and William decided they belonged.

'We'll go inside and wait,' William said decidedly. 'The division today is between old friends and new friends. We should look out of place waiting outside among people who were at school with Tom and Cynthia, or who have worked for Tom and with Robert on the farm.'

She was relieved. In the church she could sit silent, and think. The accumulated grief outside was too much for her.

There were so many already out there, lining the path and carrying wreaths or sheafs of flowers. Daniel, Thirzah and Sophie, all in deep black, stood together; Fran didn't look closely enough at the rest to identify many of them, though she recognized faces she 'couldn't put a name to'. It seemed that practically everybody who lived round about must be there. They were still united enough to care for each other. That was the Old Swithinford Fran had wanted to come home to. Her instinct that nothing must be allowed to intrude on this truly 'holy' day had been right.

As they walked up the long path between the rows of gravestones, Fran registered only two things – the boarded-over grave prepared to receive Robert, a patch of earth disturbed among memorials all bearing his family name, in the old part of the churchyard, now normally unused. That must be George Bridgefoot's doing. She wondered which of Robert's ancestors had been requested to make room for him among them.

The other thing that had twisted her heart-strings was the sight of Ned coming round the end of the church carrying a little cushion of flowers, his handkerchief pressed to his face. She thought that he must have been holding two such 'floral tributes' when he left his cottage, and that the other lay now on the grave of his own drowned fifteen-year-old son. He did not notice them, but went back to join the others waiting at the gate. Not before Fran had seen his face, though. She was glad to be going into the seclusion of the church.

In the porch they spoke to Charles Bridgefoot and Nick Hadley, who sat, apart and silent, one on each side of the door, on the medieval stone benches there. Fran deduced that they were waiting to join the Bridgefoot family, who would no doubt be coming from Lane's End with the hearse, as chief supporters of Tom and Cynthia.

It was dark inside the church after the bright sunshine. Fran made a rapid calculation that those waiting outside would fill the front of the church, forward of the transverse aisle. So she chose the first short pew behind the aisle, the same one they had sat in at Lucy's wedding. When her eyes were accustomed to the change of light, she saw Archie, cassocked and surpliced, prayer-book in hand, standing by an ancient oak bier before the chancel steps, where it would act as catafalque for Robert as it had no doubt done for his forebears for more than three centuries. It was not covered, any more than was the altar, by anything to relieve its starkness.

Across the church Fran caught sight of Jess, Anne and Eric Choppen. William had already acknowledged their presence. Behind them sat Jane Hadley, alone as usual. As far as Fran knew, the only close acquaintance Jess and Eric had had with Tom and Cynthia must have been at her birthday party; yet they had found time to come today, though it was one of the hotel's busiest weekends. That pleased her. They wanted to be part of the sorrowing community. Anne, Fran guessed, was present as a representative of her Aunt Mary. Again, what a nice thought that was, whoever's head it had originated in.

The Rector came down the central aisle and went out to the gate. The church hushed to an unnatural stillness. The pew she had chosen gave them the same view into porch and straight down the aisle to the altar as they had had at Lucy's wedding; but how different the waiting was today. She heard the tread of feet, and Archie's voice. Beth ceased her gentle, soft playing. At the church door the Rector paused while inside all silently stood.

The figure of Archie filled the pointed arch of the door, and Fran did not want to look beyond him; but as he began to move forward again, the silence was riven by a high-pitched, wailing shriek, immediately stifled, that curdled Fran's blood and made her cling to William's hand for support. Could Christ's mother at the foot of the cross have possibly uttered a more heart-rendering cry?

The coffin was being carried in front of them now, and Fran raised her eyes to acknowledge the final passing of the boy she had never known, except on that day only last September, when he had been so happy and proud in his usher's top hat and tails. She knew now why there had been a pause at the door, and why that cry had been wrung out of Cynthia. The head end of the coffin now rested on the shoulders of Charles, nearest to her, and of Nick on the far side. As instructed, both had their hands up on the coffin to steady it, and their faces laid close against the wood – a mere six inches or so from the face of their dead friend and playmate.

Behind, Tom Fairey walked alone, apparently unaware that Cynthia was having to be supported by Brian and Rosemary Bridgefoot. George and Molly followed close, and then the other friends and neighbours, two by two, in what seemed to Fran to be a never-ending line.

They reached the bier at last, and set the coffin down. The six official bearers moved to the front pew reserved for them, and Charles and Nick returned side by side up the aisle to the empty pew directly in front of Fran and William. Both beautiful young faces were white, set and strained with the effort, both physical and emotional, that they had just sustained. The church was full almost to overflowing. While the Rector waited for everyone to find a place, Fran looked at the coffin lying on the low bier and saw the one long cross made of flowers that reached the whole length of it. The emblem of suffering – so apt on this Good Friday. Not Robert's suffering, though. Wherever he was he was not suffering like those left here.

She began to let her thoughts drift away again, glad to be excused, even for a moment, from the build-up of grief around her. A latecomer at the door – Charlie Bellamy. She had braided her unruly hair into a plait taken up and over her head, on top of which was perched a tiny velvet Juliet cap, plain and demure. Her high-necked white blouse was tucked into a well-fitting, calf-length skirt, and she wore a dark blazer from which the badge of her famous girls' school had been unpicked. She walked with complete aplomb into the pew beside Charles, and Fran saw his hand move to find hers and cling to it. Well, wasn't she holding William's? What better comfort could there be for anyone than warm, close human contact? Charlie was as much her father's daughter as Charles was George's grandson. No modern inhibitions prevented them from comforting each other by touch.

Then came another late, flurried entrance, very different from the dignified one Charlie had made. Poppy Gifford had come running, and had thrown herself down on her knees beside Charlie, out of breath and sobbing. When she stood up, Charles and Charlie stood back to let her pass in front of them till she could stand beside Nick.

Archie announced a hymn. Were they really supposed to be able to *sing*? Looking at the four beautiful young folk before her, Fran found that she could.

'All things bright and beautiful . . .'

Fran shut her ears to the rest of the service, forcing her thoughts into other channels. She didn't listen to the Rector's address, except to register that it was gentle, soothing and kind. She tried not to think of Tom and Cynthia left at Lane's End alone, when the last of their closest friends had gone home. She decided that she was a moral coward, but nothing could or should induce her to go to the graveside, there to watch the bright and beautiful boy Robert had been let down six feet to a place the sunshine would never reach again. She wanted to go home.

65

It proved more difficult to leave sadness behind and turn her thoughts forward than Fran had thought it would be; part of this was because, as she had once said, she and William were like two mirrors face to face. When the light was not very bright, gloom was reflected to infinity. They were very silent as they ate a hasty lunch, neither being able to shake off sorrow.

Nor did the sight of Ned at the bottom of the garden do much to help. He had changed to his working clothes, but stood still under a copper beech tree with his back to them, gazing towards the church. They did not need telling where or what his thoughts were, as he abstractedly stroked Cat as she lay across his shoulder.

Fran was glad that she had committed herself to action that afternoon. She had no option but to fulfil her obligations, since it was she who had put them in train.

'I promised Bob I would be up at St Saviour's by two o'clock,' she said. 'What about you?'

'I'll do whatever you want me to. What else must be done besides decorating the church?'

'I think we briefed them all fairly well last night,' she said. 'All but for small details. Archie will be at church all this afternoon for the Good Friday vigil, but Beth will be at home. There's no need now for Elyot to feel like a leper down Spotted Cow Lane, but I hope he won't be seen going across there this afternoon. Most of the women will be going back to look at the flowers, once the grave has been filled in. It's too soon yet to give them anything new to wonder about. All that emotion built up this morning hasn't had its proper cathartic effect, yet. There's bound to be the usual funeral ghouls about, on the look-out for any bit of sensation. I think your first job is to go and see Elyot, to keep him from rushing across as soon as he sees Beth go home. Which reminds me – didn't you tell me Elyot had bought Beth some wedding presents of jewellery, as well as that gorgeous engagement ring? She ought to have them to wear tomorrow. She ought to find a gift-wrapped parcel by her plate.

'If I go up to Castle Hill in my car, will you go to see Elyot and make sure that little bit of business is seen to, somehow? Then come on to help me and Bob. And, darling – Ned needs occupation this very minute. Please, while I change my clothes, will you go and ask him to cut me anything the garden will yield for decorating a room? And ask him if he would be available to help Sophie in the kitchen for a rather special lunch party on Saturday. He'll be ringing his bell on Sunday, but I don't think he should be left at home alone all day Saturday. I don't know what Sophie will say, but that can't be helped. He's been hit very hard this morning. I'm sure she'll understand. Tell him I want anything he can cut at once in the boot of my car in half an hour.'

She was late getting to the church on the hill, and found Bob waiting for her outside. He was wearing such a satisfied look that Fran guessed at once that he had a surprise for her. He shyly pushed open the church door.

He must have been at work since early dawn. Not only was everything swept and polished, but the greater part of the decoration had already been done. On each side of the steps up to the chancel was a bank of pure wild beauty, constructed of beech twigs just coming into leaf, the green and the copper varieties dexterously intertwined with pussy willow, silver-grey and bright with catkins, and the first dark branches of black-thorn covered with virgin-white blossom.

Round the base of each pillar was a circle of feathery reeds and teazles, with a circle of reed-mace 'cats'-tails' forming a crown above them, their velvety brown heads standing tall and proud.

'Last year's, of course,' Bob said. 'I always go and cut some while they're at their best, but this year I hadn't got the heart to do anything with them. The cats-tails won't keep as long as this in the ordinary way – they get ripe and burst and blow millions of little fluffy white parachutes all over everything. I used to get in such a row when that happened that I stopped taking them home. But I found a way of keeping 'em from bursting. I stole a tin of Iris's hairspray and sprayed them with it. They'll last years like that.'

'Where do they come from, then?' Fran asked, running a thumb and finger from the base of one of them to the top of the spike at the end of the tail. He looked surprised.

'From the dykes and the river as run through my farm in the fen,' he said. 'I went down early this morning and took them out of the barn where I'd put them with the reeds and teazles. All the other stuff I got from the wood out here. But they still need some colour among them.'

'They're absolutely beautiful,' she said. 'Thank you, Bob.' She would have thrown her arms round him and kissed him, if William had been there. But Bob understood. Somehow, he always got the message.

'Let's look what Ned has put in my car,' she said. They found colour galore, red sprays of prunus blossoms, pink almond and ornamental cherry, and white cherry that almost made the coloured varieties look vulgar. But Ned had also supplied trails of dark ivy, as well as those of the large-leafed variegated variety. Twined round the base of the pillars, it hid the stiff stems of reeds and branches. The result was magical. She said so.

'Not so good as we can make it tomorrow morning,' he said. 'There's no sense in pulling flowers as'll wilt before you need to. There's only one thing wrong with it,' Bob said, sniffing. 'There's nothing with any scent to it. I reckon as I can put that right before you get here tomorrow. You just leave it to me.'

Fran was perfectly happy to do so. He waited patiently, not speaking till she had enjoyed it all to the full. Then he said, rather tentatively, 'I know as you've got it all in hand, but I can't help wondering if there ain't one thing as you've forgot. Won't you need the church registers?'

Fran sat down in the nearest pew, staggered that not even Archie had raised that point. She didn't know how much it mattered, but she supposed what she had promised Beth – a real wedding, not just a blessing – might possibly depend on having the registers there.

527

'Well,' Bob said, after waiting for her to answer. 'It's a good thing I know where to find them, ain't it? I should have gone up to get them only I promised William that I would never go up again by myself when nobody knew where I was. But if you'll sit here and wait, it won't take me ten minutes to get them.'

She was afraid to let him go, but she said nothing. The charm of the little church was working its magic on her. He came down with the old leatherbound book, dusting it clean, and showing her the last entry, almost a century ago. 'Where would it be best to put it?' he said. 'There isn't a vestry.'

'We need a table,' Fran answered. 'And a white cloth.'

He nodded. 'Then we could stand it on the altar slab William is so crazy about. That would please him. Will you come up to the house and see what we can raise there? I think I may have just the sort of table that would do.'

They strolled back to the house together, completely at ease in comfortable companionship. Once again she found herself marvelling at his sensitivity. There was such . . . such *innocence* about him that she felt he ought to be able to hold evil at arm's length just by being what he was, a child of nature.

But nature had a very dark side too; hadn't she experienced it only this morning? Besides, Bob himself wasn't happy. Nevertheless, he was putting everything he could into pleasing her, and two others whom he hardly knew, but whose story had intrigued him as a fairy tale thrills a child.

They saw William's car arrive before they reached the house. 'He doesn't let you out of his sight long, does he,' Bob teased. 'But then, I wouldn't, if I were in his shoes.'

'Your luck will change,' she said. 'It must be your turn again soon.'

'Yes, I reckon so,' he replied unexpectedly. 'But there's a lot of suffering to get through, first, I know. Hello, here's Charlie back, and young Charles. It's been rough on him today.'

They all went into the house together. 'Do you want us to get out of the way, Dad?' Charlie asked.

'No, not unless you want to go. We might need you. What have you been up to all the afternoon, since the funeral?'

'Just sitting in the car. Charles didn't want to go to Lane's

End with the rest of his family. And we had to deal with Poppy.'

William and Fran felt *de trop*, but no one else seemed to think so.

'Charles and Nick Hadley helped to carry Robert into the church,' Charlie explained. 'Charles hasn't got over it, yet. He didn't want to be by himself.'

The look Bellamy gave the boy was so full of sympathy that Charles responded to it.

'I don't think I could have got through if I hadn't kept reminding myself what you said the other day,' he said. 'And I keep thinking of poor old Nick. Charlie stopped with me while the worst was over. Poppy couldn't stop with Nick. They're only friends, but he'd be keen on her if he dare be. You know already about Pansy and Robert, Mrs Catherwood. Grandad told me so. So did Poppy know, but her mother and father didn't. When they got up this morning, Pansy was in such a terrible state that she blubbered it all out, and there was a most awful row. I hadn't thought she really loved Robert, but it seems she did.

'Then Uncle Vic threw one of his rages. He always smashes things when he gets into that sort of temper, and Poppy said he picked the poker up and broke Aunt Marjorie's oval mirror that had been my great-great-grandmother's. Poor Aunt Marjorie loves family things like that. He's smashed a lot of things of hers in tempers like he got into this morning. He kept asking Pansy what she thought he was going to do with shop-soiled goods like her and Poppy. Then Poppy stuck up for herself and said it wasn't true about her, and that made him madder than ever, because Pansy's always been his favourite. He just wouldn't believe Poppy. He said he was going to send them both right away where nobody'd know the disgrace they'd brought on him, and ordered them to go to their rooms, yelling at them to stop there till he'd got a doctor to see if they were pregnant. Pansy did as he said, but Poppy ran out and got on her bike and came to the funeral.

'She thinks Uncle will do exactly as he's threatened, and send them away. It won't matter much to Pansy, but Poppy is due to take her A-levels in about six weeks. Grandad had gone up to Lane's End, but I thought he was the one who would have to sort it out, so we kept Poppy till he came home. That's really why we were so long. I don't know what's the matter with Uncle Vic. He used not to be so nasty.'

'Made too much money lately,' Bob said. 'Got too big for his boots. He ain't the only farmer by a long chalk as forgets to count his blessings. Farmers never had to go to the war, you see. Nobody had wanted 'em till it started, and then everybody did. They all made more money than was good for 'em while other folks were going hungry or getting killed. There's a lot to be said on both sides. I know, 'cos I'm one of 'em. But there's a lot like Vic Gifford as seem to think making a lot of money so quick was all their own cleverness. Usually it's them as started with nothing. They'll learn, I reckon. Folks won't want us farmers when they can get food cheaper anywhere else. It aggravates me to see chaps like Gifford throwing their weight about, though.' He turned to his daughter, aware that he had been making a speech he hadn't intended to.

'Charlie, my duck, do you know where your mother kept them white lace tablecloths as were your grandmother's?'

'She said she was going to sell them, so I stole them and hid them,' Charlie answered. 'Do you want them? Whatever for?'

'Mrs Catherwood wants to borrow one for something special.'

'Come and help me find them, Charles,' Charlie said. They went, hand in hand.

Bob turned to Fran and William. 'I very nearly let the cat out of the bag then,' he said. 'The boy was so upset, I forgot they didn't know about this wedding. I was trying to take his mind off carrying that coffin.'

'It doesn't matter, Bob, honestly,' Fran said, her heart wrung again for the Bridgefoot family. 'Look! Why don't we tell them when they come back? Let's let them into the secret, so they can come to the wedding. The only thing they needn't know is why the wedding's been arranged in such a hurry and kept so secret. I'll say that the Commander is shy because he is so much older than Beth. It would be lovely to have them up at Benedict's for the wedding breakfast. Do you agree?'

Of course they did. Anything Fran wanted – William because she was the other half of him, Bob because to him she was the embodiment of a dream, the lady in the picture. He saw her as a living proof that dreams could come true. The painted version of her had been his lodestar since early childhood. He had known her all his life. To have her at hand in the flesh was a sort of miracle to him. Hope personified.

'Come and have a look at this table in the other room,' Bob said. 'I reckon it might do, but it's a bit on the heavy side.'

He led them to another smaller room across the hall, in the older part of the house. The table in question was an eighteenth-century gaming table in gleaming dark rosewood, which opened out to a green baize square, or by a cunning twist on its pedestal, to show a chess board or a backgammon board.

Fran gazed at it almost green with envy. 'Nice, ain't it?' Bob said. 'I think my mother must have picked it up at auction. We had it before I was born.'

'It's worth a fortune!' William said.

Bob grinned. 'Ah, so Iris used to tell me. She wanted the fortune. I'd rather have the table. But it'll do for what we want, won't it?'

Charlie came back, Charles carrying a bale of white lace and linen. 'Wants washing, whatever it's for, I'm afraid.' Charlie said.

'Tell 'em, Fran,' said Bob. 'William and me'll be getting the table up to the church.'

They sat like wide-eyed children, holding hands, while Fran unfolded her story. 'And *we're* invited?' Charles said, incredulously.

'You can escort me,' Fran said. 'William will be giving Miss Marriner away, and Mr Bellamy will be Commander Franks's best man.'

'Are there any bridesmaids?' Charlie asked.

'None arranged, but there can be. Why didn't I think of it before? Have you got a dress that would do – not that what you wear matters much.'

The girl nodded. 'I think so,' she said, 'though I never thought I should actually ever enjoy wearing it. We had to have a special uniform dress for Founder's Day, once we got into the sixth form. Shall I go and put it on to show you?'

She came back in a full-length dress of heavy pleated silk in deep yellow, with a huge medieval-type collar and cuffs in white. It gave her hair the colour and shine of new conkers.

Charles had closed his eyes. If the vision was still there tomorrow, he was telling himself, he would believe it; but it was too much for him tonight. Charlie saw the tears creeping out from under the tightly closed eyes, and mimed to Fran that she was going to take the dress off.

Fran reached forward and took the boy's hand.

'I'm sorry,' he said. 'I'm so frightened. It isn't possible that she can really love me, is it?'

Fran was glad she didn't have to answer. There wasn't time to tell him that Love that was worth having always hurt somewhere and somehow.

The men came back, Charlie came down in jeans and a sweater, with a pigtail down her back, and Fran realized it was getting dark.

'I want you up here as early as you can make it in the morning,' Bob was telling Charles. 'Bring your suit and change here. We have a lot of things to do before the rest of the wedding party arrive.'

'We must go so that I can get the cloth washed and ironed,' Fran said.

'I'll do it,' Charlie said. 'Have you thought about Miss Marriner's bouquet? Or buttonholes for the men? We might as well do it properly.'

Fran hadn't.

'I'm so glad,' Charlie said happily. 'Leave them all to me.'

66

Beth went down in her dressing-gown, unable to believe that this would be her last day with her father. He went towards

her, and folded her in his arms. She had to believe he was
going to keep his word.

'William called late last night,' he said, 'and left this for
you. He asked me to put it on your plate at breakfast-time.'

She began to unwrap the little parcel slowly. As if Fran and
William hadn't done enough for her, without giving her wedding presents as well! Then she read the accompanying note
. . . her first ever love letter. 'It's from Elyot, Daddy. Do you
mind if I open it?'

There were the ear-rings, emeralds set in gold; the pendant
made to match, but with a larger emerald; and a gold bracelet
watch, the face set round with tiny emeralds and diamanté. All
exquisite.

She was too overwhelmed to do more than gaze at them.
She became frightened. They *couldn't be genuine.* Elyot couldn't
be serious. But for the wedding-ring down between her breasts,
she would have thought it all a cruel jape, until she read the
note again . . .

'Daddy,' she said in a whisper. 'Just look.'

Marriner did, and a truth dawned on him. His daughter
was about to marry a very rich man, who must love her as
much as William had averred. For the first time, he believed
the story William had told him. He would be able to marry her
with joy in his heart, not just forgiveness or the magnanimity
Robert's death had forced upon him. She was looking up at
him with eyes that reminded him of when she used to sit on
his knee while he read to her the story of the Tinder-Box, and
the dog 'with eyes as big as millwheels'.

'Excuse me,' she said, and gathering up her treasures, she
ran back to her room. When Fran arrived to help her dress, she
was still sitting with Elyot's note in her hand, and his love-
gifts in her lap.

When Fran came down the stairs in her new coffee-and-
cream outfit, Sophie said, 'Anybody would think as you was
going to a wedding.'

'So we are,' Fran said. 'Not in Old Swithinford, though.'
She daren't trust herself to enlarge any further. Sophie was too
good at putting two and two together.

'Funny, that is,' Sophie said to Ned, as William and Fran

drove off in separate cars. The same suspicion crossed both minds. 'Well,' said Sophie, soothing her own somewhat hurt feelings, 'no doubt they would ha' told *us* if it hadn't been for the funeral yist'day. You may depend as they're off to a registry office. Our Rector ain't one likely to want to marry a divorced man.'

Ned nodded. 'Time they was married, though,' he said. The idea, once having taken root, continued to grow as they worked together.

When William arrived to pick up the bride, Fran was more than pleased at the transformation she had been able to achieve.

Beth was attired in a silk suit of pale blue, a pill-box hat with a matching veil sitting on top of her coiled hair. Together with the ear-rings and the pendant, the colour-scheme had the most startling effect on her eyes. They appeared to be bigger than ever, as brilliant as the sun on the sea, and of that same colour. Fran, if asked previously, would have said that Beth's eyes were 'very dark'. So they were, so deep a blue as almost to look black; but this morning they had green flecks in them. They *were* the colour of the sea. That's why they had so haunted Elyot, perhaps – till he had fallen in love with them. He had not chosen emeralds at random. They had made Beth into a sea-nymph. His two loves had been merged into one by them.

Fran left Spotted Cow Lane, as arranged, twenty minutes before William and the bride. Archie would follow her. William tactfully went out to the car with Fran, to leave father and daughter together.

'Would you like to carry this?' Archie asked, handing her a little box. 'It is the prayer-book your mother carried when she married me.'

Beth took it with tears in her throat, and lifted from the box a gilt-edged Book of Common Prayer bound in soft white leather. There was a wide bookmark of gold silk ribbon inserted at The Solemnization of Matrimony page, the ends of it hanging down. At one end there was embroidered a letter A in black; at the other, an E in brown; both, Beth realized, stitched in human hair. Beth was holding it to her heart as

Archie kissed her, picked up his clerical garments, and went to get his car.

Fran drove straight to the church, and found the others waiting there. Charlie was standing in the porch, guarding the flowers she had prepared. She had plaited her hair into a tiny crown on top of her head, and round it she had wound ropes of daisy-chains. Daisy-chains also formed a wide 'choker' round her neck, and a tiny posy of oxlips with pendant daisy-chains lay on the old stone bench, along with buttonholes made of nothing but daisies surrounded by a rosette of their own spoon-shaped leaves. No wonder Charles was mesmerized, Fran thought. Bob's daughter was the Goddess of Spring today.

Bob pushed open the church door for Fran to look inside. It was her nose that reacted, even before her eyes, to the spring-scented air. Every window-sill was packed tight with a mixture of oxlips and bluebells, their beautiful sweet-scented heads towards the interior of the nave. On the altar slab the table stood, with register and a Victorian brass standish full of ink beside it, with a goose-feather quill pen, cut to perfection by Bob. The altar was covered with a crocheted lace cloth made by Bob's grandmother, a small cut-glass vase holding the same mixture of flowers on the middle of it. It was enchanting and, Fran felt, enchanted.

When Elyot arrived, Charlie was introduced to him, and pinned her daisy buttonholes on all the men, reserving one for William. Charles's was smaller than the others, Fran noticed, and wondered why. She saw him looking down at it as Charlie pinned it through his lapel, and watched his face. It was as if he had seen a beatific vision. Under the pretence of making sure it was secure, Charlie counted the daisies with her fore-finger. Only nine of them. Oblivious of anyone else, the boy drew her to him and kissed her.

Then William arrived with Beth, and while Charlie fixed his buttonhole, he slipped the wedding-ring taken from Beth's neck in the car into Bob's hand. The ceremony could begin.

As soon as he had done his part William turned and stood beside Fran.

'With this ring, I thee wed,' Elyot was repeating after Archie.

William was holding Fran's hand. There was barely room below the knuckle for the ruby solitaire above the wedding ring and the eternity ring already there, but she had got her engagement ring at last.

Back at Benedict's, Sophie and Ned were almost bemused by the composition of the wedding party, including the Rector, that was gathered in the sitting-room. The mixture of the guests for lunch made no sense to either of them. If William and Fran were the bride and groom, as they had supposed, what were Charles Bridgefoot or Charlie Bellamy doing there?

Sophie's face set, her mouth taking on a grim line. She had reached a less pleasing conclusion. It explained why Fran hadn't told her whose wedding it was. And it accounted for George Bridgefoot not being in church yesterday afternoon – the first Good Friday, to Sophie's knowledge, he had ever missed. The tales about Charles and Charlie must have been true; the girl was pregnant, no doubt, and Esther Palmer's curse had wrought its worst so far. George must have disowned his beloved grandson, and left it to Fran and William to get the young couple married. But why was the Rector there? The only puzzle was the Rector's presence.

She waited at table with glum rectitude, so sure of the truth of her second deduction that she blinded herself with it. Every time she went back to the kitchen, she added a bit more to her edifice of conjecture. Ned could reach no other sensible conclusion. They shook their heads, mourning the stability that had been, of Bridgefoots and Faireys rooted in familiar solidarity, whatever newcomers chose to do.

Then William came to the kitchen, asking Ned to uncork the champagne he would find in the fridge in the kitchen of 'the flat'.

'And Fran wants you both to come in while we drink the toasts,' he added.

Sophie did not even remove her apron. She didn't wish the young couple harm, but she felt disloyal towards George and Molly Bridgefoot that she should be, however unknowingly, involved in their grandson's 'hole-and-corner' wedding. She and Ned stood back, away from the rest, holding their glasses as if they were afraid of being bitten by the crystal stems, as William rose to propose the toast.

'To the bride and bridegroom,' he said, and everybody stood up except the Commander and Miss Marriner. It still made no sense to Sophie when he added, 'To Beth and Elyot,' and drained his glass.

Fran caught sight of the two of them standing there 'mazed' (as Sophie would have said) and had to choke back her every-ready bubble of laughter. They stood so still and stolid that she had a momentary idea that they had been turned – not to stone, but to a couple of Chelsea pottery figures.

Then Elyot was on his feet, and all the rest sitting. The scenario Sophie had invented being so clear now to her, she had difficulty in making sense of what he was saying. He was apparently thanking everybody present, including herself and Ned. Why was Bellamy's girl marrying a Bridgefoot any concern of his? Could she be wrong? He was pulling Beth to her feet.

'And now, if you will allow us to escape,' he said. 'I propose to take the new Mrs de ffranksbridge home.'

The gasp all round the table was as dramatic as he could possibly have hoped for. They were all looking at him for explanation.

'I couldn't face going into the navy at sixteen with a name like that,' he said. 'I should have been ragged and bullied to death. But it is still my name. I signed the register with it this morning, though not even Beth noticed. I don't suppose she'll want to use it, and I certainly don't. But it will be up to her, as my wife.'

The suffocated cry as he pulled Beth towards him and kissed her came from Sophie. She had sat down in the nearest chair, struck 'all of a heap', and, just as her mother might have done, hid her face in her apron. The words that rose to her lips, though, mirrored Fran's thoughts exactly.

'May 'Im Above be praised,' Sophie said. 'That fam'ly as we all thought 'ad died out is come back to life again.'

Fran felt the goose-pimples standing out on her arms. Exactly. At Easter. First Death, then Resurrection.

67

When the news broke the next day, the effect of two such conflicting dramatic events together, both so highly charged with emotion, was enough to satiate for once the appetite for sensational news. That was something for which Fran was profoundly thankful, because while they had been at Robert's funeral on Saturday, Monica had arrived home unmistakably *enceinte*, accompanied openly by 'her man'. That the man was Roland failed to titillate palates already jaded by such rich feasts as they had just had.

Rumour had leaked out that the Gifford household was in trouble, split right down the middle with Vic and Pansy on one side, and Marjorie and Poppy on the other.

George, taking Poppy home, had done his best to calm Vic and comfort Marjorie, but he was already tired and worn out, having been subjected to much more than anybody other than Fran and William knew. Marjorie declared roundly that she had had enough of Vic and his tantrums, and might as well go and scrub floors in the hotel for a living as go on putting up with a man who had forgotten everything except his bank balance and bolstering a reputation for respectability that his family had never had.

The worm had turned with a vengeance; Marjorie the patient, meek and docile housewife took the opportunity of letting out all that she had been bottling up for twenty-odd years. She told Vic plainly that she could do without him quite as well as he without her: that 'his' bank balance was also hers, since her father had put money into getting them a start on those conditions; and that what George had given her as a present out of the sale of the Pightle had been invested in her name alone. (Not that any of these details were allowed to reach the ears of the public; Marjorie gave Vic no chance to air his woes outside the house. She made it clear to him that though they didn't live in, or very near Old Swithinford, Bridgefoot was a name to conjure with for miles around, and Gifford certainly wasn't.)

Vic, completely taken aback by his house-mouse roaring at him, sulked – especially when Marjorie went to sleep in the twins' old room. He blustered, ordering her to 'pull herself together', at which she merely laughed. Then he became self-pityingly defensive, telling her how hard he had worked for her and the twins, and look what he had got for it! Marjorie reminded him that she hadn't exactly been Curly Locks, sitting on a cushion eating strawberries and cream. After that Vic tried tearful pleading. What was he going to do if she went on like this?

'I don't know,' she said. 'It's your fault. You shouldn't have broken the mirror. Seven years' bad luck, that means. This is only the beginning of it. You do as you like about Pansy. Poppy'll be going back to school to do her exams. She wants to be a teacher. I'll see to it that she does.'

That challenge put Vic on his mettle. He booked Pansy into a very expensive riding school close to the east coast, and there the situation rested when Marjorie went home to report on Easter Monday. She was fairly sanguine of general family support.

She found Rosemary at the Old Glebe, a very tired, dejected, wan and weary Rosemary. The obligations of her friendship with Cynthia had been wearing indeed. Marjorie enjoyed telling the tale of her belated rebellion, even though the root cause of it was a sad one. In spite of herself, Rosy was amused.

'How long are you going to keep it up?' her father asked Marjorie.

'Oh, just till Pansy's gone. He'll have had enough of sleeping by himself by then.'

Rosemary didn't join in the general chuckle. 'He did break the mirror, Marge,' she said. 'You can't laugh about that. Besides, you're a Bridgefoot. You can't expect to escape Aunt Esther's curse any more than the rest can. It's fallen on Pansy. What about Poppy? I'm worried about Charles, though since last Saturday he don't know what he's doing. Then there's Lucy.'

'Don't say that!' said Molly, snapping at her. 'Esther hardly knows Lucy. Why should she want to bring bad luck on her?'

Rosemary bit her lip, and shook her head, not prepared to reply. 'I shall have to go,' she said. 'I've had to leave her by herself a lot lately, and that makes her nasty. She's safe enough to be left, but as soon as we're all out of sight she starts poking about, going through Brian's desk, and Charles's room, and my pantry and cupboards. It's horrible, knowing she's watching us and always looking for another way to upset the applecart. And somebody's stolen the key to the sideboard, so the drink bottles are always empty. She can't be drinking it, because she's teetotal, so we think she must be emptying it down the sink. Nobody else has been there, except Jane Hadley. I daren't let Brian think it's her, or he won't have her in the house again. But Brian says he's afraid it might be . . . Charles. Could it be him, Grandad? He's so upset about Robert Fairey, and so out of his head about Charlie Bellamy . . .'

'It just could be,' George said slowly. 'I don't want to think so, but if ever a boy had cause to take to drink, one way or another, he has. Don't say anything to him, though. Let things cool down first.'

Of all this Fran and William were happily unaware. Once the wedding was over, so marvellously successfully, they had no wish for anything but to be together alone at Benedict's.

They had more sense than to intrude, even by telephone, on Beth and Elyot, though they had made a point of going up to look at and take photographs of the inside of St Saviour's, and had found Charles and Charlie there. Bob had sent them to start clearing away the flowers, but they had rebelled. It was too beautiful to spoil till they really had to, Charlie had decreed. They promised to do it, but until the time came they just liked to sit there together.

To Charles, Saturday had been spent in dreamland. The whole occasion had helped him to pass the bar of youthful rebellion and subjection to the dictates of his peer-group. It was his first introduction to an adult social milieu he had only ever once before glimpsed, at Aunt Lucy's wedding. He had been surprised how little of an ordeal the lunch up at Benedict's had been to him. Everybody had treated him as an equal – in age as well as everything else. He had had his first real lesson in social grace, and learned it well. The vision that was Charlie in her jewellery of daisy-chains had been perfectly at home there. He wanted to be as easy in that sort of company as she was, or her father, if it came to that. Bob *was* obviously 'at home' there. Charles was well on his way to hero-worshipping William, and intelligent enough to see that William's friendship with Charlie's father was as genuine as that with the Commander. He remarked on it to Charlie.

'Oh, Dad's just a natural gentleman,' she said. 'It's only really a question of courtesy — treating other people as you'd like them to treat you, whoever they are. Some people seem to know the rules without having to learn them — like Dad does, or your friend Nick. *You* needn't worry. You fitted in all right. It was lovely.'

So was the knowledge that they would be going up to Benedict's again soon. Fran had asked for some 'cats'-tails' to put in a flower arrangement on her lovely staircase, and Mrs Franks wanted some too.

Roland took Monica up to see Fran and William on Easter Monday, looking happy and contented. Her rather short figure somewhat accentuated her 'bump' in spite of her well-designed maternity wear. 'The doctor says Zinjie is a big baby,' she said. 'Probably a boy. I think Dad would have rather had a girl.'

'Can't please everybody,' Roland said. 'There's always another time.'

Fran hoped so. She daren't ask about Sue.

Roland followed her out to the kitchen when she took the dirty dishes away, on purpose to give her the latest information.

'Her parents' divorce is through,' he said. 'She's upset about it, but won't say what she intends to do. She just won't co-operate with any of us. Don't worry, Mum. You can see how happy I am, even with things as they are. *Che sera sera.*'

'Then so am I,' Fran said. She had every reason to be.

Sophie retailed talk about the Great Romance, and the resurgence of interest in Esther Palmer's curse.

'Surely you can't believe in it, Sophie,' Fran said. 'You're a Christian.'

Sophie was silent. Fran didn't pursue the point. It was one of the areas where the veneer of Christianity over paganism was very thin indeed.

*

541

'Lady Day again come Friday,' Sophie said, as they sat drinking coffee on the Wednesday morning of Easter week. 'I shan't ever forget what it were like that year as Choppen first come and the Thack'rays went and my Jelly was killed and everything. It didn't seem then as things could ha' settled down like they have. It's to be 'oped as nothing like that'll never 'appen no more.'

'That's too much to hope for,' William said.

'Lawks!' Sophie answered, looking reprovingly at him. 'Ain't we 'ad enough 'appen to us just lately to last us a lifetime?'

'Well,' said Fran. 'We do have good things as well as bad ones. We should get bored if nothing ever happened. Think what there is to look forward to – there's Lucy Bridgefoot's baby due in June, and Monica's in August. And once William gets to the end of July, he'll be free for a whole year. The forecast seems good.'

Forecasting, however, is still an inexact science. 'Come Lady Day' there were plenty of straws in the wind that didn't presage all sunshine.

Bob Bellamy received notice from the bursar of the college which owned Castle Hill Farm that when his present lease ran out next year, it would not be renewed. Not, they had taken the trouble to assure him, that they were not satisfied with his tenancy – far from it. It had, however, been decided that as his farm was one of their few endowments without restrictions upon it, it would be offered for sale, with others, to raise cash badly needed. As the sitting tenant, he would, of course, be given the first refusal.

Last year, he would have been glad to be released from a farm and a place he felt so alien in. This year, he could barely face the prospect of leaving; he had grown to love everything about it (except the pictures on the walls of his extraordinary living-room), but there was no chance of him being able to buy it. Iris had taken most of the money he had made, and John's going had left the farm in the fen on his hands. There would be no alternative for him but to rouse himself from this dream he had begun to regard as reality, and go back to the farm he owned. What would it mean to Charlie? She had been so happy here, just lately. Her passionate, rebellious moods were very rare now.

That thought hurt him most. For once he was unable to foresee anything beyond the stark fact that he could not expect her to go down into the fen. There was no need for her to know, yet. Let her be happy while she could.

He put the letter away, and went to sit in the church to think things over. Winnie had produced another litter of pretty kittens. Who would feed her, once he had gone?

The church soon began to work soothing magic on him. It was full of memories and friends. He was still welcomed there by those unseen forces that nobody but himself was aware of, too. The ghosts didn't want him to leave them. Well, he would make no decisions till they were forced upon him.

It was Anne who alerted Fran to the fact that Jane Hadley was worried because her six-month occupation of the cottage she had been so happy and comfortable in would run out at the end of May.

'But she works for Eric Choppen – and for Jess as well as for you,' Fran said, somewhat indignantly. 'Surely it's in his own interests to let her stop there. I shall tell him so.'

'It isn't him you need to tell,' she said. 'The lease is to Mr Bridgefoot. All hush-hush, to save that prickly pride of hers, and from what I can make out from what little Jess tells me, it was mainly so that Nick should be able to stop on at school till he had taken his A-level exams. They'll be over by the end of May. And enquiries about lets for the summer are piling up. If Nick does get a place in a university for the autumn, she'll be on her own, anyway. I wonder what her story really is?'

'Whatever it is, she deserves better than to be made homeless,' Fran said. It was nothing to do with her, and she hardly ever saw Jane now that the chaffinching sessions had more or less come to an end. Jess pleaded too much work, keeping Anne pretty well occupied as well. Besides, Monica was in residence now, and for the foreseeable future. But she was sorry for Jane.

William was sympathetic as well, but reminded Fran that there was no need for her to shoulder everybody else's troubles.

'Haven't you got enough to do looking after me?' he teased her. 'You're a reincarnation of Alexander the Great, always looking for new worlds to conquer.'

'Wrong sex,' she said.

'Praise be,' he replied.

'OK, Professor,' she said. 'I know the next line. "Leave it to the gods."'

He looked at her more soberly than the context seemed to warrant. 'That's all you can do, honestly, my darling. What will be, will be.' What was, that very minute, was a very shy Beth ringing to ask them to be their first guests at the Old Rectory, for dinner on Saturday. 'Just the four of us,' Beth said.

'I can't think of anything nicer,' Fran replied. William looked up at her mischievously. 'I can,' he said. 'We'd better go, though. But if they've still got the megrims, we may catch it.'

'You've had the symptoms all the week,' she said. 'You caught it last Saturday, at the wedding.'

'Not you as well? I rather thought I'd given it to you, with that ring.'

'M'm. Perhaps we ought to be worried. Megrims seems endemic with us.' She avoided his outstretched arms neatly. 'I'm going to ring George,' she said, 'to ask him if he could spare time to come up and see us tomorrow evening. Oh, look! How nice. Here's Charles and Charlie with the flowers from the church. Ask them in, darling. We'll give them an early supper.'

'Is that wise?' he asked. 'We ought not to risk giving them the megrims.'

She stopped to watch the two young folk unloading the boot of Charles's car, and turned back to him with unwonted seriousness.

'I hope,' she said, 'that we may possibly immunize them against it, for a while, anyway. I'd be glad if what they caught from us is a bit of wisdom about the nature of love. That they don't need to snatch at it, and spoil it, like so many do these days.'

He could find no adequate answer. He kissed her, gravely and humbly, instead.

*

When George arrived next evening, Fran saw by his face, before he ever spoke at all, that he had something on his mind more serious than Jane Hadley's accommodation. She apologized to him for intruding on his time.

'What I wanted to say is of no great significance,' she said. I asked you to come up here because we have more chance to talk privately here than at your busy house. But it can wait. You tell me what's the matter. Sophie told me the rumour about your daughter being at loggerheads with her husband about Pansy. I feel guilty about my part in that. We perhaps didn't consider the consequences carefully enough. None of us saw that sort of consequence, did we? Is that what's worrying you? I can see something is.

He smiled. 'I still think we did right. Don't you worry your head about that. Marge is only teaching Vic a lesson I ought to have given him myself ten year ago – that there's other things more important than making money. They'll be all right again in a couple of weeks. No – it's a bit of news I had from Tom Fairey at Lane's End only half an hour ago. He rung up to tell me that he's sold out, lock, stock and barrel, and him and Cynthia are going to live at Bournemouth. Just like that. As soon as ever they can get possession of a house they went to look at on Tuesday. Never told nobody, never asked nobody.'

She was horrified, because her mind racing forward told her that whoever had bought Lane's End had been waiting for the right moment to pounce, like a cat at a mousehole. Waiting to strike as soon as Robert died, before the numbness of grief had worn off Tom and Cynthia's common sense. That pointed to somebody local, or at least in the know. Surely it couldn't be Eric and his partners, who included Elyot? It was horrible, ghoulish, revolting. She wanted to be sick.

'Manor Farms?' she said, in a small husky voice that wouldn't work properly.

To her enormous relief, he shook his head. 'Worse,' he said. 'Better the devil you know than the devil you don't. Not that Eric Choppen's any sort of a devil, once you do know him. He's a good chap. I wish it had been him, 'cos he would have bought it to go on farming it. Tom's sold out to a

545

developer who hopes to be allowed to build hundreds of little houses all alike on it. Chap name o' Bailey – Bailey Developments Ltd. Tom didn't tell me the figure, but I gather it's somewhere round the half-a-million mark. Seems to me as if Tom's got no feeling for anything except about the house. There's been a Fairey in it for more than three hundred year, and he can't bear to think of anybody else living there.'

Fran was not only absorbing the shock; she was also asking herself why the name of Bailey sounded familiar to her. She remembered.

'Oh!' she cried. 'I can't believe it! Why didn't I let Bob Bellamy shoot him? Except that would have meant Bob shooting himself as well.'

She found herself telling George what she knew about Bailey from Bob, but he already had a fair idea, having seen Bailey once or twice at meetings in the last couple of years.

'We shall do all we can to stop it,' he said. 'But money talks. There's always somebody on a council or a planning committee willing to take a back-hander if it's big enough. Bailey ain't the sort o' man to risk paying Tom the development price for farming land before he'd got things pretty well in hand. But what beats me is what did Tom want the money for?'

There was no answer to that riddle. She didn't broach the question of Jane's cottage. He was in too much distress.

'If the Lord had seen fit to take Charles instead o' Robert,' he said, 'the last thing in the world as I should ha' wanted would have been more money. There's no such thing as compensation for anything like Robert dying. I shouldn't like to be in Tom Fairey's shoes when he comes to his senses. What he's got now is blood money, it seems to me.

'You can't serve God and Mammon. Tom very likely don't believe in God no longer, so he's made his bargain with Mammon. I daresay he'll live to regret it. Specially if he ever bothers to remember what happened to God's only son. But he didn't stop to think what it would do to the rest of us. That's what aggravates me. Thank God Lane's End lays a fair way from the middle of the village – nearly as far as Castle Hill does. That's about the only bit o' comfort I can see.'

It was far from any comfort to Fran. She knew only too well now why Bailey had been trying to undermine Bob. Wearing him down so that if the time came, he would feel such an outsider that he'd be glad to go, and put up little or no resistance. Bailey Developments Ltd had their eyes on Castle Hill already.

68

Term had begun again. On the first day back at school, Nick got a note from Poppy telling him she daren't risk meeting him on Mondays for the time being, and wishing him well for the exams about to start. He was not surprised, nor particularly upset. Since Robert's death and Charles's infatuation with Charlie, he had got used to being lonely. He fixed his mind even more firmly on the long-term future, to which these exams were the key. If he was concerned about anything other than his school work, it was that his mother seemed unusually depressed. He supposed she, too, was looking forward to the time when he would be gone from her, either to a university or a job wherever he could get one. He had no obligations to Poppy, nor she to him; but his obligation to his mother he would carry with him wherever he went, and for the rest of his life.

When William was away again after a vacation spent mostly within call if not within reach, Fran was restless. She had other nebulous worries that she had not properly formulated while there had been so much else to think about. She missed the chaffinching sessions a lot. She saw Anne occasionally for a chat, but Jess hardly ever. Greg was spending more and more time away, sometimes even over weekends. Fran regretted that just when she had begun to think that she and Jess were at last getting back to their close childhood relationship, the pattern had changed again. Perhaps Jess was blaming her (and Roland) for being the cause of Greg's absences. It ought to have made Jess seek company more, not less.

The more she considered that, though, the clearer it seemed to her that the real cause of the trouble was Monica. Jess didn't like Monica, and never had done. She had been forced to swallow her 'moral righteousness' with regard to Fran and William; but the cause of that rather uncharacteristic stance on Jess's part in the first place had been her possessive jealousy, especially of Greg. It was still as strong as ever. Jess would have displayed her feelings of moral outrage to Monica who-ever the father of Monica's child had been. That he was Fran's son and another woman's husband had given her firmer moral ground to stand on than ever William and Fran had provided. The last straw was that Monica had involved Greg. It was not only because his partnership with Monica took him away a lot. It had also made him more financially secure, which in turn had given him a lot of confidence he had previously lacked. Jess had always been the dominant one in their relationship, partly because it was she who had had to keep the wolf from the door. She was resenting his challenge to her.

Elyot and Beth filled the friendship gap a lot; the 'foursome' of Fran and William, Beth and Elyot was such a happy, compatible one that it seemed to have existed always. Both couples welcomed and nurtured it.

They had been together one evening recently when Beth had suddenly announced to them, without the least sign of any inhibition, that she thought they might like to know that she was *not* pregnant.

William spluttered on his drink, and asked whether they were supposed to congratulate her, or otherwise. (As he said to Fran afterwards, it was such an impossibly improbable state-ment for Beth the Parson's Daughter to make publicly that his first impulse had been to reply 'What? No soap?')

Fran admitted to much the same reaction, but said she had wondered whether Elyot was relieved or disappointed. He hadn't left her much time to wonder.

'That being so, and our moral integrity undeservedly estab-lished,' he said, 'I propose to take my wife for a honeymoon cruise. If I bring her back pregnant, it will stop all belated speculation, and your Sophie shall be one of the first to hear the glad tidings.'

'Sophie?' said Fran. 'Whatever has she got to do with it?'

'Oh, come, Fran! I can't let her down, can I? Didn't you hear her exclaim that "the family", like the prodigal son, "was lost, and is found; was dead, and is alive again"? That puts some sort of onus on me, doesn't it?'

'And on me,' said Beth. 'You may have married the wrong woman. What if I fail to produce you an heir?'

Elyot leaned over to knock the dottle of his pipe into a large Victorian ashtray inscribed 'Prepare to meet thy God'. He looked about half the age he had done before marriage, and let his eyes linger lovingly on Beth's face before turning a pair of wickedly humorous eyes on William.

'Well,' he said, 'we can but hope. If it is so it won't be for lack of trying. I told you I could never resist a challenge, and this is one I shall positively enjoy.'

So in another few days they would be off. No packaged holiday would satisfy a man longing to introduce his new love to his old one, so there was no date fixed for their return. Fran was going to miss them badly.

Then there was Monica. Fran was growing fonder of her all the time, but getting rather maternally anxious. Monica was now fully six months pregnant, and as busy as the proverbial bee; but as Beryl Bean had observed, she looked more than 'six months gone', and 'as if she might fall to bits at any minute'. The observation made Fran uneasy, in case it might indicate some abnormality. It could not be denied that Monica was not only very large, but somewhat oddly shaped. Fran was afraid to ask questions, but Monica answered her unspoken one.

'I'm in the hands of the best obstetrician to be had for money,' she said. 'He assures me that everything is fine, and that all will be well.'

When Fran repeated that to William, he laughed at her and told her that she was, as he had always suspected, nothing but a dyed-in-the-wool old countrywoman at heart. She countered by enquiring where his wits had been wool-gathering, if he hadn't found that out till now.

It was true, because while she had nothing pressing

work-wise, and the longer she lived at Benedict's, the more strongly she felt the old house to be an integral part of the community; not, as at first it had seemed, an island linked to the mainland only by the avenue of trees across the 'front cluss'.

It was not often that she was entirely alone there, because both Sophie and Ned put in much more time than they were paid for; but there came a Friday when for various reasons she had been alone all day, and couldn't expect William home till much later than usual. She watched the sunset from the landing window, and was preparing to go down and make herself some supper when she was aware of movement at the bottom of the stairs.

'Who's there?' she called, reaching for the light switches.

It was a male voice that answered her, but not one that she recognized instantly. Nor could she interpret the words, and was slightly alarmed as she went down; but in the stairwell, by the door to the kitchen, she recognized the haggard face of Charles Bridgefoot. It was patently clear at once that he was either ill or in some deep trouble.

'Charles! What's wrong? Have you had an accident?'

He shook his head, not attempting to speak. He was limp and bedraggled, and his usually fresh and handsome face bore the traces of tears. His red-rimmed eyes told Fran that they were only the last of many shed recently.

Let explanation wait. He was a boy needing help. All the practical woman in her came rushing to the surface. She put on the kettle, and made him some strong, sweet tea. He drank it obediently, to please her.

'Now come with me,' she said, and when he didn't move, she pulled him up and led him to the bathroom, where she sat him down on a stool, as if he might have been only ten, and bathed his swollen face with clear cold water. He made no protest, even when she wetted the curls that fell over his forehead. As she handed him a towel he swayed, and she leapt to steady him. He put his arms round her waist and laid his curly head against her. She held him there for a minute before saying, gently but crisply, 'Now come and tell me what this is all about.'

He followed her into her study, sat down to the chair she

pointed to, and handed her a letter. 'This came this morning, just out of the blue,' he said, his voice hoarse and strangled. 'I've been out all day since. Read it.'

She sat down at her desk, and read.

Charles,

How can I do this to you? Only because I love you. By the time you get it, I shall have gone, without leaving you any address or any way at all of finding me. Please don't try. It would only make things worse. Nobody knows where I'm going, not even Dad. That's because I love him, too.

You have a right to know why I'm doing this, because every word I have ever said to you about loving you for ever is true. It always will be, whoever both of us end up married to. Do try to understand. I'm not the same silly schoolgirl you picked up on Boxing Day, but I'm still me. That's part of the trouble. I don't know who 'me' is. I've got to find out.

Yesterday, Dad went down the fen. Before going he showed me a letter from his landlord here. He has to give up this tenancy, because they are going to sell. It will mean him going back to the fen. He's terribly upset, but there's no other way out. He asked me what I wanted to do. I said I would tell him when he came back, because I wanted to see you first. I knew what I wanted to do, but . . . ? I'm only eighteen. You're only twenty. Your family wouldn't let us get married. If Dad hadn't had to move, there might have been a chance for us, in time. Your grandad and grandma like me. But I spell trouble for you with your dad and mum, not to mention your aunt. I blotted my copybook with them because of her. They'll be glad I've gone. They'll tell you you'll get over me. Perhaps you will. Perhaps I even hope so. I want you to be happy.

I told you once that you would have to wait a long time, because even then I knew that the one thing I could do to make myself good enough for them was to do what I had intended before I met you, be a vet. Vets are somebody. Tenant farmers aren't. So what's new?

Yesterday, while I was at home by myself, there was a knock at the door, and there stood my bloody mother. I hate her, and she hates me, always has done. I hate everything she stands for. She's a tart, a tramp, a whore, but she's still my mother. She isn't my father's wife any more, but she's still my mother.

You can't get round that, Charles. I've got her genes. My children will have them, too. For all I know now, I may still turn out to be like her, only interested in sex and money. How can I tell? I've never tried sex yet. I wish now we had, but I wanted to keep us special. I used to like to think that when we were fifty we'd still be like Mrs Catherwood and Dr Burbage, or Commander Franks and his wife. I shall never forget being with you in that church, the day they were married. Wasn't it lovely? Something for me to remember.

My mother is short of money. She planned to get some out of Dad by blackmailing him about me. About us, that is. If Dad paid up, she would keep clear, and leave it to Dad to make me acceptable to your parents; if he didn't, she'd stop around so that everybody could see what she was, and how she got her living. Now do you see why I have only one way out? There's no safety in giving in to a blackmailer. Even if you had married me in spite of her, well, your pocket is deeper than Dad's. She would have poisoned everything for us, maybe even our love for each other. I'm a sort of life insurance for her, or at least a meal ticket. I saw through her, which she didn't expect. I'm not going to let her spoil your life, or Dad's.

There's only one way I can defeat her. Disappear, and let nobody, *nobody*, know where I am. So I'm setting out for wherever I'm going now, when I've finished writing this, before Dad gets home or you turn up to try and stop me.

I'm legally an adult, and not a 'missing person'. The police won't be able to try to find me, for her, for Dad, or for you, my Charles. I can take care of myself. Remember that I have three languages besides English at my disposal.

I don't want you to forget me, though if we do ever

meet again I expect you'll have some beautiful, posh wife with you. I warn you that I couldn't be trusted not to kill her, because I shall always think of you as my Charles, as I shall always be

Your Lambkin.

The pages were smudged with inky tears, and so many muddied tears had been added that in some places the writing had almost been washed away. Fran sat holding the letter with her eyes fixed on Charles, who was leaning forward in her chair with his head buried in his hands and his shoulders heaving.

Fran was desperately fending off the pain she knew was going to strike and shrivel her if she let it, by assembling a barrage of disparate and random thoughts.

Where was the God she professed to believe in, that he should let this happen? Was Love like the Hebrew Jehovah, 'a jealous god'? Jealous of any other sort of love? Even one like this, as sweet and pure as an oxlip? As unselfish as any Christian could want? Were Love and Suffering born twins, so that where one was, there would the other be also? Did that mean that if there were no love, there would be no suffering either? Could Tom Fairey be suffering more than Charles was? Poor boy, this was the second blow to him. Robert had gone as well as Charlie – or perhaps in the other order. Charlie had gone as well as Robert. As distant and irrevocable the one as the other. Charles was speaking. She must listen to him.

'It's worse than if she'd died. I think I could have borne that. I don't think I can bear this. It wouldn't have been so bad if she didn't love me, but she does, doesn't she?

'She couldn't have written that, or done what she has done, if she hadn't loved you,' Fran said. 'It's because she loves you so much that she had the strength to do what she thought she had to.'

'How could she hurt me like this, then? So much?'

What could Fran answer? ('Yet each man kills the thing he loves . . .')

'I think she's hurting herself quite as much as she's hurting you.'

The boy uttered a low moan. 'There'll be nobody for her to go to. I've got Grandad, and her father, and . . . I wanted Mr Burbage . . . she won't have anybody. I must find her.'

'Ssh, you can't. If you could, her mother could. You mustn't try. Not for a long time yet, at any rate. All we can do is hope.'

'What for? A miracle? Is there any hope?'

Fran hadn't the courage to answer truthfully. Sophie had lived in hope for thirty years, only for it to be killed at the moment of fruition. False hope was harder to bear than no hope.

William's car-hooter signal that he was home broke the stillness. He came through the front door calling, as he almost always did, 'Sweetheart, where are you?'

Fran watched the boy crumple, and ran to William for help and succour. She pushed the letter into his hands, and fled.

Charles was unconscious only long enough for William to skim through the letter. He opened his eyes to find William sitting on the arm of his chair.

'Sit still,' William ordered. 'We'll talk when you are able to. Here, use mine.' He passed Charles his handkerchief. 'Don't hurry. We've got all night if we need it.'

'Mum will be worried. And Grandad. I ought to go home, but I can't. I can't!'

'Fran's probably phoning them,' William said. 'And Mr Bellamy. I think she'll go to see him. I'll stay here with you till you want to go home.'

He was right. It was best for Charles that William had him to himself, and best that Fran went to Bob. She found him sitting in his chair surrounded by animals, mostly cats. He detached two new kittens from his pullover, and stood up to greet her. She put out both her hands, and he held them close to his chest. She never kissed him except in William's presence, but his grip on her hands communicated his distress, and how glad he was to see her.

'How did you know?' he asked simply.

She told him, and he nodded.

'I've been so worried about them both,' Bob said. 'Did he tell you why she went?'

'He gave me her letter to read. It's heartbreaking. Was it really necessary?'

'She thought so,' he said. 'She may be right – though not because of Iris and her bloody tricks. If only she had waited to see me! I should have told her I wasn't going to let her be beat by her bitch of a mother. It's my fault as Iris is her mother, and I'd have done anything to make it up to her. Charles's grandfather would have been on her side.

'I told you them two had a love story worth taking notice of, didn't I? Like gold, it was. I loved to see 'em together. But it was nearly too good to be true, if you see what I mean, at their age. I mean, there's always a bit of dross in gold that has to be got rid of somehow, and it's come to me sitting here tonight that Charlie's got enough of me in her to know that and to feel pushed to do what she's done. Sort of putting it to the test. I reckon Iris turning up, along with that letter about my tenancy here, that I showed her, put a match to the gunpowder. Better now than later. It may turn out to be a good thing.'

'In spite of what it's doing to Charles?'

'The hotter the fire, the purer the gold, my pretty.'

Her heart lifted a tiny bit. 'Does that mean you don't despair altogether for them?' she asked, hardly daring to listen for the answer. 'I'm afraid for Charles, and I was afraid for you. That's why I came. I left him with William.'

'Then stop with me now you're here, long enough to give William a proper chance to deal with him. I shan't be able to help him, because he won't want to come anywhere near me. I shall miss him, as well as her. Charlie's my girl. I was beginning to think of Charles as part of her.'

They sat down facing each other across the huge hearth. He picked up the two kittens again, cupping them in his hands and rubbing his face on them as he went on talking, telling her the situation about his tenancy.

'There's only one thing that'll stop Bailey's little game,' he said. 'And that's for me to buy it. They offered me the first refusal. But I can't do that without selling my land in the fen. I don't want to, 'cos that's where my roots are. But I would have done, to give Charlie a chance to stop here and be happy.

I've got till Michaelmas to decide. If she ain't back by then, I should be as well being miserable by myself in the fen as here.'

'You think there's a chance she may come back?'

He shook his head. 'Don't bank on it. I ain't sure. But I ain't so knocked over by her going as I might be. I went up to the church as soon as I found out yesterday that she'd gone, and it seemed to me then as I'd always knowed them two had got a lot of misery to go through before we had another wedding in George Bridgefoot's barn. I always feel able to go on hoping up there. As if the ghosts are telling me it ain't as bad as it might be, for me or for Charlie. But I don't *know*, like I do sometimes. Don't tell Charles I said so, though, will you? I might be wrong.'

He stood up, easing one of the kittens away from his shoulder. 'Stop it. Tittles, you're tiddling my ear with your whiskers,' he said, dropping it on to Fran's knee. She played with the kitten, thinking she mustn't stay much longer, because of Charles.

Bob was putting the kettle on, whistling as he did so. He was always full of surprises, of one kind or another. His concern tonight for Charles, instead of for himself or for Charlie was strange. What other man would have taken that attitude?

'Aren't you worried about Charlie?' she asked him.

For once he didn't seem to want to answer her. 'No, not in the way you mean,' he said at last. 'She's been away at school since she was eight, and she's had to fend for herself. She's been abroad most summers, because her mother didn't want her at home. She's got too much sense to go where she can't speak the lingo well enough to get by. And I ain't worried a lot about men, because she knows all right who her man is. There'll only be danger if he gives up and marries somebody else to please his father. It's *him*, not her, as I'm worried about. It's him as is got the suffering to do. That's something I do know, and I reckon this is only the beginning of it. I wish you hadn't asked me.'

So his sixth sense was at work, warning him of something more concerning Charles. She wished she hadn't asked, too.

'And as for that bloody Bailey . . .' He turned on her the

same terrifying, glittering, tortured eyes as he had done up by the church wall the day Bailey had shot the little girl's cat. 'There's more ways than one of stopping his little gallop. I can always shoot the bugger if I have to. The first thing he'd do would be to bulldoze the church down, pretending he thought he'd bought it. Not while I'm alive and can handle a gun, he won't! I shall know a lot o' things by Michaelmas. If Charlie don't come back, I can all'us keep a cartridge for myself.'

Fran scrambled to her feet in horror, putting the tiny scrabbling kitten back into his hands. He kissed its snub little nose, and the feel of it transformed him again into the gentle giant that was his normal self.

'It ain't come to that yet,' he said. 'Don't you worry about me till you have to. Get back to William and Charles. They need you more than I do by now. I shall be all right.'

She believed him, and went home.

69

William had left her a note that he had taken Charles home, and would be back as soon as possible. In fact, he came in almost at once.

He had taken a man-to-man line with Charles, he said, not a father-to-son one. He had exposed himself and his own misery, telling him about Mac, and how he had tried to cure his pain by marrying Janice – only to be hurt worse still when she had left him. Once he'd got the boy's full attention, he'd gone on to say that even so he had never really known what agony love could bring until he had found his earliest love again, when he was already married to the wrong woman.

He had made Charles join him in a sandwich, pleading that he had had no supper himself . . . and gone on talking. Some people said you only loved once, but that wasn't necessarily true. What was true was that there was no other love quite like your first. When that got bruised, as Charles's was now, it seemed that the most natural thing to do was to let anger and pride kick love while it was down; to tell yourself that there were plenty of other fish in the sea, and go fishing for another far too soon.

That, William had told Charles, he thought a great mistake. In his case, it had made him hate and despise himself; but that's what the old saying about not being able to put old heads on young shoulders meant. Only Charles could decide what Charles would do. All William could do was to offer what experience had taught him.

'It's what most people will advise you to do,' William said. 'But any fool can offer easy, off-the-cuff advice. It gets them off the hook of having to bother about you. Real friends care enough to put their own experience at your service. That's what I'm doing now. I'm *asking* you to think before you take that line, not telling you what to do. I'm begging you to grin and bear it now, till the hollow inside you fills up again. It may even fill up with hope, though I know you don't think so now.

'You see – it seems to me that the girl who could write that letter would be worth waiting for for ever. And in your case, hope isn't just wishful thinking. You know she loves you, and wants you. If you can't bear this, what would you do if she were to come back and find you tied to somebody else? That's what happened to me. It didn't make it any better that I was fifty. Fran was still Fran, and the only woman I'd ever really wanted.

'I hadn't the advantage you have. I didn't know how much she had loved me, because the war had prevented us from finding out. I only really realized it when this old house brought Fran and me together again. I guess that's what drew you here tonight.'

Charles had nodded. To William he could say anything, now.

'I heard you call out "Where are you, sweetheart" when you came in. That's what I'd been saying all day. If only I knew, it wouldn't hurt quite so much.'

'Oh yes it would! Probably more. You can't do anything at present but wait till you get so used to the pain that it doesn't seem so bad as it did at first. It'll hurt worst first thing in the

morning, and last thing at night. You'll have to learn to cope
with it, so start now. Wherever she is, she's probably crying
for you this minute. Remember that. One day you may wake
up and find her standing by your bed. I say wait for her, at
least till you have to admit that hope is really dead. Now I'm
going to take you home. I know you think you can't face it,
but it's got to be faced. Like going to the dentist.'

As he told Fran, he daren't risk her loving sympathy
undoing any good he might have done. He had endeavoured
to fix the boy's mind on the positive, deliberately using
Charles's respect for him as an agent.

Charles found the ordeal of facing his family worse than he
had expected. His father did just what William had forecast,
taking a bluff line that Charles had only thought himself in
love and would be chasing another girl before the month was
out. The attitude of satisfaction Charles detected in Brian made
him feel so positively hostile that every implement he encountered in a day's work became a potential murder weapon. He
imagined his father skewered on a pitchfork, run down by a
tractor, poisoned with weedkiller. Fantasized violence at least
helped him get rid of some anger.

All his mother did was cry even more than she had been
doing lately, which was most of the time. Charles lost patience
with her. He couldn't see what *she* had to cry about. It was
Robert who had died, wasn't it? Not her son. He only wished
it had been. He left her to cry.

Worst of all was his first meeting with his grandparents.
Grandad had lovingly sympathized and let him cry. That was
bad enough. But Molly broke down, and said, 'It's all Aunt
Esther's curse. I didn't believe in it but I do now. It's getting
to everybody – Marjorie, and Pansy, and your Mum and Dad,
and now you. There's only Poppy, and Lucy and her baby left.
I shan't rest till it's born. We might lose both of them.'

'Strewth, Mother,' George said, almost shouting at her.
(That was getting as near to swearing as he ever did.) 'Talk
about a Job's comforter! If you don't care about Charles's
feelings, you might about mine.'

That sent Molly away, and left Grandad looking guilty.
Charles felt it was all his fault.

'Try not to take it too hard, my boy,' George said. 'Time heals all wounds. You haven't got over Robert yet, have you?'

'This is worse than that,' Charles replied, testily. 'People can't help dying. Charlie went of her own accord because she knew Dad thought she wasn't good enough for me. Not good enough to carry on the Bridgefoot line, I suppose he meant. Well, there won't be a Bridgefoot line now, because I shall never marry anybody else. You might as well get used to the idea, first as last.'

He got up and swung himself out, not wanting to see the effects his words had had on his grandad, whose fault it certainly wasn't.

But George thought it was. It had all started with him selling the Pightle, against his better judgement. He was too good a Christian to believe in any pagan curse, so it had to be just a string of coincidences which wouldn't have happened if he hadn't invited them. He would have to go and make it up with Molly, and he wouldn't tell her what Charles had said. 'Never' was a very long time. The boy would get over it, some day. He was young and strong and healthy, and man enough to be tempted by another girl somewhere, even if it wasn't that fancy one Brian had in mind for him.

George sighed. Not that marriage, or even any sort of sex, guaranteed a family nowadays. Women could please themselves, since the coming of the pill. Still, perhaps that was looking too much on the dark side. While there's life, there's hope. His knees hurt him as he went upstairs to look for Molly. He felt old, for the very first time.

The week dragged on. Tom and Cynthia Fairey left without saying goodbye to Rosemary and Brian, which hurt them a lot. Fran asked Sophie, who for once didn't volunteer the information, what people were saying about Charlie's flight, and if she knew how Charles was. Thirzah would surely have reported any news from the Old Glebe.

'There's only ever one reason why a gal goos away suddenly, accordin' to them at the shop,' Sophie said. 'Thirz' says Charles Bridgefoot's as surly as can be, and won't look nobody in the face. 'Im as was always so bright and cheerful. I must say as I should never ha' thought it o' them two as you 'ad 'ere

560

the day as the Commander married the Rector's daughter. But then, whoever would ha' thought such a thing about our Wend'?'

With Monica's 'fatherless' child due in less than three months' time, Fran let the subject drop. She was on too dangerous ground to try to defend the innocence of those other two so constantly on her mind.

Charles was, as William had predicted, getting used to the dull ache in his heart that never went away. Each day seemed endless, doubly long because he had nowhere to go, and nobody he wanted to see.

Temperance Farm was no longer home; it was only the place where he slept, and ate what little he did eat. He had nothing to say, and nothing to do.

Brian persisted in pretending that nothing out of the way had occurred, and tried to engage his son in bluff conversations about football or TV programmes. Charles did no more than grunt monosyllables in return, which enraged Brian. Rosemary barely spoke to either, though her anxious eyes followed Charles everywhere. Aunt Esther was a particular thorn in Charles's flesh, because she no longer kept to her own quarters. Rosemary had given up the fight; her aunt did more or less as she pleased, and was likely to be met anywhere in the house. She had also taken to singing hymns, in a loud, cracked voice that was so out of tune that it made even the best-known hymns unrecognizable. That sent Charles into a frenzy, and he had difficulty in restraining himself from striking her. All the misery and distress he was enduring concentrated itself into vitriolic hatred of his great-aunt. Why did his mother put up with her? Why was she letting the old woman get the upper hand?

He knew the answer. Because all of them, even his father and grandmother, now believed in her curse. They daren't offend her. When he said so to his mother, she admitted it and tearfully begged him not to cross the old woman.

He was no longer happy visiting the Old Glebe, because they were worried about him, and couldn't hide it. Lane's End was only an empty house, Castle Hill unbearable, and Nick, he knew, was revising hard for his exams. Aunt Marjorie's household, now lacking Pansy, was still an uneasy place. Perhaps they were afraid of Aunt Esther, too. Even Charles admitted that it was not until she came that things had started to go wrong.

His car reminded him most of Charlie. Sometimes it hurt, sometimes it comforted him. A faint scent of her perfume lingered there, now and then wafting up to him so unmistakably that it seemed she was there beside him. William had said that wherever she was, she was probably longing for him as much as he for her. When the scent was strong, he persuaded himself that she was thinking of him. The last thing he wanted was any other girl's perfume to interfere with hers.

One afternoon, having finished work, he drove the long way round because the thought of going home, with Aunt Esther there, nauseated him. He screeched the car to a halt when he caught up with Nick walking home. He opened the door and Nick got in. Both were thinking the same thing and it made conversation difficult. Where there had been six at Christmas, in May there were only two; but both were lonely. Nick's time was precious when he ought to spend it revising, but Charles's need and his own inclination coincided. His mother said his exam results would probably be all the better for a let-up and the renewal of the friendship she knew he had been missing. And while he was with Nick, the clouds over Charles were a little less dark.

Coming down early to breakfast one morning, Charles was surprised to find his father waiting for him in no very pleasant mood. He had been eating better since having Nick around again, and helped himself, waiting to hear what Brian had to say.

'Where were you last night?' The tone was belligerent, and Charles's hackles rose.

'Why? Out with Nick. We went for a drink.'

'What time did you get in?'

'Lateish. I went straight up to bed. What's this all in aid of?'

'Don't tell me lies. Your mother and I both heard you. I take it you brought Nick in for another drink. It won't do him much good to be roaring drunk just before his exams.'

'I don't know what you're talking about. We had a couple of beers in a pub and I took Nick home.'

'Then who finished my new bottle of gin, and half the whisky as well?'

Charles flung himself out. 'I don't know and I don't bloody care. But if I want to get drunk, I shall.'

That was the last straw for Rosemary. At Molly's insistence, Dr Henderson was consulted, and he advised sedation and anti-depressants till she got over the stress of the trauma of Robert's death and funeral. She obeyed him and stayed in bed two days, leaving her aunt on the loose.

When Charles came in late on the Friday evening, there was such a rumpus going on in the sitting-room that instead of going straight upstairs, he paused to listen. He could hear his mother crying, Aunt Esther singing or quoting by turns, and his father shouting.

> 'There is a happy land,
> Far far away
> Where . . .'

'Shut up! Shut up, you silly old fool. Rosy, it's no good! She's mad, I tell you. She must be. I am going to get the doctor, whatever you say!'

'No, don't leave me, Brian. She'll be all right soon.'

'Ha!' said Aunt Esther loudly and clearly. 'Let death seize upon them, and let them go down quick into hell: for wickedness is in this dwelling, and among them.'

Charles went in. 'Charles,' his father said, enormous relief in his voice. 'Go and ring for Dr Henderson. Tell him what's happening and ask him to come, quick.'

'"Pull for the shore, sailor, pull for the shore",' sang Aunt Esther. She stopped to eye Charles up and down, with basilisk gaze. 'The prodigal son is returned from his whoring. He shall bring down his father's head with sorrow to the grave. At evening let him return, and make a noise like a dog. Let him wander up and down for meat, and grudge if he be not satisfied, as he hath grudged me whose heart is pained sore within me. For Moab is my washpot.'

Charles, hearing his mother whimpering with fear, strode close to the old woman, who raised her stick to defend herself. But he had got near enough.

'Dad, she hasn't gone mad. She's drunk! I can smell it.'

Aunt Esther growled and tried to get out of her chair. 'Deliver me from them that give their mouths to evil, and him that framest his tongue to deceit. Let me have strength to curse my enemies till the hour of my death. Oh, thou deceitful tongue! Lo! This is the man that trusted in the abundance of his riches, and strengthened himself in his wickedness. Thou shalt be destroyed for ever and ever.' She shook her stick in Charles's face. 'Thou shalt be taken away, and plucked out of thy dwelling place, and rooted out of the land of the living. Let thy posterity be cut off; and in the generation following let thy name be blotted out.'

Rosemary shrieked, and Brian leapt to catch her as she fainted.

Charles stood helpless in front of the upraised walking-stick, afraid to leave to go to the telephone till his father had carried his mother out of hearing and danger of attack.

'Whiter than the snow! Whiter than the snow!
Wash me and I shall be . . .'

A sudden grimace contorted her face. She was gasping for breath, though her mouth went on working. Then she groaned, closed her eyes, and opened them again to say, 'My heart is smitten. I am withered like grass.'

Charles caught her as she fell forward and laid her on the hearthrug.

'Stroke,' said Dr Henderson. 'Cerebral haemorrhage, probably fatal, though she may last months. I'll ring for an ambulance. Get your mother to bed. She's just had too much to put up with lately. At least she'll get a break for a while, now.'

But Rosemary refused to be comforted. 'If she dies,' she said, 'I shall always be afraid. She died cursing Charles. And if she doesn't die for a long time . . . she said she would curse him till the hour of her death. There's no escape from her.'

'Don't be silly, Mum,' Charles said. 'Why should God listen to a wicked old woman like her? She was blind drunk on Dad's gin and whisky, and hadn't the faintest idea what she was saying. At least Dad'll believe now that it wasn't me and Nick pinching it. Her curses seem to have come home to roost.'

Brian mumbled an apology feeling guilty, but he felt no guilt towards the old woman.

'I hope the damned old witch'll die before morning,' Brian said.

70

William said he thought Fran ought not to follow up her enforced involvement in Charlie's disappearance, either with the Bridgefoots or with Bellamy. She – they – had done what they could, and both victims would come again of their own accord if they wanted to.

She had to agree. She didn't want to turn herself into Old Swithinford's agony aunt. But it was difficult to forget what Charles and Bob were suffering. Their trouble made her feel guilty at her own content, worst of all when she was lying in bed, close to William. She sometimes wondered how on earth she had got through without that warm physical contact that made her feel so safe. She was conscious of every inch of the masculine length of him, as he was of the shorter, more rounded curves of her. She tucked her feet between his, not to warm hers but just to feel his slim ankles with her toes. He threw an arm over her, often quite unconsciously stroking her cheek or her ear. This was nothing to do with the ultimate physical contact that made them one; it was the bread-and-butter part of any good 'marriage'. She was quite aware that often his mind was not with her, and that if she had asked him what he was thinking about, he would have replied that he was weighing up a bit of new documentary evidence which purported to prove that Joan of Arc was really never burnt at the stake at all, or something of the sort; and she, if he had asked her, would have had to answer that she was thinking she must change a bit of dialogue that in retrospect sounded absolutely unnatural as she had left it in her typewriter.

Such musing about what this meant to her made her ache with sympathy for all those who didn't know the comfort of it, including those like Bob and Sophie who had never known it, and those like Charles and Charlie who might now never discover its worth. Those two would have made the most of it; she thought of them hand in hand, as she had last seen them together. *They* would have enjoyed the ordinary fare – the thin brown bread and soft yellow butter – which made the jam taste even better. The young folk who stole the jam without bread and butter little knew what they were missing. Charlie's letter had made it plain that they had never tasted the jam. And from what she had gathered from some of Bob's remarks, he had had only an occasional taste of rather tasteless jam, with no bread and butter to spread it on. How immeasurably lucky she and William were! As William would say, if he hadn't gone to sleep already, 'Praise be!' Measured in those terms, Roland and Monica only had half a marriage, yet; he came as often and stayed as long as he could, but it wasn't like this. She turned over, and fitted her back into the curve of William's sleeping figure. So safe. So blessedly, comfortably safe.

It had been a very strange sort of weekend up at Temperance Farm. Brian was rather subdued as he drove Rosy to the hospital to visit Aunt Esther. Charles found the silence at home too much for him, but thought guiltily that he had taken too much of Nick's revising time already. His exams were due to begin on Tuesday. Charles, messing about aimlessly, lost ground against his longing for Charlie. He yearned for her so intensely that he considered seriously whether it was possible that anybody had ever died of love. His condition would be worse when Nick had left, in the autumn. Even Poppy would be gone to a teachers' training college.

He was glad to think that at least Aunt Esther had settled

one thing. If Nick's mother had to leave the cottage at the end of May, as Nick had said he feared, Charles felt sure his mother would take Nick in, and perhaps even his mother as well, till they all knew what was happening.

He tortured himself by remembering his first meeting with Charlie. On the spur of the moment, he picked up the telephone, and asked Bob if he could have Ginger to look after. It was characteristic of Bob that he recognized at once that the youngster's need was greater than his own. It had been a solace to him to care for Ginger, but he agreed readily to let Charles have him, and said he would bring the horse over to Temperance Farm on Tuesday.

Charles spent the rest of the weekend better for having to prepare stabling and organize a tack-room.

Sophie arrived at Benedict's on Tuesday morning early, on purpose to get there before William left for work. The moment Fran caught sight of her, she recognized a bearer of bad news. Sophie's tread was heavy, her face white, and her mien grave.

'What is it, Sophie?' Fran asked, not being able to wait till Sophie had gone through the ritual of putting her apron over her overall.

Sophie sat down at the table, still wearing her long black coat. 'Bad as bad can be,' she said. 'It's like the plagues of Egypt, one thing after another till the last as was the worst of all, when all the firstborn sons was took. First Ned's son, then Tom Fairey's, and now Mis' 'Adley's. And your own near worrying you to death. It makes you frit to think whose might be next.'

'Nick Hadley? What's the matter with him?'

'Ain't you 'eard? There was a haccident yist'day afternoon. 'E's in 'ospital, not expected ever to come round again.'

'William,' cried Fran, standing up and reaching blindly for him. He dropped his briefcase and put both arms round her to steady her. She was trembling with shock, while her thoughts rushed out towards Jane and to Charles.

Sophie sat at the table, her hands in her lap, quietly crying. Accidents recalled Jelly's death to her. Fran freed herself from William and sat down, reaching across the table to hold Sophie's hand.

'Do you know what happened?' Sophie shook her head.

'Please William, could you spare time to ring somebody to find out? We must see if there's anything we can do.' William went, and came back looking very sober.

Nick had been walking along the pavement to the bus-stop with two classmates. He had been the outside one of the three, nearest the road. A huge juggernaut van, going in the same direction rather too fast, was forced by another vehicle coming the opposite way to get too close to the pavement. Nick had turned to look, and the sudden swerve of the van had caused a faulty bolt on the wing-mirror to give way. The mirror had swung out on its long arm and caught Nick a heavy blow on the temple, just above his right ear. He had dropped like a log, and was in a coma. The prognosis was not good.

Sophie's sobbing was the only sound as they digested William's report.

''E never 'as 'ad no luck, not from the day 'e was born. And 'is poor mother! What'll she do? 'Er as brought 'im up all by 'erself, and were so proud of 'im! Why 'as 'e been took away from 'er? Why was my Jelly took away from me? Why 'as 'Im Above forsook us all 'ere in Old Swithinford? What are we done to deserve it? And Esther Palmer 'ad a stroke Friday night, getting 'erself in a temper and calling down curses on young Charles, so George told Daniel. As if the Bridgefoots 'ad ever done 'er any 'arm.'

The same questions that Job asked: the questions nobody has ever been able to answer. William and Fran didn't try. William took his coat off and went to the telephone. Nothing would induce him to leave Fran and Sophie alone that day. He had got his information from George Bridgefoot, who had not been his usual dependable self, but a bewildered and helpless old man. William had gathered long ago how fond of Nick George was, but he thought there was more than that behind the change in George. It appeared to be affecting the whole Bridgefoot family. When Fran and Sophie had recovered a little, he discussed it with them, relying on Fran's intuition and Sophie's knowledge as to whether they should offer help, and if so, what.

'You may depend upon it as they're worried about that ol' woman's wicked curse on Charles,' Sophie said.

William didn't dismiss that, and Fran had long ago thought it out for herself. Once such an idea had been planted, every coincidence fertilized it till it grew big enough to cast shadow over all common sense. Its double roots reached deep, to prehistoric paganism supported by the Old Testament.

'I think you should go to see the Bridgefoots,' Fran said. 'George knows Charles confided in us. He might want you to deal with Charles again, if he's taking it very badly. I think I must find out from somebody what's happening to Nick's mother. All of them, including Monica, know her better than I do, but none of them is as free to help as I am. I can but offer. I'll go up to Jess, first.'

Jess and Anne knocked off for their coffee-break to talk to her. Jane had been at the hospital all night. Jess had had the terrible task of breaking the news to her, and Anne had driven her at once to the hospital.

It had, they said, been an awful experience, dreadful. Jane had been dusting Monica's sitting-room when Jess found her, and she hadn't even stopped dusting for more than about ten seconds. She had neither cried nor said a word. In fact, Anne said, she had simply been herself only more so. Rigid with such unnatural self-control that Anne had been scared and shivery with superstitious fear. She hadn't wanted to leave Jane to go into the hospital alone, but her offer to accompany her had been coolly but firmly declined. 'It scared me, just to see her,' Anne said. 'Nobody ought to be as self-controlled as that. It's frightening. Utterly fatalistic. As if she didn't care about her son at all.'

'He's all she does care about,' Fran said.

Jess agreed. 'She's spent her whole life protecting him,' Jess said. 'What gave me goose-pimples was that it seemed to me she'd been expecting something like this to happen. As if she accepted that they were both doomed right from the start. You can't help those who won't be helped. The only sort of help she's ever been willing to take has been for Nick, not for herself. God knows what will happen if he dies. If he lives and wants anything, it'll be very different, I think. We can try again then, but till then, I'm sure it's kinder to her not to try. Not even to sympathize. She's been twenty years building up

569

her defences. One kind word too many could bring them all crashing down – and then where would Nick be, without her? He may be brain-damaged, or paralysed, or anything. We must wait and see.'

Fran got up and gave Jess a warm, loving hug, to which Jess responded by clinging to her longer than she needed to. This wasn't Jess the clever businesswoman. This was the Jess whom Fran, and William, and Greg loved. She was still there, under the capable modern female executive.

Fran called in on Monica on her way home. On this sad morning, Fran thought she was pure joy to behold. Her figure was getting rounder and rounder, and she seemed to find it all a great joke. She patted her 'Zinjie-bump' and said, 'Greg calls me Botticelli. Little Barrel. We're going to call our new range of maternity wear "the Botticelli range".'

Bob Bellamy had not heard of Nick's accident. He gave Ginger a good grooming, and decided he would have to make two trips to Temperance Farm, one with the horse, and one with all the essential tack in case Charles should be tempted to ride him. Bob hoped so. He did not ride himself – very few fenmen did. So he only put a halter on Ginger, and set out to walk with him. It was a good four miles or more each way, but fen folks were used to using their feet.

He enjoyed the walk. The hawthorn was bursting into bloom, and by next week every hedgerow that the syndicate had left standing would be 'white with may' as the old rhyme said. He stopped every here and there to pick a leaf bud not yet fully unfurled and pop it into his mouth to chew. 'Bread-and-cheese', all country children called it. He didn't know why – but then he didn't know why he called water-rats 'moggies' or flowering rush 'hens-and-chickens'. He had a never-failing curiosity about anything and everything like that. It hadn't been much in evidence just lately, because he missed Charlie more than he dared admit. He missed Charles as well – or perhaps it was that he missed the two of them together. He had woven them into another dream, one to match the dream-picture of Fran's high-born ancestress looking down at him with such loving eyes. 'Whoa!' he said to Ginger, stopping a moment to think about that. That was why he had connected Fran's eyes resting on William, and Charlie's on Charles, with his dream. The lady in the picture used to look down at *him* like that. If only he could travel backwards and find out, as he was sometimes able to travel forward . . .

It was Rosemary he encountered in the farmyard, a Rosemary of vastly different aspect from the one he had last seen and spoken to. He explained about Ginger, and asked if he could hand him over to Charles. She shook her head.

'Haven't you heard about Nick Hadley?' she asked, and told him. 'We're nearly out of our minds,' she said. 'Since Charles heard about Nick, he's shut himself up in his bedroom and locked the door. He won't speak or answer us, and hasn't had anything to eat or drink for more than twenty-four hours, now. He's so quiet, Brian thinks he must be asleep, but I know he isn't . . .'

Bob read in her agonized eyes her unspoken dread. 'Brian threatened to break his door down, but I wouldn't let him. I'm too frightened of what he might find, Mr Bellamy. Brian's gone to get his father. Charles has always been his grandad's boy. If he won't answer Grandad, we shall have to break in . . .' Her eyes flinched from the imagined horror.

Bob was tying Ginger's halter to the yard gate.

'Wouldn't it be better for all of you for somebody like me to talk to him?' he asked. 'I'm no stranger to him, and when you feel like he does your family are the last people you want. Will you let me talk to him through the door? And if I have to, try to get in? You needn't come. Just show me the way.'

She wondered if Brian would be angry with her, but if he was, she didn't care. Bellamy might be the girl's father, but he was kind, and seemed to understand. If Brian hadn't had such big ideas, she might have been looking forward to a wedding, not dreading another funeral.

She led Bob into the house and showed him Charles's door. She lingered, unable to tear herself away. Bob took her firmly but gently by the arm and escorted her back into the yard where he had found her.

'You stay right out of the way,' he said. 'Here, feed these to Ginger.' He fished in his pocket and produced three carrots, an apple and some lumps of sugar. 'Stay here till I come back,' he said. 'And don't let anybody else come near.'

He had no fear that he would find anything but a broken-hearted boy lying exhausted on his bed. There would be danger only if over-charged emotion turned to anger, and anger to violence. He had the extraordinary feeling that it was his own son in the locked room. He would have acted just as Charles was doing, once, if he had been in the same situation.

He tapped on the door, said who he was, and asked to be let in. When there was no reply, he said that he had brought Ginger. He heard a stifled sound.

'I'm in no hurry, mate,' Bob said, easily. 'I'll sit on the floor and wait till you open the door. Your mother's taking care of Ginger and your Dad's gone to fetch your grandad. You ain't the only one missing Charlie, you know. If you don't want to talk to me, I want to talk to you.'

The key was turned, and a distraught Charles let him in, locking the door again after him. 'Take Ginger home again, please Mr Bellamy. I shan't be able to look after him. I can't bear to think of Charlie coming back one day and not finding even Ginger where she expects.'

Bob's intuition told him how frightened Charles was, and why. He sat down on the bed, and did the one thing neither Brian nor Rosemary would have dared to try. He took the dread-filled youngster into his arms, as if he were only six, and gave him solid flesh to cling to.

It was into Brian's visit to his father that William unwittingly intruded.

He had never been into the Old Glebe House before and was immediately charmed by his surroundings, but not by the atmosphere, which was charged not only with sorrow but also with such terrible apprehension that he could not but be aware of it. He apologized for his unheralded appearance, saying Fran wanted to know if there was any way they could help. The Bridgefoots could not hide the fear that he was at a complete loss to understand.

Molly had begun to cry again. William went to kiss her, asking gently if there had been bad news of Nick. She shook her head and tried a wobbly smile. 'No, as far as we know, he's just the same. No bones broken, but the blow to his head could kill him, or leave him blind, or anything . . . they don't know yet. It's Charles we're so upset about.'

William was not sure how much Brian knew of Charles's visit to Benedict's. He used his expressive eyebrows to ask to be enlightened.

'We don't know how to deal with him,' his grandfather confessed, glad to shift the weight of decision fron his own shoulders to William's. 'He locked himself in his room yesterday, and won't come out, or answer. There ain't a sound from his room. He's been like that for more than twenty-four hours now, and Brian thinks we ought to get the police to break in.'

'The police? Whatever for?'

George said, having great difficulty to get the words out, 'They're used to dealing with suicide.'

'*Suicide?*' Willaim's voice betrayed his surprise. 'Why on earth should you say that?'

Brian launched into the tale of Aunt Esther and her curses. William was stunned. Could it possibly be that this solid-as-rock Christian family had surrendered so completely to the old woman's pagan psychological warfare?

Their three pairs of frightened eyes confirmed that they had. He didn't know what line to take, because for a moment he saw them not as the wealthiest, most repected farmers in the community, but as a medieval peasant family putting salt on the doorsill to keep out the witches. (Even he himself still 'touched wood'.) Time didn't change primitive human nature; but this contagion of fear had to be nipped in the bud now, before it became self-fulfilling.

'You're all as bad as Sophie,' he said lightly. 'You surely can't think a bitter old woman who was drunk anyway could kill even a fly with words? But if you will offer your hand to a rabid dog and let it bite you, you must expect consequences. Come on, Brian, let me go with you to coax Charles out. He's just had too much all at once.'

The relief they showed was gratifying to William. He felt he had restored them to the twentieth century. All the same, he was glad to find when they reached Temperance that Bob had done his job for him.

Bob had prevailed on Charles to keep Ginger at least for the present, and persuaded him to go and have a bath, and then get up. He was just about ready to start his walk back to Castle Hill when William and Brian appeared.

Rosemary, brimming over with the need to do something for her son, had gone inside to cook a tempting snack. Bob, with his head on one side, was contemplating a morose Brian. When the silence grew a bit too long, Bob said, 'Go easy with him, mate. He reminds me of a young hoss that has just caught sight o' the cart behind him. However hard he runs away, it still comes after him. Folks our age have got used to our blinkers. We know the cart's still there, but as long as we can't see it, we're all right. He'll come round now, if nothing else happens to make him bolt again.'

Brian, as William could see, was not very pleased to be addressed as 'mate' or given advice. He mumbled rather incoherent thanks and more or less dismissed them. William offered Bob a lift home, which he was glad to take. In the seclusion of the car, they could talk.

William was considerably concerned to learn that Bob was by no means as assured that Charles was 'out of the wood' as he had pretended to be. 'They don't know how to handle him, for one thing – at least his father don't. He'd be better if Nick were to come round, or if the old woman died. He told me he kept thinking about the old nursery rhyme, "And then there was none." He meant Robert, then Nick – then himself.'

'You can't believe this silly nonsense about the curse, surely?' William said, and flushed at the amused look Bob turned on him.

'I'm as superstitious as most fen-men are,' he said. 'But not enough to let a crazy old woman frighten me to death. She were crafty enough to hit on a way o' getting her own back. She never expected to be able to scare everybody. Well, she hasn't done it. They've scared theirselves.'

'That's nothing new, either,' William said. 'If I had time, I could give you a lecture about such things in medieval times. They caught fear from each other as well as the Black Death.

Have you ever heard about the "dancing madness"? In the fourteenth century, all over Europe people just simply seemed to go mad and started to dance, but couldn't stop. They went on till some of them dropped dead from sheer exhaustion It spread, as the Spanish 'flu did in 1918, by all accounts. It needs something else to happen quickly to stop this spreading.'

Bob was always fascinated by William talking history, and followed much more intelligently than a lot of William's students.

'Bailey's after my farm to stick another ticky-tacky estate up on,' he said. 'I shall be gone back down the fen by then, most likely, but I reckon if we begun to stir folks up about that they'd soon forget they were under anybody else's curse but that bugger's.'

'You're absolutely right,' William said, 'as usual. All it needs is a new topic to take their minds off this run of disaster. No, I won't come in. Fran went to see if anybody was looking after Nick's mother. If we're both away too long, Sophie will be dying of fright. Thanks a lot, Bob.'

'Come up and give me that lecture sometime,' Bellamy answered. 'I get too lonely now and then to believe myself. Things ain't so black as they might be.'

71

The long early summer days dragged themselves by in windless warmth, under high blue skies in sunshine that seemed to Fran so sterile as to be almost synthetic. 'Wonderful weather,' said the holiday strangers when they met at the pub or the shop. To those who knew the scene in all weathers, the 'perfect weather' this spring was a mockery. Waking every morning to it meant another day to spend in this vacuum of waiting. 'It's as if our needle's got stuck in a groove on a long, low, mournful note,' Fran said to William.

'Better than a dying fall,' he replied, and she knew he meant it literally. He knew where her thoughts were.

He was finding this end of term more than usually full of problems, and the thought that once he reached the end of July he was going to be off duty for a whole academic year was losing some of its happy anticipation.

'I know we always say that we are happier at Benedict's than anywhere else on earth,' he said to her on a Sunday morning as they lay and watched the morning mist lift to reveal yet again 'that blasted blue sky'. 'I think it's time you, at any rate, had a change of scene. Let's plan to spend next summer term somewhere else – in Cornwall or Wales or the Cheviot Hills. It may be years before we have another chance. Coming back home would be wonderful.'

So it would, providing they didn't come back to a place so caught in the waiting trap as Old Swithinford was at present. Waiting in apprehension. It was still only late May, but it seemed like five lifetimes since Easter. Some things that were pending had definite forms and time limits; it was those that were formless and lingering that hung like a veil of gloom between them and the blue sky.

Esther Palmer was still in hospital, with one side completely paralysed, and unable to speak. While she lived, Molly Bridgefoot fretted; she dreaded the day when Alex should ring to tell her that Lucy had gone into labour. She knew she was being silly, as everybody told her – but even they who laughed at her did it uneasily. Molly would have been anxious in any case, like all mothers of daughters awaiting a first child. It was waiting, guiltily half-hoping, for Esther to die that put her so much on edge.

Fran 'whittled', as Sophie would have said, about Monica's not because she feared any trouble with the pregnancy, but because after her mother's marriage and departure to the States, Sue had refused to go home to her father. She had done a round of visiting friends, keeping Roland on tenterhooks because she often neglected to tell him of her whereabouts. He was torn in two between his legal and marital tie to his unstable and insecure wife, and his desire to be with his 'Little Barrel' and its contents.

Nick still lay in a coma, with no signs yet of any recovery. Fran told herself, and Sophie, that 'time was still very young' for such a serious injury. Sometimes people lay in comas for months, not weeks, and then recovered. His mother sat by his bed, day and night, whenever the hospital would let her, her hands folded in her lap, her face immobile. She had stopped working to be able to be there, and though all her employers had wanted to go on paying her, she had politely but firmly refused to take money for services not rendered. She grew thinner and more haggard, but that was the only visible sign of her suffering. The time could be counted in days before George's lease on her cottage ran out. He had been unable to renew it because it had been let for the summer before she had ever moved in.

Nobody felt able to ask what she intended to do, though Fran had said to William that when the time came, she would risk a snub and offer temporary accommodation in Eeyore's Tail. Fran didn't want to have to worry George, because the worst thing of all was anxiety about Charles, who had broken down, mentally and physically, before their eyes.

Some days he refused to get up or speak. If his mother went near him, he pulled up the sheet over his face and refused to look at her. His father, impatient, got the same treatment except that he was sworn at from beneath the covering sheet. Brian appeared to be exasperated to the very limits of his endurance by what he chose to believe – and to say: that it was all on account of Charles's 'mooning over that Bellamy girl'. Charles himself begged his mother not to let Grandad near him, because that would only make him worse.

On days when he did get up, scruffy and unshaven, he simply disappeared in his car. Bob had been requested by Brian to fetch Ginger home, and had reluctantly done so.

Doctors summoned by Rosemary were given short shrift by Charles himself, who told them there was nothing they could do. Haggard and thin, he often staggered home very late and went straight up to bed. Then Brian raged, sure that he had taken to drink. One morning when Rosy couldn't rouse Charles into any sort of normality, in terror she shook him to wakefulness.

'I'm going to get a doctor, whatever you say,' she said. 'You are ill.'

Drowsily he lowered the sheet and replied, 'Not ill, just dying,' and covered himself again as if he were already a corpse.

In panic she rushed up to the Old Glebe, seeking Brian and other support.

'He isn't drunk,' she said, glaring at her husband.

Brian pulled away from her. 'Well then, you'd better face the truth. I've suspected it all along. Where do you think he goes? To get a drug fix, of course. And all over a bloody little tart no better than her mother.'

George looked up and angrily told his son to mind what he was saying. 'I'm going to ask Alex to come to see him,' he said. 'No, Mother, I know it's no time to be asking Alex to leave Lucy, but we can't go on like this. *I won't have it*. Say what you will, but he's my only grandson. This is my affair, and I shall do as I like.'

He told Fran all this in confidence the night the selected few met at Benedict's to see what was to be done to prevent Bailey from carrying out his development plans. With Elyot still honeymooning, Brian inventing another engagement, William abstracted, Greg away and other farmers mostly fatalistically apathetic, the group lacked positive leadership. Bob Bellamy's absence Fran was inclined to regard as treachery.

There had to be an official 'objection' made to the council. The first move was to elect a chairman. Fran had confidently expected Brian Bridgefoot to accept the task, but he wasn't present. George was looking so old that she worried about him. She did her best to make excuses for Brian, but thought he should have learned some sort of lesson from Tom Fairey. In his absence, George took the chair till they could vote somebody to the position.

'What about you, Rector?' George asked persuasively.

Archie shook his head. 'I'm among friends only, here tonight,' he said, 'so I can ask that what I'm about to say goes no farther till I have made it official. I shall not be here to see it through. With Beth so happily married, I have done a lot of thinking. You will all be too kind to say so, but I haven't been much of a success here – and the reason for that is that I am out of my own element. I hope to be offered some urban inner-city living, where what I can give is badly needed. I know what I am doing. What you need in my place is a man with a country background. Please excuse me.'

The strained silence told its own tale.

'We're wasting time,' said Eric Choppen. 'Suppose I volunteer? I would not put myself so forward if there were an old inhabitant willing and able. Bailey won't play fair. He needs an opponent who knows the tricks well enough to keep one step ahead of him. I know I made mistakes . . . I can only ask you to believe that I've made better use of the de ffranksbridge estate than Bailey would have done. I also have an office at my disposal for dealing with correspondence. But I shan't be offended if you tell me I'm still too much of a newcomer to represent your interests properly.'

The rest were all staring at him in wonder. How the leopard had indeed changed his spots! With enormous relief, George got up, and Eric put on his spectacles, motioning Anne with her shorthand pad to to his side.

At that moment, Bob Bellamy crept in, apologizing silently for being so late. Eric told him swiftly what had taken place so far.

'You'll have to get up early to keep in front of him,' Bob said bitterly. 'That's why I'm late. I had occasion to go up Lane's End way, and I see a cloud of dust rise, so I went to look. He's just bulldozed the old farmhouse down. One minute it was there, and the next all there was to see was a heap o' rubble and a cloud of dust. It was only stud and mud and thatch, but it had stood wind and weather for about three hundred and fifty year . . . Gone in less than five minutes. He wasn't there, of course – his men had "had their instructions".'

'Wasn't there a preservation order on it?' William asked.

'Not through yet, probably. The deal with Tom can't be finalized, surely?' replied George.

'Then it wasn't his to knock down?'

'Yes, I reckon it was.' George spoke quietly, but they could see what he was feeling. 'I reckon that's what Tom meant when he told me – that he'd sold the old house as a separate lot so that it couldn't be part of the development. Tom trusted his word.'

'See what I mean?' asked Choppen. 'Act first and explain after. There's no power on earth that can make him put it back as it was.'

Could the gloom get any deeper? Looking round the group, Fran decided that that there were a couple of bright spots. Eric had tonight come over to their side against a common foe; and Bailey might have been there in person when Bob arrived, gun in the crook of his arm. Things might have been a lot worse.

72

Alex was willing to oblige his father-in-law, but on two conditions. It had to be soon, and he had to have Charles's co-operation. Charles refused point blank. Rosemary, desperate, suggested William or Bob as mediators. Brian flew into a temper and vetoed Bob, so William was more or less forced to do what he could. He succeeded insofar as Charles agreed to talk to Uncle Alex so long as his father stayed out of the way, and William remained within call.

'Must get back to your Aunt Lucy,' Alex said cheerily to Charles after a three-hour chat he hadn't minded half as much as he had expected to. 'No more consultations now till you have a new cousin. William's going to take me to the station. See you again soon, with Aunt Lucy and George or Georgina.'

Brian was waiting at the foot of the stairs. Rosemary, eyes full of questioning, offered tea, hoping to be told something.

'No thanks,' said Alex decisively. He kissed Rosemary, saying, 'Get some food down Charles before he dies of starvation. Cook him his favourite snack and make him eat it if you have to pinch his nose to make him swallow.'

He waited till she had gone kitchenwards, out of hearing.

'Now take me somewhere where I can talk to you in private,' he said.

'Benedict's,' said William without hesitation, and Brian, white to the gills, followed them to the car without a word of protest.

In William's study, Alex the psychiatrist began to talk, his gaze holding Brian's. 'There's nothing whatsoever the matter with him physically,' he said. 'But that's not a lot of comfort. He thinks he's dying, and he doesn't care. Unless we can change his state of mind, he's about as hopeless a case for his age as I've met recently.'

'I don't believe it!' Brian burst out passionately. '*Dying!* Rubbish! He can't be! You say there's nothing wrong with him.'

'Haven't you heard of Africans, young and strong and perfectly healthy, just lying down and dying only because they believe themselves to be?'

'But why should Charles think that?'

'Three very good reasons. He thinks he's doomed because all his life three boys have been about together. One is dead and another in a coma resembling death. Charles says things always go in threes. That's a belief as old as the hills. He believes himself to be the third victim. He worked that out the moment he heard of Nick's accident. Then there's this "curse", He hadn't believed a word of Miss Palmer's senile ranting until the accident; but the shock knocked him off balance. To him she is the equivalent of the witch-doctor who puts a spell on the perfectly healthy African and kills him, so he has told himself that if it's fated, he might just as well give up and let it happen.

'He's willing himself to die, to get it over and done with, because as he sees it, there's no escape. And as I'm warning you, he may succeed. Not by suicide, but by just willing himself to die. To get feebler till he dies, as he knows Robert did. Because in his case he doesn't care. That's the real reason.'

William got up and poured Brian a large dose of brandy. Brian had his face down in his hands on the table, hidden from both the other men. He was shaking, and began to clench and unclench his fists, banging them on the table.

'Damn you! Damn you!' he said to Alex. 'Who are you to

sit there and tell me my son is dying? Do something if you're so clever. Get me the best doctor in London! In England! In the world! Why should I believe you, just because you're my brother-in-law? All this psychology's poppycock, anyway. I told Dad not to involve you.' He got up, and walked to the window, his knuckles showing white as he held himself up by clutching the back of a chair.

Alex looked with pity towards him. William said, keeping his voice low, 'You said as well that Charles wanted to die. Did he say so? Did he tell you why?'

'Isn't it obvious? He's got nothing to live for. If he were fifty, he might have the will to live for his farm, his heritage, his bank balance, and all the other things mature men in his position put in place of what they've lost. But a boy not yet twenty-one? I'm not talking psychological jargon – just plain common sense. Where would you expect a healthy young twenty-one-year-old's thoughts to lie? With sex, of course, and with establishing himself in the pecking-order of his peer group. He has lost his two best friends, and his girl. Not, I understand, just any girl who would to help him overcome his shame at having to confess himself still a virgin. *His girl.* The only girl. The one for whose sake he would – perhaps may – die still a virgin.'

'We can't get Robert or Nick back – but we could make an effort to try to find Charlie Bellamy,' said William.

'Would she come back if you did? Does she care for him? Didn't she leave absolutely to please herself?'

'No,' said Brian loudly. 'She went to please me. Because she knew I didn't want her in my family. Take me home.'

'You are not to tell Rosemary or your parents a word of what I've said,' Alex said sharply. 'This is no time for tearful contrition or recrimination. My wife and my child are part of your family, and as much to me as Charles is to you. You are only in the same position as Robert's mother was from the first time I arranged a consultation for her. Be a man and keep what I've said to yourself.

'I may very well be wrong. Charles is not my patient. I'm only giving off-the-cuff advice, which is what I was asked for. He may well recover completely – especially if you can trace the girl. Is there any hope at all of that?'

'Ask William. He's thick with her father. I'm not. He wouldn't help me.'

'He would do anything for Charles,' William was quick to interpolate. 'I think he loves Charles next to Charlie, like a son. He wants her back as much as Charles does, but he hasn't a clue where to start to find her. She made sure of that.'

They had to rush to catch Alex's train, Brian sitting in the back seat alternating between despair and temper. When they got back to the Old Glebe, they found George messing about outside, waiting to pounce on them, out of Molly's hearing.

William could see at once that Alex's injunction about secrecy would not be acted on. He decided he had better stay around to make sure George got a report that bore some likeness to the truth.

He wished he hadn't. Brian was beside himself with dread, fear, despair, remorse and, above all, guilt. He was driven to attack the bringer of bad news in his fright and anger, and his father, who in his opinion had invited trouble by insisting on getting his la-di-da shrink of a son-in-law instead of a proper doctor, was at hand, a readymade victim.

'As if you didn't know Alex could do no good, you bloody old fool,' Brian yelled. He poured on George's fast-greying old head all the vengeful contumely meant really for himself.

'You still want to run the show, and be boss of everything and everybody, me included. Well, you won't have the last word this time! I shall have another opinion, and get the best treatment money can buy. And when Charles is better, you'll remember that he's my son. Not just your grandson, like he's had to be till now.'

William was expecting the old man to break down, and wondering if he dare intervene. He got out of the car with the intention of trying to persuade George to go into the house and leave him to deal with Brian. But there was no need.

The old man straightened his back, held up his head and put his weight on the garden fork he had been using. 'Have you finished?' he asked his son. 'Because if you have, I've got something to say. Do you remember when you were so chuffed about Lucy doing so well for herself, and what you said that day? You as good as told me that money was about the only thing that mattered to people now. And you made me so mad that I told you there would come a day when you would find there were things as no amount of money could buy. Now you know as I spoke the truth. Charles's life is one of them things. See what your money can do!' He began to walk away.

'Where are you going?' shouted Brian to his father's retreating back.

'To where I've always gone for help in time of trouble all my life,' George answered. 'Where money don't count. To church.'

73

On the last Friday in May, Jane Hadley went early, on foot, to Swithinford, to catch a bus to Cambridge where Nick still lay unconscious. There was no change. She kissed his beautiful pallid face, and left. She went first to the main post office, to be told that there was no mail poste restante for her there, upon which information she produced her Post Office Savings Book, drew out the last remains of her meagre savings, and visited a furniture repository. Then she took the bus home, and began to pack Nick's clothes and the few things he treasured, particularly his books, into a tea-chest well lined with newspapers. She put her own few belongings into two battered old suitcases and began to clean the cottage. It was midnight when she had finished and washed all the bedlinen. She then took a bath, got dressed again and slept uneasily on the settee.

Very early next morning, a taxi arrived to collect her and the tea-chest. Having deposited it and paid for a month's storage, she went again to the hospital and the post office, only to receive the same negative answer at both places. Her busfare home left her with approximately two pounds in the world.

When Fran, next morning, which was the first Sunday in June, got up unwontedly early to drive up to the cottage to offer her refuge in Eeyore's Tall, she had gone. There was no evidence at all of occupation.

Fran retreated to the shelter of her own beautiful home and the comfort of William's listening ear. She was remorseful and puritanically guilty.

'It's what Kezia used to say,' she said. '"It's no use doing a kindness if you do it a day too late." We all knew how much Jane Hadley was up against it, and we didn't raise a finger because of her stiff-necked pride. We should have had more sense. Till I know where she is and what's happening to her, I shall have no peace. We shouldn't have let her stand us off.'

'Your family of lame ducks is getting too big,' William said. 'You can't bear everybody's troubles.'

'Put it in the plural,' she said. 'You've been doing your share, lately.'

They were interrupted by the telephone bell. It was Roland, sounding flat, tired and defeated. Sue had disappeared. 'I've informed the police,' he said. 'She may be ill, or have lost her memory. She's registered as a "missing person". I'll keep you informed.'

'So now we have an epidemic of missing persons as well,' Fran said, returning from the telephone to tell William. 'Three already – Charlie, Jane and now Sue.'

William sat down in his chair and pulled her on to his knee. He knew her in this mood, which pelican-like would feed on itself till it caused a storm of tears and self-reproach.

'Now, my darling sweetheart,' he said. 'The only way of being able to help other people is not to let yourself go under. We're just having a very bad patch. But if you are going to rely on Kezia's and Sophie's aphorisms, what about the one that says "The darkest hour is just before the dawn"? And haven't you forgotten our guardian angel? We chose to live here, you know. We wanted to be part of everything again. We've got to be prepared for the bad with the good, haven't we?'

'And the good with the bad,' she said. 'Times like this minute.' She snuggled her head into his shoulder and felt her moral courage seeping back. 'Sorry, darling,' she said. 'I'm

OK now. Just one beam of sunlight through the clouds would make a lot of difference, though.'

'Not would. Will,' he said. 'You're too big a baby to nurse for long. I'm out of practice. You should sit on my knee oftener.'

She laughed. 'Isn't that funny?' she said. 'It used to be a sort of first move in courting. You never see couples like this now, do you? Pity!'

'There aren't any first moves nowadays,' he said. 'Poor kids, what a lot they miss!'

The telephone rang again. She jumped up, but he got to it first, and came back with a half-humorous smile. 'News,' he said, 'but whether a beam of sunlight or not I can't decide. Aunt Esther was gathered to her fathers some time in the night.'

'Poor old fathers!' said Fran.

'Lucky young Charles,' said William seriously. 'It may be in time to make a lot of difference to him.'

74

'Bob Bellamy had been very much disturbed by the experience of watching the beautiful old house at Lane's End fall before the bulldozers. He could not forget it, or the awful finality of it. He sat in his chair, as always surrounded by animals, and thought about it. All that history, gone in a flash! All those worries and cares, thanksgivings and rejoicings that had taken place there, memories now with nowhere to roost. Weddings and births, deaths and funerals. Quarrels and partings, kisses and lovers' meetings – those old walls had held them all. Where had they gone? Did nobody but himself hear them crying in the wind for somebody to care that they were lost? He was sorry that he had been the one to witness their habitation vanishing in a cloud of dust. It haunted him, and added to the loneliness he was feeling more and more.

Would it be the same if Charles died? Would the younger Bridgefoots do what the Faireys had done, and leave their four hundred years of memories for Bailey to disperse? Would Bailey bulldoze the Old Glebe down, when George had died of a broken heart? Would the new houses on Bailey's Castle Hill Estate inherit the ghosts, when the room he was sitting in and the church became a cartload of dust? Well, he wouldn't be here to know.

He'd be in the fen, in his own house, neither very old nor very beautiful, but stuffed to its eaves with tales of his forebears going back long before the house was built. Tribal memories. Old Swithinford had had the same thing, until recently. Where would all those feelings for the past take refuge? At Benedict's, of course, stored there along with his dream. Perhaps at the Old Rectory, too, though Beth and Elyot might not know they were there. He would know, if ever he was invited there, and so would William.

A kitten scrabbled up his trouser leg, and he picked it up to cuddle it to his face. It cheered him up. New life of any kind always did. It also reminded him that he hadn't yet been up to feed Winnie, who was suckling five kittens and couldn't be neglected. He put on an old straw hat to enable him to look upwards in spite of the brilliant sunshine, took the food he had already prepared and his forked ashplant, and set off.

Winnie came at his call, kittens on wobbly legs following her. He picked up the kittens one by one and examined them. He had to get them used to being handled, or he wouldn't be able to give them away. Now where on earth had Winnie found a Siamese mate? Or were those two kittens with such Siamese heads and blue eyes a throw-back in Winnie's own breeding somewhere? One tom, one female. Nobody else but himself was going to have them, he told Winnie.

He was just about to leave the porch when a faint moaning sound reached his ears. He stopped to listen. An animal in pain? If so, he had to find it, if it took him all day. The sound came again. Definitely an animal in pain – *inside the church*. He remembered with guilt that he had not locked the door last night, but surely he hadn't left it open?

It was dark inside the church, after the bright light outside.

He grasped his ashplant firmly. He might need it to defend himself if it were a badly injured dog, till he could go for his gun to put it out of its misery.

The sound came again, from the shadows at the back of the church. The first thing he made out as his eyes accustomed themselves to the change of light was a pair of battered old suitcases. A tramp crept in to die? Tramps didn't often carry suitcases.

He approached with care, and saw her. She had been kneeling in the last pew, and had keeled over sideways, where she now lay moaning incoherently.

'Effendi! Effendi!' she was calling, over and over again.

He recognized her at once, though it didn't matter to him who she was, nor what she was doing there, or saying. She was an animal in pain, a human animal in the sort of pain he understood. He threw away his hat and his stick, and picked her up. She was limp in his arms, and cold.

He sat down with her in the pew, holding her against his own warmth, trying to establish how far gone she was and whether he dare leave her to run back to his telephone. He decided against it. Her head sagged on his shoulder and she had stopped moaning; but she was still breathing. He carried her into the porch, where it was warmer, and sat down with her again, chafing her cheeks and cold hands, until at last she opened her eyes.

'You're safe now,' he said, as she began to struggle. 'Just lie still. You know who I am – Bob Bellamy. Don't struggle – you'll faint again if you do. Just sit still and get warm.'

He gathered her up to make her more comfortable and to make it easier for himself to hold her close. He was wearing only a thin open-necked summer shirt and the warmth of his strong chest came through it to her face. The arms with rolled-up sleeves were taking all her weight that wasn't already resting on his knees, and when she forced her eyes to open again, the glimpse she had of his face made it seem not worth struggling to get away. She let the arm contact flow through her, thinking she was either dreaming or dead. She hadn't been in contact with another human body for so long. So long! Not at all, not even a handshake, since Nick had left her.

Memory of Nick, and of her plight, flooded back. 'Let me die,' she prayed. 'Let me die now, in such blessed warmth and comfort.'

She opened her eyes again, to find he was still there, studying her intently. 'There, that's better, my beauty,' he said, exactly as he would have done to Ginger or one of his cats. 'As soon as you feel well enough, I'm going to carry you up to my house. Just till I can get you to a doctor.'

She didn't want a doctor. She wanted to die. She shook her head, and tears she hadn't shed in the sight of another person for many years began to creep silently down her face. He guessed that her son had died and that she was only now remembering. He stood up with her, surprised to discover how light she was. He would have no difficulty in carrying her back to the house.

'Put your arms round my neck,' he said, 'and hang on as much as you can. It's a fair way and I don't want to drop you.'

The arms she raised to clasp round the back of his sturdy neck were like matchsticks; just elegant bone with no flesh. He went on talking as he might have done to a child, while putting two and two together in his mind. He knew now why she was so light to carry. She was half-starved.

He was puffing a bit, nevertheless, by the time he got her into the house, and glad to put her down in his own chair. He had worked out more or less what had happened, except that he didn't know, and daren't ask, about Nick.

'How long had you been in the church?' he asked.

'Since it got dark last night. I had nowhere else to go. Thank God it was open.'

'So no wonder you fainted! A long cold night with nothing to eat or drink. Are you still cold?' She nodded.

'I'll get you some hot-water bottles,' he said, and went into the kitchen to put the kettle on and think. He needed advice, and Fran was the obvious person to ask; but he didn't want his unexpected visitor to hear. He had to feed her, too – but you had to be careful about feeding a starving animal. He warmed a little milk, sweetened it well and laced it with rum. He tucked the two hot-water bottles beside her, one in her lap and the other at her back, and wrapped a blanket round her. He held the cup to her lips and let her sip a mouthful at a time. Then he sat down and waited till the warmth and the rum had its effect. She slept. He wasted no time in ringing Fran.

She was as relieved as she was appalled at his story. He had been quite blunt in telling her the details. He had a homeless, destitute, starving woman on his hands, in a lonely spot like Castle Hill. What was he to do? Had Nick died?

No, said Fran, George would have known, and said so. She would ring the hospital and find out, and let him know. If she didn't ring, it would mean there was no change. Better not for Jane to hear the bell, yet. But what was he to do with her, tonight? Where was he to take her?

Fran's answer was as instantaneous as it was decisive. 'Nowhere. Keep her where she is. She intended to disappear. Let her. Who'll know?'

'But Fran – what will people say?'

'She was Bert Bleasby's housekeeper for about eighteen years. Why shouldn't she be yours for a month or so? Keep it dark till she's well enough to let on that it was all arranged. Nick's accident had prevented her from telling any of us. So I won't come up unless you ask me to. At least that way she'll be fed, and have a bed.

'I did go up to see her this morning early, to offer her temporary accommodation in our flat. I expected to be snubbed, because she has never been known to accept charity. If you offer her a job, it won't smack of charity. For the time being, concentrate on getting her well again.'

He wasn't at all sure about Fran's suggestion, though only on Jane's behalf. Poor and plain as she appeared, she had not been born to a life of hard work and penury, that he could swear. Dare such as he offer her either work or charity? Not that it mattered to him what folks said; he had nothing to lose. Neither, if it came to that, had she. He had thought at first that she was a lost and injured animal, and so she was. He wouldn't have been expected to turn an animal out because of what folks said, would he? Fran was right.

When she woke, she was much better, but shyly tongue-tied. He was at her side at once, lifting her out of the chair on to her feet.

'There's no change in Nick,' he said, 'and the bathroom's upstairs – lean on me and I'll show you. Fran Catherwood knows you're here and thinks you ought to stop till you've got over last night. Nobody need know, but it's up to you. Fran'll come and get you if you don't like the thought of stopping with only me here. But you're welcome, if you do want to stop.'

He opened the bathroom door for her. She actually almost smiled. 'Mr Bellamy,' she said. 'Could I have a bath? And another drink?'

He bestowed on her the amused grin that had first endeared him to Fran.

'That means you've decided to stop,' he said. 'Good. I'll get a bed ready for you. My daughter's room is empty.'

In the hope that he might one day find her on the doorstep, he had kept Charlie's room well aired and the bed made up. It couldn't be damp after a spell of such hot weather. Since she had decided to stay, he thought she should go to bed at once. He could take her something to eat. He opened the wardrobe door and found what he hoped for. Charlie had not taken her dressing-gown.

Outside the bathroom he stopped and called that he had left a dressing-gown on the floor by the door. Then he sat at the bottom of the stairs listening for her, just in case. He heard no ghosts there today, because he had other matters to think about. He wouldn't mention them to her, anyway.

She came towards him wearing the dressing-gown, and the sight jolted him. She was too tall for it, or it not long enough for her, so that from her knees downward her thin legs and feet were bare. He couldn't imagine Iris ever letting a man see her like that. But this woman was a lady, not in the least embarrassed – because it never occurred to her that there was any reason to be. Or that he might be. Consequently, he wasn't. Even his natural shyness had so far been absorbed by her needs.

'Don't come down. Go and get in bed straight away. When did you last have a proper meal?'

'I can't remember,' she said, truthfully.

'Then you mustn't eat much. Will you mind if I bring something in to you once you're in bed?'

Bed, after last night in the church and the night before on a settee, could not be resisted. She didn't care whether she ate or not. She shook her head.

He opened another door to a large, airy, beautiful room with a single divan bed in it. She didn't undress any further, having no night clothes of her own, but fell on to the bed as she was and pulled up the eiderdown.

She still wasn't at all sure that it wasn't all a dream. Tenant farmers were men like Bert Bleasby, weren't they? Creatures, like most other males, to be kept at bay. She had been treated like a queen. When would the spell be broken?

He knocked at the door. She called to him. 'I don't want anything to eat, after all. I'm afraid I couldn't swallow anything solid.'

Just as he had expected. He hesitated no longer, but pushed open the door and went in. He set down the tray, took her under the armpits and set her higher on the pillows. Then he sat down on the side of the bed, and took the bowl and spoon from the tray into his brown hands.

'Open your mouth,' he ordered, and to her own surprise she obeyed. Soft, sweet bread and milk, made with today's fresh milking. He fed her till the little bowl was empty. 'Now sleep till tomorrow morning,' he said.

The window showed that it was already getting dusk. He bent down and tucked the eiderdown close round her face. Like a cat, she turned her head and rubbed her face against his hand in gratitude. Then she began to cry, letting go of the pent-up grief and worry of the last terrible weeks. Once started, she couldn't stop. He sat down again on the bed beside her.

'Cry it out,' he said. 'I won't leave you, if I have to sit here till morning.' He sat as quiet as a sleeping kitten, big man though he was. He was still there every time she opened her eyes, until the surety of her feeling of absolute safety got the better of her and she didn't bother to try to open them again.

75

He didn't go to bed himself that night. He wanted to be ready dressed in case of emergency, but there was none. Almost as soon as it was daylight, he went up to the church to get her suitcases. The morning mist forecast another hot day. The drought would soon be serious.

He always did most of 'the yard work' with the animals himself, and this morning did it with a will. He wanted to be back in the house before his unexpected guest woke. He briefed his men that he might not be out at work with them today. He could afford a bit of time off because it happened to be the little lull that came between hay-time and harvest. He didn't want to think beyond that. In spite of the drought and his neglect of the farm since Christmas, it looked well. He had grown to love the place, but saw no way of saving his occupation of it. However, he had more urgent problems on his hands this morning.

He made a tray of tea, cut some thin bread and butter, and soft-boiled an egg. When he knocked on her door, he found Jane wide awake, alert and purposeful. When she saw the tray, she actually smiled. (Few people other than Nick would have thought she could, nor was she aware that she had done.)

'I don't remember ringing for room-service,' she said.

His heart rose. His task might not be so difficult after all, if she could both smile and joke.

'I shan't feed you this morning,' he said, 'but I'm going to stop to make sure you eat it. And to talk to you, if you're well enough.'

She nodded, and began to eat. He told her what Fran had said. She considered it, delicately nibbling to savour the almost forgotten luxury of a meal prepared by any hands but her own. Then she nodded.

'On conditions,' she said. 'It would be much more than I ever hoped for. The first condition is that I work here only for my keep and a bed. I shall look after you, not the other way round like this.'

He looked crestfallen. It gave him enormous pleasure to care for anything alive, and at present he had only animals; but she couldn't be expected to know that.

'Secondly, I feel very bad about the way I have let all the others down who gave me work when I needed it so badly. Would you agree to me doing as much as I could for them as well? And thirdly, it can only be a day-to-day contract. What will happen when – if – my son comes out of hospital, I daren't allow myself to think.'

'He would be welcome here,' Bob said. 'There's plenty of room. Till I have to leave the farm next year, anyway. But it takes two to make a bargain. It's off unless I pay you a fair wage. If you like, you can have your own sitting-room. I never use the other rooms. And I shan't ask questions. What you choose to tell me's a different thing.'

'Go away,' she said. 'I'm going to cry again.' He went.

She came downstairs before he had finished his own breakfast and fed all the domestic animals. He was suddenly shy again. 'I went up and fetched your suitcases,' he said. 'And I found this on the floor where you'd been sitting. It was screwed up, so I opened it. I think it must be yours. That's why I said what I did about not asking questions. I'm sorry I read it.'

He laid before her a crumpled piece of paper. It was a first draft of an 'insert' in three top national newspapers which had cost her the bulk of her savings, and to which there had been no response.

Effendi. Have mercy on your proud disgraced one, who pleads not for herself but for him who bears your name and is near to death. Box 234.

Beneath the English, it was translated into Arabic script, in which she had wanted it printed.

She looked up at him, the line of her mouth set hard again and her head held high.

'It was an appeal to my father, when all other hope had failed. He didn't answer.'

Bob couldn't bear the pain in her voice. 'Perhaps he didn't see it,' he said.

'He reads those papers. He reads Arabic script. That's why I used it, to attract his attention. I shan't bother him again. Thanks to you, I am no longer destitute,' she said, adding, 'Don't blame him. I'm the culprit, not he.'

For what? For producing Nick. Anger flared in Bellamy as he thought of Charlie, and of the way Choppen had dealt with the same situation.

She read his eyes and said gently. 'Times have changed. And he was – is – a very proud man. But thank you.'

She screwed the scrap of paper into a ball and tossed it on to the fire which, in spite of the heat, smouldered always on the huge hearth. It was a gesture of dismissal of all that lay behind her, and as that Bob read it.

He was awed. A woman such as she, to have come to this. To being his domestic help, and still retain that courage and such dignity!

'Do you want to go and see Nick today?' he asked. 'I can spare time to take you, till it rains again.'

His kindness kept threatening to undo her, but she hadn't enough money left for many bus fares. Again he saved her embarrassment.

'After lunch then,' he said. 'Go back to bed till then.'

Ned was already in the kitchen when Sophie arrived that same Monday morning.

'We prayed for rain, yist'day at church,' she told Fran. 'This 'ere dry weather's getting real serious for farmers.'

'May's been too hot,' Ned agreed. '"A cold May, for corn and hay" is how the saying goes.'

'Ah,' Sophie countered, 'but it'll be all right if we get some rain soon.

> '"A dry May and a leaking June
> Makes the farmer whistle a merry tune."'

She was not giving Ned best where a bit of country lore was concerned.

'The Bridgefoots ain't got much to whistle about,' Ned said sadly.

'We prayed for Charles in church as well,' Sophie said. 'And Nick 'Adley. The Rector preached a beautiful sermon, more like we're used to, about having faith in miracles, like Elijah and the widow's son, and Jairus's daughter being raised from the dead.'

'We need a miracle,' Fran said. 'A whole shower of them.'

'You never know what the day will bring,' said William, coming in to tell Fran he was going.

'A cloud no bigger than a man's hand would be enough to give us all hope,' she said, and they all dispersed to their particular tasks.

Fran, sitting at her typewriter, thought back over the conversation, which their common knowledge of the Bible had maintained on two levels at once. Ned and Sophie had understood its metaphorical meaning as much as she and William. She sighed. There wasn't much hope that the future occupants of Bailey's Lane End Estate would get the same amount of solace out of TV jingles.

Early in the afternoon, she had a call from Bob Bellamy, whose voice couldn't hide suppressed agitation. He needed her advice again and asked if she could possibly spare time to go up to Castle Hill.

'What's wrong?' she asked, dreading that his answer would be bad news of Nick.

'Nothing *wrong*,' he said. 'Might be something right.'

'On my way,' she said. Anything hopeful would be more than welcome.

Jane greeted her shyly, and thanked her. Fran looked at Bob for explanation of his appeal for her help. He told her.

He had lent Jane Charlie's dressing-gown. She had found a letter in one of its pockets, obviously opened, read, shoved there and forgotten. It was in French, and therefore beyond Bob; but Jane had read it and said it was a letter to Charlie offering her a job as an au pair. The significant thing was that it bore an address and telephone number.

'I don't know that she took that job or if that's where she is,' Bob said. 'But I reckon we ought to try it, don't you? Only we mustn't raise anybody's hopes. That's what worries me. We've got to keep it to ourselves till we know.'

Fran felt dizzy. 'A cloud no bigger than a man's hand,' she had said. This was it. 'We should waste a week getting letters there and back,' she said, 'so we must make contact by phone. They wrote in French, so one must suppose they don't speak English. We need a French speaker. Mrs Hadley?'

'Far too rusty. Besides, if she is there, whoever rings has to tell her about Charles. It should be somebody she knows well.'

'I can read French,' Fran said, 'but I couldn't conduct a conversation in it to save my life. And I wouldn't want to be the one to have to tell her about Charles, if I could. But we must find somebody. And without wasting time.'

'What about William?' Bob asked.

Fran gawped at him, speechless. One never thought of William as anything but himself plus history. *But of course!* Medieval history at his level meant he was as conversant with French as with English. Besides, as she knew quite well, he spoke it, quite literally, idiom and all, 'like a native'.

'He'll be in his room,' she said. 'Can I phone him from here? I'll ask him to get home at the first possible minute.'

'I'm taking Jane to the hospital,' Bob said. 'Couldn't we save time by meeting him somewhere?'

By the time the sun went down, there was a long streak of 'mackerel sky' betokening rain overhead; and William had promised to be at Heathrow by noon next day.

After he left, Fran sat alone in her study, incredulous at the extraordinary workings of fate. Whichever path her thoughts took, she came to the place where they stuck on a silly, superstitious, half-held but entirely optimistic assurance that Aunt Esther would take the contagion of bad luck with her to her grave that very afternoon. That what had happened to Jane had led so quickly to Charlie being located was only a coincidence . . . but then William said history was made up of coincidences. Like a series of fish-hooks, he said, one thing causing another.

There might be real clouds in the real sky for the first time for weeks, but the metaphorical clouds were surely lifting. Perhaps they would soon dare to look forward again.

She thought back to her visit to Castle Hill. It was only two days since Bob had discovered Nick's mother in the church. Now, already, she had noted they were 'Bob' and 'Jane' to each other; that the big room was cleaner and tidier and more homely than she had ever seen it; and that there had been a smell of delicious cooking in the air there. If only they had found Nick no worse, she thought that for the moment she dared not ask for more.

When the telephone bell roused her from her reverie, she was almost afraid to answer it, but George Bridgefoot sounded glad.

'I thought you'd like to know that we have a new grandchild,' he said. 'Both well, thank God.'

She gulped. The fish-hooks were working. 'Congratulations!' she said. 'What is it?' There was a pause that was a fraction too long. 'A girl. Big and bouncy and named after me. Georgina. How do you like that?'

So there had been as much disappointment as his Christian philosophy would allow. Three granddaughters, but still only one grandson. Did she dare ask after Charles? Of course, she must.

He had refused to get up since Saturday morning. Rosemary had insisted on sending again for the specialist from Cambridge whom Brian had engaged after Alex's visit. He had been this morning, but had said nothing new.

Reluctant to lose a willing ear, George chatted on. They hadn't had much sleep last night, waiting for news of Lucy; and Aunt Esther's funeral – service at the chapel, interment in the new part of the churchyard – was arranged for two o'clock this afternoon. Rosy had had a very busy morning.

Following the fashion left from Victorian days, the visit of a doctor meant cleaning the bedroom, changing the bed and 'sprucing up' the patient as far as possible. She had made Charles take a bath and shave, and he had stood by the open window till his bed was ready to get into again.

'If only it would rain, I'm sure I should feel better,' he had said.

'So should we all,' George said. 'If we could only get enough of a shower to lay the dust, it'd be a blessing. It makes everybody feel lifeless. Charles sleeps most of the time. I hope he will this afternoon, because we've got to leave him by himself while we're at the funeral.'

Fran heard the wistful half-invitation for her to stand in. He was thinking that his grandson should not be left alone in his present state of mind. She volunteered at once.

By two p.m. William would be on his way back with what they hoped might be a panacea for Charles at his side. If only their remedy worked! Fran felt a chilling frisson run down her spine when she remembered that it had been Saturday that the news of Miss Palmer's death had reached Temperance Farm. Death was in the air; the crisis had come; Charles was about to give up.

Sophie was leaving early to attend Miss Palmer's funeral, in company with most of her generation. She had never had much to do with the deceased, and what she did know of her she disliked intensely; but 'respect for the dead' was part of Sophie's creed. It was one of the few remnants of the past Fran was glad to have shed.

At one fifteen she left a scribbled note for William suggesting that he take Charlie straight to Temperance instead of going to Castle Hill, and set out. If William had made good time, they could get there before anyone else returned from the funeral.

Charles was sleepy, though he raised his eyelids and courteously acknowledged her presence. He didn't want to talk. Fran sat by his window. It was not that she feared leaving him by himself, but that she didn't want to be by herself in a house geared to, and gearing itself up for, death. The first drops of rain spattered on the window and the air immediately cooled. She hoped it was only a shower, because a funeral in a downpour was enough to shake anybody's nerves.

The rain had calmed her restless charge, and she was almost at dozing point herself when William softly opened the door and stood back to let Charlie in. The girl was as brown as a nut, thinner than she had been, but, in spite of her long journey, fresh as a daisy. Fran had no time to escape, and William crept silently to her side.

Charlie went to the side of the bed and leaned over Charles.

He turned on to his back, but did not open his eyes. He frowned as he sniffed the faint elusive scent that reminded him of oxlips. He didn't want to open his eyes in case it went away. Charlie bent nearer, and Fran had a momentary glimpse of huge eyes about to brim over.

'Charles,' the girl said. They could hear the tears in her voice. She didn't attempt to touch him.

'Lambkin?' he said, unbelieving. 'My lambkin?'

Fran knew they ought to go, but to move now would break the magic spell.

Charlie took from a little bag she was clutching the dried-up wisp of the daisy buttonhole she had made Charles at Beth's wedding.

'I took it as a keepsake of you, Charles. Look!' He watched, still spellbound, as she dropped it on to the floor, and set her foot on it.

'Nine daisies,' she said, but she got no farther. He held out his arms, and Fran and William crept out and shut the door.

While William and Bob had been engaged in tracking down Charlie's whereabouts, Jane was at the hospital. The doctor had asked to see her. The blow to Nick's head was causing pressure on the brain, which could only be relieved by surgery. There were risks, of course, not only for his life, but that he might be rendered permanently handicapped, either physically or mentally or both.

For the first time, she was afraid; till now she had been stoically fatalistic, expecting nothing more than that her son's life would end in the same doomed way it had begun and had had to be lived. But three days of having a multitude of little human-kindnesses thrust upon her had broken down twenty years of stoic self-discipline and independence. She had begun to rely on Bob already, and wished him by her side now to help her bear this added burden. It was she who had to make the crucial decision whether or not to risk surgery. She asked for, and was granted, forty-eight hours to make up her mind.

But she must not allow herself any delusion that she was not still facing an inimical fate alone; at this very moment Bob was helping William to trace and bring home his missing daughter. Her brief respite from desert-island solitude was over. She should have known that her refuge was only a temporary one. She would be neither needed nor wanted once Bob's daughter was home. She regretted telling Bob of her plea to her father, and her angry declaration that she would never bother him again. For Nick's sake, she might have to.

On her way to the car park, she called, without hope, at the post office.

A letter with a London postmark awaited her. She tore it open and read it. 'Effendi' had been abroad on a diplomatic mission, and only by chance had seen her appeal on his return. He hoped it was not now too late for him to help. He thought it wise to say no more at this juncture than that if she would name the place and time, he would meet her, without prejudice, he hoped, on either side. It was too much to expect that they would be able to leap over a gap of twenty years easily, but nevertheless, he would sign himself still her loving 'Effendi'.

She went into the telephone kiosk outside the post office to steady her trembling and to read the letter again. Diplomatic from beginning to end, she thought, cynically. The letter was not the warm, loving, forgiving, welcoming response she had secretly hoped for. But . . . she had to be fair. She had given him no chance till now to show any sort of feeling towards her. She had hurt him; she had left him; she had never tried to make contact with him. She could hardly blame him now for being cautious.

She had known, from glimpsing his name in newspapers occasionally, that he was still active in high diplomatic circles. Her mother was already dead by the time of her own downfall. She could have made contact with her father through London at any time in the last twenty years, but apart from her iron resolve not to, she had considered it very unlikely that so attractive and eligible a man had not remarried. She was no wiser about that, even now.

Her thoughts were chaotic. If Charlie had not been found, her instinct would have been to ignore her father's belated reply and trust to the shelter of Bob Bellamy's wings. It was not herself, though, but Nick she had to think of. She must not be too proud to accept financial help, if nothing else.

Common sense and resolution returned to her. She went back into the post office and sent a telegram, suggesting a meeting at the main reception door of the hospital tomorrow at eleven a.m. 'Decision urgent,' she added.

Bob needed no telling, when she met him in the car park, that something was amiss. He wasted no time in getting out of the city, and at the first opportunity stopped the car. The hand he felt for was cold and shaking. He put an arm round her, and pulled her head on to his shoulder. 'Now tell me,' he said.

She longed to pour out everything, but she had had just enough time to think ... If she told him the truth about her father, the social gap he would imagine would prevent Bob from continuing to treat her as the waif he had picked up in the church. Besides, if Charlie proved to be hostile to her and she had to leave Castle Hill, her father would provide her with the excuse of doing it with dignity, and without appearing to discard Bob's kindness and hospitality. He had his dignity, too, and she wanted him to keep it. He was all too vulnerable to that kind of wound.

So she told him about Nick, and asked him to drive on. She wanted to be where she could be quiet, and think.

He had more or less forgotten Charlie in caring for Jane by the time Fran rang to tell him what had happened up at Temperance Farm. Fran promised that Charlie would be taken home to Castle Hill in time for bed, if Bob didn't mind her spending as much time as she could this evening with Charles.

He went back to tell Jane. They had discussed her problem from every angle. He begged her to be strong and opt for surgery, now, at once.

'While I'm still here, and you're here too,' he said. 'How could you manage by yourself? He may need a man to lift him. We've got to take the risk.'

What an extraordinary thing for him to say, she thought. As if the decision itself was partly his responsibility.

'Will you be all right if I go up and feed Winnie?' he said. 'Or would you rather come with me? I don't like leaving you worrying by yourself.'

'You forget,' she said. 'I've been by myself, except for Nick, for nearly twenty years. I've had to make every decision by myself. So while you've gone, I'll move my things out of Charlie's room. Where to?'

'The big bedroom at the back,' he said. 'You can get to that up the back stairs if you want to be private.' He wasn't in the least 'fussed' about anything; in her uncertainty and anxiety, his matter-of-factness had calmed and heartened her. Briskly, she set about moving her things and leaving Charlie's room just as she had found it, taking her few belongings up to her new quarters.

The bedroom was very large, and felt a bit empty and lonely, but from one of its windows there was a view across to the little church. She saw Bob come out of the porch of it carrying his hat in his hands. She forgot Nick and Charlie in watching him, wondering what on earth he could be carrying with such care in his hat.

She was not to know that he had been sitting in the church consulting his sixth sense on her behalf, and at the same time considering where the events of the day had left him.

Charlie would be happy now, but not at home with him for long. If she eventually married Charles Bridgefoot, he had no need to bother much about her future in terms of money. To put it bluntly, she really didn't need him any longer. Jane, and Jane's son, did. If keeping a roof over their heads *here* meant selling his fen farm, then it would be sold. He and he only could buy Castle Hill at farmland price. Bailey would raise his bid, but he thought he could trust the college to keep its word. He could but try.

Jane was sitting waiting with their supper ready when he came in. He went up to her and emptied his hat into her lap — two six-week-old kittens with Siamese blue eyes in tabby-striped heads with black ears and black pointed noses. They were adorable, looking up at her with anxious, frightened innocence. Then, reassured, big brother put out a paw and knocked little sister over. She grabbed his ear in her tiny mouth, and Jane could have sworn that she winked. It was so funny that Jane threw back her head and laughed, the sound of it ringing through the big room like music. He had never heard her laugh, or barely seen her smile, before.

He had already started on the sandwiches. He swallowed his mouthful and his face cleared. 'To hear you laugh like that is worth a Jew's eye,' he said. 'Don't move, or they'll be frightened. Have a sandwich.' He was as pleased as a child. His kitten ploy had worked.

'I'll go up before Charlie comes in,' she said. 'She'll want you to yourself.' In the event, that had proved to be an unnecessary precaution against any difficulty. William had briefed Charlie in any case, and tonight it would not have worried her if she had found her father keeping a harem. Not that the Jane she remembered remotely resembled a seductive houri – but a 'plain Jane' about the place was exactly what was required. The last thing her Dad needed was any reminder of her mother, Charlie thought.

76

Next morning, Jane stood on the steps of the hospital, waiting. She was still painfully thin, but a few days of good food and rest had made her skin less sallow and her general appearance less haggard. She had washed her hair, so that its very slight suggestion of a wave gave it more bulk, and the day was warm enough to allow her one cheap summer dress to look at least clean and neat. She watched her father coming towards her, tall, upright and handsome, his well-cut suit and polished shoes marking him as a well-to-do city gent. His hair had turned grey and he had thickened a bit round the waist, but his bearing and mien were still those of a man used to giving orders he expected to be instantly obeyed.

He approached the steps on which she stood, consulted his watch and prepared to pass her by. There was no sign of recognition.

'Effendi,' she said. Never had she been more grateful for the cognomen. She could not have uttered the word 'Father'. He swung round and stared at her.

'Jane?' he said, haltingly. She nodded, longing to turn and

run. He didn't know her, and he didn't seem to want to. There had been nothing resembling pleasure on his face. He put out his hand and she took it, but he did not release hers. He held it so tightly that she could not withdraw it, and in the silence his face lost some of its inscrutability.

He bent over her hand and kissed it. 'My dear,' he said, 'this is a very public place.'

He turned, and began to walk away. Was he abandoning her — and Nick — just like that? Her heart-strings had been twisted at the sight of him, but . . . it was too late. She didn't belong to his world any longer, was part of a simpler, cruder, more honest world than his. Where total strangers could and would help each other. Let him go . . . except for Nick. She clenched her teeth against unbidden tears.

He had stopped, though, and was beckoning her to follow. She had forgotten that in his world he expected underlings to follow where he led.

'We can't talk here,' he said. 'I drove down, so my car is in the car park. We'll go out to one of the villages and find a quiet place.'

The large pleasant dining-room of the inn was still empty when they sat down. He was in complete command of himself and the situation.

'Where shall we start?' he said. 'Please remember that I know nothing.'

'What do you want to know?' she said.

'The essential things. Your mother was dead, and I had had to go away. When I got back, you'd gone. Everyone had presumed that you were joining me. All I ever knew was what you told me in the note you left. You were pregnant, and for my sake you must disappear. It isn't easy to do that, so I knew you must have had help – presumably from the father of your child. I did try to trace you – please believe that. But you had left no clue at all. I hoped, until I gave up hope, that you would at least let me know you were safe.'

She nodded. She believed him.

'I gather that the child lived?'

She could only nod again; he was still living, if lying inert like a wax image could be called that.

'My grandchild. Boy or girl?' For the first time, his eyes belied his expressionless face.

'Nicholas – after you,' she said. She was unprepared for his next blunt question. 'Whose child is he?' There was no diplomacy now. His professional calm had been shaken.

'I was so young, Effendi. So silly. So flattered to get that sort of attention. And you had left me in his charge . . .'

She thought for a moment that he might be going to have a stroke. His face suffused with blood, then turned grey. She watched it grow old before her eyes.

'Are you telling me the truth? My best friend, almost as old as I, with children of his own nearly your own age?'

She looked down at her hands in her lap. They were already beginning to be less rough and work-worn. When she had next week's wages, she would buy some hand-cream. Think about anything rather than look up at her stricken father . . . though of course she must. It was he, now, who needed help.

'So you see, Effendi, why I had to disappear, and how I managed it. It would have meant ruin for him and disgrace for you. And there was poor Aunt Tessie, his wife. How could I let her suspect? It would have killed her. He was deputizing for you, and had everything in his hands. I might as well have been put into the diplomatic bag.'

'He is dead,' he said, dully. 'Thank God for that. And to think how I grieved for him! I presume he provided well for you and the child?'

She shook her head. 'He gave me all he could raise in cash,' she said. 'I wrote to Oxford to say that I shouldn't be taking my place there, and then hid – in London. The money lasted till Nick was born . . . – in a hospital in the East End. There really isn't much more to tell. Times just after the war ended were very hard, as you know. How could I work, with a baby? There were thousands like me, much more used to work than I was. I was afraid that if I even applied for help, I would be asked questions that would give away my connection with you. I managed. I shouldn't have asked for help now, but for the accident.'

'What accident? What has happened, my dearest?' he said.

The endearment raised the sluice. Her story flooded out, telling him everything; from the first terrible realization of her plight, alone, without qualification or experience, apart from the baby. In Cambridge she had seen Bert Bleasby's advert for a housekeeper in the local paper. She had not known that such a place, such primitive conditions, or such a boor of a man could exist in England, but by that time she had no resources left, and it did provide food and shelter. Bleasby had one overriding characteristic which had been of use to her: he would do anything to avoid actually parting with money. She had made her bargain with him, for just those basic needs and no wages. For what else she or Nick needed she had been forced to seek casual work in the fields and orchards. It had grown easier as time went by. Once Nick started school, he acquired two special friends whose families thereafter had more or less kept him clothed and fed, as well as giving him what few treats he had. She had never been afraid of Bleasby taking any advantage of her, because she had been aware from the start how much in awe of her he had been. With a cynical smile she told how she had learned by trial and error how to cook, and what hard work was. By that time, her employer knew he had got the best of the bargain, and which side his bread was buttered on.

The lunches her father had ordered were placed before them, and pushed aside uneaten. He never took his eyes from her face and she saw him wince time after time at her calm, uncomplaining recital of fact. She spared him nothing but the last act of the drama, stopping her tale at the point of Nick's accident. It was pity for her listener that staunched the flow of words just there.

'Have I hurt you very much, Effendi? Forgive me. None of it was your fault. I had to tell you, though, before we went back to the hospital.'

'I want to see my grandson,' he said. 'Come, let's go.'

Standing by Nick's bed was an ordeal for both, each tortured by what might have been. Nick's placid, handsome face was proof enough of his parentage on both sides.

Despair struggled against raging anger in the man's heart, as he writhed under the indubitable truth, so plain in Nick's handsome features, of his protégé's treachery. Nick was almost a double of the young aristocratic friend whom he had befriended and encouraged, helped and promoted, and whose early death he had mourned so sincerely. Since then, he had cared for the welfare of his friend's widow and his two legitimate sons, while all the time nobody had been caring for this one, or his mother. He could only do his best to make some recompense now. If it was not too late.

He produced his card and requested a consultation with the doctor-in-charge. Jane was amused to see it work the same kind of magic as it always had done. The busy doctor would see him at once.

'Stay with the boy,' he told Jane. She obeyed, and sat down by the bed as she had sat so often before, except that this time she began to talk softly to him. She had so much to tell him, now that her silence had at last been broken.

When her father came back, he had regained his usual mien of high authority, but before leaving the bedside he bent to kiss his grandson's forehead. Then he led Jane out to the privacy of his car.

He had acted without her consent, he said, because he feared that her pride might still get between them, and that she might reject his proposal. It had been agreed that he should arrange for Nick to be transferred to a London clinic run by the best brain surgeon in England, whom he knew personally. The clinic was in easy reach of the spacious service flat he had recently acquired pending coming retirement.

'Whatever he needs he shall have,' he said, 'including attendance after surgery if that proves to be necessary. And his grandfather's company whenever possible. Jane, will you come to me too?'

She had read somewhere what a philosopher had written, that you must have chaos in yourself to give birth to a star. In those few seconds before she answered, the chaos that had been in her mind so long gave birth to order. Confused anxieties and unformed apprehensions suddenly took on clear outlines, and began to fit together into a whole. She knew now what she had been afraid of for so long, and had not dared to look in the face. It had been *the inevitable parting from Nick*.

He had had to grow up and, one way or another, he would soon leave her, finally, of course, for another woman. She saw with great clarity why she had been so fatalistic about the accident – if he were to die, it was only the dreaded parting come too suddenly, and too finally. But she knew now, with a blinding flash of faith, that he wasn't going to die. He was going to live to fulfil all the promise he had shown, however long the process of recovery took.

But the time for parting had come. The long interval of his coma had already separated them. She must allow the umbilical cord to be cut and let Nick take his new first steps alone. It all made such sense.

She laid her hand over her father's as it clutched the rim of the steering wheel, and she met his eyes unafraid.

'Effendi,' she said, 'I knew you'd be able to work miracles for me. But Father . . . you were right when you wrote that we shouldn't be able to leap lightly over the last twenty years. You can see, and I have told you, what I have become – a hardworking countrywoman. I shouldn't and couldn't fit into your world, now. But Nick can, and will. He'll make you proud of him. I robbed you of so much. Let me give some of it back to you. I'll come to visit often, but Nick must have the chance to live his own life. Please.'

'And what about you, my dearest? What will you do? Let me buy you your cottage. Somewhere that Nick and I can come and visit.'

She kissed his hand as a gesture of gratitude for the offer, but shook her head.

'Some time, perhaps, but not yet. I think I have a great debt to repay first. You haven't heard the very last bit of my story.' It was almost more than he could take, but she continued to give him all the details.

'So don't you see, Effendi? "A friend in need is a friend indeed." It is less than a week since he found me in the church. I never knew such loving-kindness could exist. I had to work out why, in his case, it did. In the first place it's because he's such an extraordinary character, though completely uneducated except in all the things that matter. Then I saw how lonely he was, and that his need to have something to give to was almost as great as mine to be given to. I can't just abandon him now to his loneliness again, and go off transformed into a fairy princess. Nor at all, I think, till the crisis about his farm is resolved.'

She found herself telling him everything she knew about Bob, describing in detail the strange house, the plethora of animals, how he had quite literally spoon-fed her, how he had offered to sell his birthright to secure Castle Hill for Nick to come back to, even the incident of the kittens. He listened, only here and there interposing a question.

'No,' he said, when she had paused. 'You mustn't leave him. I can see why you are telling yourself that you must repay him. But that isn't the real reason why you won't come away, is it? You love him, don't you?'

Shock took her breath away, and colour flooded up and over her startled face. She hid it in his shoulder. When she looked up at last, the proud jut of her chin was back, and her straight gaze met his without flinching.

'I didn't know, Effendi. But I know now. He mustn't know and he won't guess because it would never cross his mind as a possibility. He's such a humble, simple man. So I'll just go on being his paid housekeeper. He'll think I need caring for more than ever now that Nick has to be in London – which is all I shall tell him, if you don't mind.'

'As long as you let me help somehow,' he said. 'Tell him as much or as little as you please. Are you sure he has no dreams concerning you?'

'If he ever has, he'll never tell me,' she said.

'Then when the right time comes, you must tell him,' he said.

He left almost at once, and went his way to start making the necessary arrangements for Nick's transfer. Jane went back to Castle Hill a very different woman from the one who had set out that morning. Several new ingredients had been added to her recipe for life.

77

'That girl,' said Sir Rupert Marland to George, 'has a kind of uncanny magic about her.'

George agreed. If Sir Rupert had declared he could see a halo round Charlie, George would not have disputed it. She had become the darling of the Old Glebe and Temperance Bridgefoots, even Brian. (In private, George had told Brian he was proud to have a son big and wise enough to admit his own mistakes.)

The reason for Sir Rupert's observation was that Georgina Teresa appeared to have made up her mind that one way or another, she was going to be the star of her own christening. She was now seven weeks old, and as Lucy was determined to have her christened in Old Swithinford church, there had been a fair amount of pressure put on her to get the ceremony over before harvest season began.

It had never ceased to fill George with wonder when the ears began to change colour and overnight a field of barley was ready to be cut; after which there would be no let-up, day or night, it seemed, until they could say that all was safely gathered in. In these days the huge tractors and ploughs followed the straw-balers in, and the landscape became patchworked with varying earthcolours until the golden panorama disappeared – far too soon, in George's opinion. Brian was jubilant when they reached that stage, but his father had never got used to it.

'We hadn't used to *start* harvesting till August,' he would say wistfully. 'My old Dad used to say, "If you ain't started reaping on the twelfth of August, you can on the thirteenth." And it went on right up to the end of September, in them days when you had to tie the sheaves by hand and then stouk 'em and cart 'em and stack 'em and thresh 'em.

'But didn't them stouked fields used to look a picture! And a stackyard full o' corn-stacks, all thatched against the rain till you could get a threshing-tackle when your turn come round. Now it's all over and done with and ploughed up ready to start again in three weeks. But you can't put the clock back. Not that I should want to, if I could. We get bigger yields for half the work. But I miss the feeling of it. It don't *feel* like a proper harvest used to.' He was in the sort of seventh heaven on this Sunday, though, with family and friends gathered together under his own roof. The immediate cause of Sir Rupert's remark was that Georgina Teresa, who had behaved herself reasonably well in church, was now demonstrating the power of her lungs. She had been passed from mother to one grandmother after the other, and finally to her father, but still she bawled.

Then Charlie stepped up and relieved Alex of the red-faced, yelling infant, and with one hand supporting the little bottom in a firm grip, with the other she pressed the tiny head close to the spot between her shoulder and her neck. Georgina gave a final gasping little sob or two, stuck her fist up to her mouth and went to sleep. Charlie handed her back to Alex and went to find Charles.

'How on earth did she do that?' asked Lucy.

'Well, I know the theory, but I've never before seen it put so effectively into practice,' Alex replied. 'The baby gets frightened and misses the safety of the womb, where it can feel its mother's heart beating. She used the pulse in her neck, and it worked.'

'I don't wonder,' said Sir Rupert. 'I'd start to bawl myself if I thought she'd cuddle me like that! Your Charles is a lucky young blighter.'

George looked across at the young couple, now sitting side by side at Fran and William's feet. Charles lacked the bronzing that work in the fields usually produced at this time of the year, but otherwise he was himself again.

'She's agreed to marry him, but not yet,' he told Sir Rupert. 'She's only just nineteen, and Charles not yet quite twenty-one. As far as I'm concerned, it couldn't be too soon. She's agreed to an official engagement when he's twenty-one, but that's all. She's old-fashioned, in some ways.'

Sir Rupert studied her thoughtfully. 'Does she give her reasons?'

'Yes,' George said. 'It isn't financial, because at twenty-one I shall make Charles a partner and he'll come into what I've already settled on him. And she wants him as much as he wants her. She just says she knows what will make them happiest in the long run. I asked her to tell me what she meant, if she could, and she said she couldn't really explain except that it was "a feeling" like her father gets sometimes. He's a very out-of-the-ordinary sort of chap. She said she had thought a lot about it, and tried to tell me. She said there was never any doubt from the moment they met that they were made for each other, but she had to find out if she was good enough for him. And she said she wants them to be like them two from Benedict's when they're that old. She's worked it out that part of William and Fran's secret is that they didn't rush things – she talked a lot to William in the car when he was bringing her home. She said they'd learned to love each other in a dozen different ways before they ever went to bed together, and that they respect each other. She's insisting on going ahead with training to be a vet – only now she'll try to do it in Cambridge. She wants to earn Charles's respect, she says. She's old-fashioned in a lot of ways.'

'But she's in front of the times in others,' Sir Rupert answered. 'This women's lib business is going to mean there are going to be a lot more female professionals in the future. Though it's a long training. Is she old-fashioned enough to keep him waiting so long?'

'I'm on her side, though I hope it won't take too long. You know, I think there was a lot to be said for a bit of proper courting. Only I want to see the Bridgefoot name made certain of before I go.'

'I don't think you need worry,' Sir Rupert said, his eyes still on Charlie. 'She'll find a way. I'd say she's a girl in a million.'

78

By the third week in July, harvest was in full swing. The weather was ideal for quick gathering and garnering, and the sun blazed down through long days on combines, tractors, trailers and balers. Farmers and labourers alike turned brown or red according to their colouring and went home late in the evening to sleep the few hours of the short nights as if they had been drugged.

It was difficult for those who were not immediately concerned with getting in the crops not to feel themselves part of it. William had said goodbye to his room in college for his sabbatical year. For the first few days he lazed, unable to believe that he had time to do nothing; but the fever of harvest in the air made him restless, wanting to be part of it. Fran was wallowing in nostalgia, anxious to be out and about to enjoy it, so they walked and drove about, offering themselves as couriers and carriers of messages, food and drink, replacement parts of machinery, and even the odd clean shirt to replace a sweat-sodden one for George who wouldn't work without a shirt at all, as Charles did. His fair skin turned rose pink, then red, peeled horribly and then tanned. As Fran said, it didn't prevent him looking like a young Greek god. Very often they would find Charlie working by his side, though only when her father had no need of her as driver or odd-job man.

Greg was taking a break before the whole load of responsibility descended on him, and went about dazed with the beauty of the landscape. He tossed off watercolour after watercolour, confidence in his own ability growing every time he brought off a picture just as he had intended it to be. Jess and Anne were putting in extra time because the hotel and sports centre was booked to capacity.

Beth and Elyot came home while the harvest fever was at its height, looking relaxed and happy, though wondering why they had stayed away so long, considering how beautiful England was, especially the Old Rectory. They strolled up to Benedict's on the day after their return, and sat in the garden drinking tea and eating Sophie's feather-light choux buns filled with cream and raspberries fresh from the garden.

'It's good to have you back,' Fran said. 'You'd be surprised what a gap was left when you two went away.'

'If we were playing the game of "Book Titles",' Beth said, 'I'd ask you to cap that remark with one.'

William and Fran looked at each other, and then almost shouted simultaneously, '*Three Came Home*?' Beth, blushing delightfully, nodded.

'Whatever are they a-playing at out there?' Sophie asked of Ned who came within earshot of her at the kitchen door. 'A-hugging and a-kissing of each other like long-lost cousins, as you might say. I told 'im they ought to put their 'ats on Too much sun on your 'ead ain't good for nobody. They're a-going on as if they're all got sunstroke.'

Among all this sort of excitement, several things had happened that without harvest-fever would have taken on far greater importance than they had done. For one thing, Charlie had got her place at Cambridge's Veterinary School. Great plans were afoot for a combined twenty-first birthday and engagement party at Christmas.

Then during William's first week of freedom, Roland had arrived with two pieces of news. One was that Sue had at last been traced – working with Mother Teresa in India! He was honest enough to say that he didn't know how to view that revelation – whether to be even more worried or whether to jump for joy. One thing it most certainly meant was that she would not be around, throwing either a real or a self-induced fit, when Monica came to full term. He had had a long talk with Sue's father, who had advised him to live his own life and let Sue live hers, since it was quite clear by now that there was no telling what she might do next and that she would listen to nobody. As a result of this, and at her father's urging, he was seeking to join a firm of architects in Cambridge, and was hopeful.

Bob Bellamy was having to harvest two farms at once, almost thirty miles apart. The prospect had not worried him, because it was a long time since he had felt so full of content and vigour. Since the days of his youth in the fen, when women would still sometimes carry out hot meals to their menfolk at 'dockey-time' and keep up a constant supply of cold tea in bottles hung down the dykesides, his personal needs had never been so well cared for. He came in from his fields on Castle Hill to meals ready and waiting, and after the long day went back to the house to find there was nothing left for him to do. Jane had fed all the animals, including Winnie, laid out clean clothes for him and often had a bath already running when he appeared, sweat-streaked and coated with dust, over the doorstep.

On the long days spent down the fen, it was an even greater treat to get back . . . though once on his native holding he regretted that it was likely to be the last harvest he gathered there. Time was flying by and he now had only weeks to make his final decision.

In the second week of harvest, Jane had to leave him to go and be in London while Nick had the vital operation. All preliminary testing had led to a favourable prognosis.

'How long will you have to be away?' Bob asked.

'No longer than I can help, in the middle of harvest,' she replied. 'But I must go to be near him, till it's over. At least a week, I think.'

'Where will you stop?' he asked anxiously.

She hated lying to him, but there was no alternative. She said she had booked a room in a cheap hotel almost next door to the hospital.

He looked uneasy, even distressed, and more than usually bashful as he asked, 'Will you have enough money? For food, I mean, and bus fares and such? And things to take Nick if – when – he comes to and knows you again? Let me give you some.'

'I promise to ask if I need any. But you've been paying me well and keeping me, so I've saved quite a bit. And don't say "*if*" Nick comes round. He will. I know it. So do you, don't you?'

His reply satisfied her. 'Do you think I should let you go by yourself, harvest or no harvest, if I had any doubt at all? Not likely! When you come back, we shall soon be making plans where to put him till he's on his feet again. Whatever happens about the farm, I shall be here till next Lady Day. Let's take one day at a time.'

She had to promise to ring as soon as there was any news. He took her to the station and insisted on giving her two five-pound notes. It made her feel mean and guilty, so to be deceiving him; but the alternative of telling the truth, and creating an embarrassing situation that would end by her having to leave him altogether, she could not contemplate. His presence surrounded her like a perimeter fence, so that in his ambience she felt utterly and completely secure. She had never expected such comfort, and reminded herself every day that if she wanted to give more than he wanted to take, she was still far happier than she had ever expected to be again.

Her father awaited her at Liverpool Street in a chauffeured limousine, and she was whisked off to a flat of unimaginable luxury. This time, the conversation flowed more easily between them. 'Effendi' had been going to see Nick every day, keeping a careful check on everything he was paying for, for one thing, as he said, but really because he couldn't keep away.

'I was afraid of retirement,' he told her. 'Now I have another object in life. Well, two, though you won't let me look after you. Tell me more about your life with your man from the fens.'

She was quite happy to do so, and recounted details of the harvest season as he had never heard them before, from the inside, so to speak. She told him of her delight in her two kittens, Ali and Baba, as she had named them. She was still a bit tense and nervous, and to talk about familiar things helped a lot.

He waited till she had settled down a bit before informing her that the operation on Nick was arranged for not the next day, but the day after that. She wondered why she had been inveigled there a day too soon. She was not left long in the dark. She had to have time to become his daughter in appearance.

'So if you don't mind me saying so, my dearest,' he said tentatively, 'I suggest that we spend tomorrow shopping for clothes. You can hardly be seen going into that palace of a clinic in such garments as you are wearing now. We'll buy you a complete new wardrobe, and then stuff all your present ones into those unspeakable old suitcases and put them down the rubbish chute.'

'No! No!' she cried, alarmed at the suggestion. 'That would give the game away when I got back, and let Bob know how I have been deceiving him. Oh, Father, I am sorry – I didn't give it a thought that I should be letting you down. Of course I would love to go shopping with you for some new clothes, but I must keep my old ones to go back in – and the suitcases. He was so afraid that I might not have enough money. He thinks Nick is in a National Health hospital and that I'm staying in the cheapest hotel close by. I shall have to leave any new clothes here. He insisted on giving me these' – she produced the two five-pound notes from her purse – 'just as the train was leaving.' She looked down at them, then at the opulence all round her, and burst into tears.

He was very patient, very kind. She apologized. 'I never thought I should hear a woman cry at the thought of new clothes,' he said wryly. 'I think I'm jealous. You must love him very much.'

'Don't laugh, Effendi. You don't know him yet, and I haven't had much chance to love anybody but Nick till very recently. Love isn't a limited quantity, in any case. There's plenty left for you.'

'I wasn't laughing. I'm only afraid of you getting hurt again. Buy yourself something new with his ten pounds, and see what effect it has on him. And while you're about it tomorrow, I think you should get something done to your hair, too. Have it nicely washed and set, and buy yourself a bit of make-up.'

She wondered, rather shaken, just how badly she had been neglecting herself, and what a scarecrow she must look. In her sumptuous bedroom, she viewed herself in her mirror and, seeing herself through her father's eyes, was aghast.

The subject of her appearance was, as her father had hoped, enough to distract her from too much worry about Nick as the hours passed. Her father's bounty seemed to her limitless, as they shopped in the most expensive places. With Bob's ten pounds, she bought a well-cut, plain 'natural' linen suit. With her hair trimmed, styled and set, the mirror showed her a very different Jane when dressed next morning for her visit to the clinic. Nick still lay supine, but he was warm under her lips as they turned to leave. She dared not look forward. Thinking backwards over only two days, she heard Bob's voice reassuring her. It was much more comforting than the consultant's measured tones.

When she rang Castle Hill the next night, she could only manage three words before crying into the telephone. 'All is well,' she said, and when he said nothing in reply she knew that he was too moved to answer her. She put the telephone down.

The first night she was away, Bob sat in his chair with a lapful of cats, and faced the fact that he had not known how much he would miss her. Charlie had taken over her duties, so he was not missing what she did for him. He was missing her. The second evening was worse, and the third worse still. After Charles had fetched Charlie away, he sat again with his animals, physically tired out and rather despondently looking across at her empty chair till he fell asleep.

He was back in his childhood dream again, standing under the picture at Benedict's, looking up at the beautiful lady who seemed always to look down on him with the wonder of love in her eyes. She could have been Fran, except that Fran never looked at *him* like that. No woman ever had done.

The telephone bell disturbed him, and he answered it. She only spoke three words, but the sound of her voice had made his heart lurch. He had, of course, been expecting the vital news of Nick, but altogether it had overwhelmed him. Now that the operation was over, Jane would soon be back. He sat down again, fell asleep almost immediately, and went back into his dream, though something was different this time. He struggled to wake, and though still half-asleep knew what the difference was. The pictured lady had had Jane's face, not Fran's. Now he knew why he was missing her. He loved not Fran less, but Jane more, and in a very different way.

He sat long with Bonzo's head on his knee and Jane's kittens in his lap. There were ghosts with him tonight. The worst of them was the remembrance of that too smart, too made-up, too sexy creature he had once called his wife.

Charlie came in radiant, even before he told her the good news about Nick. He was glad to know she would be happy in the future, though he wouldn't be now. Not without Jane. In the picture or out of it, she was the high-born lady, as inacessible in real life as in his dream. He had always known that she was a lady, far above him. He stroked Bonzo's head, and said, 'You love her as well, don't you, old fellow? She'll come back to us for a little while. Till she meets somebody of her own sort. Then you and me'll go back down the fen. You and me and the cats.'

But every time he stirred in his sleep that night, he heard Jane's voice saying, 'All is well.' It was too much of an omen for a full-blooded fenman to ignore. In spite of himself, he found himself whistling as he set out for another long day's work.

Four days later, he went to meet her at the station. He recognized the battered old suitcase before he recognized her. The face that for so long had shown her desperate anxiety and grief for her son had changed shape and colour. Her eyes were alive as he had never seen them before. Her expression told him that, as he would have phrased it, she was no longer having 'to set a hard heart against hard sorrow'. The plain Jane who had gone away looking like what she was – a domestic help – had come back looking younger, smart and happy. Apparently as pleased to be back as he was to have her 'home'.

Once in the car alone with him, she confessed to being glad to be out of London. 'I wouldn't live there now,' she said, 'for all the tea in China.'

'You don't half look smart,' he said. 'I didn't recognize you at first. I'm so glad Nick's going to be all right.'

She flushed. 'Bob,' she said. 'I do hope you don't mind. I felt so terribly shabby going to that London hospital that – I spent your ten pounds on this outfit I'm wearing. I'll pay you back a bit at a time out of my wages.'

He laughed from pure joy. 'Ten pound?' he said. 'You should see the stubs in my chequebook. Iris wouldn't have been seen out in a frock that cost less than fifty! Don't you ever mention that ten pound to me again. But you're like Charlie. You make whatever you're wearing look expensive.'

She didn't know how to deal with compliments like that. She knew only that she was utterly, deliriously happy to be back in his ambience again.

She changed her new suit as soon as they got back to Castle Hill and started work at once. Things had been restored to the status quo ante by suppertime.

There was such an air of serenity about her now that it

affected the atmosphere. She had always had what to him was the blessed boon of stillness and silence, giving him what he had never had before, companionship that left him time for his private world of dreams. If only it could last!

'It's so quiet,' she said. 'Till you've had to endure London for more than forty-eight hours, you don't know what a boon quietness is.'

'If you think this is quiet,' he replied, 'you should see the house on my farm down the fen. When harvest's over and I can spare the time, I'll take you down for a day. Will you come?'

Of course she would. She would have gone to the world's end with him. She blushed furiously at her own thought that the place she really wanted to go to with him this minute was to bed.

79

Jane was under no illusions that her secret could be kept much longer. She would have to visit Nick as soon as he had regained comprehension enough to recognize her; she had to find out from day to day how he was, for which she would have dearly liked to have talked to her father. Instead she rang the hospital, and used the telephone to her father when both Bob and Charlie were out of the way. The reason for all this deception was the result of the long talk she had had with her father the evening of the day Nick had had his operation, after she had put the telephone down on Bob.

Her father had expected her to be in a state of nervous exhaustion after the long suspense of the day, but once she had spoken to Bob, she had let herself go and wept. They were tears of relief and joy, of course, as well as the brimming over of those held back through so many years of hardship; but they were more. Now that the great milestone of Nick's possible death had been reached and passed, she was forced to consider the road ahead. How ironic it was that after all those years of striving in penury, she was now being offered a life of ease and luxury that she no longer wanted.

Her father had offered her residence with him, or whatever she fancied wherever she wanted it. He had always been wealthy and had made a lot more money, for which he until lately had no satisfactory use. He told her so. The question of money need never worry her again, and it would help him to clear his conscience that he had been so blind, and so wrong in his judgement in the past, if she would now let him do everything he could to help her. What, he had asked her, did she want?

Her answer was unequivocal. She wanted Bob Bellamy. The one thing his money couldn't buy her. If she were still penniless, she said, Bob's love of giving might have led him to love her; but if he knew the truth, he would withdraw at once. She had felt it from the first – he had a sensitivity that made it impossible to deceive him for long. She guessed that he had already placed her above him and out of his reach.

'I could be so happy with him,' she said. 'And I believe I could make him happy. But how can I do it without hurting his pride? Fate's against me, Effendi. There's no time to let him get used to the idea. He's completely at ease with the Professor up at Benedict's, or the Commander – and with their wives. He's accepted them as friends, though they have almost had to force their friendship on him.'

And once having launched into the subject she told him everything, about Bob again and his offer to sell his family land in the fen to provide a place for Nick – if it had been necessary to care for a cripple or a brain-damaged son. Now that Nick was going to recover, he would leave the farm and all he had grown to love so much to the mercy of the developers, and creep back to his native black land to live in solitary kinship with nature.

'Either way it will break his heart,' she said. 'And mine. And mine!'

He let her cry it out, and then began to ask a lot of pertinent questions. It had been a difficult story for him to have to listen to, though as usual his face gave nothing away.

'It sounds to me that if anyone deserves you, he does,' he said. 'I hope I'll meet him, one day. I think it is your pride that has to be overcome, not his. And money talks to other people, if not to him. Trust me to do what I can. But if I do my bit, the rest will be up to you. You haven't lacked courage till now. I suggest you go back and manage to make yourself indispensible to him.'

When August had only a few more days to go, the weather began to cool a little. Bob, standing to watch the sunset at the back door, remarked that it was likely they would get the heatwave over without a storm.

Most of the harvest was now in, and work slackening up a bit. A note from Eric Choppen, in his capacity as secretary of the 'Antidevelopment Group', announced another meeting, at the hotel, on Friday evening.

'I'll go,' Bob said to her, 'but there's nothing I can do now to stop Bailey if he wants this. I've had my fen farm valued. Once, it would have bought this twice. But it is sinking, and powerful mechanical implements and artificial fertilizers have altered the value of this sort of land. My son, John, foresaw all that. I didn't. So I can't raise enough money on that to keep this. If you and Nick had been desperate, I'd have had a mortgage to make it up; but you won't need it, or me. I shouldn't want to be left here by myself with you and Charlie gone, anyway. Is'll be better back down the ol' fen.'

'When are you going to take me down the fen?' she asked. 'While this lovely weather still holds?'

'You're going to see Nick tomorrow,' he said, 'and I've still got a few bits of work I must see to. Then there's that meeting Friday night. We don't want to have to rush back. Let's go Saturday. Pack a picnic with plenty of grub. We can make tea or coffee in the old house. It's empty 'cos none o' my men'll live in a place like that – but I shall. I keep a primus stove there to make my own dockey on when I'm down there all day. It's the right time of the year to see the fen.'

She met her father the next day, and together they went to the hospital. Nick was still being sedated, but his smile told her he knew who she was. Next week, said the sister, he would probably be able to talk to them.

As they drove to the station, her father told her what he had been doing.

'Have a happy day on Saturday,' he said. 'Next time you go, perhaps Nick can go with you.'

'Don't you want to see the fen, Effendi? It's probably just as good as the desert. Bob says it has a fascination of its own.'

'So has the desert,' he said. 'You loved it once.'

'Never again!' she said. 'Give me Old Swithinford any day.'

He was delighted by her reply. She could actually laugh about it now. Her bitterness had run its course.

Bob came back from the meeting on Friday in a slightly worried and puzzled state of mind. He told her what had happened. They had drawn up an official protest about Bailey's plans for Lane's End, but hadn't mentioned the threat to Castle Hill. So he had brought it up, saying he feared he could not save it, but he thought they ought to try to prevent Bailey from getting his hands on it. Then Choppen said he had been into it, but understood that the matter might not arise. The college was considering an offer for the sale of it as it stood.

'I don't know what to make o' that. It means the college has gone back on its word to let me have first refusal. And it might mean Bailey's getting hold of it by the back door. Still, I shan't be here.'

Next morning, Jane put on one of the new outfits her father had bought, a plain soft flowered two-piece with a low-cut sleeveless top. She had filled out enough to allow her to show her neck and shoulders again, though this was the first time she had dared to wear it. Its expensively cut lines did a lot for her figure. She wondered if Bob would notice it, and had her temporary explanation ready. In the event, it was she who was surprised. She had never before seen him dressed in 'casual wear'. She was used to him always in what he called his 'working clobber', complete with a hat of some kind, or in a lounge suit as for last night's meeting.

He came down the stairs in casual trousers and a white shirt, carrying a woollen pullover. The open-necked shirt with sleeves rolled above his elbows showed him deep-bronzed by sun and wind, and his hair, fresh from a bath, stood up blue-black and wavy. He was talking to Bonzo.

'No, not today, mate. I shall have plenty of time for you soon.' He wasn't looking at her. 'Ready?' he said, and picked up the picnic bags and baskets without further comment. But once in the car, he began to tell her a bit what to expect from 'the fen'. She sat by his side, adoring him and wondering why he didn't know. She had great difficulty in keeping her mind on what he was telling her. He was, she realized, remarkably well informed.

They passed through three or four fair-sized villages, and out to a spot from which the road dipped quite suddenly for so flat a landscape. On the top of the hill he stopped the car for her to take in the view.

'This is where "the Fens" start,' he said. 'Look all round, but specially east – to your right.'

It caught her unawares. She had seen that inverted blue sky with its rim resting on the earth or ocean before, and had felt trapped beneath it in the desert as the sand stretched away to the horizon. She had no feeling of being trapped here. Just one of infinite space, infinite freedom, infinite possibility.

'If you were higher up,' he was telling her, 'you could see the sea, that way. There's nothing between us and the coast but the horizon.'

'I don't wonder you love it,' she said.

He let in the clutch without answering. They went on in silence, now gently downhill all the way. Waterways everywhere. He began to explain the system of drainage, and why here and there the banks of the waterways were so high above the road. Along by the side of a real river, now, he said, not a man-made 'cut'.

They turned off the main road into a much narrower one between a patchwork of fields, some with corn still standing, some green with potato and sugarbeet crops, some just golden stubble.

'My land starts here,' he said, and a couple of hundred yards further on he pulled the car to a halt at the foot of a rickety wooden bridge over a wide drain. 'The bridge ain't really safe for much weight,' he said. 'But the house is on the other side. We shall have to walk over. I drive over when I'm by myself, but I'm not risking you.'

She stood on the bridge and leaned on the old wooden rail. Everything she had ever heard about the black, treeless, cold, ugly, miserable fen was utterly refuted. The neglected old house stood in a garden full of fruit trees, with its front to the junction of three waterways. On the western side of the one they were standing over, huge beautiful trees lined the bank, their reflections perfect in the still water. 'Black poplars,' he told her. That side of the 'river' was, he said, still more or less an undrained fen, now a nature reserve. There were reeds and rushes and a considerable amount of wildlife. It was, she decided, incredibly beautiful, but more than that. It was so quiet. The only sounds from anywhere were those of nature. Peace. Unutterable peace. And over them as they stood there was that incredibly wide sky offering both freedom and protection, while on every side the flat land held out lush, fertile promise. And hope.

'I'm glad you like it,' he said. 'But it ain't always like this. Especially in winter. There ain't many spots like this, either. But this is mine, and I do as I like with it. I think I shall live here. The nearest house is nearly a good half-mile away, and this bridge is private property. Nobody but me has a right of way over it, so there's no danger of unwanted visitors, unless they come by water. Or on their skates if we have a hard enough frost.'

They went down the other side of the bridge. 'The old house used to have a big garden,' he said, 'but I ain't bothered with it while I've been at Castle Hill. This year it was getting so rough I ploughed it up and sowed it with wheat. Just to please myself, like. I've cut some of it with a scythe and tied the sheaves and made a few stouks on it to remind myself of what harvest used to be when I were a little old boy. I know most folks think I ain't right in the head, but it don't hurt nobody else, and it pleases me. There's less than two rood on it.'

She didn't understand what he meant, but grasped the fact that she was hearing the true voice of the fenman in its own right, untrammelled by education.

He began to whistle, taking things from the car and selecting a place for their picnic. He took her into the kitchen of the empty house, lit the primus stove, filled the kettle and showed her the toilet facilities. When she went back to him, he had built a stook in the shape of a horseshoe for them to lean their backs against while they ate, and spread rugs over the stubble to sit on.

'That frock's too grand for this,' he said. 'But I'm glad you wore it. I shall remember you always looking like you do now.'

'Not like you found me in the church?'

'Both,' he said. 'You needed me then. You don't now.'

She couldn't find an answer, so they began to eat. 'Stop there,' he said, when their meal was done. 'I'll pack everything away.'

She sat looking at him as he fished in his pocket for his shut-knife and said he'd get the old punt and go along to cut her some cat-tails and reeds. In a state of content troubled only by yearning, she watched him pole the flat-bottomed old boat along, till he drew in close by where she sat. He left most of his cuttings in the boat, but brought up a selected handful.

'I found you a reed-warbler's nest,' he said. 'I'll bet you've never seen one like that before. You needn't worry, they've done with it.'

She marvelled at the tiny nest slung between three reeds, and watched huge lazy butterflies float over her. He sat down by her side again and began to strip thin, bendy rushes to reveal white, pliable pith. In no time his brown clever hands were creating a woven basket, complete with handle, from the pith. Then he filled it with flowers made in the same way.

'My mother used to call these "Kate Carney" flowers,' he said, 'after some Irish actress, she said. But I reckon fen children have been making 'em since before ever any actress was ever heard of in these parts.'

He arranged them round the side of the basket, and then tucked a wonderful white water-lily in as a centre-piece. When it was all to his satisfaction, he set it aside and began to make little sailing boats out of the long pointed reed leaves.

She was so disappointed she wanted to cry. She was sure

he had intended the little flower-filled basket for her. Had he turned too shy to give it to her?

She excused herself, and went into the house till she found her courage again. She had promised her father she wouldn't fail for want of it.

When she went back, he was lying on his back with his eyes closed. She stood over him, looking down. He had been half-asleep, and half into his dream. But there the lady stood, by his side, looking down at him — alive, but with that ineffable look in her eyes that the artist of long ago had captured. Bob shut his eyes again, to photograph the moment for ever in his mind.

She sat down again beside him, taking off the jacket of her suit. He forced himself to open his eyes and sat up on his elbow to give her the little basket, laying it in her lap. He saw the tear fall into it as she set it aside, and he lay back again.

Then she stretched out beside him, leaned over him, and kissed him. He didn't move. So she kissed him again, and incredibly began to unbutton his shirt. When she had bared his strong, hairy chest, she laid her head on it to listen to his heart. It was pounding as much as any woman in love could have wished. With a great sigh, she tucked herself up close to him and awaited his response. It was everything she could have wished for.

They lay in a wonderland of disbelieving content till the sun had slid down the western sky to the horizon.

She took the opportunity of confessing how she had been deceiving him about finding her father, and why Nick had been moved to London.

Telling himself that magic never lasts longer than moments, he began to talk, as well.

He poured out his love for her, and his belief of how hopeless it was. He explained to her his sixth sense, which had warned him from the moment he had picked her up in church that whatever the circumstances appeared to be, she was so far above him as to put her right out of his reach. All he had ever hoped for was the chance to be of service to her.

'I'm only a peasant,' he said. 'I still don't know who you are, except that you are my "lady" now and for ever. My pagan goddess. All I ask is to be allowed to worship you, though I shall always remember that just this once I held you in my arms. When I come back to live here, by myself, this spot will be sacred to me. Like the little church on the hill is I think I had better move out from Castle Hill as soon as I can, and leave you with Charlie, till my new landlord takes over. I had a letter from him this morning. He wants to come and see what he's bought. And me.'

'What's his name?' she asked.

'I don't know. I didn't bother to look. It didn't matter to me this morning. I still had this one day with you, and I wasn't going to let him spoil it. I believe it was Gordon.'

She put her head back on his chest, and heaved a sigh of utter content. 'Hadley-Gordon,' she said. 'Double-barrelled. And Bob – you haven't got a new landlord. You've got me instead, if you want me, that is. You are your own new landlord. It's a wedding present, from Effendi – my father. Everybody calls him Effendi since we lived in Khartoum years ago, because his name is Gordon, and everybody used to call General Gordon of Khartoum "Effendi". It seemed to fit my father, so it stuck.'

There had been no response so far from Bob, except for the tightened clasp of his arms around her.

She drew a deep breath. 'I don't think he thought I should have to go as far as proposing to you, though I did promise him I'd do my best to make you believe how much I love you. So will you marry me, please, Bob? It's the only thing I want, now.'

The sky exploded into millions of dancing stars.

'No, Bob, not here,' she said.

'Why not? I reckon peasants like me have made love among the barley sheaves for thousands of years, worshipping their goddess. So what's wrong with me worshipping mine? This is our sacred place.'

Why not? Love is a timeless, boundless mystery.

80

On that same Saturday afternoon, William and Fran sat in the sunshine in the garden at Benedict's, chairs close together, in a state of expectant apprehension. Late the night before, Roland had rung to tell Fran that Monica had gone into labour, and that he was summoning all obstetric and midwifery help forthwith. Fran warned him that it would probably be hours before anything whatsoever happened and told him not to panic.

'Fat lot of good that piece of advice is!' he said. 'Monica's father's in such a state already that you might think it was him having the baby. If he weren't in the other half of the house, I think I'd have had more sense than to tell him. But, thank goodness, he has to be out till after lunch tomorrow, if he'll be made to go. I'll keep you posted, Mum.'

Fran smiled. He might just as well have said outright that he didn't want her there either. So she had tried to keep calm, and had succeeded in showing no sign of any anxiety until after tea next day.

'Do you think I might ring to see how things are going?' she asked William.

'I wouldn't, sweetheart,' he said. 'You can't do anything to help, here or there, can you?' He smiled at her, a little dubiously. 'You know much more about such things than I do. This is the first time I've ever been through this, remember,' he said. 'I really didn't appreciate how long it took. Poor Monica.'

'Poor Roland,' she answered. 'I'd like to bet Monica isn't suffering half as much as he is. After hours and hours, men who care begin to feel guilty, and tell themselves it's all their fault, and they'll never let it happen again.'

'I don't think I could have stood it,' he said.

'It's only the price of love,' she said. 'Do you mean you wouldn't have wanted to pay it? Isn't love worth it?'

'How can you ask, Fran? But the thought of putting you through a long day like this . . .'

'Darling, don't! You're torturing yourself, now. They won't let it be too bad for Monica, and Roland will be with her, if he can take it. It's Eric I keep thinking about. He's there by now, and probably torturing himself with fear. He's only had two women he really loved, and lost one of them. It's the other he's worried about now. Every minute will be an hour to him . . . There's the telephone!'

She was up and gone before William had heaved himself out of his chair, and came back shaking her head.

'No news, yet. That was Eric. Just as I supposed. He's all by himself, and says he can't take it much longer. Can he either come up here, or will we go down to be with him? I said we'd go.'

'As if there was any doubt,' William said. 'I'm glad there's a chance for us to be on the spot as well.'

She looked her gratitude for that 'us'.

So they gathered in Eric's sitting-room, and tried to act normally. Monica's bedroom was too far away for any sound to come through the old walls. Conversation was difficult and half-hearted. Eric suggested asking for supper to be delivered from the hotel, but none of them wanted anything more than he had in his fridge.

'Where's the champagne, Eric?' Fran asked.

He looked guilty. 'I – I daren't tempt fate, Fran,' he said. 'It's here, but I haven't done anything with it.'

'We are acting rather like a lot of old hens,' Fran said. 'Why don't we take the opposite line, and actually offer an invitation to Lady Luck? Go and find it, and put it in the fridge. It can't be long now.'

It would at least give him something to do. When he came back, they drew their chairs together in a close arc facing the empty grate, with Fran in the middle, silently acknowledging and accepting the comfort of each other's presence.

It was almost nine o'clock before they heard the click of the door behind them, to let Roland in. Three heads turned as one, unable to interpret what they saw.

Roland was white and dishevelled, with his hair falling over his forehead, but his triumphant dark eyes belied his weariness. In each of his arms lay a little white bundle.

Nobody but he moved. He came up behind his mother, and she turned to take the nearest bundle from him.

'Your new grandson, Mum. William Gregory Wagstaffe.' Then he lowered the other into Eric's arms. 'And your new granddaughter, Eric. Annette Frances.'

'Twins?' said William in an strangled voice.

Next instant, Fran leapt to her feet and shoved the baby she was holding into William's unprepared keeping. She was just in time to grab the other from Eric before he keeled over. She handed it to Roland, and caught Eric, pushing him back in his chair. He came round at once, to find Fran sitting on the arm of his chair with her arms round him. She bent and kissed him. He turned his face into her, and wept.

Roland, embarrassed, was not sure what to do.

William looked away, and then down at the bundle Fran had thrust upon him, staring at the crumpled little red face lying now in the crook of his arm. It was the first time in his whole life he had held a newborn baby, and he was finding the experience more than he had bargained for.

How incredibly like Fran that funny little face was! A real Wagstaffe.

Then the baby opened its eyes, and in the way of all newborn babies, searched for something to try to focus them on. They appeared to be finding William's shock of white hair a very satisfactory object.

William was returning the baby's gaze. Named for him, as if it were truly his grandson. Which in effect it would be. He was moved by a feeling he had never had before, nor had ever expected to have. He caught one of the little waving hands in his and opened out the tiny fingers. They closed at once round one of his own. He couldn't believe it. Five perfect little fingernails, on five perfect little fingers already able to grip. A miniature miracle of perfection. He could only look across at Fran and Eric through very blurred eyes.

Fran left Eric to go back to Roland. She took baby Annette from him and looked at her son somewhat accusingly. 'You must have known!' she said.

'For months, of course. We daren't tell anybody – just in case. And we've had a devil of a fight with the doctors, to get our own way about them being born here. But we've won, and everything's fine. Especially Monica. You can go and see her soon.'

Fran cuddled the baby for a moment, and then took her back to Eric.

She went to relieve William of his charge, but he was reluctant to let go of the little marvel in his arms; so she knelt down beside him, and he pulled her to him, kissing the top of her head as she bent to kiss the dark Wagstaffe fuzz on the baby's head.

'Aren't they wonderful?' she said.

William Burbage, Ph.D. (Cantab), Professor of Medieval History, seasoned lecturer, renowned author, sometime Spitfire pilot, searched his extensive vocabulary for a word adequate to answer her with. There wasn't one.